In a time of fear, the One Who I Promised
will come to the raka, bearing glory in her
train and justice in her hand. She will restore
the god to his proper temple and his children
to her right hand. She will be twice royal, wise
and beloved, a living emblem of truth to her
people. She will be attended by a wise one, the
cunning one, the strong one, the warrior, and
the crows. She will give a home to all, and the
kudarung will fly in her honor.

*—From the Kyprish Prophecy,
written in the year 200 H.E.*

OTHER BOOKS BY TAMORA PIERCE

TRICKSTERS

TRICKSTER'S CHOICE
TRICKSTER'S QUEEN

TAMORA PIERCE

FANTASY

TRICKSTER'S CHOICE   Copyright © 2003 by Tamora Pierce
    Publishing History: Random House Hardcover, September 2003
                                Random House Trade Paperback, September 2004
TRICKSTER'S QUEEN   Copyright © 2004 by Tamora Pierce
    Publishing History: Random House Hardcover, September 2004

First SFBC Science Fiction Printing: March 2005.

Published by arrangement with Random House Children's Books,
a division of Random House Inc.
1745 Broadway
New York, NY 10019

Visit The SFBC at http://www.sfbc.com

ISBN 0-7394-5145-6

Printed in the United States of America.

CONTENTS

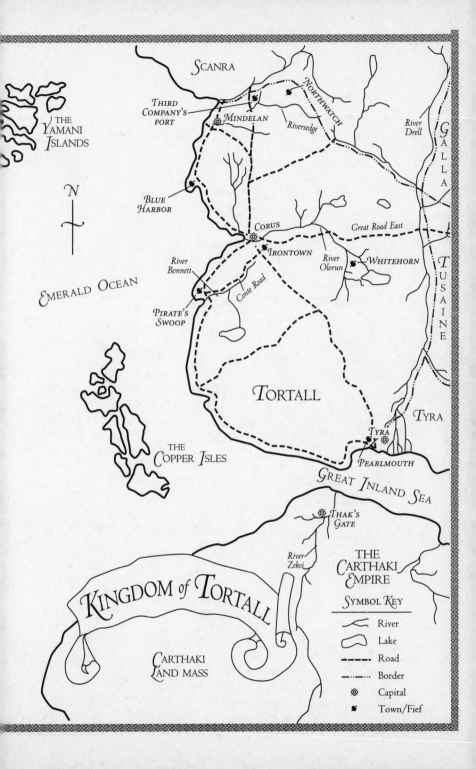

SCANRA

THE
YAMANI
ISLANDS

THIRD
COMPANY'S
FORT

MINDELAN

NORTHWATCH

Riversedge

River
Drell

GALLA

N

BLUE
HARBOR

EMERALD OCEAN

CORUS

Great Road East

River
Bonnett

IRONTOWN

River
Olorun

WHITEHORN

Conté Road

TUSAINE

PIRATE'S
SWOOP

TORTALL

THE
COPPER ISLES

TYRA

TYRA

PEARLMOUTH

GREAT INLAND SEA

THAK'S
GATE

River
Zekoi

THE
CARTHAKI
EMPIRE

KINGDOM of TORTALL

SYMBOL KEY

River

Lake

Road

Border

Capital

Town/Fief

CARTHAKI
LAND MASS

THE COPPER ISLES

Tanair Castle,
village, and estates

Lombyn Island

Kellaura Pass

Dimari

Ikang Island

Azure Sea

Jerykun Island

Ambririp

Imahyn Island

Yimosuat

Kypriang Island

Gempang Island

The Plain of Sorrows

Galodon

The Long Strait

Rajmuat

Moriji Cove

Tongkang Island

Sea of Kypriang

Birafu Estates

Emerald Ocean

Malubesang
Island

Fajurat

N
W   E
S

Symbol Key

—— River

∧ ∧ ∧ Mountain

THE DISTRICT OF RAJMUAT

1. THRONE HALL, ROBING PAVILION, PAVILION OF DELIGHTFUL PLEASURES
2. GRAIN GATE, GATE OF CARTS
3. GATE OF GOLD, GATE OF BRONZE
4. GATE OF VICTORY
5. RITTEVON ENCLOSURE AND GRAY PALACE
6. GATE OF THE SUN, GATE OF THE MOON

TRICKSTER'S
CHOICE

To Phyllis Westberg,
for knowing the best time to fire me and
for giving me the best rewrite advice
I've ever gotten:
read aloud

CONTENTS

from *The Luarin Conquest:*
New Rulers in the Copper Isles
by Michabur Durse of Queenscove,
published in 312 H.E.

In the bloody decades before the year 174 of the Human Era, the Kyprish Isles were locked in strife. Rival branches of the royal house traded the throne on a number of occasions. In turn the crown had lost control over the warring houses of the *raka*, or native, nobility. Scholars said of those years that only the jungles prospered, for the trees and vines fed on the blood of the raka. During this time the Isles exported more slaves than imported them: victors sold their enemies into the Eastern and Southern Lands, only to enter slavery in their own turn when they lost the next battle.

Queen Imiary VI of the house of Haiming made repeated attempts to negotiate peace among the raka. Her efforts failed. She was overthrown after twelve years of rule. Her successor and murderer, Queen Dilsubai, also a Haiming, favored those nobles who supported her shaky claim to the throne, and imprisoned their rivals. The glorious days of the copper-skinned warrior queens of the Isles were over.

On the mainland, the pale-skinned easterners called *luarin* by the Kyprish people saw the disorder, and the wealth, of the Isles. Rittevon of Lenman, younger son of a lesser noble house in Maren, found opportunity in the Isles' disorder. He raised funds and allies among the realms of Tusaine, Galla, Tortall, Maren, Sarain, and Tortall's southern neighbor Barzun.* For an army he summoned younger sons, adventurers, and mercenaries, all bought by the promise of the Isles' wealth. With them came battle mages trained in the arts of war at the university in Carthak. Rittevon and his chief ally, Ludas Jimajen, son of a Tyran merchant clan, placed their souls in pawn for the gold that

---

*Barzun was conquered by Tortall in the year 378 h.e., giving Jasson III of Tortall control of the eastern coastline from Scanra to the southern delta of the River Drell.

bought the services of their battle mages. They bought all the raka nobles they could in advance, promising them status when Rittevon sat the throne.

The first assault came in stealth on April 5, 174 H.E. The invaders struck not the capital at Rajmuat, where rival Haiming cousins fought over the crown, but the stronghold of the noble house Malubesai, on the southern island that bears their name. This most powerful clan was taken completely by surprise. Their homes were left in ruins, their warriors in mass graves, and their descendants in chains, all at the hands of the luarin mages.

For the next seven years, luarin ships and armies ranged the islands from Malubesang to Lombyn, from Imahyn to Tongkang. Lesser raka nobles and various clans, seeing how the wind blew, offered their allegiance to the conquerors. These became the lesser nobility of the Isles, allowed to retain lands, freedom, and lives, but taxed into poverty after their strongholds were destroyed. For the greatest raka nobles and the royal house of Haiming, the luarin offered only slavery or death. On Midsummer's Day 181 H.E., the first Rittevon king was crowned as ruler of the newly renamed Copper Isles.

The domination of the raka people continued. The luarin nobles—once tailor's sons and blacksmiths, landless younger sons and mercenaries—took for their new houses and fiefdoms the names of the land and the old noble houses. More luarin arrived to settle and do business. Marriage among the raka was encouraged for the luarin lower classes, producing a multitude of part-raka servants and slaves. The luarin were there to stay.

Like most who lose such struggles, the raka declared that only war in the Divine Realms explained the failure of their patron god, Kyprioth, to defeat the luarin. The luarin priests taught, and the raka people believed, that Kyprioth's divine brother and sister, the war god Mithros and the Great Mother Goddess, had overthrown him. It was these gods, the priests of both races said, who took the right to govern the islands, while they gave Kyprioth lordship only over the local seas, to keep him occupied under their eyes.

Soon after the last battle of the luarin conquest, an ancient priestess gave voice not to her own prayers, but to the banished god Kyprioth. His promise was passed from raka slave to raka freeman, from raka mothers or fathers to their part-luarin children. Kyprioth told his people that the efforts of the luarin kings to erase the Haiming line had failed. One branch of the old royalty yet survived. The Queen's prophecy is his promise that, from that surviving branch, the One Who Is Promised would come. She would be the Queen with two crowns, chosen by the god to lead the Isles and those who love them to freedom once more.

1

PARENTS

March 27–April 21, 462 H.E.
Pirate's Swoop, Tortall, on the coast of the Emerald Ocean

George Cooper, Baron of Pirate's Swoop, second in command of his realm's spies, put his documents aside and surveyed his only daughter as she paused by his study door. Alianne—known as Aly to her family and friends—posed there, arms raised in a Player's dramatic flourish. It seemed that she had enjoyed her month's stay with her Corus relatives.

"Dear Father, I rejoice to return from a sojourn in our gracious capital," she proclaimed in an overly elegant voice. "I yearn to be clasped to your bosom again."

For the most part she looked like his Aly. She wore a neat green wool gown, looser than fashion required because, like her da, she carried weapons on her person. A gold chain belt supported her knife and purse. Her hazel eyes contained more green than George's own, and they were set wide under straight brown brows. Her nose was small and delicate, more like her mother's than his. She'd put a touch of color on her mouth to accent its width and full lower lip. But her hair . . .

George blinked. For some reason, his child wore an old-fashioned wimple and veil. The plain white linen covered her neck and hair completely.

He raised an eyebrow. "Do you plan to join the Players, then?" he asked mildly. "Take up dancing, or some such thing?"

Aly dropped her pretense and removed her veil, the embroidered cloth band that held it in place, and her wimple. Her hair, once revealed, was not its normal shade of reddish blond, but a deep, pure sapphire hue.

George looked at her. His mouth twitched.

"I know," she said, shamefaced. "Forest green and blue go ill together." She smoothed her gown.

George couldn't help it. He roared with laughter. Aly struggled with herself, and lost, to grin in reply.

"What, Da?" she asked. "Apart from the colors, aren't I in the very latest fashion?"

George wiped his eyes on his sleeve. After a few gasps he managed to say, "*What* have you done to yourself, girl?"

Aly touched the gleaming falls of her hair. "But Da," she said, voice and lower lip quivering in mock hurt, "it's all the style at the university!" She resumed her lofty manner. "I proclaim the shallowness of the world and of fashion. I scorn those who sway before each breeze of taste that dictates what is stylish in one's dress, or face, or hair. I scoff at the hollowness of life."

George still chuckled, shaking his head.

"Well, Da, that's what the students say." She plopped herself into a chair and stretched her legs out to show off her shoes, brown leather stamped with gold vines. "*These* look nice."

"They're lovely," he told her with a smile. "Which 'they' is it that proclaim the hollowness of the world?"

Aly flapped a hand in dismissal. "University students. Da, it's the silliest thing. One of the student mages brewed up a hair treatment. It's supposed to make your hair shiny and easy to comb, except it has a wee side effect. And of course the students all decided that blue hair makes a grand statement." She lifted up a sapphire lock and admired it.

"So I see." George thought of his oldest son, one of those very university students. "Don't tell me our Thom's gone blue."

Now it was Aly's turn to raise a mocking eyebrow at her father. "Do you think he even notices blue-haired people are about? Since they started bringing in the magical devices from Scanra, he's done nothing but take notes for the mages who study how they're made. The only reaction I got from *him* was 'Ma better not see you like that.' I had to remind him Mother's safely in the north, waiting for the snows to melt so she can chop up more Scanrans." Aly had left a pair of saddlebags by the door. Now she fetched them and put them on a long table beside George's desk. "The latest documents from Grandda. He says to tell you no, you can't go north, you're still needed to watch the coast. Raiding season will begin soon."

"He read my mind," George said crossly. "That cursed war's going into its second year, your mother's in the middle of it, or will be once the fighting warms up, and I stay here, buried under paper." He indicated his heaped desktop with a wave of a big hand and glared at the saddlebags. "I've not seen her in a year, for pity's sake."

"Grandda says he's got an assistant trained for you," Aly replied. "She'll be here in a month or so. He *is* right. It's no good holding Scanra off in the north if Carthak or Tusaine or the Copper Isles try nipping up bits of the south."

"Don't teach your gran to make butter," George advised her drily. "I learned that lesson before you were born." He knew Aly was right; he even knew that what he did was necessary. He just missed his wife. They hadn't been separated for such a long stretch in their twenty-three years of marriage. "And an assistant in a month does me no good now."

Aly gave him her most charming smile. "Oh, but Da, now you've got me," she said as she gathered a wad of documents. "Grandda wanted me to take the job as it was."

"I thought he might," George murmured, watching as she leafed through the papers she held.

"I told him the same thing I did you," replied Aly, setting documents in stacks on the long table. "I love code breaking and knowing all the tittle-tattle, but I'd go half mad having to do it all the time. I asked him if I could spy instead. . . ."

"I said no," George said flatly, hiding his alarm. The thought of his only daughter living in the maze of dangers that was ordinary spy work, with torture and death to endure if she were caught, made his hair stand on end.

"So did Grandda," Aly informed him. "I *can* take care of myself."

"It's not the life we want for our only girl," George replied. "My agents are used to living crooked—you're not. And whilst I know, none better, that you can look after yourself, it's those other folk who worry me, the ones whose business it is to sniff out spies." To change the subject he asked, "What of young what's-his-name? The one you wrote was squiring you about Corus?"

Aly rolled her eyes as she sorted documents into stacks. "He bored me, Da. They all do, in time. None of them ever measures up to you, or Grandda, or Uncle Numy"—her childhood nickname for her adoptive uncle, Numair, the realm's most powerful mage—"or Uncle Raoul, or Uncle Gary." She shrugged. "It's as if all the interesting men were born in your generation." She scooped up another pile of documents from the desk. Soon she had the various reports, letters, messages, and coded coils of knotted string in four heaps: decode, important, not as important, and file. "So you can forget what's-his-name. Marriage is for noblewomen with nothing else to do."

"Marriage gives a woman plenty to do, particularly the noble ones," George said. "Keeping your lands in order, supervising the servants, using your men-at-arms to defend the place when your lord's away, working up your stock of medicines, making sure your folk are fed and clothed—it's important work, and it's hard."

"Well, that lets *that* straight out," she told him, her eyes dancing wickedly. "I've decided that my work is having fun. Somebody needs to do it."

George sighed. He knew this mood. Aly would never listen to anyone now. He would have to have a serious conversation at another time. She was sixteen, a woman grown, and she had yet to find her place in the world.

Aly rested her hip on George's desk. "Be reasonable, Da," she advised, smiling. "Just think. My da and grandda are spymasters, my mother the King's Champion. Then I've an adopted aunt who's a mage *and* half a goddess, and an adopted uncle who's a mage as powerful as she is. My godfathers are the king and his youngest advisor, my godsmothers are the queen and the lady who governs her affairs. You've got Thom for your mage, Alan for your knight"— she named her oldest brother and her twin, who had entered page training three years before—"and me for fun. I'm *surrounded* by bustling folk. You need me to do the relaxing for you."

Despite her claim to studying the art of relaxation, Aly had sorted all of the documents on her father's desk. She set the important pile in front of him and carried messages to be decoded to the desk that she used when she helped George. There she set to work on reports coded in the form of assorted knots in wads of string. Her long, skilled fingers sorted out groups and positions of knots in each message web. They were maps of particular territories and areas where trouble of some kind unfolded. The complexity of the knot told Aly just how bad the problem was. The knots' colors matched the sources of the trouble: Tortallans, foreigners, or immortals—the creatures of myth and legend who lived among them, free of disease and old age. Most immortals were peaceful neighbors who didn't seek fights, since they could be killed by accident, magic, and weapons, but some were none too friendly.

George watched Aly with pride. She'd had an aptitude for codes and translations since she was small, regarding them as games she wanted to win. She had treated the arts of the lock pick, the investigator, the pickpocket, the lip reader, the tracker, and the knife wielder in the same way, stubbornly working until she knew them as well as George himself. She was just as determined a student of the languages and history of the realm's neighbors. How could someone who liked to win as much as she did lack ambition? His own ambition had driven him to become the king of the capital's thieves at the age of seventeen. Her mother's will had made her the first female knight in over one hundred years, as well as the King's Champion, who wielded the Crown's authority when neither king nor queen was present. And yet Aly drifted, seeing this boy and that, helping her father, and arguing with her mother, who wanted her daughter to make something of her life. Aly seemed not to care a whit that girls her age were having babies, keeping shops, fighting in the war, and protecting the realm.

Perhaps I *should* let her work, George thought, then hurriedly dismissed the idea. She was his only daughter. He would never let her risk her neck alone in the field. It was bad enough that he'd taken her to some deadly meetings in earlier years, meetings where they'd had to fight their way out. If she'd asked to try the warrior life as a knight, one of the Queen's Riders, or one of the battle-ready ladies-in-waiting who served Queen Thayet, he would have found it impossible to refuse. His wife and Aly's adoptive aunts would have had many things to say to him then, and none would be a blessing. But she wanted to be a spy in the field. That he could and did refuse. He'd lost too many agents over the years. He was determined that none of them be his Aly.

He looked up, realizing that she had given him a weapon in her pursuit of fun. "What would you have done, mistress," he asked sternly, "if you *were* a spy and I needed you to go out in the field, with that head of hair acting as a beacon?"

Aly propped her chin on her hand. "It comes out in three washings, first of all," she informed him. "Second, if I was in Corus or Port Caynn, it would make no never mind. The apprentices and shopkeepers' young there pick up university fashions straightaway. Any other big city, I could just say it's the newest style in Corus. Or I'd say that they'd remember the hair and never the face under it, just like *you* taught me." George winced. Aly pressed on, "If none of that eased your flutterings, Da, I'd say that's what razors and wigs are for." She brightened. "I'll wash it out right now if you've a field assignment for me."

George got to his feet. "Never mind. Leave your poor hair alone. It's near suppertime."

When Aly stood, he came over to put an arm around her shoulders. At five feet six inches, she fitted just under her tall father's chin. George kissed the top of her very blue head. "I'm glad you're home, Aly."

She smiled up at him, all artifice and playacting set aside. "It's always good to see you, Da."

That night they ate with Maude, the Swoop's aging housekeeper and Aly's former nursemaid. Maude clucked over her hair, as Aly had known she would. She loved to make Maude cluck. Then she could remind the old woman how much she had changed from the Maude who had once disguised her young mistress Alanna as a boy and sent her off to become a lady knight. Maude always got flustered by that. Alanna was now a legend and a great lady of the realm. Maude could say it was fate that had made her open-minded back then, but she knew she was being inconsistent when she said it.

Aly liked to tease her nursemaid, not to mention everyone else. Her father knew her tricks and enjoyed catching her at them, which was fine. She knew most of his, too, because he'd taught them to her himself. She disconcerted most people, from the many boys who came calling once they'd noticed her mischievous eyes, ruddy gold hair, and neat figure to the hardened brigands and criminals who carried information to her father. She could even make her brothers yelp like puppies if she worked at it. Her twin, Alan, was particularly vulnerable, since she knew his mind nearly as well as her own.

The only person she left alone was her mother. Lady Alanna of Pirate's Swoop and Olau, King's Champion and lady knight, known throughout the

Eastern and Southern Lands as the Lioness, did not startle well. She had a temper and her own particular way of doing things. Alanna showed a sense of humor only around her husband. Aly knew her mother loved her two sons and lone daughter, but she was seldom home. She was forever being summoned to some crisis or other, leaving her children to be raised by her husband and Maude.

Not that her children required any more raising. Aly was sixteen, almost an adult and ready for adult work, as people were forever reminding her. Aly sometimes felt that everyone in her world had more exciting things to do than she did. She hadn't seen her mother, Aunt Daine, or Uncle Numair since the Scanran war began a year before. In the last month, while Aly had been in the capital, her grandparents were constantly advising the king and queen, so much so that she couldn't impose on their hospitality any longer. Her brother Thom, two years older, thought mostly of his studies. Her twin, Alan, who'd begun his page training three years late, was kept busy by the training master. She had seen him twice during her visit, and only for brief periods of time. She had felt left out, even as she had understood that for the time being, Alan belonged to his training master more than he did even to his twin sister. Rather than distract him from his training, she left him alone. Alan was like a cat: he would return to her when he was ready, and not one moment sooner.

All of the young men she had not flirted with and discarded were as busy as her brothers were. They prepared to march north when the mountain passes opened, as they would any day, or else they had left to guard the realm's other borders. None of her family would allow Aly within coughing distance of the war. So back home Aly had gone, feeling restless and in the way. At least Da would use her for paperwork, which was *something*.

Sometimes she thought she might scream with boredom. If only Da would let her spy! As she decoded reports and summed them up for him, she tried to work out a plan to change his mind.

On Aly's third day home more reports arrived. One of them was sealed in crimson, for immediate review. She deciphered it: the code was one of many she had memorized, so she required no book to translate it. Once done, she read what she had written and whistled.

George looked up. He sat at his desk, reading letters from Tyra. "Somebody would tell you that's unladylike," he pointed out. "Not your dear old common-born Da, for certain."

"No, not my dear old common-born Da," she replied, smiling at him. "But this is worth whistling over. Somehow our man Landfall's made it to Port Caynn. He's hiding out there, with important messages for you."

George's brows snapped together. "Landfall's supposed to be in Hamrkeng, keeping an eye on King Maggot," he replied slowly, using the Tortallan nickname for Scanra's King Maggur.

Aly reread the message, noting the apparently insignificant marks that marked it as coming from one of their agents, not a forgery. "It's Landfall, Da," she said. "I taught him this code myself, before we got him into Maggur's capital four years back. He kept saying it was a hard day for the realm when a little girl was teaching code."

George thought it over, rubbing his head. "Landfall. Either he was found out and escaped in time, or . . ."

Aly finished the sentence for him. "Or what he has is so important he could only carry it himself. Maybe both. He must have come down by ship."

George got to his feet. "Well, I'd best see what it's about." Landfall was one of a handful of agents smuggled into Scanra in the years before the war. He was vital enough that he reported only to Aly's grandfather Myles or to George. "Be a good lass and handle these papers for me? I shouldn't be gone more than a day or two—I'll fetch him back here. Have Maude get one of the hidden bedchambers ready."

Aly nodded. "You'll get muddy, riding to Port Caynn now," she pointed out.

George kissed her forehead. "It'll do me good to get out in the field, even if it means getting some of the field on me. I'm that restless."

Aly waved goodbye from the castle walls as her father rode out of Pirate's Swoop, two men-at-arms at his back. The ride *would* do him good. She only wished he could go all the way to her mother's post at Frasrlund in the far north, where he clearly longed to be.

Aly returned to his office in a gloomy mood. Would she ever find someone to love as much as her parents loved each other? She would miss such a partner dreadfully if they were separated, she supposed, just as her parents did. At least she would have someone to talk to, someone clever who didn't gawp at her and ask her what she meant or, worse, be shocked by her. It wasn't much fun when the only people who could keep up with her were either related or at least ten years older than she was.

The day after her father's departure Aly heard the horn calls that signaled the arrival of a friendly ship in the cove. Normally she would have run to the castle's observation platform to see who the new arrivals were, but she was in the middle of a particularly difficult bit of translation: code entered as pinholes in a bound book. If she was not careful, she would flatten the delicate marks, ending up with gibberish instead of a message. She stayed at her task until she heard hooves in the inner courtyard. Gently she set the book aside and went into the main hall, then out through the open front door.

Whatever she had expected, the scene in the inner courtyard was not it. Hostlers gently led her mother's warhorse, Darkmoon, toward the stable. The big gelding limped, favoring his left hind leg. Aly eyed the rest of the arrivals. Ten Swoop armsmen who had gone north with her mother the year before helped servants to unload their packhorses before taking them to the stable. The horses looked thin and salt-flecked, as if they'd been at sea. The men-at-arms looked much the same. So did Aly's mother.

Alanna of Pirate's Swoop and Barony Olau, King's Champion, watched Darkmoon as he was led away. The Lioness wore loose, salt-stained buckskin. There was salt in her copper hair, and she had lost more weight than the men. Aly knew her mother hated ships. She would have been sick throughout the voyage.

Aly trotted down the steps and kissed her mother's thin cheek. "What brings you here so unexpectedly?" asked Aly. "Is Darkmoon all right?"

Her mother looked up at her: even wearing boots, she was slightly shorter than her daughter. Fine lines framed the Lioness's famous purple eyes and her mouth, marks of long weeks in the open air, summer and winter. There were a few white strands in her mother's shoulder-length copper hair that Aly could not remember seeing before.

"He pulled a tendon," Alanna replied wearily. "Our horse healers did their best with him, but he needs rest. His Majesty gave us a month's leave. Where's your father?"

"Off," replied Aly. It was the family's code phrase that meant her father was on spymaster's business. "He should be back soon—it was just a quick trip to Port Caynn."

Her mother nodded, understanding, and gave Aly a brief hug.

"Why didn't Aunt Daine heal Darkmoon?" Aly demanded. Daine, the Wildmage, spoke with and healed animals as easily as she took their shapes.

"Your aunt is having a baby shape-shifter within the month," replied her mother as the men carried her packs into the castle. "If she doesn't change below the waist whenever the child does, it might kick its way out of her womb." Alanna shuddered. "It wasn't even worth asking her, not to mention it made me queasy to see her go from bear to donkey to fish every now and then, while her upper half remains the same. Darkmoon will be fine with rest." She walked toward the castle steps, limping slightly.

"What happened to you?" Aly demanded, keeping pace. "You're hobbling like . . ." She'd been about to say, "You're old," but her throat closed up. That wasn't so. Forty-two was not old, or at least not *that* old.

"I took a wound to the thigh last autumn," Alanna said tersely. "It troubles me some yet."

"But you're up to your ears in healers!" Aly protested. "You're one yourself!"

Alanna scowled. "When you've been healed as much as I have, you develop a certain resistance. You know that, or you should. *What* have you done to your hair?"

Aly tossed her head. "It's the latest fashion in Corus," she informed her mother. "It's the height of sophistication."

"It's as sophisticated as a blueberry," retorted Alanna. "Aren't you a little old for this kind of thing?"

"Why? It's fun, and it washes out. It's not like the world revolves around my hair, Mother," Aly said sharply. Why did this always happen? Home not even half a day, and her mother had already found something to criticize about her.

"Fun," Alanna said, her voice very dry. "There ought to be more to your life than fun at sixteen."

Aly rolled her eyes. "*Someone* has to enjoy themselves around here," she pointed out. "It certainly isn't you, forever riding here and there for *serious* work. You're always so grim!"

"You're *sixteen*," retorted Alanna. "When I was your age, I was two years from earning my shield. I knew what I wanted from my life, I knew the work I wanted to do—"

"Mother, please!" cried Aly. They hadn't seen each other for a year, but already they had returned to the last conversation they'd had before Alanna left. "Must you be so *obsessed*? I know all of this already. When you were my age you'd killed ten giants, armed only with a stick and a handful of pebbles. Then you went on to fly through the air on a winged steed, to return with the Dominion Jewel in your pocket and the most beautiful princess in all the world for your king to marry. I'm not you. If you were here more, you might have seen that much for yourself." She wished she hadn't made the accusation, but if anyone could make Aly lose control over her tongue, it was her mother.

Guilt pinched the girl as Alanna's shoulders slumped. "That's not what I meant," Alanna said. "That's not what I want. At least, it would have been nice, to have you do as I did, as far as getting your shield is concerned, anyway. But the whole point to doing as I did was so you could do something else, if you wanted to. It's just that you don't seem to want to do anything." She massaged one of her shoulders, watching her daughter. "Look, hair is, is hair, I suppose. If you want it blue, or green, or leopard-spotted . . . Who am I to say what's fit for a girl?"

She walked into the castle. Aly turned to see the hostlers and men-at-arms regarding her with reproach. "She's not *your* mother," she told them. "You try being the daughter of a legend. It's a great deal like work."

Aly didn't expect to see Alanna at the supper table that night, but the servants did. A second place had been laid, and Alanna was already seated when Aly entered the smaller family dining room.

"My first solid meal in days," Alanna informed her daughter as Aly took her seat. "I threw up all the way here on that cursed ship."

"It's still too wintry to ride?" asked Aly, accepting a bowl of oysters in stew from a maid.

Her mother had already begun to eat. Once she'd emptied her mouth she replied, "Not if I didn't mind getting here by the time I'm supposed to be back at Frasrlund." She ate with quick, efficient movements. "Seasick or no, the boat was faster. It's going to be a long summer. I admit, I will be the better for some time here."

"Then King Maggur means to fight on, despite losing his killing devices?" Aly inquired.

Alanna mopped out her bowl with a crust of bread. "He's still got his armies and his ship captains. If all there was to Maggur was that disgusting mage of his, we'd have beaten him like a drum last year. Could we not talk about the war? I've done nothing else for months."

Aly stifled a sigh. There were so few subjects she could safely discuss with her mother. Unless . . .

It had been over a year since their last talk. In that time she'd honestly tried to find something to do that would please her father, without success. Perhaps she had gone at it the wrong way. It had never occurred to her before to enlist her mother's help.

"You know what you were saying before, Mother?" she asked as the maid set a roasted duck between them.

Alanna carved it briskly, serving herself and Aly while Aly dished up the fried onion pickle that went with the duck. "I barely remember my own name at the moment," Alanna replied. "What did I say before?"

"That I needed to find work." Aly arranged her onions in a design on her plate. "As it happens, there is work I like, work I'm good at. And it's as important as warrior's work; I think you'd be the first to say as much."

Alanna looked up from her plate, her purple eyes glinting with suspicion. "Out with it, Aly," she ordered. "You know I have little patience for dancing around a thing. What's as important as a warrior's work?"

Aly put down her knife and folded her hands in her lap, where her mother couldn't see them. Making sure the proper casual spirit was in her voice and face, she said, "I would like to serve the realm as a field agent. With the war making a hash of things, I bet I could make my way into Scanra. We need more agents there. Or Galla, or Tusaine. We're about to lose one of our Tusaine folk—well, not lose, gods willing"—she made the star-shaped sign against evil on her chest—"but we have to pull him out of Tusaine, and we'll have to replace him—"

Alanna set down her knife so hard that it clacked as it struck her plate. "Absolutely not," she snapped. Her face was dead white. Her eyes burned as brightly as the magical ember-like stone she always wore around her neck.

Aly leaned back in her chair, startled by Alanna's vehemence. "I beg your pardon?" she asked politely, buying time until she figured out what she'd said wrong *this* time.

"No daughter of mine will be a spy." Alanna's tone made the word *spy* into a curse.

"But Da's a spy," Aly pointed out, shocked.

Her mother fingered the glowing stone at her throat and replied slowly, "Your father is a unique man, with unique talents. They are put to better use in the service of the realm than in his old way of life. I am grateful for that. He also has people of like mind, training, and background to help him in what he does. People better suited than his daughter."

"You're trying to say Da's no noble, no blueblood of Trebond," Aly said, finding the point that her mother tiptoed around. "You're trying to say spying is not a noble's work. But Grandda is a spy, too—what about him?"

"Your grandfather distills the information your agents gather. He serves as the visible spymaster so your father may work undisturbed," said Alanna. "That's different."

"You wanted me to have work that means something to me," protested Aly.

"Not *this* work, Alianne. I have to endure it when your father does it. I don't have to accept it from you." Alanna sighed and leaned back in her chair. "Spying is not fun, Aly. It's mean, nasty work. One misstep will get you killed. If you were hoping I'd talk your father around, you were mistaken."

"But that's what I want!" cried Aly, frustrated. "You're always after me to do something with my life. You tell me, make a decision, and I have! I help Da with it all the time and nobody objects!"

"Then I should have done so," Alanna said. "And I should have done it years ago. You're right—I was never around for your growing up." She pushed her chair back from the table. "While I'm here, I'll try to make up for it a little. We'll use our wits, see what we can do." Wincing, she got to her feet and walked past Aly. She stopped, hesitated, then rested a hand on Aly's shoulder. "I've been a bad mother to you, Aly. But perhaps I can help you find your way, at least."

She took away her hand and walked stiffly out of the room. The maid pursued her, after giving Aly an annoyed stare, to remind Alanna that she'd barely had anything to eat.

Aly stared at the goblet beyond her plate. She knew that tone in her mother's voice, the one that had crept in as Alanna spoke of Aly "finding her way." Aly was to be her current project. Every time she was at home, Alanna seemed to require a task, something to keep her hands busy until her next summons to kill a giant, round up outlaws, fight a noble who challenged the Crown's judgment, or take part in a war. During her last stay she had gone over every inch of the Swoop's walls with masons, remortaring stones and building the walls higher by a full yard. The household had spent weeks cleaning out stone dust after she left.

Aly had no interest in being a project, liking herself as she was. Frowning, she considered her choices as she drummed her fingers lightly on the table. She could stay and have her mother talk at her until Da returned. Then she could sit about decoding reports by herself, feeling underfoot and alone, until her parents remembered there were other people in the world. It had happened before. The prospect was not enticing.

Her parents needed time to themselves. As it was, George would probably have to visit the spy Landfall, especially if the man was tucked away in a secret room for safety. It also occurred to Aly that she might not like the result when Da learned she had tried to enlist her mother's help. It was very hard to make Da angry, but that might just do it.

They deserve time alone, together, Aly told herself virtuously. I will give it to them.

She got up from the table and went to her father's office. If she applied herself, she could finish the rest of the correspondence that evening and leave her father with nothing to distract him when he returned. In the morning, she would sail her boat, the *Cub*, down the coast to Port Legann. She would even leave a note so that her parents wouldn't worry. She often sailed alone, and winter in the south had been fairly mild. The sea might be a little rough, but she could handle it. If the weather turned bad, she would take shelter with the dozens of families she knew along the coast. And it was early enough in the year that pirates wouldn't have started their raids yet.

She would sail to Port Legann, visit Lord Imrah and his tiny, vivid wife, and give her parents the time alone that they deserved. She would also avoid being turned into her mother's project. Alanna's energy was a fearsome thing. A few days before her mother left for the north, Aly would return to bid her farewell. If a tiny voice whispered at the back of her brain that she was running away, Aly ignored it. Her plan really was for everyone's good.

She finished the decoding and paperwork, leaving her summaries in a neat stack on her father's desk. That night she packed a small trunk. As the sun first drew a silver line along the horizon, she carried it down to the *Cub*. By the time the sun was clear of coastal hills, Aly was plowing through the waves, shivering a little in her coat. She imagined the result when her mother found her note on the dining room table. If her mother's past reactions were any indication, she would curse the air blue that Aly had dodged her plans. Then Da would return, Aly's parents would bill and coo like turtledoves for three weeks, and by the time Aly returned from Port Legann, both of them would be in a better frame of mind, ready to welcome their only girl-child. Aly liked it. This was a *good* plan.

For two days she enjoyed her sail and the solitude. Shortly after dawn on her third day out she rounded Griffin Point and found she had miscalculated. A clutch of pirate ships, their captains not aware that the raiding season had yet to begin, had destroyed the town that lined Griffin Cove. Aly tried to turn the *Cub*, but the wind was against her. They surrounded her before she could get her ship out of the cove.

By midmorning a mage was stitching a leather slave collar around her neck. It would tighten mercilessly if she tried to escape beyond the range of the mage who held its magical key. The captain of the ship that had sunk her beloved *Cub* watched as the mage finished the collar. "I want her head shaved," he snapped. "Nobody's going to buy a blue-haired slave."

Three weeks later, Rajmuat on the island of Kypriang, capital of the Copper Isles

Aly huddled in the corner of the slave pen farthest from the door, knees drawn up to her chest, arms wrapped around her knees, forehead on her arms. She was barefoot. Her hair was now only the finest red-gold stubble. She was dressed in a rough, sleeveless, undyed tunic, with a rag that served her for a loincloth. The pirates' leather collar had been exchanged for one that would keep her in the Rajmuat slave market until she'd been sold.

After three weeks, two of them on a filthy, smelly ship, her body was skinnier and striped with bruises. There was also a purple knot on the back of her head. That was a gift from one of the pirates, who had not expected her to know so many tender spots where her nails could inflict serious pain. To anyone inside or outside the pen, she looked as cowed as any slave about to be sold for the dozenth time.

Aly's brain, however, ticked steadily, working through what was likely to happen and what she could do about it. Tomorrow the slaves in her pen were to be sold. Escape from the pen was not impossible, but it would have required more time than she had, and there was the nuisance of her leather collar to consider. Her best bet was to be sold. She could then leave her new masters, acquire money and clothes, and take ship for home.

It was the selling part that most concerned her. At her age, she would be considered ripe for a career as a master's toy. This was not acceptable. She wasn't sure what she wanted to do about her virginity yet, but she did know that she wanted to give it up when *she* chose.

To that end she had eaten little until now. The other slaves had thought her mad for giving away half of the pittance they were fed, but Aly did not want to be as shapely as she had looked at home. The head shaving had been a blessing, though the pirates hadn't meant it to be. Anything that made her look odd and troublesome would help her to avoid masters who might buy her for pleasure.

Aly watched her companions over her arms. They clustered around the gate, knowing supper was on its way. When it came, she would get a last chance to make herself as undesirable as possible without actually cutting off important body parts.

The slaves stirred. Keys rattled. The gate groaned as it was pushed open from outside. The slaves shrank from the guards armed with padded batons who entered first, to hold them back. Cooks tossed a number of small bread loaves onto the floor. Next they set down pots of weak porridge. The slaves surged forward with the wooden bowls they'd been issued on their arrival.

The strongest captives kept things orderly at first. They held off the rest as they helped themselves and their friends. Only when they retreated did the others descend like starving animals to seize what remained.

Aly deliberately flung herself into the flailing mass of limbs, offering herself as a target for any elbow, fist, knee, or foot that might help to make her look ugly. She fended off the worst blows with tricks of hand-to-hand combat taught to her by her parents. The rest, accidental or weak, sharp or soft, Aly endured. Her skin would have few white patches left when she was done. The rest would be bruised, cut, and scratched, the signs of a fighter.

A white starburst of pain opened over her right eye. An elbow rammed her lower lip on her left, splitting it. She didn't see the fist that struck her nose, but through the bones in her head she heard it break.

Blood rolled down the back of her throat. Heaving, Aly struggled out of the crowd. She stumbled back to her corner, her face blood-streaked and her lip swollen to the size of a small mouse. Once she had the pen's wooden walls at her back and side, she clenched her teeth and molded the broken cartilage of her nose so that it wouldn't heal entirely crooked. The pain made her eyes water and her head spin. Still, she was pleased with herself and with the slaves who had unknowingly helped to mark her.

A while later someone's foot nudged her—it belonged to the big woman who'd been thrown into the pen two days before. Aly blinked up at her with eyes swollen nearly shut.

"That was stupid," the woman informed her as she crouched beside Aly. In one hand she offered a crust of bread soaked in thin porridge. In the other she held a bowl of water and a rag. Aly examined the bread with the magic that was her parents' legacy. It seemed unlikely that anyone would try to poison her, but checking was a reflex. She saw none of the green glow of poison in her magic, and accepted the food. As Aly maneuvered a scrap of soggy bread through her swollen lips, the woman gently wiped dry blood from her face.

"You'll have a nice fighter's scar on the brow, little girl," she remarked. She spoke Common, the language used throughout their part of the world, with a rough accent that Aly couldn't place. It was Tyran, maybe, but there something of Carthak in the way she treated her *r*'s. "And a broke nose—they'll brand you as quarrelsome," the woman continued, cleaning Aly's many cuts. "No one will buy you for a bed warmer now, unless they're the ones that like women in pain."

"For them I'll look like trouble. I'd be a dreadful bed warmer," Aly told her with an attempt at a grin. The effort made her wince. She sighed and popped another piece of bread into her mouth, although it was hard to chew and breathe at the same time.

The big woman rocked back on her heels. "You *planned* this? Be you a fool? A bed warmer gets fed, and clothed, and sleeps warm."

"With a good owner," Aly replied. "Not with a bad one. My aunt Rispah used to be a flower seller in Corus. She told all manner of tales about masters and servants. I'll wager it's worse when you're a slave with a choke collar." She fingered the leather band around her neck. "I'd as soon not find out. Better to be ugly and troublesome."

The woman got back to work on washing the blood away. "So were you always mad, or did it come on you when you was took?"

Aly smiled. "I'm told it runs in the family."

Think of this as a sort of divine present from me to you. It could almost be letters from home. I don't want you thinking that all kinds of dreadful events are taking place in your absence. I hope you appreciate it. I wouldn't do this for just anyone. The man who spoke in Aly's dream had a light, crisp, precise voice, the sort of voice of one who could annoy or entertain in equal measure. That voice didn't mumble, or speak in dream nonsense. Aly was completely and utterly convinced that it was a god who spoke to her. Now she knew why her mother had once answered a question about how she knew when a god was a god: "Trust me, Aly, you know." Aly knew.

Darkness cleared from her dream vision to show her Pirate's Swoop. It was the clearest thing she had ever seen in her sleep. She felt as if she had become a ghost who watched her mother. Alanna sat on a merlon atop the observation deck on their largest tower. Out on the Emerald Ocean, the sun was just kissing the horizon. Shadows already lay over the hills east of the Swoop.

Alanna rested a mirror on her thigh: an old, worn mirror that Aly recognized. Thom had given it to their mother when he was small, when he'd thought her the kind of mother who liked mirrors with roses painted on the back. Ever since, Alanna had used the mirror to magically see the things she wanted to find. Aly felt a hand squeeze her heart seeing her mother still using Thom's childish gift.

Alanna picked up a spyglass and trained it on the southern coast, despite the poor light of the fading day. After watching through the glass for a time, she set it down and grasped the mirror. Violet fire, the color of Alanna's magical Gift, bloomed around the glass. On the mirror's surface Aly saw only gray clouds.

Her mother cursed and raised the mirror as if to smash it against the stone of the merlon. Then, gently, she lowered it back onto her lap and returned to the spyglass.

Footsteps. Ghost Aly turned to see her father walk right through her. He rested a big hand on the back of his wife's neck and kissed her under the ear before he asked, "Nothing yet?"

Alanna lowered the spyglass and shook her head. "I thought she'd come home in time to say goodbye," she said, shaking her head. "I have to sail tomorrow, George, I can't wait."

Aly looked down at the cove, where three ships flying the flag of the Tortallan navy lay at anchor. All were courier ships, built for speed. The king wanted his Champion in the north as soon as he could get her there.

Poor Mother, thought Aly. She'll throw up for the whole voyage. But she's going anyway, to get back to her duty. And she put up with it coming south, to give herself as much time with Da and me as she could. Now she thinks I don't care enough to see her and tell her goodbye.

"What of the mirror?" asked George.

Alanna turned vexed eyes up to him. "I'm getting nothing from the mirror, but there are a hundred reasons for something like that."

"Like you being exhausted?" George inquired gently.

Alanna rolled her eyes. "Don't start with that again, George."

"And why not, when it's true?" he demanded. "If you won't speak to the king, perhaps I should."

Tired? Aly thought, startled. Alanna the Lioness *tired*? Impossible.

She looked at her mother's face and saw lines she hadn't noticed before, at the corner of those famed purple eyes, at the corners of the Lioness's mouth. Aly remembered that her mother was almost forty-three.

"Field duty is a lot less tiring than serving as Champion during peacetime," Alanna told him. "And I won't have you saying anything to anyone." She sighed. "But it could be the reason I can't find her when I scry. I was never that good at it to begin with."

"If she's not home by the time you sail, I'll see to it she visits you in the north, to apologize for worrying you."

"I'm not *worried* worried. Aly can take care of herself. I just—bah." Alanna leaned back against her husband. "Thank all the gods the war is winding down. Will you write to me when she comes home?"

"I'll send her with the letter." George kissed the top of his wife's head. "Don't forget, Alan would have told us if there was anything to worry about. He can always tell if Aly's in trouble. Remember the time the horse threw her and she broke her head. Alan knew of it before Aly got conscious."

Alanna smiled reluctantly. "I'd forgotten that." She reached for her mirror. "Maybe I should give it one more try."

"And tire yourself more? I think not." George took the mirror from her hand and tucked it into the pocket of his breeches. "Why don't you go get ready for supper? Maude had them cook all your favorites."

"All my favorites? They'll have to roll me north, I'll be so fat." Alanna collapsed her spyglass.

"Ah, but you'll puke it all up on the trip, so eat away," George said in a falsely comforting voice.

"That's disgusting," said his wife drily. She turned and left him alone on the observation deck.

Only when she was gone did George pull a rolled scrap of paper from his pocket. When he read the message, the lines of his craggy face deepened and his broad mouth went tight. Ghost Aly read over his shoulder. It was a brief message in code from Lord Imrah of Legann: *She's not here*.

George crumpled the paper in his hand and stuffed it into his pocket just as Aly sensed her ghost self fade.

When Aly woke in the morning, she felt beaten all over—and so she had been, she remembered, by slaves fighting for supper. Her eyes were watering. She swiped at them with her hand and winced as she touched the sensitive bruising that ringed them, the legacy of her broken nose.

Had she really heard a god in her dream? Why would any god show her visions of home? She hadn't understood that comment about "letters," or the one about her absence. She wished she had tried to tell her parents that she was fine and would be home as soon as she could get away. It hadn't even occurred to her, she'd been so caught up in what her parents said. She did know that she *would* sail north as soon as she got back, to mend bridges with her mother.

Get sold, learn my way about, get free, get home, she thought, grunting as she struggled to her feet. That's simple enough. I'll make it up to her.

Please, Goddess, she prayed to her mother's patron deity, let me get sold to people I can escape from in one piece.

You asked me about slaves. They mean different things to different countries. There are slaveholders throughout the Eastern Lands, though slaveholding is an uneasy subject from Tortall to Maren, for one reason or another. Slaves are expensive, that's the thing to remember. You need vast lands to make slavery pay. They're a sign of wealth in the Copper Isles. Owning slaves there says that the master is as rich as any Carthaki lord. In Scanra, slaves are a sign of your skill in combat. It's the big farms like those in Maren, and in the Carthaki Empire, that need slaves all the time, to work their huge fields. And there's little their majesties can do about it. We buy back Tortallans taken captive if they can find them, but pirates strike and flee, selling some of their load here and some of it there. They're careful. They have to be. If they're caught, their punishment is painful and fatal.

—From a letter to Aly when she was twelve, from her father

2

TRICKSTER

May 4–6, 462 H.E.
The house of Duke Mequen Balitang, Rajmuat, Kypriang Island, the Copper Isles

Dressed in a light cotton tunic and leggings in the Balitang house colors of red trimmed with blue, Aly sat on a bench in the front foyer of the Balitang family's rambling town house. She was there to answer the door in case anyone came during the night. In a chest across the entryway was the pallet and blanket she would lay out for herself later. At the moment she was wide awake and planning.

Her hands were as busy as her mind. Deftly she used pliers and wire filched from the house blacksmith to shape a lock pick. It was part of a new set to replace those that had been taken by her pirate captors. She would be whipped if she was caught with pliers or lock picks, but she didn't intend to be caught. They were the next element in her plan to return home. With them she could open the smith's locked cupboard where he kept the special saw that would cut the metal ring off a slave's neck. The saw would break both the ring and its magic, a spell that would choke her if she attempted to leave the city.

With one ear cocked for the sound of anyone's approach, Aly reviewed her plans. Once free of the collar, she would disappear into the depths of the city. Already she was armed with a sharp knife she had stolen from the kitchen on her second day in the house. The law forbade all slaves to carry weapons, but Aly didn't care. She would always prefer the risk of getting caught with a forbidden weapon to the risk of getting caught without one at a moment when she would need it. With a knife and lock picks a girl of her talents could easily find decent clothes and a cloth to cover her stubbly head. Properly dressed, she could make her way through the marketplaces and help herself to enough coin to buy her passage on one of the many ships that sailed out of Rajmuat harbor every day. Her father had trained her well; she meant to prove it to him. Maybe when she returned he would be convinced that she could take care of herself as a field spy.

Her plan to discourage buyers who wanted a girl for their bedchambers had worked so well it was a little eerie. She had shown the market a sullen, scowling face that added to the impression made by her cuts and bruises. They marked her as a fighter, and trouble. Still, she had expected to get *some* bids. None had been offered—none at all. Even those who might like to break a troublesome slave had not blinked when they saw her. After two days of no offers, and the puzzled looks of both her fellow slaves and her sellers, Aly's owners decided to get rid of her. When Ulasim, the head footman to Balitang House, and Chenaol, the cook, purchased an expensive pastry chef, the slave sellers had thrown Aly in for free, to thank them for their custom.

To Aly's surprise, Ulasim and Chenaol kept her. It seemed they needed a slave-of-all-work, someone to obey the orders of everyone in the house. She stayed busy, but Mequen and his wife, Duchess Winnamine, believed that a well-fed slave was a harder worker. Their policy of kindness extended to clothes and even to healers. Aly could now breathe through her nose, although it would show the sign of the break all her days. The scar in her eyebrow was also hers for life.

Aly almost regretted the need to leave this interesting household. Its sheer size had not impressed her, despite the fact that the Balitangs hired or owned over a hundred servants and slaves in this great residence alone, not counting the family men-at-arms. Her adoptive aunts and uncles in the Naxen and Goldenlake households boasted as many servants, and the Tortallan palace had four times that many people to keep it in order. It was the makeup of the Balitang household and the family that intrigued Aly. If she hadn't known her parents would be worrying, she might have stayed on for a while to see what kind of people the Balitangs were. After years of lessons in the Isles' history, detailing the thorough job of conquest done by the luarin, or white, ruling class, she had expected to find all luarin in service and all the brown, or raka, folk as slaves. She had also expected that, as a luarin and a slave, she would need to prove over and over her ability to find tender spots on a raka tormentor's body before he or she decided to leave her alone.

Instead the pure-raka cook, Chenaol, had taken Aly under her wing and introduced her to a household that contained a majority of part- and full-raka servants and slaves, in addition to pure-luarin slaves like Aly, purchased as they came into the Isles' markets. As head cook, the wickedly humorous raka woman ran the kitchens with a firm brown hand and a sharp brown eye, supervising luarin, part-raka, and full-raka servants and slaves. She made it clear to all who came through her door that Aly was to be left alone.

"They gave her away, poor lass," Chenaol had told the household. "She's got enough on her plate without you lot tormenting her." It seemed Chenaol's word was law, regardless of her ancestry. Aly admired the woman. Chenaol was in her mid-fifties, a tart-tongued woman with sharp eyes. There were a few gray streaks in the coarse black hair she wore in a braid down her plump back. Her skin was the coppery brown shade of a full-blood raka, creased with light wrinkles about the eyes and mouth. Busy as she was, she still found time to show Aly the ropes in the rambling mansion.

The strangeness of this household didn't end with Chenaol. Ulasim, the brawny head footman, was also a full-blood raka. Of the Balitang's chief servants, the housekeeper, the steward, the coachman, and the healer were pure luarin and free, as was Veron, the commander of the men-at-arms. The chief hostler, the elderly Lokeij, was a full-blood raka slave who didn't seem to notice the collar around his neck, and half the hostlers who served under his eye were free and of mixed parentage. If the raka of the Isles were oppressed by their luarin masters, it was a thin, watery oppression in the Balitang household.

Already Aly had learned that the duke, the master of this house, had taken one of the raka nobility as his first wife and married her best luarin friend for his second. His choices might not have been worthy of note in another man, but Mequen was a descendant of the luarin ruling house, the Rittevons. Did this mean the luarin attitude was softening toward the enslaved raka, or did it simply mean that Mequen Balitang was far enough from the throne that no one cared whom he married? Sadly, Aly wouldn't get the chance to find out. Her parents would be fretting. She was going home, even if she had to manage all the arrangements herself.

Her escape would have been easier if she could just visit one of Da's Rajmuat spies, but Aly didn't dare. Spies were not to be trusted. Her identity was a vital secret in this new, hostile world. Tortall's enemies would pay any sum for her in order to use Aly against her family. They might even suspect that Aly knew something of her father's work. If that happened, they would squeeze her like a lemon. With those stakes, an agent might give in to the temptation to sell her for a profit. Even a faithful agent's communications to George might be intercepted. Aly had to get out of this one on her own.

There was a chance that her family might locate her first. Mother couldn't find her, if Aly's dream had been true, and the god had made her believe it was. It had been too vivid, too clear, and too convincing for her to deny it. So Mother couldn't scry her. Her father or Uncle Numair might track her down. Normally she would have expected Aunt Daine to have animals out to search, but Aunt Daine was in the process of having a child. Even the Wildmage couldn't attend to things while carrying a baby that changed shape constantly.

Still, Aly wasn't going to wait for rescue. She would free herself. If that didn't convince her father she would be a good spy, nothing would.

Sudden hammering on the house door made her jump. She hid her tools and went to see who was outside. A big white man and two men-at-arms, all soaked to the skin from the warm, pouring rain, strode into the hall. Aly greeted the first man with the deep bow of a slave to someone who was clearly a luarin noble, her palms together before her chest. His men had brown and reddish brown skins, marking them as warriors from either the lesser raka nobility or the bulk of the regular population of the Isles.

"I know it's late and doubtless they've retired for the night," the luarin nobleman said gravely, "but I'm afraid you must rouse the duke and duchess. Tell them Prince Bronau Jimajen has come with news of great import for them. *Royal* news."

Aly took the prince's sopping cloak and went to rouse Ulasim. The likes of her didn't visit Duke Mequen and Duchess Winnamine in their personal quarters. When she gave Ulasim Bronau's message, the big raka went pale. "See the prince to the azure sitting room," he ordered as he struggled into his tunic. "Show his men to the kitchen to be looked after. Ask Chenaol for refreshments for His Highness. Hurry!"

Aly spread Bronau's cloak before the kitchen hearth to dry as she passed on her orders to Chenaol. The cook sniffed. "Remember, you have the right to refuse if he invites you to his bed, girl," she advised as she set out a tray and a bottle of wine. "His Grace will back you. He lets no one force his slaves. Not that many turn the prince down, though. When he visits the summer residences, he goes through maids like grease, a different one in his bed every night."

Aly nodded and ran to show Bronau to the sitting room. He took a chair with a sigh as Aly hurriedly lit candles, then the braziers that gave these city homes their warmth. As she worked, she reviewed what she knew of this man from the reports. Bronau was not of King Oron's immediate family, but he was the brother-in-law of Princess Imajane, the king's sole daughter. His older brother, Rubinyan, had married the princess. Everyone who knew him said that Bronau was a good man in a fight, a commander who had the respect of his men and the affection of the king and his family.

Aly glanced at him as she got the braziers going. He looked taller than he actually was, being only three inches taller than Aly. He had a warrior's build, with broad shoulders and heavily muscled thighs, fierce gray eyes, and winged brows over a nose that had been broken once. He wore his reddish brown hair in waves to his shoulders but kept his beard closely trimmed. His big hands carried an assortment of weapon scars. The main flaw in his comeliness lay in the mouth framed by his beard. His lips were thin almost to the point of invisibility.

Like most luarin nobles, he wore the fashions of the Eastern Lands, remade for a jungle city: elegant blue silk hose and a blue linen tunic over a semisheer shirt of white lawn. The tunic was embroidered in the raka style along the collar and hems in a silver design of coiling dragons. He was dressed for an elegant spring party. His blue leather shoes were not meant for walking or riding in the rain, and he wore jeweled rings on every finger, a gold earring with a diamond bauble in one ear, and several gold chains on his chest.

He caught Aly's eye and smiled, his face lighting with humor and tremendous charm. "I know. I'm scarcely attired for the weather."

Aly gave him a sidelong glance, that of a woman who likes what she sees. He probably saw that look all the time and surely expected it. He smirked at her.

"It's not for me to say, my lord prince," Aly murmured. The relationship between Tortall and the Isles had always been unsteady. She would get a measure of this man now so that she could add to her father's notes about him when she returned. Their people seldom got the chance to talk to one of the most powerful men in the Copper Isles.

Bronau's eyebrows came together with an almost audible snap. "Come here, girl," he said, beckoning.

Aly obeyed. There was little danger that he might try anything improper. Under slave etiquette, another man's slaves were to be left alone, unless the master or the slave involved indicated otherwise.

The prince gripped Aly's chin with his hand and inspected her face. "Not a drop of raka blood in you, is there?" he asked, curious.

"No, my lord prince," murmured Aly, keeping her eyes down.

Bronau released her. "I don't like the precedent, keeping luarin slaves. It gives the raka ideas. See here—if these raka dogs bother you, don't hesitate to tell Duke Mequen," he told Aly sternly. "He looks out for the slave women, and you can't trust the raka to behave themselves unless they know there's a whip close to hand."

"My lord prince is too kind," Aly said, bowing once again. Bronau obviously didn't know that Chenaol, who could juggle razor-sharp cleavers with ease, had discouraged most problems of that sort. "If you will excuse me, I will bring some refreshment to you," she murmured.

Bronau nodded and settled into his chair, watching the embers in the nearest brazier. Aly fetched the pitcher of wine and the tray of fruit, cakes, and cheese the cook had put together to the sitting room. As she set the tray where Bronau could reach it, then poured him a glass of wine, she made sure that nothing in her manner told him that she was interested in giving him more than food and drink. It wouldn't take more than the right look and the right smile with this man. She would be in his lap with his hand under her tunic before she could sneeze. Chenaol was right: Bronau had a flirt's air. When Aly got home, she'd suggest to Da that they try one of their female agents with him. Bronau might tell far more than was prudent to a pretty, listening ear.

Once he was served, she left him. She fetched a mop and set to work cleaning up the water the guests had tracked onto the marble floor of the hall.

She was nearly finished when Ulasim raced down the steps from the family quarters. He slowed when he approached the azure sitting room, straightened his tunic, then went in to the prince. Both men emerged a moment later, to climb upstairs.

Aly watched them go. She'd give much to know what Bronau told the Balitangs. He'd said "royal business"—was that code for problems with the king? It could be. Oron was insane. Most of Rittevon House was these days. Aly's own mother had been forced to kill a Rittevon princess years before, when that lady started to kill people with an axe. The present Isles king was her uncle, a fearful and unstable man who turned on favored courtiers overnight.

Eavesdropping was not an option. If she were observed anywhere but at her post by the door, she would be questioned. Instead she finished mopping the floor. Later she would see what she could learn to take home to her da.

The next day the duke and duchess summoned the household to the hall where they held parties. It was the first time that Aly had seen any of the Balitang family but her master and mistress. Chenaol named them for Aly. The proud, brown-skinned girls, imperious sixteen-year-old Saraiyu and small, intense, twelve-year-old Dovasary, were the daughters of the duke's first marriage, to a raka noblewoman. His two full-luarin children, a four-year-old girl, Petranne, and three-year-old Elsren who was still awkward on his short, rounded legs, were by Duchess Winnamine. Other relatives who lived in the house were present, cousins who served Winnamine as ladies-in-waiting, a great-aunt, and the duke's uncle.

Duchess Winnamine sat on the dais, her elegant hands neatly clasped in her bronze velvet lap. Her brown eyes were only slightly accented with kohl, her brown hair dressed in curls that were tied up, then threaded through a velvet net on her head. Her sharp, straight nose and neatly curved mouth gave evidence of a strong will. She wore pearl drops in her ears, a gold chain around her neck, and only three rings, which was restraint in jewelry for an Islander. Many wore rings on every finger and several earrings, men and women alike.

Duke Mequen rose to his feet as the last to enter closed the doors behind them. He was about five feet ten inches tall, with the solid build of a man who rode a great deal but spent little time practicing weapons skills. His dark eyes were set under perfectly curved brows and framed by laugh lines. His nose was broad and straight, his mouth wide, his chin square. He wore his dark hair clipped short to draw attention away from the fact that it was retreating from his forehead. He was somberly dressed luarin-fashion in a black linen tunic over a silvery shirt and gray hose, with a ruby-hilted dagger at his waist, a signet ring on the index finger of his left hand, and a gold hoop ring in one ear. Aly liked the look of him. She already knew from his servants that he was a fair man, if unconventional in the way he ran his home and chose his wives. Now she could also see that he was well mannered and thoughtful, always nice traits to find in a noble.

Slowly his people quieted. Mequen looked them over, hands clasped behind his back. "I'm sure you've heard rumors," he said, his deep voice clear throughout the room. "His Majesty is no longer confident about my loyalty. He has invited me to prove it with expensive presents. While he evaluates these presents, my family and I are invited to visit our estates on Lombyn Island, where we must stay until he feels better about us."

Shock raced through the people like a physical thing. Some of their families, free and slave, had worked for the Balitangs for generations. Because the duke was uninterested in court intrigues, they had believed the king would never turn on him.

"This breaks our hearts," Mequen said, his sorrow plain on his face and in his voice. "We are forced to sell lands and slaves to give the king the reassurances he requires. And those we can take with us are dreadfully few. Our Lombyn holdings, the inheritance of Duchess Sarugani"—the mother of his older daughters—"are small." He glanced at his steward. "Our chief sources of income are not gold and gems but sheep, goats, and rabbits. We cannot live there as we are accustomed to do. We cannot feed you all."

By now some of the women were crying. Husbands wrapped their arms around their wives. Children clung to their parents.

The duchess rose. "We will do our best to see you are cared for," she said, her calm voice flowing over them. "Our friends have asked to hire or purchase many of you. We will separate no families. We will sell you to no one known to treat his people badly. As soon as provision has been made, you will be told. It will be soon. We must be on our way in just a week."

The duke took up the explanation. "Should no one we trust offer for your service, we have sent for a matcher, one with connections and the magical Gift to see what your aptitudes may be. He will examine you and obtain new places for you. That begins today." Mequen let out a deep sigh. "Some of you will come with us. Many of you already know who you are. For the rest, tell the steward if you desire to stay with us. But remember, we go to a rougher way of life, far from any town. We will have few amenities, less food. The highlands are colder than our jungles, the land inhospitable. Think it over." He paused, then nodded. "May the gods bless you. May they grant us all voyages to safe harbors."

Chenaol shook her head, her mouth in a tight line. "It's back to the slave brokers for you, Aly girl, unless the matcher sees you have special skills."

"And you?" Aly asked, not worried in the least. She needed just two more nights to complete her picks. Once she was rid of her metal collar, she could bid farewell to the Balitangs and the Isles alike.

"I stay with Lady Sarai and Lady Dove," Chenaol replied. "Forever." She left the room with the other departing servants, a short, round raka woman dressed luarin-fashion in an orange gown.

A curious way to put it, Aly thought as she mingled with the servants. Not "with the duke" or "with the family," only with the two daughters of the first duchess. The raka duchess.

The longer Aly stayed here, the more she saw how frayed the relations between the full-blooded luarin and the full-blooded raka were. A push from the right people might throw the entire country into civil war. That was news worth taking home. Too often in the past the Copper Isles had meddled in Tortallan affairs. Perhaps its rulers needed something to keep them busy.

The next morning the slave matcher summoned all those who had not found other homes as yet. Most were the less skilled workers—hostlers, lower-ranking footmen and maids, slaves whom the carpenter and the smith would not need in the north, and Aly. After the family's friends and well-wishers had made their selections, over forty slaves remained.

"How does this work?" Aly whispered to the boy who carried messages for the house as they lined up before the matcher. "I never heard of it before."

The boy wasn't surprised. Everyone knew Aly was fresh-caught out of Tortall. They never thought to wonder how she spoke Kyprish, the language of the islands, so well. "He looks at ya," he whispered. "He's got the magical Gift and all. He's looked at the owners that hire through 'im, too, so he can match folks that go good together. Not that we'll have much luck, us not having skills. 'Less he sees a talent. Sometimes they can, the Gifted matchers, anyways."

Ulasim led them into the grand hall. People had come and gone over the last day to remove paintings, tapestries, and candelabra for sale. All that remained were the tables and chairs. They would be carried off in the morning.

Ulasim lined the slaves against the wall, his brown eyes alert for any sign of misbehavior. The matcher stood next to chairs occupied by Duke Mequen and Duchess Winnamine, waiting. He was a plump black man in typical raka garb: a wraparound jacket and sarong, both made of serviceable tan linen. He shaved his head but grew a tuft of beard, which he stroked as he talked to the Balitangs. Now Mequen nodded to him. The slave matcher started at the far end of the line.

Aly watched from under her lashes. After he had bathed each slave in the pale orange fire of his magical Gift, the matcher conferred with Mequen and Winnamine. Slowly he worked his way through the slaves until he was closer to Aly. She measured his Gift. He was powerful enough to notice her magical Sight. Doubtless he would try to do something with her because of it.

She had the Sight from her father, but its force was her mother's legacy; magic ran strong in Alanna's family. George used his Sight to tell when he was being lied to or when someone held out on him. Sometimes he could also recognize one who would be his friend or his enemy. It was different for Aly. Her sight enabled her to see immediately whether the person she looked at had magic or godhood; whether that person was ill, pregnant, or lying. It also revealed the presence of poison in water or food. All she had to do was concentrate on how she wished to see something. Her power made it possible for her to clearly discern the tiniest of details, things invisible to the normal eye, or to see far into the distance. A new master might value it for as long as she stayed with him or her. Aly was unimpressed by her skill. She would have preferred to have the all-purpose Gift wielded by her mother and her brother Thom.

The matcher had come to Aly's neighbor. She closed her eyes against the glare of his Gift as the man weighed the young slave. Finished, he addressed Mequen and Winnamine. "I'll keep him with the others, see if he can be trained. I'll send your percentage of his final sale when it's made."

"Very well," Winnamine said. "We've heard good things about your training school."

"It's to my advantage to treat them well," the matcher replied. "It always pays off." The messenger left. Finally the matcher came to Aly. "Look up into my eyes, girl," he said, his melodic voice kind. "This won't hurt."

Aly met his gaze. The slightest hint of orange fire grew around his hands. Then the matcher hiccuped. "What?" he began to say.

Something changed. Inside his round frame Aly saw another body, compact, lean, wiry. Under his face lay another: square, the strong chin covered in a short beard, a brief nose broad at the tip, sparkling dark eyes, and short hair. This was *not* an internal aspect of the matcher; this was something else.

Well, well, Aly thought, amazed. I have a god.

Gold light spread from the matcher's body, flaring out around him like a sun. The Balitangs stepped back, shielding their eyes against the light with their hands. Vast, bell-like tones that sounded vaguely like speech rang out, the effect so powerful that Mequen and Winnamine dropped to their knees.

Aly felt no urge to kneel, nor did that light hurt her eyes as it did those of her owners. She gazed at the being who had come to occupy the matcher's body and leaned back against the wall, crossing her arms over her chest.

"Hello, there." A crisp, light voice, not the matcher's, came from the man's lips. "I apologize that we weren't able to meet earlier. I hope your journey here wasn't too harrowing."

"It was delightful," Aly said with her best nice-girl smile. "All lovely and serene, like sleeping on lilies, only without the bees in my nose. You spoke to me in my dream."

"I did," the god said, averting his eyes in a falsely modest way. "You'll get more. I don't want you to get homesick."

"But that's so *thoughtful*," Aly said innocently. "I'd thank you, but I just don't have the words. Until I find some, you might tell me just who you are supposed to be. Won't that be lovely?"

"Dear, you're being deliberately obtuse," the god inside the matcher teased. "You know a god when you see one. You may call me Kyprioth."

Aly thought swiftly. She didn't recognize the god's name, which didn't necessarily mean anything. Gods' names and importance varied from country to country. "Why would I want to call you anything, sir?" she asked, still in her character of a sweet young girl.

"Because I might be of use to you. In fact, I already have been." Kyprioth reached into the matcher's jacket and pulled out a tiny ball of light. "You sent a prayer to my sister, the Great Goddess, in the matter of who would purchase you. I intercepted it, since I took care of that little matter myself. You may have the prayer back."

Aly frowned at him, forgetting her impersonation. She looked at the strong, wiry hand inside the matcher's well-padded one. "You did what?"

Kyprioth smiled. It looked extremely odd under the matcher's unmoving features. "I made certain that you would go to the Balitangs and no one else. I fixed your seeming so that no one else would bid on you."

Aly scowled at him. "Do you mean I got my nose broken, my eyebrow scarred, and the rest of me all battered for *nothing*?"

"The eyebrow scar is quite dashing," Kyprioth told her earnestly. "I'll fix your nose if you like."

Aly covered her nose with a protective hand. "No. I got this nose the hard way, and I'm keeping it."

"Well, keep this, too," the god said, thrusting the light-ball at her. "Use it to appeal to the Goddess another time."

Aly reached out and took the ball. It oozed into her skin like water into sand and vanished. She rubbed the spot, looking the god over. "What have you done to them?" she asked curiously, nodding to the kneeling duke and duchess.

"They're talking to a Great God," Kyprioth assured her. "Not me—they wouldn't listen to me—but to my brother. They can't see or hear us, if that's what you're worried about. He's telling them that they are beloved of destiny and are meant for great things in this world. They are to be wise and accept their banishment, for their time of greatness will come."

Aly raised an eyebrow at him as she mentally listed the other Great Gods that this one might be. "Won't Mithros mind that you borrowed his seeming?" she wanted to know. "All the legends *I've* ever heard say he objects to it. Strenuously."

"What he doesn't know won't hurt him," Kyprioth said blithely. "I happen to know he's dealing with the start of a war on the other side of the world just now. Both sides are invoking him, of course—silly mortals. Don't you want to know what his seeming is telling them about you?"

"Not interested," Aly replied, smiling at the god with easy good humor. "I have plans."

"Very like your father, manner and all," Kyprioth informed her with a pleased smile. "I can't believe he hasn't the wit to put you to some proper work."

"You talk like you know him," Aly remarked. This was starting to get interesting.

"He and I have done quite a bit of business together."

"He never mentioned you," Aly said. "At our house, we usually share what gods are monkeying about with us today."

"Of course he never mentioned *me*," Kyprioth answered. "What sane man wants the people around him to know he's favored of a trickster? They might suspect that my favor causes certain interesting events in their lives, don't you think? Your father knows there's no point in mentioning something he can't change."

"I'll tell him you said so," replied Aly, her mind in a whirl. Her father would definitely have to explain *this* to her. She couldn't wait.

"Actually, you won't," said Kyprioth. His speech was clear, crisp, and fast, a promise of amusement in every inflection. It was the kind of voice that talked people into doing mad stunts. It made Aly very wary of him. "At least, not right away," he amended. "I have a small wager for you first. Play this out for me, and I'll deposit you at the cove at Pirate's Swoop. I'm the local sea god, among other things."

Aly raised an eyebrow. "Why should I dance to some trickster's tune?"

Kyprioth chuckled, a rich, warm sound. "Oh, my dear, I'm not *some* trickster," he informed her. "I'm *the* Trickster. Kyprioth is the name I have here in the Copper Isles, in addition to rule over our seas. Don't you even want to hear my wager?" He leaned close to Aly and whispered, "It's made to order for a girl with your skills."

Aly shrugged, hiding her sudden interest behind a mask of boredom. "I suppose I won't be rid of you until you tell me, so talk away."

"It's simple," he assured her. "Keep the children of this family alive through the end of summer. Do that, and I'll send you home as the gods travel. You'll be here one moment and there the next."

"And if I can't? If I lose?" Aly wanted to know.

"You'll serve me for an entire year," Kyprioth replied. "If you're still alive. I can't make any promises. If things go really badly, you might be killed by accident."

Aly twiddled her thumbs, pretending to ignore him. She wanted him to raise the stakes.

Kyprioth sighed. "I'll convince your father to let you be a field agent. I'm a god—I can do that."

"You can't force him," Aly said. She spoke from long experience with her father.

"No. But he'll pay attention if I tell him how good you are on your own," he explained. "I have a feeling you have a real knack for this. And I'll grant him a boon as well."

"I'm a slave," Aly reminded him. "These people won't listen to me."

"They will now." Kyprioth beamed at Aly. "That's why I needed my brother's seeming. He's telling the duke and duchess that he's chosen you, someone their enemies will overlook, as his messenger. That they will come to no harm if they listen to your advice. Sooner or later, of course, you'll have to prove to them you're worth listening to, but I'm sure you'll have plenty of chances for that. Have we a wager?"

Aly considered it, rubbing her hand over her short-cropped hair. From her true dream she knew Mother had already gone north for the summer's fighting, and making things right with her had been the only reason Aly was prepared to rush home. On one hand, the wager meant she would have to follow the Balitangs into exile. On the other hand, what better way to prove to Da that she could manage the work? Even if he wouldn't let her spy, he might attach her to the king or queen as a sort of bodyguard, to keep an eye on things. He'd know her ability if Aly showed him that she was able to keep a family in one piece when they were out of favor with a notoriously unstable king.

She might never get another chance like this. Her father would be hard put to argue with a god's assessment, especially if that god was the Trickster. Aly grinned. Even Da couldn't refuse her if she did it. He was very good about admitting when he was wrong. "We have a wager, then, under those terms," she told Kyprioth. "But I'll need help."

The god grabbed her stubbly head in both hands and kissed her forehead. Aly yelped: the kiss sent something like a shock through her. "You'll get it," Kyprioth said. "On Lombyn." With that he was gone.

If you've a story, make sure it's a whole one, with details close to hand. It's the difference between a successful lie and getting caught.

—*From* A Workbook for a Young Spy, *written and illustrated by Aly's father and given to her on her sixth birthday*

3

THE RAKA

The Long Strait and the Azure Sea

People out of favor with King Oron did not waste time in farewells. The king had slaughtered entire households, down to the last dog, once he decided he could not live with his fears. Two days after Aly entered into her wager with Kyprioth, the Balitangs loaded their belongings onto several cargo ships and prepared to set sail.

Only Prince Bronau came to see them off that humid morning. He kissed the duchess on both cheeks, embraced the duke, and kissed Lady Saraiyu's hand. Aly barely glimpsed this. Her new charges, Petranne and Elsren, did not care for ships, or the early hour, or Aly herself. Their governess and nursemaids had gone to other households along with seventy-four other servants and slaves. Winnamine assigned their care to Aly as the reason they had kept her with them. Neither the duke nor the duchess had summoned her to discuss the visitation from the god they believed to be Mithros. Instead they hid their thoughts behind polite, distant faces and told Ulasim that Aly would mind the little ones.

Aly hung on to Petranne and Elsren as they jerked and shrieked in her grip. At last she gave up trying to hear. She read the adults' lips, as she'd been taught by her father.

"I'll try to get word of events to you as often as possible," Bronau assured the older Balitangs. "The king's none too healthy. Things could change suddenly if he passes on. If Hazarin takes the throne, for instance."

"Don't speak of such things," Mequen told Bronau. "It could be taken for treason."

Winnamine rested a hand on the prince's arm. "*Try* to be careful, Bronau."

The prince grinned, then walked down the gangplank as the crew prepared to cast off. The Balitangs waved farewell. Bronau stood on the edge of the dock, watching as the ship weighed anchor.

"Come on, you raka dogs, put your backs into it!" yelled the luarin captain to his sailors. "'Less you want a touch of the whip to smarten you!" It was how many luarin in Rajmuat who were not part of the Balitangs' circle addressed their raka slaves and servants. Aly thought it was a foolish way to talk to someone who might be inspired to throw one over the rail into a shark-infested sea, but she would be the first to admit she did not have a conqueror's heart. She couldn't see who would profit by keeping the original owners of a country ground into the dirt.

Elsren broke out of Aly's hold and ran toward the rail. Still clinging to Petranne, Aly seized the boy by his shirt with her free hand and dragged him back. "I want Jafa!" wailed Elsren, tears running down his plump cheeks. Jafana had been his nursemaid. "I hate you!"

Aly sighed and wrapped an arm around him. "I know, and I'm sorry," she replied. "In your shoes, I'd hate me, too, but we're stuck with one another." She looked at Petranne. Tears rolled down the little girl's cheeks. "Sometimes being a noble isn't much fun, is it?" she asked. Petranne shook her head.

Aly glanced at Mequen and Winnamine. They waited at the rail, none of their feelings on display as the ship drew out into the harbor. As Elsren calmed, Aly studied the city, not having seen it when she first arrived. Rajmuat was splendid, full of peaked gates and three-level temples, each with a spiked tower thrust into the sky. White or rose pink walls contrasted with the dark green of the trees that lined its streets. Homes also sported peaked roofs and intricately carved eaves, those on wealthy houses traced in gold or silver.

Something else reflected the sun, too, pricking Aly's eyes with swords of light. She looked up. High above the city Stormwings circled like vultures over a carcass. Aly shivered. These part-human, part-metal immortals feasted on the rage, fear, and death spawned by human combat. Their wings, each metal feather shaped precisely like a bird's, were the source of the bright flashes of sun on steel.

"They always know." Winnamine spoke quietly. "The Stormwings—they always know when unrest is starting. How can they tell?"

Mequen put an arm around her shoulders. "We don't know if they do, my dear," he replied. "Maybe they just know that it's a sure bet in Rajmuat. There *will* be fighting in the streets, if he doesn't appoint an heir soon, or if something happens to whomever he appoints. We're going to be well out of it."

"We *hope* we're well out of it now," replied the duchess.

Aly knew she had a point. Sometimes King Oron did recover from his fears. Sometimes he didn't. Sometimes he got worse. If Kyprioth was dragging Aly into the Isles' affairs, they might well be growing.

At least the Balitangs wouldn't miss life at court. They occupied themselves with charity work, fashions, books, and music, not politics, court, or trade. They kept their own accounts and oversaw the work of the household. Aly suspected that they would settle quietly into rural life, given half a chance. If she was to win her wager, she had to ensure that they would get that chance, at least until the summer was over.

She wondered why a Great God would take such a brief interest in the family. In her experience, once a god took an interest in a mortal, that mortal was stuck with that god for life. Still, that wasn't Aly's problem right now. Safeguarding this family, without calling notice to herself, was her problem. If anyone were to find out that the daughter of the Tortallan king's Champion and his assistant spymaster was summering in the Copper Isles, she wouldn't live long enough to collect on that wager. The thought made her grin as she turned her face into the fresh sea breeze. At long last she had a real challenge, and she meant to enjoy every moment of it.

The captain never made good on his threats to smarten his raka seamen with his whip. The ship glided up the Long Strait. The warm, damp winds drove them gently north along the long, slender neck of water that separated Kypriang, the capital island, from Gempang Isle in the west. Dolphins, always a sign of good luck, sped alongside the vessel, watching its occupants with mischievous eyes and what looked like mocking smiles.

The Long Strait was another world compared to Rajmuat's crowded streets and busy docks. Limestone cliffs rose high on either side, threaded with greenery and falling streams, capped with emerald jungles that steamed as the day warmed up. Brightly colored birds soared to and fro, indifferent to the ships that ploughed the blue waters. From the Gempang jungles came the long, drawn-out hoots of the howler monkeys.

"Tell me a story," demanded Elsren after his afternoon nap.

"Yes, a story," Petranne insisted, sitting up against the rail with her legs crossed. "A *new* story. Jafa only ever tells the same ones."

"Did not," retorted her brother. Petranne stuck her tongue out at him.

Aly listened to the howler monkeys and smiled. She sat cross-legged in front of the two children, keeping one hand in Elsren's belt. She had spent the morning dragging him from under the crew's feet. "Once the most beautiful queen in all the world had a menagerie," she began, thinking wickedly how Aunt Thayet would screech if she could hear this story again. "In it were those self-same monkeys you hear all around us, the howlers. Now, the queen was often out and about, and the only things she liked better than coming home were her reunions with her beloved king, and an unbroken night's sleep." Softly she told them about menagerie keepers who sold places in the palace gardens near the queen's balcony the nights after her return, then roused the howler monkeys to break the silence with their loud, penetrating calls. Woken from her sleep, the hot-tempered queen would race onto her balcony, bow and arrows in hand, in an attempt to shoot the beasts no matter how dark the night. Those who watched from below rejoiced in the fact that their queen slept without a nightgown.

"Of course, the king's spymaster put a stop to it, once he knew," Aly concluded seriously. "He made the keepers use the money they'd made to build another enclosure for the howlers, where they wouldn't disturb the queen. But there are still men who will swear by every god you know that they truly have the most beautiful queen in all the world."

Petranne and Elsren stared back at Aly soberly. Finally Elsren said, "That one was new. Tell another!"

"Yes, another!" pleaded his sister. "That was a good one!"

"You're from Tortall, aren't you?"

Aly turned to look for the source of the new voice. The older girls, Saraiyu and Dovasary, stood nearby, listening as Sarai fanned herself. There was no way for Aly to read what they thought in their level eyes or polite faces. It occurred to her that, being half-raka, these girls must have learned to hide their feelings well. They would have heard the people of Rajmuat and the rest of the Isles speak with careless cruelty of their mother's people. They may even have heard some of that cruelty from nobles of their own class.

Dovasary continued, "Your Kyprish is very good—you barely have an accent."

"Thank you, your ladyship," Aly replied meekly. She knew her accent was not Tortallan. Her teachers had come from Imahyn Isle and had pronounced her Kyprish as perfect. The Balitangs spoke with a Rajmuat accent.

"My sister asked you a question," Saraiyu said imperiously. "Are you from Tortall?"

Aly bowed her head, every inch of her the perfect servant. "Yes, your ladyship."

Dovasary plopped herself down beside Elsren and pulled him onto her lap. Aly disentangled her fingers from his belt. "Then you know stories of the King's Champion there, the one they call the Lioness!" she said eagerly. For the first time since Aly had seen her, the younger girl's eyes were alive with interest. "Tell us some!"

"Is she really ten feet tall?" asked Petranne.

Saraiyu settled neatly beside Aly, disposing her cotton skirts perfectly. Waving her fan, she asked, "Is the Lioness as good with a sword as they say? The duchess made me stop my sword lessons." Her voice turned frosty as she spoke of her stepmother. "She said they were unladylike."

Aly scratched her head to cover her confusion. Can I talk of Mother as if I'd never seen her in my life? she wondered. No—as if I'd seen her once or twice, at a distance. They'll expect that. When Chenaol and Ulasim had first brought her to Balitang House, the steward had questioned her about her origins. Aly had claimed then that she'd been a merchant's daughter and a maid at Fief Tameran, south of Pirate's Swoop. The household there had been close to the Grand Progress several years ago. Everyone would have turned out to see the monarchs, the prince and princess, and the King's Champion ride by.

Now she folded her hands in her lap. "The Lioness is really that good with a sword, your ladyship," she replied to Sarai, this time acting the role of a polite servant. "King's Champion isn't a title for decoration. Every time a noble demands a challenge to settle a matter of law, the Champion must fight and win for the Crown."

"What happens when she loses?" asked Petranne.

Aly looked at the child, startled. "She doesn't."

"But everybody loses sometime," Sarai told Aly.

"Not the Lioness," Aly said, her mind scrambling. Mother lose? How could she? "Not since she's been Champion, that I know of." Remember, you only know the stories, she ordered herself.

"She must have lost sometimes, when she was training, maybe even when she first got her shield," Dovasary pointed out. "And Tortall's at war—she could be killed in that."

Aly's pulse raced. She fought to sound natural, to keep from showing her distress at the idea. "Oh, well, training and that, everyone loses," she said with a shrug when she was sure of her control. "But the war's a year old already, and the Lioness is hale enough. She visited her home just before I was taken." If Alanna was killed in the fighting this year, she would die without Aly having said goodbye.

"Tell us," begged Saraiyu, leaning forward, her dark eyes eager. "Tell us how she came to be the Champion. Tell us how she found the Dominion Jewel. Tell us *everything*."

Aly only had time to tell them the story of how the Lioness had brought the Dominion Jewel home to her king. Then Duchess Winnamine declared it was time for the children to study. Even Elsren had lessons in counting to do. Aly remained topside, relieved of her duties for the time being. She stood at the rail, enjoying the calls of colorful birds, the clear blue water under the ship's prow, and the sheer loveliness of the spring day.

She registered movement along the cliff tops on either side of the strait. Aly sharpened her Sight for a good look. Her fingers clenched on the rail as she realized that she saw hundreds of copper-skinned raka, men and women alike, dressed in the traditional wrapped jacket or round-collared tunic, and the tied skirtlike wrap called a sarong. Some wore garments that were richly decorated and jeweled, with more jewelry on their fingers and at their throats. Others wore plain colors with embroidery and strings of beads for ornament.

The women drew their straight black hair away from their faces in a double-domed style, much like that of Yamani women, while the men wore head-bands, turbans, or hats. The raka groups were of all ages, from the smallest infants to the oldest adults. They stood in silence, as far as Aly could tell, watching as the Balitang vessel passed by.

She turned to look back down the strait, to check whether the natives watched all shipping out here. Two vessels earlier had overtaken the three that carried the duke's household. No other ships followed in their wake, and nowhere did she see people on the cliffs behind them. The raka left as soon as the duke's ship drew out of easy view.

She tugged at a sailor's arm as he coiled rope on the deck. "Do they always do that?" she asked, pointing at their audience. "Come and see boats go by? They don't look like they mean to attack."

The half-raka man looked at her, then at the cliffs. "No," he said quietly, "they do not do that. They prefer to remain unseen when the luarin pass." He touched Aly's slave collar. "Do not draw attention to it," he said, nodding toward the duke and duchess, who sat at a small table in the bow playing chess. "The luarin get uneasy when the raka do things they don't understand."

I want to understand. Aly thought it, but she did not say it. She doubted that the sailor would confide in her. One thing seemed obvious: something about these ships drew the interest of many people on the two islands. The raka faces, when she used her magical Sight to better examine them, were expectant and eager. The sailor had told her the watchers were not typical. Something about the duke's party drew their attention.

His servants? Aly wondered, drumming her fingers on her thigh as she turned the matter over in her mind. Or his oldest daughters? Mequen was a Rittevon, a lesser one, but still of the line of the luarin conquerors.

Belowdecks she heard Elsren yell, "I want *up!*" Aly's rest time was over.

Before she fetched the child, Aly took one more look at the cliffs. The raka they had passed were leaving, returning to their jungle towns and their luarin masters' estates.

That night after supper the duke and duchess read to their younger children from a book of raka myths. Aly returned to the ship's rail to watch the cliffs around their anchorage, a small cove on Kypriang's lush western shore. The night, warm and damp, folded around her like a blanket. With her magical vision she didn't need light to see the raka, standing or seated on rocks that overlooked the cove. It seemed they required no light, either. Lamps burned only aboard the trio of ships that rocked on the gentle waters. The moon had just begun to show its rim over the mountains that formed Kypriang Isle's spine.

"They're our people, too." Twelve-year-old Dovasary rested her hands on the rail as she came to stand beside Aly. She spoke in Common, not Kyprish.

"Our mother—Sarai's and mine—was a raka. Sarugani of Temaida. Her family was of the older nobility, from before the luarin came, but they don't have a title higher than baron now."

"They're lucky to have that much. None of our raka family talks about who they were or what they did before the invasion," Saraiyu remarked quietly. She came to lean on the rail on Aly's other side. "They must have seen their friends being slaughtered or sold. They would have beggared themselves with the conquest taxes rather than suffer the same fate."

"You're half luarin yourself," replied Aly, her voice idle, her attention apparently on the shoreline. "Begging your ladyship's pardon."

"That would be the half that cousin Oron seems determined to murder or disgrace," Sarai pointed out. "Even a madman should have more care for his own blood kin, particularly given the nest of vipers at court."

Aly smoothed a hand over the rail. "Forgive me for saying it, but your ladyship comes close to treasonous talk," she murmured. "I'd as soon be with the part of the family that's exiled but alive."

"You won't betray us," Saraiyu replied casually. "I don't know about Tortall, but here the entire household is executed along with the suspected traitor. Then they sell the one who reported their masters, if they're known, to Carthak."

"Ouch," said Aly, meaning it. "That's not the way to create support among the lower classes."

"The thinking is that a servant of traitors who turns the traitors in is doubly treasonous, to her master as well as the king," Dovasary explained. "They like to nip that sort of thing in the bud."

Sarai turned to face east, watching the moon rise, leaning back on the rail with her elbows and rump. The torchlight slid along her long, barely hooked nose and over a full, sensual lower lip, then flickered along the curved lines shaped by her plain pink luarin-style gown. It lent sparkle to her brown eyes and caressed her perfectly arched brows and high cheekbones.

"Is it so hard, being half raka?" Aly wanted to know. "All Rajmuat—even a fresh-caught luarin slave like me—knows the lady Saraiyu is considered one of the beauties of the city."

Sarai's smile was crooked. "By men, and the raka nobility, and some of the luarin houses, yes, I suppose." She looked at her sister. "It's not vanity, Dove. I can count as well as the next person."

Dove shrugged. "I didn't utter a word."

Sarai made a noise that in a less attractive girl would have been labeled a snort. "And yet, when it comes to marriage, it's amazing how many luarin families discover marriages that were arranged when their sons were in the cradle. Marriages their young men had never *heard* of until then. Particularly the higher-ranking luarin nobles. I can't help but notice how many young men give way when they learn their mothers don't care for the color of the future bride's skin, however beautiful she may be."

Dove sighed. "And the raka nobles are wary around us because we've got Rittevon blood in our veins. They don't want to lose their sons the next time the king thinks his relatives are plotting against him."

"Dovasary!" whispered Sarai, shocked.

The younger girl leaned around Aly to look at her sister. "I have ears, Sarai, and people hardly ever notice me. I know what I hear. The raka don't want to risk the Rittevon insanity for their grandchildren."

Aly grimaced. She'd once overheard one of Tortall's young knights, a Bazhir, tell Grandfather Myles, "Oh, I'm considered wonderful when it comes to letting and losing blood for the Crown. But marriage? Even jumped-up merchants who weren't barons a generation ago won't let their daughters marry a Bazhir, whatever their wealth and standing."

I suppose I'd best remember what the Bazhir at home endure, she thought, before I go looking down my nose at the luarin. You really should have a clean house at home before you start picking at the way your neighbor does the dusting.

"What does a slave know of treason and kings anyway?" asked Dove. Her dark eyes were now intent on Aly's face.

Aly shrugged. "I was a maid in a nobleman's castle when I was taken," she replied. "*My* ears are as good as anyone's."

"I don't see how any Tortallan girl would want to be a maid, not with all the choices you have, compared to us," Sarai remarked. "If I lived there, I'd join the Queen's Riders, and learn to ride and use a sword and bow like they do. Or maybe even become a knight like the Lady Knight Keladry. The raka ladies of old knew how to fight. In the last great battle against the luarin, on the Plain of Sorrows, a third of the Kyprin warriors were female."

"And the whole army got thrashed," Dove reminded her sister mercilessly. "The conquerors had more battle mages, and more catapults, and ballistas, and liquid fire. It didn't matter how many women fought with the raka that day. They died just as easily as the men."

"You're so *prosaic*, Dove. Oh, look, the raka." Sarai pointed to the rocks about the cove. The moon was above the mountains now, a huge pearl in the indigo sky. By its light the people on the cliffs were clearly visible. "They've been doing that all day."

"Sarai?" called Winnamine. "Dove? It's time to sleep."

The two girls rolled their eyes at one another. "No late nights for us," Sarai remarked drily. They went below.

Aly turned back to watch the sea by moonlight. The older Balitang girls struck her as being much like falcons, always hooded and tethered, not able to hunt as their hearts desired. It was such a waste, keeping fiery girls like this in the background, not letting them forge their own path in the world. She'd like to see what these two would accomplish.

Two mornings later their ships emerged from the Long Strait into the Azure Sea, the body of water that lay between Imahyn and Lombyn Isles. Aly grinned as the captain jubilantly announced that the sea god Kyprioth was smiling on their voyage. Apparently this was the quickest, smoothest passage of the strait the captain had ever made. Duke Mequen finally stopped the man's recital of how unpredictable the passage could be, a tale of crosscurrents and wind gusts, with a reminder that he might annoy the god by too frequently mentioning his name.

Aly wasn't sure how easily annoyed Kyprioth was, but she was distracted from her thoughts as the Azure Sea emerged from its veil of morning fog. Its bright blue waters were clear. Vividly colored fish darted through its depths, circling a population of sea turtles, dolphins, and the occasional eel. The sun burnished the tops of the waves to the color of gold.

Elsren leaned precariously over the rail. "Gull boats!" he cried. Aly seized his luarin-style tunic, securing her adventurous charge. A multitude of boats was gliding toward them from Imahyn, Ikang, and Kypriang Isles. They were as colorful as the fish, with brightly colored sails, prows and sterns fashioned in long, pointed curves, and every inch of outer hull decorated and painted. Raka sailors, both men and women, dressed in no more than vivid sashes and sarongs, steered the graceful craft as they stared at the Balitang ships.

"Have you ever seen anything like this?" Mequen asked the captain.

"Never," the man replied, sweating. "*Never.* And I grew up on the Azure Sea."

"They're unarmed," Winnamine commented. She had a spyglass raised to her eye. "I don't see a weapon anywhere."

As the Balitang ships sailed north, the fleet of colorful boats parted before them. Elsren and Petranne clamored for a place in the bow. With Aly to keep them from falling overboard, they waved gleefully at the raka and loudly admired the rainbow bevy of ships. With the dignity suited to their more advanced years, Sarai and Dove came forward to stand with Petranne and Elsren, watching as their mother's people approached.

Aly sharpened her Sight until she could see the raka's faces. The sailors stiffened when the older girls showed themselves; some pointed to them. The raka flotilla swerved, its ships forming two polite lines. Then, one by one, the ships glided past the Balitang family's ship, one on either side of their bow. The raka merely glanced at the three luarin faces—Aly's, Petranne's, Elsren's— then fixed on Sarai's and Dove's light brown ones.

It's not us who brought the raka out, Aly thought. It's Sarai and Dove. The two half-raka girls. The two girls whose mother came from an old noble house—a *raka* noble house.

"If you are wise, you will say nothing of this to anyone," Winnamine said from behind them, her melodic voice soft. "Ever. Do you all understand? The king would not like to hear that we drew so much attention from the raka."

Sarai shrugged. "Nobody cares what the raka do," she replied, gazing at the people who sailed by. "Especially not the king."

"You never know who is watching," persisted Winnamine. "Don't encourage them. Go below."

"When Papa says." Dove didn't even look at her stepmother.

Aly knew Winnamine was right. It seemed that she could start to cover her part of Kyprioth's wager here and now.

"My ladies, my apologies, but this scares me," she whispered, the picture of an alarmed slave. "I've not been here long, but, well, back home there's stories of your king. This could get your house and those raka in trouble with him. We'd all pay for that, in blood, most like."

Sarai glanced at Aly, confused. Aly looked at her and shrugged, suggesting that it was just her opinion.

Dove sighed. She grabbed Sarai's hand and towed her older sister below.

"Well done," murmured the duchess.

Aly looked up three inches into the duchess's face. "The wisdom of what you said was just a little slow in reaching their brains," she offered.

"We both know it was the suggested threat to the raka that convinced them," replied Winnamine. She rubbed her temples. "They liked me well enough when I married their father, but now they're old enough to be difficult, just because I tell them things they don't wish to hear."

Aly thought of her own mother and winced inwardly. "It's hard, living in the shadow of a respected woman," she told the duchess.

Winnamine looked at her sharply. "Very wise, for a girl Sarai's age. Perhaps the One who appeared when the matcher looked you over chose well," she said, referring to the god's visit in terms that Petranne and Elsren wouldn't understand. "He said you were clear-sighted, and would see a way for us out of all this."

"I'm sure I won't need to do any such thing," Aly replied cheerfully. "You'll hardly know I'm here."

Winnamine shook her head with a rueful smile, then watched the raka craft that continued to sail by. After a moment she returned to Mequen. Tired of the spectacle, Petranne and Elsren followed her.

Aly remained in the bow, leaning on the rail. It was embarrassing to think that rather than truly expressing her independence, she had been difficult with her mother just for the sake of being difficult, because she was sixteen and stubborn.

That night they anchored in the harbor at Ambririp, off the northeast point of Imahyn Isle. The family slept ashore at a proper inn. Mequen's and

Winnamine's servants took care of the younger children. Aly remained with the rest of the household, the servants, slaves, and men-at-arms. They set up a communal supper on the beach near the dock where their ships were anchored.

Chenaol took command of the meal. True to what she'd told Aly about staying with Sarai and Dove, the raka woman had turned down other nobles' offers of higher pay and more leisure time. Now she sent Ulasim and two other men to the Ambririp market with a list. Three more servants dug a fire pit in the sand and hung a metal cookpot over it from an iron tripod. Once the men returned with Chenaol's ingredients, she set to work, shredding a chicken and cooking it in water, cutting up hard-boiled eggs as the meat simmered. One of the cookmaids chopped shallots, spring onions, garlic, and chilies. Another ground them into paste along with cut ginger, lemongrass, and lime juice. Once the broth was ready, everything went into it, including bean sprouts and bean-flour noodles.

Aly refused the hot sauce they offered her when her bowl was filled. She had tried it once in Rajmuat, at her first meal among the Balitang staff. They had roared with laughter as she gulped water to put out the fire in her nose and throat before finally showing her that yogurt or bread worked better to ease the bite. She'd laughed, too, once she doused the fire. Even now she grinned as they teased her about picking out the visible pieces of chili pepper. Finishing the contents of her bowl, Aly thought that perhaps she was getting used to Isles cooking. This dish made her eat only twice as much yogurt and bread as the raka, instead of her usual four times that amount.

Afterward some maids washed up. Everyone gathered around the fire, luarin, part-raka, and raka alike. Back in Rajmuat the free servants and the men-at-arms each had their own hall. They didn't mingle with the slaves. Here, Aly saw, they felt too lonely and out of place to separate into their usual groups. A leather bottle was passed from one person to the next as each took a large drink of its contents. When it came to Aly, she sniffed, caught the unmistakable odor of liquor, smiled, and handed it on.

"That's arak, girl," Chenaol said comfortably, relaxing against a sack of rice next to Aly. "Distilled palm sap wine. It's good for you. Warm your belly, lighten your burdens."

Aly smiled. "But my belly's already far too warm from supper," she joked. "At this rate, I'll open my mouth one day and burn the trees down." That drew a laugh from the others.

Chenaol shrugged. "More for me, then," she said, and took a healthy gulp.

The skin made two more rounds of the household. The men and women from Rajmuat were homesick, though most agreed that life with the Balitangs was better than that with other noble households. Aly was startled to learn that many of the servants, including Ulasim, and a handful of men-at-arms were actually from the Tanair lands on Lombyn. This would be their first return home since the death of the first duchess, Sarugani.

At Balitang House the chores had been unending, and most of the staff had been too exhausted to talk at the end of the day. If they did talk, it wasn't to the new, junior slave. Here Aly was one of them. Now she got the worm's-eye view of the Rittevon court, told by those around her after they had gossiped with Rajmuat's other servants and slaves.

They were united in their belief that King Oron would die soon. The old man had been failing in health and mind over the last five years. Hazarin, the sole remaining child of King Oron's first marriage, was the rakas' bet to inherit the throne. They thought Hazarin was as peculiar in his ways as his father, with an affection for huge meals and strange drugs. His next relative was his half sister, Princess Imajane, but under the luarin law no woman could succeed to the throne. Last of all there was Dunevon, born the same year as Elsren, child of the king's third wife.

"Oron's wives don't seem very lucky," Aly remarked. The people around her burst into laughter.

"You're right enough there," the head footman, Ulasim, replied with a grin. He was in his forties, a hard-muscled raka with direct brown eyes, black hair pulled back in a horsetail, a mustache, and a chin beard. His nose had met someone's fist, elbow, or knee far more often than Aly's had. He was a hard man, but fair, and the household respected him. He told Aly, "See, His Majesty starts to think his wives have lovers, and, well . . ." He drew his thumb across his throat.

"Maybe Lombyn's best for us," remarked one woman, her face shadowed.

"You haven't been there," Ulasim informed her. "It gets *cold* on the Tanair plateau. No jungle, the birds all drab little things . . ."

"There's condors," argued a hostler. "And crows."

"And *big* drab birds," retorted Ulasim. "It's in the middle of nowhere, not a town worthy of the name for miles. I was born on those lands. I know."

"Then why did you come?" demanded a maid. "You had plenty of offers to serve elsewhere."

Ulasim looked into the fire, his face somber. Finally he said quietly, "The duke's the best man I've ever served. I came to his house with Duchess Sarugani, and I never regretted it. These are good people. I won't turn my back on them." He looked around the circle, meeting everyone's eyes. He stopped at Aly. "Maybe you think we'll be left in peace out there. I don't. They'll need all the friends they can get." He took another drink of arak.

He'd be a good man to have on my side, Aly thought. If I can get him there without him thinking I'm up to something. That will be interesting.

She turned to Chenaol. "Did *you* know the first duchess?" she asked. Chenaol had the same Lombyn accent, dulled by years in Rajmuat, as Ulasim.

Chuckles sounded around the fire. "She was a handful," Chenaol admitted. "I worked for her relatives, House Temaida—that'd be the lesser nobility, the raka, Aly. Anyway, Sarugani came down from Lombyn and stayed with us when she was presented to the nobility. I was assistant cook for the Temaidas then. We got friendly because she liked my herb garden. I asked to go with her when she married, and the family agreed. She was spirited, always up to something. She had half the luarin nobles as well as the raka chasing her. And the present duchess, she and Sarugani were like sisters."

"You'd never know they were raka and luarin, they were that close," someone murmured. "Her Grace doesn't care what color your skin is."

"Now, Sarugani was fearless in the saddle." The head hostler, Lokeij, was present, a white-haired old raka slave everyone knew would never be sold. The family hadn't even suggested that he be put up for sale. "Ride anything in the stable, broken in or no. She made those luarin biddies cackle, riding in breeches like a proper woman of the raka."

"It was her riding that did her in," Ulasim went on. "Lady Dove was five, or a bit short of that, and Lady Sarai was nine. The duchess went hunting one day with friends. The horse failed in a jump—broke her neck and the beast's legs. My lord was nearly a ghost for long after. We looked after him and the young ladies till his aunt Nuritin moved in. *She* woke him up."

"Gave him an earful, told him he was a disgrace," said the raka healer Rihani with a grin. "Told him he was neglecting the girls and his house, he'd no male heir, and he'd let himself go to seed. Hounded him until he started to live again. Convinced him he'd best marry, since he wasn't getting any younger and he'd no son and all. That's when he realized what a treasure Lady Winnamine was."

"*Luarin,*" said Lokeij, shaking his head. "Always getting themselves into this male heir mess. We raka know better. It isn't the equipment the clan chief's got, it's up here." He tapped his forehead. "The old king wouldn't be such a fool if he broke with luarin custom and made Lady Imajane his heir. *She'd* get the country in order."

"Hush!" someone whispered. Aly saw Lokeij jerk, as if he'd just taken an elbow in the ribs. "It's treason to talk so—a whipping at the very least!"

"So all those raka turned out to see Sarugani's girls." Aly used a tone that implied she didn't believe what she was saying. She wanted to steer the talk away from possible treason, as well as learn a little more about the family. "Is that it? Seems to me they were more interested in how beautiful Lady Sarai is. How important was her mother, anyway?"

The raka present exchanged glances. Finally Ulasim said quietly, "She was just from an old raka family, that's all. Personally, I think these raka knew of the duke's disgrace. How often will they see anyone who isn't raka being sent into exile? He is related to the king, after all."

Aly could have pointed out that other luarin nobles must have gone into exile, but her instincts told her it was time to shut up. It was always difficult to probe for information gently, without causing others to think she might know more than was safe.

Ulasim got to his feet as nimbly as if he'd never touched the arak. "I don't know about you, but we sail at dawn, and I'd like a proper sleep."

Aly sighed to herself. She would have to teach these people better ways to steer someone away from a dangerous line of thought. Ulasim might as well have shouted that she'd touched on a secret.

The footman's words signaled the other servants and slaves. They, too, rose and went to their hammocks aboard the different ships.

As Aly helped Chenaol carry the cooking tools back aboard ship, the cook told her, "Free raka—the ones who don't work for the luarin—keep their reasons to themselves. They don't trust us city folk, and we fear them. Every time they revolt, and they do, now and then, the luarin usually execute all the raka they can catch. That would include us. So people get jumpy when you ask too many questions."

"You don't keep any ties with your families?" Aly asked as she stowed the last of the herbs. She turned to look Chenaol in the face. The woman blinked. Liar's sign, thought Aly. That's what Da calls it when someone blinks during questioning.

"Seldom," Chenaol replied, blinking again. "Mostly we keep to our city family. Off to bed with you, then."

Aly obeyed, though it took some time for her to sleep. She was going through her memory, trying to see if she had ever known the proportion of Copper Isle raka to the luarin. And what secret was so important that even slaves and servants with drink in them wouldn't hint at it?

You do your bit, and then you get to pretend to be part of the scenery. You sit and you sweat and you hope that all those who are paid to go out and show their faces and do the bloody work don't foul everything up. The waiting for others to act on your information will give you the belly gripes, but that's what agents do. And I advise you not to pray as you wait. You don't know who will answer, times like that.

—*From* A Workbook for a Young Spy

4

THE ROAD

Lombyn Island, Tanair Castle and village

They set sail once more at dawn, baking quietly in a sudden burst of early summer. By midmorning Lombyn was in view, an island nearly as long and wide as Gempang, but far more mountainous, with a ribbon of green jungle at the mountains' feet, pine forest above, and then bare rock. Somewhere behind those granite barriers, Aly knew, was the Tanair estate, part of Sarugani's dowry and Sarai's inheritance. It was as safe as any of the Balitang holdings, since it belonged to Sarai and not Mequen, which made it less vulnerable to seizure by the king. As a refuge, it might just work, Aly thought.

Their ships were closing on Dimari's harbor when Aly noticed movement in the skies. Winged horses rode the columns of warm air that rose along the cliffs of Lombyn, their immense, batlike wings outstretched, their manes and tails fluttering as they climbed and descended. Aly adjusted her Sight. Above the jungles and mountains she saw even more of the great creatures, all colors of horse from solid black to solid white, roan, buckskin, bay, chestnut, piebald, odd-colored, flea-bitten, dapple, a universe of horsedom in the air of Lombyn. She gasped in awe, thrilled to see these great immortals playing in midair. Did Aunt Daine know there were so many in the Isles? Winged horses were rare in Tortall. Aly had seen a handful of the smallest kinds, no bigger than starlings, and only one of these big creatures. Hurroks, the predatory fanged and clawed variation of this breed of immortal, they had aplenty, but their milder cousins were scarce.

"In the old times, the *kudarung,* what you would call winged horses, nested in all of our Isles." Ulasim, dressed for the day in a sleeveless cotton tunic and breeches, had come to lean on the rail next to her. He squinted up at the fliers, a hint of a smile on his face. "They are sacred to the raka, the sign of our royal house, and its messengers. Then foreign mages banished the kudarung to the gods' home with the other immortals, without asking our thoughts on the matter. They left us only songs and paintings to remind us of their beauty. Kudarung are found in all sizes. Those are just the biggest of them."

"I'd heard they are different sizes," Aly murmured, entranced. "How prideful of those mages, to banish them without asking you." She remembered something she'd read in some of her father's reports. "But they're back now," she pointed out, her tone one of harmless interest. "So do they serve the Rittevon kings? I mean, you said they were royal messengers."

The smile Ulasim had brought to the rail vanished. His mouth flattened into a tight line. At last he leaned over the rail and spat into the water. "You speak lightly of serious things, Aly. Five of the kudarung were captured by Crown mages and forced to breed. So yes, the luarin king has kudarung as messengers, but they did not come freely to him, as they did to our queens." He turned to Aly, his brown eyes sharp as they rested on her face. "There will be more raka than luarin, in the Lombyn highlands," he said. "You should speak more carefully there. None of the raka are so tame as we let the luarin believe." He turned and went below, leaving Aly to consider what he had said.

They docked in Dimari, Lombyn's main port, around noon. Once again the family and a handful of body servants went to an inn to rest. The slaves and servants unloaded possessions from the ships, then packed them in wagons purchased by servants who had left for Dimari the day the Balitangs knew they were going into exile. Some wagons were already loaded with foodstuffs. Near them the servants had penned or cooped domestic animals. The duke had planned ahead, Chenaol told Veron, the luarin who commanded the household men-at-arms. Life was harder on the plateau where Tanair stood, the crops less plentiful. The duke had purchased supplies in advance, to keep the family and their attendants from placing a burden on the local folk. One of the island's merchant caravans had already been engaged to carry extra supplies in when they made their summer rounds. Not only would the family not create a burden for the people who had farmed Tanair for centuries, but they meant to expand what was grown and herded to the benefit of everyone.

"What *is* Tanair, exactly?" Aly asked the cook as she struggled to push a crate onto a wagon of kitchen supplies. "I mean, I know it's a fiefdom, but no one's said if there's a town anywhere near, or a river . . ."

"Tanair Castle is a tower with outbuildings," Chenaol replied with grim good humor. "Inner wall, outer wall. Then there's the village around it. Inti and Pohon are two other villages on the plateau. There's some luarin blood in the Tanair folk and some in Inti, which stands on the road leading to the western ocean. There's no luarin blood in Pohon. It used to be that any part-luarin who wandered into Pohon never wandered out, so the luarin stay away. Word gets around."

"How charming," Aly murmured.

Chenaol shrugged, her dark eyes twinkling in their folds of flesh. "Pohon folk are a righteous lot—or maybe *destructive*'s a better word. They're so cut off up there that they don't realize the luarin are here to stay, and breed. Maybe when they've had the chance to meet our ladies, they'll change their—Oh, curse it, those idiots will smash my peppers, mauling them about that way. You there!" she yelled to two dockhands as they slung baskets into a wagon. "Those aren't hay bales!"

Interesting, Aly thought as she continued to load the kitchen wagon. Chenaol had almost let something important slip. Why would the Pohon folk change their minds about luarin when they met "the ladies"? What about Sarai and Dove would change minds, and why did the cook want the Pohon minds changed?

Aly felt as if she was reading a book from which every second page was missing. She needed to learn more about the raka and their politics.

The next morning masters, servants, men-at-arms, slaves, and animals set out from Dimari, bound for the Turnshe Mountains, which formed Tanair's eastern border. On the first day they rode through lush, settled lands owned by luarin and farmed by raka. The people labored in the sun and heat, men and women alike wearing only a tied sarong tucked up to keep them out of the mud. This was one of the most fertile parts of the Isles. Everywhere that Ali looked she saw rice paddies, the plants covering the brown water in which they were planted in a green mist. They also passed coconut and bamboo planta- tions. Struggling to keep Elsren and Petranne from falling out of the covered, padded wagon where they would spend the rest of their trip, Aly did not envy the raka and part-raka who labored everywhere. When overseers descended on the slaves with whips raised, Aly had to look away. Without the Balitangs, she might have been one of those slaves, laboring in filth and being punished if she displeased a man with a whip.

This was the way most of the world lived, on slave labor. Tortall didn't en- courage it, any more than Tusaine, Galla, and Tyra did, but some people in those countries did own slaves. Everyone ignored the working slave popula- tions of the great farms of Maren. Aly just wasn't used to it. To her the slaves looked very like the convict gangs who labored on Tortall's roads and in its quarries and mines. At least those people had committed crimes to get a sen- tence of hard labor.

Overseers or no, when the Balitang wagons passed the farms, the raka straightened to watch them pass. Dark-skinned full-bloods or varying, light- skinned mixed-bloods, all shaded their eyes and looked on in silence as the wagons rattled by. Free raka, not wearing slave collars, dressed in colorful sarongs and light tops, stood by the road to see them. There they remained as the caravan, encircled by Veron's twenty men-at-arms, passed by in all its clatter. Others watched in the villages, from trees and upper-story windows of houses, on bridges and on rocks in the rivers. None of them said a word. All returned to their tasks as the last goat and man-at-arms went by.

Aly itched to question them but, trapped in the wagon with Elsren, Petranne, the duchess's maid, Pembery, and the house's mildly Gifted healer, Rihani, she had to accept it as an itch she couldn't scratch. That vexed her. Grandfather Myles always said it was impossible to have too much information. Aly agreed from the bottom of her heart as she watched those stony, copper-skinned faces. She would not sleep easily until she knew what was on the raka's minds.

They spent the night at a village inn and set out once more at dawn that day and the next. On their third day out of Dimari the road entered dense jungle. It was like being enfolded in a vast, warm, damp woolen cloak under the trees. The ground actually steamed in the early morning as the land gave up moisture under the warming sun. Here the raka appeared at the head of turnoffs that led to their villages. The deeper into the jungle they went, the fewer raka men wore sarongs or shirts in the heat. Many wore only a loincloth; they carried farm and woodland tools or hunting spears.

The men-at-arms rode closer to the wagons, but Aly saw no hostility on those raka faces. None of the onlookers so much as moved when they passed. What draws them to stare at Dove and Sarai? she wondered endlessly, until she wished she could just yank the questions out of her head and bury them under a rock. If the raka among the duke's people knew, they were not saying. She ought to know: she took every opportunity to drift near them when they weren't aware of her, listening in on their conversations. Many were as spooked by the local raka as Aly. None would speculate on what made them flock to view the Balitangs.

With the sun directly overhead they stopped on the road for a cold lunch of bread, dates, and sticky rice dumplings stuffed with beef and steamed in banana leaves. Aly expected Elsren and Petranne to complain at the rough fare, but they regarded the food and life in the wagons as an adventure. Elsren promised that as long as Aly produced new stories, he and his sister would behave.

"You have a happy nature," Aly told them as she cleaned Petranne up after lunch.

The four-year-old beamed at her. "I'm having fun," she informed Aly. "Aren't you having fun?"

Aly grinned at the girl. "Actually, now that you mention it, yes, I am. I've never seen jungle before."

"We have lots," Petranne explained as Aly scrubbed Elsren's upturned face. "There's hundreds and hundreds of islands, and they *all* have jungles on them."

"And have you seen them all?" Aly teased. She had spoken only half the truth to Petranne. The jungle, with its myriad flowers, trees, vines, and birds, was a gorgeous place, even if it was so humid it was hard to breathe. Aly could look at such beauty all day, except that she also knew the dangers of such thickly wooded ground. Jungles—any forest, for that matter—limited her field of vision. They offered outlaws too many opportunities for mischief. The fact that the raka could be so quiet in their movements, never giving away their presence until the Balitangs rounded a bend in the road and saw them, made Aly's nerves fizz with alertness. One of these times the raka around the bend might not be so friendly.

After lunch the raka witnesses vanished. Aly discovered she disliked that even more than she disliked having scores of raka silently watch the Balitangs. Their caravan passed a number of openings where roads and trails led away from their road, but they saw no one. As far as Aly knew, the jungle raka might be up to any unpleasant thing.

Their caravan traveled about ten miles before a horse on the lead wagon picked up a stone in her hoof. Mequen commanded their group to halt, which for Aly meant permission to climb out and look around. She stretched as she hobbled down the line of wagons and animals. Her entire body felt cramped. Not only had Petranne, Elsren, Pembery, and Rihani decided to stretch out for a nap, but Dove and Sarai had joined them, filling the wagon bed as full as it could get.

The kinks worked from her back, Aly observed the jungle, thinking. Something wasn't right. This was more than the absence of raka watchers. What was it? She knelt, pretending to tie a sandal lace, as she examined their surroundings.

When in doubt, her mother had said during hunts and rides through bandit country, use your ears. Aly used hers. Leaf movement: some, in a slight breeze. Tree movement: no, the breeze wasn't strong enough. Moving water: the burble of the stream along the right side of the road. Feet in leaves: a couple of the men-at-arms crouched by the stream for a drink of water.

She heard no animals. Where were the calls of howler monkeys and the chatter of parrots? Where were the rustlings of mice and shrews in the leaf clutter? The jungle should have been alive with wildlife sounds. The hair at the back of her neck prickled. Something was very wrong. The raka who had vanished from the roadsides knew it, and now she did, too.

Aly looked up and down the length of the train. She didn't want to go shrieking to the duke and duchess. They would listen, but she would also draw the attention of the other servants and slaves, and she had been bred from the cradle not to draw attention. She needed to encourage someone else to voice concern at the silence.

At the back of the train, where the cows walked on tethers, five men-at-arms, some part raka, one full raka, had clustered to talk. There was tension in every line of their bodies. They would do.

Aly strolled up to them. "I know I'm new here," she began. The five men turned to stare at her. She smiled at them shyly. "It's just, you know, I'm a country girl at home, and my old dad taught me a few things."

The one named Fesgao, Veron's second-in-command and a pure-blood raka, raised angled brows. His ebony eyes were calm and level. His nose followed a straight line down from his forehead; he had high cheekbones and a square chin. Dressed in Balitang tunic and breeches, he was solidly muscled. His sword and dagger were plain but of good-quality steel. Aly guessed him to be thirty or so, younger than Ulasim and more reserved than the head footman. "And why should we be interested in what your father taught to you, little girl?" he inquired.

"Because Da taught me the same thing you have noticed," she said. It was a guess, but judging from the way two of the men looked up at the trees, it was a good guess. "Or do all your birds and mice and monkeys take a nap this time of day? Back home, we hear silence in the woods, and we arm up."

"And do you know woods?" asked Fesgao.

"I know the ones at home," she said. "I know them as well as Da."

The next moment Fesgao gripped Aly by the arm and drew her to the front of the line of wagons. Mequen and his sergeant, Veron, were idly talking while they watched a servant unharness the mare who had taken the stone in her shoe. The old hostler, Lokeij, waited with a fresh horse, his lined, monkey-like face worried as he looked at the lame mare. The other slaves liked to tease him that he thought of each and every Balitang horse as his own child.

"Fesgao, what's this?" demanded the sergeant. "And who's this wench?"

"A country girl who hears the same thing we do," said the raka, letting go of Aly.

"And what does she hear?" asked Mequen, his steady brown eyes on Aly's face.

She bobbed an awkward curtsey. "Nothing, Your Grace," she replied, keeping her eyes down as she acted the same country girl she had pretended to be for Fesgao. "Back home, in the woods, when the animals go silent, oft-times it's because robbers are waiting up the road."

"I'd like permission to scout ahead, sir," Fesgao said to Veron. "We five are country-bred like her. In the city streets you know I follow your lead without pause. Here . . ." He left the word hanging in the air as he met Veron's gaze.

The sergeant, a luarin, scratched his head and sighed. "Forgive me for saying it, Your Grace, but he's right. I'm not a raka jungle runner. Fesgao is."

Mequen looked at Aly. Now she returned his gaze in an un-slave-like manner, silently reminding him of a god whose voice had driven him and the duchess to their knees. After a moment Mequen focused his gaze on Fesgao. "What do you recommend?"

"If we may scout ahead?" asked Fesgao.

"Go," Mequen ordered.

Fesgao hand-signaled to three of his companions. They faded into the brush on the left of the road. Aly couldn't even hear them once they vanished from sight: these men were good.

Fesgao and the other part-raka guard started for the right side of the road. Suddenly Fesgao stopped and looked at Aly. "Do you wish to come and see for yourself?" he asked, an ironic twinkle in his eyes.

Aly shook her head. "*I'm* no warrior," she said, still the country girl.

Fesgao let the tiniest of smiles reach his lips. Then he and the other man-at-arms skipped over the brook and vanished into the jungle.

Mequen looked around, his eyes assessing their company. "Sergeant, have your people on their horses, bows at the ready. Ulasim," he called cheerfully. "A word, if you please?"

The footman, who'd been talking to Chenaol, walked over to them. "Your Grace?"

Mequen lowered his voice. "Quietly—*quietly*—get the bows and spears out. Give them to any of the servants who can use them." He glanced at his wife by the wagon, and added, "Sarai and Dove as well. We may have a problem, but tell everyone to behave as if this were normal." As Winnamine sighed, Ulasim bowed. He ambled down the line of wagons, looking for all the world like a man taking a leisurely stroll, but he managed to speak to all of the free servants.

"It will take me days to undo the wildness that your putting weapons in the girls' hands will stir up," Winnamine told her husband softly.

"We may need that wildness out here," Mequen replied. "Winna, we aren't in Rajmuat now. We aren't living a round of parties and concerts and hunts. Perhaps the rules of Rajmuat no longer apply."

Aly started to ease back, keeping her head down, pretending to be invisible, since they seemed to have forgotten she was there. "Aly," said the duke.

She cringed and halted. After a moment she remembered who she was supposed to be, and bobbed a curtsy.

"Did the god warn you?" Mequen asked quietly. "Are these King Oron's assassins?" He and his wife watched her intently.

"Your Grace, I don't need the god for something as plain as this," Aly said, her voice just loud enough for them to hear. "Frankly, I'd as soon not trouble him any more than I can help. Gods . . ." She chose her words carefully. "Gods complicate things." It was the understatement of her life, to judge by the havoc her mother's Goddess and her Aunt Daine's god relatives had wreaked.

"Here I'd hoped they would simplify them," Winnamine remarked with a sigh.

Aly grinned. "That wouldn't be very interesting," she said.

The duchess raised her eyebrows. "I do not like interesting things," she said, amusement in her eyes even though her tone was one of reproof. "They tend to bite painfully."

A thought caught Aly's attention. "You know, Your Grace, we might make some noise, to distract the robbers," she said. "Something to account for our still being here." She nodded toward the horses. Lokeij was almost finished hitching up the fresh cart horse.

Winnamine went over to the old man and whispered in his ear. Lokeij nodded and walked down the line with the limping mare. A moment later Aly saw two menservants go to work on one of the wheels of a supply wagon, cursing loudly. Lokeij stopped to confer briefly with Ulasim, who came trotting up to the duke and duchess, a worried look on his face.

"Your Grace, my lady," he said, puffing slightly as Veron rode up to see what was going on, "forgive me, but one of the men says we have trouble with one of the wagons."

"What do you mean, a wheel's coming off?" cried the duchess, the image of appalled nobility. "We can't loiter here! We'll never reach the inn by dark at this rate, and I simply cannot sleep in the open!"

Within moments the caravan was transformed, giving the appearance of an anthill that had been kicked. The men removed the wheel as others clustered around to see what the problem was. Veron's men-at-arms quietly armed themselves and mounted their horses, drawing in closer to the wagons. Ulasim and a couple of the servants moved down the length of the train. As they passed, Aly saw the gleam of weapons set within easy reach.

She started to head back to the children, but Winnamine called, "Stay, Aly. Pembery is exhausted—she never sleeps well when she travels. Help me to untangle these silks."

Aly returned to the lead wagon. Winnamine did indeed have a heap of embroidery silks on her lap where she now sat on the wagon seat. She also had a drawn crossbow at her feet, hidden from view by the horses and her skirt. Startled, Aly glanced at Winnamine, then accepted a tangle of threads. "I want the girls to have decent marriages among their peers, which they won't get if they act like raka highland savages," Winna told Aly quietly. "But I never said I expected all women to be helpless and unable to defend their families."

"Yes, Your Grace," Aly murmured as she made a mess of the thread.

The duchess smiled. "Of course. You come from the land of fighting ladies like Queen Thayet, the Lioness, and Keladry of Mindelan," she remarked, laying an emerald strand flat on the seat beside her. "Doubtless you feel naked without a weapon in your hand."

Aly frowned at the mass of silk in her lap. "Your Grace, you only hear about the fighting women because they make the most noise," she told the duchess. "Most of Tortall's women wouldn't touch a sword if you begged them to. We have all sorts of females among us, you know."

Winnamine raised perfectly plucked brown eyebrows. "And which sort are you, to be the god's chosen?" she asked, her voice a whisper.

Aly shrugged. "I'm the confused sort." That answer startled a chuckle out of Winnamine.

Fesgao and his men eased out of the jungle and over to the lead wagon. Mequen and Sergeant Veron came to stand with the duchess and Aly. Fesgao brought a stick with him. He used it to draw a rough map in the dirt of the road.

"There's fourteen of them, on either side of the road just before it crosses a bridge," he told them. "This creek joins a bigger stream there. It's maybe a mile ahead." The other four men-at-arms nodded their agreement.

Mequen asked the question that Aly wanted to ask: "Are they fighters, or local?"

"Poor men, Your Grace," said another scout. "And women—two of them, anyway. The weapons are either old or they're farm weapons. They're not royal killers, just renegade jungle raka."

Aly could feel the relief that rose from the duke and duchess.

"Well, if we go forward, now that we're warned, we can fight them off," said the duke. "Or we can fall back to town and send the local soldiers to clean them out."

"They'll vanish from the area if they think we know they were here, Your Grace," said Veron gruffly. "Then the raka dogs will go after the next prey to cross upwind of them."

Aly scratched her head. In for a calf, in for a bull, she thought, and said, "I don't know if this could work, Your Grace, and I hope you forgive my boldness, but what if you send men to come up on their backs?"

"We could strike from behind," Fesgao said. If he'd taken offense over Veron's remark about raka dogs, his face did not show it. "And you could attack from the road. They would be caught between us."

Veron looked at Aly and shook his head. "From the lips of infants shall the truth come unadorned," he said, quoting a proverb. "If we are willing to risk casualties, Your Grace, we could be sure this rabble won't harass our supply caravans in the future."

"Instruct your men, sergeant," Mequen said. "How long should we wait until we set out?"

Within moments Fesgao and the other scouts, along with two of Ulasim's footmen who could shoot, had vanished back into the jungle. Winnamine counted slowly to one hundred while orders traveled down the line of servants and wagons. The wheel was put back on its wagon; Aly was ordered to sit with the children and keep them calm. No one considered giving her a weapon. In every slaveholding country it was illegal to give weapons to slaves.

Instead, Aly got Petranne and Elsren to lie flat on the wagon floor as part of a brand-new game, seeing how long they could hold perfectly still no matter what they heard. As she waited she murmured stories to keep them calm, feeling the weight of the knife she had stolen in Rajmuat heavy under her waistband. Dove and Sarai, bows in hand, covered either side of the wagon, pushing up the canvas just enough so that they could see out and aim.

As the wagon rumbled forward, Aly remembered her father's long-ago advice not to pray. Now she wondered, Was that how it started with you and Kyprioth, Da? You praying, and him answering? I mean to ask you that, when I come home this autumn.

The bumpy ride seemed to last forever. Elsren and Petranne had just begun to complain that Aly wasn't making sense when the wagon jolted to a stop. They heard yells and the crackle of bodies in the brush. Two arrows punched through the canvas wagon cover. Aly pushed Elsren and Petranne tight against the base of the padded seats, where arrows couldn't reach them. Pembery and the healer, Rihani, huddled against the other bank of padded seats, keeping their heads down as the maid whimpered and Rihani mouthed prayers. Sarai, her lovely face grim, shot her crossbow and reloaded it. Dove watched through her opening in the canvas, her small hands trembling on the stock of her bow. Someone outside screamed; others yelled. Aly heard the clang of metal on metal, and a crash in the woods.

The noise stopped for a moment. Then Veron and Mequen shouted orders. At last Ulasim opened the canvas door into the wagon. "It's clear," he told everyone inside. "Rihani, you are needed. My ladies, your father wishes you to attend him. Aly, also."

"I'll look after the little ones," Pembery said gratefully. She gathered Elsren and Petranne into trembling arms. Both children tried to wriggle free, clamoring to see the battlefield as the maid clung to them.

Aly followed Sarai and Dove to the head of the wagon train. They had halted just before the bridge. Some of the dead lay in the jungle on either side of the road. A few of the household staff and men-at-arms sported wounds, but none of the Balitang party lay among the bodies as far as Aly could see. Fesgao, Veron, and the rest of Fesgao's party of men-at-arms were forcing six bandits to their knees, binding them in ropes while other men-at-arms leveled weapons at the captives to prevent their escape.

Aly's temples began to throb. She had not considered this possibility, that robbers might be captured. The neatest solution would have been if they'd all been killed or if those left alive had fled. What would the duke say? He was a sensible man. He should realize there was no question of letting the captives go. They would only rob the next group to come up this road, or else they would get reinforcements and attack the Balitangs again.

Aly clasped her hands tightly behind her back so that no one would see them shake. The Balitangs could not turn back with captives in tow. They would never reach the safety of the village they had left that morning, with its royal fort and soldiers, by dark. The duke's people would be under constant attack along the way from would-be rescuers. At their present crawling speed, they would need two days to reach the next royal outpost. The local families would have plenty of time to steal their men back. If the Balitangs kept the captives until they reached Tanair, it would mean six more people who must be fed and guarded. The duke could spare neither guards nor food. If he enslaved the robbers, Aly wouldn't trust them, particularly not if the new slaves got word of their whereabouts to their families.

There's just one solution, Aly thought as the duke and duchess watched her sidelong to see what, if anything, the god would order her to say. She couldn't let them know that her particular burden of a god had given her a wager, not instructions. She also couldn't bear to tell them what they had to do, what her father, grandfather, and mother would have told them they *must* do. They had to execute six impoverished men.

"Let's kill these raka swine," Sergeant Veron said, inspecting one bandit's rusty sword. His eyes were gray ice. "Make sure their kin think twice before they attack luarin."

Duchess Winnamine looked at her husband and nodded, her face an emotionless mask. "My dear, it's the only solution."

Mequen shook his head, troubled.

"No!" cried Sarai, who might one day be faced with such a choice. "We can't do murder, and that's what it is, murder!"

"It's survival," Ulasim said gently. He was there in his capacity as the head of the male servants and slaves.

"Forgive us!" cried one of the bandits, a haggard-looking man in his forties. "We would never harm the la—"

"*Silence,*" ordered Fesgao, his dark eyes flashing.

"We swore a vow, on the altar, that all we would take is food, when you have so much," babbled another bandit.

"None of the others would help or even stay to hear it done," the man next to him added. "They did not come to see you pass. They retreated into the jungle to hide their faces in shame, but they know how it is with our village. They know we are desperate."

"The lord took everything for the tax, *everything,*" explained the first man who had spoken, talking fast. "Our children cry, their bellies empty. So we swore the vow before three villages. Our people would have killed us otherwise, had we harmed the la—"

Fesgao stepped forward and slapped the man, rocking the bandit back on his heels. "Keep your mouth *shut,* you fool," he hissed.

Aly pretended to be concerned with one of her fingernails. Something besides the normal treatment of criminals was going on here. Fesgao had twice stopped these men from saying one particular word, one that began with "la." Ladies, again, she told herself. He stops them from saying "ladies" in front of the luarin nobles. And these ladies aren't just important to the local raka. Fesgao also thinks the ladies are important. She wrote these thoughts on the growing list in her head of things to investigate.

"Their families will come to free them, unless they know their men are dead. They will fear us, and stay well away, if we do it," the duke said reluctantly.

"Make them slaves," suggested Dove. Everyone turned to stare at her. "Then sell them at the next army post."

Aly whistled silently. Now there was a solution she hadn't considered. She eyed the small, dark twelve-year-old with new respect.

"You can't enslave them," Sarai argued. "Look at them. They're poor, half starved. What is their village like, if the men look this bad? Papa, we'd make their lives worse, not better. Their families need them to hunt, and fish—"

"And rob, and kill?" Winnamine asked, cutting her off.

"Why do we even discuss this?" demanded Veron, his voice hard. "These dogs attacked members of the royal family. By law they must die. If we had time, we ought to hunt down and burn out their nest—in fact, we should report it at the next royal fort. This sort of lawlessness only gets worse if your first response is a soft one."

The adults debated it further. Aly thought the duke was about to order Veron and his men to kill the captives when Sarai interrupted again. "Give them a choice, Papa," she begged. "Death, slavery, or free and *loyal* service to our family. If they pick service, we'll have six more fighters—"

"Who will kill us as we sleep, begging your ladyship's pardon," Veron interrupted. "Your offer speaks well of your heart, but you will put us in danger."

"Make them swear by Mithros," retorted Sarai. "Or one of the raka gods."

"People have broken vows to gods before," Winnamine reminded Sarai gently. "If the god is busy elsewhere, it might be too late for us when the god finally punishes the oath breaker."

"Make them swear in blood." The quiet suggestion was Dove's. "If that's what they choose. No one breaks a blood oath. We can trust them if they swear that way, and if they don't . . ." The girl shrugged.

Those who broke such an oath died as their own blood boiled in their veins. No mage, however powerful, had found a way to prevent that. The gods had decreed it, and so it remained, a promise no one would dare to break. Aly looked from Dove to Sarai, a peculiar emotion stirring in her heart. She wasn't sure what it was, beyond respect for both girls, but it was powerful and troubling. She put it aside for the moment and looked to Mequen for a decision. The duchess and Ulasim nodded. When the duke looked at Aly, she nodded and ignored Veron's confused look. He would be asking himself why she was even present, let alone why his master seemed to want her opinion.

Before anyone could stop him, the man who had first spoken had wriggled over to Sarai. Awkwardly he leaned forward to touch his forehead to Sarai's shoe. "You are as gracious as you are beautiful," he whispered.

Aly bit her tongue. It was Dove who had truly found a way to keep these men alive. She glanced at Dove, who met her eyes and shrugged. "She's prettier," the younger girl murmured as she passed Aly on her way back to the wagon. "Everyone always goes to her first."

The oaths were given, the bandits untied. When the wagons rolled on, they did so with six new men and a parchment that bore each former bandit's thumbprint in his own blood. If their families attacked, the men would tell them the bargain they had made, and invite them to live at Tanair.

They camped beside the road at sunset and moved out at sunrise. It took the better part of the day to reach the royal fortress at the foot of Kellaura Pass. Only as they approached the fort did the local raka emerge again to watch them go by.

Inside the fortress walls, the Balitangs spent a day bathing in hot springs, sleeping in clean beds, and eating meals that were not cooked in a single pot. Another day of plodding brought them through the pass, watched at different points by silent raka, and into the high plains country on the far side of the mountains. They stayed the night at a second royal fort, among soldiers eager for fresh faces and news from Dimari and the capital. The raka waited beside the road that led the Balitangs northwest, watching them without a sound. They made Aly's flesh creep. At home people waved, or called their greetings or insults. She wished the raka would say *something*.

Two days later they passed through a ring of high-thrust rocks and clefts onto a broad, grassy plateau. Here a log palisade encircled a hill: their new home, Tanair Castle and village. Aly complained of stiff muscles to Pembery, Rihani, and the younger children, then hopped out of the wagon. She walked alongside it as they approached Tanair, taking the chance to view what she thought of as her summer home. The twenty-foot-high palisade did not inspire her with confidence, though the fifteen-foot-deep trench that lay before it, with its flooring of jagged-edged rocks, had promise. The wooden bridge to the village gate was sturdy enough to take the weight of their wagons, but wooden bridges could be burned or destroyed in a hurry. That wasn't too bad.

Inside the palisade lay the village, built around the foot of a raised earthen table capped by a stone wall. Aly swept her eyes over the village as they walked through, her busy mind ticking off details that might be useful later. The streets were clean and the houses sturdy, built half of wood and half of stone. There was plenty of space for herd animals and flocks if they had to be brought inside the palisade in an attack. The place had two smithies, which meant Tanair had a certain level of prosperity, and the people who lined the main street to greet their caravan looked capable enough. The colors ranged from pure luarin white to pure raka copper brown. Unlike the people of the lowland jungles, these villagers dressed for warmth in wraparound jackets and leggings, many of them brightly colored and embroidered. There was an inn with a proper stable, which meant that travelers came and went, and that money fed the village coffers. There were sheds and outbuildings, too, and temples for the luarin gods and the raka gods on opposite sides of the street. Aly liked it. People with a good life would defend it more vigorously than people who were beaten down by their masters and their fates.

The wagon train climbed up the earthen table and through the gate in the stone wall, into Tanair Castle's outer courtyard. It was on a direct line with the inner gate, which revealed Tanair to be an ancient five-story tower with outbuildings. Aly had thought Pirate's Swoop was plain, but at least they had three towers, connected by the castle's wings. Lady Sarugani's family may have been ancient, but plainly they were not wealthy. The soldiers who lined the stone wall were old men and boys in their midteens.

Aly rubbed the back of her neck. Well, it's a challenge, she thought. If I can keep these people safe here, I'll be able to handle anything Da could throw at me later. And who knows? Maybe King Oron will forget us. All I need is to keep the children alive for the summer, after all. It might take him that long to remember he sent the Balitangs away.

You promised me help! she thought to Kyprioth as she helped Elsren and Petranne out of the wagon. The sooner the better, if you please. I can't see everything at once!

There is no better spy than a slave. No one notices them. They may go anywhere, look into anything, if they are careful. They can ask questions that would be suspicious coming from others, because everyone believes a slave is stupid, even given evidence he is not.

—From a letter to Aly when she was ten
from her grandfather, Myles of Olau

5

SETTLING IN

The realization that life as it had been lived in Rajmuat must now change struck the family, servants, and slaves as they looked over the grounds of Tanair Castle. In the outer courtyard lay stables, storage sheds, a carpentry workshop, a dovecote, a mews, and a small kennel. Within the inner courtyard the broad stone keep was supplied with a kitchen attached to it on the ground floor, a barracks for the men-at-arms, two wells, and a blacksmith's forge.

"But where do we sleep?" one of the Balitang servants asked.

"In the main hall, on pallets," Chenaol told them. "This castle was part of Duchess Sarugani's dowry when she married His Grace. When the family stayed here, servants and slaves slept together in the main hall, on the floor."

When some of the free servants protested that they would not sleep among slaves, Chenaol shrugged. "Before the family built the upper stories, my mother said *they* slept in the main hall, too," she said. "Their quarters are right overhead now, where the hearth fire warms the upper rooms."

A shriek from Elsren called Aly back to her charges. She calmly ended a hair-pulling dispute between the boy and his sister, Petranne, and gave both of them things to carry inside. Petranne tried to shove the box she held back into Aly's hands. "We're not *slaves*," the four-year-old said.

Aly looked at the thick gray clouds that raced over the sky, then shrugged and set the box in a cart. "All right, my lady, but don't come crying to me when the storm wets your dolls. That's the box they're in," she replied, slinging rolled blankets over one shoulder and a heavy pack over another. "Come on, my lord Elsren."

The boy turned, stuck his tongue out at his sister, and marched toward the castle door, manfully hauling a small basket. Petranne caught up with them as they entered the castle. In one hand she carried the box with her dolls in it; in the other she carried a basket with Elsren's wooden toys.

Everyone worked fast to get their belongings into shelter. After her last trip inside, Aly lingered on the steps to the keep's main door. Thunder growled in the distance. She gnawed her lip, trying to remember if she had found all of the children's things.

"So, Aly Bright Eyes," said Ulasim, coming to a halt beside her. The weight of the box he carried made the heavy muscles of his arms bulge, though he stood as if it weighed nothing at all. "Wishing they'd sent you back to the Rajmuat slave pens?"

Aly glanced along the line of his back. His tunic, pulled tight by the weight of the box, revealed extremely heavy muscles for someone who was a head footman. She raised an eyebrow. "Are you?" she asked, curious.

"I savor the delights of civilization," he informed her, his long mouth in a crooked line. In some ways he reminded her of Da. "I'm spoiled, that's all. I'll recover."

"But for you this is home, isn't it?" Aly wanted to know. "Aren't you glad to be home?"

Ulasim shook his head. "Tanair isn't my home. I'm from Pohon."

He'd startled her. She let him see it. "And you work for luarin? Chenaol says the people there hate luarin."

"They do. It's a long story. I will wager you a gigit that Elsren is now at the top of the stairs, ready to tumble down. He *is* three. They have a talent for such things at that age."

He was probably right. Aly raced inside, deliberately running with her knees together as she flung up her heels, the awkward run of a maidservant who hated it. There was no need for anyone here to see that Aly could be swift, that she normally ran with the wide-open stride of someone who had been trained to it. She meant to give the household as few reasons to ask questions about her as possible.

Elsren wasn't near the stairs on the second floor of the keep, but he had found and unsheathed one of his father's daggers, testing it on the wooden floor. Aly took the weapon, scolded Elsren, then threw the screaming child over one shoulder and climbed up to the third story. She plopped Elsren on the floor of the small chamber he would share with Petranne, next to a heap of his toys. As he started to play with them she got to work making the beds.

She was nearly finished unpacking when Pembery came for her. "His Grace and the duchess wish to speak to you in their rooms," she told Aly.

Aly curtsied to her and trotted downstairs, mentally listing all she had to do before she could sleep that night. Bathe the children tomorrow, she told herself. By the time Petranne and Elsren finish supper, they'll be so worn out they won't even be able to sit upright. Little monkeys. No wonder Mother spent so much time away, if Thom, Alan, and I were half as lively as these two. And I need to find that missing trunk of clothes. Ulasim might know what happened to it....

She knocked on the closed door that was the entrance to the suite of rooms shared by the duke and duchess. "Come in," Mequen called.

"Close the door behind you," added Winnamine.

Aly bowed to her masters, wondering what was going on now. Their rooms—sitting room, bedroom, privy, solar—were only half unpacked. Lightning flashed through cracks in the closed wooden shutters, and rain thudded against them. The keep was so old-fashioned that none of the windows had glass, which was still too expensive for all but the greatest lords, let alone the raka nobility. Candles burned on branches set on tables; cressets of burning coals lit the main hall and stairs. Winnamine was kneeling beside a crate in the sitting room, taking out neatly folded clothes, while Mequen stood before the hearth.

"We're going to free you, Aly," Winnamine announced.

Aly held a finger to her lips to hush the duchess, then went to the door that opened onto the servants' stair. It gave way stiffly, and the landing and stairs were covered with dust and cobwebs. She closed it again, reassured that anyone who might have thought to eavesdrop from there would have left a mark. She couldn't depend on that reassurance in the future. The servants would be cleaning the back passages soon, for access to the rooms on the upper levels. She went to open the bedroom door. The bedchamber was undisturbed except for trunks and boxes piled by the door, to be unpacked as soon as the room was cleaned. She left that door open so that no one could sneak in and eavesdrop. She wanted to do the same with the servants' stair, but their conversation would echo through the stone corridor if she did.

"Forgive me, Your Graces," she said, bowing to her owners. "I'd prefer that no one overhear."

Winnamine raised her eyebrows, then continued, "My lord and I have discussed it. It's not right, keeping a slave collar on the god's messenger."

Aly rubbed her nose gently. This should have occurred to you, she scolded herself. True, she hated that metal ring. It was a constant annoyance, chafing her tender skin, pressing on her throat when she turned over in her sleep. The Balitangs had changed the radius of the magic on the collar for the greater spaces of Tanair, but even so, if she had to go farther than five miles from any member of the family, it would choke her until she returned to them or died.

And she needed the cursed thing.

"I thank you, Your Grace, but no," she told her mistress. "Truly, I don't require freedom just yet."

The duchess froze in the middle of lifting tunics from the chest. The duke turned slowly. Their brown eyes, his deep-set in folds of flesh, hers even under perfect brows, locked on Aly.

"This isn't our attempt to rid ourselves of you," Mequen told her. "You may masquerade as a servant, that's all, free to go wherever you like."

Aly sighed. "May I sit, Your Grace?" she asked. "I've been running up and down those stairs all afternoon. My feet are killing me."

Both of them stiffened momentarily, half offended that a slave would sit in their presence. It was Mequen who thawed first. "How thoughtless of us. Sit, please." He took one of the chairs for himself. Winnamine looked at her husband, raising her brows. He shrugged and flicked his eyes at Aly. Aly grinned, having read, "Are you mad?" and "She is the god's messenger" in their silent exchange. It was a good marriage when a couple could communicate easily without speaking.

The duchess carried the stack of clothes into the bedchamber, then returned. Only when she sat down did Aly do so. It might have been too much to ask her to return to a room where the slave was already seated.

Aly took a deep breath and leaned forward, bracing her arms on her knees, a position her da favored when he needed to explain things. "Servants aren't free in a way that's useful, Your Grace. People expect servants to be loyal. Everyone knows that if a servant dislikes a master, he finds a better one. Nobody expects a slave to be loyal or clever. We hear things servants won't. And if slaves turn up somewhere they don't usually go, everyone assumes their masters ordered them to go there. I really am far more use to you as a slave."

Duke Mequen frowned at her. "But every slave wants to be free."

"Actually, some don't," Winnamine remarked in a thoughtful voice. "I've overheard them say that servants always risk finding themselves in the street with no money and no way to get proper work, while a slave is cared for all his days."

"If the slave has a good master," Mequen pointed out.

"There's another thing to consider," Aly told them. "I need answers to questions no one will answer for someone who's luarin, and free. Me being a slave solves that little problem. Even free raka feel superior to a luarin slave."

"That's . . . very subtle," the duke remarked slowly. "Tell me, Aly, who were you in Tortall?"

"I was a maid at Fief Tameran," she said, gazing at him with wide, innocent eyes. She had chosen Tameran because it was a holding she knew as well as the Swoop. "I was visiting my sister at Bay Cove when the raiders got me."

"What sort of maid?" asked the duchess. "You seem rather more knowing than the usual run of servant."

"General," replied Aly, her voice casual. "Minding the other servants' children, helping in the kitchen when we had guests, sewing, gardening, the like. As for the knowingness, well, I've always been nosy, I suppose. We were schooled—by the queen's decree, all Tortallan children learn their letters and sums. I learned a bit more than that. As for the rest . . ." She shrugged. "It's just the way I am. Maybe the god made me smarter."

"You were free, but you wish to remain a slave," the duke said, as if he did not believe that he had heard correctly the first time.

"Once I have served the god, he's promised to send me home," Aly told him. It wasn't even a lie. "He won't need me forever, I'm sure."

Winnamine inspected her fingernails. "Then we'll reassign Pembery and give you her place," she said.

Aly winced. "You'll make her into an enemy I don't need, Your Grace," she replied. "And you'd be hobbling me. The god's told me what I must do. To keep you safe, I need to know this ground like I know my home. What I need for now is to range outside the walls. Can't I be given a herd to work? Goats would do best. They can graze anywhere. No one questions a goatherd clambering all over the land."

"You should have something to excuse your wanderings inside the wall as well," suggested Mequen. "What if at night, when everyone's indoors, you carry our messages for us? Thus we shall have reason to talk to you privately, when we give you notes to carry to the rest of the castle and the village."

Aly stared at him, startled. She hadn't thought the duke would have a talent for this kind of thing, but it seemed that he did. "Perfect, Your Grace, and thank you," she said, bowing in her chair. "I hadn't thought of that." The best secrets are those kept in full view, she thought to herself. Everyone will see me running the Balitangs' errands, and no one will think twice about it.

"But surely even looking after the little ones would be better than herd work," objected Winnamine.

"Not for my side of the god's bargain, begging Your Graces' pardon," explained Aly. "I need to learn how easy it would be for killers to strike the plateau. A herd will give me a reason to wander." She gnawed her lip and added, "If you wish to help me, I would be grateful if you would take the magic off my collar, so it won't choke me if I go more than five miles from one of you. A tablet of parchment would help, too, so I can make a map of things."

Silence fell for a moment as the couple considered what she had said. Mequen frowned in thought, then asked, "Why does the god take an interest in us? He didn't really say, except to tell us we have a great destiny."

Aly wanted to reply that the god had tricked them and that their children were his object. But then she would have to explain to these nice people that they were in the hands of a trickster, not Mithros. It would be far better for Aly if they didn't know about Kyprioth and his wager. "I don't believe gods are very forthcoming with things like answers, Your Grace," she replied. "I've yet to hear of one that was, anyway."

"Well," the duchess said, getting to her feet, "goats and messages it is. I'm afraid you must be demoted, Aly." She rummaged in a box that sat on a nearby table and produced a booklike tablet of parchment sheets stitched together. "Use this. What have you got to write with?"

"Charcoal's best, Your Grace, and easy for me to get. Thank you," Aly said, fitting the tablet into the front of her tunic.

"Send the housekeeper to me, and I will arrange for your change in station," Winnamine said. "Report to His Grace or me here after supper for our messages. And let us know what we may do to help."

"Aly, come here." Aly obeyed, standing in front of the duke. He touched her metal collar with one finger and murmured a phrase in old Thak, the dead language favored by mages for spoken spells. The metal felt a little cooler on Aly's skin when Mequen dropped his hand. "There you are. You may go, then."

Aly bowed and left.

Worn out by settling in, the entire household made an early night of it after their arrival at Tanair. On her pallet in Elsren and Petranne's room, Aly dreamed of crows.

This dream felt real, but not in the same way as that dream of her parents. There she could not feel a thing. In this dream she sat in the fork of an immense tree, its bark rough on her skin. She heard the wind in the leaves overhead and smelled apple blossoms from somewhere. She was surrounded by crows who hopped from branch to branch above her, on either side, sharing her own branch. One flew at her, tugged her sleeve, and dropped back to the ground. Another struck her back with his claws, making Aly hang on to the tree trunk. The crow yanked her clothes, then fell away. Another darted up to pull at her leggings; one more took her right little finger in its beak and felt along its length. When its tongue tickled her, Aly pulled free. She sensed no harm in them, only great curiosity.

The one who had mouthed her finger now gripped her wrist gently with its beak, working its way up until it tasted cloth, then back down to her hand. It wandered over Aly's lap to her left side to repeat the procedure. Its fellows glided by to tug at Aly's clothes and hair. It seemed to be an inspection of some kind. The only one who did not touch her and jump back to the branches was the one who went from exploring her hands and arms to her ears, making her giggle.

"That *tickles*," she said, lifting the bird down to her lap. Something had splashed or marked its back feathers with a white mark like a wave, a mark that sparkled faintly in Aly's Sight. "Vexed a mage, didn't you?" she asked the crow with a grin. "Were you tickling him, too?"

The mage was just crotchety, said a voice in Aly's head—Kyprioth's voice. *Our friend here has an excess of curiosity about humans even for a crow.* A new crow settled on the branch across from Aly. Unlike the other birds in the tree, this one wore sparkling rings on each talon and a necklace of sparkling gemstones. He blazed with godhood in Aly's Sight.

"Hello, Kyprioth," Aly said drily. "I take it all this is your idea?"

Most certainly, the bejeweled crow informed her in the god's crisp, kindly tones. *You asked for help, my dear. I have wagered that these crows will not be able* to keep you *safe from human predators until the autumn equinox. They will teach you their language, so they can spy for you.*

Aly scratched her head. Somehow, when she had dreamed of one day creating her own spy network, a flock of crows had not been part of her imaginings.

The crow who'd run afoul of a mage jumped from her lap to her shoulder. Gripping her flesh through her tunic with his powerful claws, he ran his beak through the inch-long brush that was her growing hair.

"That tickles, too, you know," she told him. The crow continued to preen her. To Kyprioth she said, "If I have a wager with you, and the crows have a wager with you, where's the trick? Whenever there's a trickster about, there has to be a trick, everyone says so. What's yours?"

You don't have to worry, said Kyprioth, his tone entirely smug. *You're only here for the summer, remember? This is going to be my greatest trick ever, pulled off under the noses of mortals and gods alike, but it will take some time to put it in place. In the meantime, your new friends here will teach you useful crow sounds. You in turn will teach them to understand necessary human sounds.* He preened his chest feathers. *At least, I think the crows will teach you. Do you accept the wager, my cousins?* he asked the crows.

Will you keep your word about food? A crow's voice sounded in Aly's mind. It sounded like the speaker was a senior male. *There's barely enough in this high, flat place to keep two small flocks fed, let alone fifty more of us.*

I will ensure that you are all fed, Kyprioth reassured them. *You can't win the wager if you're starving.*

One female said, *I am not certain. You know how stupid two-leggers are.*

We are two-leggers ourselves. That voice was light, young, and male. It came from the crow on Aly's shoulder. *Or are you standing on your wings? We know they use counting words, just like us, and they have words for different kinds of predators. They are as much kin to us as Kyprioth there.*

You have always been too fond of those creatures, Nawat, said another female crow. *It isn't right.*

This seems like a lot of trouble to go for a wager, added a new male crow.

If it's too much for you, I suppose I could take my wager to the ravens, Kyprioth remarked, cocking his head this way and that, as if he weighed up the crows. *Or the magpies. I thought you would find the stakes worth your while, but perhaps the ravens will like them better.*

We want the wager, snapped the female who had said she was uncertain. *Even if it takes forever to teach a stupid human.*

The crows shrugged their shoulders. *That means "very well,"* Nawat told Aly. *It means they agree.*

"What are your stakes?" Aly inquired, thinking they must be something special to cause the crows to jump when they saw their chance of winning slip away.

Nothing that concerns you, the stern female snapped. *So don't start thinking you can steal it for yourself. Now. We begin with numbers.*

Aly looked around for Kyprioth. He was gone. She shook her head and paid attention to her lessons.

Aly rose at dawn, her head buzzing with crow sounds. She scavenged a lunch from the yawning kitchen staff and went out to take charge of her goats. She had some experience at herding, from working with her friends who herded the Swoop's animals when she was younger. Time and education as her father's daughter and as a lady had put an end to the friendships, but at least she could manage fifteen goats.

The air was cool when she left Tanair, but she could tell the day would be warm, even hot. Except for puddles and damp grass, no traces of last night's thunderstorm remained. She led her charges up into the rocky ground just north of the point where the road entered the Tanair plateau. Grass sprouted everywhere between the granite boulders, which made the goats happy. Perched on the rocks, Aly could see the road and the palisade that enclosed castle and village, which made her happy. She could also see the two-man guard Veron had placed to watch the road and alert the castle if anyone came that way.

Once she was settled, Aly put aside her pack and walking stick. In all the stories of gods she had heard, she had learned that if a god wasn't somewhere else in the world, and the speaker was of interest to that god, all that person needed was to speak the god's name. "Kyprioth, I need to talk to you," she said quietly. "We are overdue for a private conversation."

"I'm touched," the familiar crisp voice remarked.

Aly turned. For the first time she saw the god standing on his own, not covered with someone else's form. She had seen the outlines of this shape in the matcher's body, so she guessed it was one he liked. He was only two inches taller than Aly, lean and wiry like a dancer, shoulders erect, bearded chin up. He had very short salt-and-pepper hair that was more salt than pepper. It extended all the way down to frame his mouth and face in that trim beard. His nose was short and broad, his eyebrows shaped in pointed arches. Leagues of mischief gleamed in his large brown eyes. He wore a Kyprin-style wrapped coat of green cloth. It was hung all over with charms, pins, brooches, and bits of jewelry. The native sarong covered his legs, the material made of intricate patterns woven in many-colored threads. The patterns shifted when Aly looked at them, making her dizzy. Even the knot over his left hip appeared to move in its many turns and folds. It seemed to be intertwined with fine silver, gold, and copper chains. His sandals were leather studded with copper. There were rings made of copper and studded with gems on all of his fingers and several of his toes. His lone earring was a copper hoop with beads on it made of colored stones.

"Well, here I am," he prodded. "Speak up. I can't do this often. I don't want my divine siblings to learn I'm suddenly spending more time here in the last few weeks than I have in the last couple of centuries."

"I don't understand," Aly said, frowning.

"You don't need to," replied Kyprioth. "Too much information is bad for you mortals. Just look at your history if you want proof."

Aly made a note to ask the raka servants about Kyprioth and his relationship with the other Great Gods. She had a feeling it might be important. Changing the subject to keep him off balance, she said, "You're a god. Why not make yourself young and handsome?"

"I like myself this way," he informed her as the goats crowded around, sniffing him. "I look amiable and inoffensive, like an elder statesman, don't you think?"

"No elder statesmen *I* know," Aly retorted with a grin. "Ours all wear breeches or hose, like decent people." To the goats she said, "Get along with you! You'd think you'd never seen a god before."

"But they haven't," said Kyprioth, his voice smoothly reasonable. "And I like goats. They have so much talent for trouble. Aren't you happy with the crows?"

"The crows are delightful," Aly told him. "But they won't be enough. We need a mage, a real one, you know. Rihani's sweet, but mostly she knows healing. There's another healer in Tanair village. We've got a few who can shed light or start fires among the people who came up from Rajmuat, but if a real mage attacks, we are cooked cats. Unless you can make a mage out of me. A good one, of course."

"But you said it yourself, no one notices a slave," the god said reasonably. "You would be noticeable as a mage, particularly to other mages."

Aly scowled at him. "You were listening."

Kyprioth grinned at her. "Don't you wish you were a god? We can eavesdrop wherever we like and no one knows. Think how useful that skill would be for you. You don't need to be a mage, my dear. Your particular, *peculiar* array of talents is what interests me," he explained. "You really are quite exceptional, you know."

"Piffle," said Aly. "Da has dozens more skilled than me."

"Not necessarily, Alianne of Pirate's Swoop," Kyprioth replied. There was kindness in his voice. "You come of exceptional people, and you are a fitting heir to them."

"They don't think so," Aly pointed out. "And I agree. I'm the family layabout. Don't those four children deserve better?"

"Now you talk as if you believe all that nonsense you've been told about your unwillingness to work. We both know you aren't unwilling at all." The god lifted Aly's chin with a strong brown hand. "You were marked by fate from birth, just like your parents. Accept that, and see what you can accomplish here, on your own. It's going to be an interesting summer."

"Speaking of that, what am I here to protect them from?" Aly wanted to know. "You never said."

"All sorts of things." Kyprioth's voice was tart with exasperation as he released her chin. "Really, Aly, you have an imagination, *and* a sense of the real world. You shouldn't have to ask. Their family is out of favor with a monarch whose grip on sanity is loose, they've been sent to live in country far from any serious kind of defenses . . . would you like me to add a flock of hurroks or a herd of robber centaurs? Spidrens, perhaps? Rival nobles looking to gain favor with King Oron?"

Aly sighed. "No, thank you, the normal run of perils should be enough—"

He was gone, as if he'd never been there. Aly looked at the grass that had been under his feet: it wasn't even bent. "He'd be impossible to track," she told the kid that was leaning against her leg. "Aren't you supposed to be frolicking, or something?"

The kid butted her thigh.

"Shoo," Aly ordered. "I need to map this ground."

She was eating her lunch of bread and cheese when a crow flew down and lit a few feet away. Aly sat up as he stared at her. When he flicked his wings out in a settling-down gesture, she saw the white rippled streak on his feathers.

"Nawat?" she asked. "That's what they called you, isn't it?"

He replied with the wing shrug that was crow language for "yes."

Aly tossed him a chunk of the heavy brown bread. "So are you here to test me on what I learned?" she asked.

The crow gripped the bread in a talon and gulped down a piece. He answered with a rattling caw that startled the kids so much, they leaped over one another. Aly shook her head at the silly youngsters and searched her memory. "Five?" she guessed.

A wing shrug. She had gotten it right. Nawat voiced another sound.

"Hawks," Aly said with more confidence. "What's 'men'? Two-leggers, like me." She looked down at her chest. "Only flatter."

Nawat finished the bread and walked over to her. Gently he stretched his head forward and pecked her lightly on the bosom.

"Stop that!" Aly said, pushing him away. "I don't let males of my own kind do that, I'm not about to start with you!"

Nawat replied with a croak that Aly recognized.

"Men?" she asked.

The wing shrug. Nawat spoke two sounds that Aly correctly identified as "five men." At least I'm learning a new language during my summer holiday, she thought humorously. So Mother won't be able to say I wasted my time completely. She handed the crow some more bread.

That night she ate with the slaves and the six bandit men-at-arms in the castle courtyard: the soldiers refused to let the new recruits eat with them, blood oath or no. The servants ate in the kitchen, since they ranked higher than the slaves. The family and their attendants ate in the great hall.

Summoned to carry messages for the duke and duchess to people in the village, Aly slipped her first map to the duchess for recopying in ink. In return she took Mequen and Winnamine's messages and carried them down to Tanair village. Most were invitations to visit the Balitangs at the castle, written to the headman, the town's artisans and healers, and the priests of the different temples. It was nearly dark when Aly returned to the castle to take up a chore of her own.

As she passed through the castle gate, she saw that Sergeant Veron was in charge of the night guard. Tonight she waved to him as she trotted through the gate to the inner courtyard.

Veron frowned down at her, his gray eyes puzzled. "You are the slave Aly, are you not?" he called down to her.

"I am, Your Honor," Aly called back cheerfully. "Just taking messages about for Their Graces. Don't mind me."

She suspected that he was one of those people who was not happy until he could fit someone into a proper category, after which he could ignore them. He confirmed her suspicion by nodding and turning back to talk to one of his men.

Aly walked on through the open gate to the inner courtyard, where she stopped and bent to retie her sandal. As she did so she gave the courtyard ahead a quick glance. The slaves with no work to do lounged around a small fire, gossiping with a handful of off-duty men-at-arms who weren't too proud to be seen in their company. No one else was in that courtyard. A look through the gate to the outer courtyard showed no change since she had passed through. Soldiers paced the walkway on top of the wall, keeping their night's watch. Veron stood there, too, staring at the village below.

Straightening, Aly scratched her head, stuck her hands into her pockets, and strolled into the shadows at the base of the inner courtyard wall. No one had seen her. Moving noiselessly but casually, as if she had every right to be there, she walked in the shadows to the guards' barracks.

The nice thing about sergeants in command was that they had ground-floor rooms, often with windows. Because it was warm for spring, Veron had left his shutters open for the cool evening air. Silently Aly pulled herself up onto the sill and swung her legs inward, waiting to make sure she wouldn't bump anything before she lowered herself to the floor. As she straightened, she did that inner twist of mind that let her Sight adjust. Now the room was as well lit to her gaze as it would be to a cat at night.

At first glance she found none of the safeguards that a wary man would set to alert him that someone had broken into his things, like a hair over the crack where the lid met the bottom of his chest, or a powdering of chalk or flour in front of it, or across the doorway. The lock on the chest was child's play. It required only three of the picks she'd stuck into her loincloth before the mechanism opened. Aly ran her hands gently through the folded clothes without disturbing them, checking for anything unusual. Da had taught her this trick, along with the art of picking pockets, using things with bells attached until she could search without ringing a bell. All she found were letters from Veron's home, neatly bundled and tied up with ribbon. Aly undid the ribbon to scan the letters. They were ordinary missives from parents and siblings, full of home news. Her Sight found no signs of code spells; none of the letters themselves was in code. She folded the papers as she'd found them, and retied them in the same way. Next she tested the depth of the chest against its height on the floor to check for hidden compartments. There was none.

She searched the room as she had the trunk, checking each possible hiding place on the bed before leaving it as she had found it, unwrinkled and straight. Quickly she moved on to the sergeant's shaving gear, chair, and table. She rapped the legs of the furniture to see if any held secret compartments. About to give up, Aly noticed a darker spot over the shadowed door.

With the hearth stool to stand on she could reach the area. She took down a slim, dark wood box that had been set on the door's thick frame. The lock was simple. Aly had it open in a trice. Inside were sheets of thin parchment, a reed pen, and ink that glowed with some kind of spell. With them she found a stick of clear blue sealing wax and a seal: a tiny eye over a spread-winged osprey, symbols for the intelligence service of the Copper Isles.

Gingerly Aly returned the box to its proper place. She placed the stool in the dents in the earthen floor where it had stood before the fireplace. Then she eased herself through the window and into the safety of the shadows outside.

Her suspicions about the sergeant were right. He was King Oron's spy in the Balitang household. He might not even be the only one. Should she let the duke and duchess know? Or should she keep that information to herself for now? They might insist on getting rid of Veron, and that wouldn't be practical. Aly knew from her upbringing that the spy you know is present is always preferable to the unidentified spy. Veron could be watched. He might lead her to other royal spies within the Balitang household, or even help her to locate spies sent by enemies other than the Crown.

It was the kind of thinking that always gave her mother headaches, a way of looking at several different possibilities for each situation. To Aly and her father it was a fine game, but Aly had learned early on that Mother hated it. That was a shame, because it was far more interesting that anything her mother might play at on horseback.

Still turning possibilities over in her mind, Aly drifted through the gate into the outer courtyard. A glance at the stables revealed that a lamp burned in the chief hostler's quarters. Why wasn't Lokeij out with his boys, among the group in the inner courtyard? The old raka was a sociable man, much given to telling fireside stories until moonrise.

Aly padded into the stables. They were empty but for the horses, who drowsed as she passed. Silently Aly walked into the one-story addition that housed the tack room, the stable boys' dormitory, and the chief hostler's quarters. She kept to the wall, where there was less chance she would step on a loose board. The murmur of voices from Lokeij's room was too low for her to make out what was said. Aly hesitated, then shrugged and opened the old man's door.

Lokeij, the cook Chenaol, the man-at-arms Fesgao, and the head footman Ulasim all sat inside. They had the look of old friends having a nice evening's chat, complete with drinks and a bowl of dried fruit and nuts to share. Aly blinked. All four were pure raka. She had known before that it was unusual to have so many pure-blood raka in the best positions in a luarin household. Only now, seeing them, did she realize that all four main servants here at Tanair were purebloods. Was that a nod to the older girls' heritage, or was it something more? Perhaps it was both, she thought.

"Good evening," she said with a smile. "This looks cozy."

Lokeij grinned at her, his dark eyes, framed by multiple wrinkles, twinkling with amusement. "Surely old friends may sit and talk when their work is done."

"Old friends who number two free servants, a slave, and a man-at-arms, all seated together?" Aly crouched by the door and wrapped her arms around her knees, curious to see what she might learn. "You're very relaxed in your standards for company."

"Why do I not think you are here for a drink?" Fesgao asked, pointing to the pitcher and a wooden cup.

Aly smiled crookedly. "I'd as soon gulp down a mouthful of fire," she replied.

Chenaol laughed and slapped her knee. "You won't get to like it if you won't drink it," she told Aly.

"But I'd like the use of my tongue until I die," retorted Aly. "I think it would eat away at the tongue of anyone who isn't raka."

"So then, curious Aly, why are you here?" Ulasim wanted to know.

Aly looked at each dark face, wondering if she was getting herself into trouble. She sighed. She needed some real answers, and she had to start somewhere. She had a feeling that these four people were more important to this household than their positions seemed to be. "Just who *was* Duchess Sarugani to the raka?"

"That is a question we will not answer," Fesgao replied. "Why do you ask?"

Then you just answered it, Aly thought. She was *very* important to you and yours. "I like gossip about my betters," she replied blithely. "And I was spooked by all those people watching us. Do they line the roads and sea lanes for every family that goes into exile?"

"Who knows why country raka act as they do?" asked Chenaol with a shrug. "Most of the time they laze, hunt, and fish. The household of an exiled duke—a Rittevon duke—was a show for them."

Ulasim leaned back and laced his hands behind his head. "Duchess Sarugani was of the lesser raka nobility," he told Aly, his eyes sharp on her face. "No raka ever married so high before. It stands to reason that people would take interest in her and her daughters."

Aly got to her feet, wincing as muscles she hadn't used in some time protested the change in position. Goat herding had not been so much work the last time she had tried it. "Oh. I didn't think of that," she said lightly. "It looked to me as if there was some big mystery about it all."

"Curiosity killed the cat," Fesgao remarked, his dark eyes unreadable.

Aly rolled her eyes. Why did everyone say that to her? "People always forget the *rest* of the saying," she complained. "'And satisfaction brought it back.'" She looked at the pitcher of arak. "Though if that's all you mean to drink, I doubt I'll come to be curious with you very often."

Their chuckles followed her out into the stable. Aly whistled a tune softly as she passed the sleeping horses. The raka had gracefully turned her questions aside, but they weren't good at facing down open queries. What they had said about the first duchess was true, but it was only part of a larger truth. From the way they had avoided her gaze, and from the stiffness of their movements, Aly was almost certain that Sarugani had not been minor raka nobility at all. Plans to do away with entire noble houses were usually flawed, as her readings of history had taught her. There were always second and third cousins tucked away in corners, waiting for the right time to announce they were of the supposedly dead house. Or those cousins neglected to wait and died as the result of a premature announcement. Had she money to wager, Aly would bet it all that Sarugani was the daughter of old, powerful raka nobility, probably even a very well hidden seed of the royal line. If that were so, then Sarai and Dove were doubly royal, raka as well as luarin. If *that* were true, if the mad king ever learned of it, no Balitang would be left alive.

The four raka whom she had just left seemed much friendlier since they'd left Rajmuat. During the long journey here she had overheard slaves and servants alike wonder why servants of Chenaol's and Ulasim's rank and qualifications had chosen the Balitangs' exile. Lokeij, of course, had been too old to sell, for all his skill as an hostler. And here they were, teamed with a real soldier who was also a pure-blood raka. Fesgao's quiet competence and leadership had impressed her during the bandit episode. Seeing these four together had crystallized things for Aly, giving her a working theory as to why these people had remained with Mequen and his family. They were guarding the hidden treasure that was Sarugani's daughters. If trouble came, Aly would have their help to protect two of the children, at least.

She stepped into the courtyard and frowned. She had forgotten another very important question. She would ask it at another time, though. Too many questions might make the four raka conspirators think Aly was an unhealthy person to keep around.

As she walked into the keep, she heard children crying, "Aly, Aly!" Elsren and Petranne, who had been seated at the foot of the main stairway, hurled themselves at her. Dove and Sarai came in their wake, more sedate, but with the same eagerness in their eyes.

"A story!" clamored Elsren. "Mama said you might tell us a story if we were good and we were!"

"Please," begged Petranne.

"The duchess didn't actually *say* Aly would tell you a story," Sarai reminded her. "She said to ask Aly, *if* Aly wasn't too tired. Aly looks pretty tired to me." She turned her brown eyes on Aly, who saw wistfulness in them.

Petranne, who had hugged Aly enthusiastically, drew back, plucking coarse hairs from the front of her gown. "You smell of goats," she said, wrinkling her nose. She was very much the finicky young noblewoman.

"I don't care!" Elsren cried. *"Please,* a story?"

Aly looked at the four young Balitangs and told herself that if she was to keep them alive, she ought to get to know them. "Actually, I'd like a story of my own," she said, towing the younger children to a bench against the wall. "And then one for you."

"And then bedtime," Dove told Petranne and Elsren. "Aly rises very early now."

"What story did *you* want to hear?" asked Sarai. She settled on the floor gracefully, tucking her bronze-colored skirts around her long legs. Aly could see how Sarai would attract boys. Apart from her connection to the royal family, she was lovely in a sensual way, her nose long and curved, her upper lip a perfect arch over a full lower lip, her skin a creamy shade of golden brown. Her eyes were large with frivolously long lashes, tucked under delicate eyebrows. She wore her shining dark hair combed smoothly back and coiled into a knot of braids from which curled locks dangled. Hers was a face of passion and sensuality, one that promised a happy, if maddening, time for any male who took her interest.

Elsren and Petranne curled up on either side of the bench with Aly, leaning against her as they pleaded with their eyes. Dove found a stool and set it next to Sarai, folding her hands neatly in her lap once she was seated.

"Well, it doesn't really have to be a story," Aly said, putting an arm around each of the younger children. "I was just curious about a god somebody mentioned to me—Ky—Kyprioth. Do you know anything about him?"

The older girls traded wary looks. Finally Dove said, "I don't see how it could hurt. He's one of the old raka gods. He's the sea god here, except maybe to the luarin. The raka say he used to be the patron god of the Isles."

"Some people say that he played one trick too many on Mithros," Sarai added. "He is a trickster god. The Isles deserved one in those days, with all the clans fighting, and every island against its neighbors. You can see why people might think a trickster was running it all."

"The Mithran priests say that all the fighting among the raka weakened Kyprioth's power, so when the invaders came from the east, Mithros and the Great Goddess came with them, and threw Kyprioth from his throne," Dove told Aly. "The raka believe he'll regain his throne one day, and return the rulership of the Isles to the raka."

"Where did you hear that?" asked Sarai, curious. "I never heard anyone say anything about his return."

"That's because you attract attention," Dove informed her older sister. "I go out of my way *not* to attract it, so I hear more things. People forget I'm there."

"Oh." Sarai shrugged. "I hate being quiet. It's so very boring."

Aly, shaking her head at Sarai's indifference to what she might learn this way, saw that Dove was shaking her head as well. For a moment their eyes met—hazel slave's and brown-black noble's—in perfect understanding.

Then Petranne yanked Aly's sleeve. "Now a story?" she asked, her voice teetering toward a whine.

The moment gone, Aly searched her memory for a tale. The information about Kyprioth she would consider later, in a quiet moment of her own.

"Once in a kingdom far away, a girl with a knack for handling horses came to a large fair held in the capital of Galla," she began.

"Will the Lioness be in this one?" asked Sarai eagerly. "Will there be battles?"

Dove kicked her sister gently. Petranne scowled and said, "Hush!"

Aly waited until Sarai was quiet again, then continued. "As I was saying, she came to the fair seeking work. . . ."

Frasrlund, on the Vassa River, Tortall's northwestern border
As soon as Aly's eyes closed, a vision presented itself, very different from those times when the crows taught her their language. This was one of Kyprioth's "letters from home" dreams, like the one in which she'd seen her father talk to her mother, with Lord Imrah's note in his pocket.

Now she rode high in the air, seeing the landscape below like a shadowy map. The place looked familiar. It was Frasrlund, Tortall's northern harbor city, an island at the mouth of the powerful Vassa River. In more peaceful times she had visited it often, though never with such a good view of the place.

The skies were dark, but the night was lit with torches, their flames driven nearly flat by a hard wind out of the east. Cities of torches lighting thousands of tents lay over hilly land on both sides of the Vassa. Torches burned also on the ramparts of the city, isolated from the armies by the tumbling river.

Frasrlund had been under siege by King Maggur of Scanra since the previous year. Now the Tortallans had driven Maggur's army back across the Vassa. The flags on the southern side of the river were Tortallan, those on the northern side Scanran. So the city was yet to be freed completely. That would come when Maggur either no longer held the northern throne or else signed a treaty promising to leave Frasrlund to Tortall. Until then the Tortallan army could not retreat. The minute troops were moved away from Frasrlund, the Scanrans would swarm over the river again, to encircle the prize and try to starve its people into surrender.

Stalemate, Aly thought, shaking her head. They can't drive us off, and we can't leave the city to them. Splendid. Mother must be bored out of her mind.

Thinking of her mother, Aly suddenly found herself inside a large canvas tent, lit by oil lamps and warmed by charcoal braziers. Alanna the Lioness sat at a rude camp table, writing reports.

Men clamored outside. Alanna grabbed the longsword that rested on her table and swept the blade from its sheath. Aly clenched ghostly fists in worry. She couldn't see how an enemy might get so close to the tents that housed the army's commanders, but there was no sense in Mother taking chances. Immortals, mages, or spies might well get near enough to do real damage here.

Alanna reached for her shield, then spun to face the door. The flap burst open and a tall man with black hair and a black, trimmed beard entered in a swirl of wind and cold air. Aly recognized King Jonathan, as her mother did. Alanna dropped her shield and knelt, placing her sword at her side.

King Jonathan IV, co-ruler of Tortall with his queen, Thayet, bent and scooped his old friend up into his arms. "Alanna, I'm so sorry," he said as he hugged her. "Is there any news yet?"

Alanna stepped back from him, confusion on her too-honest face. "News of what?"

"Myles hasn't been able to find a trace of her in Corus," the king said, pulling off his riding gloves. He investigated the contents of a steaming pitcher and poured its warm cider into a cup. "I've got the Bazhir looking around," the king added, "but we've had to be discreet." He drank and poured the cup full again. "Gods help us if our enemies find out she's missing."

Alanna turned her sword's hilt in her hands, her violet eyes on her king. "Thayet's missing?" When the king stared at her, blue eyes astonished, Alanna guessed, "One of the princesses? Really, Your Majesty—"

"Mithros," whispered Jonathan. "I thought you knew."

Alanna's hands tightened on her sword. She scowled at Jonathan. "Knew *what?*"

Jonathan rubbed his forehead and dropped into one of the empty chairs. "I thought George . . . Alanna, look, put the sword away."

Aly could see her mother was trembling. "Am I going to need it?" she asked, her voice tart. She went to her desk and picked up the sword's sheath, keeping her back to Jonathan. "Spit it out, Jon."

"It's Aly," the king began.

"She went to Port Legann . . ."

"Actually, it seems she never arrived there," Jonathan said, leaning forward on his chair. "She's missing."

Aly saw her mother's shoulders go stiff. She slid her sword into its sheath. "But George knows," she commented softly. "So *that's* why he hasn't written she's home. I thought maybe the letters went astray."

"He's looking for her. So have Myles and Gary and I. As soon as Numair settles Daine and the baby at the palace, he's going to search, too." He looked at her face and sighed. "I'm assuming George didn't want you upset—"

"Of course he didn't," Alanna said, putting her sword on its stand. "I hate it when he goes all chivalrous on me. I'm not some fragile blossom who can be distracted by—by bad news from home."

"He knows I need you here," said the king. "Not distracted. And everyone will notice if you go looking for her. You're too visible, remember. You don't want our enemies to realize your daughter, my goddaughter, is missing."

"I'm not a fool, sire." Alanna fought to speak calmly: Aly could see it in her face. She tried to touch her mother's shoulder, even hug her, but her arms passed through Alanna's body. The Lioness rubbed her arms as if she felt a chill and told the king, "I know we have enemies. All of us whom Aly calls family. Has anyone besides me scried for her?"

"I have," said the king. "So has Numair. We've found nothing. Numair's tried crystal, flame, water . . . they turn gray or they vanish when he does. All I see is fog. Look for her if you wish, but I think something, or someone, is hiding her from us. You have to pretend nothing's wrong, understand? For Aly's sake."

"Yes, I *do* understand," Alanna said quietly. She lifted her sword and drew it half out of its sheath. The metal sparkled with purple fire. Aly hadn't realized why her mother had always insisted there be three inches of mirror-bright blade near the hilt of her swords. Now she knew the answer: her mother was using the blade as she would a mirror, as a tool to scry with, not just as a weapon. "And I'll be calm. I'll pretend everything's just lovely. I know Aly has the tools to survive. She can defend herself, she's cleverer than I ever was, and she has all those things George taught her. I have to believe she's alive, and she's doing her best to stay that way." She scowled at the gray fog that raced over the surface of her blade, and rammed it into its sheath. Turning, she glared at her king. "May I be alone now, sire?" she asked. "I need to write to my husband."

The king was getting to his feet as Aly's surroundings faded. Encased in a fog, the sight of her mother's quarters gone from view, Aly heard a familiar light voice in her head. *I believe you didn't think she'd be worried. I believe it never occurred to you that she knew what you could do, let alone that her hope would be that you could protect yourself.*

She always treated me as a feckless child, Kyprioth! Aly retorted silently.

An impression you encourage, as I recall, the god reminded her.

The fog vanished. Aly sat in the crows' tree, surrounded in the night by crows.

We could be sleeping, trickster, one of the crows informed him. *Instead of laboring to teach a two-legger.*

One crow, with a silvery streak on his back, walked over to Aly and sat in her lap. *She's learning,* Nawat told his brethren. *Listen to how well she does. Aly, what is the noise for twenty?*

6

OF GOATS AND CROWS

Aly woke in the morning with a headache. While the other slaves and servants who had shared the great hall floor roused, she put away her bedding, gathered her day's meals in the kitchen, and took the goats out. Today she led them to a spot in the hills north of her previous day's grazing site so that she could survey a new part of the ground she might have to defend.

Once the goats were settled, she ate bread and cheese. The food and the crisp morning air cleared her head. Feeling a bit less worn, Aly washed her face and cleaned her teeth at a spring tucked between two rocks. She marked it on her map. If the afternoon was as hot as it promised to be, she meant to take a proper bath. She regretted the absence of soap, but unless she was ready to plod back to Tanair, she would have to manage without. Besides, Aunt Daine disapproved of people who used soap in a water source.

For a while Aly simply lazed, warming up in the sun, watching the goats, and thinking of her visions and dreams. She was just as glad not to be going home for a couple of months. By the time she returned, her mother would have forgiven her father for not revealing that Aly was gone. When Alanna was in a temper, anyone with sense was happier someplace else. Her father would survive—he could always laugh away her mother's bad moods—and Aly would come home when the storm had blown over.

She wished that her mother or the king had said what kind of baby Aunt Daine had birthed. No one could even magically tell the child's sex while it was in the womb. It had shifted both sex and shape constantly, pummeling poor Daine with everything from elephant feet to ostrich claws.

"I'm glad *I'm* not a shape-shifter," she told the younger goats, who were grazing nearby. "Well, there are advantages, but having a baby doesn't seem to be one of them."

Aly was studying the map she had made the day before when a shadow momentarily blotted out the light on her tablet. She looked up, to see a lone crow gliding overhead. At last he landed on a rock nearby and stayed there, flicking his wingtips. It was the crow's way to say, "This is my territory." Aly saw the white streak that marked him as Nawat, by far the most encouraging of her crow teachers.

"Nawat, it's too nice a day for more lessons," she called to him. "Didn't we do enough last night?"

Nawat hopped down beside her, still flicking his wingtips. Overhead Aly heard the voices of nine more crows. They flew toward the cut where the road led east, naming the things they saw, starting with calling Aly and her herd of animals *possible food*. They also identified Nawat, a badger in the rocks, the human-made wide trail through the barrier edge of the plateau, a herd of deer retreating to the mountain forests, and a lack of humans on the deer's trail.

Aly was quite pleased with herself. She had understood every sound they made. "I must be the best student you ever had," she remarked. Looking from the sky to Nawat, she saw the marked crow had opened her pack and was eating some of her bread.

"Now see here," Aly began. Then she remembered that Kyprioth had promised the crows would be fed. "He better not have told you *I'd* supply food for all of you," she complained. She picked up the roll he had picked at and tore it into pieces. Slowly she sat next to him and offered a piece with her fingers.

Nawat accepted the offering, stuffing it and the remaining bread into his large beak into the pouch under his tongue. Once his beak was full, he flew off. Aly dusted off her hands. "You're welcome!" she shouted after the retreating bird. When he was gone from view she picked up the parchment tablet and got to work.

In the days that followed, crows flocked to Tanair in their family groups. Nawat led them to Aly so they would get a good look at her. Once they were all familiar with her, the crows spread out over the plateau, relaying what they saw back to Aly through messengers, or describing the land during her dream lessons. These came at night, when Aly learned their speech as the crows learned hers. In the morning Aly rushed to write down all the crows had told her, forming a rough picture of the plateau from their descriptions. Nawat was always there to help, day and night.

She was startled by the complexity of the crow language. She also enjoyed their company, both in her dreams and out in the fields. She had always liked the glossy black creatures. Like Kyprioth, they were tricksters, stealing laundry, causing dogs to chase them until the dogs were exhausted, and trying their luck by interfering with pigs at their meals. Now she found their wicked sense of humor extended to their dream conversations with her. Only Nawat would not tease Aly, by day or by night. She seemed to fascinate him.

While the sun was up, as the crows described what they saw in the distance, Aly familiarized herself with the nearby village and farms. She struck up conversations with bakers, smiths, mothers, and herders. She helped women to hang laundry and tugged stubborn clumps of weeds or large rocks from the paths of farmers' ploughs. She held straps for harness makers and chased thieving dogs. The people were suspicious and wary of her. She expected that and didn't force herself on them. The important thing was that they got used to seeing her around.

A week after her first encounter with Nawat, Aly was mapping the ground on the southwestern side of the road when he told her that people were coming. Aly thrust her tablet between two stones and grabbed the staff that was the only weapon she was permitted as a slave. A few moments later she heard the approach of horses.

It was Sarai and Dove, dressed for riding and flushed after a morning gallop. Behind them rode their bodyguards: Fesgao and another man-at-arms. The girls swung out of their saddles and shook the stiffness of a hard ride from their bodies.

"We thought you could use company," Sarai remarked, unhooking a canteen from her belt. She opened it and drank greedily, letting water spill over her cheeks. If she was aware of the two men watching her, she gave no sign of it.

Aly looked at the girls. "Not to say that I'm not honored, my ladies, because I am, but it's hardly fitting for you to come see the goatherd," she pointed out in her best good-servant manner.

Dove sighed. "We're desperate, Aly. If we have to work in the stillroom one more day, Sarai will bite someone's head off. Then Papa would be disappointed in her. We thought a gallop would air us out."

"I hate stillrooms," grumbled Sarai as she took the saddle from her mare. Dove unsaddled her own mount. It seemed the girls planned to stay awhile. "If I have to stew up any more smelly plants, I will *scream*." Sarai placed her horse's blanket on the grass and sat on it. Aly watched Fesgao and his companion as they dismounted at a distance to leave the girls and Aly in relative privacy.

"Sarai is happier on horseback," Dove explained. "I don't mind mixing up spices and medicines, but it's hard to concentrate when Sarai starts to mutter."

Sarai plucked out the jeweled pins that held her coiled and braided hair in place. She set them in a pile beside her and pulled her heavy black hair out of its style as she lay back on the blanket. Once down, she arranged it in an ebony fan around her head. It was still wet from a morning's wash. "You could take my place, Aly. I'm sure Rihani would be happy for you to work in the stillroom. I'll tend goats."

"My heart just stopped dead with anticipation," asked Aly. "But no, I cannot leave the goats. They would bleat for me. I would hear their cries with the ears of my heart."

"You weren't really a maid, were you?" asked Dove. She had settled on a rock that overlooked the valley and the guards' position. "You don't talk like you were a maid."

"I'm an educated one. Most of us Tortallan common-born are, these days." Aly kept her eyes on her map as mentally she kicked herself. She could not act like her old self here. Just because there was no age difference between her and Sarai, and only four years between her and Dove, she could not treat them as equals. It didn't matter that on her mother's side her blood was far bluer than that of descendants of a ruffian lot who had invaded the Copper Isles scarcely three hundred years ago. "They insist on it. All children attend school for five years to learn to read and write and figure. The priest said I was his most promising student," she added proudly, the country girl praised by an educated man.

"King Oron says that your king and queen will regret educating their people one day," mused Sarai. She turned her face up to the sun. "An educated populace makes trouble, that's what he thinks."

And he's as daft as a Stormwing, Aly thought. Aloud she said meekly, "It's not my place to say, my lady." Motion drew her attention as Nawat landed beside Sarai. He poked his beak through the shimmering heap of hairpins. "Lady Sarai, look out."

Sarai sat up and yelped to find a crow so close to her. The bird snatched two jeweled pins and bounced back, steadying himself with his wings as the girl scrambled to her feet. "Give those back, you!" she cried, reaching for him. He leaped away again and again, leading Sarai on a chase across the grassy meadow. Aly gathered up the other hairpins before he returned for those as well.

"He's not at all shy of humans," Dove remarked from the rock where she sat, her arms clasped around her drawn-up knees.

"He isn't a normal crow," Aly admitted. She hid a smile. The crow jumped higher and higher each time Sarai lunged, but he never actually took flight. Aly knew he was tormenting the girl on purpose. "Perhaps he's someone's runaway pet."

"Oh, no," Dove replied. "It's illegal to keep crows as pets. Well, not illegal as in a law written in books, but the raka get really upset by it. Even luarin won't defy the custom."

"Why not?" Aly wanted to know. She knew two people at home who kept pet crows.

"They're sacred to Kyprioth," replied Dove. "Since tricksters have to be free to create mischief, the raka say it's bad luck to the house to hold a crow against its will."

"Well, nobody's holding this fellow now," Aly pointed out. "He just seems to have adopted me."

"I give up," Sarai told them, panting, as she returned. "He can keep them."

She collapsed on the blanket and fought to catch her breath. Aly wordlessly leaned over and poured the other pins into Sarai's lap.

"Kyprioth will be pleased," observed Dove. "He likes bright, shiny things, they say." She looked at Aly as Sarai began to braid her hair once more. "Do you have other stories about Alanna the Lioness?"

A jerk of her hand left a smear of charcoal on Aly's map. She painstakingly rubbed it off the parchment. Guilt flooded her veins as she remembered her mother's worry in the dream. "Why such interest?" she asked, glad she didn't blush easily. "I mean, forgive me, ladies, but I can see why the little ones are interested. All that fighting, and adventure. Children love heroic stories. You aren't children."

"It isn't just children who need heroes," Sarai replied, shocked. "Don't you see what she's done for women, for all women? The Lioness, your queen, Lady Knight Keladry, they're living proof that we have a warrior spirit, too, that it hasn't been bred out of the luarin blood. The Lioness is a true hero. She protected her country when no one else could, man or woman. Mithros, she found the Dominion Jewel, she's killed giants and monsters to defend those who can't fight them! That *proves* that we can do things men do. Not in the same way, perhaps, but we can still do them!"

"Everybody needs heroes, Aly," Dove added. "Everybody. Even grown women. Even slaves."

Aly looked at the younger girl. Dove's small, dark face was alive with enthusiasm. Keen intelligence shone in her dark eyes, and fire burned in her tawny cheeks. Something about her reminded Aly of the Lioness herself, though she would be hard put to name it. "Even the raka, my lady?" she asked.

"Especially the raka," Sarai told Aly.

Dove shrugged. "There's room enough in the Isles for both peoples, if only everyone could be brought to see as much."

Fesgao approached them and bowed. "My ladies, it is almost noon. Your father will be concerned."

Groaning, Sarai and Dove got to their feet, saddled their mounts, and rode away. Dove turned in the saddle just before they reached the road, and waved goodbye to Aly.

The dust had settled from their departure when Nawat returned. He walked over to Aly and dropped the two jeweled hairpins into Aly's lap. She grimaced and wiped crow saliva from the pins.

"Thank you, but slaves don't own jewels," she told him. "I would get in trouble if I'm caught with these. I'll give them back to Sarai. But it's sweet of you to want to give me a present, though," she said hurriedly. Without thinking, she reached out and ran a hand along the crow's glossy back. "I'm sorry," she said, pulling away. "I forgot you're wild. I didn't mean anything by it."

Nawat climbed onto her lap and gently ran his beak through Aly's growing hair. She closed her eyes, relaxing in the sun.

Hours passed. Gray clouds slid across the sky while Aly, Nawat and the goats prowled the countryside. By late afternoon rain began to fall. Aly wrapped her map book in oiled cloth, whistled the goats in, and led them home. Nawat flew overhead, perching under the roof of a village barn as Aly took her charges through the castle gate. She was soaked clean through. She wanted nothing more than dry clothes and a hot meal.

She put the goats in their outer courtyard pen. Entering the inner courtyard, she found the slaves and the six former bandits huddled under the eaves of the barracks and the kitchen. All stared miserably at the sky. The rain showed no sign of letting up. Unless they found room in the stable, they would have to eat in the wet, doing their best to keep rain out of their bowls.

The door to the keep opened to frame Duke Mequen, flanked by his duchess and Ulasim. "This is ridiculous," he said. "All of you, come into the hall. We'll manage for tonight, but I'll see to it that we get more tables and benches for the future. From now on, this household eats together."

"The servants won't like that," Lokeij murmured in Aly's ear.

She looked at the old hostler. "They'll learn to live with it, I suppose," she replied. "Somebody told me that's how it used to be done in older castles—the household ate and slept all together. It's only been the last two centuries that nobles took quarters of their own and the servants had a separate hall to sleep in."

Lokeij gripped the back of Aly's neck with a friendly hand. "A word of advice. Slaves aren't so knowledgeable about history," he murmured. "Not raka slaves, not luarin slaves, unless you've been specially educated and sold as a tutor. Are you a tutor?"

Aly smiled at him. "That's so sweet," she replied. "My da always said my brains were too big for my head."

Lokeij looked into her face, his rheumy dark eyes inspecting her almost pore by pore. "If I were you, little parrot, I'd rub dirt in my bright feathers and work harder to pass for a sparrow," he said.

Aly spread her tunic, streaked with grass and mud stains. "The goats have taken care of that, don't you think? I'm sparrowing already. Chirp. Tweet." She winked at him and entered the castle. She wanted to change to her spare set of dry clothes before supper and to return Sarai's hairpins.

That night, when she dreamed her crow lessons, Nawat was not there. Instead the senior female crow took over. In addition to teaching Aly new sounds and hearing Aly's explanation of sounds and behaviors made by humans, she introduced Aly to the new crows who had come to Tanair.

Aly saw no sign of her friend the next day, either. She heard and easily interpreted the calls of the crows, but Nawat had become company for her, out alone with the goats. She missed him as she took shelter under a tree from the daylong drizzle. With Nawat to talk to, she wouldn't have been so aware of the cold and damp. To warm up she tried some of the hand-to-hand combat exercises she had learned, but soon found that mud and wet grass made for tricky footing. More often than not she went sprawling, which amused both the goats and the crows.

When she returned to the castle at the end of the day, she found that long tables and benches had been placed in the main hall. There was an order to the seating. The duke and his family were on the dais, near the big hearth. The servants were arrayed at a long table set at right angles to the left of the dais. The men-at-arms who were not on duty took their seats at the first long table to the right. The slaves had lower tables—those with special skills like carpentry and smithcraft on the right, with the soldiers, general slaves like Aly, and the slave maids on the table below the free servants.

The new arrangement did not sit well with everyone, particularly the free luarin servants and the men-at-arms who had come with the family from Rajmuat. Ulasim and the fifteen other full- and part-blood raka seemed perfectly comfortable. Aly was just happy to be warm, dry, and sitting down.

Once the weather cleared up the next day, Dove and Sarai began regular visits with Aly after they and their guards took a morning ramble through the country around their new home. Sometimes they brought Petranne and taught the four-year-old to ride her pony, as her guard guided it on a lead rein.

Aly welcomed their company, particularly since Nawat had not returned, neither in her dreams nor during the day. She soon saw that, on the older girls' part, her attraction lay in her stories of Tortall, those too bloody or full of bedroom gossip for Petranne and Elsren. In exchange, Aly extracted Isles gossip from her visitors. Sarai knew most of the luarin and raka nobility, as she had been presented at court. Her descriptions of life there were precise, cutting, and without illusions. Dove seemed to have spent her time in Rajmuat in different circles, among the capital's intellectuals and more worldly merchants, studying politics, trade, and the affairs of foreign nations.

The more time she spent with those girls, the more respect Aly had for them. They would have been at home in the circle of clever, observant women that were Aly's adoptive aunts. More than once Aly caught Dove eyeing her after she'd asked a question that a slave might not be expected to ask. She had to wonder if Dove, at least, did not suspect there was much more to Aly than a metal ring around her neck.

Sometimes the Balitangs stayed long enough to eat lunch with Aly. More often they visited for a short time before they returned to the castle and the duties Winnamine had set for them. With only a fifth of the servants who'd worked at the Rajmuat house, every member of the family was now required to help with chores. Mequen met with villagers, supervised repairs to the walls, and oversaw the building of new sheds and sleeping quarters within the castle walls. Sarai and Winnamine plied their needles, not on ladylike embroidery and tapestry work, but on plain sewing for the household. Dove, who loathed needlework, worked in the stillroom and learned to spin. When the older girls described their labors to Aly, they spoke as if work were an adventure. Aly hoped they would feel the same when winter made it impossible to leave the castle.

Twice a merchant caravan came to Tanair with supplies. On both visits Aly saw the merchants reach the Balitang lands through the road in the rocks. The crows warned her ahead of time so that she could look over the merchants and decide if they were a threat or not. They were always welcomed at village and castle, both for the items they carried and for the news of the realm.

Two weeks after her arrival at Tanair, Aly was drowsing in the late morning sun when the crows set up a racket that made her jump to her feet and draw the stolen knife from her waistband. She couldn't tell what they were saying—none of their sounds were those she had been taught. Skeins of shrieking birds flew by, bound for the southern road, where they circled and dove at a man who walked there.

Aly sharpened her Sight until she saw the newcomer as clearly as if he stood before her. A young man of her age, he carried a sack over one shoulder, one not big enough to hold what he might need for life on the road. His luarin-style tunic and leggings were patched and darned, showing plenty of wear. He was barefoot, and he walked in an awkward manner, as if he had not really mastered the use of feet. The strangest thing about him was the way his skin looked to her Sight: feather patterns showed under every inch of bare flesh.

Curious, Aly told the goats "Stay," and trotted down to the road. Something about that feathered pattern was very interesting.

"Hello, Aly," the newcomer said in a pleasant baritone as she approached. His skin was dark, but not raka brown—more like her da's coloring than a raka's. His eyes were brown, long-lashed, and deeply set on either side of a long, thin razor of a nose. His cheekbones were sharp, his chin square with a hint of a point. His mouth was long and slender, the lower lip fuller than the upper. He wore his short black hair tousled, as if he'd combed it back with his fingers. He was nearly six feet tall, with a wiry build. The way he moved, Aly half expected him to leap straight up into the air at any moment and not come down. The feather patterns under his skin were even clearer to her Sight up close than they'd been when she first looked at him. She thought that if she touched him, she might *feel* feathers, as if he'd pulled a human skin on for a disguise.

He'd called her by name. "Do we know each other?" she asked.

"I looked different before." The newcomer knelt and placed his sack in the roadway. "I am sorry I have been away so long," he added, undoing the knot and spreading out the cloth. "I had to practice this shape. It is not what I am used to. I am used to it now, though." He looked up at Aly. "I am here to serve you and the two-legger queen-to-be."

Aly peered into his face. If he wore another shape normally, one with feathers . . . "Nawat?" she whispered.

Nawat smiled at her, his entire face lighting up. "I did not want you to see me fumble like a nestling," he explained. "This shape, and the talking, are hard. My friends say I am even sillier than a nestling." He waved up to the crows whirling over their heads.

"But . . . are you a mage?" Aly asked, tucking her knife back into her waistband. "A, a shape-shifter? A god?" But I would have seen those things in him, she thought, completely bewildered.

"I am Nawat Crow," Nawat replied. "*They* could do this, if they wished." He looked up at the crows again. "They do not wish."

Aly sat on a boulder at the side of the road. "Aunt Daine never said crows could make themselves into humans."

Nawat shrugged as birds did, thrusting his shoulder blades up from his back. "We do not give away all our secrets." He smiled. "I can help you better this way. I learned to make arrows for the two-leggers." He gestured to the contents of his open satchel. "They prize arrows, and no one makes them by the stone sticks where you live."

"Castle," Aly murmured, nibbling her lower lip as she tried to work this all out in her mind. She nearly had control of her thoughts when she made the mistake of truly looking at Nawat's satchel.

"Goddess save me," she whispered in awe, picking up a feather as long as her forearm, stippled in a pattern of gold and soft black. "This is a griffin feather! And this one, and this . . . How did you get these?" she asked. "They're worth a fortune. Everyone knows you hit what you shoot at with griffin fletching."

"They are sparkly," Nawat said. "The griffins shed them. I thought if I brought you a present that was made of discarded things, no one would punish you for having them."

Steel glinted through the heap of shimmering griffin feathers. Carefully Aly pushed them aside. At the bottom of the pile she found strips of metal, shaped like bird feathers. She gulped. With a trembling hand she lifted a feather a handspan in length and drew its tip along the corner of the cloth satchel. The corner fell neatly away, as if sliced by a razor. "*Stormwing* feathers?" she whispered, meeting Nawat's deep-set gaze. "You're carrying *Stormwing* feathers?"

Again that shrug. "They molt," Nawat replied. "The feathers are shiny. I collected them and washed them," he added.

Aly was glad to be sitting down. Neither griffins nor Stormwings liked others to approach their nests or flocking grounds. Her own mother would rather face a company of hill bandits than a nesting griffin. "What did you mean, the two-legger queen-to-be?"

"She lives with you in the stone sti—the castle," Nawat corrected himself. "She flocks with you sometimes, when you sit with them." He pointed over Aly's shoulder. When she looked back, she saw that the goats had followed her and were grazing beside the road.

"So much for telling you to stay," Aly remarked, more to herself than to the goats. She turned to watch Nawat again. He means Sarai or Dove, I bet, she thought. That's why Kyprioth wagered me that I couldn't keep the children alive. He wants a half-raka queen, and he fears he won't have a contender after this summer.

"Are you not glad that I came?" Nawat asked, a worried look on his handsome face. "I will help you better this way, with arrows, with the crows. I will be your friend."

The word hit Aly's own heart with all the force of an arrow loosed from a bow. She had no real friends here. Spies don't have friends at all, she told herself, but Nawat's offer was impossible to resist. She was lonely. Nawat at least wouldn't penalize her for being luarin, Tortallan, a slave, or her parents' daughter.

"Put those away," she told him, pointing to the piles of feathers. "We'll go eat lunch and figure out what story you will tell the Balitangs, so they'll take you on as a fletcher."

"I cannot say I am a crow?" asked Nawat, tying his satchel up once more.

"You can, but they'll think you're mad," Aly said. "They won't let you near the family unless you have a story they will believe."

"You will tell a fine story," Nawat said cheerfully. "You do well with such things."

Aly grinned. "Thank you for the compliment," she replied.

"It is my first," replied Nawat. "I am glad my first compliment is a good one." Aly looked at him to find his eyes twinkling with mischief. Aly shook her head with a smile. It would be good to have a friend who was a crow. They knew how to have fun.

She worried about taking a stranger who was not raka home, but her worry turned out to be useless. The castle's part-raka bowyer, Falthin, was a single man whose son had drowned at sea two years before. Nawat reminded him of his lost child. Falthin took the young man into his village home eagerly, particularly when he had seen the treasure trove of feathers Nawat brought with him.

Hearing about the newcomer, Duke Mequen, Sergeant Veron, and Ulasim each went separately to Falthin's shop or to his home to meet Nawat. All returned with good things to say. Nawat's singularly innocent, friendly nature opened doors for him that the feathers did not.

Aly overheard Ulasim tell Lokeij, "The boy is a bit simple, but good-hearted—no threat to us as far as I can tell." At some point during the summer she would find out what precisely Ulasim meant by "us," but for now she was glad that no one seemed to think Nawat was dangerous. She did wonder if Kyprioth had done anything to smooth the young crow's way, but if he had, Aly saw no traces of it anywhere.

Nawat also drew a good deal of attention from the castle and village girls. Whenever Aly returned for the day with her goats, she would find one or two girls lingering around the bench where Nawat worked, outside Falthin's workshop, where the fumes from the glue he used would disperse in the open air. Often one of those women was Sarai, who told Dove in Aly's hearing that she thought Nawat "adorable." For some reason that soured Aly's mood, until she realized that Nawat treated Sarai with the same friendly grace he showed to every other person in Tanair. He kept his most wicked glances and murmured jokes for Aly. She wasn't sure if this was a good thing or not, but she was pleased to get something from him that Sarai could not.

The hardest thing to remember is to keep your mouth closed. You'll be tempted to say what you know, or mention that you've met folk you've no right to meet. Keep your counsel, hold your tongue. Good listeners live longer. And keep in mind it's harder to keep your mouth buttoned on the things you know more about than those you're with.

—*From* A Handbook for the Royal Intelligence Service, *by George Cooper, given to Aly for her tenth birthday*

7

CONVERSATIONS

Three weeks after the family's arrival at Tanair, Aly took her goats up into the rocky ground just east of the castle, nearly three miles north of the road that led to Kellaura Pass. Chenaol's nine-year-old great-niece Visda, who tended one of Tanair village's herds of sheep, led her flock to graze near Aly's. She led her dogs, who clearly thought they could herd so much better than these two-leggers.

When Sarai and Dove came with their bodyguards at midmorning, the four girls started a game of skip-rope on the bare ground next to a watering hole. Sarai was taking her turn, with Aly and Visda to spin the rope, when the crows who watched the road set up a racket. Aly dropped the rope and clambered onto a rock to hear them better. Once she could translate what they said, she slid back to the ground where the other three girls waited, staring at her.

"Lady Sarai, might I ask a favor?" she asked in her best well-trained-slave manner. Adding a trace of the attitude of one who is versed in secrets, she went on, "I may not say as yet how I know this, but a party is riding this way from the pass. It is led by a warrior in armor, and numbers twenty soldiers and five others—attendants, I believe. You are a swift rider. Will you carry word of this to His Grace, your father?"

Sarai raised her thin brows. "We have men on guard where the road enters Tanair, Aly," she pointed out.

"Three miles south of us, my lady," Aly replied. "The crows do not believe these men are hostile, but a little more warning is always useful."

"*You* speak to the crows," Sarai remarked in disbelief.

Aly smiled and bowed, now the mysterious mage. "Say rather, my lady, they speak to me." It's the truth, too, she thought, waiting for the young noblewoman to make up her mind. For once it would have been useful if I were

Mother, she added ruefully. When she tells people to do things, they snap to. Of course, she isn't a slave in a hostile country.

"Has this got anything to do with Papa and the duchess's talking to you every night behind closed doors?" asked Dove.

Aly glanced at the younger girl, all thoughts of her mother gone. "Oh, my lady, you give me far too much credit," she said, meeting Dove's stern gaze with amusement. "As if the likes of them would have serious talk with the likes of me." Behind her humorous mask she mentally kicked herself. She had to remember that Dove was quick and perceptive!

Sarai beckoned to Fesgao, who waited at a slight distance with Dove's bodyguard and the horses. The raka led Sarai's mount forward with his own. She swung herself into the saddle. "You'd better keep up," she told Fesgao. With that, she kneed her mare into a trot, then a gallop. Fesgao urged his mount after Sarai, who rode as if she were a centaur and one creature with her horse.

"She's the best horsewoman I know," Dove remarked as her guard brought her mount. "If Mother could ride like Sarai, she'd be alive now. Sarai never would have tried that jump, not without knowing what lay on the other side." She mounted and followed her sister to the castle, her guard at her side.

Aly turned to Visda. "Watch my goats for me?" she asked.

The girl nodded. "The dogs won't mind," she told Aly with a grin.

Aly raced up into the rocks, bound for the ones that afforded a clear view of the distant road. As she climbed, she realized that she needed to cut herself free of the goats. She had covered all of the ground reachable with a herd in tow. Today she'd been lucky to have Visda there when the alarm sounded. Otherwise she might have been forced to leave the goats, risking the loss of some, if not all. They couldn't afford to lose a single animal, and she needed more freedom of movement.

Panting, she approached the highest point of a giant slab of granite. Once there, she lay down until only her head rose above the stone, noting the crows scattered among the rocks and trees between her position and the road. Now that she was visible to them, they fell silent. Here came the new arrivals, clothed luarin-style in tunics and breeches, their armor and weapons glinting in the sun. Their pack animals were heavily laden, as if for a long march or a long stay. At the head of their double column rode a helmeted man in light armor. Aly sharpened her Sight to get a better look, as the Balitang men-at-arms who were posted to watch the road motioned for him to stop.

She instantly recognized the leader. Silently she wriggled back from her vantage point until she could turn over and stare at the sky. Prince Bronau. Why was he here? Had he come as the duke's friend or as a servant of the Crown? If so, what were the Crown's orders?

She hummed to herself, thinking. If Bronau had been ordered to capture or kill the duke and his family, he hadn't brought enough men. He knew how many trained soldiers the duke had, because he had seen them off on their journey north. For all he knew, the duke might have added new fighters on the way. Aly smiled. Actually, the duke had done just that, binding the six bandits to him with blood. Their families had trickled up to Tanair, solidifying the former bandits' allegiance to the duke, who now fed and housed them.

Carefully, she rolled onto her stomach and crept back to her vantage point, bringing her magical Sight to bear on the prince once more. Bronau looked to be in a good mood, joking with the roadside guards as they waved him on. The guards' messenger was already leading his horse out of the shelter of the rocks. As soon as he reached flat ground he rode off at a gallop, carrying the word of the new arrivals to the duke and duchess, not knowing that Sarai would be there before him.

Aly continued to inspect Bronau's party. The servants who rode behind the prince also looked relaxed and comfortable. If Bronau's errand was a violent one, surely his attendants and soldiers would be more wary. These soldiers looked as if the only thing on their minds was shedding their armor on this hot, sunny day.

Aly slid down the granite slab. She wouldn't know anything more until tonight, when she could collect the gossip at Tanair.

The duchess, however, had other plans. Aly and Visda were about to eat lunch when one of Lokeij's boy hostlers rode up on Winnamine's own gelding. "Her Grace asks for you to attend her, Aly," the lad told her, dismounting. "I'm to take the goats and you're to report to Her Grace in the keep. Hullo, Visda." When Aly blinked at him, caught off balance, the boy rolled his eyes and thrust the reins at her. "I know you're practically fresh-caught, but even you ought to know better than to keep the mistress waiting."

"Oh—yes, of course," Aly stammered. She mounted the gelding clumsily, so that the two watching her wouldn't mention how curiously at home Aly was on horseback, and set out, with much flailing and rein tugging, back toward the road. Only when she knew Visda and the boy couldn't see her anymore did she kick the horse into a gallop.

She slowed when she came within view of Tanair's walls but kept the gelding at a trot up to the castle, allowing herself to bounce on his back like the greenest of riders. Lokeij himself took the reins from her as she tumbled from the saddle. "You need practice," he told Aly, grinning.

"Not on your life," she gasped, as if she had never had to ride before. She lurched into the keep.

Dove waited for her at the door. "*She* wants you," she told Aly, and towed her into a small room off the main hall. Normally it was a study, but Winnamine stood there now with a basin of steaming water, a towel, soap, and a clean tunic and leggings.

"Thank you, Dovasary," she said. "Close the door behind you." Dove obeyed. Winnamine turned to Aly. "Wash up, please," she ordered. "I have just promoted you to maidservant. You'll serve the wine right now, while my lord entertains Prince Bronau, and at table tonight. Ordinarily I would do it myself, but we have no housekeeper now, which means I must make all of their sleeping arrangements."

"Could not Ulasim . . . ?" Aly inquired.

The duchess shook her head. "Ulasim is off with the men cutting wood for our fires. How could he know we were to have company? Which means I must take charge of our servants and make room for Bronau and his train. Besides, if you are to be our advisor, now is a good time to start. I would like to know what you make of Bronau's presence. You may see things with your fresh gaze that His Grace and I would not, having been friends with the prince all our adult lives."

"The duke does not expect me to wait on them?" Aly wanted to know.

"No," Winnamine replied calmly, "but I can't arrange this any other way. He may be polite and ask you to stand where you can't hear them, but at least you'll be able to form an impression of the prince. Is he hiding anything, is he uncomfortable, is he frightened . . ." Winnamine sighed. "I wish he'd given us warning!"

"I'm honored to serve, Your Grace," Aly told her mistress smoothly. "It won't matter if His Grace asks me to stand out of earshot. I read lips."

Winnamine put her hands on her hips and looked down the three inches between her eyes and Aly's. "Well! Now there's a bit of luck! Or maybe not luck, with a god involved. You read lips. Amazing."

Aly grinned. "I thought you might feel that way about it, Your Grace," she replied.

"I am grateful for any advantage," the duchess confided. "What a mess! Let's have that tunic off, Aly." As she helped Aly to pull the dirty tunic over her head, Winnamine continued to speak, thinking aloud. "We'll give the second floor to him and his servants. My lord and I will share with Sarai and Dove. His men will have to sleep in the new guest quarters. We haven't got enough beds, but I won't quarter them on the villagers. Our people work hard enough to feed and house themselves. I wish Bronau had known what a burden he was placing on us. Chances are he didn't know how small this place is. At least you don't need a comb."

Aly soaped her hands and arms. "Why me, Your Grace?" she asked. "Why not a regular maid? You asked for me before I told you I read lips."

The duchess rubbed cream onto her hands. They were trembling. "We've tried to put a good face on it, for the servants, and the children, but Aly, we are in mortal peril. Two years ago . . ." Her voice shook.

Aly looked around the room and spied a pitcher and cups on a tray. The pitcher held water. She poured some into a cup and offered it to Winnamine. The older woman took it with both hands and drank. When she had composed herself, she said evenly, "His Majesty dreamed that his son Hanoren turned into a rat and bit him. Hanoren and all his household were nailed to crosstrees along Rajmuat harbor." Her mouth twisted bitterly. "Needless to say, shipping fell off badly that year."

Aly started to say she knew the story, but held her tongue. It was not something a country maid would have heard.

"Now my lord and I are out of royal favor," Winnamine said, returning her cup to Aly. "The king might still dream about us. And here is Bronau. His could be the breath of wind that knocks us into Rajmuat harbor."

Aly removed her leggings and pulled the clean clothes on, watching the duchess through her eyelashes. "Is this your only reason for calling on me, Your Grace?"

Winnamine twisted a handkerchief in her fingers. "Bronau is amusing, charming, and careless. He goes after what he wants. When he doesn't want it anymore, he drops it. We live on the edge of the king's suspicions, Aly, and Bronau doesn't think. The god says we must trust your insights. I mean to place you where you will get them." She got to her feet and left as Aly straightened her clothes.

Watching the duchess go, Aly glimpsed a flicker of orange the shade of Dove's gown as the door opened. She wondered how long Dove had been listening. If Dove was going to make a habit of it, she ought to learn that anyone who looked at the opening between door hinges would see a color that didn't match that of the door.

The duchess returned with the wine tray, two pitchers, and cups. "Don't kneel, just bow. Serve the prince first," she told Aly. "The pitcher with the mermaid on the grip is for Mequen. The wine in it is well watered. Fill Bronau's cup as often as you can, of course. Wine always loosens his tongue, another thing that makes him a perilous friend."

Aly nodded. Balancing it carefully, she carried the heavy tray up the stairs to the family's private chambers.

A footman let her into the duke's sitting room, now given over to the prince. Mequen and Bronau sat in chairs on either side of a table, perfectly relaxed. Aly bowed and set the tray down, ignoring the duke's questioning eyes. She poured out a cup of wine from the unmarked pitcher for the prince and one from the mermaid pitcher for the duke. Mequen accepted the cup with a slight frown. "Will Her Grace not be joining us?" he asked, obviously puzzled.

"She is finding quarters for His Highness's servants and guards," Aly said with a polite bow. "She sends her regrets."

Mequen's frown deepened. "Then why does she not ask the house—" He stopped abruptly, then sighed. "I had forgotten. We no longer have a housekeeper." To Bronau he said, "I didn't realize what a spoiled creature I had become until we had to make do with twenty-odd servants and slaves instead of over a hundred. I think you'll like this vintage, Your Highness." To Aly he said, "Stand by the far wall, please, Aly. Out of earshot."

As she obeyed, Bronau asked, "Do your people expect us to drink ourselves under the table, sending up two pitchers?" He and Mequen touched cups and tasted their wine.

"Actually, I've been drinking the local brew, to help the villagers make a little extra coin against the winter," the duke replied easily. "It's crude stuff, but if I don't drink it after I buy it, they'll return my money. Proud people, these highlanders. I won't subject you to it. What you have is a proper wine laid down by my father."

"It has a southern taste," Bronau admitted, drinking. "You coddle your people, Mequen."

"It would be different in Rajmuat," Mequen admitted. "We're isolated here, and must depend on these folk to get us through the winter."

Aly took her place and read the men's speech on their lips. She also employed her Sight to catch any lies.

"King Oron has turned that suspicious gaze on *me* now," Bronau told his friend. "The old man gets stranger with each sunrise. He's hiding in his quarter of the palace, has been for weeks. All of his food is tested for poison. He had your old friend Athan Fajering executed for—are you ready for this?—wrong thoughts."

Mequen turned white under his summer tan. "But Athan was his chancellor for eighteen years!"

Bronau nodded. "He was also an enemy of my dear sister-in-law Imajane, and my charming brother Rubinyan. You know Rubinyan has never been that fond of me," Bronau continued. "When Oron started to watch me, I started to think that Imajane and Rubinyan might well decide to inform him that I have 'bad thoughts,' too."

Mequen sighed, shaking his head. "I wish that you and Rubinyan would reconcile. It grieves me that my two best friends are at odds. And I think you wrong your brother, suggesting that he is turning the king against you. Rubinyan is a good man," he said earnestly, almost pleading. "He is reserved, and hard to know, but he is a wise and strong ally."

Bronau shook his head. "You always think the best of people, Mequen. If he is so good, why didn't he come to see you off?"

After a few more attempts, Mequen gave up trying to get the prince to see his brother in a kinder light. "One day, mark my words, you'll change your tune about Rubinyan," he said.

"The two of them are isolating that old fool Oron," Bronau said after his fourth cup of wine. "Soon he'll see only Imajane and Rubinyan, and one day they'll come to tell the court he's dead. They also spend plenty of time with Prince Hazarin," the prince confided. "I have to hope they don't turn Oron's most likely heir against me."

"Don't be ridiculous," Mequen assured him. "Hazarin likes you. He always says the rest of court's much too grim when you're away."

"The rest of the court is terrified of Oron," Bronau replied with a laugh. "They don't dare twitch."

At last Winnamine came to say a hot bath awaited Bronau. Mequen shooed Aly out. She gathered up the wine tray and cups while he and Winnamine told Bronau they would see him at supper. Once they were outside, Winnamine put the tray on a side table and indicated that her husband and Aly should go upstairs. She led the way into the sitting room of what had once been Sarai and Dove's chambers. Neither girl was in sight.

The duke and duchess took seats as Aly checked the door to the servants' stair. She could hear the maids preparing rooms for the prince and his servants. To be on the safe side, when she closed the door, she pulled the carpet up until it covered the space where the door didn't quite touch the stone floor, and stuffed the rag she used as a handkerchief in the keyhole. Then she covered the crack under the main door. She found a dust cloth and stuffed a corner of it into the keyhole. Then she opened the door to the older girls' bedchambers so that she would see if anyone came in that way. At last she nodded to her masters.

Mequen looked at his wife. "My dear, why send Aly to wait on us?" he wanted to know. "I know you were busy with your domestic arrangements, but surely one of the girls with experience waiting on the nobility would have served." He smiled kindly at Aly. "Though you did a creditable job."

"Aly isn't used to Bronau as we are, my dear," Winnamine explained. "She might see what would be hidden to us. And she has certain useful skills."

"Useful?" Mequen asked, raising his brows at Aly.

"I read lips, Your Grace," Aly said meekly. "And I can tell you that the prince is telling the truth about why he came."

"What? How could you possibly know that?" the startled duke demanded.

"Liars blink more when they lie, or they look away while they answer," Aly explained. She did not want anyone to know about her Sight if she could help it. Only a fool told all of her secrets. "The prince is frightened." She looked at the duke. "Did you see he was sweating when he talked about the situation at court?"

Mequen raised his eyebrows. "All of us sweat when we think of the royal court," he said drily. "I am so accustomed to it that I didn't even notice. Truly, the god blessed us when he sent you." He held Aly's gaze with his own. "But he didn't bless you, did he?"

"I am Your Grace's servant," Aly told him, wide-eyed and earnest.

"Very courtier-like," remarked the duke. "One would think you a practiced associate of kings."

Aly had to shoo him away from this line of thought. She beamed at him. "So many compliments from Your Grace tonight!" she said, allowing her lashes to flutter. "I will become conceited, and the other servants will be hurt that they have not drawn your gracious attention."

"Aly, the Players lost a star performer when you didn't elect to train as a professional fool," the duchess said with a smile.

Aly shrugged comically. "The Players' loss is Your Graces' gain," she said, then added as a deliberate afterthought, "Mine, too, of course." She looked at the duke. "Truly, Your Grace, why fidget over what use the god makes of insignificant me?"

"Because I receive better service from someone who is happy," replied Mequen. "Because you are not insignificant, however much you may jest about it. And we know so little about you, except that bright Mithros says you will guide us through great trouble. Don't blame a man for curiosity, messenger." He looked at his duchess and sighed. "Well, my dear?"

From the corner of her eye, Aly saw orange cloth in the crack between the door to the bedroom and the wall. She really would have to suggest better ways for Dove to eavesdrop.

"We can accommodate them. Barely," Winnamine replied, bringing Aly's attention back to the duke and duchess. "We're putting his men-at-arms up in the new barn. They're not at all pleased, but they have no choice. What of our people? Shall we send them out of the great hall at mealtimes?"

Mequen shook his head. "Perhaps if Bronau sees how limited our space is, he'll rusticate somewhere else. Besides, our people earn their place in the hall through their work."

Realizing they had finished with her, Aly murmured a farewell, bowed, and went to the main door of the suite. Carefully she returned the rug to its correct position and removed the dust cloth from the keyhole.

"You'll remember to pour the wine at the head table at supper, won't you, Aly?" asked the duchess.

Aly turned and bowed. "Of course, Your Grace."

First she ought to see to her goats. When she went outside, she found the inner courtyard awash in Bronau's people, as well as anyone from Tanair who had a reasonable excuse to be present. The only quiet place was the spot near the guard barracks where Nawat worked at his bench in the sun, gluing feathers to arrow shafts. For once he wasn't encircled by admiring females. Aly hesitated, then walked across to him.

Nawat didn't even look up from the painstaking task of setting a goose feather in its bed. "Your feathers are ruffled," he said.

"Well, it's very exciting, having visitors and all," she said, looking at the new arrivals.

"You act like a flock when a snake crawls by," the crow-man pointed out. "If that is excitement, it is not the good kind. Do you wish to mob them, to drive them away?"

"I couldn't even if I wanted to," she informed him, smiling. For all his human guise, he was still very much a crow. Impulsively she asked, "Did you get a look at him? The prince?"

"The one with fox-colored hair? He came to see me work." Nawat looked up at Aly and grinned, white teeth flashing against his tanned skin. "I did it badly."

"What do you make of him?" Aly wanted to know. "Or did you not have time to get a sense of him?"

He replied with a wing shrug, then said, "I do not need time. I know a hawk when I see one."

"A hawk?" she repeated, thinking he had recognized Bronau's hunter bird look.

"A hawk," Nawat said firmly, his eyes on his work once more. "He will drive you off your own kill and steal your nestlings. He *should* be mobbed, before he steals any of yours. Shall you and I mob him?"

Aly tugged her ear, frowning. Somehow Nawat didn't have the same view of hawks as that held by people who'd been born human. "Unlike a hawk, Bronau comes with a flock of soldiers. You and I are outnumbered."

"We could mate," Nawat suggested eagerly. "In a year our nestlings would be large enough to mob anyone we like. In two or three years we could have still more nestlings, until no hawk will venture near our territory. Shall I court you? Do you like grubs or ants better?"

Aly smiled, finding him both silly and lovable. "It takes longer for human nestlings to get big enough to mob," she explained, wondering if Aunt Daine's conversations with animals were like this. "And I'm too busy to court. I've the goats to fetch, for one."

"I will be here," Nawat said placidly, returning to his work. "In case you change your mind about mating."

Aly brought her animals in early, then spent the afternoon idling around Bronau's people. All of them were relieved to be away from the king. They spoke of the arrival of more Stormwings, and of the many noble families who had decided to summer in the country. Only those who feared that the king would consider their departure suspicious had remained at court. Prince Hazarin was the only noble who acted as he had always done, drinking and attending parties in the pleasure district night after night.

When Bronau joined the Balitangs for supper, he brought gifts for the family. For Mequen and Winnamine he had newly published sets of books, which they received with true enthusiasm. A soldier marionette went to Elsren, a gorgeous doll dressed in Yamani fashions to Petranne, and a history of Carthak to Dove.

For Sarai, Bronau produced eardrops that were clusters of tiny peach-colored moonstones the same golden tint as her cheeks, and a gold necklace with a matching pendant. Sarai was overwhelmed. She immediately removed her white pearl eardrops and donned the new ones in their place. When she fumbled with the catch on the necklace, Bronau offered to help. Sarai lifted the heavy braided coils of her hair so that he could see better. With the necklace fastened, he turned Sarai to face him as she beamed at him.

"Lovely," Bronau said with a tender smile. He took Sarai's hand and kissed it.

Aly, standing behind them on the dais, looked at the wine tray she was holding, her mind working busily. Prince Bronau had brought gifts nicely chosen to appeal to each Balitang. It might just be coincidence that his gift to the oldest, marriageable daughter of the house was the kind of token a girl would see as an indication of special affection. It might also be coincidence that his gift had given Bronau a chance to touch Sarai, and Sarai an excuse to let him.

Aly glanced at Dove. The twelve-year-old held her book open to a detailed map, but her eyes were on Bronau and her sister. Mequen and Winnamine had also seen the exchange between their oldest daughter and their friend.

A footman collected the books, doll, and marionette as kitchen servants brought out the food. Aly poured wine into the cups of everyone on the dais, then took up the water pitcher. It was customary to dilute supper wine. She used less water for the prince, duke, duchess, and Sarai, and a good bit of it for Dove, Petranne, and Elsren, then took her position behind the prince and the duchess.

The servants passed along the dais, starting with the prince and ending with Elsren, offering a loaded tray to everyone. The older diners selected the things they wanted, while the healer Rihani chose Petranne's and Elsren's meal. The offerings were a mixture of foods of the Eastern Lands, Southern Lands, and raka kitchens. Aly recognized the salad of long beans, chilies, coconut, shrimp paste, and garlic, having sampled it in the leftovers from a meal back in Rajmuat. There was a noodle salad, another favorite raka dish adopted by the luarin, this one with garlic, chilies, cashews, peanuts, and celery. There were chicken dumplings, dates stuffed with curried jackfruit, and pickled asparagus.

Looking at it all, Aly shivered. She had eaten a great deal of rice since her arrival in the Isles, to the point where she was beginning to feel a bit grainy. It was hard to trust local fare when there was always a risk that some bright bit of red or green would set her mouth afire, but the diners here, luarin and raka, ate this strange selection as easily as her own family consumed meals of apple frit-ters, fish pasties, and venison. The chief change to the Balitangs' diet since their arrival at Tanair was the absence of seafood, which was otherwise the backbone of Isle cooking. She was grateful for the lack. There were too many volcano-blast chilies in the seafood dishes of the Copper Isles.

During the meal Bronau relayed news of the capital. He described recent plays, performers, and books, and news from the Eastern and Southern Lands. Aly took it all in, noting that Scanra continued to attack Tortall, despite heavy losses and rumors of rebellion among Maggur's lords. The luarin free servants listened to every word, as did Sergeant Veron and some of his luarin and part-luarin men-at-arms. The raka and many of those who were part raka seemed indifferent. Bronau's people looked around at their surroundings, obviously unimpressed.

If you think we're countrified now, Aly thought evilly, *wait till they bring out the dishes made with goat's milk. That should put a pickle up your noses!*

Petranne and Elsren were soon squabbling, their bellies full. Their nurse-maid had to gently scold them several times. Dove was intent on Bronau's con-versation, but what she made of it Aly couldn't tell. Sarai, too, was listening to the prince, her lovely eyes shining in admiration. Like Dove, Winnamine and Mequen listened with polite interest but without giving away their thoughts. Aly approved. After her observation of the prince, she no more trusted him not to repeat anything the Balitangs might say than she could trust him not to repeat what other nobles had told him since the Balitangs' departure. Though their remarks were cruel, Bronau didn't seem to notice that his gossip upset his hosts. Sarai's admiring mood evaporated as she listened to what their fellow nobles had said of them. She folded her napkin into small pleats, her lips pressed tightly together. The duke and the duchess toyed with their wine-glasses, their eyes glittering.

As Aly was pouring the last cup of wine for the meal, Bronau half turned to get a better look at her. "I know you," he said with a smile. "You're the little luarin slave who opened the door, the night I brought the king's news to my friends. You've risen in the world, from doorkeeper to wine pourer."

Aly bowed. "I do all manner of chores now, Your Highness," she mur-mured. "I would not have had this opportunity in Rajmuat."

"I'll bet it's not as exciting here as in the capital," the prince said. "If my memory's right, you had more of a Tortallan accent then. Did it rub off in the jungle? And your hair has grown more. The color is most becoming." He was teasing her, his gray eyes dancing.

Aly knew what she was expected to do. She did it, bridling and smiling at the prince. "I've learned ever so much more since I first saw Your Highness," she told him, acting the flattered female. Privately she supposed that Bronau was well enough, as men went, though he was much too old for her—he looked to be in his mid-thirties. Smile as he might and wink as he did when he straightened in his chair, Aly was unmoved. He did have nice hair, charm, and elegance, but he was lipless, shallow, and direct. He would bore her within a fortnight. Queen Thayet had once teased Aly that she would never find a man who could keep her attention for very long. Aly hoped that wasn't true. For now, she considered ways to avoid Bronau in case he invited her to share his bed.

"Sleep with him?" Chenaol asked when Aly mentioned it, once she had returned to the kitchen with the wine tray. "As I told you early on, you can say no. His Grace lets his people make their own choices."

"I thought the nobility would bid their servants to please their guests," Aly remarked as she sat down to a meal of leftovers.

"Not His Grace. If they're willing, and they're protected from getting themselves with child, they may do as they please, and His Grace will defend them," Chenaol replied. She was greasing her favorite wide cooking pot, the one like a large bowl. "But he won't have anyone forced." The woman looked Aly full in the face. "Why do you think people are so loyal to this family?" she asked quietly. "Because *all* are people in this house—raka and luarin, slave and free. The first time Petranne slapped a slave and called her a lazy cow, the duchess spanked her, and took away her dolls for a month. Petranne said she'd heard it at a friend's house, and the duke ended the friendship. There are good luarin here, Aly-who-knows-so-much."

Aly gnawed on her lower lip, then murmured, "And of course, there are Duchess Sarugani's heirs." She knew it was a risk to say it, but with the household aflutter with the new arrivals, the raka might accidently reveal more than they had before. Aly hoped to catch them off their guard.

"Why do you say 'heirs'?" Chenaol demanded, her voice soft. Her small brown eyes were sharp as she looked at Aly. "Under the luarin, only males inherit."

Under the luarin, Chenaol had said. Aly stuffed a rice ball into her mouth and chewed as she thought. So Chenaol knew of the old law, the law under which the females could inherit—females such as Sarugani's daughters. Aly had once heard a man-at-arms figure the population of the Isles was one white among six brown. Did that number cover the mixed-bloods? Where might they stand if the raka chose to take back their home?

She was reaching for another rice ball when a sharp knife pricked the delicate skin under her ear. She was filled with admiration. She hadn't even seen Chenaol palm the blade. "Is that the boning knife, or a chopping knife?" she asked politely. "If you press hard and cut down, I should bleed to death quickly. Of course, I'll make a mess."

"You're very calm for someone who's about to get her corpse dumped somewhere for the crows to eat," whispered Chenaol.

"Now, this simply will not do." A white, bright figure in the shape of a man appeared, seated across the table from Aly. Elsewhere in the kitchen everyone froze in place, eyes and chests unmoving. Only Aly and the cook were free. "Chenaol, my dear girl, stop that." The bright figure spoke with Kyprioth's crisp, cheery voice, accented just now with impatience. "I send help, and how do you thank her? We won't get very far if you kill a luarin who can be of use."

"Bright One, she's a royal spy," Chenaol snapped. "Too curious by half, sticking her nose in everywhere . . ."

"She is *our* spy, not the Crown's," Kyprioth informed the cook. "Imported for your purposes with not a little trouble on my part, I might add. I'll take that." The knife vanished from the cook's hand to reappear in front of the god's light-shape.

Aly glared at him. "I was handling this," she informed Kyprioth. "I didn't need you."

"Yes, but you're so careful about asking around that our wager will be done before my people realize you can help," Kyprioth said reasonably. "Chenaol, why has it taken you so long to realize that Aly is someone special? Think of all the things you can do with her to help."

Chenaol glanced at Aly, then at Kyprioth's glowing form. She held out her hand. "You and your games, Bright One. It would be so wonderful if you ever once gave a body a hint about what you had in mind. I'll take my knife back, please."

"She isn't very respectful," Aly pointed out, interested. She couldn't be angry with Chenaol. In her shoes, Aly would have killed such a nosy slave on the road to Tanair.

"Respect is hard to get when you're a trickster," the god said mournfully. "People are so often inclined to think the worst of one."

Aly propped her chin on her hand. "I can't imagine why," she retorted. "Give the knife back."

"I mean to be sure that she won't murder you when my back is turned," argued Kyprioth. To Chenaol he said, "If you kill this spy, I'm not getting you a new one."

"You should have told us," the cook repeated.

"I expected you to work it out," snapped the god. "*I* wouldn't have let a royal spy get a whiff of our girl. Really, must I do everything?" Without so much as a flicker he was gone. The knife was back in Chenaol's hands. The other servants and slaves in the kitchen began moving about again, unaware that they had been held captive for a short time.

Aly watched Chenaol for a moment before she said, "I'm glad he's not *my* god."

The cook gave her the thinnest of smiles. "As long as his eye is on you, girl, you are his. Mountains give way before that one does."

Aly shrugged. "All gods are like that. You can't reason with them." Hastily she added, "Or so I've heard." She knew it from her mother, the Goddess's own warrior, and from her Aunt Daine, a demi-goddess in her own right, who had met far more gods than any human would think healthy.

Chenaol sighed. "And so you are a spy."

Aly winced. "Please keep your voice down."

"I'll have to tell the others," Chenaol pointed out, eyeing the edge on her knife. "They feared that we'd have to kill you, when all of us like you so much. Fesgao insisted we give you a chance." She put down the knife. "At least the god didn't steal this. He's as bad as a crow for taking things. I got my cooking knives from my mother, and she from hers."

Aly rubbed the back of her neck. "Then raka inheritance is through the mother's line," she confirmed.

"Yes, of course. And the oldest child inherits. We don't care if it's a boy or girl."

Aly looked around. No one was within hearing. Most of the staff had gone back to the main hall, where Bronau's minstrel was tuning a lute. A shimmer of bells told her some of the staff had brought out their instruments. She murmured, "So under raka law, Sarai and Dove are their mother's heirs. And their mother *was* royalty, wasn't she?"

Chenaol got up and poured herself a cup of arak. She sat and propped her feet on a little stool. "The last of the house," she replied, as quiet as Aly. "You know, some of the luarin nobility have taken up the custom. The first child inherits, whatever sex it may be."

"But not the royal line," Aly reminded her.

Chenaol lifted her cup in a silent toast. "Anything can change," she said, and drank.

Aly was drifting off to sleep when she heard steps approach her in the dark main hall. She waited, a hand on her stolen knife. Feathers rustled as two shadowy figures dropped pallets on either side of her. Aly caught the drift of jasmine scent from her left, and soap mixed with aloe from her right. "You're supposed to be in your parents' room," she whispered to Dove and Sarai.

"But you're more interesting, and it's too hot upstairs," Sarai whispered.

"Can I bear the compliment?" Aly asked. "I'm not telling Lioness tales all night."

"It really is too hot up there," Dove said. "And we're not used to such close quarters. We can tell you stories, if you like. Since you're not from here."

Aly yawned as she thought quickly. "I'm too tired for a long story," she told the girls. "But I'd like to know what your mother was like."

"She came from the old raka blood, the nobility before the luarin conquest," replied Sarai, her voice dreamy in the shadows. "She was light, and color, and fun. She had a laugh like small gold bells. Every day was a holiday with her. She and the present duchess were best friends. I suppose that made it easier for Winnamine to take her place." Her voice had turned bitter.

"If she was trying to replace your mother, would she and your father have waited years before they wed?" Aly wanted to know. "I heard it was one of your aunts who made him remember he owed it to the family to remarry."

"What's *your* mother like?" asked Sarai abruptly. "You're so cool and thinking all the time—is that how your mother is?"

Aly had wondered what she would say when this question was asked. The obvious lie, that her mother was dead, felt too much like an ill-wishing to her. Her mother walked dangerous roads too often for Aly even to lie about her fate.

Instead she told a different falsehood. "I never knew her," she replied. "I'm told she is a traveling musician. Her company spent winters in town, and she'd live there with my father, who's a merchant. Only, the year after she had me, she stopped coming."

For a moment both girls were quiet. Then Sarai whispered, "Aly, I'm sorry. We never meant to pry."

Aly put a small quiver in her voice and replied bravely, "I hardly ever think of it. Da's so good to us." Softly she added, "She didn't leave because of my sisters. Only me."

"Do you *mind?*" someone growled nearby. "We have work in the morning, in case some of us have forgotten."

"Aly, forgive us," whispered Dove as she lay down on her pallet.

"I'm your slave," Aly replied. "You have the right."

Sarai murmured, "No, we don't." The sisters fell silent.

And that should be the end of *that* kind of question, Aly thought, satisfied.

Essence spells. We carry our essence everywhere, in our skin, in our hair, our nails. This means that everything we touch picks up some of ourselves. The longer the contact, the more essence is transferred. Thus, if you get clothing someone has worn when he or she has been active, or hot, or upset, that clothing will supply you with more than enough essence to work a spell. Mages favor essence spells for things such as locks and keys, because such spells can be linked to the owner alone. They are foolproof. They work if the owner touches something in a hurry, while under stress, in the cold. And there are ways to go around such spells.

—*From a lecture on basic magical theory by Numair Salmalin at the Royal University at Corus, attended by the thirteen-year-old Aly*

8

A SPY'S WORK

Aly rose before dawn, as usual, since the duchess had not suggested that she give up her daytime work. She emerged from the kitchen wing to find Nawat seated on the rim of the well that served the cooks. He was surrounded by crows. The birds had found seats on the well's cover, Nawat's shoulders, the ground, the kitchen garden fence, and even the archery targets set up between the barracks and the garden. All of the birds looked as pleased as any human to be up so early, with the sun just showing above the eastern horizon. They sat or stood or walked, feathers ruffled against the early morning chill, eyes half shut with sleep. They stirred as Aly moved through them. Nawat turned to look at her.

"My clan has come," he explained. "We will mob the Bronau hawk if you ask it. He is a danger to humans and their nestlings."

Aly scratched her head. What was she supposed to say to *that*? Certainly she agreed. Her wager depended on keeping the Balitang nestlings alive this summer. Bronau was one of the factors that put them at risk.

"It's not so easy among two-leggers," she explained, wondering how she could explain human politics to her feathered allies. "We can't drive him off. We'll put the nestlings in more danger if we do."

One crow made a croaking noise that sounded like a variation on the call to attack and kill.

"Then let us kill him and his flock," Nawat said brightly. "He cannot kill or steal anyone if his bones are scattered between here and the mountains."

Aly sighed. "Nawat, it's not just Bronau. These soldiers who follow him? They are not his entire flock. He has a vast flock that will come to destroy everything where he was killed, understand? His brother, his sister-in-law, the king . . ."

Nawat regarded her with puzzlement, head cocked to one side. The other crows had the same expression and tilt to their heads.

"Humans do these things differently." Aly knew she sounded feeble, but she was unsure how to explain matters so that they would make sense to them. "They aren't as consistent as crows. Rank and alliances change among humans all the time, inside the flock and outside. And if you hurt one of their kin, they'll punish whole families, even whole towns. You are here to help me, and I am here to keep the Balitang nestlings alive all summer, yes?"

Nawat smiled. "Yes, Aly."

"Then you must trust me when I say that mobbing the prince would place them in even more danger," Aly told him, now feeling weak and peculiar. She wondered if Aunt Daine ever felt this way, and if being able to speak animal languages made times like this easier for her aunt. "If we are vigilant with the nestlings, if we never let them stray from our eyes, we can hold them safe without mobbing anyone." She rubbed her forehead, which had begun to ache. "Will you tell your friends, Nawat?" she asked. "And I will explain to you about humans and royalty later."

"Yes, Aly," Nawat told her with that particularly sweet smile. It was a smile that could divert her attention from Kyprioth's wager, so she thrust all thought of it from her mind and went to collect her goats. She was leading them through the village gates when she heard the crows take flight from the castle. For a while she turned and walked backward to see the birds soar above Tanair, delighting at the sight of their iridescent blue-black feathers in the early light, and the graceful sweep of their wings. Soon they were gone, some to the trees among the eastern rocks, others to the fields that supported Tanair. She only hoped they hadn't left large, white, streaky signs of their presence for the household to find when they went outside.

Aly walked on, savoring the fresh morning air and the promise of warmth to come. The weather here was nearly perfect: warm to hot days, and cool nights. She walked among fields that showed signs of crops coming in, down roads lined with wildflowers and the occasional tree. There were worse places to spend the summer, she decided as she led the goats into the rocks about the Dimari road. With Bronau's presence to keep her alert and with the understanding that Kyprioth would not have troubled to involve Aly and the crows if he'd anticipated a peaceful summer, she knew she could pass a few interesting, pleasant months here. She *did* like a challenge.

Aly settled the goats in the rocks above the road to Dimari. Once they were happily grazing, she sat to peel the casing from her morning's cold sausage. "Kyprioth," she called teasingly. "I'll share my breakfast with you."

"Spare me." The god appeared atop a nearby boulder, dressed as a raka with his usual scrambled collection of jewelry and sparkling ornaments. He sat casually, his arms looped around one bent knee, so the jewels in his bracelets caught the morning sun. "Sausage has no appeal for me whatever."

Aly sighed. "It's cooked, silly."

Kyprioth turned his face into the wind. "Cooked or raw, sausage is not the food of the gods. Why are we talking? My brother and sister won't stay occupied with other wars forever, you know."

Aly examined her fingernails as if she weren't interested in her next question: "Are you looking to start a war here, sir?"

Kyprioth grinned, white teeth flashing against brown skin. It was a grin that was the essence of mischief, with none of the sweetness of Nawat's smile. "A fine effort and well executed. May I remind you that you never call me 'sir'?"

Aly grimaced. Tiny slips like that betrayed an impersonation.

"Why should you care?" the god went on. "You have but one task between now and the autumn equinox: to keep the Balitang children alive. War isn't a concern for you."

Aly leaned back against a tree, her eyes on the goats rather than the god. "You see, that's what I wanted to ask you about," she explained in her friendliest manner. "It's just that I worry Chenaol will believe I am here for a bit longer than the summer. I would hate to disappoint her when I go. She might even believe that *you* might keep me here."

"Oh, no, I will do nothing of the kind," Kyprioth said. "I doubt that Chenaol takes it that way."

Aly sat up on her knees and looked at the god. "Good," she said. "A wager is sacred in the Divine Realms—anyone knows it. If you try to change the terms we've agreed to? I'll bring the matter before your fellow gods, including the two whose attention you least want to draw. The two who kicked you off your throne. Don't even think of pulling the wool over my eyes."

He vanished from his rock to reappear in front of Aly. "The thought never crossed my mind," he said, and kissed her on the forehead. "A wager's a wager." He vanished, making the air pop where he had been.

Aly shook her head, then stood and stretched. "I should feel relieved," she mused aloud. "And yet, somehow, I don't."

She dozed for a while in the sun. When she woke, it was to a crow's announcement of riders on the road south from Tanair. Aly sharpened her Sight and saw a noble riding party below her: Prince Bronau, Duke Mequen, Duchess Winnamine, Sarai, and Dove were out riding. The prince called a mocking challenge, which Sarai accepted with a whoop, nudging her horse into a gallop as the prince spurred his own mount. They thundered down the southern road, Sarai like a warrior out of legends, her hair springing from its pins. Two bodyguards followed the racers at the gallop, while Mequen, Winnamine, Dove, and their guards kept to a lively trot. They waved to Aly, who waved back, as they rode on.

Aly stretched out her leg tendons, touching her toes as she turned things over in her mind. Did Bronau think Sarai might be a bride for him? The prince was a younger son, which meant his pockets might not be very deep. Did he think Sarai had money? Through enthusiastic eavesdropping, Aly had discovered that Balitangs inherited by luarin law. Elsren would get the bulk of the duke's lands and wealth at his death. Sarai and Dove would split their inheritance from their mother, Tanair and a few other small estates. They would not be wealthy brides.

She heard footsteps, quiet but not noiseless, among the rocks to her left. Aly bent casually and picked up two of a small pile of stones she had made before her nap. Back at home she had learned to throw rocks from the village boys, until she could kill rabbits or dent heavy wood with the force of her throw.

"She rides well, our Sarai."

Ulasim stepped out from between the rocks. Aly looked him over. Today he wore homespun and moved as easily in the rough garments as her own father moved in his clothes. Aly noticed something else: the outlines of dagger sheaths against his sleeves and on his breeches where they fell over his calf-high boots. Ulasim hadn't worn blades before.

"She does ride well," Aly said. "I suppose you've talked to Chenaol."

"Of course," said Ulasim. "We are all in this together."

"This," Aly said musingly, guessing that he spoke of the conspiracy among the Balitang raka. "Tell me, did you ever want to put Sarugani on the throne?"

Ulasim shook his head. "The time wasn't right." After a moment's hesitation, he added, "And she wasn't right—more heart than head, when everyone knows the head is what matters when dealing with the luarin. It matters, too, that she had no royal blood through the luarin line, which will bring more of the part-raka to our cause. Our lady has the Rittevon blood as well as the ancient Haiming blood, and she is wiser than her mother. The people will love Sarai as queen." He fell silent for a moment, then said, "We have waited a very long time for this. We shall have only one chance—if we fail, the luarin will see to it that we cannot rise again. That is why so many came to see her. They know what is at stake. They have prayed for this chance for generations."

The head hostler Lokeij rode up on Duke Mequen's hunter. The old raka used no saddle, Aly realized, and no bridle. Her estimation of the tiny man rose several notches. She would have shrunk from riding such a big horse with full tack, let alone with none.

Lokeij dismounted easily and set the horse among the goats to graze. Then he lay down atop a rock, apparently there just to bask in the sun. Ulasim picked up a stick and whittled on it. It seemed they were waiting.

Aly put her rocks back in their pile and practiced head and handstands on the soft grass.

She had just progressed to walking on her hands when Chenaol arrived through the rocks, panting from the exercise. "I told them," she informed Aly as she collapsed beside the girl.

"I noticed," Aly said with a grin. "Who else did you tell?"

"Fesgao," replied Chenaol, fanning herself with one hand. "Veron's got him in charge of the watch today, and he dares not leave."

Somehow Aly wasn't surprised to hear that Fesgao was part of the conspiracy. She hesitated for a moment, then shrugged. *Time to get my feet wet,* she thought, and said, "Veron is the king's spy. He keeps his papers and coding materials in a box set on the lintel over his door. Have you someone who can watch him, and intercept any reports he might try to send out? Not Fesgao—he's too obvious."

"One of my stable boys will do well at such work," said Lokeij. "Boys are less obvious than men, and these boys are forever trailing behind the men-at-arms when I've no work for them. It will be easy."

"Should we tell His Grace?" asked Ulasim.

Aly shook her head. "The duke and the duchess do not need to know," she replied. "I will tell them when it is necessary."

Lokeij turned his head to stare at her. "They listen to you?" he asked, plainly startled. "But they only know you as a slave."

Aly grinned. "Your friend appeared to them as Mithros and told them to listen to me," she explained. "They think I'm his messenger."

"That explains . . ." Chenaol's voice trailed off as she considered what this information did explain.

"Fesgao said that you suggested he check the forest for bandits on the way here," Ulasim remarked. "He wasn't sure if there were people abroad, having been in the city so long, but you convinced him."

Aly shrugged.

"Well!" Chenaol said, more pleased than she had been the previous night. "Things should go better, now that we have a proper spy. We're ready for anything."

"Anything but a mage," Aly pointed out, lying back and linking her hands behind her head. As clouds scuttled by, she added, "The healer Rihani is good only for healing, and only a certain amount of it, at that. A true mage, come here on King Oron's behalf, could crack us wide open. Speaking of the king . . ."

Lokeij leaned over and spat to one side.

"Satisfying, but not useful," Aly said. "If spit made a difference, you raka would have had the Isles back as soon as everyone got to know the luarin. With regard to the king, if he has one of his bad twitches, Veron and his boys won't be enough to hold off a royal assault. And you can't count on Veron. Like as not, he'll just open the Tanair gates like a good dog. Have you raka made your own provisions for warriors? Patrols of the plateau? If outsiders infiltrate this area, you should stop them before they reach Tanair."

"But why?" Ulasim wanted to know. "Surely it's enough to retreat to the castle. We're safe inside the walls."

Aly shook her head. "If they trap us in the castle, then we are well and truly *trapped*," she explained. "It would be far better for any assassins the king sends to vanish before they reach Tanair. That way, when the king asks what happened to his soldiers, His Grace can say, 'What soldiers?' without even needing to lie. What he doesn't know won't hurt him."

Lokeij whistled. "Make the king's warriors vanish if they come . . . what a deceitful turtledove you are."

Aly smiled at the sky. "Oh, don't," she replied in the tones of a flirtatious court lady. "Stop, I insist. Your flattery makes me blush."

"Have we the warriors?" asked Chenaol slowly.

Lokeij cleared his throat. When the other raka looked at him, he raised his eyebrows. They nodded. The old hostler turned his eyes on Aly. "There are some fighters up here, waiting," he explained. "In the villages. Over the last three years they have come, young men and women, nearly sixty in all, to train and to wait. The elders will be happy the time has come to put them to use. They hunt, they fight, and they flirt with their daughters and sons." He smiled. "They are also very good at riding, scouting, shooting, and building walls. They have their own mounts, and can live in the open air."

"The crows will help," said a voice from nearby. Nawat had come up soundlessly to stand near a boulder. "We will teach your fighters as we taught Aly."

Aly didn't even see Ulasim leave his place, the man was so fast. He jammed Nawat against the boulder and put a knife to his throat. Nawat twisted, an arm moving. Ulasim went down on his knees. He bent over, gasping, dead white under his coppery skin. Nawat jumped five feet in the air to the top of his boulder. Two long strides took him across the rocks; a short jump put him on a tree branch over Aly's head.

Chenaol went to Ulasim. "What did you do?" she demanded. "If you've killed him . . ."

Nawat smiled at her from his leafy refuge. "I only pecked him with my fingers. He was rude to try to cut me. I will help Aly do whatever she must. He should know that."

All three raka stared at the young fletcher. "What *are* you?" demanded Lokeij. "You aren't raka."

"Isn't he?" Aly asked lazily, watching Ulasim and Chenaol through her lowered lashes. "What is he, then? Luarin?"

Ulasim straightened with a grimace. He patted Chenaol on the shoulder, reassuring her that he wasn't stabbed, then stared at Nawat. Ignoring him, Nawat picked something off the tree trunk, eyed it, then ate it. His eyebrows shot up. He looked around, found a twig and broke it off, and used it to root in a crevice of the tree bark.

Ulasim wiped a hand over dry lips and crouched a little, holding the spot in his side where Nawat had struck him. "Not luarin," he said at last, wonder in his eyes and voice. "But not raka, either."

"Does it matter, if I give your warriors the secrets of the crows?" asked Nawat. He brought his twig close to his face. A grub squirmed on the end of it. He popped it into his mouth and thrust his twig under a new piece of bark. "We have a wager with the Bright One, too, the god of tricks," the crow-man explained as he wriggled his twig. "To help Aly, we must help the nestlings. Surely it makes no difference what I am. You humans worry about proper names too much."

Chenaol looked at Aly. "Do you vouch for him?"

"Why not ask your god?" Aly demanded in return. "The crows were his idea."

Ulasim rubbed his side. "Things were simpler in Rajmuat," he complained. "Nawat, tonight you'll meet with Fesgao and me in the guard barracks. We must work out patrol schedules and decide how your crows will communicate with our fighters. And come down out of that tree. You're making my neck hurt, and your eating habits make my belly squirm."

Nawat jumped to the ground, then found a rock to sit on. "No more knives?" he asked Ulasim.

"No more pecking?" Ulasim retorted.

Nawat looked at Aly. "I cannot teach the raka as we taught you. We will sort that out."

"I leave it in your capable hands," Aly told him with a smile. She looked at the raka conspirators. "Any other royal spies in the household?"

"Just Hasui, and she's in the kitchen under my eye," Chenaol replied with a firm nod. "I prefer not to kill her, if it can be helped."

"No, don't," Aly said. "It'll leave you short-handed in the kitchen. For another, we can send the wrong information through Hasui and Veron to their masters. Knowing who is your spy can be quite useful." She scratched her head, reviewing all the things they had discussed. There were plenty of factors to keep in mind, and she wanted to make sure that they had covered the most important ones. She had always expected her first job as a spy to be a simple matter of watching targets and sending reports on their behavior. Da would never thrust a green spy into a political swamp like this one for her first assignment. She grinned. She would have a tale to tell him when she went home!

Ulasim was staring at her. "What?" she asked.

"Where did you learn to think this way?" the raka asked slowly. "We would have killed Hasui outright if Chenaol had not said she would be controlled in the kitchen. Killing Veron would break no one's heart. He's too fond of whipping raka to get them to move. We never would think to make the spies pass on bad information. And it never occurred to us that a castle might be a trap."

"Oh, the god fiddled with my mind," she replied wickedly. "They're fond of doing things like that. You never know what they'll get up to."

"I do not believe you," Ulasim replied, an amused glint in his dark eyes. "No god ever needs to know such tiny things. Who are your people?"

"Tortallans," Aly informed him. "Merchants. Harmless. Unless you count my mother, who was a Player. What of Prince Bronau's people?" she asked, changing the subject. "Are any of them more than they seem to be?"

The raka looked at one another and shook their heads. "They just got here," Chenaol reminded Aly.

Aly yawned. "I'll have a look around, then. Perhaps Her Grace will excuse me from pouring the wine tonight. You might want to keep a constant watch on them, too. After all, they might find the weapons hidden in the storerooms under the stable."

Lokeij cursed eloquently. "You can't know about them! I've got the stables watched all the time!"

"I didn't know until now," Aly replied easily, enjoying the joke she had just played on the old man. She ignored Lokeij's muttered curse, though she stored it in her memory as a useful one to know. "It's a central location, after all, and the raka linger there all the time."

Ulasim whistled softly. "Our friend picked well when he picked you."

Just don't get used to me, Aly thought at she smiled at him. I don't mean to be here after the autumn equinox.

Chenaol looked at the sun. "I'd best get back," she told them. "Those lazy wenches will slack on the cooking if I'm not there." She set off among the rocks. Ulasim murmured quietly to Lokeij, then stood aside as the old man mounted his horse as nimbly as a boy. Aly looked around for Nawat—he was nowhere to be seen. Like any crow, he seemed to have the ability to come and go unnoticed, something that didn't involve magic, only animal craft.

At last Ulasim was alone with Aly. "Tomorrow I will send Visda to you. She and her dogs will graze her herd with yours every day after this. She will tell no one what you do once you have settled the flock. This way, should you need to leave your post, she can look after the goats as well."

Aly nodded. "Good idea. I thank you."

"Also, what are your preferred weapons?" he wanted to know. "Can you use any, O child of merchants?"

Aly raised an eyebrow at him. "You don't believe what I told you of my family. I'm hurt. Maybe even crushed." Ulasim was unmoved. She delayed by reminding him, "It's my life if I'm caught with weapons, you know that. Slave owners don't arm slaves." She wasn't sure if it was wise to let anyone know of her skill with knives.

"Then you must not be caught," Ulasim replied coolly. "Have you been to the shrine between the stable and the wall?"

Aly shook her head.

"The flagstone before the altar can be lifted. What shall we leave there for you?" He smiled thinly.

Aly nibbled her lower lip. It would be nice to have more blades than just the stolen one hidden in her bedroll. She'd always teased her father when he complained about the magic that alerted the king and queen of people carrying hidden weapons. She had liked telling him that he sounded like a child without his favorite blanket. Now she understood his feeling of vulnerability. Like Aly, he could fight hand to hand at need, but daggers were what he loved. He'd taught that love to her. "Daggers?" she asked. "Good ones, as flat as may be, with sleeve and leg sheaths? They would be a blessing."

"Merchants," Ulasim remarked drily, referring to her false background again. "Yes, of course I believe you. I must, mustn't I? You *are* Kyprioth's chosen, so the truth drips from your tongue like honey from the comb."

"Again you are suspicious," Aly told the raka, shaking her head in sorrow. "You wound me so deeply." She liked Ulasim. He was smart.

"I can see that," retorted Ulasim. "Daggers we shall provide you, under the flagstone tonight." Aly relaxed, looking at the clouds again, but the raka was not finished. "And since you are so busy watching the plotters who creep up behind us, I will assign a guard to you. Someone who won't look out of place with the goats." His voice was firm, his eyes direct as Aly sat up and groaned a protest. Ulasim said firmly, "At the very least he can run your errands."

Aly sighed. "What about a girl?" she asked, "or a woman? Less conspicuous and less likely to stir up gossip."

Ulasim stiffened. Aly made a face at him. "Sarai told me your women fought together with the men in the raka armies," she said patiently. "It seems reasonable to guess that the raka who aren't under the luarin eye continue to train their women to fight. I can understand your not wanting folk to know. This way, the luarin think the number of raka who might give them trouble is half of your actual force. But *I'm* not going to tell, and a female won't be noticed as much as a man."

"I will see to it," he said. He started to go, then turned back to face Aly. His dark eyes were puzzled. "I suppose I must trust the god's opinion of you, but you still worry me. He is a trickster, when all is said and done."

"But I'm not," Aly assured him, the picture of earnest youth. "Why, I'm just as true and honest as dirt. And I'm even more charming than dirt."

Ulasim winced. "Thank you for describing yourself in such unforgettable terms," he said. "I see you and the god are well matched."

Aly watched him go. Ulasim is their general, she decided, thinking about the roles each raka played. Lokeij is in charge of communications and storage for weapons and supplies. Fesgao must be their war leader, used to straightforward combat. And Chenaol . . .

She plucked a grass stem. She supposed every army needed a chief cook who was quick with her knives, but surely there was more to Chenaol than that. Did she command the women of the raka? What could she do that the men could not?

Aly's memory showed her an image of Chenaol talking to the merchants who stopped by Tanair from time to time. She was accepting boxes from them, boxes that Aly had seen open in the kitchen: knives. No one questioned a raka cook in the purchase of knives. And it would be easier to smuggle longer blades to a cook than a man-at-arms watched by a luarin superior. Aly smiled. Chenaol was the raka armorer. That was why Ulasim has said "we" when he talked of giving me knives, she thought. He may plant them, but he'll get them from Chenaol.

Truly this was a fine morning, Aly reflected as she stretched and thought. Now she had human allies and their resources. With Bronau in residence and the king's disfavor, the Balitangs' luarin and raka alike had an excuse to strengthen their defenses. Any of them who had been waiting for "someday" to come would know that day was nearly upon them. They would be razor-sharp, with no need for Aly to sharpen them, and, unlike the crows, they would understand that Bronau might serve as a lightning rod to draw the king's wrath.

Aly gnawed a grass stem. The raka and the crows were prepared for attack by armed fighters both from within and without. However, they still could not withstand a strong magical attack. Somehow they would have to produce a mage.

Once again Aly brought the goats in early. After they were safely penned, she waved to Nawat, who was fletching arrows near the archery butts, and entered the keep in search of the duchess. She found the lady in the small bedchamber where Petranne, Elsren, and their nursemaid slept, giving her son a bath while the maid toweled his sister dry.

Aly bowed. "Excuse me, Your Grace," she said.

Winnamine looked up at her. Her hair had escaped its severe domed style to curl around her face and neck. Her indigo linen gown was water-spotted, and she was flicking drops of water into her gleefully squealing boy's face.

"Pembery," she said to the maid, "would you get some more drying cloths? I fear both Elsren and I will need them."

The maid curtsied. "At once, Your Grace," she murmured. She wrapped Petranne in a cocoon of cloths and trotted from the room.

"Your Grace, Hasui, one of the kitchen slaves, will take my place as wine pourer tonight," Aly murmured in Kyprish. Neither Elsren nor Petranne spoke it very well, though Dove, Sarai, and their parents did. "There are some things I must do in your service. And I will need to report to you and His Grace later, once the prince has retired."

Winnamine's eyes sharpened. "You will be careful?" she asked, keeping her voice low as she, too, spoke in Kyprish. "You will take no risks that might endanger us?" Unconsciously she grasped Elsren's hand in hers.

"Your Grace, no one will even know what I did," Aly assured her.

"Mama, why are you talking that way?" demanded Petranne from her corner by the fire. "Only raka talk that way."

"But the raka are our people, too, dear," Winnamine told her daughter. "We honor them by learning their tongue. They were here long before our ancestors came."

"But Aly isn't raka," the girl pointed out. "She's luarin."

"She honors our raka friends, too," Winnamine said, absently soaping Elsren's back.

Aly bowed and left the watery room. She had no interest in explaining the language of conquest to a four-year-old, and knowing Petranne from the journey to Tanair, she was aware that the girl would stick to the subject until the end of time if not muzzled.

She retreated to a small closet off the servants' stair and changed into the dark, long-sleeved tunic and leggings she kept hidden there. She had stolen them from the Balitang storehouse back in Rajmuat and hidden them for special occasions. She then wrapped a length of dark cloth around her face and head until only her eyes showed. By the time she finished, the household was assembling for the evening meal. Aly hid in the closet where she kept her prowler's clothing until she heard no footsteps on the servants' stair for a good space of time. Pocketing the lock picks she also kept there, she emerged carefully and peered into the main hall around the door behind the Balitangs. Hasui, cleaned up and dressed to serve at the dais, poured Bronau a cup of wine as Aly watched. Supper had begun.

Quickly Aly counted the prince's household in the hall. Everyone was present, eating with the duke's servants. Satisfied, Aly climbed the keep stairs, past the floors where the prince, then the Balitangs, slept. When she reached the fourth floor, where Bronau's household stayed, she got to work on the servants' trunks, using her picks with care.

By the time the first course was over downstairs, she had uncovered two royal spies among the prince's servants. She didn't flatter herself that it was her skill that made the discovery so easy. Anyone who searched their baggage would have seen it. Both men carried unusual supplies of paper, as well as the general code book issued for the Isles' lower-level spies. Aly had memorized its contents over a year ago, when it had become the new general code for the Isles. Swiftly but expertly she checked each nook and cranny on the floor where the servants might have hidden more surprises.

That chore done, she padded down to the second level and used her picks to enter the prince's rooms. She searched his two menservants' belongings first. They, too, carried more than their share of writing paper as well as one book. Their volume was *The Perfect Servant*, a popular book of advice for those who worked in a higher capacity in a house or fiefdom. These men did not report to the Crown, however. One of them had already started his next report to his master. Using the faint marks in the book on service, Aly swiftly deciphered the greeting on the document: "To my lord Rubinyan."

She raised an eyebrow. So the Crown used Bronau's general servants to spy on him, while his older brother bought the services of Bronau's body servants. What kind of bad feeling existed between these two? She couldn't imagine Alan or Thom hiring anyone to spy on her. Of course, neither of them was eyeing a feeble king's throne.

She left the servants' belongings exactly as she had found them and proceeded to Bronau's private writing case. The magic on the lock blazed in her magical Sight. The case wouldn't open if she tried the various unlocking words that she knew. There was also no keyhole in the lock, which didn't surprise her. Bronau struck her as the kind of man who was careless with keys, even important ones. He wasn't the sort to fuss with complex things, either.

Aly peered more closely at the lock, shifting her Sight to read magic. The signs on it turned dark and appeared one at a time, over and over, until she identified what each meant. The case had been locked with an essence spell, the perfect thing for a man who didn't like the bother of keys or details. Fortunately for Aly, she had studied these matters under very fine teachers. An essence spell was quite easy to break once recognized.

Aly reached for Bronau's riding gloves, which he had thrown on his bed in his rush to dress for supper. His hurried servants had left them right where a bright girl would find a use for them. Aly took a glove and turned it inside out, then pressed a leather fingertip to the lock. A line appeared through the middle of the device. The lid opened. Carefully she turned the glove right side out and replaced it in the exact spot she had found it. Her father had drilled her in such habits over the years, during exercises where he would send her out of the room, shift the things in it, then summon her back to replace everything as it had been. When she was little it was her favorite game. Now it was habit to remember the exact placement of anything she moved.

Aly knelt on the floor and raised the box's lid. The first seven letters inside were addressed to businesses: a draper, a moneylender, a cobbler, a horse coper, a jeweler, an armorer, and a bowyer. In them Bronau wrote that he was aware of the sums that were owed to them. Aly leafed through the papers and found the bills he had mentioned. Reading how much he owed to these people, she raised both eyebrows. This man spent more on shoes than Maude did to supply Pirate's Swoop with food for a month.

Aly paused to listen for outside sounds. Hearing only the faint noise from the great hall, she returned to the letters. Bronau wrote the merchants that his debts would be paid, within the year, with interest, and he swore it by Mithros. He also wrote that they would be well rewarded for their patience.

Aly arranged the letters neatly and put them aside with their bills. Prince Bronau seemed very confident he would be able to pay his creditors in full, even the moneylender. And he'd taken the risk of dragging a god's name into it. The receipts all had "fourth notice" or "fifth notice" written on them, and the dates covered the last four years.

How *did* he intend to pay? Aly wondered. None of Bronau's people had said that he'd snagged himself a very wealthy heiress. From what Aly knew, the money would not come from his brother and sister-in-law. Now he was out of favor with the king, and yet he was strangely confident. These letters were dated two days ago. Sarai was no heiress, not the kind that Bronau needed. From the notes on their bills, the prince's creditors were about to haul him before Mithros's altar, where lawyer-priests would strip Bronau of all he owned.

Aly looked at the next sheet of paper in the box. It was covered with scratch-outs and rephrasings. It seemed to be a letter to an old friend, chatting of this and that. Aly read it over twice, eyed the scratched out words, and nearly groaned aloud. The letter was in the most simple-minded code in existence, the very first code she had memorized. It was based on *The Book of Mithros*. Nearly every household in the Eastern and Southern Lands had a copy, even if the residents took some other god as the center of their belief.

"Duke Zeburon," she translated, "though you are both on the Royal Council, I have reason to know you are no friend to my brother R. We might find common ground between us, with the end in mind of ousting R. from his position."

That was as far as Bronau had written. The rest of the box held empty paper and *The Book of Mithros,* but Aly checked it all, just to be sure. There were no other signs of code or magic. Carefully she replaced everything as she had found it. After a double check of the room to make sure it looked as it had when she broke in, she left by the servants' stair, changed into her normal homespun tunic and leggings, and walked into the kitchen.

The prince has given me plenty to think about, she thought, scrounging leftovers. As soon as the house is quiet, I'll make sure the duke and duchess are thinking, too.

Aly was dozing by the kitchen fire as the staff began to carry the dishes out for washing. Pembery woke her with the message that Their Graces had errands for her. Aly grumbled a reply and trudged up the servants' stair once again.

The duke and duchess awaited her in the sitting room of their new quarters. To Aly's surprise and discomfort, Sarai occupied the chair next to her father.

The older Balitangs correctly read the rigid set of Aly's body. "Sarai is of age," the duke said gravely. "She will have to learn these things to survive. We have already told her of the god's message to us."

Aly pressed her lips together. "The more who know, the more you risk" was a motto she'd memorized practically in her cradle. Still, Sarai was Aly's own age. That had to be old enough to be told there were mysteries afoot. Resigned, Aly swept the room with her Sight, wondering if Mequen and Winnamine had thought the thing all the way through. As she suspected, she caught a flicker of movement in the gap between the door to the main stair and the floor. Immediately she heightened her magical ability to see color and detail and identified the eavesdropper. She crossed the room silently and yanked the door open. Dove stumbled into the room and almost fell. Aly caught her by one thin arm.

The duchess started from her chair, then settled back into it, biting her lower lip. Mequen scowled at his daughter. "Dovasary, it is the most common of all behaviors to listen at doors," he told her. "As a lady, such coarseness is beneath you."

As she covered the crack under the door with a carpet and stuffed a cloth scrap from the duchess's sewing basket into the keyhole, Aly glanced at Dove to see the effect of the duke's words. Dove looked at Aly and rolled her eyes, then went to stand before her father. "You told me curiosity was healthy," she said. "Is that confined only to books and nature? Sarai would just have told me anyway. I'd have made her."

"As if you could!" her older sister snapped.

Aly ignored their debate as she filled in the cracks under the remaining doors and plugged their keyholes as well. Just to be on the safe side, in case one of the spies who had come with Bronau had the nerve to dangle on a rope outside the window, she closed and barred the shutters. When she finished, the discussion was over. Dove wore a tiny smile of satisfaction as she pulled up a chair next to Sarai.

"Are you ready?" Aly inquired. The duke nodded. Aly said, "I searched the belongings of the prince and his servants tonight," she informed her listeners.

Mequen frowned.

"Your Grace?" Aly inquired.

"I'm not sure I approve," he replied quietly. "He is a friend, a guest in my house. He is entitled to his privacy."

Aly caught the glance traded by Sarai and Dove, one that showed exasperation over their father's unbending good manners. The duchess showed only concentration as she seemed to focus on the neat stitches she set in her sewing.

Aly thought the duke's scruples were sweet, if unrealistic. Da had always told her that noble honor hindered those who had it as much as it helped them. "Your Grace is an honorable man, and I respect that. However, I am charged with the safety of you and your family. Honor of the type you describe is a luxury." Before he could order her never to do so again, she held up a hand. "Before you speak, Your Grace, you should know that the prince already enjoys no privacy whatsoever. His attendants include Crown spies. His body servants are both in his brother's pay."

"*Rubinyan?*" whispered the duke. He gripped the arms of his chair with white-knuckled hands. "Ridiculous! He would no more spy . . . Rubinyan is as much my friend as Bronau. He is a good man. They don't get on, but it is temperament, not politics."

"Unless you are connected to the royal family and the court," Winnamine pointed out, keeping her voice low. "Then politics and temperament are never separated."

"I cannot believe it," repeated the duke. "I will not believe it."

At least he knows the difference between "cannot" and "will not," thought Aly. "Would Your Grace like proof of what I say?" she asked. Da had warned her that sometimes people refused to believe even when evidence was waved under their noses, but she thought she should offer.

Mequen shot her a startled look. "Aly, no, of course not. You are the god's messenger. You would not lie."

I would if I thought it was for your own good, Aly thought as Winnamine patted her husband's arm.

"This might be Imajane's influence," the duchess murmured. "She has seen so many conspiracies in her own family that she would suspect them of anyone. Wouldn't you, growing up as His Majesty's daughter?"

"True, true," whispered the duke, but Aly could see his eyes. Mequen was too intelligent not to see that it was sensible for someone near the throne, like Rubinyan, to watch a powerful, charming fellow courtier, even if that courtier was his own brother. The duke also had to be thinking that if Prince Rubinyan suspected his brother, he might suspect anyone, including Mequen himself. "Why am I surprised?" he asked, and sighed. "That is the way of things at court. Everyone spies on everyone else."

Aly could see that the duke understood her. No wonder Da prefers to work with clever people, she thought. They can work out the obvious without openly speaking of it. She said, "There's more, Your Grace. I took the liberty of going through the prince's writing case."

"Aly!" cried the duke, shocked. Winnamine hurriedly put a finger over her husband's lips, to remind him to keep his voice down. The duke tightened his mouth, then leaned forward and fixed Aly with his sharp brown eyes. "Nobles do *not* read one another's mail."

"I would not know, Your Grace," replied Aly smoothly. "I *was* a servant. *Now* I am a slave. It's a matter of survival for us to know what our masters know."

"I don't believe I noticed before, but you have perfect grammar," remarked Dove. "Isn't that odd for a slave who was once a maid?"

"The god chose me for my skills at mimicry, my lady," Aly replied. That was not a lie at all, she virtuously told herself.

"I take it you found something in Prince Bronau's case, or you would not have raised the subject," Winnamine said.

Aly nodded. "His Highness is greatly in debt," she told them.

The duke batted this aside with an impatient hand. "He is always in debt. Really, Aly, if you waste your time with small follies . . ."

She named the sum she had added from the receipts, stopping the duke in midsentence. The duchess went pale. Sarai gasped.

At last the duchess said, "He'll spend the rest of his life repaying that."

"He says not, Your Grace." Aly then told them of the letters he had written but not yet sent—letters to his creditors that promised repayment within a year. She then repeated the contents of the partial letter to Duke Zeburon, offering an alliance against Rubinyan.

"Papa, whatever it is, I'm sure he can explain," Sarai said hurriedly, anxiety in her eyes. "Perhaps he believes Rubinyan doesn't trust him. Perhaps he just wants to make sure he has friends, in case Imajane ever turns the king against him. It's just more of that jockeying for power you always say goes on at court."

"And the money?" asked the duchess, inspecting her sewing.

"He must have an heiress he's courting," whispered Sarai, looking down at her lap. "Perhaps Lady Tyananne. She's come out of mourning. And the Ianjai family wants to marry into the nobility. No one will mind a merchant wife, not if she's married to someone as popular as Bronau is." A tear rolled down her cheek and spotted her gold velvet lap.

Aly, pretending not to notice that Sarai wept, asked the duchess if she had messages for her to carry. Her task was done. She had reported what she had learned, and unless they asked her opinion, they had to decide for themselves what to do with that information. She had no opinions of her own, so she wouldn't try to influence their thinking. Bronau was still a threat. She did make a mental note of the fact that if she wanted to influence Mequen at some point, she could appeal to his honor, just as she could appeal to Sarai's love of adventure and excitement.

Winnamine dismissed her. As Aly pulled the carpet back into place and removed the cloth from the main door's keyhole, she glanced back at the silent Dove. The girl was sketching the carved whorls in the arm of her chair with a finger, her brow wrinkled, deep in thought. Aly saw no distress on that small face, only calculation.

It's those who are overlooked by the folk around them you want to watch. They see more than they tell, and they think more than they talk. You want them for your friend. You don't want them asking questions about you.

—From a letter to Aly from her father when she was nine

9

LEARNING THE GROUND

In the morning Aly visited the shrine between the stable and the wall. There, under the promised flagstone, she discovered six knives, all of a finer make than her stolen one. Chenaol knows how to pick a blade, she thought admiringly as she tested them on the fraying hem of her undyed goatherd's tunic. One, as long as her middle finger in the blade and wickedly sharp, had a sheath that hung by a cord. When she put it over her head, the knife and sheath slipped between her breasts under the band she wore. All that showed above her tunic collar was the kind of cord from which might hang a religious pendant of some kind. Two perfectly flat knives fit in sheaths under her leggings so well that they barely left a mark on the cloth over them; two more flat knives and their sheaths went under the sleeves of her tunic. The most substantial she could wear in her waistband at her back or carry it with her lunch and water bottle. She put it into that bag and moved one of her leg knives up under her waistband at the middle of her back, where she could reach it in a hurry.

The raka conspirators had revealed more with this gift of weaponry than perhaps they intended her to know. They were desperate for help. They knew they were unused to the world of armies, spies, and nobles. The god's gift of Aly must have seemed like the answer to their prayers.

"It's not fair, you getting their hopes up, when you know I'll be gone in the fall," she muttered to Kyprioth as she collected her goats. The god chose not to reply. Aly shook her head. Perhaps before she left she could teach the raka the potential dangers of any move they might try against the king. She led her animals out of the castle walls.

Aly and her flock were halfway through the village when the little shepherd girl, Visda, joined her, along with her sheep and the boy who had summoned Aly to Tanair the day before. "Aunt Chenaol says we're to graze with you," the girl confided, waving to the baker as they passed. "And if you're called off sudden, me and Ekit"—she jerked a thumb at the boy, who stuck his tongue out at her—"we'll take both flocks. Well, me and Ekit and Grace and Arak," she added, naming the shaggy herd dogs. "Aunt Chenaol says you're doing important work for the One Who Is Promised, and we should help you—"

Aly halted and stopped the girl. Bending down, she drew Ekit over so that he could hear as well as she whispered, "Never repeat that, either of you, all right? Not to anyone. Even if you hear others talking about me. Not even if your friends say it. For that matter, if 'the One Who Is Promised' means who I think it does, you must *never* speak of her that way again. *Never* let on that you know more than what you need to know to herd animals, understand?"

Visda scowled. "I *know* that," she said crossly. "Great-aunt Chenaol made us promise. But you already know."

Aly sighed. "Look—the fewer times you say anything aloud, the better your chances that no one will hear you who shouldn't. Understand? Enemies can't report what they didn't overhear. Now, what shall we talk about?"

"Sheep, goats," Visda replied brightly.

"Dogs," added Ekit.

Aly grinned at them. "Better."

With a wave to the town men who stood morning watch on the gate, they passed out of the village and onto the dusty road. Visda began to skip, Ekit to run with one of the dogs. "I love summertime!" Visda told Aly. "All the bees, and the flowers, and the sun, and no one to stop us from running!" She raced ahead gleefully, trying to catch Ekit, her bare brown feet thumping against the road. The sheep, resigned, picked up their trot, along with the goats.

Aly shook her head, smiling, then ran to catch up with the children.

Their little group settled among boulders. The goats ate grasses tucked between stones, while the sheep grazed on more level ground just below. The dogs placed themselves where they would spot a stray the moment it wandered off from its fellows. Once the animals had settled, Visda and Ekit removed hand spindles from their packs and clumps of wool combed and rolled for spinning. As Aly climbed higher into the rocks to get a more commanding view of their surroundings, the boy and the girl began the painstaking work of spinning thread, just like the children who minded flocks throughout Tortall.

Aly had finished her breakfast when she heard the thump of bare feet on the rock just behind her. Resting a hand on her leg knife, she looked back. Nawat crouched on the rock, smiling at her. "Would you like a grub?" he asked, offering a plump one. "I got it just for you."

Aly struggled to think of a diplomatic reply. "We humans don't eat grubs." Remembering stories she'd heard from some of her father's agents, she added, "Not when we don't have to."

"But these are juicy and filling," Nawat assured her. "I saved the best of them."

Aly gulped. Her breakfast bread and cheese rolled in her belly. "Let the grub live to make more grubs," she suggested.

Nawat sighed. "It is hard to mate-feed someone who will not eat."

Aly leaned back and looked at the sky. A winged horse soared overhead, flying, it seemed, for the sheer joy of it. "We're not to the mate-feeding stage," she informed Nawat lazily. "We barely know each other."

"What if I filled my mouth pouch and spilled it for you?" Nawat asked. "Would you take food that way?"

"I would *lose* food that way. I'd throw it up," Aly retorted, amused and nauseated at the same time. "Aren't you supposed to be making arrows?"

"I am supposed to be finding goose feathers," he said comfortably, apparently unhurt by her refusal of his offer. "But my friends are getting them for me so I may see you." He reached over and ran his fingers through Aly's hair. "None of the other human females are so easy to preen."

The movement of his hand was soothing. "Are you preening other females?" Aly asked, warm in the sun.

"Only little ones, for practice," Nawat explained. "The old ones chitter—giggle—and bounce if I try. It's annoying. You don't giggle and bounce. I like that."

"You keep trying to preen the ones who giggle and bounce, and you might find yourself preening one of them for the rest of your life," Aly teased. "Their fathers and uncles and brothers will see to that."

"Humans do strange things," Nawat told her with a sigh. "I must go soon. My brethren call that they have my feathers."

Aly strained to hear, but Nawat's ears were better than hers. She heard only goats, sheep, and Visda's humming.

"The raka did as they told you they would," Nawat continued. "Yesterday their warriors began to leave the villages here. They took horses, food, shelters. Some moved into the forest at Pohon, others into the woods and cliffs outside the village of Inti. More rove the fields. Fifteen made their camp a mile on the other side of the road, in the rocks. They will keep watch for those who come through the mountains."

Most of these were words and concepts Aly had taught the crows in their dream lessons. One was not. "How can you tell they are raka?" she asked. Perhaps he had gotten the idea that *raka* meant "human." "Am I raka?"

Nawat shook his head. "Crows know the raka," he said. "They are our people. Time long past, when the first nest had given birth to the first flocks, Sky, our goddess, laid green eggs in her nest. The Dawn Crow, her mate and our god, was very confused. They hatched to become our brothers and sisters, the raka. In time they stopped hearing the voices of Sky and the Dawn Crow, and turned to Kyprioth to serve, but they never forgot their brothers and sisters the crows."

Aly shook her head. "I had no idea. I'm glad to know the patrols are out, though."

Nawat smiled. "I knew you would want to know they do as they say. They respect tricks you will do for them."

Aly sat up to protest that she did not do tricks, but Nawat was clambering down through the rocks to the road. Crows flew in from the east, circling him. He was nearly gone from Aly's view when they began to rain feathers down on his head.

Aly leaned back on her rock to think, without success. All her mind would produce for her was the memory of Nawat's fingers as they passed softly through her inch-long hair, and a repeating thought: "This place gets stranger every day."

Some time later she heard the distant thud of hooves. She sat up. A party trotted by on the road below, trailed by guards. Prince Bronau rode with his hosts again, or rather, with Mequen, Sarai, Dove, and their guards. They were almost gone from sight when the prince and Sarai broke into a gallop, riding hard down the strip of empty earth.

Aly propped herself on her elbows. Apparently Sarai had recovered from her unhappiness over the possibility that the prince was looking for a rich wife. It was either that or the prince had flirted enough to make her forget. Aly shook her head. She hoped Sarai wasn't too infatuated with Bronau. Aly's instincts shrieked that the prince was trouble looking for a place to happen. She did not want it to happen on her watch.

Once they were gone, Aly slid to the ground. What was the good of having knives if she was too out of shape to use them? She needed to exercise, and to keep exercising. When she found a level patch of grass, she began her stretch routine, loosening all of her muscles, a group at a time. She followed those with routines for hand-to-hand combat: punches, kicks, pivots, leg sweeps, blocks, elbow and palm strikes, tucks and rolls. She was lost in it, feeling her muscles warm up and loosen, when a crow nearby gave the call that meant "friend."

Aly looked around, wary and waiting. A tall raka woman moved out of the shadow between two large boulders. Crossing her hands, Aly gripped her wrists, ready to release the straps that secured her knives. "Good morning," she said pleasantly in Kyprish, every nerve of her body quivering despite her relaxed appearance. "I don't believe we've been introduced."

The woman leaned on the six-foot-long staff she carried. "I am Junai Dodeka, daughter of Ulasim Dodeka. I am here at my father's request, to keep you alive."

Aly inspected the newcomer. Junai was four inches taller than Aly and lean, covered with wiry muscle. Her cheekbones were sharp enough to cut with, her nose the same shape as Ulasim's. She wore her straight black hair braided and pinned tightly down. She dressed in a faded olive-green tunic and loose brown breeches. Her feet were bare.

This woman was clearly a fighter. There were knife scars on her hands and arm muscles and on her right cheekbone. Dagger sheaths made lines against the cloth of her breeches and waistband. She also wore leather and metal wrist guards and a leather band around her neck, a rough guard against a knife to the throat.

"I don't know how much a stick is going to do as a weapon," Aly remarked casually.

Junai spun the staff until it was level, then twisted the hand grip at the center. Blades twelve inches long sprang from each end of the staff, turning it into a double-ended spear.

"Well," Aly said, raising her brows. "Of course, that is a very different matter." She looked at the older woman—she was in her middle twenties, Aly guessed—and decided to try a theory she had in mind. "I don't suppose *you* know of any mages we might recruit?"

Junai took a step back. "What makes you believe there is a mage here, luarin, or that I would know of such a one?"

Aly leaned against a tree and thrust her hands into her breeches pockets. "My gracious, whyever would I think such a thing?" she asked, batting her eyes as she clasped her hands under her chin. "Well, let's see. We're attacked by bandits just on the other side of the mountains—we brought some with us, did you know? They're sweet, in a starveling way. Yet here we are, on this lovely flat plateau, with thriving farms, and raka who aren't nearly so ragged and thin as most of the ones who watched us come here. Tanair is just a fat goose ready for the plucking, yet no one speaks of bandits. Ever. No one mentions raids in the past, or patrols—your father had to be nudged into setting patrols out in the open lands, to look for royal soldiers or assassins. Back home, bandits huddle in isolated places, waiting to make their fortunes by taking them from others. Oh, wait, I forgot. There are no bandits at home where a strong mage is to be found. Did I miss anything?"

Junai stopped leaning on her spear and began to spin it, hand over hand, casually. "Father was right. You are clever. So take my advice. Don't ask about our mage. She hates luarin. She'll burn your face off if you come near her. Doubtless I would perish in your defense. There are ways to live without mages. You have the god's favor, I am told. It will serve you better than she will."

Aly rubbed her nose and looked Junai over. "So if this mage sees to the bandits, how am I to have faith in *your* ability to protect *me*? I'd think your only fighting practice would be from mock battles with people you've known all your life."

Junai bared teeth in a menacing grin. "I was a caravan guard for seven years," she informed Aly. "You want to try me?"

"No," Aly said, waving an arm in dismissal. "I'll take your word for it." She let the conversation end. Junai had told her more than she had planned to. Certainly she had not meant to agree that a mage lived on the Tanair lands, but that much she had done openly. She had also told Aly that her orders to guard Aly's life were more important than her fear of the mage. The mage was raka, probably a full-blood, if she hated luarin with such unmixed passion. And since Pohon village was notorious for its hate of luarin, chances were the mage lived there. Aly had scouting to do, then, before she approached this mage herself.

Aly went back to her exercises. The sun was almost directly overhead when the riding party returned to the castle. Aly heard the beat of their horses' hooves as she searched for a stray kid among the rocks. When she found the youngster and returned him to his mother, she discovered that one of the riders and her bodyguard had come to join her. A horse idly cropped grass where Aly had set her knife-throwing targets. A guard lingered near Visda and Ekit, talking with the children. There was no sign of Junai, but Aly guessed that the woman was around somewhere, watching.

She rounded the horse and stopped, looking at Dove. She had spread a blanket to sit on and was placing food on it. Aly had thought that if any of the Balitang girls wanted to investigate Aly after learning she represented a god, it would be Sarai, the oldest, who had one foot already in the adult world. Yet here was her younger sister, meek in a pale green riding costume with no embroideries or ornaments at hems and collar. She sat cross-legged in loose, comfortable breeches, a napkin on her lap as she gazed at the meal she had laid out. She wore her black hair in multiple long braids under a sheer head veil, the style favored by maidens in the Isles.

"I thought you might tire of bread and cheese," Dove remarked, looking up at Aly. "And *I'm* tired of Bronau mooning over my sister when he thinks the duchess isn't looking. I know Sarai's just keeping her hand in at flirting, but it makes me queasy to watch."

Aly sat on the grass beside the blanket. "Your ladyship honors me," she said, wondering what the girl was up to.

Dove didn't look at her. "What honor? I doubt my father lied to us and you aren't really the god's messenger. If you *are* the god's messenger, don't you have a particular standing which has nothing to do with the collar on your neck? Oh, curse it, Chenaol forgot the butter." She tossed a roll to Aly. This was not the rough brown bread that Aly normally brought to her duties with the goats, but a white bread studded with dates, raisins, and bits of fig.

"Even if your father didn't lie, and he doesn't strike me as the kind of man who does, it would still look very odd if you socialized with me," Aly explained.

"I'm not socializing." Dove picked up the open book at her side. "I'm the shy little sister, seeking time to read alone with enough people close by that my bodyguard won't fret." She looked at Aly. "It was my idea."

Aly studied her companion and helped herself to a handful of olives from a small crock. She'd heard people talk of Dove. The household had decided she was the intellectual one, without the warmth, charm, or dash of her older sister. Certainly Dove liked to read, but Aly had also noticed that the girl was both curious and observant.

"There's little I can tell you," Aly said, spitting an olive pit onto the grass. "I don't know myself why the god called on me." Except that I'm to keep you alive through the summer, she added to herself.

"And if you did, you wouldn't tell us," said Dove, eyeing dried slices of mango. "Being the close-mouthed sort. Is there anything you need? Information about the family, Tanair . . . ?"

Aly shrugged. Just because Dove wanted to test her didn't mean that she couldn't test Dove back. "I could use the best maps you can find of this area," she said. "I know nothing about the layout of the ground here, and that could be very troublesome. I'd like to see the other two villages and the road down to the western sea, but for now I can manage with maps. Copies will do, if you have only one original, but they should be good copies, no mistakes."

Dove shook her head. "Papa gave Sarai and me the maps for all our mother's lands, since they are our inheritance. And the bailiff has extras. I'll get a set for you. You'd tell Papa and the duchess if we're in danger from Bronau, wouldn't you?"

Aly picked up a sausage baked in dough, country food from the Eastern Lands. She looked it over, wondering if Chenaol had spiced it in the Isles way and if she would regret taking a bite. "Do you have a reason to distrust His Highness?" she asked. She took a careful bite of sausage. It tasted just like those at home.

Dove nibbled her mango. "I don't trust anyone who feels you should like them because they love themselves so much," she said tartly. Aly snorted, spraying crumbs on the grass. "Don't laugh," Dove told her. "It's true."

"I wasn't laughing at you," Aly said when she had swallowed the rest of her mouthful and taken a drink of water. "I was laughing because you put it perfectly."

"He thinks if he smiles at you and gives you presents you won't notice he can't keep his mouth closed," grumbled Dove, appeased. "If we were in Rajmuat and the king's spies heard the way he talks, we'd all be under arrest. Does he believe there aren't any spies out here?"

"We'll just make sure they don't have the chance to report anything," Aly assured the girl. "That's the nice thing about being all tucked away like this. We can control what information comes into these lands and what information leaves them." She passed a sausage roll to Dove. "Try one of these, and tell me which members of King Oron's family are still alive."

In the days that followed, Aly settled into her expanded role among the Balitangs and the raka conspirators. Junai became a silent, constant presence from the moment Aly left the main hall in the morning until she reentered it at night. Wherever Aly spent her days, Junai was at hand, looking on as Aly tended goats, talked to Visda and occasionally Dove, and practiced her hand-to-hand combat.

The raka patrols were now visible. Aly would look up from studying the maps Dove had brought, to note distant groups of riders, mounted on nimble ponies. They skirted the farms and wound through the estate's rocky eastern border. Sometimes younger riders came with them, to practice fighting and tracking away from the gaze of the duke's and prince's men-at-arms.

Aly traded on and off with Hasui as wine pourer on the dais. Every second night she searched the rooms occupied by Bronau and his attendants for new letters. Bronau's spies wrote nothing, having no way to get correspondence out of Tanair, but the prince himself wrote every day, preparing letters that offered alliances to nobles who were not friends of his brother. Aly memorized each noble's name, knowing that Bronau would send these calls for aid as soon as the opportunity came. She wanted to know whom Bronau felt was safe to approach.

When Aly took pouring duty, Bronau always made sure to say hello to her. He also flirted constantly with Sarai in the dining hall. Fesgao and the servants said that he did so at all other times as well. Everyone saw how Sarai responded to Bronau's compliments and teasing, obviously flattered by the man's charm and attention. At night, as Aly recited what news she found worth the family's time, Sarai listened without comment. She could not keep the trouble from her face as Aly quoted Bronau's latest piece of correspondence, any more than her parents could. Only Dove showed real curiosity and appreciation of what Aly had learned.

Bronau did not neglect Mequen and Winnamine, so his dealings with Sarai caused few ripples apart from idle speculation. Aly heard the servants' and slaves' observations when she and the chief raka conspirators—Ulasim, Chenaol, Lokeij, and Fesgao—met over a late supper in the kitchen. They talked softly over drinks and snacks while most of the household listened to music in the great hall. Ulasim summed up the patrols' reports for his three comrades and Aly. Chenaol had the day's gossip and discoveries from the servants and the villagers, where her own family played a vital part in everyday business. Lokeij and his stable boys shared news from visitors to the stables, as well as Tanair's herdspeople, while Fesgao passed on the gleanings from the prince's and the Balitangs' men-at-arms. Sometimes Nawat joined them if the crows had seen anything of interest. Aly was surprised at first that the raka accepted Nawat so readily, until she overheard Chenaol tell Fesgao that their prophecy had mentioned the help of Kyprioth's crows. Between the reports from the people and the crows, Aly had as perfect a spy network as her da could have put together.

So far there was little of interest to discuss: crop news, deer and elk sightings, human movement such as the route followed by the daily riding party, and bedroom intrigues between the locals and the royal guests. Aly was confident that she would know about danger before it got very far. With so much information coming in, she felt more like Aly of Pirate's Swoop every day.

One night Aly finished her day's report to the Balitangs. She turned to go when the duchess stopped her. "Aly, can someone else take your goats tomorrow?"

Aly nodded.

"The prince wants to see our villages," explained Sarai. "Inti and Pohon. We thought you might want to come as well."

"You did want to see more of the plateau," Dove said. Normally she kept silent during these reports. Now she gave Aly a tiny smile and returned to setting out the chessboard for her nightly game with Mequen.

"I'm having the maid pack some of Rihani's potions to bring to the villages," the duchess added. "That will explain your presence. We'll have soldiers, but you can say I didn't wish to entrust the bottles and jars to a ham-handed warrior."

Aly smiled. "Thank you, Your Grace," she told the duchess. "I await your orders in the morning." Finally, she thought. A chance to ferret out the mage at Pohon!

She rose at her usual time so that she could take the goats down to Visda, then returned to the castle. Waiting in her cleanest tunic and breeches, a small cloth bag with a few necessary items slung over her shoulder, she watched the men-at-arms at their morning combat drill. There was a quiet, grim competition between the Balitangs' and Bronau's men. Neither side was at its friendliest. Blows that should have been taps hit with authority and pain. Looking around the courtyard, Aly noticed Junai in the shadows, her eyes intent on the sparring men. No doubt her guard was considering new fighting techniques.

One person Aly hadn't seen yet that day was Nawat. Perhaps he worked outside only at dawn, when things were quiet, and went back into Falthin's bowyer shop when the courtyard got busy. Aly tried to pretend she wasn't disappointed, but her illusion fell to pieces when she saw Nawat walking toward her, leading two saddled and bridled horses. He was smiling at her in a way that made her throat tighten just a little. She coughed to clear it.

"I am to ride with you," Nawat explained when he reached her. "Workers in the villages gather wood for bows and arrow shafts, and I must collect it. We will ride together and our crows will visit us."

"They'll probably frighten the horses," Aly said, accepting the reins Nawat offered. "Falthin certainly gives you plenty of time away from work."

"He says I am young only once," Nawat informed her. "He says that when I choose a mate he will help me with the bride price. Do you have a bride price? What is a bride price?"

He might as well have touched her with a branding iron. Aly jumped. Had she been someone else's daughter she might even have shrieked. As it happened, she was saved from having to answer by the arrival of the prince, the duchess, the older girls, and their guards. Lokeij himself brought out Sarai's mount, and winked at Aly and Nawat.

I suppose he *thinks I'm interested in bride prices, too!* Aly thought, indignant. She would have to explain things to Nawat, so he would know how very uninterested in such things she was. For now she had a performance to give. As far as anyone here knew, Aly had not spent much time in the saddle. To that end she dragged herself onto her shaggy chestnut mare, every inch of her the ignorant servant rider. The horse bridled, pranced, even reared twice. Aly stayed on while she pretended to be on the verge of falling off, flopping here and there as the mare worked off her early-morning fidgets. It seemed that the horse figured out that she was experienced. Once the chestnut calmed down, Aly took the basket of potions from the duchess.

As they set off, Aly and Nawat rode between the nobles and the men-at-arms. Snatches of conversation came back to Aly: talk of weather and crops, hunting and books. More than once she heard the prince tell Sarai, "When you return to the capital," as if they were on Lombyn for a holiday. Today for a change Aly watched from close quarters as the prince and Sarai had their daily gallop, their bodyguards following. The duchess, confident the pair would never be out of sight of their guards, remained with Dove and the main group of riders.

As a riding companion, Nawat was perfect. He sat his mount as if born in the saddle. Aly supposed it was because in many ways he was as much an animal as his horse. Staying close to Aly, Nawat pointed out the land's features as they rode across it. Aly memorized them all, placing them on her mental copy of the Tanair map: roads and trails, creeks, springs, farms, stands of trees and of rocks where enemies might hide, herds of animals, clumps of wild berries and fruit trees. She also saw that the raka who labored in the fields stood at attention as Sarai galloped by and bowed to the duchess. They watched Dove from the corners of their eyes. Aly hoped their restraint was due to the Tanair conspirators' warning them not to show any favor to Sarai before outsiders.

It was almost noon when they reached the village of Inti, astride the road that cut down through cliffs and waterfalls to reach the western coast of Lombyn. Inti itself was set on a mound of raised earth. To Aly it was the second most dangerous point on the Tanair lands, a less obvious route into Balitang territory. Ulasim had assured her that his people were aware of the problem. The road was watched. Inti's villagers kept messenger doves to carry word of an enemy's approach to the castle. There was also a large flock of crows in the trees around Inti and the road west. They bawled wary greetings to Aly and Nawat, then reported normal activity.

At Inti even Bronau could not ignore the rakas' behavior. The villagers stopped whatever they did to look on in silence as the headman and elders came to greet their company.

I suppose I should be grateful they don't have signs up proclaiming, Welcome to the One Who Is Promised, Aly told herself. She made a mental note to ask Ulasim and Chenaol how many noble luarin knew of the prophecy.

The raka remained silent as the duchess gave half of the contents of Aly's basket to the village midwife, then followed the village headman to his home. There the headman and the elders offered the nobles herbal tea, coconut custard, sticky rice, rice flour cakes, cassava melon slices, and banana fritters on woven grass platters. They ate seated on the headman's broad porch as the townspeople looked on.

Aly knelt just behind the duchess and Sarai, within earshot as Bronau sipped his tea and quickly set the cup down. "Murky stuff," he whispered to Sarai in Common, his eyes dancing merrily. "Do you suppose they scooped it from a swamp? Perhaps we'd best check for slugs and salamanders. They eat anything that doesn't eat them first, these wild folk."

Aly doubted that he even realized he was insulting their hosts; he was simply bent on flirting with Sarai. To her credit, she kept her eyes down as a blush mantled her golden brown cheeks. Let Bronau think the blush was maidenly confusion. Aly, seeing the girl's trembling hands, knew it for rage. She glanced at the raka elders. From the flashing eyes of three of them, she knew they understood Common as well as their own language.

I need hand signals, she thought, putting it on her mental list of things to do. In case I have to tell the family things without speaking aloud. Right now she wished she could ask Sarai to steer the prince away from his present line of chatter. She was wondering if she would have to spill tea on the man when Dove said, "Your Highness, perhaps these elders would like to hear news from Rajmuat?"

With everyone's attention now on him, Bronau was happy to perform the role of the great man for the townspeople. He patronized them, explaining the most obvious things, but at least he was no longer making fun of their hospitality. I love that girl, Aly thought, passing the banana fritters to Dove. The younger girl met her eyes. Her mouth twitched slightly in a tucked-away smile.

The visit ended with an exchange of politenesses between the duchess and the village elders. The Inti raka stood in silence as the nobles mounted up and rode on their way.

"That was odd, don't you think?" Bronau asked Winnamine as they left

Inti behind. "Did you see how they stared? Surely they've seen luarin nobility before. And they weren't chattering as they always do, in that dreadful language of theirs."

"We are still a novelty here," Winnamine replied, her face and eyes serene, with no hint of any emotion but pleasant interest. "Remember, these are highlanders. They hardly ever see *anyone* new, let alone of the luarin. Really, my dear, the tea and the food were perfectly safe. We all took our share. You insulted them by not taking any."

"I would have insulted my belly even more," Bronau said with a grin. "Just because I keep pigs doesn't mean I eat their slop."

A chill rolled off the raka among their men-at-arms. Bronau had not even tried to keep his voice down.

"For our sake, Bronau, will you be gracious to them?" Winnamine asked playfully, resting a light hand on the man's sleeve. "We have to live with these people for the time being."

Bronau took her hand and kissed her fingertips. "For you I will risk it, Winna. But don't be so resigned. Once I return to the capital, I will use all my influence to bring you back to civilization." He turned to Sarai. "After all, the young men don't know what they're missing while you are here."

As they rode on, Nawat drew closer to Aly. "Raka aren't pigs," he murmured. She wondered if Falthin had told him to speak quietly, or if Nawat sensed that it was a bad idea to be overheard. "Why does he speak of them that way?" the crow-man wanted to know. "They are humans, just like he is."

"I don't think he sees them as just like him," Aly explained.

"He is foolish, then," said Nawat. "There are more raka than Bronaus."

They rode on to Pohon, on the north side of the plateau. Once again the farmers stood up from their work to watch them pass. Aly, sharpening her Sight, noted that the closer they rode to the village, the more farmers had weapons close at hand in the fields. She also noticed that the men-at-arms had closed ranks and moved up to ride two deep on either side of the column, enclosing it on three sides. They entered forested land beyond the fields, until they came to Pohon. These villagers were different from those of Inti, except for the mute attention they gave Dove and Sarai. They accepted the duchess's medicines without thanks. Their eyes were hostile when they looked at the men-at-arms, sullen as they regarded the prince, the duchess, Aly, and the luarin maid. Aly wondered if they remembered that their precious Lady was half luarin.

In the confusion of greeting the elders, Aly asked Winnamine to excuse her, implying that something she had eaten had not set well in her belly. When the duchess looked at her with the tiniest of frowns, Aly raised an eyebrow. Winnamine's eyes crinkled with mirth, then she gravely nodded her permission.

Carrying her cloth bag and the empty medicine basket, Aly slipped into the shadows along the sides of a village house and put on the disguise she had packed into it: a beige head scarf such as farm women wore, tied at the nape of her neck, and a jar of brown skin tint, made of sap, that she could wipe off quickly. She smeared it on her face, arms, hands, and the tops of her feet where the leggings did not cover the bare skin. At the last moment she remembered the back of her neck, a mistake her father told her was often the death of spies. She hoisted the empty potion basket onto one shoulder as the raka women did, and sauntered through the area between the houses. Nearly everyone was gathered before the headman's porch, where the nobility sat. Aly walked away from them.

Somewhere around Pohon there was a mage. Aly hoped it would be here, within the palisade walls. She kept her head down as she ambled along the beaten paths that were streets and walkways, keeping an eye open for any house that was decorated with the colors of a raka mage: red and purple braids, and green threads strung like spiderwebs in small wooden circles. People might visit a mage in her house for the treatment of their illnesses, or the mage could be elsewhere, helping a woman in labor while the midwife sat with the dignitaries at the headman's residence. If the mage was away, Aly's Sight would show her where the mage could be found.

She did see magic. Its white fire gleamed everywhere, in signs written on doors, windows, ladders, and wells, on the sides of jars and baskets, scratched in garden dirt. She didn't know what they were for; the raka used very different signs from the eastern mages. From experience Aly could guess at their meanings and file in her memory the signs that obviously were for house blessing, disease, or fire prevention.

When she reached the rear wall without Seeing even a hint of a mage, Aly chewed her lip. She had prowled all over Pohon without luck. She had to return to the duchess's party. Certainly she didn't want to get left behind. Her disguise wouldn't stand up to close inspection. The raka's hate for the luarin was a nearly solid thing. It discouraged plans to stay the night.

She turned. Three raka men and two raka women blocked her path.

"So what is it?" asked one woman, a dark, feline creature who radiated contempt. "You thought raka are so stupid they wouldn't notice a stranger prowling our village?"

"What are you nosing about for?" demanded one of the men. "Plots, weapons, treachery?"

"Or just something to steal?" asked the biggest man. "As if you luarin left us anything of worth."

Aly crossed her arms to hide her movements as she freed her wrist knives. "Actually, I'd meant to talk to you about that," she said cheerfully. "I thought I'd make a list, tell you what I need . . ." She lunged right, clearing that side of her attackers' line. They charged her and halted, clear of the two blades she now held like the expert she was, one pointed out, one pointed back. She waited, her feet well placed, her balance perfect. It was important that she be careful. Killing one of these people would create more ill will for her and the Balitangs.

The big man came at her, tossing a long knife from one hand to the other like a market-day tough. Aly darted in, knocked the knife flying while it was between his hamlike hands, and jammed the edge of one of her blades up under his chin. His eyes flicked left. Aly snapped out a side kick that forced the man sneaking up on her to stumble away, protecting his bruised arm. On both feet again, she hooked the big man's legs and yanked his feet from under him, dumping him onto his back. She jumped and landed on his belly with both knees, knocking the wind from his lungs.

A woman threw herself on top of Aly, who rolled away. The woman hit the big man instead, slamming the breath from her own lungs. Aly jumped to her feet and waited, her eyes on one of the men and the other woman. They closed in on her, blades out.

A knife cut the air between the two advancing raka to strike the earth just ahead of them, quivering, planted in the dirt. As the man looked back to find the thrower, Junai advanced, slowly turning her weapon hand over hand. When she passed the two on the ground, she smacked the woman on a kidney with her staff, drawing a yelp of pain. Junai kicked the man in the ankle, her boot slamming a sensitive bunch of muscle. The man swore. The woman facing Aly backed away from Junai, hands raised. The third man, trying to get around her, went down face-first, Nawat on his back.

"Don't kill him," Aly told Nawat quickly, not sure what the crow-man would do. "Let him breathe." She looked at Junai. "Are you going to scold me now? I was handling things myself."

"How did you do it, back there?" Junai inquired, brows raised. "No magic, no smoke or mist, you were just gone. And I wasn't born yesterday."

The woman who held up her hands looked at Junai, then Aly. "She's *that* one? But she's luarin!"

"Don't talk to me, talk to the god," Junai replied casually. "That is, if you think you'll like the way he answers. All of you, memorize her face. Don't let this happen again." She looked at Aly and sighed. "They're getting ready to leave."

Aly tore off the head cloth and began to rub the sap off her bare skin.

"How did you leave?" Nawat wanted to know. "Even *I* lost you until I heard the village dogs bark about a fight."

Aly shrugged, finding clean spots on the cloth to take off each patch of color. "That's what I do," she told him. "That's why I'm here." She resheathed her knives, then picked up the basket she had dropped.

"Do you speak only dog, or the language of all animals?"

"All animals," Nawat replied. "Is that good?"

"It could be," Aly replied. Passing the two on the ground—the woman who lay, both hands pressed to her kidney, the man clutching his ankle—she stopped and smiled. "It was ever so lovely to meet you," she said politely. "Let's do it again. Don't let me see that cheap brawler's trick a second time," she added, nudging the man with her foot. "Any decent fighter will take you when you don't have hold of your weapon."

She tucked her disguise into her cloth bag, stowed it in her basket, which had been tossed aside in the fight, and walked back to the horses. By the time she and Nawat reached them, and Junai faded to wherever Junai kept herself, the nobles had said farewell to the Pohon elders. Only when they had ridden out of the village did Aly relax and review how she had done. Not so well, she decided. She was rusty. She had used too many flashy moves of her own. She needed to practice more.

As they turned toward home, Nawat fell back. He was on foot now, the wood and arrow shafts he had collected in the villages bundled and strapped to his horse's back.

Dove joined Aly. "Did you see how they were, in the villages?" Dove asked, keeping her voice low. "The prince wasn't even *trying* to be discreet at Inti. No wonder the raka hate us."

"Us?" Aly repeated.

Dove looked sideways at Aly. "The luarin. We stole their country, killed most of their nobles, put thousands in near slavery, and made the rest complete slaves. I'd hate us, in their place."

"But you're not the same," Aly pointed out. "You and Sarai are half raka."

"Some villagers in Pohon saw the luarin half before the raka half," retorted Dove. "I noticed, even if you didn't."

"Oh, I got a good idea of it," Aly murmured.

Sarai let out a cascade of laughter. The prince smiled. Clearly he'd said something to amuse her.

"She's half in love with him," Dove said, her eyes on the man who rode between her sister and stepmother. "They'd do more than talk if the duchess left them alone."

"Only half in love?" To Aly it seemed as if Sarai was head over heels.

"She can't forget his money problems," Dove commented. "I'm not helping. Whenever she starts to gush I mention his debts. And she's no fool. She knows she has no fortune, just some land. So why does he court her? She's forgotten all about the boy from Matebo House who made up to her in Rajmuat. It used to be I couldn't get her to shut up about him. But Bronau pours on the honey, and Sarai goes all gooey-eyed."

Aly saw it then, as clearly as if she'd read Bronau's plans in one of his hidden letters. "Dove, Prince Hazarin is next in line for the throne, isn't he? Then who's after him—Princess Imajane?"

Dove shook her head. "Female. She can't inherit under luarin law. Hazarin doesn't have children—and the way he lives, nobody expects it. His only heir is Prince Dunevon, and he's just three. He's the only child of Oron's third queen. She's dead. I suppose Oron would put Dunevon under the guardianship of Hazarin or Imajane and her husband. Or just Imajane and Rubinyan if Hazarin was king."

Aly smoothed the reins over her hand. That matched reports on the kingship of the Isles she had read at home. "And if something happened to Hazarin and Dunevon?"

"No, they're healthy enough," Dove said automatically. Then her golden cheeks paled. "Papa. Papa's next in line."

"Sarai would be a crown princess," Aly pointed out, her voice soft. "So would you, and Petranne. Elsren would be a prince." Aly hesitated, then continued, hoping she did not make a mistake with this girl. "Rubinyan married into the royal family," Aly reminded Dove. "Maybe Bronau wants to do the same."

Dove chewed her lower lip. "This is too deep for me. We need to tell the duchess. Though if she likes Bronau . . ."

So Dove, at least, now thought of her stepmother as an ally. Aly was relieved to hear it. "She likes him, but she knows he is not as careful as she would like," she told Dove. "Her Grace would listen."

"Why did he come?" Dove whispered, glaring at Bronau. "We're in trouble enough with the Crown. We don't need more of the king's attention."

"I don't believe the prince thought about that," Aly replied. "Only about what he wants."

Supper that night was over in the main hall. The conspirators, Nawat, and Aly had just finished their night's meeting. Aly was about to leave to report to the Balitangs when Ulasim grabbed her arm.

"Just what did you think you were doing, in Pohon today?" he asked quietly. "You gave Junai the slip. You left your companions to walk through a notoriously hostile village alone, for what reason? To learn they have nothing? That under the luarin they are nothing, when once they gave birth to queens?"

Aly glanced at the hand on her arm, then looked at Ulasim and raised an eyebrow. He met her gaze, his grip still firm.

"Surely Junai told you I can take care of myself," Aly said very gently.

"Not against a group," Ulasim told Aly. "Why? The god cannot watch you always. No god can. And you are too wise to take foolish chances, Aly of the crooked eye."

"Don't call me that," Aly replied. "It hurts my feelings. And Pohon isn't so badly off, not with five arms caches that I could see on a casual walk. There is also that herd of very fine horses recently moved outside the wall. I am assuming that was so we couldn't notice how well mounted the Pohon raka are. I didn't get into any of the barns, but blaze balm has a distinctive smell."

Ulasim's eyes went wide. His hold on Aly tightened.

Aly sighed and grabbed his little finger, forcing it back against its normal curve. "Now, be nice. You might startle me into breaking your finger," she pointed out as beads of sweat formed on Ulasim's forehead. "Think how unfriendly that would be. It's not like you don't trust me, after all. I *am* the god's chosen."

Ulasim let her go. She released his finger. "I'm Tortallan, remember?" she asked. "As long as the Balitangs and I live out the summer, I don't care what the raka are up to. I'd move the blaze balm, though. Bronau's served in combat. If he smells it the Pohon folk will be in trouble with the Crown. *I* was looking for a mage."

Ulasim massaged the finger she had bent, eyeing her with respect. When she said "mage," his eyebrows shot up. "Junai said you'd been at her about that. We told you, there isn't one."

"And I took it as a nice, polite lie between allies," Aly said reasonably. "But our guest's presence makes me uneasy. The longer he stays, the more likely he'll draw attention this way, attention nobody wants. My task here is quite simple, Ulasim. *I'm to keep this family safe.* That doesn't mean dealing with a threat when it actually comes; it means preparing for them in advance. For that, I require a true mage, not a healer with a few extra spells, like Rihani. The raka have one. I need her."

Ulasim sighed, and rubbed his forehead. "She doesn't live in Pohon. And you must be patient. Junai is working on her."

Aly leaned against a nearby wall and stuffed her hands into her pockets. "*Junai* is working on her?"

"And others," mumbled Ulasim.

"Why is Junai important enough that this recluse will speak with her?" Aly pressed, knowing there was a secret here, and wanting it.

Ulasim smoothed his hand over his short, neat beard. "Because Ochobu is her grandmother. But I wouldn't count on her help, Aly. I really wouldn't. She said when she disowned me that it would take a miracle for her to even come downwind of me again."

Now Aly knew the secret. "Your *mother?*"

"Who cast me out," Ulasim explained. "My father was dying, and she summoned me home. I didn't feel I could leave the young ladies. Mother never forgave me."

Aly straightened and dusted off her tunic. "Well, we'll just have to think of a miracle, then," she told Ulasim. "Or rather, I will. You think of what to say to her when you see her again."

Ulasim grabbed Aly's arm, gently this time. "Don't ask the god," he begged. "You don't know what he might do."

Aly smiled grimly. "Don't worry," she reassured the tall man. "I already know better than to call on gods casually. But there are miracles, and there are *miracles*. I just need to think of one."

Midsummer's Day, June 22, 462 H.E.
Trebond, in northern Tortall

It was another of those not-quite-dreams that Aly knew Kyprioth had sent. The Kyprioth dreams always felt like everyday life, except that she was a ghost and the dream ended before dawn in the Copper Isles.

This dream had a familiar background: the towers of her mother's former home, Trebond, rising on a bluff just to the west. The ghost Aly stood in a woodland clearing that was filled with creatures one expected to see in dreams. A handful of Stormwings, one of them a glass-crowned queen, perched in the trees. Beside them stood a basilisk, a seven-foot-tall lizard-like immortal with skin like beads of different shades of gray, lighter on its back, darkening to thunderhead gray on its belly. A gray pony stood beside the basilisk, thoughtfully cropping grass. On her back perched five tiny monkey-like creatures, pygmy marmosets, nibbling on raisins as they looked around. Wolves, squirrels, golden eagles, horses, ponies, and dogs lined the edges of the clearing, the squirrels and the dogs tucked behind the horses, where they kept an eye on the wolves.

Among the humans Aly recognized her foster uncle Coram, Baron of Trebond, and his wife, Aly's aunt Rispah. With them stood a tall older man with silver-blond hair and tanned skin. A peculiar creature Aly knew as Bonedancer—a kind of bat-bird skeleton—rode on his shoulder, peering this way and that, fascinated with its surroundings. As Aly watched, the skeleton took flight, soaring on bone wings with invisible feathers, to land on the pony with the marmosets. One of them politely handed the skeleton something to eat.

Present also were Onua Chamtong and Sergeant Ogunsanwo of the Queen's Riders, the former Rider commander, Buri, and her new husband, Raoul of Goldenlake and Malorie's Peak. Aly saw her own mother, and Lord Wyldon of Cavall, one of the commanders of the northern armies. Lord Wyldon stood on the far side of the clearing from Alanna and eyed her much as the squirrels eyed the wolves. Aly's grandmother Eleni was at the center of the clearing, dressed as a priestess of the Great Goddess. Aly's grandfather Myles was there, too.

Near Eleni were Numair and Daine, dressed in their finest clothes. Between them they held a blanket like a hammock, each of them gripping two ends of it. The blanket writhed as if a score of creatures did battle for room inside it. Once a pair of hooves thrust through an opening. A moment later a snake's tail fell out of one end.

Aly's father rode into the clearing on a lathered horse and slid from the saddle. He rushed over to kiss Daine's cheek and clap Numair on the shoulder, then looked at his wife. Aly's mother eyed her husband strangely, her violet eyes cold. She jerked her chin up in some kind of challenge. George frowned, then went to her. He leaned down and whispered something in her ear; Aly saw her mother's mouth shape the words "Not now." George straightened, puzzled. Aly, too, was puzzled. Why was her mother angry with Da?

"I'm sure they'll be here any moment," Daine told Eleni. "Ma said the Great Gods ag—" She and Numair buckled, the weight in the blanket hammock suddenly large and rounded. A moment later they could raise the hammock again. Daine smiled apologetically at Aly's grandmother, who eyed the surging blanket as if it were dangerous. "Baby river horse," Daine explained with a blush.

"I can't begin to imagine nursing her—him—it," Eleni said, fumbling.

"It's a challenge," replied Daine, determinedly cheerful as she and Numair struggled to keep the squawking contents of the blanket steady.

The air behind Eleni shimmered silver. Two people stepped through. One was a man, over six feet in height, clad only in a loincloth. His skin was green-streaked brown; from his curly brown hair sprouted a rack of antlers that would have made an elk proud. His companion was gowned all in green, with a mist-fine green veil over her hair and face.

These were Daine's parents, Aly realized in wonder. These guests were divine ones: the hunt god Weiryn, whose territory included the mountains of Galla and Scanra, where Daine had grown up, and his wife, Sarra, Daine's mother, known as the Green Lady. After she had joined Daine's father in the Divine Realms, Sarra had become a minor goddess of healing. She appeared to those who lived in and around the village where, in her mortal days, she had raised Daine and served as a midwife. Since the two were restricted to the Divine Realms after their involvement in the Immortals' War, Aly could only guess that they had gotten special permission to cross over on Midsummer's Day for the naming of their grandchild.

The gods nodded to Eleni, who curtsied deeply to them. The other humans in the clearing bowed or curtsied as well. Daine and Numair could do nothing but nod. Their child's latest shape change had sent quills shooting through the fabric of its blanket.

"Now, this will not do." The Green Lady raised her veil, revealing a pretty face crowned by blond hair. Aly could see how, as a mortal, Sarra had won the love of a god. Sweetness shone from her face and eyes and turned her voice into music. "Really, dear, you must be firm with children."

Daine's mouth curled down wryly. "It's hard to reason with a six-week-old, Ma."

"We did try," added Numair, his gaze sharp as he looked at his mother-in-law. "Every way that we could."

Sarra walked over and reached into the hammock blanket, pulling out a wolf puppy. It turned instantly into a young giraffe, then a gosling. Whatever shape it took, Sarra held it firmly. "Now see here, youngster," she informed her grandchild, "you ought to be ashamed, wearing your parents out all the time. And this kind of thing isn't good for you. You'll exhaust yourself before you're ten. Enough. Choose a shape and a sex and stick to it, right now." She listened for a moment, then shook her head. "Five years at least. Learn the limits of one body. Then, if you're good, you may try others. Now *choose*."

A moment later she held a human baby girl in her hands. The child looked up at her with wide, solemn eyes. Sarra gave her to Daine. "She'll be good now," the goddess told her daughter. "And in the future, don't shape-shift while you're pregnant. It gives them the wrong idea."

The naming proceeded from there.

Sergeant Ogunsanwo, Onua, and Aly's mother and father served as godsparents for the new child. Afterward the guests came with gifts and good wishes for the baby. Numair and Daine stood as if a boulder had been lifted from their shoulders, beaming like the happy parents they were. Aly couldn't imagine what it had been like for them, with a newborn that changed shape so often. Aly had cared for human and animal babies and had been exhausted by them even when they didn't shape-shift.

Throughout the ceremony and the party, Aly watched her parents. Alanna was stiff near her husband, though obviously happy for her friend Daine. When George touched her elbow and they wandered off under the trees, Aly followed them, worried. What had vexed her mother *this* time?

"Lass, what is it?" George asked once they were out of earshot of the others at the naming celebration. "You seem angry."

"Angry?" Alanna glared up at her husband. "How would you feel if you found out one of our children had disappeared and I was keeping it from you?"

George's shoulders slumped. "You heard."

"I should have heard it from *you*, George! Not the king! She's my only daughter, you knew she was missing—"

George rested his hands on her shoulders. "You were in combat. I want you to concentrate on staying alive. I thought for sure I'd have found her by now. I thought—"

"But you've asked?" Alanna's anger evaporated. She gripped her husband's tunic. "Sent out your whisperers, asked for a girl of her look?"

"I dare not." Aly's father's voice was soft. "I dare not, my darling. If our enemies knew she was out there—we cannot risk it. The king's been scrying for her, but it's as if she's clean vanished."

Alanna rested her forehead against George's chest. "I've been scrying, every night, every morning, any moment I can. But if she were dead, surely His Majesty or I would have seen it." She looked up. "Have you asked Alan? Twins often know if the other's in trouble. He—"

George laid a gentle finger over her lips. "I did. He only knows she's not hurt or frightened. Alanna, what of the Goddess? She's your patron."

Alanna shook her head. "I've prayed, without a whisper of a reply. Nothing. Perhaps she's busy elsewhere, I know I'm not her only supplicant—"

Aly flinched. A few tears rolled down her mother's cheeks. George gathered Alanna into his arms. Alanna dried her face on his tunic, then turned her head so that she could speak and he would hear. "I want to hunt for her myself." She cut off her husband as he drew breath to speak. "I know. I said I *want* to, I didn't say that I could. I'm noticeable. And there's still a war to fight. Maggur's like a rabid wolf, at his most dangerous when he's cornered. But then I think of our Aly—"

Aly's vivid dream faded. She woke. A castle dog sat beside her, surrounded by the shimmering glow that marked a god's presence.

You were about to try to get word to them, so they won't worry, the dog-Kyprioth said into her head. *Save your efforts. Any paper you send out of Tanair will vanish. Any courier will forget the message. Our wager is between you and me alone.*

"My mother is *worried,*" Aly whispered, not wanting to rouse the sleeping servants. "She shouldn't be thinking about me, only about the war. She could get killed if she's distracted."

The dog licked its chops. *We had a bet, Alianne of Pirate's Swoop. I won't risk interference from your parents or their patron gods.*

Assassins approach a problem differently from soldiers, you see. They can't lay siege, they can't offer an honorable fight. In their trade numbers are dangerous. An assassin's advantage lies in folk missing him when he's about. He hits hard and fast, then goes. Once you've tried to kill the first time, the target has the wind up. Failure the first time means it'll be that much harder to get close a second time.

—Told to Aly when she was eleven,
in a conversation with her father

10

ASSASSINS

Through the rest of June Aly's goat herding was often interrupted by visitors: Dove, occasionally Sarai after her morning ride, various raka. Junai never appeared, not even to eat lunch with them, though Aly always knew where her bodyguard was. One day even the duchess came. She brought Petranne and Elsren for a picnic on the hillside, sharing their lunch with Visda and Aly as well as her own children, and talking about her own country upbringing.

The raka who stopped by always had questions about Sarai and Dove. What were they like? Were they haughty? Did they know the ways of the raka, or had their hearts been taken by the luarin? Aly tried to build their sympathy and liking for the girls. At the very least, if the family were attacked some night, the raka might be convinced to hide Sarai and Dove.

Aly's supper routine was the one she had fallen into after Bronau's arrival. One night she would pour the wine at the head table. On the next she searched Bronau's correspondence and that of his servants. Both routines were followed by meetings with the raka conspirators and Nawat to exchange information. Once all that was done, Aly collapsed happily onto her pallet, usually falling asleep in the middle of plans to ferret out the elusive mage.

On her nights at the head table, Aly noted that the prince got more and more restless, though he did his best to hide it from Sarai. The two of them still rode every day, with the duchess or the duke as chaperons. The rides got longer. It seemed the prince needed more and more exercise to keep from exploding. Even a game of chess with Mequen tried his patience.

A week after their trip to Pohon, Aly sat with Visda and Ekit over the last scraps of lunch. She was about to practice her combat skills some more when the calls of crows filled the air. Aly listened and translated their sounds: a peaceful caravan of some kind, probably merchants, was coming down the road from Dimari.

Turning the goats over to Visda, Aly went to get a look from the rocks above the road. She had almost reached the summit of one boulder, where she could watch without being seen, when someone clasped her ankle and yanked her down into a crack between stones. Aly twisted hard to free herself as she slid down, then jammed herself against her would-be captor's side and arm, pressing one of her daggers to his throat as she kept him from reaching one of his. The young raka who had grabbed her stared down at her with emotionless eyes. Aly looked him over. This was her first encounter with one of the raka who watched over the plateau.

She patted the man's cheek. "You would belong to the patrol, yes? Lovely to make your acquaintance. I feel so looked-after."

Cloth slithered on stone as Junai slid down to their location. "It's her," Junai explained to the raka, her voice very dry. "Don't let the silly mannerisms fool you." She looked at Aly. "Were you on your way somewhere?"

"Nice meeting you," Aly told the raka warrior, then climbed back up to the higher rock, Junai at her back. Just below the summit Aly flattened herself on the stone and belly-crawled the rest of the way, keeping her head low until she just crested the top.

It was a merchant caravan. Aly recognized most of the carts and people, who had come to Tanair twice this summer. There were faces she did not know: three full-blood male luarin, a part-raka man, and a beautiful luarin woman. The woman was a charmer, Aly thought, sent as a temptation for men. The four unfamiliar men were hard-looking fellows with their share of knife scars. Aly watched as their eyes flicked restlessly over their surroundings. They seemed more wary than alert. Though they wore only belt-knives openly, she could also see the print of hilts against their shirts and breeches. Their bulging belt purses and saddlebags were guaranteed to hold even more tools for bloody work, unless she had lost her grip on her education entirely. These were not the tougher breed of merchant who followed Lombyn's jungle and mountain roads. These were killers.

Aly did her mental trick that allowed her to see distant objects in detail. Now the unfamiliar traders were as clear to her vision as if they stood right before her. One, a luarin dressed in a buckskin tunic and breeches, drove the lead wagon with Gurhart, the chief merchant, beside him. Something about the way he held himself told Aly he was the assassins' leader. He looked to be five feet eight inches tall, with short brown hair. He was olive-skinned, dark for a luarin, with green eyes and a round scar on his left cheekbone. The remaining three male strangers, two full luarin, one a half-blood, rode as guards, their crossbows set easily on their thighs. Their tunics and breeches were unremarkable shades of brown. Two had brown hair; the part-raka had black hair. All three were lean and muscular, with swords in plain sheaths that had seen hard use.

The standout was the woman, but Aly guessed she was meant to divert attention from the men. She wore her blazing red hair coiled and pinned at the back of her head. She sat beside the driver of one of the other wagons, looking around at the scenery. Her eyes, as restless as those of the other assassins, were blue. Her dress almost matched her eyes in color. Despite the pampered smoothness of her skin, the woman had strong arms and capable hands.

Aly turned her gaze to Gurhart, who ran the caravan. He was part raka and a decent enough fellow. Over his other visits Aly had been careful to talk to him, presenting herself to him and his people as an eager young girl who desired news of the world beyond Tanair. Gurhart, flattered by her attention, had told her more than regular news. Aly knew the names of his wife and children, how much he had made the year before, and how often he'd come to Tanair before the Balitangs made it worth his trouble. From those talks Aly knew Gurhart was no more able to hide his troubles than three-year-old Elsren. She saw no discomfort on the merchant's round face now, no unease or suspicion. That didn't necessarily mean the new members of the caravan were all right, she told herself. It might just mean that Gurhart had been short of hands, and these five had shown up. She wondered how many of Gurhart's original crew of workers had vanished before he'd hired these hard folk.

Aly watched as the caravan passed, then slithered back down her rock. Only Junai waited at the bottom. The young raka had left to spread the word of the caravan's arrival.

"Dish out more stew, Mama, there's guests for supper," Aly told Junai. She returned to Visda and asked her to take charge of the goats, then set off toward Tanair at a trot. She had not gone far when the sound of hooves greeted her. One of Lokeij's stable boys approached on horseback. He led the mare Aly had ridden before, the chestnut called Cinnamon.

Remembering she was not supposed to ride well, Aly clumsily pulled herself into the saddle and turned Cinnamon toward the castle, with a word of thanks for the boy. The caravan overtook her at the village gate. Aly dismounted and led Cinnamon through the village with a word of greeting for those merchants she knew from their previous visits. From their responses, Aly gathered that word had reached them that the castle was full to the rafters. The merchants were unhappy at the prospect of having to find lodging in the village, but they were used to roughing it. So much the better, Aly thought as she walked through the castle's outer gate. Fewer people would spent the night inside the castle's walls, which meant fewer people for her to watch. Those five newcomers would be enough of a problem.

Lokeij awaited Aly by the stable, a look of concern on his old monkey's face, contradicted by his gaudy red sarong. He nodded toward the gate to the inner courtyard. Gurhart was there with two wagonloads of goods, talking to the duchess, Chenaol, and Ulasim.

Aly walked into the stable leading the mare. When Lokeij joined her, she said, "Assassins came with the merchants this time. You'll need to alert the others. Where's our family?"

"The ladies play chess with the prince and His Grace," Lokeij replied instantly, meaning Dove and Sarai. "The little ones are having baths in the kitchen. You saw Her Grace." He trotted out of the stable.

Aly unsaddled Cinnamon and groomed her. Her hands trembled slightly, but that was probably just the excitement that came with a real challenge. She had done this sort of thing before, twice, with her Da when killers had gotten into a place he was guarding. The nice thing about Tanair Castle was its lack of space. It limited the ways that assassins, trained to attack in the dark while the household slept, could approach their targets.

Ulasim and Fesgao arrived together with Lokeij. Ulasim checked to make sure no one could see or hear them in the depths of the stable, then nodded to Aly. "What do you have?" he asked.

Aly leaned against the stable wall. "Five strangers are with them," she replied quietly. "They look like professional assassins to me. By now, they'll have smuggled themselves into the castle on those wagons I just saw outside the keep. Either that or they might be hiding in wait for an ally who's inside to let them in after dark." She described the probable assassins in detail adding: "I worry that there could be more hidden in the carts, and that maybe they turned some of the regular merchants to their side. Can your people search the wagons and take anyone we don't know? Just to be on the safe side."

"You speak as if we will not find them." Fesgao was the quietest of the four raka leaders, but Aly had come to value the few things he chose to say. Did he value her in the same manner? she wondered.

"These are professionals," Aly replied. "The first thing they learn is to get away from their transport, in case some bright-eyed young thing like me suspects something isn't right."

"Then how do you suggest we catch them?" asked Ulasim. He looked down at Aly, his dark eyes impossible to read. "Is it the plan we discussed? Move the family to a safe place after supper, and set our people where these murderers will attack at night?"

Aly nodded. It was a good plan, arrived at by mutual agreement among the raka conspirators, with only the occasional nudge or suggestion from her. Its success depended on the loyalty of the raka, but the Balitangs—at least

their two elder daughters—had that, and none of the conspirators wanted anyone to realize their interest lay solely with the older girls.

"I'm afraid we'll have to include the prince, too. I'm *sorry*," Aly said as the
three rakas' eyes blazed. "But they might be here just for him, and not care who
else gets killed in the meantime. I'd as soon not risk it."

Lokeij spat on the stable floor to show his disdain for the prince. "What
of the prince's servants?" he wanted to know. "We didn't account for them
when we planned this."

Aly looked at Ulasim, their general, to see what he would decide. "Urge
the prince's servants out to the barracks for a nighttime drink and game of
dice," Ulasim said after a moment's thought. "We can guard them in there
safely enough. Our extra fighters will go on the fourth floor in case the assassins try to come down from the roof." He looked at Aly. "Unless we should
guard the roof now?"

Fesgao answered, "They mustn't think we know they're here, in case there
are more we haven't identified. We must act normal. Usually we never go up on
the roof."

"If we leave the roof and the servants' stairs open, we'll control their main
line of attack. We can draw them all out right away," Aly added. "We don't
want to spend the rest of the summer jumping because one got away and is
waiting to finish the job."

"And we don't want any escaping to carry word to Rajmuat," said Lokeij.
"If that's who sent them."

He looked at Aly, who shrugged. "We should know when we question
them," she told him.

"We can do this," Ulasim said firmly. "We get our fighters in place while
the family and the prince dine. Then we pick these gutless shadows up like rats
in a trap, so they'll never trouble us again. The plan we have is a good one.
Let's set it in motion."

The three men walked off to do their parts of the plans they had
thrashed out with Chenaol and Aly over their many nighttime talks. Aly
watched them go. She had faith in them, she realized. They hadn't been
raised to protect themselves and those in their care as she had been, but she
felt good knowing they were on her side. She wished Da had fifty like them
in his service.

When Aly passed through the kitchen, Chenaol nodded to her. Her staff
was busy with supper preparations. Looking around, Aly noted there were
fewer knives in sight than usual. She suspected she would find them on the
persons of those servants and slaves approved by the four raka conspirators.
When Chenaol herself tossed Aly a roll to nibble, Aly saw the cook's tunic go
flat against a cleaver-like shape tucked into the woman's waistband.

A stroll across the courtyard showed Aly a selection of raka men and women drifting into the stable. She recognized a number of off-duty men-at-arms, including the six former bandits who had been captured on the road. Others were villagers. Some were raka she had never met, part of Ulasim's extended force. Aly slipped around behind the stable and entered through a back door. Lokeij stood lookout there.

Both of them listened as Fesgao gave instructions to the new arrivals as they lounged around the horses' stalls. ". . . *quiet*, understand? Stop by the kitchen door. Chenaol has things for you to carry, to hide weapons and give you a reason for being there. Go up the stairs a few at a time before and during supper. Don't poke along, but don't rush."

"What of Veron and the men on guard duty? Shouldn't they be told?" someone asked.

"They'll be at the gates. Let them stay there in case this is only part of the attack," Fesgao replied. "We'll keep this just among us for now."

Aly nodded approval to Lokeij, who winked. The raka leaders had trained their people well. The old man followed her outside. "Too bad you don't have this organization in Rajmuat," she whispered to Lokeij.

The old man raised his thin, hard brows. "But we shall," he replied, his voice quiet. "We guarded our ladies—the girls and Sarugani—in that sinkhole for longer than you've been alive, Kyprioth's mouse. The bigger part of us went to other houses when we were exiled. Our folk recruit more people in the city even now. They know we will come again, and they mean us to have help when we do."

Aly smiled. "I don't know why the god bothered with me," she told Lokeij.

"Because you have the crooked eye, and the memory, and you can talk to the luarin," Lokeij said promptly. "We see four or five paths where you see twenty. Will you go with our family tonight?"

Aly nodded. "I won't be of any use in a fight among all those warriors," she replied. "But I'd like to have at least one assassin alive at the end, if you can manage."

Lokeij nodded. "One day you have to tell us who you were before slavery. Why it is you are so knowing, so young."

Aly shrugged. "I'm the god's chosen," she reminded him.

"True," Lokeij replied, "but the gods never build without a foundation. A crooked eye like yours takes years of work." He glanced at Aly's clothes. "Were I you, I'd clean up. You pour the wine tonight."

Aly looked down at herself. Her tunic was streaked with horse sweat. She grimaced and ran to find her spare clothes.

At supper, Aly watched everyone from her position on the dais. She couldn't tell whether the raka members of the household were excited or nervous. Their faces, ranging in color from dark ivory to coppery brown, looked just as stoic as they always had. Centuries of luarin rule had taught the native islanders iron control. The prince's servants, and the rest of the household behaved normally, chattering and eating heartily.

In the shadows by the main stair, Aly glimpsed movement, but only because she looked for it. A few raka used that route to the upper stories. Most relied on the servants' stair behind the stone veil of the wall. By the end of the meal every raka fighter who did not eat with the family was in position.

Aly saw no reason to alarm the Balitangs until they'd finished supper. They were halfway through the dessert sweets and cheeses when Aly murmured to the duke and duchess, "We must place you in the study opposite your present quarters, for your safety. If you can gather the children and the prince and go there, acting as if you are engaged in some leisure activity, I would appreciate it. No one must think there's anything out of the ordinary."

The duke gave the tiniest of nods while the duchess looked down. As Aly returned the wine to the kitchen, she heard the duchess say gaily, "I have a game we haven't played yet. My dears? Your Highness? It's one that you won't have played in quite this fashion."

I love that woman, Aly thought as she set down the pitcher. She is never at a loss.

Chenaol joined Aly. "My girls know their places. Ulasim has men on the exits. Come down here once the fighting's done, and I'll have your supper ready."

Aly grinned at her. "You have a nice idea of what's important," she told the cook. "Try not to kill any more of them than necessary. They have to be questioned."

Chenaol drew the cleaver from her waistband as Aly walked back into the great hall. The kitchen servants were on their way to Chenaol as the tables emptied. No one was interested in music that night. Aly suspected that everyone felt tension in the air, even if they didn't know the reason for it.

Aly climbed the stairs, searching the shadows for shapes that didn't belong. By now she could have found her way through any part of the keep in pitch darkness. Tonight she saw nothing unusual. She hadn't expected to. The enemy might use the servants' stair or the fifth-floor storeroom as a hiding place from which to launch their attack, but that meant the risk of someone from the household tripping over them before it was time to strike. Aly expected the attack to come from the roof. She would use that route in the assassins' place. How many people looked up? If her instinct was right, they'd be there now, waiting for lights to go out below, knowing the shutters would be left open for cool night air to flow through the keep. Once the household seemed to be abed, the assassins would use ropes to climb down the tower's sides and swing into their prey's bedrooms.

Aly reached the third-floor landing and the family's present bedrooms. By now the enemy would know that the prince had the ducal rooms and the Balitangs occupied the third floor. Since they were obviously professionals, Aly knew they would know their targets' sleeping arrangements well before their attack. Ulasim stood by the stairway, a long dagger in each hand.

No one wanted to speak more than necessary, in case the assassins were already inside the keep. Ulasim pointed to the floor, jerked a thumb at the ceiling, and nodded. Everything was ready on the second and fourth floors. Fesgao lounged in the shadows near the door to the family's sleeping quarters. He nodded, too: fighters were hidden inside. Aly pointed to the door of the small room by the stair that served as the children's tiny schoolroom, and raised her brows. Ulasim nodded. The family and the prince were there. Carefully Aly opened the door just enough to slip inside.

"Why is *she* here?" Bronau demanded softly.

"She is as useful in a fight as I am, Your Highness," Lokeij retorted. "We want her out of harm's way." He clutched a double-headed axe in his gnarled hands. Aly expected the old raka to fall over with its weight, but he stood easily, balanced on the balls of his feet. Behind him stood the healer Rihani, her arms around Elsren and Petranne. They stared silently at everyone. Elsren sucked his thumb.

Lokeij was not the only armed man in the room. Both the duke and the prince held drawn swords. "I don't like hiding like this," growled Bronau. "I'd rather fight them myself."

"And leave my wife and children protected only by Lokeij?" asked Mequen. "It's not as satisfying as engaging the enemy in the field, old friend, but it's important to me."

"I could defend *myself* if I had a sword," Sarai reminded the adults, her voice sharp.

Bronau smiled at her. "I would love to see you with a sword in hand," he said. It was clear he thought she would make an adorable picture rather than a combat-ready one. "With a gold hilt and gold armor to match. You could be one of the lady knights of old at the Midwinter Masquerade."

"*And* you haven't had a sword in your hand in four years," murmured Dove.

"Whose fault is that?" snapped the older girl, darting a sharp glance at her stepmother.

Aly crouched by the keyhole in the door. Outside she heard the first signs of trouble. "Hush!" she ordered as she put her ear to the opening.

"Mequen, you are indulgent of your slaves, but surely you won't let this one give orders as if she were one of us!" exclaimed Bronau, outraged.

The duchess held her finger to her lips to silence him.

Aly put an eye to the keyhole, mentally adjusted her power, and exercised her Sight to see as much of the story as she could. Fesgao was gone from his post at the bedroom door. Thumps came from the family's bedroom, and a cry from overhead. She tried to see the stairs, but the keyhole limited her field of vision to the joining of step and floor, something her Sight could not change. Just once she wished she could scry in a mirror or crystal like her mother and Uncle Numair, so she could know what was going on.

From the stairwell Aly heard a scream. Behind her someone gasped—Petranne or Elsren. Ulasim came into view at the foot of the stair, a killer's descending sword trapped between his long, crossed knives. He twisted away to free his weapons; as the assassin's sword dropped, Ulasim lunged in with a backhanded dagger swipe. Aly saw blood, enough to tell her that Ulasim had cut the assassin's throat. The assassin tumbled limply down the stairs past the raka footman. Ulasim checked to make sure his opponent was dead, then ran upstairs once more.

The fighting seemed to last forever, though Aly knew that it was her own worry and impatience that stretched the passing time. She sent up prayers to Mithros for the Balitang servants, along with frequent reminders to Kyprioth that if she was to do as he wished, he would have to keep the people who worked with her alive. Finally, the noise from the upper floors and across the hall faded. There was a long silence. Then Fesgao emerged from the family's bedchamber, his clothes slashed in two places, a bloody longsword weighing down his left arm. Behind him came the raka who had been hidden in the bedroom. Ulasim walked onto the floor from the direction of the stairs, his long, sweat-soaked hair hanging in his face. Three more Balitang fighters moved into view, carrying bodies wrapped in sheets over their shoulders. They laid them on the floor.

Ulasim said huskily, "We think we have them all."

Aly let the prince and the duke out first, then the duchess, and Sarai. She glanced at Lokeij, then nodded toward Dove, Rihani, Petranne, and Elsren. He nodded in reply, indicating he would guard them until they were certain the keep had been scoured of the enemy.

"Until we're sure," Aly told Dove. The girl sighed and took a seat. Rihani's smile was bright with gratitude. Aly closed the door on her way out, ignoring Petranne's cry of indignation.

"They came in on ropes, through the windows, Highness, Your Graces," Ulasim was telling the nobles. "They were on the roof, as we guessed they might be."

"Why didn't you take them on the roof?" demanded Bronau as he and the duke sheathed their swords. "You would have spared us some anxiety!"

"We have but one door to the roof. Only one may go through at a time, Your Highness," Fesgao said with a properly respectful bow. "They could have picked us off as they liked, and we could not be certain all of them were there. As it happens, they were not. My lads report there are still others outside." He looked at the duke and the duchess. "You appear to have been their targets. Perhaps the children, too, since they sleep here as well."

There was a clatter on the stair. Veron, with the men-at-arms who had been on guard duty, charged up, swords bared. Ulasim and Fesgao put themselves between the nobles and the men-at-arms.

"Your Grace, I heard fighting," the sergeant panted, ignoring the two raka between him and his master.

Mequen raised a hand palm out, a calming gesture. "Our servants defended us, Veron. Apparently assassins were smuggled into the keep during the day, or rather, they smuggled themselves."

"I feared it was bandits," the sergeant replied. He looked around at the bodies, then knelt and uncovered a face. "I'll have a word with my boys, letting these get through the inner gate," he promised. He looked up at the duke. "With your permission, I'd like to search the keep, top to bottom."

"Tell me something first," asked Ulasim, his face stern. "Tell me you did not know of this attempt."

Veron's jaw muscles clenched, then relaxed. When he replied, he spoke to Mequen. "No, Your Grace," he replied quietly. "I did not know of it."

Ulasim glanced at Aly, who gave the tiniest of nods. Veron was telling the truth; her Sight confirmed it, though she would tell the others that he showed none of the signs of a liar.

"What is this?" Mequen demanded, his voice sharp. "Why should Veron know assassins had come? You make it sound as if he would have helped them."

Ulasim and Fesago regarded Veron with unflinching eyes. The sergeant flushed beet-red, hesitated, then knelt, his eyes on the duke. "Your Grace, forgive me," he said, shame-faced. "Somehow these men have learned I am ordered to report your actions to the Crown. I am Your Grace's servant, but the King is also my master." After a moment Veron added, "Surely Your Grace understood that watchers would be present in your household."

"Kill the traiterous dog," Bronau snapped, gray eyes flashing. "A man should have but one master. You pay him; he should be yours alone."

Winnamine rested a gentle hand on her husband's arm. "We should not decide this now, when so much of pressing importance must be attended to right away," she murmured.

Mequen lifted her hand to his lips and kissed her fingertips before he released her. "Wise as ever, my dear," he said.

Aly nodded to Ulasim and Fesgao. They moved aside so Veron could see the duke better. Mequen told him, "Very well. Do as thorough a search as you and your men can perform."

"I trust you didn't take all of your guards off the gate," Prince Bronau said with a smile.

Veron stiffened. Really, Aly thought, for a prince he's got no tact. The duke trusts Veron to do his job properly, royal spy or no. Bronau could at least have trusted the duke's judgment.

As Veron led his men back down the stairs, Aly realized that the prince would make a dreadful husband for Sarai. Bronau would encourage Sarai to be even more headstrong than she already was, if she didn't kill him for condescending to her desire to be a warrior.

The nobles walked into the family's bedroom. Fesgao and Ulasim accompanied them. Aly took a moment to memorize the faces of the three dead men—assassins often came in families—before she went inside. There she sighed. The wide, pretty chamber was a shambles. Multicolored raka hangings, embroidered cushions, tapestry frames, pillows, comforters, bolsters, and curtains from the main bed, all were hacked and covered in goose feathers speckled with blood. Four assassins lay sprawled on the floor, weapons still in their hands.

The fifth knelt beside the door between two impassive raka. His arms, wrists, and ankles were bound, his mouth tightly gagged. Blood streamed down his face from a cut in his scalp. He was the man Aly had identified as the leader. His green eyes were stony as they met hers.

She looked at the other bodies. Here were two of the merchant's regular employees as well as two more strangers. The count of dead outside included two of those she had recognized as assassins as well as one of the merchant's people. Where was that redheaded woman? Was it possible that she wasn't an assassin but a spy, trying to root out secrets in the village at that very moment?

Sarai bent and picked up one killer's sword, easily taking its weight in her delicate hand. She held it upright. "No maker's mark on the hilt," she commented to herself. "But if this isn't royal foundry work, I don't know swords."

Bronau chuckled. "Sarai, you startle me. How would you learn that?"

Sarai lowered the blade slowly. Aly was impressed. She knew swords were heavier than they looked. It took control and strength in the wrist and arm to do what Sarai was doing.

The duke wandered over to the bed. He was idly brushing at feathers, looking around, when a heap of curtains a yard away shifted. Up came the missing woman, her teeth bared in fury, a long knife clutched in her hand.

Aly felt as if she were struggling through honey, she was so slow. Like Aly, Ulasim, Fesgao, and the prince all stood on the wrong side of the bed, closer to the door than Mequen. The duchess gasped. Mequen scrabbled at his sword hilt.

But Sarai, the killer's weapon still in her hand, lunged across the gap. Her arm stretched out in a long, ferocious thrust that pierced the woman through. Swiftly she braced a foot against the assassin's body and freed her sword, then cut the woman's throat, just to be sure.

The sixteen-year-old looked around at the rest of them, brown eyes wide, blood on her hands, face, and clothes. "It's so messy," she murmured in surprise. Then she fainted.

Aly, trembling, went to her and knelt. Using her Sight, she confirmed the girl hadn't been wounded or poisoned. Though it would serve me right if she had been, Aly thought, furious with herself. Idiot! I shouldn't have let *anyone* come back in here until I checked the room. That's *my* job, and I was too over-confident to do it!

Feathers and cloth rustled as Winnamine joined her. She had found a pitcher of water and handkerchiefs. She wet a handkerchief, wrung it out, and began to clean her stepdaughter's face. Aly soaked and wrung out other handkerchiefs and began to wipe Sarai's hands as the girl began to come around.

When Sarai opened her eyes, Winnamine gave her a tiny smile. Her mouth trembled. "Obviously halting your sword lessons was a mistake," she murmured to Sarai. "It's a crime not to encourage such an aptitude."

Sarai stared at her stepmother. "But I fainted," she whispered.

"After," said Winnamine. "You fainted *after* you'd done the important thing." She bit her lip, then continued, "We shall find you a teacher in the morning. In fact, though it may be too late, I may study swordcraft, too. And Dove . . . ?"

Sarai gulped, tried to speak, and could not. At last she cleared her throat and said, "She hates swords. She does like to shoot, if she doesn't have to shoot animals."

"Archery it is," Winnamine said. She blinked over-bright eyes, then leaned in, and kissed Sarai's cheek. "Thank you for saving his life." She took a deep breath, then rose and went to see how her husband was.

Sarai looked at Aly. "If I'd known that all it would take to start my lessons again was killing someone . . ." Her voice and humor failed. Her eyes overflowed. "Did I do the right thing?" she whispered.

Aly cleaned blood from Sarai's other hand as the other girl wept silently. "You did better than me," she replied softly. "I just stood and stared. But I wasn't needed. Sarai, balance a murderess's life against your father's. This entire household would prefer the duke to an assassin."

"There's one who disagrees," Sarai remarked as she struggled to sit up. She pointed to the last living killer. He'd made no sound as the drama had unfolded. Now he stared blankly into the air.

Aly sighed. "Will you be all right?" she asked Sarai.

A hand reached down: the duke's. Sarai took it, and let her father pull her up into his arms.

Aly stood and went to Fesgao and Ulasim. Bronau had gone out to the landing, where he inspected the dead men. "Perhaps he should be reminded that his servants are missing," Aly murmured to Ulasim, "and that if he wishes to see to their welfare, he should go to the barracks? I don't want him noticing me any more than he already has."

At a look from Ulasim, Fesgao went out into the hall. He bowed politely to the prince and spoke to him as Ulasim and Aly watched. "She was beautiful, our Saraiyu, wasn't she?" Ulasim inquired, his mouth barely moving as he whispered. "Like Gunapi the Sunrose, goddess of war and molten rock."

"She was," Aly admitted. Her eyes stung strangely. The last time she had seen so perfect a fighting move was when her mother had battled pirates at the Swoop.

"Without you, all might have been lost," Ulasim told Aly suddenly. He picked up one of her hands and pressed it to his forehead. "We owe our lives to you, and our thanks to the god for you tonight."

Aly yanked her hand from his grip, unnerved by his intensity. "Ulasim, calm down," she said, forcing amusement into her voice. "I just alerted you about some assassins, that's all."

He surveyed her from his greater height. Aly had expected him to be offended by her light brush-off. Instead he smiled. "I always forget, you are not of us. We think you are raka in your heart, but no. You are newly come. No one teaches a slave the laws that govern the Isles. Had these *sisat*"—he pointed to the still-living assassin with his dagger—"killed even one Balitang or the prince, then every raka man, woman, and child of Tanair village and castle would die. That is the luarin law governing such things."

"Oh. But these are luarin assassins, and I'd bet whatever I own that they were sent by the king," Aly pointed out. "If he sent them, surely he wouldn't enforce that law. . . ." Her voice trailed off as she registered the grimness on Ulasim's face. "Even if he sent the assassins himself?" she asked, wanting badly for it not to be true and fearing that it was.

"The idea is that if any member of the luarin nobility is killed, the nearest local raka must have helped the murderer. At the very least, the courts would say that the local raka did not die to stop the killers," added the duke. He stood behind them, one arm around Winnamine, one around Sarai. Both he and Sarai looked mournful. "It's insane, but Oron is quite mad. The law itself comes from the time of the luarin conquest. It's how they broke the spine of the raka rebellion. Some of us have laid petitions before the courts to have the Conqueror's Laws repealed, to no avail." He shook his head.

Aly stared. That is just not right, she thought. To murder people who had nothing to say about it, just because they were near? She understood why there were such laws. They were made to fit a conqueror's logic, used to keep a captive people under control. She had just never matched the law to the faces of people she knew, like the Balitang raka.

I don't want to get involved with this country, she thought as she looked at the floor. I must go home soon, before I get so wound up in their lives and injustices that I'll never want to leave.

The prince trotted down the stairs, two of Fesgao's weary men following. Fesgao himself walked back into the bedroom. "Aly? What do you recommend for this man?" he asked, nodding to their prisoner. "Torture?"

Startled at the suggestion, she met his eyes and realized that this was yet another test. She made a face at him. "Any amateur knows torture is chancy at best. People do still lie under torture. What you need is truthdrops."

Fesgao gave a tiny smile and went to find Rihani. Aly looked at Ulasim. "So I may look forward to these little exercises until I die, is that it?" she asked brightly. "Or will you decide I'm not some luarin brute before I am, say, fifty?"

Ulasim wiped one of his long daggers on a cloth. "Oh, more like forty, I'm sure," he replied casually. He flipped the dagger up casually, caught it by the hilt, and in the next motion cut the gag from the last assassin's mouth. "Who sent you?" he asked.

The man stared at the raka, expressionless.

"Once we have truthdrops in hand, you will speak," Ulasim pointed out. "Keep your pride and tell us now. Don't wait for magic to force you."

The man leaned forward and spat on the floor.

Fesgao returned from the room across the hall with Rihani in tow. She held a small, uncorked vial in her hand. Aly was startled by the healer's steely gaze. Normally Rihani was as fierce as pudding. "Open his mouth," Rihani ordered.

A band of green fire locked around the assassin's throat and tightened, vanishing into his flesh. The man choked. Green fire coated his mouth in Aly's Sight as his face got redder and redder. The veins bulged in his throat and forehead as he fought for air. Within a moment he was dead.

Aly bit her tongue to keep from shouting her frustration at the lost opportunity. "*This* is why we need a mage who is not just a healer," she said quietly, looking into Ulasim's face. "And I should have seen that coming." She turned and ran down the servant's stair before she gave in to the temptation to shout. It was time to get some cool air.

Sloppy! she thought as she strode outside. Sloppy not to check the room for assassins before I so much as let a Balitang set foot outside that protected room. Sloppy not to think he might have a silencing spell on him before we set it in motion. What else have I missed? There are ways to stop a silencing spell. And Sarai shouldn't have had to kill anyone!

I have to be sharper, she told herself, gently thumping her head on the keep's stone wall as a reminder. I won't get lucky a second time.

The inner and outer courtyards crawled with Bronau's and Mequen's men-at-arms. They were looking for anyone suspicious, turning the buildings upside down in their search. Three guards from the merchants' caravan lay dead at the entrance to the kitchen wing. Bronau's and the Balitang soldiers searched the bodies. Laid out in front of the barracks, awaiting proper burial, were two of the castle's own, one of the former bandits and one of the official men-at-arms. Aly murmured a prayer to the Black God for their rest in the realms of the dead, then wandered back toward the keep.

She heard voices behind the kitchen wing, where a tiny garden had been built for Tanair's ladies. A small door opened directly to the servants' halls inside the tower. Its torches cast light onto two dead merchant's guards lying on the path that led to the carefully landscaped garden. Two of Ulasim's servants stood beside them, but their attention was on the fig tree that shaded the walk.

Intrigued, Aly walked over to see what was going on. The two dead men were the first that night who had not been killed by blades. Both lay facedown, with dents between their shoulders and their heads twisted askew.

"Please come down," a Balitang hostler was saying to the tree. "You have already unnerved us enough for one night, *duan*." The title meant "honorable sir," used to a man who was not a noble. "Ulasim will wish to know what you did here."

Aly looked up. Nawat, perched easily on a branch that should not have held his weight, gazed down at her. With his dark, long-nosed face surrounded by leaves and growing figs, he looked like some wilderness god.

"*Now* what are you up to?" Aly demanded as her conscience pinched her. She should have told Nawat what was going to happen tonight so that he could have decided whether or not he wanted to be caught up in human quarrels.

"I am up to nothing," the crow-man said cheerfully. "Those two were going to mob you through that door." He pointed to the door into the keep. "I stopped them."

Aly knelt beside the dead men. Their necks were broken. The dents in their backs looked like the prints of bare feet. She glanced at his: they were bare. "How did you do it?" she asked her strange friend.

"I saw it," said another servant, one of the footmen. "We had the duty here. They was coming at us, and all of a sudden he leaps up in the dark, and hits one in the back with both feet, kicking out, like. Then he did it to the other. And then he jumped into the tree."

Aly stared up at Nawat. He must be very strong to break bone with jumping kicks from a standing position, she thought. Well, crows are very strong. "You could have been hurt," she told him. "They might have killed you."

The hostler snorted. "Not him!"

Nawat's gaze was steady as he looked down at Aly. "They were going to mob you," he repeated firmly. "I mobbed them. Only I added a hawk thing. When the hawk strikes, he breaks the head of the prey. I did that."

Aly rubbed her temples. "Thank you," she said. "Will you come down now? I think we have them all."

Nawat smiled brightly at her. "I will come down for you, Aly." He jumped down as lightly as a cat. Aly patted his cheek absently and let him come along as they patrolled the rest of the castle grounds.

It was hours before the castle's residents calmed enough to go to bed. Aly was in the kitchen, finishing a very late supper, when the duchess's maid, Pembery, found her. "His Grace wishes to see you in the ground floor study," she told Aly, and yawned. "Don't take forever. I can't go to bed until the family is settled."

Aly sighed. She would have liked to go to bed herself. Instead she found the duke in the small room where she had cleaned up the day Bronau had arrived. There was a bottle and a glass on a table by the duke's hand, but the contents of the glass were untouched. The duke himself was staring at a branch of candles, drumming his fingers on the arm of his chair.

Aly bowed. "Your Grace wished to see me?" she asked.

"Veron says the merchant Gurhart tells us that all of his people who became particular friends of the five newcomers are also among the dead," Mequen replied. "A search of their belongings has revealed gold *seratudus* and a death order under the Crown's seal."

"I'm sorry to hear that, Your Grace," Aly told him softly.

Mequen nodded. "Gurhart swears by his own blood there are no other assassins among his people," Mequen continued, his dark eyes weary as he gazed at Aly. "He says he knew nothing of the assassins' true purpose in taking work with his caravan. Some of his people had vanished, so he was forced to hire these. I think we must assume those who disappeared while they were in Dimari were killed by the assassins, so that Gurhart would be forced to take them on."

Aly nodded. It was what she had expected they would hear. Hauling goods out to the back of beyond was not a trip anyone enjoyed. The road was hard and its dangers were greater than the coastal routes. Gurhart would have leaped at the chance to replace his missing people, and assumed the vanished workers had simply decided not to go to Tanair.

The duke's voice, husky with exhaustion, hardened. "What I find interesting, god's messenger, is that you did not warn us that danger was on the way. Instead, as far as my wife or I could learn from Ulasim or Fesgao, *you* observed the newcomers with the caravan and viewed them as a danger. It argues, you see, that the god has placed you here not as his oracle, but as his warrior."

"Oh, no, Your Grace," Aly said, gleaming with innocence. "I'd break a nail on one of those dreadful swords. I just have a memory for faces. Maybe I saw one of the assassins back in Rajmuat. Well, he'd no right to be with a Lombyn caravan, had he? Unless he was up to no good, of course. I said as much to Lokeij, who thought it worth passing along."

"And that is another thing," said the duke. "How is it that I find my chief defenders here in the keep are servants and off-duty men-at-arms, not Veron and the men on watch? It was perfectly obvious that Ulasim and Fesgao were in command here, and that they consulted you. I will have the truth now, if you please."

Behind her mask of wide-eyed harmlessness, Aly cursed. She had walked head-on into his next hard question. She thought fast. "I only noticed something odd, as I said," she lied. "And I wasn't sure of Veron, being a royal spy and all. He was carefully watched, I assure you. We made certain he sent no reports to the Crown after he reached Tanair. As for using the servants, it stands to reason that anyone Veron picks for regular night duty is probably someone loyal to him alone, willing to admit Crown servants with orders against Your Grace."

"That those men are mostly the pure-luarin men-at-arms is not a factor?" Mequen wanted to know.

Aly sighed to herself. Why couldn't this man have been stupid? Instead she replied, "Your Grace would have to inquire of Ulasim and Fesgao. Perhaps the ones with raka blood look up to Your Grace for marrying a raka the first time around."

"And producing half-raka daughters in the Rittevon royal line?" asked the duke very quietly.

Aly looked down and twiddled her thumbs. He was in possession of far too much of the whole picture for her comfort. "Your Grace's servants are devoted," she said.

Mequen scowled. "Are you incapable of giving a straight answer?" he demanded.

Aly grinned at him. "Not always, Your Grace," she replied impishly.

Mequen drummed his fingers on his leg. "We would be dead tonight were it not for you people of our household," he said at last. "Be sure I will not forget it." His gaze hardened. "*Any* of it, Aly."

She scratched her head. "You know, Your Grace, this will go so much easier for everyone if you accept the god's gifts without question," she reminded him. "Take it from me, you'll just give yourself headaches this way."

Mequen smiled. "So I will. I suppose inquiring into your origins comes under the heading of questioning the god's gifts."

Aly bowed her head meekly. "Oh, undoubtedly, Your Grace."

"Very well. You are dismissed—with my thanks."

Aly was about to open the door when she thought of something else. She faced the duke. "Your Grace also owes thanks to Lady Saraiyu," she said, not sure if she was overstepping her bounds.

"She will have her sword lessons again, if that is what concerns you," replied Mequen. "After tonight, I think your Tortallan king is wiser than we are, to allow women to take up arms. Sleep well."

A noble maiden must convey dignity and chastity without appearing to think about either one. Let common-born girls tussle in the hay with their loutish swains. The future of your family's bloodline and your future lord's bloodline should be your greatest concern. Let no man but one of your family embrace you. Let no man but your betrothed kiss any more than your fingertips; let your betrothed kiss you only on fingers, cheek, or forehead, lest he think you unchaste. And never allow yourself to be alone with a man, to safeguard the precious jewel of your reputation. No well-born maiden ever suffered from keeping her suitors at arm's length. Your chastity will make you a prize to your future husband's house and an honor to your own.

—*From* Advice to Young Noblewomen, *by Lady Fronia of Whitehall (in Maren), given to Aly on her twelfth birthday by her godsmother, Queen Thayet*

11

MIGRATIONS

To be on the safe side, Aly suggested to Ulasim that he might want to question Gurhart, to see if he told the head footman the same story he had given to the duke. She looked on as Ulasim and Fesgao interrogated the man using truth-drops. Gurhart's answers were the same as those he'd given Mequen. It was just a safety measure, but Aly was determined not to be overconfident again. She had been virtually sure of Gurhart's innocence. He was too terrified to lie, and he should have been. Anyone but Mequen would have confiscated all Gurhart owned and demanded lives as well. Here in the Isles, the duke didn't even need to have the executions approved by a royal court, as he would in Tortall. On his own lands in the Isles, the luarin noble had the rights of a king. Bronau would have demanded everything, but with Sarai to plead with him for clemency, he gave way.

Aly also made sure to be on hand as Veron, Fesgao, and the men searched the caravan board by board. As she had expected, they had found nothing in the assassins' gear to indicate who had hired them. As professionals, they had stripped themselves of anything personal before they joined Gurhart on Lombyn.

Returning to the castle after the search, Aly was joined by old Lokeij. He looked none the worse for his late evening. He was teasing her for her yawns as they wandered into the inner courtyard. There one of the corporals put the off-duty armsmen through sword drills. Today their numbers included Sarai, paired off with Fesgao, and the duchess, who was learning the beginning drills under the corporal's instruction.

"Is she not beautiful?" asked Lokeij softly as he watched Sarai parry and disengage with catlike grace. "Like Gunapi—"

"The Sunrose, the goddess, I know," Aly interrupted, watching the girl and her partner. "If she doesn't keep her guard up, she'll be skewered by someone who knows what he's doing."

Lokeij looked up at Aly with a frown. "You know so much about it, I suppose."

Aly opened her mouth to say she knew plenty about swordplay, then closed it. Finally she said, "I watched lots of armsmen practicing. I even saw the Lioness fight."

"Who?" asked Lokeij.

Aly stared at the little man. Who had not heard of her mother? "The King's Champion of Tortall," she informed him. "The first female knight in over a century. The Lady Alanna of Pirate's Swoop and Olau."

Lokeij shrugged. "A luarin," he said dismissively. "I only pay attention to them when it's a matter of survival or of protecting my lady's girls." He rubbed a hand over his bristled chin thoughtfully. "So she's good, this Lioness?"

"She's never lost a fight as King's Champion!" Aly said, offended by Lokeij's disinterest. This was her *mother*, a lady acknowledged by all to be poetry with a sword in her hand. She looked at Sarai just as Fesgao sent the girl's sword flying into the air. "Your Sunrose has a way to go to beat Alanna the Lioness."

She walked on to the castle, feeling wistful. She'd never had to say more than her mother's name to describe her before. She was truly away from home, to say "Lioness" and not have every person within hearing turn to listen. *This is a terrible time to find that I miss her,* Aly thought, picking up her step. *There's nothing I can do about it until autumn.*

To shake off her mood Aly went to Chenaol and begged for chores. She was setting the dais table when Sarai walked into the great hall from outside, straggle-haired and sweat-soaked. She massaged her sword wrist wearily. Aly guessed that Sarai hadn't practiced as much as she'd meant to since her last official lesson.

She was about to call out a suggestion that Sarai wrap her arm in hot, damp towels when Bronau emerged from the study near the staircase. He halted Sarai with a touch on the shoulder and murmured in her ear. Sarai looked up into his face, startled, then glanced around with the look of someone checking for her parents. Aly knew that look very well, having often used it herself. She held perfectly still. With the afternoon's light fading, the dais was in shadow, and so was she.

Sarai nodded and whispered to the prince. Then she continued her climb up the stairs, while Bronau retreated into the study and closed the door.

It had been open before, Aly realized. The prince had been sitting in there, waiting for Sarai to return.

Once the table was set, Aly returned to the kitchen and took Chenaol aside. "Let Hasui pour," she murmured to the cook. "I have things to do."

Chenaol nodded and beckoned to Hasui. Aly left to wash up.

She ate in the shadows at the foot of the stair, her supper cheese and venison slices jammed into a cut roll. All seemed normal on the dais. Bronau, seated between Winnamine and Sarai, plied the duchess with his usual easy flow of conversation and compliments. He seemed to ignore Sarai next to him.

Sarai, too, tried to pretend interest in Dove, seated next to her, and in her food, but she wasn't good at it. A blush mantled her cheeks. She had put a jeweled chain as a band around her forehead, with a citrine droplet dangling at its center. Citrines glinted from her earlobes. Her pale yellow silk dress had a neckline properly meant for court dinners, not country ones. A gold chain with a large gold-tinted pearl drew attention to the shadow between her breasts.

Aly shook her head. If ever a girl was dressed for an assignation, it was Sarai. Aly could have taught her a thing or two about sneaking away to meet a man. Everyone in the room suspected, particularly her parents. She couldn't wait to see how the girl would get away from her family.

Getting to her feet at the end of the meal, Sarai stumbled, bumping into Bronau. He fell sideways against Winnamine as the duchess raised her wine cup to her lips. Wine spilled down the front of Winnamine's rose-colored gown.

As servants, Bronau, and Mequen scrambled to help the duchess, Sarai quietly ducked out through the servants' door behind the dais. Aly had guessed that would be her way out. She entered the passage through another door under the shadow of the stair. On this level the hall passed around the outer wall, allowing servants to bring dishes or messages to the dais without being seen by everyone in the room. The servants' stairs to the upper floors also ended here. The ground floor level had two exits, one directly into the kitchen, one to the outdoor area where Nawat had brought down the pair of would-be assassins.

To the left of the outside door lay the ladies' garden, a small green oasis with a fountain, flowers, and trees tucked between the castle and keep walls, in a spot that drew sunlight every day. Its edges were planted with pines and ferns, which made it seem like part of a forest. The plants also gave Aly cover to hide in as Sarai arranged herself on the broad lip of the fountain. With the approach of night the garden was deep in shadow. The only light came from torches on a walkway on the outer curtain wall. In these conditions Aly got so close to Sarai that she could hear the girl's dress rustle as she fidgeted. Aly settled down to wait.

The musical part of the evening's entertainment in the great hall had begun when Bronau came down the flagstone path. "Sarai, my dear." His voice was warm and soft, intimate.

Sarai's dress whispered as she got to her feet. "Your Highness, good evening."

Bronau chuckled. He kissed Sarai's hand and sat on the lip of the fountain, pulling her down beside him. "That was very clever. I'm not sure Winna will thank you, but I don't believe anyone noticed you left in all the excitement."

"You said you had something important and private to discuss," Sarai pointed out shyly.

"But I am distracted by the music of your voice, those lovely eyes, the sweet curve of your lips . . ."

Aly couldn't see, but she didn't need to. Sarai's quiet gasp, cut off abruptly, and the rustle of silk, painted a clear picture of a kiss. Oh, dear me, Aly thought, shaking her head. Making up to your host's daughter—bad prince! Now, why do you suppose he's doing it on the sly? He's not married, and her parents are his friends. He could probably get permission from His Grace to court Sarai.

"My lord prince!" Sarai was definitely flustered. "It's so improper!"

"I know. I apologize." Bronau's voice was a little hoarse. "My feelings carried me away. To watch you ride, to see you among your devoted subjects, like a true queen—none of Oron's wives were as graceful or as gracious as you. Don't look so alarmed. No one can hear us."

"But you talk something like treason, Your Highness," Sarai warned gently. "I am no queen, only the daughter of a disgraced nobleman."

"But if I asked you to be queen of my heart?"

Aly crinkled her nose with distaste. She had sighed over speeches like that one in the stories she had read and the romantic ballads she had heard. In real life they sounded tawdry. He was a prince of the realm, nearly twenty years older than Sarai. How could he talk like a minstrel performing for ladies in a bower? Did he think Sarai had no brains or honor?

"Your Highness, why have you not asked my father's permission to address me in such terms?" Sarai asked. Her voice was small but firm. "He is your friend. So is my stepmother. For that matter, you used to court Winna."

"Ah." Bronau's chuckle had an embarrassed sound. "To be honest, I hadn't meant to get so carried away, truly. But my feelings . . . The affection I had for Winna was that of practicality. She was a widow and my friend, I had found no true love, so I offered her a marriage of friendship. I thank the gods now that she preferred Mequen."

Don't fall for this dolt, Aly silently begged Sarai. I'll bet he wrote all these pretty speeches down and memorized them so he could make any maiden swoon all over him.

Unaware of his hidden critic, Bronau continued to talk. "I escaped love for years, only to be plunged into it when I thought myself immune. I need to know from your own beautiful lips: would you be averse to a union with me? You would be queen of my heart in truth, and I would put the world at your feet."

Sarai's hesitation was marked. Aly raised an eyebrow, fascinated. Back in Tortall, she herself had sighed with the feelings of kisses and strong arms, yet she was still practical. The boys who had courted her had called her cold-blooded. Now it seemed that she and Sarai had that in common: that their hearts could be racing as their heads remained cool. "Your Highness," Sarai murmured at last, "I cannot bring glory to your name. Tanair and a few estates like it are my only inheritance. You have seen how poor it is."

"I care nothing for your fortune, Sarai," Bronau said. There was enough passion in his quiet voice to almost convince Aly. "So I am an impractical fool. Certainly Rubinyan and that human Stormwing he married think so. But I would rather have a woman I loved than the plumpest heiress in the Isles. Unless . . ." His passion faded audibly, with a trained actor's precision. "The difference in our ages . . ."

"Oh, no, Highness, that's not it at all!" Sarai's emotion was not calculated. She spoke from the heart. "How could I—a man so alive as you—"

There was the movement of cloth, the catch of breath, sighs and murmurs. Aly pushed back her cuticles, then carefully cleaned under her nails, waiting for conversation to start again. Bronau would do no more than kiss Sarai, not when there was a chance a sentry would look down from the parapet and see them.

At last Bronau asked, his voice rough, "Will you marry me, enchantress? Will you let me make you queen of the world?"

Sarai was panting. Aly envied her; she liked kissing, too.

At last Sarai managed to say, "Your Highness, I am not free to choose. If my father says I may . . . He's your friend, he won't refuse us if that's what we want."

Bronau hesitated. At last he said, "I cannot ask him. Not yet. I am under suspicion, as are you. Oron might see a union between us as a threat."

"He sees everything as a threat," Sarai reminded him.

"When I am in favor at court again, I will ask Mequen for your hand—if you wish to give it." Another stifled gasp. Aly wondered if they were going to do this all night.

"I'll go back first," Bronau said. "Give me time to reach my rooms before you return. And thank you, for giving me hope."

Judging by the movement of shadows beyond her screen of ferns, Aly suspected Bronau kissed Sarai's hands, then her mouth, one last time before he left the garden. Now she also noticed that the ground under her was damp. The duchess would skin her for getting another tunic dirty.

"That wasn't very wise," a small, clear voice—Dove's—announced. "And it was *extremely* improper, letting him get you alone. People would say you aren't very well brought up."

"What do you know?" Sarai retorted, sounding like a cross sixteen-year-old, not a gently bred maiden swept away by her lover's kisses. "You're only twelve. And you're not in the least romantic."

"Good." Firm steps sounded on the earth. A rustle of cloth announced that Dove was sitting by her sister.

"Besides," Sarai added, "I *had* a chaperon. Didn't I, Aly?"

Aly giggled and stood. "How did you know?" she asked.

"I just guessed," Sarai replied. She and Dove were making sure her hair was tucked up and neatly pinned once more.

"Why did you let them do that?" Dove wanted to know, bending around Sarai to glare at Aly. "It was so shameful."

"Hmph," Sarai replied with a sniff. She tugged a lock of hair out of Dove's hold when she tossed her head. "Wait until you're my age and the blood's hot in *your* veins. He's very handsome, and charming—"

"And he's *old*," Dove interrupted. "It was disgusting."

"He's a man of the world," Sarai informed her sister, her nose in the air.

"So he's twice as likely to get you pregnant as a boy your own age who loves you and doesn't know what he's doing. That's what Chenaol says," Dove snapped.

"Dovasary Temaida Balitang!" cried Sarai, shocked. "Never say Chenaol told that to *you*!"

"No," Dove said, her chin thrust out mulishly. "She said it to one of the maids who's got one of Bronau's servants chasing her, but it means the same for you, doesn't it?"

"He never mentioned his debts," Aly pointed out, brushing a clump of moss from the front of her tunic.

Sarai drooped and sighed. "No, he didn't. And he didn't talk to Papa first. But Aly, I think he's serious about the marriage."

Aly propped her chin on her hands. "I do, too," she admitted. "And it makes me uncomfortable. I hope it makes *you* uncomfortable. Or wary, at least."

Sarai laughed. "I don't need to be wary," she said, elbowing Aly. "I have you and Dove for that."

Aly smiled evilly at Sarai, showing teeth. "But not for explaining to Their Graces where you have been since supper. You may tell them Dove and I were present, of course, but we won't be there to sweeten the discussion for you."

Sarai looked from Aly to Dove, who gave her a grin identical to Aly's. "I'm going to read in the library for a while," she told Sarai. "I'll come upstairs later."

Aly inhaled deeply. "I believe I'll enjoy the cool air for a bit," she said, her voice light. "Summer nights are *so* lovely."

"All right for you two," Sarai told them sharply. She got to her feet. "I may as well get it over with. And I'll remember this!" She flounced down the flag-stone path.

"She always surprises me," Dove remarked. "She didn't try to tell you that you're a slave, so you have to go with her."

"No, she didn't, and she could have," Aly admitted. "Most *would* have."

Dove sighed. "That's Sarai for you. Just when you want to shake her until her teeth rattle, she does something like that." She stood. "I really do mean to read for a while."

"And I really do mean to sit," replied Aly. She watched the younger girl leave, her soft leather shoes making no sound on the path. Sometimes talking to Dove was nearly as good as talking to Da or Aunt Daine.

She remembered the time her mother had caught her kissing at a party for Prince Roald's engagement, and grinned. The boy had fled, not wanting to deal with Aly's mother when she seemed so displeased. "Now look what you've done," Aly had reproved Alanna when the boy was out of earshot. "It'll take me weeks to train another one to kiss like I want him to."

"Kisses are serious things," Alanna had retorted. "You talk of them as if they're party favors."

Aly had kissed her mother on the cheek. "They're serious for *you*, Mother," she'd said. "They're party favors for me."

It was worth the scolding that followed, about Aly's lack of seriousness, to see the shock on the Lioness's face, and to see her mother realize that kisses didn't *have* to be serious. Of course, when Alanna had been in her best kissing years, Aly remembered, most people had thought she was a boy. Boys were never as free with kisses among other boys.

She sighed. They had the blood of Trebond in their veins, yet she and her mother were so different. She wondered if Alanna had ever noticed that. She definitely needed Da to remind her that life could be fun.

"Was he mate feeding her?"

Aly looked up at the fringe tree across the bowl of the fountain. "Nawat," she said, resigned more than surprised. Of course he would be here.

Nawat leaped to the ground and circled the fountain to sit next to Aly. "Is that mate feeding?" he asked. "It didn't look as if he transferred food to her tongue pouch, but it is hard to tell in the dark. I've seen other humans do it, only not this close to me. They do it in shadows, as if it's a secret."

"It's kissing," Aly explained, her mind half on how she had missed his presence in the tree and half on what she was saying. "Two people touch lips. It's mating behavior, but it's not mate feeding. It's—"

Nawat turned his head sideways and pressed his lips to Aly's. His mouth was soft and warm, his breath lightly scented with spices, his smell clean, with hints of beeswax and wood oils from his work. Aly's usually distant and ob-serving mind focused completely on the feeling of his mouth against hers. She dimly felt Nawat hesitate. Then he brushed his hand against the side of her neck and cradled the back of her head as he deepened the kiss.

Someone laughed in the distance. Aly jumped to her feet as if launched from a catapult. "Yes, you've got the idea, but you should really practice on someone else," she told him, trembling from head to toe, furious with herself because, after all, she *had* been kissed before. "Somebody who isn't so busy, or, or busy . . ."

Nawat looked up at her, smiling slightly. For the first time there was something in his gaze that was human, and very male. "You said *busy* twice," he pointed out.

"I'm very busy," Aly retorted. She stopped and caught her breath. What was the matter with her? She was no blossoming girl-child, with no experience or sense of proportion. She calmed down. "But you can see, it's not mate feeding. Still, it's very serious, Nawat. You shouldn't go around kissing just anybody."

Now she sounded like her mother. Aly turned and strode down the path, away from the crow-man. She was doing her best to pretend that she was not running away. How could she care enough about this to run from someone who became a human male through sheer curiosity, who would eventually tire of it and return to his own shape? And why did she care if he wouldn't be around one day?

The next morning the merchant caravan left for Dimari. Aly and Ulasim, along with thirty raka and part-raka, surrounded the caravan when it reached the area where the road east cut through the rocks at the edge of Tanair. Gurhart and his people obeyed orders to step away from their mounts and wagons, plainly terrified of these masked and hooded riders. As soon as the travelers were seated under guard by the road's edge, Ulasim's people began to search the wagons and horses. Following Aly's instructions of that morning, they combed through the caravan, then its people.

Aly, sweltering in her mask, followed Ulasim up and down the line of carts, horses, and people. She took care of the tricky bits herself as she taught Ulasim what she knew of caches and secret hiding places. Bronau's letters to his creditors were in Gurhart's own mailbag, as were letters from the Balitangs, their servants, and their men-at-arms. Aly glanced over these in case she had missed anything, but they were straightforward enough. Soon they found the other letters, Bronau's to his brother's enemies, and all of the reports sent out by the royal spies and Rubinyan's spies. Those were confiscated and burned. Aly would not risk word of anything unusual finding its way to Rajmuat. The merchants would tell what they had seen and could remember, but the worst piece of information they possessed was that Bronau sheltered with the Balitangs. Unless any spies in the caravan were very good and had been able to read the coded documents, they would have no other information that might alert a suspicious spymaster.

When the searchers finished, they helped the merchants to reassemble the caravan, then saw them on their way. No one would get the chance to sneak back and tell the castle's spies that they had been robbed of information.

"You scare me sometimes, little one," Ulasim remarked as he watched the caravan's dust settle in its wake.

Aly yanked off the stifling hood that had covered her face and slave collar. "You're going to make me conceited," she replied with a grin. "I'm going to blush, I know it."

"My people are not happy about Bronau's pursuit of our lady Sarai," he told her as the raka patrols returned to their day's work. "The Jimajen line is as corrupt as the king's."

"Tell them not to fret," Aly said. "Sarai's no fool."

Not long after she dozed off that night, Aly saw a glowing figure walk through the soft gray curtain between her and dreams. It was Kyprioth. Although the god appeared in her mind's eye only as a glowing figure with arms and legs, she was still sure it was him.

"Hello, there." His voice sounded in her ear, clear, friendly, and crisp. "Would you like to go for a short trip?"

"Am I going to be tired in the morning?" she demanded. "You know, I do work during the day."

"And you shall be as fresh for it as a sea breeze," Kyprioth replied. "Look."

Aly looked. There was her body, deep in slumber on her pallet. She stood on air beside the god. "Very well. What kind of trip?" she asked.

Kyprioth put a strong, surprisingly real arm around her ghost self's waist and told her, "You'll see. It's going to be instructive, trust me on that."

He bore her up through the keep's walls and into the open sky beyond. The ground, just touched with silver under the waning moon, raced underneath them, mountains, jungle lowlands, the sea. Lombyn Isle passed into the distance behind them. Below lay the Azure Sea, black in the moonlight.

"Why do we travel this way?" she inquired, feeling confused. "You show me what's going on in Tortall through dreams."

"I don't care about Tortall," replied Kyprioth. "But I do love my Isles, and I love to see them at night. You may as well appreciate the view. Tell me they are not beautiful."

"They're lovely," Aly said, and yawned. "Can I go back to bed now that I've admired them? My skin gets dry if I don't get my beauty rest."

Kyprioth didn't even bother to reply. He carried her over the eastern side of Imahyn Isle and down the long axis of Kypriang at a speed that would have made Aly dizzy if she had been in her body, instead of dreaming.

Ahead lay the lights of Rajmuat, spread over the harbor hills. The city was ablaze with light, its people milling in the streets. Kyprioth and Aly popped through the palace roof, landing inside a huge bedroom even more brightly lit than the streets. Courtiers gathered near the door, murmuring to one another. Priests of the Black God, the god of death, stood beside a great bed at the heart of the chamber, silent, waiting.

At the center of an expanse of heaped pillows, linen sheets and goose-down comforters lay an old, emaciated man with silvery hair, black eyebrows, and stubbled cheeks. Aly had seen sketches of him in Tortall: King Oron. His lips were stained black. At his side a healer lifted away a basin filled with blood and bile. She shook her head at the nobles who stood nearby.

The man who stood nearest to the old king wore a circlet crown. "Prince Hazarin," Kyprioth said to Aly.

The healer jerked around as if she'd heard. Her eyes widened as she looked in their direction. She shivered and hurried out of the room through a small side door.

Next to the prince stood a woman who also wore a circlet crown. She would be Princess Imajane, King Oron's only surviving daughter. She was beautiful in an icy, razor-sharp way. Aly looked at her for a moment, then turned her gaze to the third person there who wore the circlet, a yawning boy Elsren's age: Prince Dunevon. Imajane held the sleepy child upright.

Behind her stood a man Aly had glimpsed during her early days with the Balitangs: a tall, balding man with chill gray eyes, a thin, straight mouth, and hair that was silver on top of his head, shading to black at the ends. There was a resemblance between Rubinyan and Bronau, though Rubinyan was fifteen years older. He stood behind his wife, Imajane, his calculating eyes on the king.

The dying man struggled to sit up. As Prince Hazarin assisted him, the courtiers surged forward.

Aly was unimpressed by Oron's oldest living son. Hazarin was in his mid-forties. At six feet one inch, he towered over every other man in the room, but his commanding height was offset by his bulk. He had a round face and a belly that spilled over the cloth-of-gold raka sarong he wore in defiance of the lu-arin court's dress code. He combed his hair straight back from his face, which accented his soft, blobby features. A small, spade-shaped beard framed his full, pouting lips.

"His vices are the table and anything that he may smoke, drink, or breathe in," Kyprioth told her. "He has a wife who begs him for a child, but she will get none. His loins are barren from a child's disease, contracted when he was a man. He thinks Rubinyan is the wisest man on earth, except for his taste in wives. He detests his half sister, and she him. He doesn't want to be king."

"Attend, all," croaked the dying Oron as Hazarin supported him in a sit-ting position. "I hereby name my son Hazarin to be king after me." He glared at Hazarin. "If I were you, I'd get me an heir. I—"

"Excuse me," Kyprioth said abruptly, and vanished. The next moment Aly saw him again, this time inside Oron's body.

"A great monarch comes," Oron said, his voice suddenly full and commanding. "A sunrise of glory for the homeland, harbinger of new power and might in the councils of the Emerald Ocean, when the fields are reaped of the invading plague!"

The god left the king's body and mind as easily as he'd entered. Oron collapsed, gasping for air. The surrounding courtiers all murmured and stepped back, uncertain and afraid. Rubinyan whispered in Imajane's ear as Dunevon started to cry.

"I love deathbed prophecies," Kyprioth confided to Aly. He'd returned to his spot beside her. "They always put the cat among the pigeons."

"I don't suppose you'd want to confide this grand plan of yours to me," Aly asked playfully. "Come on. I know you want to brag how smart you are." No one in the room seemed to be able to hear her. "Tell, Kyprioth."

The god shook his head. "You probably won't be here for it," he told her. "If you keep the children alive, you'll be on your way home in the fall. Besides, it's dangerous to say some things outright."

Aly sighed. She didn't enjoy being left in the dark.

Kyprioth patted her shoulder. "It's too serious for you anyway," he added.

"You're not letting me have fun," she retorted, pouting.

The healer returned. She shooed the courtiers to their posts by the door, walked around the king's family, and made Oron more comfortable. He grabbed her arm, struggled to tell her something, but failed. Slowly he went limp.

"The king is dead," Rubinyan said as the healer drew the sheet over the dead man's face. He turned to face Hazarin. "Long live the king!" He bowed deeply to the former prince. Imajane curtsied low. The courtiers followed them in salute to Hazarin.

Kyprioth chuckled, rubbing glowing hands together. "The first act ends," he told Aly as he put his arm around her waist. "The next begins."

"Except you won't tell me what it is," Aly said as they soared through the palace roof. "It'll be like leaving before the play's over. Why can't you just tell me how you want it to come out?"

"Because you suffer so prettily, dear," Kyprioth informed her as they leaped into the starry night.

In the morning Aly took the goats out. She was still feeling cross that she couldn't see where the god's long game might lead him, and the Isles. Rather than visit briefly with Nawat, she nodded to him as she had done the morning before, and bustled past his workbench. For a moment his smile caught and held her attention. She dragged herself away. Every time she looked at the crow-man, her lips remembered the feel of his. And she saw him so often when she was at the castle! It was too distracting. She refused to think about it. At this rate, she would become yet another girl who lingered by his bench when she was free of work. Surely she had more pride than that!

That night, in her report to the Balitangs, she told them of Oron's death and Hazarin's ascension to the throne. She assumed that the god had wanted her to pass the information along.

"That poor old man," Winnamine said. "At least he's out of his misery."

"That poor old man had hundreds murdered, Winna," Dove reminded her softly. "He's out of *our* misery, which is more important."

"But Hazarin!" exclaimed Sarai. "He's a disaster. And he can't have children. If he could, one of his mistresses would have given him some by now, even if his wife's barren."

"She isn't," Aly said. *"He* is. The god told me." She knew that she ought to feel bad about concealing the true identity of the god who really tampered with the Balitangs' lives, but she didn't. Their ignorance was healthier for Aly. She couldn't tell how they might react if they learned that Aly knew their god was not Mithros. She didn't want to find out.

The duke and the duchess now exchanged looks. "It's Dunevon, then, and a regency council, should he succeed Hazarin while still a child," Mequen remarked slowly.

"Or Imajane will get herself appointed regent," Winnamine pointed out. "Should anything happen to the king, of course. Which we pray it will not."

"Should we tell the prince King Oron is dead?" asked Dove, deliberately not looking at Sarai. "With Hazarin on the throne, Bronau is back in royal favor. He'll want to leave for Rajmuat right away." Sarai gave Dove a glare that would have peeled stone.

"Speaking of Bronau, young lady," Mequen said, turning to look at his oldest daughter. Sarai looked up at him. "You are a girl of sense and proper upbringing. This news about the king changes a few things."

"He wants to marry me," Sarai informed her parents airily. "He said so. There were enough eavesdroppers"—she glared at her sister, then at Aly—"to tell you that's the truth."

"But you need to keep things in mind now," said Winnamine. "More than the fact that he's in debt and you are no heiress."

Sarai thrust her chin out, the image of sixteen-year-old stubbornness. "What sorts of things?"

The duchess sighed. "Once Bronau courted me, remember. I learned a few things about him. He is ambitious. What can the Balitangs—disgraced, impoverished, exiled—offer an ambitious man? Seemingly nothing, except that with the king dead, your father is one step closer to the throne. Whoever marries *you* is one step closer. Bronau needs money, but in a pinch, a possible future queen might do, particularly if your father is no longer an obstacle. And he loves both of you."

Sarai shook her head. "He loves me. I *think* he does, anyway."

"Daughter, love is wonderful, but Bronau need not marry for it," the duke said gently. "Countless women at court and in Rajmuat, married and not, will happily give him all the love he requires." Without taking his eyes from Sarai he added, "He has taken the maid Pembery to his bed every night he has been here."

Sarai's eyes blazed. "I hate you!" she cried. She threw down her hoop and fled the room.

"She told me she just liked the kissing," Dove said plaintively. "I thought she was playing at being in love with him, not serious."

"No, but she is proud. It hurts her pride to think he's taken someone else into his bed when he's supposed to be pining for her," said the duchess with a sigh. "We build up pretty pictures of men, when we want to be in love. We hate to have them ruined."

Now Aly could, and did, slip away. If Bronau didn't have ways to get court news in a hurry, she would eat her pallet. He would leave them soon, which could only be to the good.

Three days later a dust-covered messenger with a guard of royal guardsmen arrived from Dimari. Word had reached the island's governor through a network of mages who communicated through scrying glasses, mirrors, and other devices. They served the Crown throughout the Isles, passing information far more quickly than normal methods carried it. The governor's message threw life at Tanair into a bustle, as everyone learned what, until now, only the Balitangs, Aly, and the raka conspirators knew. Oron was dead. Hazarin would be crowned soon, and he wanted his friend Bronau at his side. By nightfall that day the prince was ready to set out the next morning at dawn.

Hasui poured the wine while Aly waited in the shadows under the main stair. She watched Sarai as the girl picked at her food. Just as Aly had expected, Sarai left halfway through supper, making excuses to her parents and Bronau as she fled the hall. Aly moved to wait by the door that led from the servants' stair to the ladies' garden.

As the household left the main hall after the meal, Sarai, cloaked and wearing a maid's head scarf, emerged from the keep. Without a sound Aly followed her to the garden.

Bronau was already seated on the lip of the fountain, the picture of male dejection: head down, hands clasped loosely between his knees. He jumped to his feet when he saw Sarai, and crossed the ground between them in four broad strides, sweeping her up in his arms and kissing her fiercely. Sarai hesitated, then her arms went around Bronau's neck. She kissed him with the same passion he gave her.

Aly eased into a wall niche to watch. This was better than any drama that

Players acted out for an audience. And this *was* a drama. Sarai played the desperate maiden, yearning for her forbidden lover. Bronau was the older, jaded man who had found his heart's desire when he ceased to look for it. By now Aly was certain that the indignation Sarai had shown her parents over their assessment of Bronau's motives came more from Sarai's belief that they thought her a child than from a broken heart.

At last the man and girl separated, though they held onto one another's hands. "I swear to you, this is temporary," Bronau said, his gray eyes intent on Sarai. "I don't know if I can bear a separation, but this is our grand chance. Hazarin is my friend. He'll recall your family from this desolation, and he'll speak for me to Mequen. Then I can court you in the proper manner, not in this hide-in-the-corner way."

"Speak to Papa now," Sarai pleaded.

Bronau shook his head. "When I have only my name and little more? Mequen would be a fool to let me have you when there are wealthier men who can offer you proper estates and all that your loveliness deserves. But if Hazarin grants me the things he has always claimed will be mine when he comes to the throne, then I won't be a second son; I'll be a wealthy man in my own right. I will dress you in pearls, then, and little else." He embraced her again.

This time when they stopped to breathe, Sarai told Bronau, "You'll find some other woman at court, I know it. One who's sophisticated, and rich. You'll forget all about an ignorant girl like me."

"You are wrong. I will not ask for your promise now, but you will see I mean what I say," Bronau told her. "Give me some token of yours, to keep near my heart."

Aly twiddled her thumbs. She tried to remember the passionate speeches that had been addressed to her. Had they been this nonsensical? Would she have swallowed them?

Perhaps when I was twelve, she thought, then grinned. Being the daughter of the Lioness and of a spymaster, she hadn't been romantic even then, well before she'd had extensive dealings with the people who made up her father's world. For a moment she saw Nawat's face in her mind's eye. He would never say such things to her, or to any girl!

She banished Nawat's face from her thoughts and watched the lovers. Bronau was tucking the citrine drop Sarai wore as a pendant into his belt pouch. There were more kisses, more avowals of undying passion. When they heard the duke in the distance, calling Bronau, Sarai fled through the rear entrance to the garden. Aly kept to the base of the keep wall as she followed the girl.

Sarai waited for her on the keep's front steps. She sat there, head propped on her hands, staring at the activity around the barracks and the torches that lit the darkness. Aly sat beside her without a word.

"I wouldn't have done it if I hadn't known you'd be there," Sarai remarked without looking at Aly. Her lips were swollen with Bronau's kisses. "Knowing you're watching helps me to keep my head. Otherwise I might well end up on the grass with my skirts around my waist, like those maids he tumbles."

"He seems very passionate," Aly said idly, running her fingers through her cap of hair.

Sarai sighed. "He kisses so much better than the boys in Rajmuat."

"Do you want to marry him?" Aly wanted to know.

"I'm not sure." Sarai frowned. "I daydream about it, but it is just a dream. Papa and Winnamine aren't sure of him. That has to weigh with me."

"They're his friends. They ought to know," Aly pointed out.

"Well, he's leaving tomorrow. I won't have to worry about it for a while," Sarai remarked, and sighed. "Maybe I'll see if that handsome Nawat has decided to be interested in me yet. He's only a commoner, and an odd one at that, but it might be fun, teaching him how to kiss."

Aly scowled as the other girl stood and went inside. She wasn't sure that Sarai ought to practice kissing on someone who might not realize it was just a form of amusement. Worse, what if Nawat fell in love with Sarai? Aly knew that Sarai was very much aware of her position as a noble. She would flirt and have fun, but when her father reminded her of her duty to her family, Sarai would do it. She would marry for the betterment of her family.

Aly decided Nawat had to be warned. She told herself that she didn't want that innocent heart of his broken by a noble beauty trying her wings. Aly refused to admit that she had any personal reason to warn him. It occurred to her, briefly, that she had been much like Sarai back at home, flirting with boys and men just because she was bored and liked kisses. The thought was not a comfortable one.

No one expects a woman busy at her sewing to pay attention to what's being said around her. Never mind if a man's mother and sisters showed them they heard everything while they stitched, he'll still think a woman who plies her needle saves all her brains for the work. You're a far better spy hemming sheets than if you clank with daggers.

—*From a letter to Aly from her father, when she was fourteen*

12

THE MAGE OF POHON

Aly rose at her usual hour the next day, but instead of immediately leaving with her goats, she waited. When Bronau's party rode out she collected her herd and followed. She had resigned herself to the fact that the men were likely taking secret communications with them. These were not merchants, who could be frightened by hooded warriors. Aly didn't worry about any report Veron might smuggle out with Bronau's company. With a new king on the throne, the royal agents throughout the Isles would await instructions from their masters before they made any reports that might offend the new government.

Aly tracked the prince and his group to the road out of Tanair, watching them until even their dust was gone. She silently wished them a dangerous voyage and death at sea, then took her goats on to graze. When Aly and the goats reached Ekit and Visda, she found that Nawat, Ulasim, and Junai waited there along with the shepherds. Ulasim was already riding a horse, while Junai held the reins for three mounts, including the mare Cinnamon.

"Did you sigh over the last of his horse's droppings?" Ulasim wanted to know, smirking. "You watched him go for long enough."

"Aly doesn't like him," Nawat pointed out. "Aly thinks he will come back and try to eat the nestlings."

Aly grinned at the crow-man and looked at the two raka. "So lovely of you to pay a call," she told them. "I wish you'd sent your messenger ahead, so I might have prepared refreshments."

"You will have your jokes," replied Ulasim. He looked like a bronze raka idol in the saddle. "Mount up. We go to Pohon. My mother has agreed to meet us—that is, you. It's going to be a long morning."

Junai revealed the thinnest scrap of a smile, the first sign of any emotion Aly had ever seen on her face. "You have no idea how long," she said.

Aly raised an eyebrow at her bodyguard. "Your grandmother's that charming, is she?"

"Come see for yourself," Ulasim said. He looked at Nawat, who was idly picking insects from a tree's bark and eating them. "Your presence will not help. I told you so back at Tanair."

Nawat bird-shrugged. "Mages do not worry me."

Aly clumsily mounted Cinnamon.

"There is no need to keep doing that," Ulasim told her wearily. "Lokeij says you can ride well."

"Then keep that to yourselves," Aly retorted. "It suits me that our associates not be aware of all my skills." To Nawat she said, "You were scarred by a mage once. Shouldn't that make you wary?"

He cracked a beetle between his teeth. "It was the Pohon mage who did it," he said. "She makes funny noises when her sheets are in the mud." He looked up at Aly. "The red ants are spicy. Would you like one?" He offered her an ant with his normal cheerful smile, but the look in his eyes was that of the human male she'd seen the night he had kissed her.

Horrified, Aly realized she was blushing. She *never* blushed. "I thank you, no," she replied, turning Cinnamon. To the two raka she said, "Let's go, then. Visda, Ekit, I'm sorry, but the goats—"

"We are ready," Visda said with a grin. "Have fun with the mage."

Aly followed Ulasim and Junai to the road. "This mage," she asked the raka, "she's decided she will join you?"

Ulasim snorted. Today he dressed as a raka in a homespun wraparound jacket, embroidered in dark colors, and a highland raka's leggings. His long hair was tied back in a horsetail. "She has only said she will talk to you, and I wouldn't put it beyond her to change her mind. Do you know how annoying it is that you can do that?" he asked Nawat, who trotted along next to them, his bare feet scarcely making a sound on the dirt road.

"I am running." Nawat's voice was as relaxed as if he sat on his workbench, fletching arrows. "It is not as good as flying, but it is exercise."

"Yes, but—does he bother you?" Aly asked the two raka. To Nawat she explained, "I don't want to make any raka uncomfortable, you see, and maybe you would."

"We are cousins," said both Nawat and Junai. They halted and stared at one another. Both looked startled and pleased.

Finally Junai said, "Everyone knows what he was. And crows and raka are both the children of the crow god and goddess. Our legend says the first humans were hatched out of the great crow nest. We made a mistake in the egg and shed our feathers."

"Then there have been other crows who turned into people?" asked Aly. She couldn't help but think that *someone* could have mentioned that earlier.

"Rarely," said Ulasim. "But there are tales, just as there are tales of those raka who turned to crows rather than die. Do we stand here all day, or do we get on with things?" He sent his horse down the road. Aly and Junai followed, Nawat trotting along between the two women.

"Am I no longer the goatherd?" Aly wanted to know.

"Her Grace says you need to be able to move," replied Ulasim. "Our ladies wish to ride far and meet their people. Her Grace wishes to spend more time at the castle, minding the younger children and preparing the household for winter. You are to bear Saraiyu and Dovasary company, with their bodyguards, and Junai."

Aly nodded. That would work. As always, she was grateful to the duchess for seeing what was necessary. "Now, this mage is your mother?" she asked. "Junai's grandmother Ochobu?"

"She hates luarin," replied Junai as her father's face went stony. "She has agreed to talk, not to help. That will be a matter for your persuasion, unless you intend to have the god command her."

"If I were you, I would call on the god," Ulasim informed Aly dryly. "She is sworn to him. She must obey. You? We will be lucky if she does not scorch you. But you insisted on seeing her, and she is a powerful mage, powerful enough to guard this entire plateau."

Aly drew herself up in the saddle, miffed. She was the daughter of George Cooper and the Lioness, after all. It was a pretty sad thing if she had to depend on a god to step in whenever a little diplomacy would do the trick. "Have we brought presents for her? Sometimes a properly offered gift appeases even the most stubborn people."

"It would not appease her," Ulasim replied, grim-faced. "She is a cross-grained, bitter, cruel old hermit."

"She says the sweetest things of you, too," said Junai. "I think you are both too proud to apologize, Father." To Aly she said, "He's right about a gift, though. Grandmother would only make it explode in your hands."

"Here," said Nawat, reaching a hand to Aly. "She might like this." He passed her something hard.

Aly looked at the thing he'd given her. It was a rock, some kind of granite, bright and sparkling in the sun. "Nawat," she asked wearily, "why have you given me a stone?"

"It is sparkly," Nawat informed her gravely. "Females like sparkly things, just as crows do."

Junai made a noise that sounded very like a snort to Aly.

Aly sighed. She ought to have known that his reason didn't make sense to her in the least. "Not human females, Nawat."

"That's not exactly true," Ulasim told her in a choked voice that sounded as if he was trying not to laugh. "Rubies, emeralds, diamonds, all of those things sparkle, and human females love gems."

Aly shot the footman a look that said, *Don't confuse him!* She tucked the rock into her belt purse. "I'll explain later," she told Nawat, who watched her with worried eyes. "Thank you for trying to help me."

When they rode around the walls that encircled Pohon, Aly relaxed. She was not sure the villagers had forgotten her last visit. Instead Ulasim and Junai led her and Nawat deeper into the forest, following a narrow road. They passed into the lands behind the village, riding under tall, ancient trees alive with birds and squirrels. It was a perfect summer day, not too hot even on the open road, with gentle breezes carrying the scents of pine and leaves to Aly's nose.

At last they reached the top of a ridge that looked down into a small, cup-like hollow. At its bottom was a rough log house, hung about with charms, signs, and wind chimes. A creek raced past it, shaped with stone by human hands to form a deep pool before it reentered the trees. A line of drying clothes hung in the sunshine behind the house, a homely touch for a mage's domain. A pair of cats lounged in front of the door, watching them with eyes turned amber by the sun.

Nawat grinned. "It's washing day," he observed.

Aly frowned at him. "Leave the wash alone. You're not a crow anymore."

"No," he replied. "I am a mateless human." He sighed, trying to look forlorn.

"Stop that," Aly warned. She kneed Cinnamon down the path toward the cottage. Halting in front, she and her companions dismounted.

A tiny creature flew over to sniff Aly. She sighed in wonder. It was a miniature flying horse, a bay mare, bat-winged and perfect, its body no larger than her hand. "Where did you come from?" she asked softly.

"They nest here," replied Ulasim as other winged horses flapped around them. A piebald stallion glided over to Nawat. "The old woman puts up with any nonsense if it doesn't come from a human being," the raka continued bitterly. "Sometimes I think—"

He was interrupted by the piebald stallion. The tiny creature reared and neighed, pawing the air in fury.

"Maybe he remembers me," Nawat remarked. The stallion flew at him, hitting him in the face with his wings. "Stop it! My mother had nestlings of her own to feed!"

"You took one of their nestlings?" asked Aly, horrified.

"Several," replied Nawat, trying to shield his face. Two more winged horses flew in to attack him. "They make a very—ouch!—good meal for hungry young!"

"Why did you come if you made an enemy of the little kudarung?" Ulasim wanted to know. He and Junai backed off, leading their mounts away from the small winged creatures. "Is there *anyone* hereabouts who likes you?"

Nawat yelped as four more winged horses swooped at him from a clump of bushes, where they seemed to gather. Aly giggled as they dove at him, kicking, biting, pulling his hair and clothes, smacking him with their wings. "I thought they wouldn't remember!" he cried in answer to Ulasim. "It's been weeks, and I was a crow!"

Aly dismounted and handed her reins to Junai, then ran laughing to Nawat's rescue. "Stop that," she ordered as more of the small winged horses swarmed out of the brush. "He isn't a crow anymore." She gently tried to bat them away from Nawat. "How did you even recognize him? He's not here to take nestlings." She grabbed the piebald stallion as he tried to nip at Nawat's face. "He's quite a reformed—ow!" The tiny stallion twisted in her grip and fastened his teeth in one of her fingers, drawing blood. Aly dropped him. The stallion flew at her face. Aly squeaked and ducked.

More of the winged horses appeared in answer to their fellows' enraged calls. Half of them descended on Aly, the rest on Nawat.

"I think they believe you are a crow, too," Junai called as the still-amused Aly protected her head with her hands. The creatures bit her hands and gouged her head with hooves and teeth, battering her with their wings.

"Will you *help* us instead of gawping?" demanded Aly, trying not to laugh. She didn't want to hurt the tiny immortals, but their assaults were painful, and she had business here. She could hardly impress Ochobu Dodeka if she was too busy fighting off winged pests with long memories.

"But it's the most amusing thing I've seen all year," Ulasim replied in a strangled voice. Speaking appeared to destroy his control; he collapsed in laughter. Junai simply watched, a tiny smile on her usually still face.

Aly flapped her open hands, trying to push the small kudarung away. Nawat covered his head with his arms. "They're clever, aren't they?" he asked Aly, wincing. "To know I'm a crow even in this shape."

"I don't care how clever they are," Aly replied. She yelped as a kudarung bit the rim of her ear. Grabbing the animal, she tried to tug it free, but it refused to let go. Not wanting to hurt it or tear her ear, she had one course of action left to her. She ran for the stream, and dove into the part that had been shaped to form a deep pool.

The water, coming from the mountains, was bone-achingly cold even on this summer day. She lunged to the surface and gasped, her teeth chattering. Water sprayed all over her as Nawat jumped in, shedding kudarung as they saw where he was bound.

Aly swam to the edge of the pool. She was about to climb out onto the land when a small flock of kudarung attacked, driving her underwater. She found Nawat there, forced under the surface as she had been to escape their tormentors. They shot up for a deep breath of air before the immortals descended. On her next trip for air, Aly looked around quickly. There, on the bank near the shallow upper stream, she saw a likely weapon. She ducked underwater and swam toward it, her head aching from the chill and the kudarungs' assault. When she came up again, the large branch was a yard away. She lunged and seized it, wading into the shallow water above the pool. There she stood, batting her persecutors away with the branch.

Nawat joined her, to huddle at her side. "They are not very forgiving," he observed.

Aly lifted a foot and shoved him back into the pool.

Above the shrill, furious calls of the kudarung she heard laughter as harsh as any crow's bawl. She turned to find its source and saw an old woman barely five feet tall. The newcomer was dressed like the highland raka women in a bright wraparound jacket and long skirt, both thickly embroidered. The fire of a magical Gift shone from beneath her skin in Aly's Sight. The old woman had a long nose, eyes like upside-down crescents framed by wrinkled flesh, and a mouth as straight as Junai's. White locks combed to either side sprang from her hairline at the center of her forehead. The rest of her short, curling hair was the color of steel shot with threads of black and white. Her laughter had a jeering quality.

"Ochobu Dodeka, is this how you treat your guests?" Aly demanded, swinging her branch at the kudarung. "We're here to talk to you. Call these things off before I hurt one!"

"I don't want to talk to *you*," the old woman replied with a grin that showed teeth. "And they aren't pets, to come and go at my command." She looked at Junai and Ulasim. "*This* is the god's messenger?" she demanded, her black eyes snapping with scorn. "If you're listening to this luarin sisat, you haven't a prayer of success. I won't go with you to die!"

Aly sighed. It was time to work. She handed the branch to Nawat, who was climbing out of the pool. When he took it, Aly went to Ochobu. The kudarung who had concentrated on swarming Aly turned to continue their attack on Nawat.

"Am I mistaken?" Aly inquired mildly, leaning her head to clear water from one ear. "You're refusing to help us."

"If they are helped by such as you, they are beyond hope," retorted the old raka. "They would do better to take the road as roaming Players, amusing the luarin nobility."

Aly leaned her head to the other side to clear the water from that ear. In her politest tone she inquired, "So you must approve the work roster, before you will deign to help? Must the ones who risk their lives among the luarin every day bring each and every tool they choose for your inspection first?"

Ochobu scowled at Aly. "No one asked you."

Aly dug in her ear with a finger. "Your *god* asked me, Ochobu Dodeka," she replied, still polite, knowing that the old woman expected her to show rage. "And do you know what? It will be for nothing," she informed the raka with her friendliest smile. "Because as long as you and others like you find only obstacles, you can put off actually having to *do* something. You can just talk about it and dream of someday. We'll all die of old age. You raka will still have the luarin boot on your necks. After a while, *raka* won't mean 'people' any-more—it will just mean 'slave.'"

"I could blast you where you stand," Ochobu whispered, her eyes deadly.

Aly wrung out her tunic's hem. "Go on," she said cheerily. "Do your worst. Of course, the god might object." She gave Ochobu a moment to think and then another moment to act. When it was clear the raka mage was not going to kill her, Aly called, "Nawat, stop playing with the little horsies. We're going back to Tanair."

"I would gladly stop playing with them," Nawat called, swinging his branch around him to keep the kudarung at bay. "They are the ones who will not stop."

Ochobu looked over Aly's shoulder, pushing her lips in and out, as if she were thinking. Aly concentrated on wringing out as much of her tunic as she could reach. Finally Ochobu bared her teeth and whistled sharply. A handful of kudarung flew away from the swarm. The old woman whistled twice more before the rest broke off their assault and returned to their clump of brush.

Ochobu looked at Ulasim and Junai. "Did the pesky crow have to come?" she demanded.

Aly smiled graciously. "I like the crow."

The old woman looked at Aly, then at Nawat. "Stay away from my drying lines," she warned.

Nawat treated her to his beaming smile. "I am a man now. Men do not drag cloth in the mud."

The mage snorted, then looked Aly over. "Were you any other god's mes-senger, I wouldn't believe you," she said drily as Ulasim and Junai led the horses across the creek. "But our god *would* pick a luarin."

"You choose tools for a task by their crafting, not their look," a crow said crisply from a nearby tree. He flapped over to land on a barrel in front of the cottage. "A smith's finest hammer will be streaked with soot." Like the Kyprioth-crow of Aly's first Isles dream, he wore gem-studded rings on his talons and a gaudy jeweled necklace around his throat. He shone in Aly's Sight.

"So you really chose this wench," Ochobu said.

Kyprioth ruffled his feathers. "Stop trying to quarrel with me, or I will leave you to the Rajmuat luarin. Do you think Oron was bad? He will be as nothing compared to Hazarin, Imajane, Rubinyan, and Bronau, believe me. If we're to change things, it must be now. The Chain's time has come."

Aly frowned. "What's the Chain?" she asked.

Kyprioth turned a ring on one claw with his beak. It was Ulasim who answered. "My mother and her friends," he said, meeting the old woman's eyes with defiance. "A network of raka mages, spread throughout the Isles, waiting to take back what was theirs."

"You said it might not be so," Ochobu remarked wearily to Kyprioth. "You said we might fail."

"Every human effort has that chance," replied Kyprioth. "We gods can't change that. Besides, it would be very bad for your characters if you had things easy all the time."

"I told my children that. They didn't believe me any more than I believe you." Ochobu walked over to a bench next to her door and sat between the cats. "We wouldn't be in this state if you had turned the invaders away three hundred years back."

Kyprioth leaped off the barrel in crow form and landed on the ground as a man, in his human jewelry, jacket, and sarong. He stood before Ochobu, sparks in his dark eyes. Aly took a step back, feeling his presence as a pressure on her body and mind, like a heatless sun. Ulasim and Junai shaded their eyes as they looked on. Only Nawat seemed unconcerned. He squatted on the ground, dripping, as he ate selections from a column of ants.

"You do not think gods may be routed from their thrones, and thrust into the outer parts of the Divine Realms?" Kyprioth asked Ochobu softly. "You do not believe a god may be so battered in combat with his land-hungry brother and sister that he might need centuries to heal? Do not speak of what I should have done, Ochobu Dodeka. You were not at my side on that battlefield."

Aly wished she could go anywhere else. This was too personal for her. For the first time she felt like a true intruder in the Copper Isles. *This* was the reason he toyed with her and the Balitangs, this ancient loss. Kyprioth's playfulness had made the stakes seem small, as if he had meddled with her life for his own amusement. Now she had the truth of it, that the tide was turning in the Copper Isles. She was a pawn, the Balitang children just one more piece, on a board that stretched over miles and years.

Ochobu slid down to kneel before Kyprioth, tears streaming down her face. She had borne even more of the god's power than had Aly, Ulasim, or Junai.

Aly rested a hand on the old woman's shoulder. "Maybe she snaps at you because she's afraid," she told Kyprioth, though she didn't quite dare to look into his face. "You gods know you have centuries to turn the tables. We humans don't. We have short lives that can be made shorter with the stroke of a sword."

Burning fingers gripped her chin, forcing her to look up. Aly jerked away from the painful touch. When Kyprioth grabbed her chin a second time, it didn't hurt. Her knees quivered as she met his bottomless gaze, but somehow she managed to remain on her feet.

"Dear heart, you are wasted in Tortall," Kyprioth told her softly, his eyes showing her suns and waves that swamped islands, volcanoes, and shivering cracks in the earth. "One of us would have put a fire like yours to use sooner or later." He let Aly go and regarded Ochobu. "Old woman, let's have a cup of tea, for old times' sake."

Aly helped Ochobu to stand, but she didn't go with Kyprioth and Ulasim when they followed the woman inside. She stayed in the sun, drying out with Nawat as Junai unsaddled and groomed the horses. It took a while for her head to stop spinning from that long look into the god's eyes.

A flicker of light at the cottage's open doorway told Aly that the god had left. Ulasim and his mother remained inside for a while longer, talking. Junai and Aly practiced their combat exercises and Nawat tried to catch fish bare-handed in the stream. At last Ulasim left the cottage, saddlebags hung over one shoulder. He and Junai got to work saddling their horses and the sway-backed mare that ambled out of the shelter of the trees when Ulasim left the house. Ochobu finally emerged, carrying a pack. She thrust it into Aly's hands, then walked over to the clump of brush where the tiny kudarung nested.

"Nawat, put that down," Aly told her friend, who had secured a wriggling fish. "We're leaving."

"But I just caught it," Nawat complained. "I knew I could."

"You still know you can. Let the poor fish go," Aly retorted. "With all the bugs you've eaten today, you can't possibly be hungry."

She heard a sound and turned, frowning, to see what was the matter with Junai. Her usually stoic bodyguard was actually trying not to giggle.

"If you only knew how *strange* that sounds," Ulasim remarked. "You sound like her mother." He nodded at the red-faced Junai.

Nawat sighed and released his captive back into the stream.

Aly shook her head and strapped Ochobu's pack to the back of Cinnamon's saddle. "Well, he *has* been eating a lot of bugs," she said, knowing that didn't explain anything.

Ochobu returned and mounted the swaybacked mare. Three adult kudarung flew in her wake, all of them pitch black with white stars on their muzzles. "They make good messengers for short distances," Ochobu told Aly. "And if you or the crow bothers them, you can carry your own messages."

Aly rubbed her sore ear and winced. She had bumped the deepest bite. Holding her much-smeared handkerchief to the wound, she said, "I never bothered them in the first place."

"I will not bother them if Aly says not to," added Nawat. To her he whispered, "Not until we have enough nestlings of our own to mob them back."

"We're not *going* to—" Aly began in a heated whisper, trying to deny that they would mate and have nestlings, but realized it was useless. This was just one of those ideas Nawat would have to outgrow, since words didn't seem to change his mind on the subject.

"Let's go," Ulasim ordered. "There is work to be done at home."

They rode together out of the hollow and back down the road. When they reached the fork that led to Pohon, Ochobu reined up. "Junai, ride in and let Pilia know I am gone," she ordered. "Ask her if she will keep an eye on things and feed my animals."

"I cannot," Junai replied. She pointed to Aly. "She is my charge."

The old woman glared at her granddaughter. "You think I cannot protect your luarin pry-monkey?"

"Sorry, Grandmother," Junai said quickly. She kicked her gelding into a trot and headed for Pohon.

Aly watched in awe, then turned to Ochobu. "Will you teach me how to do that?" she asked. "She never listens to me."

"I will not," said Ochobu, following Ulasim down the road. "Converse with me only when you must, luarin. I may have to treat with you, but we will not be friends."

Aly shrugged and let mother and son ride far enough ahead for them not to suspect she was eavesdropping. Ochobu might never like her, that was plain. So long as they could work together until the equinox, Aly didn't care if Ochobu liked her or not. The old woman had every reason to hate white skins, after all. *At least I don't have to share a small castle with her over the winter,* she thought happily. She watched as Nawat ran into the woods a little way to examine something that had caught his eye. He would return when he felt the need.

It occurred to Aly that in her eagerness to get *any* kind of true mage to Tanair she had never asked anyone what kind of power Ochobu had. Obviously the old woman was strong, to stop bandits from preying on the villages of the plateau, and protective magic was certainly the most important thing for the Balitangs to have. Still, Aly could put Ochobu to better use if she knew the mage's strengths.

Aly let her mind drift, absorbing forest sounds: songbirds, rustling creatures, squirrel disputes, Nawat's steps among tree litter. In the distance a crow family discussed the location of a dead animal supper. An eagle's distant shriek reached her ears, and the whisper of wind in the pines. She closed her eyes, adjusted her mind to bring into play the more complex aspects of her magical Sight, then opened them.

Ochobu's Gift had been visible from the moment Aly first saw her. Gifts always appeared in her vision as a series of ripples in the air around the mage, as if he or she gave off heat. Now Aly's deeper Sight discovered more specific powers that appeared as images that glowed then faded over the round curve of Ochobu's back. She saw a mortar and pestle, a handful of plants, a storm racing over the open fields of the plateau, a charm that turned away harmful magics, a bowl of water for scrying.

"Stop that," Ochobu called over her shoulder, startling Aly out of her calm state. "It tickles."

When they got back to Tanair, Aly had a quick talk with the duchess about the morning's events. "So you're saying we have a mage now," Winnamine said when Aly was done. "And we need to make her part of the household, without raising a fuss."

Aly bowed. "Exactly, my lady."

Winnamine stared into the distance for a moment, her lips moving as she thought. At last she looked at Aly. "Rihani's never been comfortable as our sole healer. She is a wonderful herbwife, but has little experience with serious ailments. I think she'll be relieved if this Ochobu takes over, and she can be of use in making medicines. I also know my woman, Pembery, is less than delighted with looking after Elsren and Petranne during the day. Rihani may take her place, and Pembery shall wait on Sarai and me. And you, my dear, are being promoted again. It is time Dove had her own maid."

Aly grinned. "I serve at Your Grace's command," she replied, thinking that the duchess would have made a fine general, with her delicate way of rearranging her troops. From what Aly knew of the household, everyone whose job had just changed would like the new arrangement. The change for Aly herself meant that she was now free to ride anywhere that Dove might choose to go.

Once the duchess met Ochobu and explained things to Rihani and Pembery, Rihani took Ochobu to the keep's infirmary. Aly helped the footmen to move the duke's and duchess's things back to their old rooms, now that Bronau was gone. After the adult Balitangs were resettled and the older girls' rooms restored for their use, Sarai took charge of Aly's wardrobe. Dove ordered a hot bath for her new maid. "Because you should look nice, and not shed goat hair on my things," she said primly, her eyes dancing with mischief.

Aly stuck her tongue out at her young mistress and happily climbed into the tub. The main thing she had missed about home, after her family, was the luxury of a real bath. After weeks of washing in ponds or from a basin full of water, a hot bath was bliss.

Aly soaked until the water began to cool. She washed her scant inches of red-gold hair twice, scrubbed until she was crimson with cleanliness, then dried herself with a proper cloth. She noticed that she had put on some weight with the Balitangs, but the meals of leftovers, bread, and cheese had still not brought her to the weight she had at home.

"Try these," Sarai ordered, opening the dressing room door and tossing in gowns and shifts. "Can you sew?"

"I can sew," she told Sarai, thinking, Da made sure of *that*. "Of course, I require the usual tools for it."

"Use my box," Sarai offered. "Dove replaced her sewing things with ink and pens and paper. You'll need to take these clothes in—you're too big for Dove's hand-me-downs, and too bony for mine." She grinned at Aly and closed the door.

Aly spent the rest of the afternoon stitching Sarai's castoffs to fit her thinner frame. Once she had a complete outfit—a cotton shift and an amber-colored gown—she dressed and hurried downstairs in time to pour the supper wine. Afterward she joined the family in the duke and duchess's chambers, Sarai's sewing box balanced on her hip. There she sat and sewed, a perfectly natural evening's occupation for a lady's maid. Once Rihani took Elsren and Petranne up to bed, the family shifted in their seats to look at Aly.

"I thought you objected to promotion," remarked the duke. "You told us that people would notice a servant being somewhere that she shouldn't."

"I've kept my goatherd's things just in case," Aly said. "For now, acting as Lady Dove's maid will take me to the places I need to go as long as I continue to wear my collar."

There was a rap on the door. Without waiting, Ochobu came in and closed the door behind her, sealing it with a line of magical fire visible only to Aly. "To foil eavesdroppers," the old woman explained gruffly. She nodded abruptly to the Balitangs, then took a seat uninvited.

Aly sighed internally at the old woman's pride, then told the duke, "Your Grace, this is Ochobu Dodeka of Pohon village. She is the mother of Ulasim, and a true mage. Ochobu, I present His Grace Duke Mequen Balitang." Aly glared at the old woman until she bowed to the duke from her seat. "Her Grace has already made Ochobu's acquaintance," Aly continued. "Ochobu, may I also present Lady Saraiyu, and Lady Dovasary."

The old woman looked the girls over with sharp eyes. Then she bowed, but to that she added the raka gesture of respect, her arms crossed over her breasts, palms on the opposite shoulders. The girls, startled, responded with the same gesture.

To the duke Aly said, "Ochobu is sent by the god to help to protect you." She crossed her fingers behind her back, praying that no one here would mention which god was involved. She had forgotten to tell Ochobu that the Balitangs believed it was Mithros who had taken an interest in their fate.

"When Aly said she'd found a true healer and herbwife, I nearly collapsed with relief," the duchess told the duke with a smile. "Rihani is good with herbs and lesser ailments, but I've been living in fear that someone would break a leg or some great sickness would reach us. We would be in real trouble." To Ochobu she said, "You are thrice welcome among us."

"I could do no less, lady," Ochobu replied stiffly. "I served the family of the first duchess, and it is my honor to serve her daughters."

"I would like to learn from you, if it's agreeable," Winnamine said. "Unless you prefer not to have someone underfoot? I know many healers don't. Rihani will assist you, of course, but I think the more I can learn, the more useful I will be."

Aly couldn't decipher the look that Ochobu gave Winnamine. Finally the old woman said, "Most luarin do not ask. They order."

"We are not of that sort," Mequen replied, his deep voice quiet. "In this house the raka are respected, as my first wife was respected. Winnamine was also Sarugani's friend."

"We can gather herbs when we go out riding, like we did for Rihani," Sarai told Ochobu. "If we know what to look for, we will."

"Riding?" asked the duke, raising his brows. "Are you not needed here? Lessons, getting our house in order for winter . . . ?"

"We have summer chores well covered," said the duchess. "The girls feel they didn't really get to know the local people on their rides with Bronau. Everything was formal, and country matters bore him. I'd like to stay home with the little ones. I feel I've been neglecting them." When Mequen still frowned, the duchess touched his arm. "My dear, the girls will have plenty of time for lessons once winter starts. The villagers say we may be confined to the castle for days at a time. Let them ride now, while they can."

Mequen took Winnamine's hand within his. "Very well." He looked at the girls. "Behave and obey your guards, or you will be confined to the castle grounds until spring, do you understand? We are not in Rajmuat any longer. Trouble can find us here easily."

"Yes, Papa," said Dove meekly.

"Yes, Papa," echoed Sarai.

Aly glanced at Ochobu. The old mage watched the duke, her eyes and face unreadable. Still, thought Aly, she isn't cursing or spitting on the floor because he and the duchess are luarin. It's a start.

In a time of fear, the One Who I Promised will come to the raka, bearing glory in her train and justice in her hand. She will restore the god to his proper temple and his children to her right hand. She will be twice royal, wise and beloved, a living emblem of truth to her people. She will be attended by a wise one, the cunning one, the strong one, the warrior, and the crows. She will give a home to all, and the kudarung will fly in her honor.

—From the Kyprish Prophecy, written in the year 200 H.E., discovered in Duke Mequen's books by Aly

13

LADIES OF THE RAKA

The next morning, after Pembery and Aly helped them to dress and make up their room, Sarai and Dove took Aly to breakfast, then to the stable. They passed Nawat, seated in the sun as was his habit, carefully gluing feathers to shafts. Aly stopped for a moment, fascinated with Nawat's fine touch as he set the fletchings in glue. Sarai returned and dragged her away.

Lokeij's stable boys had already saddled Sarai's gelding, Dove's mare, and Aly's mare Cinnamon. Fesgao, two of the other men-at-arms, and Junai were already mounted, waiting for them. Aly clambered as awkwardly as she could into the saddle and made a small business of wriggling to settle herself. Their party rode through Tanair at a walk. Many of the people who were out wanted to greet the two Balitang girls personally. Aly was careful to sit her mount like a sack of flour, keeping up the pretense that she rode badly.

Once they were clear of Tanair's gate, Sarai cried, "Let's go!" and kicked her gelding into a gallop. Fesgao and one of the men-at-arms followed her, catching up before she was too far ahead. Dove did not even twitch her mare's rein for a faster gait. Aly, Junai, and the other man-at-arms stayed with her.

"I thought she just did that to show off for Bronau," Aly commented.

"No," Dove told her, and sighed heavily. "Every summer, when we go to our mountain estates on Tongkang, she gallops everywhere. She loves to ride. I think she'd do anything in the saddle if she could, including sleep."

"That talent could be useful," Aly pointed out.

"Wait till your behind starts to hurt, *then* tell me if it's useful," advised the younger girl. "I really admire Winna. All those rides with Bronau, and never once did she let on she's got saddle sores."

"She wants Sarai to like her *that* much?" Aly was surprised. She knew that the duchess wanted her stepdaughters' affection, but she hadn't guessed how far the lady might go for it.

"Well, a little," Dove admitted. "They get on well enough anymore. Mostly Winna came for Bronau." She frowned, her small dark face intent on her thoughts. "Winna likes him well enough. I mean, you could tell, she laughed at his jokes, and they talked all the time, but—Aly, she doesn't trust him. I don't think she even knows how little she trusts him. She never let them escape their bodyguards on our rides."

"Interesting," Aly said thoughtfully, sharpening her magical Sight so that she could keep an eye on Sarai and her escorts, still galloping down the road. "She doesn't think he'd dishonor Sarai, does she?"

"I don't know," Dove replied. "What I know is that Winna understands the prince as well as anybody, even better than Papa. Her not trusting him to behave honorably, that worries me. Doesn't it worry you? Because I don't think we've seen the last of His Highness, not at all."

Aly looked at the twelve-year-old. "You're very observant," she remarked.

"And cold," Dove said, her mouth pulled down in distaste. "You didn't say cold. Everyone does."

"But you're not cold," Aly replied. "You've learned to hide yourself. To hide in plain sight."

"Like you," Dove pointed out.

Aly grinned. "You have to admit, it's very useful."

Dove chuckled. When she did, her face lit with a powerful light. "Do you play chess?"

"A little," replied Aly, who could almost beat her grandfather, one of the finest players in Tortall.

"Good," Dove said cheerfully. "It's getting harder to lose so Papa doesn't realize what I'm doing. I can tell him I'm teaching you."

After their return to the castle, Aly laid out clean clothes for Dove, then went in search of their new mage. She found Ochobu in the rooms set aside for the healer and any patients at the back of the kitchen wing. The old woman was hanging up bunches of dry herbs next to those Rihani had already prepared. Shelves along one side of the infirmary, once empty but for Rihani's collection of salves, liquids, and tools, now bore a collection of medical and magical tools, substances, and books.

"What do you want?" Ochobu demanded, stretching to hang a bunch of dried mint from a beam overhead.

Aly leaned against the door frame and smiled. "I wanted to see how you were settling in. I confess, I thought you'd prefer to live in a hut behind the stable than here within luarin walls."

Ochobu glared at her. "If I say I will do a thing, I do it," she informed Aly stiffly. "I have come to safeguard the lady Sarai, and to help you win your wager. If the Balitang children survive the summer, there will be one less luarin in the Isles at least, and you are a particularly annoying one."

Aly raised her brows. "So the god told you of our bet. Does Ulasim know?"

Ochobu shook her head. "The god spoke to me in the night. He says you are only a temporary irritation. He thinks that with the summer over, the luarin rulers will have sorted out the kingship. The lady who may or may not be our promised one shall be safe for the winter." She poured juniper berries from a bowl into a mortar and began to mash them, releasing their piney scent.

The mention of the end of the wager itched Aly. Being called "a temporary irritation" was also quite annoying. "There are too many of us to kill, you know," she pointed out, thinking she was starting to talk like her father. "Too many who have been here three centuries."

"Do you think I don't know that?" demanded Ochobu, pausing in her work to scowl at Aly. "I'll have to get used to luarin, even if they aren't you."

"You will if you don't want a massacre," Aly said, holding the old woman's eyes with hers. "If you don't want to mark your return to power with killing. How much luarin blood will you discard? Half-bloods? You'd murder your own lady, then. She'd object to the murder of her luarin father and stepmother in any case. Quarter-bloods, eighth-bloods? How much do you count as being too much?"

"Stop it," growled the old woman. "The raka people are not like the first three Rittevon kings, slaughtering those who would not bend the knee to them. We are not murderers."

"That's not what I learned at my da's knee," Aly retorted. Her mental image of people executed by righteous natives was too awful for her to let Ochobu's prejudices stand without argument. "The raka used to kill all the time. Your nobles and your rather temporary queens in the years before the luarin came were so busy battling each other that you didn't have the strength to fight off an invasion. By the time you banded together, it was too late."

"I *know* that," Ochobu growled, mashing her berries with ferocity. "*All* of us who inherited this mess know."

"Is a mess what you mean to give your new queen?" Aly wanted to know. "How can she be sure her people will stand behind her? Or will you put a dagger in her back for the crime of not choosing a father the raka will approve?" Aly inspected her fingernails. They would need work if she was to continue as a maid rather than a goatherd. "Personally, I think you might do well with Sarai on the throne—"

"Silence!" Ochobu interrupted, glaring at Aly. "No names!"

Aly raised an eyebrow at her and waited.

Ochobu laid her pestle aside. "We have lived too long as tenants on lands that our foremothers owned. I know that. I know what is at stake. I can see for myself that a certain young woman is royal in two bloodlines, and that seems to fit the prophecy. But I am no lapdog, trained to roll onto my back for you or any other luarin. I am here to make up my own mind."

Aly brushed a speck from her sleeve. "Then let me tell you something I've observed. Those you call luarin here, including the ones who are part luarin, part raka—they aren't citizens of the Eastern or Southern Lands. They see themselves as Kyprians. They took your land's names for their own. They've made the Isles prosper. I think they've earned the right to stay, if they don't side with the Rittevons when the time comes."

"Is that the god speaking through you?" Ochobu demanded, her eyes flinty. "Or just you?"

Aly fought the urge to give Nawat's wing shrug for a reply. "I assume the god picked me for my opinions as well as my skills, however temporary I might be. I am an outsider. Sometimes we see more clearly than those who live inside the problem."

"I'll be better off when you leave," Ochobu complained. For the moment she sagged, the lines of her face deepening. "You've given me a headache. Go away."

Aly went.

She took lunch with the Balitang women and spent the afternoon with Sarai and Dove as they played with Elsren and Petranne. After Winnamine summoned the two older girls to their newly begun weapons training, Aly occupied herself with household mending and a quick search of Sergeant Veron's rooms, to read his latest reports to the Crown. Once she had finished, she asked Chenaol to heat water for the sisters' baths, then laid out the girls' supper dresses. Bored with nothing to do but mend clothes, Aly wandered over to the window to look out over the inner courtyard.

Below her Dove and the men-at-arms practiced archery. Aly leaned her elbows on the sill to watch and nearly yelped before she caught herself. Someone had come up with a new game.

Nawat stood against the wall, relaxed and alert. Before him two men-at-arms were preparing to shoot. Dove stood behind one archer with a handful of arrows, while the duchess held arrows for the second archer. Aly's mind told her that the duchess would hardly consent to murder just as the first man shot. The second man shot immediately after him. Then both set fresh arrows to the string and shot steadily, arrow after arrow, one at a time, until they had exhausted all the extras held by the duchess and her stepdaughter.

Nawat caught them all with grace and ease, snatching the arrows from the air as if he had all day to do so. When the archers finished, he gathered the heap of arrows at his feet and carried them back to their owners.

He's so *fast*, Aly thought in awe. *I* couldn't do it, and I'm no slouch! She sighed, wishing Da were here to see it. He'd taught her to catch daggers in midair, but this game was much more hazardous.

The game was not done. The men-at-arms repeated the experiment with javelins, then hunting and combat spears. Nawat caught them all, moving so fast Aly couldn't follow his hands. She cheered him and the men-at-arms on.

When the bell rang to remind the household it was nearly time for supper, he looked up at the applauding Aly and waved. "This is my favorite game," he called to her. "Do you want to play?"

"I wouldn't dare!" she cried, laughing, before she retreated into the room. She'd seen men catch knives before. She had seen the finest archers in the Queen's Riders draw an outline in arrows of someone positioned against a wooden fence or wall, just to show they could do it. She had never seen anything like this.

Sarai and Dove ran in. Sarai smiled at Aly. "You should have *seen* your face! Did you know he could do that?" she asked as she collapsed on her bed.

Dove unstrung her bow, shaking her head. "He's amazing," she said, coiling her bowstring.

"You know, maybe this horrible old place isn't so bad," Sarai told the ceiling. "Not if these wonderful men keep showing up."

Aly raised an eyebrow at her. "I wouldn't try kissing him," she warned. "It wouldn't be what you expect."

Sarai wrinkled her nose. "Aly!" she complained. "I found out he eats bugs! I'm not kissing a man with bug breath!"

Aly blinked. I don't remember him tasting of bugs when he kissed me, she thought. I'd better pay more attention next time.

Her mind promptly reined her up. This was highly improper. There would be no next time. Her task was looking after the Balitang children, not mooning over someone, particularly not a crow turned man.

Even if he *could* pluck arrows from the air.

The next morning Aly, still on a goatherd's hours, walked out of the keep into the dawn. The sun had just cleared the walls to light the inner courtyard and the young man who straddled a bench there. Aly stopped to watch him carefully glue pieces of feather onto the wooden shaft.

Nawat looked up at her with a smile that lit his eyes. "You are beautiful in the new light," he told her. "If I were the Dawn Crow, I would bring you the sun to hatch as our first nestling."

Aly blinked at him. Her heart felt strangely squeezed by some powerful emotion. She bit her lip to distract herself from a feeling that made her horribly unsure. "Have you been kissing anybody?" she asked without meaning to, and gasped. She had let words out of her mouth without thinking, which was not like her! Worse, they were such personal words, ones he might feel meant personal feelings she did not have! This was the kind of thing that other girls said, those girls who were not bored by all the young men who had courted them. How many handsome fellows had sighed compliments to Aly while, unconcerned, she had mentally wrestled with breaking a new code? At home she never cared about her suitors enough to worry if they kissed other girls. She scrambled to blot out what she'd said. "Not that it's any of my business, but you should understand, people have a way of kissing for fun, without it meaning anything serious, and I'd hate for you to think someone wanted you to mate-feed them just because they're kissing—" Stop babbling, her mind ordered. Aly stopped.

Nawat's smile broadened. That disturbing light in his eyes deepened. "I have kissed no one but you, Aly," he assured her, serious. "Why should I kiss anyone else?"

Aly gulped. You can continue this conversation, or you can talk about something less . . . giddy, she told herself. Less frightening. "You know I won't always be around," she said abruptly. "I don't belong here, really."

"Then I will go with you," Nawat said. "I belong with you."

He doesn't know what he's saying, Aly told herself. He doesn't know what that means.

She looked at him, arms folded, trying to keep any extra feelings from leaping out. "What are you doing?" she asked, to change the subject to anything less dangerous. Then she grimaced. He was fletching arrows, as always.

She glanced at his bench, then bent down. He was fletching, but these arrows were heavier, and the feathers he used were not bird feathers, but Stormwing. "How did you cut them up?" she wanted to know, genuinely curious. More scraps of cut-up steel feathers lay on the bench.

Nawat pointed to a long piece of what looked like black, chipped glass. "Shiny volcano rock," he told Aly. "Chip the edge until it is sharp. That cuts Stormwing feathers. They come from the heat of the place where Stormwings were born."

Aly touched the glassy blade. "Obsidian," she said. "That's its name."

"Yes," Nawat replied. "Shiny volcano rock." He set a length of steel feather into a thin groove filled with glue and held it in place.

Aly didn't see a single cut on his hands, though the feathers were lethally sharp. "Won't they be too heavy for the glue?" she asked.

"I shaped the glue. It holds Stormwing feathers," Nawat answered.

"Stormwings really are born in volcanoes?" Aly inquired, curious.

"In the beginning time, when they were first dreamed," replied Nawat, setting another piece of steel feather in its slot. "Now, if carrying an egg does not kill the mother, they are born from steel eggs." He looked at Aly and sighed, his dark eyes wistful. "The eggs are too heavy for a crow to take."

"You've already taken enough from Stormwings," Aly told him, pointing to the small pile of glinting feathers beside his bench. "You could have been killed."

"There is a trick to it," he replied, and blew lightly on his fletchings. Holding the arrow shaft before one eye, he squinted down its length. "Perfect," he declared, and set the arrow down.

"It seems like a lot of trouble and risk when goose feathers are safer to work with," Aly remarked. "What is a Stormwing-fletched arrow for, anyway?"

"They are mage killers," replied Nawat. "No matter if the mage is powerful, if he has great spells to protect him. A Stormwing arrow will cut through illusion and magic."

Aly whistled softly, impressed. "Take very good care of those, then," she told Nawat. "We might find a use for them."

"I made them for you," Nawat said, giving her that radiant, innocent smile. "They are yours, for a day when they will help you." He offered a finished arrow shaft to her.

Aly smiled at him despite the goose bumps that rippled along her skin. "Keep them until they're needed, please," she told him. "My archery skills aren't very good."

"You could practice," Nawat pointed out.

"I'm a slave," Aly explained. "Slaves who are caught with weapons are killed."

"Then do not be a slave," he said, matter-of-factly. "Fly free."

"Not just yet," she replied. "I'll see the summer out first."

Five days later a well-guarded messenger arrived on the plateau. Crows and raka patrols encircled and held the small group until Veron and the castle guard arrived. As the Balitang men-at-arms approached, the raka guards scattered to make Veron think they were robbers and not fighters who had been assigned to keep new arrivals away from the Balitangs until they were searched.

Aly and her riding companions, out on the road west of Tanair, heard the crows' alarm. They arrived at the eastern road at the same time as Veron. Aly murmured a suggestion to Fesgao that he join in the search. If the new arrivals were royal assassins, Aly suspected Veron would take them to the Balitangs. With Fesgao involved, she knew no killers sent by the Crown would go undiscovered.

She watched as the men-at-arms questioned the strangers, looking for anything unusual. None of them lied in answer. As it turned out, their errand was a normal one. They bore thank-you gifts from Bronau, purchased in Dimari before he sailed. They also brought letters from those friends who had been writing to the exiles all along, as well as letters from those who had decided it was safe to correspond now that Hazarin might recall them to the capital.

After supper, Winnamine, Sarai, and Dove played soldiers on the floor with Elsren and Petranne. Pembery, Aly, and Rihani worked on sewing as the duke opened the letters and read them aloud to the family. Aly saw that Winnamine, normally so controlled, could not keep a tiny, sarcastic smile from her lips as people who had been silent for weeks now proclaimed their affection for the Balitangs. Sarai's toy soldiers acted fiercely as she struggled to control her anger with such fair-weather friends. The duke shook his head sadly as he read. Dove practiced that staple item of a young noblewoman's studies, a facial expression of polite interest that gave away none of her true feelings. Aly silently applauded Dove's skill. The twelve-year-old was much better at that polite control than Sarai.

For herself, Aly could only give a mental shrug as she stitched. It was human nature for people to protect themselves from a monarch's temper. That went triple for everyone who lived under the king's eye in Rajmuat.

There was news, too, from the Eastern and Southern Lands. Aly barely listened to the word from Carthak. Emperor Kaddar and his empress were still dealing with that realm's far-flung malcontents, though Kaddar's grip on his throne grew firmer with each passing year. She was far more interested in news from the Eastern Lands, though she pretended the same indifference as she had for Carthak. The Scanran war continued, but the end was in sight. There were rumors that unhappy clansmen had secretly reached out to the Tortallan monarchs, offering peace in trade for their king's head. Aly hoped that Their Majesties, ably assisted by people like her mother, would choose to hammer the Scanrans for a while longer. It would ensure that fresh Scanran attacks would not take place for at least another generation.

After the duke had read all the letters he wanted to share, he opened the trunk from Bronau. Once again there were new books for him, the duchess, and Dove. There was a wooden pull-along knight on horseback for Elsren, who abandoned his soldiers, and a new doll for Petranne, who immediately did the same.

For Sarai there was a gold necklace, its fine chain decorated with citrine drops along its length, and a matching bracelet. The older girl put them on immediately and went to the duchess's looking glass to admire them. "He remembered how much I like citrines!" she told them all.

"Huzzah for him," muttered Dove. Aly, the only one who heard, grinned.

Mequen shifted uneasily in his chair. Winnamine reached over and rested a hand on his arm. "So my old friend courts you, Sarai," the duke said, watching her with concern in his eyes. "Of course, his friends have suggested that he marry for years, but we thought . . ."

"Oh, Papa, it's not serious. He's just flirting," Sarai replied.

"That's very different from what you've said before," the duchess pointed out.

"Well, I'm sixteen, and giddy," Sarai told them mischievously. "My husband had best be faithful to me alone. Bronau isn't likely to do that. Besides, unless King Hazarin gifts him with offices or estates, he's not very wealthy."

She went to kneel beside her father. "Don't fret, Papa," she said, her face turned up to his. "I'd never do anything without your approval." She looked at Winnamine, hesitated, then said, "Or yours, Winna."

Aly looked down, not wanting anyone to realize she had seen the sudden happiness in the duchess's face. It made her feel very much an outsider. She missed her mother, prickly though she was.

The July days that followed were filled with hazy summer heat that made even the lightest cottons stick to their skins. Despite the temperatures, Aly did not give in to the urge to laze. She sewed, cleaned, and helped Sarai and Dove to amuse the younger children so that Rihani could help to put up herbal teas and medicines against the winter. At night Aly met with the raka conspirators, Ochobu, and Nawat, going over what news had come in that day from crows, people, and Ochobu's scrying bowl. They discussed fresh arrivals in the valley while the raka filled Aly in on who in the Isles might support them in times of trouble—the nature of those times left carefully undescribed—as well as who it was who might turn on them.

Each day Sarai bounced away from the breakfast table, Aly and Dove following at a sleepy distance. Outside they would find their mounts and guards waiting by the stables. Some days they had instructions: errands to run for the duchess or mushrooms, berries, and herbs to collect for Chenaol and Ochobu. Other days Nawat came with them, to collect wood for arrows or simply to keep the girls amused.

"Falthin is an easy master indeed," Sarai remarked on Nawat's third such ride with them. She looked at him sidelong through her lashes and made her mare prance so that Nawat might look at her hips if he chose. Aly just shook her head, remembering that she had flirted just as much when she wasn't working for her father and grandfather. She wished that Sarai had something serious to do with her time instead of wasting it in the enticement of a man who didn't see her as a potential mate.

Not, she told herself hurriedly, that she cared if Nawat *did* look at Sarai as a potential mate.

"Falthin the bowyer tells me I am only young once, and the winters indoors are long," Nawat replied, his eyes not on Sarai's hips but on Aly's face.

Their group often carried medicines brewed by Ochobu and Rihani to the villages of Inti and Pohon. If they were not invited to take their lunch with the wealthier families, they found shady brookside places to eat their bread, cheese, and whatever else Chenaol might have packed for them. Afterward they would doze, cool their feet in the water, talk, or sew. If it wasn't too hot, they practiced hand-to-hand combat and weapons skills with Aly and Junai. Aly loved the long, slow days, filled with the buzz of crickets and the sight of blindingly white clouds scudding over the turquoise sky. Summer was as beautiful on Lombyn as at Pirate's Swoop. She barely missed the stacks of reports at home, the bustle of messengers coming and going, or her fair-weather round of visits to relatives and foster relatives.

As lazy as the time could be, Aly never forgot who her companions were. Everywhere they went, the raka turned out to look at the Balitang girls. Sarai always stopped to say hello, to learn their names, admire their children, and listen to their old people. The girls would be offered cups of the villainous Kyprian tea, which they had to accept or risk offending their hosts. Drinking it, Aly always wondered if it could be used to remove varnish from furniture.

She had hoped that the novelty of watching Sarai might wear off, but she reckoned without Sarai or the raka. Like Aly's mother, Sarai detested going home by the same route she had taken to leave it. She led them along tracks Aly would have sworn were game trails, past small farms, hunters' cabins, and mining and lumber camps on the plateau's edge. They chatted with people Aly suspected were poachers and others she knew were smugglers. Sarai greeted women dyeing cloth and men tanning hides. Aly would not have suspected that so much of the plateau was taken up by farms, or that Sarai had a talent for locating them all.

Despite her reservations about the raka mounting a successful rebellion, Aly had to admit that Sarai showed promise. She had the same air of genuine interest in people's lives that Queen Thayet had shown when Aly had accompanied her godsmother on trips. Sarai cared for the people, and they responded. Looking at her, their faces were bright with hope. Aly could only pray that their hopes were fulfilled, for them and for Sarai.

One day they rode to Inti. When they got within view of the village, Aly, who had been using her Sight to eye the road ahead, made the girls halt. Thirty-odd people were camped on the village outskirts. As they stopped, a raka patrol melted out of the trees on the northern side of the road. Their leader rode out to meet Fesgao. The two men spoke briefly. Fesgao then brought his horse around and came back to their group.

"They are raka," he told the girls. "They have come to see the lady." His long eyes flicked up to Sarai's face, then away. To Aly he said, "It is well. They came up from the coast, and have no taint of the assassin to them."

"Then let's say hello," Sarai declared. "It's the least we can do, if they've made that horrible climb up the western road."

Aly still didn't like it, but she had no choice. Sarai had already urged her gelding forward. As they approached, the raka patrol vanished under the trees once more, while the raka in the camp gathered on either side of the road. Watching Sarai approach the nearest of them, Aly sent a hurried call to Kyprioth for help.

Let them see their ladies, the god replied. His voice boomed in the empty air, coming from the open sky. The raka from the camp immediately dropped to their knees. Sarai hurriedly controlled her mount and Dove's as the frightened horses began to plunge and fight the rein. The guards' mounts held steady, though white showed all the way around their eyes. Aly's Cinnamon calmly helped herself to mouthfuls of grass. "Let them greet Saraiyu and Dovasary," Kyprioth went on, "and return to speak of them in their home villages, with hope."

As Sarai dismounted, Aly directed an angry but unspoken remark to the god. *It was a* private *question. Why did you have to make such a revelation of it?!*

Because this is part of the biggest trick I have ever played, the god said for her ears alone. *Because they must be heralded with signs of divine favor. I just showed them some.*

You upset the horses, Aly retorted silently. *Show-off.*

Now you begin to understand me. The god's private voice was filled with amusement. *I knew it would happen sooner or later.*

Sarai passed her reins to Aly. She started forward, then turned to glare at Dove.

Aly nudged Cinnamon closer to the younger girl. "I'll hold your mare," she offered.

"What are we getting ourselves into?" Dove whispered. "If word of things like this gets back to the palace, we'll be cooked in front of its gates over a slow fire."

Despite her concern, she dismounted and gave her horse's reins to Aly. Fesgao and the rest of the guards were getting down from their mounts, too. Aly sighed and did the same for them. She knew better than to even ask Junai to hold the horses' reins. Junai would say, quite properly, that as a guard in an uncertain situation she had to keep her hands and her attention free.

The raka bowed low to the girls, arms crossed over their chests, palms to their shoulders. These were poor people, Aly noted, with scarcely an unpatched jacket or sarong to their names. Their numbers encompassed all ages and both sexes, from people so old they were carried in stretchers to babies still at the breast. Aly observed the crowd as the guards watched those closest to the Balitang girls, alert for assassins who might have slipped by the patrol. All went quietly. Once each raka had said hello and told Sarai a little about him- or herself, they bowed, collected their belongings, and quietly left their camp.

"They appeared overnight from the coast," said Inti's headman when they finally reached the village itself. "They haven't been any trouble, but they said they meant to stay until they saw you. I don't see what I could have done."

"Next time, send word," snapped Fesgao, his normal calm disturbed by the unexpected encounter. "We could have brought more guards with us."

On their way home, Aly dropped behind to ride next to Fesgao. Softly she asked, "Is there any way to keep such groups from coming? It attracts attention."

The man shook his head. "The raka have lived without hope for so long," he explained. "I cannot blame them for wanting to see it with their own eyes."

"If you think these girls will let you foment a rebellion in their names, you will get a rude awakening," Aly cautioned Fesgao. "They and their parents are loyal to the Crown."

"Ah, but is the Crown loyal to them?" asked the raka. "That has yet to be seen."

Fort Mastiff, Tortall, on the Scanran border

This was yet another of her dream visits to Tortall, Aly realized, coming from sleep to wakefulness in the air above a large, new, wooden fortress. It flew the flag of the realm of Tortall, a silver sword and a silver crown on a blue shield. Beneath it flew a scarlet flag with a golden cat rearing on it, the banner of the King's Champion, Alanna the Lioness.

Aly could see her famous mother below, planted solidly at the center of a ring of onlookers. She was dueling with someone. From the fighters' quilted tunics and absent helmets, Aly judged that this was a practice session, not a real fight, though both her mother and her opponent wielded live sword blades. There was a risk.

Aly drifted down, curious about who might be mad enough to take on her mother, even for practice. By the looks of things, Alanna was overmatched. Her opponent was nearly six feet tall, broad-shouldered, with muscled legs revealed by cotton breeches. Sweat-soaked brown hair, cut short at the nape of the neck and across the forehead, framed a face tanned in the sun, and brown-hazel eyes, a dreamer's eyes, with ridiculously long lashes. Those eyes were steady as they watched the Lioness's sword.

"Go, Kel!" someone yelled from the sidelines. "Youth and skill!"

"Age and treachery!" bellowed a large man on the far side of the ring. Aly knew him. Lord Raoul of Goldenlake and Malorie's Peak was one of her adoptive uncles, a big man who kept a short, brown-skinned woman in the circle of his arm even as he urged his friend Alanna on. Aly recognized the brown woman as yet another of her adoptive aunts, Buri, married to Uncle Raoul less than a year.

"Youth and skill!" cried another man Aly knew well, Nealan of Queenscove, her mother's former squire. "Don't let that old lady cut you, Kel!"

"Whose side are you on?" Alanna demanded, her eyes flicking over to Neal. "You were *my* squire!"

Her opponent surged forward as the Lioness's attention wavered, her blade slicing the air in an overhand swing. This had to be Keladry of Mindelan, Aly realized, fascinated. Since Aly had been eight or so her mother had spoken continually of Keladry, the first girl to go for her knighthood since Alanna. For a while Aly had been jealous of the girl, thinking her mother was more interested in Kel than she was in Aly. Only in the last few years had she realized her mother simply understood Kel better than she understood Aly.

Kel bore in on her smaller foe fast, but Alanna came up and under Kel's attack, smacking the bigger woman hard in the ribs. "You've been using that pig-sticker of yours so much, you've forgotten how to wield your Griffin," Alanna taunted. "You've gotten lazy!"

Griffin, Aly thought, then remembered. Mother said Kel had named the sword Alanna had given her Griffin.

Kel lunged in again, her sword blade tangling with the Lioness's, until the two women were locked together, hilt to hilt. Now Kel brought her superior height and weight to bear, forcing the Lioness down and back. "Lazy, is it?" Keladry said, panting. "I'll give you laziness, shorty."

Alanna laughed and sprang free of the tangle, darting around to swat Keladry on the behind with the flat of her blade. "Age and treachery!" she taunted Kel.

Kel stood back and, gasping, saluted Alanna with her weapon. "I guess I need to work on my sword skill after all, Lioness," she said, accepting someone's water bottle. She nodded toward the gate. "I think we have company."

A tall gray figure—Tkaa the basilisk—strode through the gate, holding his long tail off the ground as a lady would hold the train to her gown. From crown to tail he was covered in dust that turned his beaded gray skin to gray-brown.

"Tkaa," cried Alanna, running to greet the newcomer. "Whatever brings you here?"

The basilisk bent his head so that he could whisper into her ear. Aly dropped down until she was close enough to hear him. "I bear news from your husband." Tkaa's voice was like the whisper of flutes. "He asks me to tell you that he's got real word at last, from Rajmuat. You must not worry if he disappears for a time."

Alanna seized the basilisk's paw. Aly, looking around, saw that everyone else was keeping a respectful distance from the unlikely pair.

"Aly?" whispered Alanna. "He's got word of her?"

Tkaa nodded.

Alanna turned and walked speedily back to her quarters, the men shifting out of her path. Like Aly, they knew the set look on Alanna's face meant she didn't want to talk to anyone.

"Please tell me you have good news." Lord Raoul had walked over to greet the basilisk. "Whatever it is. She's been as jumpy as a horse covered in ants all summer."

"I sorrow to hear it," said the basilisk. "I can tell you that diplomats from Scanra are in Corus to negotiate a peace treaty."

His information was greeted with a shout from the people who had followed Raoul to say hello to the newcomer. Aly's dream began to fade as men and boys ran to tell their fellows Tkaa's news.

Aly opened her eyes. She lay on her pallet in the great hall. Looking at the torch that still burned to light any late comings and goings on the main stair, she saw that it was the middle of the night, with a few more hours to go until dawn. A fresh torch set by the stairs always burned out just before sunrise.

Someone nearby snored. Aly heard a dog's claws scratch on the stone flags as their owner dreamed of hunting. Farther off she heard a rustle of mice.

She stared into the dark. Da was coming to Rajmuat, she realized. He would track her to the slave pens, then to the Balitangs' town house, then to Lombyn. It might take him weeks. He could not use his Kyprish agents. He would have to question people without seeming to question them. He would be looking for a girl with hair, not one shaved bald, but sooner or later he would find Aly and want to take her home.

She'd go, of course. She hoped he could wait till the equinox, so that her bet would be done with. And then she'd return to the safety of Pirate's Swoop. If all went as it was supposed to, Da would then let her do field work.

And what happens to the Balitangs then? she asked herself. What happens to the raka?

She wouldn't think of that. Da needed her. Mother missed her. And there were her brothers, her grandparents, and her adoptive family. She could see them once the Balitangs were safe, if she didn't go home with Da right away. There was an idea.

Back to sleep. The only result she would have from worrying about it now was daytime exhaustion from lack of a proper night's rest. Da would come when he came.

If you're to lie to a god, and sometimes it's fair useful, do it with the truth. They smell lies on two-leggers, or they see it, or whatever it is they do. But if all you're telling them is whatever part of your lie that's truthful, they'll accept it. The gods don't see what's always in our minds. Mayhap they'd go mad if they knew everything we think as we think it—I know I would. Besides, mortals were granted the right to make our own choices when we were shaped. So if a god's got no reason to be suspicious, he won't enter your mind to find that you've only spoken half the story.

—*Daine Sarrasri, daughter of the Gallan goddess The Green Lady and the hunt god Weiryn, to her fifteen-year-old adopted niece, Aly, during a discussion of the Immortals' War*

14

PIVOT

The first group of outland raka had been gone three days when another came in. They, too, would not leave until after they had seen Sarai. Five days later a third group arrived at Inti. This one was the largest yet, a regular caravan from the coast that masked its real purpose by carrying sealskins, whale oil, shell buttons, salt, beads, and dried seaweed to trade.

To support their story of coming to Inti on business, Sarai sent a villager for her father and Ulasim, who could ride to Inti and do business for the family. She told her companions they would spend the night in the village, since she had so far met only half of the caravan's members. Their group took supper with the newcomers and introduced them to Mequen and Ulasim when they arrived with their guards.

In a gesture of goodwill, Inti's headman gave up his home to the Balitangs for the night. Inside at last, Aly set the pallet they'd found for her at the foot of the large bed shared by Sarai and Dove. Exhausted by watchfulness among a crowd of unknown raka and by a secret but thorough search of their wagons and gear, Aly plunged into sleep as soon as her eyes closed.

Kyprioth awaited her in the glowing form he'd used to show her King Oron's death.

"What now?" Aly demanded crossly. "I have enough on my plate at the moment, without you dragging me all over the mortal realms."

"You will be glad to know this by the time we are done, my dear," the god informed her. "It is the pivot on which all else turns. I've yet to meet a spy who didn't want all the information he—or she—could stand."

"You could at least pretend to be sorry you bothered me," Aly grumbled as the god passed a glowing arm firmly around her waist.

"And deprive you of whining?" he asked as they shot through the roof of the house, into the open sky beyond. "I *have* noticed how careful you are not to complain to those you serve. I thought it only fair to let you berate me a little."

"That wasn't berating you," Aly said darkly, even as she savored their passage over velvety land and watched the brilliant stars overhead. "When I berate you, you'll know it." She sighed dramatically. "Not that you'll care."

"I won't," Kyprioth replied as they soared over the Azure Sea. Far below, a long, sinuous form arched up along the water, scattering it in diamond drops in the starlight. Kyprioth crooned a greeting to the whale, who called back as its tail popped free of the water, then passed into it again. "Though I know that I will prize the way you phrase yourself. I am certain that you will be more than eloquent at the art of berating."

Aly replied with a rude invitation not commonly offered to a god, startling a peal of laughter from Kyprioth. "Whatever else I may say of you, and I'm sure there will be plenty, at least you have a sense of humor," she added.

"I *am* a trickster," he replied in a modest tone.

Gods, Aly thought. They always insist on having the last word.

All too soon the journey was over. They settled into the king's bedroom in the palace at Rajmuat. The curtains over the terrace doors were drawn against the night air, cooler here above the harbor. The chamber was dark except for one small lamp by the door to the outer room and another by the door to what looked like the privy. Servants slept on pallets all around the room, ready to jump up to do the king's bidding if he needed anything in the night. On the bed King Hazarin slept alone, pouting even in his dreams. He labored to breathe, releasing the occasional snore.

"He ate richly tonight," Kyprioth observed in a tone of mild interest. "Venison in wine sauce, pork with a pineapple and honey gravy, buffalo coconut curry, sticky coconut peanut rice with currants and almonds, five different wines from the Eastern Lands . . ."

"He *always* eats like that?" Aly wanted to know, awed.

"The richer, the better," replied Kyprioth. "He insists on at least five coconut dishes at every meal, though healers keep telling him a lighter diet would be better. It's really a toss-up as to what kills him first, his heart or an apoplexy of the brain. Actually, I have a bit of a wager on with my cousin the Graveyard Hag about that."

He went quiet. Hazarin bolted upright in bed, his eyes open and staring as he fought to breathe. His plump hands went to his head. He uttered a strangled noise loud enough to wake two of the sleepers around him. As they struggled to their feet, Hazarin fell back on his pillows, eyes wide. He stared blankly upward as his hands flopped down. He gaped endlessly as the anxious servants felt his throat and his wrists. The woman who held his wrist looked at the man who touched the big veins in Hazarin's throat. The man shook his head, then cocked his head to put his ear over Hazarin's open mouth.

The woman turned to look at the other sleepers. "Wake up, you fools!" she snapped, her voice low and cutting. "Something's happened to the king!"

Blankets flew as the sleepers roused in a panic. Within moments they had silently lit more lamps. One man thrust a blanket under the edge of the main door, to keep the light from showing outside. Aly understood what was going on. These were the acts of people who might die if anything questionable took place in the room where the king slept. They all gathered around Hazarin, some making the star-shaped sign against evil when they saw the king's face.

"He's dead," the man who had listened for the king's breath told his fellows. "I don't know why, but he is."

"We must call a healer," said a young maid. As she turned toward the door, one of the men grabbed her arm.

"Idiot!" he snapped, keeping his voice low. "What if it's poison? Who will be blamed? He was fine when he rose from supper, fine when he came to bed—"

"He mentioned a headache," interrupted the woman who'd been the first to wake.

"Not a headache bad enough to call the healer," retorted the man who had stopped the younger maid. "Now he's dead. If it's poison . . ."

"They'll say it was one of us," murmured someone else. "They always do."

None of them said another word. Silently they collected their belongings and fled through a door to the servants' stair hidden behind a tapestry. The last to leave blew out the lamps.

"They'll have gone to ground in the city by dawn," Kyprioth remarked to Aly. "And they'll escape Rajmuat by noon, if they have any sense. Stay here. I have a wager to collect from the Graveyard Hag. I told her it was folly to bet on a Rittevon king actually having a heart."

"Wait," Aly said. The god bent his glowing head down to listen. "Why don't you tell those poor people his death was natural? That they can't be blamed?"

"I could, if you want them to return and be tortured anyway. The new regents will want to make sure his death was accidental. Healers make mistakes, after all. Actually, since I'm in a good mood . . ." He touched a finger to Aly's forehead, sending a small shock through her. "Find the king's healer. Tell her this would be a good time to catch a ship for Carthak." Then he vanished.

The magic he had placed on Aly told her where to find the healer on duty. The woman slept in a nearby chamber. Aly tried to grab her by the shoulder and shake her, but her hand passed through the healer's flesh.

"Excuse me," she said.

The healer twitched.

"Excuse me," Aly said loudly into the healer's ear. The woman sat up with a yelp, passing through Aly.

The healer glanced around.

"Right here," Aly told her. "Don't I glow, or something?"

The healer gasped. "I meant no offense, Goddess—"

"I'm not a goddess," Aly interrupted. The gods hated it when someone who wasn't a god took the title. "I'm a messenger. King Hazarin just died. I think it was ap—ap . . . that thing where blood vessels in the brain explode."

"Apoplexy," muttered the healer, scrambling out of bed. "If I warned him once . . ."

"He's beyond warning now," Aly informed her. "Perhaps this would be a good time to leave the country. Before they find him."

"I must warn his servants," protested the healer, going to her door. "We'll all be questioned, to ensure he wasn't poisoned."

"His servants are warned," Aly said flatly. The healer turned and stared at her. "They're leaving right now, and they didn't think to tell you. Grab your essentials and run."

As the woman scrambled to pack, Aly returned to the dead man's bedroom. Kyprioth was still absent, but Hazarin's ghost sat by his former body, smiling. She could tell it was the king: he looked as if someone had painted his complete portrait on sheer cloth, except that no painter would have done a picture of Hazarin in his nightgown.

"You're very cheerful for a man who's dead," Aly remarked.

The ghost looked at her. "But I'm well out of it," he explained. "All the plotting, never knowing who's a friend and who isn't, wondering if the food I eat is poisoned or if someone's buying grim spells to use against me. It's done. Are you the Black God?"

"No," Aly replied, "I'm a mortal. The god I—" She hesitated, not wanting to say it, but she had to give *some* explanation. "The god I serve brought me here, to see what happens."

Hazarin shook his head. "It's a bad business, meddling with gods," he told Aly wisely.

"I know," Aly said ruefully. "If it helps, you died a natural death. That's what my god said, anyway."

"I would have died of something," Hazarin replied. "Really, I suppose I signed my death warrant the day I made Dunevon my heir, with my sister Imajane and her husband as regents, should I die before Dunevon came of age. My spies told me this afternoon that Imajane's looking for death spells. This was a much better way to go, and probably everyone will think she had me killed anyway." He grinned at the thought.

"You don't sound upset," Aly remarked. "If *my* half sister looked to have me killed, I'd be *very* upset."

"Not at all," Hazarin replied. "We weren't raised to *like* one another. My father thought that if we did, we'd band together and get rid of him."

"It doesn't sound like a happy way to live," Aly murmured.

"Now you know why I'm glad to be out of it," Hazarin told her. "It's—" Abruptly he stood and bowed at the door. Aly glanced at it over her shoulder and turned. A tall shape, robed and hooded, made all of shadows, was standing there. "I am ready to follow you, Great One," Hazarin told the shadow that was the Black God. "This girl says she's mortal."

Though Aly couldn't really see much of the god's form in the dark room, she was convinced he looked her way. She didn't want to die with so much left unfinished. This god could take her now if he wished to do so. Trembling, Aly knelt. She felt a warm, comforting pressure on her shoulder, as if someone had squeezed it. When she looked up, Hazarin's ghost and the god were gone, leaving behind the shell of Hazarin's body.

Time passed. Kyprioth finally returned at dawn with a glowing chess set. He and Aly played until a guard, concerned by the lack of activity in the royal bedchamber, cautiously opened the door. He cried the alarm. As Kyprioth and Aly watched, people came and went. Other guards were called to search for the missing servants and healer.

At last another healer arrived, a blond, cross-looking man. He was rumpled, as if they had dragged him from bed to see to the dead king. He was just finishing his examination when the icy princess Imajane and her husband, Rubinyan, arrived. Like the healer, they looked as if they had rushed to pull on their elegant clothes.

"Well?" demanded Imajane sharply, her blond head high. "Was it poison?"

"It was the poison of rich gravies, fatty meats, and too much cursed coconut, as he was warned time after time, Your Highness," retorted the healer. "He died of apoplexy. Don't think you can torture another answer out of me, if you please. Not only am I the head of the guild, but he was not my charge. The healer who had him in care is gone. Fled, I should imagine."

Imajane glanced at the captain of the guards. "The servants fled as well?" The captain bowed. "Find them and the healer," Imajane ordered in a crisp, elegant voice. "Search wherever you must." She looked at her husband. "My dear?"

"All things seem plain enough." Rubinyan spoke firmly in measured, deliberate tones.

Aly shook her head in pity for Hazarin. Except for Dunevon, these people were his only family, and they obviously didn't sorrow over his senseless death. "We must ensure that the servants do not gossip," Rubinyan continued. "Until we can make certain that the change of rulership is complete. Dunevon must be crowned as soon as possible. We need the Mithran High Priest. He can do it quickly now, and we can stage a ceremony with all manner of pomp later."

"Certainly Your Highnesses can and must crown the new king before all else," said the healer, drawing a sheet over Hazarin's face. "But it is well past dawn. There has been too much coming and going here. By noon the whole city will know the king is dead." He flung the terrace curtains wide and yelped, staggering back, eyes wide with terror. "Who needs servants to bugle the news?" he cried, pointing.

Imajane and Rubinyan moved forward to see what had frightened the man. Stormwings perched on the terrace rail, males and females alike, their bare, human chests streaked with filth and caked with dark fluids, their steel wings and claws gleaming in the early-morning sun. They grinned broadly, steel teeth glinting, and spread their wings, sending darts of reflected sunlight and an unspeakable smell into the room.

"Got something for us?" one of them asked. "Dead kings always mean trouble, fighting in the streets, with plenty of hate and dead bodies. A meal for us."

"Not today," Rubinyan said firmly. "Order will be preserved." He yanked the drapes shut.

"You've trouble at your backs, mortal, and you're too full of yourself to notice!" shrieked a female, her voice cutting through the heavy brocade drapes. "If I were you, I'd watch for the Trickster's choice!"

Aly looked at Kyprioth. "Do they mean me, or just the changes you're setting in motion?"

"They're Stormwings," replied Kyprioth evenly. "They're just stirring things up."

Aly raised an eyebrow. "Somehow I don't believe you."

Kyprioth shrugged. "And that hurts me," he said in a blithe tone. "You have no idea how much that hurts me."

Time passed. The Mithran High Priest and his acolytes hurried to the palace. There, in the throne room, Aly and Kyprioth looked on as the three-year-old Dunevon was prompted through a brief coronation. Aly felt bad for the little boy, who was just Elsren's age. Dunevon looked thoroughly terrified. He obeyed Imajane's orders, acting his part like a trained pony in front of as many nobles and guild leaders as his regents could find. At last he sat perched on the immense teak throne that dwarfed him, a small, pearl-bedecked crown on his dark curls. On his right, his half sister and regent, Imajane, held Dunevon's diamond-crowned scepter. On his left, his co-regent, Rubinyan, held a pillow with the bared sword of the king's justice on it.

Bronau stood in the third rank of the nobles before the dais. He was unhappy, the look in his eyes murderous as he stared first at Imajane, then his brother. This was not the laughing, charming man who had spent so many days with the Balitangs. Looking at him now, Aly saw him as a volcano on the edge of explosion. Imajane and Rubinyan saw it, too. Their eyes continually flicked to Bronau throughout the proceedings.

Once the last hymns were sung, Imajane stepped forward. "We have a new king, to ensure our safety as we take our beloved former king to his resting place," she proclaimed, her voice ringing through the stone hall. "Now must His Majesty, and his subjects, give way to the condition of mourning, in honor of our beloved Hazarin, and to cleanse our souls of sorrow."

Imajane beckoned the Black God's High Priest forward from the first rank of notables. It would be his duty to see to Hazarin's burial. As he stood before the dais and proclaimed the order of the funeral rites, Aly turned to Kyprioth. "It just occurred to me: if it's afternoon here, it's afternoon in Lombyn. I have to get back, before they bury *me*."

"They won't," Kyprioth said blithely. "Ochobu won't let them. Just enjoy the performance. How many royal funerals have you been to?"

"Why keep me dawdling?" inquired Aly at her most patient. "The Balitangs should know they have a new king, again."

"There are a few more things you should see," Kyprioth replied. "We'll just wait."

"I don't *want* to wait," Aly said firmly. "I need to get back. If something happens to any of the Balitang children while I'm kept here, our wager is finished. You can't say I lost if something happens to them when you have me a whole country away."

"Nothing will happen. The wager stands," Kyprioth told her.

"I'm *bored*," she informed him. "I bore easily. I do *not* wish to loll about here while everyone talks and eats and does whatever other silly things these luarin pests do for fun."

"There, at least, I can help you," Kyprioth said. He raised a glowing arm and wrote a sign in the air. Shadows wrapped around her.

She drifted for some time. At one point she thought she was waking up inside her own body. She heard Ochobu say firmly, "I can do nothing here."

"No more should you." Aly struggled to open her eyes: that was Nawat's voice. What was he doing in Inti, where she had gone to sleep? He had stayed at Tanair that day. "The god has her fast," the crow-man continued. "He will give her up when he is done with her." Into Aly's ear he whispered, "If he does not give you back, my flock and our kinfolk will make him suffer."

Aly struggled to reassure him, and to say his breath didn't smell of bugs in the least. In the end, the darkness in which she floated pulled her back into its depths.

Finally her awareness returned. Now she was standing in a luxurious child's room. Expensive gilded and painted toys lay on the floor. A pair of hounds barely out of puppyhood wrestled for control of a silk table runner. Dunevon, clad all in black velvet, giggled and clapped his hands as he watched. Half-eaten marzipan fruits, candied violets, and raisins lay scattered on the rug around the boy.

Aly didn't like that. From her own experience with Elsren and Petranne, she knew it was bad to give a child so many sweets. Didn't the little king have a nursemaid, someone to look after him properly? Aly thought very little of those who dressed a little boy in expensive velvets, then left him to play on the floor. She looked around for the god, but Kyprioth was nowhere in view.

Wood creaked. A tapestry bulged. Someone pushed it aside to enter the room: Bronau. He was holding a wooden marionette in one hand.

"Uncle Bronau!" cried Dunevon, running to him. "How did you come in? Was it magic?"

"No, just a secret door," Bronau replied, catching the boy king up in one arm. "It's *our* secret now." He jiggled the marionette invitingly for the child. "I told you I would bring you a present. I wanted it to be a surprise, just between us. Is Your Majesty pleased?"

"I'm not a majesty," replied the king, pouting. For a moment he looked much like his dead half brother. "Hazarin's a majesty. I'm a highness. I keep telling them, and they keep doing it wrong."

Bronau chuckled, that rich, seductive sound he had so often lavished on Sarai. "Don't you see, Hazarin had to go away. Before he left, he made you a majesty," he explained. He looked around nervously.

Aly didn't like Bronau's manner. His charming mask often slipped, to reveal tension-bright eyes and tight jaw muscles. He was up to no good.

"Where's your cloak, Dunevon?" he asked.

The boy pointed to a clothes press. "But it's summer. I don't need a cloak in summer."

"We're going sailing," Bronau told him, offering the child his best smile. "I have a wonderful ship waiting in the harbor."

"Sailing?" asked the boy, clearly delighted. "Can we go see the howler monkeys at home and winged horses and maybe a kraken?"

Bronau crossed the room, still holding the boy. "I'd prefer to avoid the kraken, Your Majesty," he said, fumbling one-handed to open the press. "But there will be monkeys, even merpeople. Perhaps, if you're very good, a herd of winged horses. There's one on Imahyn Isle, did you know that?" He scrabbled through layers of clothes until he produced the cloak. Once the press was shut, Bronau stood Dunevon on it and put the cloak over the child's shoulders, tying it securely.

"Can't we go in the morning?" asked Dunevon. "This cloak's *hot*."

Bronau chuckled without humor. "Actually, sire, it must be now. Uncle Rubinyan and Aunt Imajane want to send me to Carthak. If I go there, I'd never see my favorite little king again. I'd rather take you sailing now." He raised Dunevon's hood and tightened it until the child's face was barely visible.

"But it's too *hot*," complained the boy, flailing under the garment's heavy folds. "I don't need a cloak. I don't want to go sailing now. Aunt Imajane promised I could have jugglers if I ate all my supper."

"Well, I have supper waiting on the boat," said Bronau, picking the boy up once more. "We'll find you jugglers even if you don't eat your supper. Dunevon, just hold still and do as you're bid!"

"I don't want to!" wailed the boy, his eyes filling with tears. "I want jugglers now, and my belly hurts!"

Bronau clapped a hand over Dunevon's mouth. "That's not all that will hurt if you don't be quiet!" he snapped.

The two dogs had stopped their play when Bronau came in. Dunevon's greeting had told them this was no stranger, but their manner changed the moment he began to cry. They barked shrilly, advancing as their young master fought Bronau's grip. Suddenly Dunevon shuddered with the effect of too many sweets on a young stomach. He vomited into the hand Bronau held over his mouth.

The man reacted just as Aly would have done: he swore and dropped Dunevon, holding his drenched hand out. "You disgusting little brat!" he cried, trying to clean himself on a tapestry. "You did that on purpose!"

Dunevon ran across the room, screaming as he wept. The door burst open, revealing a handful of guards. Beyond them Aly saw a bottle of wine and a pair of dice on the floor, explaining why they hadn't checked on their king until now.

"Halt in the king's name!" cried one of them, fighting to get clear of his fellows so he could draw his sword.

"Halt!" yelled another guard.

Bronau looked at Dunevon. The boy was out of his reach now. The guards planted themselves between him and his quarry. He started to draw his sword, reconsidered, then fled through the secret door. The guards poured after him, leaving the sick king to scream alone.

"Is he mad?" whispered Aly. "He just tried to kidnap the king!"

"Not mad, necessarily." Kyprioth's glowing form materialized beside Aly. "Hungry for power, which Imajane and Rubinyan will never give him. If he can't get it here, he will try to find it elsewhere. Those who search for him will bring power in their train, power they will bring to bear on anyone who tries to help Bronau. So, now, Aly of Tortall. We come to the days when you shall win or lose our wager—"

He stopped abruptly as two bright forms appeared before them, shining so fiercely that Aly shaded her eyes. They solidified until she could tell that they were male and female, and make out their features. The man, black-skinned and powerfully built, a crown like the rays of the sun blazing on his head, wore gold armor and carried a spear. The woman was bare-breasted in the style of the priestesses of old Ekallatum, with a bell-like skirt hanging from its bodice. The crown atop her tumble of dark, wavy locks blazed silver like the moon. Immense snakes twined around her bare arms.

"Brother, what is it that you do here?" they demanded, their attention on Kyprioth. Aly clapped her hands over her mouth to prevent herself from screaming. The divine voices and presences tore through her ghostlike body, shredding her like ancient silk.

Mithros—he could only be Mithros, Aly knew—added, "We left you the seas that cradle this place, and the seas alone." His voice rolled like horses at the stampede, hammering Aly's ears. Daggers of pain thrust into her skull as she fought to keep from fainting.

"We have been occupied with affairs on the other side of this world. Now we return to find you in the Rajmuat palace, which is no part of the sea." Aly's mother had described the Goddess's voice as the belling of hounds and the bugle of hunting horns. To Aly it was more like the shriek of triumphant eagles and the slow, whispering glide of snakes on rock. Her knees wanted to give way, *demanding* that she kneel. She would not do it. It was one thing to kneel to the Black God, who would take her in hand one day. It was another to kneel to the pair who had done the raka such a terrible wrong when they supported the luarin conquest.

Aly fought. She trembled as she summoned all of her willpower to stay upright. They were gods, but *she* was not sworn to them. She would *not* collapse in a heap.

"Should brothers and sisters suspect wrongdoing at every turn?" asked Kyprioth. "Are you so unsure—"

Aly kicked him. Later, when she was herself again, she would question her sanity, and wonder how his glowing body felt the kick from her insubstantial leg. Right now she saw only that all three brilliant heads turned their attention to her.

She followed her instincts. She smiled, bowed deeply to the Great Goddess and Mithros, and said in a tone her father would know quite well, "Begging your pardons, O Great Gods, ruler of we mortals, but I ask that you forgive my father's friend and patron." Kyprioth *had* said he'd worked with her da, after all. Remembering to speak only the truth, she continued, "At present I am deeply interested in the politics in Rajmuat—*vitally* interested, I should say. If my time here is to be well spent, I should understand how things work. These Isles have long been a factor in Tortall's politics—" She cut herself off carefully. She dared not play this too broadly, or they might suspect a rat. Humbly she continued, "What am I saying? You are the Great Gods. You know what there is here to know. Forgive me, I beg—I am flustered, standing before you. You divine brother Kyprioth is my father's patron. He has been helping me to understand the Isles. Since I was stranded on Lombyn with the mortals I presently serve, Kyprioth generously gave me this chance to observe the change in kingship." There, she thought, wondering if her insubstantial face was sweaty. I spoke only the truth.

She kept her head down; the light of the gods' faces hurt her ghostly eyes in any case. Glowing fingers pressed her chin up and forced her to gaze into eyes as green as emeralds, as measureless as the Royal Forest in high summer. "I can look into your heart, Alianne of Pirate's Swoop," the Goddess said, her voice making Aly shiver. "I can see if you lie."

Aly stepped away from that hand, whose touch burned even her unreal body. Once again she bowed respectfully. "Great Mother, you know I speak the truth," she said, choosing her words with immense care. "You could see the lie on me. If you know the family I serve, you understand how important it is that they know of Hazarin's death and Bronau's treason." Not for nothing had she listened to Aunt Daine! "Forgive me, Great Mother. I don't mean to be disobliging. Your divine brother Kyprioth knows the danger to the family I serve. He brought me here to see these things at first hand."

It was hard to read the Goddess's alabaster features in the blaze of her glory. Still, Aly could have sworn the Goddess raised her brows and pursed her mouth. Aly knew that expression from her mother: Alanna looked that way when she had a suspicion that someone was not being honest with her. "Your mother is dedicated to me," she pointed out.

Aly bowed yet again. "That is true, Great Goddess, but I am too much like my father. I must follow his path, in service to the Trickster."

"You are very like your father," the Great Mother said at last, her voice shuddering through Aly. "It is the kind of prank he *would* play."

"No prank, Goddess," Aly assured her. "What I do here is entirely serious."

"Enough," said Mithros impatiently, his voice sounding in the marrow of Aly's bones. "The Teasai on the other side of the world strike their gongs in the call for war. Their women beg you, my sister, for the strength to fight their city's enemies." To Kyprioth he said, "When we made peace nearly three human centuries past, you lost your eminence here. Do not think we will take it well if you break that peace."

"Brother," Kyprioth said reproachfully as he spread his hands, the picture of glowing innocence, "surely I know when I have been beaten."

The universe around them wrenched. When Aly could see clearly again, Mithros and the Goddess had vanished.

She looked at Kyprioth. From the movement of his light-shape, she could tell he was stroking his beard in thought. She poked his glowing ribs with her ghostly elbow. "You owe me," she informed him.

"I know that," Kyprioth replied slowly. "Well, never let it be said that I do not return favor for favor. Shall I free you from our wager? Take you home and speak to your father on your behalf? Then neither of us will owe the other."

Aly pursed her lips. "How can I trust you?"

"I owe you. Even tricksters must pay what they owe."

Aly thought about it. To be home again, without this metal ring around her neck; to have Da give her the chance she yearned for—those would be fine things. The Scanran war was dragging to its end. Soon her mother would return, as would Aunt Daine and Uncle Numair and the baby. There would be hot baths and the newest fashions. As the warriors came home the capital would light up with celebrations. Aly could read books, laze about, dress like a girl of property once more. She could even speak her mind instead of manipulating people.

She smiled and shook her head, trying to imagine the butterfly self she was among the men of the court. Instead she saw Winnamine and Mequen, Sarai and Dove, Ulasim and Chenaol. Nawat would come back to Tortall with her, but Lokeij and Junai would not. And Kyprioth had hinted Bronau would bring danger to Tanair.

"No," she said at last, "a bet's a bet. You don't wiggle out of this one that easily. And if I win the bet, you pay what was wagered, *and* you still owe me."

Kyprioth sighed. "You drive a hard bargain, Aly."

Before she could ask him if he was trying to pull the wool over her eyes, he swept her up in a glowing arm and shot into the air, through the palace roof. They were on their way north again.

Something occurred to her as they rose into the air over the city. Her mother was the Goddess's chosen. Why hadn't the Goddess known she was missing? Aly knew her mother wouldn't have wasted all this time, knowing she could call on the Goddess and not doing so. Kyprioth, Aly realized. "Why hasn't the Goddess come for me?" she asked the god. "What did you do? You can't tell me that Mother hasn't been praying to her for a glimpse of my whereabouts."

"I wasn't going to deny it," replied the god. "You know I dare not let my sister find out what I'm up to. I would be *thousands* of years coming back from where she and my brother would send me. One of my friends keeps your lovely mother company. She catches your mother's prayers and keeps them for me."

"You'd better hope Mother never finds out, or you'll have worse than your sister and brother to contend with," Aly told him. "You don't want the Lioness hunting for you."

"I know that," Kyprioth said. "I assure you, I am being quite careful."

Aly said nothing more as they traveled. Instead she reviewed the various combinations of results that might come from the events she had just witnessed. Bronau had planned to ask Hazarin to recall the Balitangs. Now Hazarin was dead. How friendly would Imajane and Rubinyan be to the Balitangs?

She dared not underestimate Bronau. He was now more dangerous than ever, as a man on the run and in disgrace, possibly declared a traitor. Whatever had driven him to such a harebrained stunt? Surely he knew he couldn't escape the palace with a three-year-old, even if he did know secret passages?

Why hadn't Bronau waited? Once his brother and sister-in-law were settled in their regency, they would have been less vigilant for unrest. Bronau could have gathered and bribed followers in his own time, ensuring his ability to seize power without taking unnecessary chances. Now he would be hunted the length and breadth of the Copper Isles. The new regents would view all of his friends with suspicion. The Balitangs would be among the first to draw their attention, since they had housed Bronau only weeks before.

The raka would need more patrols at Tanair. She would have to talk to Ulasim and Fesgao about that. With Ochobu and Aly to make sure no spies were brought into their ranks, the raka could expand their unofficial army.

She hardly noticed when she popped back into her body. Her planning stopped only when true sleep washed over her.

You asked me why the king doesn't just call on the gods for help with Scanra. We mustn't get too dependent on the gods. On the day before King Jonathan's coronation, the Great Mother Goddess spoke of a crossroads in time, when not even the gods can predict how things might go. At such times they must step away and let us deal with things. It's a blessing, in a way. It evens the balance and saves us mortals from being the gods' puppets. Still, it's hard to think of it as a blessing when you're frightened, you don't know why, and all you want is for the god to tell you what the bad thing is so you can hunt it down and kill it.

—*From a letter to Aly when she was fourteen, from her mother*

15

WINGED MESSENGER

When Aly woke at last, her muscles screamed in protest as she tried to sit up. Her mouth tasted disgusting. Her teeth felt as if they had a thick coating of slime. She was lying on a cot in a house that had whitewashed walls.

"How long?" Her question emerged from her throat as a croak. She looked around stiffly. They had brought her back from Inti and put her in Tanair's makeshift infirmary.

Nawat, asleep on a chair by the door, was startled into wakefulness. He raced across to Aly and touched her face. "I am very angry with the god for keeping you so long," he said, his dark eyes worried.

Aly smiled at him. "It was very instructive, though," she whispered.

Nawat kissed her swiftly on the mouth, then raced out the door. When he returned, he brought Ochobu with him.

"How long was I away?" she asked the old mage.

Ochobu sat on the cot's edge and lifted one of Aly's eyelids. "Five days," she said. She checked Aly's other eye. "We carried you home on a litter. You need a bath." She rose and looked down at Aly, her old eyes as unreadable as a god's. "Is it bad, what he showed you?"

"Bad enough," Aly admitted. "I'll need to talk to Ulasim and the others right away. I don't care what they're doing. Are Their Graces about?"

"The duchess and the children help Chenaol to put up fruit and vegetables against the winter," Ochobu replied. "The duke is in the village. He oversees all the new building here."

"They can wait until tonight, I think," Aly said, rubbing her temples. "But I need Ulasim, Chenaol, Lokeij, Fesgao, and you, as soon as I'm cleaned up. We need to prepare for serious trouble."

For two weeks after Hazarin's death and Bronau's attempt to kidnap

Dunevon Aly roamed. She covered Tanair's castle and village on her own, then rode all over the plateau in the company of Sarai, Dove, and their guards. It was a relief to leave the keep each day. After hearing the circumstances around Hazarin's death, Aly's news about the change in government and Bronau's rashness, Mequen and Winnamine seemed burdened, as if someone in the house had died. The adults understood that a nation with a child king was vulnerable to rebellion and trouble from its enemies. Sarai was furious that Bronau would frighten a child so badly. Dove's opinions stayed behind the younger girl's dark eyes.

Ulasim had recruited another raka patrol, but the harvest had begun, and every hand was needed to bring it in. Tanair winters were harsh. The crops had to be brought in and food laid up. Aly understood the thin line between poverty and starvation. Harvest at Pirate's Swoop was always a scramble, one in which the baron's entire family worked in the fields. Despite knowing that, Aly had to struggle to hide her impatience with the raka. Bronau was on the loose, with the regents searching for him. If she had an army to keep the Balitangs safe, she would still wonder if she had planned for everything.

Aly calculated the time it would take Bronau to reach Lombyn. It would be a week if his passage was as swift as the Balitangs' had been. To that she added a handful of days on the road, assuming he landed on the western coast, or a week if he came from Dimari. When a third week passed with no sign of the renegade prince, Aly relaxed slightly. Perhaps Bronau had been captured. Or perhaps he had decided that Tanair was the first place his enemies would look for him.

Waiting for something to happen, Aly met with the raka conspirators each night to review their arrangements and hear their news. She also visited Nawat to hear what the crows had to report. Only with Nawat could Aly enjoy the summer's calm. The nights were getting cool, but it was warm at Nawat's side. Once he finished with the news, he taught Aly the names the crows had for the stars, the different types of cloud, and the moon. The only thing that had the same name for crows as it did for humans was the constellation known as the Cat.

"My mother knew the Cat," Aly confided. "At least, that's what she told me when I was a little girl. That the star-Cat became a mortal one, and taught her things as she grew up. It was my favorite story, even if it wasn't true."

"Why should it not be true?" Nawat asked. "The Cat is a god of sorts. He makes his own decisions to help or to hinder two-leggers." He put an arm around Aly.

She leaned into his hold, not thinking, then tugged away. "Nawat!" she exclaimed. "What is that supposed to be?"

"Don't you like it?" he asked. "Fesgao does it to Tulpa the miller's daughter, and she nestles against him."

"I'm not Tulpa," Aly insisted. "Besides, I can't be distracted." She got to her feet hurriedly and thanked all the gods that she did not blush as easily as her mother did. "Nestling is *very* distracting."

"I know." Nawat got to his feet, resting his hands on her shoulders. "You are Aly, who guards us all." He bent down and kissed her slowly and sweetly. Aly clung to him because she was afraid to try to stand on knees gone to jelly. At last Nawat released her. "Good night," he said cheerfully. He walked out through the inner courtyard gate, on his way home to Falthin.

Aly remained where she was, a hand pressed to her lips, for a long time.

Realizing that if Bronau came they were as prepared as they could be, Aly threw her energies into the winter preparations at Tanair. There was plenty for everyone to do, from the duke and the duchess to the child who brought in the eggs each day. The older Balitang women and their twenty servants and slaves worked at the tasks of the season: boiling and jellying, peeling and cutting, grinding and sealing, smoking and pickling. Mequen was everywhere, helping to get the crops in, the wood cut and stored, and making sure Tanair was weatherproofed. Like the village children, Elsren and Petranne helped their families. Each night Petranne showed Aly her day's work, presenting the wads of lumpily spun wool with as much pride as if they were the finest thread. Elsren collected baskets of pine cones to use as kindling, losing half of them on the way home.

Weapons training was the only thing to continue uninterrupted. Sarai worked on more complex battle dances. These were combinations of footwork, thrusts, blocks, and chops meant to be used until she could do the sequences without thought in response to a real attack. Winnamine still labored to master the most basic battle dance, but she practiced ferociously, ignoring blisters and aching muscles. Dove's archery improved daily. She could now shoot a cluster of five arrows in a circle no wider than her stepmother's hand. All the same, Dove never got so good that Nawat couldn't catch her arrows. Aly grinned to see grizzled veterans consoling the twelve-year-old, assuring her that they, too, could not loose a shot that Nawat didn't catch.

One morning, as Aly rode out with her young mistresses and their guards, she noted clouds along the western edge of the mountains. "Let's make it quick," she advised. "We take the medicines to Pohon and back. That looks like rain to me."

"You worry too much, Aly," Sarai scoffed as she mounted up. "Those clouds are miles away."

"Aly is right," Fesgao told his mistress firmly. "To Pohon and back, no farther. Storms move fast up here. You should know this by now."

Sarai put up her nose and galloped her mount through Tanair's open village gate. Aly watched Fesgao gallop after Sarai and shook her head.

"She'll calm down," Dove told Aly as the two girls rode out of Tanair. Nawat followed them at an easy trot. Ochobu had commissioned him to gather roadside herbs for her that day. "She just doesn't know what she thinks about Bronau going so wrong. The only way she knows to deal with it is to ride hard."

Aly grinned and glanced down at Nawat. "I don't suppose you'd flirt with Sarai?" she asked the crow-man. "She thinks you're handsome. You could clean the bugs from your teeth."

"And you aren't old and stupid like Bronau," Dove added.

"I am too young for Sarai," Nawat replied soberly. "I am not even a month old. Sarai is ancient compared to me."

Aly and Dove giggled. "Oh, tell her that when I'm there to see," Dove begged. "I want to watch her face when you do."

They caught up to Sarai and Fesgao five miles outside Pohon. The other two riders had reined up at the spot where a barely used track met the road.

"Sarai, no!" cried Dove, exasperated beyond her usual calm. "Can't we, just *once,* go somewhere and return *quickly?*"

Nawat raised a finger, his eyes sharp. "Hold."

Aly held very still, listening. Why had the usually polite Nawat voiced something like an order? Then she heard it, the raucous clamor of dozens of crows in the East. She strained to hear, but many of them called different things, some of which she had never been taught. "What—" she began.

"A winged four-legger comes from the mountains that hold the morning sun," said Nawat. "She bears a fledgling two-legger on her back. They seek the stone sti—the castle."

Aly frowned. "Winged . . . a kudarung. A big one, to carry a child on her back."

"That's a royal messenger," Sarai commented, her perfect brows knit in disapproval. "Only the Rittevon line may call on winged horses as messengers. I doubt that Dunevon would think of using one unless he wanted a ride."

All three girls wheeled their mounts and raced to Tanair, their guards on their heels. Nawat was left behind to make his way on foot.

They had to slow to a trot through the village. By then Aly had already spotted the new arrivals: a boy or girl of ten, clad in shearling garments against the cold of the upper air, strapped to a large gray mare with a white mane and tail and huge, bat-like wings. Messenger and mount sailed over the girls' heads. With an adjustment to her Sight, Aly could see the winged horse badge of the Rittevon family—they would never use the raka word kudarung—on both the messenger's tunic and the chest piece of the kudarung's harness.

The pair set down within the castle's inner courtyard as the girls and their guards rode through the gate. Ochobu's three tiny kudarung darted from the kitchen to circle the gray, looking like blackbirds against a thundercloud. Dove tumbled off her horse's back and raced inside to alert the duchess. Sarai ordered Veron to find the duke. Aly slipped off Cinnamon and took the three mounts to Lokeij and his stable boys.

"You know what the luarin say, don't you?" Lokeij murmured as he watched the messenger unbuckle the straps that held her to her mare. "Deadly news rides horses that fly."

Aly sighed. "If only the Rittevons use them as messengers, I can see how people might think that."

"The custom is an old one, from the time before the kudarung were banished to the Divine Realms," Lokeij said. "Our people had all but forgotten, until they returned twelve years past. Once the kudarung came here in flocks, all sizes of them, to nest and rear their young."

Aly washed her hands in a bucket of water, the picture of idle innocence. To Lokeij she said quietly, "Someone implied to me they served the old raka monarchs freely, but that King Oron had to capture some and breed them for his service."

"It was farsighted of Oron, may we live to spit on his grave." Lokeij grinned, revealing all the gaps in his teeth. "When Sarai takes power, the people will see the kudarung come to her freely. They will see she holds the crown by right."

"Don't say that aloud, even to a friend," Aly warned. "The less it's mentioned, the less chance someone will overhear who shouldn't."

"Cautious Aly of the crooked eye," said Lokeij with a chuckle.

"If you keep sweet-talking me so, I'll charge you before the duke of turning my poor frivolous head," Aly replied, batting her eyelashes at him. "An incautious spy is soon dead. And don't start asking again who I was before I ended up here."

"You think that others don't wonder?" Lokeij asked, his eyes glittering with interest. "That Their Graces don't ask how many tiny signs and tricks a god could teach a mortal in a short time?"

"What I think doesn't matter," said Aly as she shook her hands dry. "I just live my life at the god's beck and call."

Lokeij snorted his disbelief.

Aly waved a lazy hand at him. "Now, if you'll excuse me, I'm going to snoop."

Once the duke arrived, he and Winnamine retired to their private rooms with Sarai and the messenger. They didn't ask for a servant to attend them. Aly idled in the great hall, restacking logs on the hearth, until Sarai appeared at the top of the stairs. "Aly, have Ulasim find this girl a place for the night," she called, urging the messenger down the stairs. "Papa and Mama have asked for you to bring some wine."

Aly obeyed, summoning Ulasim for the messenger and going to Chenaol for the wine. When she reached the duke's rooms with the tray, Sarai took it, then poured cups for her father and stepmother. Winnamine offered the messenger's letter to Aly. All three Balitangs looked haunted.

Aly took the letter and scanned it. The seal was the Rittevons': a winged horse triumphant, rearing on its hind legs, wings outstretched. The writing on the document was firm and elegant, though it was not in the professionally smooth hand of a scribe.

My dear Mequen and Winna,

I regret that this letter brings no good news to you. King Hazarin is dead of apoplexy. Dunevon, my lady's half brother, is now king, with Imajane and me as his regents. That would be tragic enough. Hazarin was in his prime, and no kingdom ruled by a child is stable. There is worse news, however. My brother, in madness or folly, attempted to kidnap Dunevon, to what purpose I cannot guess. He has been formally charged with high treason. Our agents seek him throughout the realm. Already we have learned that my brother is attempting to create rebellion among the outland nobility. This cannot be allowed.

I am concerned that he may seek refuge with you and your family, as he did when he incurred Oron's disfavor. For the love you bear me, will you ask him to come to Rajmuat, to answer the charges? If he comes of his own accord, I may be able to smooth things over with the king's council. Should his enemies take him, I fear for my brother's life. He has always said you and Winnamine are the coolest heads in the family. I agree. If you can persuade him to return, Imajane and I will be forever in your debt. We are reversing Oron's charges against you. Soon you will be able to return to Rajmuat. I cannot envision keeping the Midwinter Festival without my best friends there. With thanks from Imajane and from me,

Your friend Rubinyan

Aly reread the letter. *Rubinyan says he's worried,* she thought, *but he never calls Bronau by his name or implies that he cares for him. And he doesn't ask the Balitangs to come home now, when he is as good as king himself, for all that he calls them "friends." Does he want them to serve as bait for his brother first?*

She returned the letter to Mequen. *Of course His Grace will do it,* she thought, watching the duke's troubled face as he rolled the letter up into a tight scroll. *He has faith that Bronau can explain his way out of this, or that Rubinyan will save him from the gallows. But he can also tell that something is not right here.*

Mequen tapped the rolled letter against his leg. "He sent this by winged horse," he said at last. "It's a private letter from him to me, but he used royal messengers for it. Is he mad? In the reign of Hanoren the First, it was ruled that no regent may take on the prerogatives of the Crown. That includes the use of winged horses."

"He wanted the news to reach us as quickly as possible, with all the distance between us," the duchess explained. "He thought you would understand. And it does involve the attempt on Dunevon."

"I do not like it," replied Mequen. "It is most improper."

"Perhaps Aunt Imajane wished us to get the letter quickly, and she granted the use of the messengers?" asked Sarai. "She is as royal as Dunevon, even if she can't inherit."

Aly folded her hands in front of her. "Will Your Grace tell this to the household?" she asked politely. "Let them know that the prince's next visit may be . . ." She chose her words carefully. "Different," she finished.

The duke and duchess traded glances. It was Sarai who replied. "Is this the kind of thing servants should know?"

Aly looked at her. "If the prince comes and there is a fight, they'll be involved," she pointed out. "And some of the servants . . ." She stopped. Light was growing in the room, casting the family and the furnishings into high relief. The source of it, she realized, was her.

With a mental sigh she silently asked Kyprioth, "Will you stop playing games?"

"You want them to listen, don't you?" asked the god. "Keep talking."

Aly resigned herself. I must be sure that my next task in life can be handled without gods, she told herself. To the Balitangs she said, "You have servants who will be useful if things go wrong. Ulasim, for one. Ochobu. Royal spy or not, Veron must be warned that Bronau may come armed, with soldiers on his tail." Aly went silently to the door to the servants' stair to reveal Dove, who had been listening again. Aly beckoned her inside and closed the door. "Lady Dove should have been here already, to further her instruction about the world she must live in."

"Dove, eavesdropping is a slave's trick," the duke told his younger daughter.

Dove looked down. "I'm sorry, Papa," she replied, though she was clearly not.

Aly looked at the family. She still gleamed with power lent to her by the god. "I advise you only because I want to ensure nothing happens to you. I want to keep you and your children safe, and I cannot do it alone. I am not the sort to go dashing around with a sword in each hand."

The duchess pursed her lips. "When you put it that way, of course, we must listen," she said drily. The glow that blazed from Aly faded.

"Find those you think must know and send them to us here," Mequen instructed. "We will explain."

Once she'd found Ochobu, Veron, and Ulasim, Aly left it to the duke to share the news. She wandered down to the kitchen. There Chenaol and the kitchen staff were feeding the messenger, bombarding the girl with questions. Chenaol winked when she saw Aly. The cook would get any scraps of information the messenger might have.

Aly nodded to Chenaol and went outside. Near the stable, the winged horse and Nawat stood forehead to forehead. Nawat's lips moved. Aly watched, fascinated. What *was* Nawat doing?

"They speak, as winged creatures will," Lokeij said. He had appeared at Aly's elbow. "Whatever news the kudarung has, Nawat will hear it."

Aly ran a finger under the metal ring on her neck. It bothered her more than usual tonight, having picked up bits of hay during her day's work.

"Annoying, isn't it?" Lokeij asked. "Now you feel like a raka. Even those who do not wear a metal collar have felt luarin rule chafing for nearly three centuries."

Aly raised an eyebrow at the old man. Here was another chance to make the point she had tried to impress on Ochobu: the greatest problem with the raka's and Kyprioth's plans. "I know luarin rule irks you," she replied evenly. "So let me ask this: does it bother you that blood will be shed to remove *your* collars? That the luarin who try to do their best by you, who only inherited the mess the Rittevons have made, may die to ease the collar off your necks?"

"Do you speak of our lady's family, or of Prince Bronau?" asked Lokeij. "The Jimajen house is known for its brutality to their raka. We will rejoice if Jimajen blood is shed."

Hands in his pockets, Nawat left the winged horse to the meal of oats Lokeij had supplied and sauntered over to the hostler and Aly. "She says that the winter rains will come late in the jungles," he told them. "The fishing is off. She says also that the free kudarung know the old blood is present here, on Lombyn. When the time comes, the kudarung will gather to salute the new queen."

Aly thought this over. A powerful symbol of someone's right to rule was always useful: the appearance of the Dominion Jewel had once convinced Tortallans that Jonathan was the rightful king. She nodded. "Thank her, please. We are honored that the kudarung will help us."

"It will be as it was before," Lokeij whispered, eyes bright with awe. "The rightful queen in Rajmuat, and the kudarung soaring in the skies."

"She isn't on the throne yet," Aly cautioned. "Don't let your dreams outrun your common sense." She took another look at the kudarung, who had folded her wings as she ate greedily. Still thoughtful, Aly returned to the castle, absently running a finger around her slave collar.

When Aly left the tower the following morning, she found Nawat at work outside, as usual. Crows were perched all around the inner courtyard, on every space they could find. There must have been thirty of them.

Nawat greeted her with his warm smile, the one that always got an answering smile from her. "My clan will roost here for a time, until the weather says it is the season to fly down to warmer country. They say they will be sure to empty their bowels off the sides of this nest." With a wave of his hand he indicated the castle walls.

Aly looked at the crows, then at the young man carefully attaching sharp Stormwing fletchings to a heavy arrow shaft. "Another mage killer?" she asked. For the first time she noticed that despite his deftness and assurance, he always worked slowly with the razor-edged Stormwing feathers.

"There are all kinds of mages in the world, and sometimes they run in packs," Nawat replied.

Aly nodded. Looking at the circle of crows, she asked, "Will we need so many?"

Nawat bird-shrugged. "They are my clan. If they are not needed, they will watch the game."

Aly raised an eyebrow as she turned her gaze on him. "Is this a game to you?" she asked.

Nawat looked up. His dark eyes held hers. "You are never a game to me, Aly. And hawks are never a game to crows."

"But you aren't a crow now," she pointed out softly.

"A crow may put on human shape or crow shape, but we remain crows," he replied firmly. "Hawks, too, are the same, whether they are born in human nests or hawk ones. The nestlings must always be protected. Since you have chosen to protect these, I and mine will protect you."

Aly nodded, blinking her eyes against sudden tears. She couldn't think of a thing to say in response to such a declaration of complete friendship. Instead she rested her hand on Nawat's shoulder. His warm fingers covered hers for a moment. Then he returned to his fletching, and Aly wandered out through the gate to inspect the Tanair defenses.

She walked down through the village, waving to the baker and exchanging greetings with the innkeeper's wife. Visda and Ekit raced by, surrounding Aly with goats and sheep. She grinned as they swirled out through the village gate on their way to pasture.

Except for those early risers and the sleepy-looking men-at-arms on the wall, Aly had the ground to herself as she examined the village defenses. Duke Mequen had worked on the wall along with other projects all summer. Much had been done since their arrival, shoring up what was left of the ancient stone wall and bracing the palisade just outside. More than anything Aly wished they'd been able to build the stone wall to the height of the log one. If an enemy came at them with battle fire, the palisade would burn, and the stone walls wouldn't stop anyone. Aly understood why more hadn't been done. The duke could only call on those of his men-at-arms who weren't on duty and the few villagers who didn't have crops to harvest or winter preparations of their own. It didn't make Aly feel any better. She would just have to pray that no enemies came with battle fire, or that those who did fell into the ditch in front of the palisade. If they burned the wooden barrier, the villagers would have to retreat within the castle walls and expect to lose everything outside them.

Aly trudged back up to the castle. Perhaps Ochobu could fireproof the palisade. She wanted to be certain the duke could summon the villagers inside the walls and warn the valley herders to hide with their stock. They needed ways to heat barrels of oil or water and get them onto the walls to dump on any attackers . . .

Enough, she told herself, leaning her forehead against the stone of the outer courtyard wall. They'll only let you do so much. His Grace and Veron will have plans laid to bring folk inside the castle and defend it. My job is to twiddle my thumbs and wait for something to happen. If I'm to do that, I may as well go sew winter clothes. I can only act on what information I have, as I have already done. Now it's a matter of waiting.

I *hate* waiting.

"Kyprioth," she called silently in a teasing voice. "Kyprioth, Kyprioth, Kyprioth. Don't pretend you aren't nearby. All this is too important to you. Talk to me."

"You are getting to know me a little too well," the familiar voice said wearily. "What is it?"

"Oh, don't be grumpy," she told him, still being playful. "Isn't it a grand thing that I do know you so well? Now, tell me—something's about to happen, isn't it? The reason why you brought me here in the first place."

"Well?" demanded the god.

"What is it?" Aly wanted to know. "What's coming? I could use a hint. My working blind isn't precisely useful, you know."

"All I see is a coming together of lives and possibilities. Anything could happen."

"Just a little hint? You're a god, you must have some notion," she replied, prodding him.

"I DO NOT." Suddenly the god's voice boomed in her mind as it must boom in the minds of the Balitangs and the raka. Aly locked her knees. She would not drop to the ground, no matter how much Kyprioth sounded like a Great God to her just now. She stubbornly remained on her feet as he continued, "It is the hour of mortal choices. It is your turn to dictate the course of fate. I can do no more."

Just when she thought he was finished, that he'd made his portentous announcement and gone away, she heard him say, much more quietly, "Besides, my brother and sister have returned. Well, I knew they would. Don't betray my trick to them, Aly. Keep them thinking this is just another human squabble."

"Thanks ever so," she thought to him. "I'll do as much for you one day. And you still owe me."

When her sense of Kyprioth's presence faded, Aly sat at the base of the castle wall. She had her answer, in a manner of speaking. Things—events—were unfolding, and now the humans would have to do their part. The gods had to let the dice fall as they may.

Wonderful, Aly thought, leaning her head against the wall. Might I have the Graveyard Hag's dice right now? Aunt Daine says they're weighted with lead, so the Hag wins every roll. I don't mind cheating at a time like this.

A shadow passed over her. Aly looked up to see the kudarung and her rider in flight, on their way back to Dimari.

Three afternoons later the crows at the pass shrieked the news that eleven armed riders were on the road to Tanair. Crows and a raka patrol followed them to the village to make sure that none of the visitors left their group unnoticed.

Nawat was working at his bench when the crows proclaimed the news. "They say that Bronau is with them," he told Aly. She helped him by holding a piece of leather flat on the bench while Nawat cut it up for laces. "The hawk is coming."

Aly nodded. "I have to let go," she warned him. Nawat sat back. Aly released the leather, then ran to report first to the duchess. Winnamine took Aly to the duke, who was reviewing the harvest totals.

"We'll let him in. Bronau can relax, and tell his side of the story. I want to hear what he has to say," he told Aly and his wife. "We owe him that. And I am sure he will do the right thing, once he's had a chance to think it over."

Aly carried word to Chenaol, and thus to Sarai and Dove, who were helping the cook to strain seeds from newly made jelly. To their credit, the girls finished their tasks before they raced to their rooms to change clothes and to move things so their parents could sleep on the third story with them. Bronau would have Winnamine's and Mequen's rooms, but the fourth floor was no longer available to his men-at-arms, as it was full of winter stores. Even Bronau would not suspect his friends did not want his soldiers living among them. Instead they would sleep in one of the new buildings, under Veron's eye.

Aly was cleaned up and wearing a dress by the time Bronau entered the great hall. Mequen and Winnamine waited there to meet him, as did Sarai. Dove had refused to greet the traitor, using words just that blunt. From her position behind Sarai, Aly watched as Bronau handed his outer coat and gloves to one of the house slaves. He approached his friends with his ready smile.

"So grim," he said teasingly. "Whatever can you have heard?" He kissed Winnamine on both cheeks and gave Mequen a man's brisk hug. He took Sarai's hand and kissed her fingers with comic elegance, his raised brows and twinkling eyes drawing a smile from her in spite of herself.

"We've heard dreadful things, my lord," she explained shyly.

"Come up to our rooms and talk," offered Mequen. "Aly, refreshments, please."

Aly curtsied and went to the kitchen. Chenaol had already assembled a tray for her. "Ten men-at-arms, Fesgao says," the cook reported in a whisper for Aly's ears alone. "They've been riding hard. If ten's all he's got, His Grace could simply kill them all and ship Bronau back to Rajmuat. Or kill Bronau and send his pickled head to the regents. It's a good way to make sure there's no more trouble."

"The duke wants to keep it friendly," Ochobu said icily. She was seated at a table, clutching a mug of tea with knobby fingers. "Whoever heard of a luarin that wasn't ready to shed the blood of others? And this is a fine time to have such qualms, when killing the Jimajen prince would simplify things."

Aly grimaced. "Things are not precisely friendly between him and the prince," she pointed out, though privately she agreed that their lives would be far easier if Bronau and his men were dead. The duke was not that kind of person, however. "His Grace says that if Bronau grovels a bit, it will be all right. He says Rubinyan would never order the death of his own brother. We're to wait and see."

"The duke's too good for this, you know," Chenaol said, glaring at Ochobu. "For that luarin snakepit they call the royal court. He always was."

"He's soft," the old mage said harshly. "And he doesn't know anything about the house of Jimajen. They will turn on him with a smile and a razor in their hands."

"Aly." Lokeij stood at the kitchen door, beckoning. Aly went to him. "Something's off," whispered the hostler. "None of these came with him before—not the men, not the horses. And he's brought no body servants. Warn the duke."

Aly nodded and took the tray from Chenaol. The change in attendants could be entirely harmless. Perhaps Bronau hadn't cared to burden himself with body servants when he was on the run. Perhaps they'd been captured. Perhaps his usual warriors had been unable to follow him when he escaped Rajmuat.

I hate *perhaps*es when lives are at stake, she thought as she climbed the stairs. And I'd as soon handle a jar of acid on a bumpy road than try to guess what folly Bronau will commit next.

Once more she poured out wine for everyone in the duke's sitting room, even Sarai. She also murmured Lokeij's news into the duke's ear as she served him. Mequen nodded and gestured for her to take her place behind the duchess. "You can speak before Aly," the duke assured Bronau. "Whom would she tell it to? The grass?"

Bronau smirked at Aly, then addressed his friends. "There was something wrong in Hazarin dying so unexpectedly. I don't suspect my brother, of course," he said, grinning, holding up a hand to stop the protest he expected Mequen to make. "Imajane, though—she doesn't show the madness, but would you care to wager that it skipped her and got every other member of the Rittevon family?"

"Even Dunevon?" asked Winnamine with a smile, offering Bronau the pastry dish. He accepted one and wolfed it down. Aly wondered when he had eaten last.

"Oh, who knows?" asked Bronau. "He's only three, poor lad. Winna, it would break your heart, the way they keep him. No boys his own age in that tomb of a chamber, their servants in place of his . . . I'd never use a child of *my* blood so." He glanced sidelong at Sarai, who ducked her head shyly. "But Imajane is as cold as the ocean deeps. It would never occur to her that Dunevon's a child more than he is a king."

"But you tried to kidnap that king," Mequen said gently. "Bronau, Rubinyan has written to us."

"Ah," said the prince. "So that is why you regard me with such reserve today. It was a rash act, I see that now. I wasn't thinking of anything but getting the boy to safety. If they killed a reigning king, will they stop at murdering a child?"

"I cannot believe Rubinyan would be a part of either crime," Mequen replied stiffly.

Bronau hung his head. "No, no, of course not." He turned his feverish eyes on Winnamine. "Don't you find it suspicious that Hazarin's servants and healer vanished all at once? I'll wager *they* could tell some stories."

"These are all good points," said Mequen, "but until the charges against you are dismissed, you can only sow disorder with such talk." Nothing about him suggested that he knew the true fate of Hazarin's servants and healer. "You must answer to the king's council and clear your name. If the misunderstanding cannot be dismissed, Rubinyan may have to make some gesture. Send you into exile, perhaps, or imprison you at the Stronghold. But your friends will seek your pardon."

"Return and stand trial," suggested Winnamine. "You'll slip the rug out from under them. By running, you only create more doubt in people's minds. Once the council sees and hears you, and knows you felt that you did your duty by the Crown, I think you'll find more allies than you suspect."

Bronau chewed on a fingernail, the picture of a guilty child. "Do you truly think so?"

"Of course," Winnamine replied, resting a hand on his arm.

"Men on the hunt for other men, particularly a man known as a fighter, like you—such hunters do make mistakes," Mequen reminded his friend. "If you're caught, if you fight, some dreadful accident might happen. You might be killed by an overzealous armsman before you can speak to the council at all."

Aly refilled glasses as the conversation went on. Daylight faded into sunset. Mequen and Winnamine came at Bronau in close order, persuading, joking, and debating. They did all they could to sow a gentler, more thoughtful mood in their rash friend.

The turning point came when Bronau looked at Sarai. "And what of you?" he asked. "Do you think I am a criminal?"

She lowered her eyes. "My lord, how could I think you a criminal? It is your life, I fear for . . ." Her eyelashes fluttered like butterflies. "—And your future," she added in a shy whisper.

Oh, she's good, thought Aly in admiration, remembering Sarai's fury when she heard of Bronau's kidnapping attempt. She's very good. I could turn opponents to her queenship right around by just giving her time to work on them.

Mequen eyed his daughter and his friend. At last the silence created by Sarai was finally broken by the supper bell. Mequen asked, "Will it help if I go to Rajmuat with you? Rubinyan will listen to me, I think, and the two of us can talk to Imajane."

"Papa!" cried Sarai, alarmed out of her maidenly distress.

"My dear, I don't think you could return before the passes close for the winter," Winnamine said, her hands clenched in her lap.

"This is more important," Mequen explained gravely to his wife and daughter. "If only one of us goes to Rajmuat, it won't seem as if we are forcing our way back into favor. If I must wait to return until spring . . ." He shrugged.

Bronau stared at Mequen. "You would do that for me? They could arrest you."

"I don't believe Rubinyan will allow that. And yes, I will go, if it helps to ease the trouble between the two of you," replied Mequen, his gaze sober. "The realm needs you and Rubinyan both. We can't afford dissent in the family that rules the Isles, not with a child on the throne and our Carthaki friends eyeing us like a ripe plum to be picked."

"Of your goodwill, give me a day to discuss it with my people," he said, voice and body weary. "They have been with me over many hard miles. They deserve a chance to decide if they will return and share whatever happens to me."

"Of course you may have the time," Mequen said, getting to his feet. He went to Bronau, who stood and embraced him. "And you should rest before you return. You look worn to the bone."

Bronau looked at Mequen, then at Winnamine and Sarai, obviously puzzled. "It hasn't occurred to you, has it?" he asked. "Should anything happen to Dunevon, *you* would be king. You—"

Mequen put a hand over his friend's mouth. "Please don't speak of that again," he said gently. "*Ever*. Haven't you noticed? Kingship in the Copper Isles drives people mad. I don't want it, for myself or my family. And in case you've forgotten, when I first married, the king had me swear before Mithros that I would never seek the crown. I keep my word."

Bronau hugged Mequen impulsively. "You were always better than the rest of us," he said, his voice thick. He let Mequen go and stepped back. "Now. Where may I clean up? I must tell you, I haven't had a true meal in days."

Aly took Bronau to the duke's bedchamber, where he would sleep as he had on his last visit. Once he was supplied with hot water, soap, and drying cloths, Aly returned to the family. The door was unlatched. She entered the room to find that Sarai had gone. The duke and the duchess were in each other's arms.

"I'm sorry," Aly said when they looked at her.

The duchess had been crying. She muttered an apology and went to the washstand to splash water on her face.

"It's all right," Mequen replied. With Bronau no longer in view, the duke's true feelings were easier to read. His shoulders drooped, and the lines on his face were deep with care. "We must go downstairs in a moment in any case."

Aly hesitated. What she had to say would distress him, but she needed to say it. "Forgive me, Your Grace, but should you not make him swear before the god to behave? To abide by your direction?" she asked, trying to tell him to do it without making it a direct order. She didn't think they trusted her enough to accept orders, even if she went against her training and gave them. "If he panics, there's no telling what he might do. An oath would rein him in."

Mequen sighed. "Aly, if you were noble-born, you would know that would be an intolerable insult to an honorable man like Bronau. To ask for such a vow implies I do not trust him. Do you wish to spark the very kind of outburst that got him into this mess? Leave the nobility to handle the nobility."

Aly blinked at him. Just once she wished she could speak her mind, to tell him that she, too, was noble-born, and some nobles could not be trusted as far as they could be thrown. She was sorely tempted to point out to him that Trebond blood was bluer than that of any Kyprish luarin. Instead she put such unwise answers from her mind, came about, and tried another tack. "Your Grace, he has a point. They might well imprison *you* if you returned." *I would*, she thought, but did not say aloud.

Mequen shook his head. "Rubinyan and I have been friends since boyhood. He would never do such a thing." When Aly opened her mouth again, he raised a hand to silence her. "Enough of plots and plotting. Don't you have the wine service at supper?"

Aly had been dismissed. *Never mind that I speak for the god,* she thought with a mental sigh. *Never mind that I am trying to keep him and his family from harm.* Aly turned and left the room without so much as a curtsy to her master.

16

BETRAYAL

Aly woke the next morning with the other servants, having taken forever to sleep the night before. Yawning, she rolled her pallet and stored it, then cleaned up for the day. Once presentable, she joined the line for breakfast. Chenaol was serving. When Aly reached the cook, she asked Chenaol to remind everyone to watch Bronau and his people.

"That's easy enough," Chenaol said drily, keeping her voice soft. "They amble about the courtyards like this was a friendly visit. Just look at that." She pointed to one of the kitchen slaves, who flirted busily with two of Bronau's men at the outer door. "They act like they haven't a care in the world. That's just not right, not with Princess Imajane at their tails. She's not nearly as kind as Oron—she once had a man flayed when he spat on her shadow. Any idea of what the prince means to do?"

"He's thinking," Aly murmured as Chenaol filled her bowl with porridge. "It will take him a while, since thinking isn't something that comes naturally to him."

Chenaol laughed hard and long. Aly smiled reluctantly. "I'm glad *you're* amused," she said, and went off to eat her meal in peace.

She was almost finished when Ulasim found her. "The duchess asks for you," he told her. "Hurry—they just sent the order for the ladies' and the prince's horses to be saddled. Lokeij will have yours ready."

Aly gave her empty bowl to the slaves who washed the dishes, then climbed the stairs to the family's quarters. The duke sat writing at his sitting room desk. Aly heard the voices of Winnamine, Sarai, and Dove in the bedchamber.

"Your Grace sent for me?" she asked Mequen. He hadn't, but she wanted to gauge his mood and his thoughts.

The duke raised his head. "Bronau has asked to remain here a week, to rest his men and the horses," he said quietly. "Then he and I shall return to Rajmuat, to straighten this out. He understands that he went astray. He says Rubinyan will hearken to me more than he will to Bronau, and I fear that's true. In the meantime, he's riding today with my lady and the girls."

Aly cocked an eyebrow. "Did he swear?" she inquired. "Did he swear to behave?"

Mequen's eyes hardened. "Enough. You do not know him as I do. I will hear no more of this, understand? Things are different for nobles than for commoners. If you cannot believe that, at least pretend to do so."

The bedchamber door opened. Out came Winnamine with Dove and Sarai, all dressed for riding and carrying bows and quivers. "Aly, there you are," the duchess said. "Come—we're going to hunt with the prince. Where were you this morning? My maid helped both girls to dress, but she was not happy."

Aly shrugged. "I assumed that I was back in the great hall, since the young ladies were with Your Graces and Your Graces' servants," she said, bowing to the duchess. "Will you forgive me?"

"Yes, of course," said Winnamine, pulling on her gloves. "It never occurred to me that you wouldn't see your place is with Dove now."

"Come *on*," urged Sarai. "Bronau's waiting."

They passed the day as they had during the prince's first visit. He galloped with Sarai, then rode with the duchess, Sarai, and Dove. Aly, the ladies' bodyguards, and Junai followed close behind. Bronau told jokes and talked about Dunevon's coronation, relating the list of those who attended and what they wore. As far as Aly could tell, Sarai and the duchess hung on every word. Dove rode silently as she listened. Above them crows swooped and cawed. From their calls Aly knew who was nearby and whether they were raka, members of the Balitang household, or strangers.

The group returned with partridges for that night's supper. Aly took the birds to Chenaol, while the Balitang women went to play with Petranne and Elsren before they went to their weapons practice. With free time to spend, Aly did the rounds of the castle. She spoke first to the girls' raka defenders, telling them of the duke's and Bronau's plans. Nawat reported that the crows had seen nothing suspicious on the plateau, which made Aly feel a little better. Her relief did not last very long. Bronau's presence itched more than a rash. She could barely sit still, not when her instincts were shrieking.

Sarai and the duchess came out in the late afternoon sun to practice sword skills with the men-at-arms, while Dove joined in the archery practice. Bronau looked on, smiling like an indulgent uncle. Dove was stringing her bow when Nawat approached. He slid a handful of arrows into the twelve-year-old's quiver. Dove's eyes went round. She gazed at Nawat in awe, one of the few times Aly could read clear feelings on the girl's face. Each of Nawat's arrows was fletched with griffin feathers. It reminded Aly once more that Nawat had been a crow for most of his life. No two-legger would have given precious grif-fin fletchings to a child, let alone a girl.

One of the footmen came for Aly. "His Highness and His Grace play chess," he informed her. "They wish you to serve wine."

Aly followed the man back into the castle, her mind busy. Perhaps Bronau would get caught up in the game and say something she could use to persuade the duke to let his friend return to the capital alone. Instead the two men spoke of the past. Mequen and Rubinyan had been pages and squires together. Bronau had served under Mequen's command in the royal navy, then com-manded the naval escort that had carried Mequen on diplomatic missions to Carthak. The men discussed Isles politics, Carthaki history, and music. They discussed players and compositions for so long that Aly wanted to sleep where she stood. Every now and then, when Bronau said something funny or engag-ing, the duke would glance at Aly, as if to say, "You see? He is a good man and a good friend."

Aly kept her face pleasant and refilled the cups as they emptied. Prince Bronau had shown on too many occasions that he was reckless and unreliable. He probably was a good friend to Mequen, but that meant very little in a dan-gerous political world.

The chess game ended; the men went out to practice sword skills with Veron and Fesgao. Aly stowed her pallet and belongings in the room where Sarai and Dove currently slept, then went downstairs.

Nawat met her in the great hall. "My brethren have come to roost here for the night," he informed Aly. They stood aside as Elsren and Petranne clattered by, pursued by their nursemaid. "The light is going. They say all remains quiet on these lands."

Aly nodded. "My head aches, though," she told him. "If all goes well, why am I tense?"

Nawat ran his fingers gently through Aly's short hair, preening her. "That is your task," he replied simply. "Most humans think the appearance of quiet *is* quiet. They do not see that sometimes the enemy is as quiet as the serpent. Only when it has stolen all of their eggs will they know bad walks in the quiet as well as the noisy."

Aly leaned against the wall, looking up into Nawat's deep-set eyes. "I thought you were worried about hawks."

"Those as well," Nawat answered. "But a hawk I can see. While I watch the hawk, who is to say the serpent is not behind me?"

Timidly Aly reached up and ran her fingers gently through Nawat's hair over one ear, preening him in return for the first time. "I wish the duke were as wise—or as clear-sighted—as crows."

Nawat was bending down to Aly when Ulasim called from the stair, "Aly? Lady Dovasary is calling for you." Nawat made a face and kissed Aly lightly on the nose, then left the hall. Aly tried to scorch Ulasim with a glare, but the big raka only returned a polite, meaningless smile. She stuck her tongue out at him as she trotted by on her way to Dove's room.

The day had cooled rapidly, enough that Sarai and Dove both wore woolen dresses to supper. Aly and Pembery loaded the braziers in the girls' rooms with charcoal and set them alight so that they would be warm as they slept. Then they followed their mistresses downstairs.

Bronau's men-at-arms ate supper with the Balitang household, then retired to their quarters. The family's servants and slaves played music and sang, relaxing. At last the Balitangs went upstairs. Aly helped to undress Dove, then spread her pallet near the door of the master bedroom. After she donned the shift she slept in, Aly refastened the sheaths of her knives around her ankles and arms. Her sleep would be uncomfortable, but she dared not risk a night without them. Once that was done, she talked with Dove as Sarai read. From the sitting room, they could hear the murmur of conversation between the duke, the duchess, and Bronau.

At last the girls' parents came in and went into the dressing rooms to change clothes, with the help of Pembery and the man who waited on Mequen. The servants laid out their own pallets at the foot of the master bed as the duke and duchess slid under the cool linen sheets and a light coverlet. Sarai and Dove lay on cots placed on the far side of the bed, between Winnamine and her dressing room.

Aly looked around. Something wasn't right. Mequen was about to blow out the last candle when Aly said, "Wait, please." She went into the dressing room and returned with his unsheathed sword.

"Aly," Mequen said, his eyes sharp with anger. "You really go too far—"

Winnamine laid her palm against his cheek to silence him. "Humor us, my dear. Keep it close."

The duke sighed in exasperation. "Gods, save me from the nerves of women!" he snapped, flinging himself back against his pillows. Then he sighed and sat up. "Thank you, Aly. I know your concern is for our welfare."

Aly placed the sword on the table with the candle. She angled its hilt so Mequen would find it instantly if he reached out in the dark. "Good night, Your Grace," she said, and blew out the candle. Using her Sight, adjusted for the dark, she found her pallet easily.

Sleep would not come. She tried to keep still, so as not to wake the others, but her body trembled with nerves. When she slept in the great hall, she could hear everything outside and in. She also had freedom to move downstairs. This room felt like a trap.

Aly heard the whisper of cloth on cloth through the crack under the door beside her. She pressed her ear to it, straining to hear. The sitting room on the other side was closed. She had watched Sarai shut that door, putting a heavy wooden barrier between the bedchamber and the main stair. What had made that stray noise, mice? The old tower had its share, but this sound was not mouselike.

She heard a thump, then a creak. Someone was definitely opening the sitting room door. "Your Grace!" Aly whispered, scrambling to her feet. "Wake up!" She lunged for the door and braced her shoulder against it, cursing the absence of locks on the family's rooms. What could she use to barricade the entry besides her own weight? Behind her she heard people scrambling out of their blankets.

As Aly braced her shoulder against the door to keep it shut, someone pushed on it from outside. It edged open. She scrabbled for purchase on the floor with her bare feet, without success, and leaned into the door with all of her weight. It wasn't enough. The door slammed open, smashing her against the wall behind it. Pain seared through her as her back hit stone with a crack. Aly groaned and shoved the door away from her. She sank to the floor, fighting to stay conscious.

Someone in the room threw the water pitcher: Aly saw it fly through the open doorway. A man yelped outside; the pitcher shattered on something hard. Mequen shouted orders to his wife and servants. Then Bronau, clinking in a chain mail shirt over a leather tunic and breeches, walked in. He carried an unsheathed sword in his hand. Three of his soldiers, wearing mail and carrying torches, followed.

The duke's manservant, howling in rage, attacked with no better weapon than an iron candelabrum. Bronau ran him through, then thrust the dead man off his blade with a booted foot. His men spread out behind him. Mequen had grabbed the sword Aly had left for him. He now stood between Bronau and the women of his family. Winnamine placed herself in front of Sarai and Pembery, another iron candelabrum in her hand like a sword. Aly couldn't see Dove behind the bulk of the master bed.

"I didn't want this, Mequen, Winna," Bronau said, pain and regret in his voice. "Not a fight. We're all friends, aren't we?"

"Friends don't call at midnight with swords in hand," Mequen retorted.

"Swords don't have to come into play," Bronau said with his charming smile. "We can work this out. All you need do is declare your claim to the throne. Once you are crowned, you'll abdicate in favor of your oldest daughter and her husband—me. You'd like that, wouldn't you, Sarai?" he asked, his voice honey-sweet. "To be queen, clothed and jeweled as your beauty deserves. It could be a step forward for your mother's people. I know you have a sentimental attachment to them." Bronau looked from Mequen to Winnamine. "Don't make me do this," he pleaded.

"Our servants will be at your back momentarily," said the duke. "You can't believe you and ten men can take my daughter and me."

"Of course not. That is why the forty other warriors I've recruited came onto the plateau after sundown," Bronau informed them. "I *did* notice all those idle raka warriors riding to and fro when I visited here. My lads are combat veterans, not peasants or slaves with arrows and rusty swords. Your gates are now open to my armsmen—I'm afraid we had to kill some of your guards to do that."

"We have a mage," snapped Sarai. "You won't defeat her so easily!"

Bronau smiled as if she were a clever student who had given a good answer. "I thought you might have one by now. I have three. They are keeping your old woman busy, if they haven't killed her yet. Mequen, be sensible. I don't want to kill you. You're going to be my father-in-law."

Aly got her feet under her. She leaped onto the back of the closest man-at-arms. Wrapping her right hand around his chin, she yanked his head back and dragged her left-hand knife across his throat. He choked, staggered, and toppled backward, crushing Aly under his body. She squirmed madly, trying to free herself.

"Papa!" cried Sarai as Winnamine held her back.

Mequen lunged with his sword, chopping at his old friend. Bronau parried the blow with a half-turn, pushing Mequen's blade aside. Mequen kept his sword moving in a sidelong cut that bit into the belly of Bronau's second man-at-arms. The wounded man dropped his torch. Mequen used a bare foot to sweep the soldier's feet from under him, dumping him onto it. The body smothered most of the flames as Mequen blocked another of Bronau's strikes.

Pembery shrieked and hid under the bed, begging the gods for help, as Winnamine and Sarai threw everything they could reach at the third of Bronau's soldiers. Aly cursed as she struggled to free herself of the corpse that weighed her down. The remaining man-at-arms advanced on Winnamine and Sarai, shielding his face from the rain of vases, plates, and cosmetics jars. Aly saw no sign of Dove.

"Don't kill the girl!" shouted Bronau as he hacked the bed curtains by mistake. Mequen cut a long, shallow slice down Bronau's leg, cutting through leather into flesh.

Aly got her right hand free. In it she held a knife. Clenching her teeth, she rose halfway under the dead man's weight and threw the blade. It struck the last man-at-arms on the cheekbone, opening a gash there. He glanced toward Aly with a snarl.

The moment his attention shifted to Aly, Winnamine slammed her candelabrum across his face. The armsman's nose broke with a dull crunch. Ornate metal leaves opened cuts in his eyebrows, cuts that blinded him with blood. Winnamine hit him twice more with all her strength. The soldier's knees gave way.

As he dropped, he lashed out, cutting Mequen's leg. Mequen glanced down and stabbed him through the throat. Then the duke's feet slipped in the armsman's blood. He fell across the downed man's body. As he fought to rise, Bronau ran him through.

"Papa!" Sarai shrieked. She darted past Winnamine and grabbed her father's sword. Facing Bronau, she brought it up to the ready position. "He is your *friend*!" cried Sarai.

Bronau stepped back, raising both hands, though he kept a grip on his sword. "He would be the first to tell you that when a crown's at stake, friendship becomes a luxury." He pointed to Mequen. "I've seen men survive worse. Only swear that you'll marry me and be my queen, and I'll call one of my mages to heal him."

"He lies," Aly croaked, Seeing it in Bronau.

"I know that," snapped Sarai. "His lips move, don't they?" She lunged, her sword aimed at Bronau's heart. He stepped back, half-pivoting, as her sword cut a bright line across his mail. Sarai caught herself, pivoted, and lunged again.

Bronau seized her blade in gauntleted hands and wrenched it out of Sarai's grip, tossing it aside. As she stumbled, he shoved her onto the bed. "We can do this nicely, or not," he informed her calmly, "but you are going to lead a revolt at my side."

Aly wriggled free of the body that had pinned her. She gripped a knife in her left hand and jumped for Bronau's back, grabbing for his chin with blood-slick fingers. Her hand slipped. Instead she hooked her fingers in his nostrils and pulled, then stabbed blindly. Her dagger scraped bone, not flesh. She'd gotten his jaw by mistake.

Bronau roared and threw himself back, slamming Aly against the unforgiving stone wall. Her ribs cracked. Still she clung, raising her left hand for another slash. He wrenched the knife from her grip, breaking more of her bones, then slammed her into the wall again. Aly's vision went dark. She hung on for her life and dragged on his nose, keeping his head back.

Something thudded into Bronau. Aly couldn't see what it was. He went still, wobbling on his feet. Something else hit him. Aly groped the man's neck until her swelling fingers hit two long, slender shafts buried in his throat. She freed Bronau and shoved him forward. He dropped onto his face. Bracing herself against the wall, Aly looked across the bed. Dove stood on its far side, a bow in her hand. A few griffin-fletched arrows lay on the coverlet where she could reach them.

"Papa," whispered Sarai. She lurched off of the bed without so much as a glance at the man who would have made her queen, and ran to her father's side. Dove dropped her bow and did the same.

Winnamine grabbed a shirt and knelt beside the girls. Carefully she laid the wadded-up shirt on Mequen's bleeding wound and pressed down with it. "Pressure slows the bleeding," she whispered.

Aly seized a goosefeather bolster from the bed and used it to beat out the small fire that had spread from the second man-at-arms's torch. She used what was left of that to light candles, then stumbled through the study and battered the door to Petranne and Elsren's rooms.

"Who is it?" asked Rihani, her voice shaking with terror. The two younger children were crying.

"Aly. The duke's cut in the belly. Come see to him."

"I don't know if I can help," Rihani protested.

"I'll find Ochobu!" snapped Aly. "Just keep his grace alive!"

She heard furniture scrape. Weeks ago Rihani had been told that, if an attack came, she was to barricade the door, to keep the younger children safe. When the door opened, and Rihani saw Aly, she nodded.

Aly didn't watch her enter the duke's bedroom. She raced down the stairs to the main hall. Her broken left arm hung by one side, limp and bluish purple. Sharp pains stabbed her right side, where she had broken ribs. She prayed they wouldn't puncture her lungs, then ignored them. Without Ochobu, Mequen would die.

Ochobu was not in the great hall. The room was in chaos as Ulasim and a few armed footmen fought nearly thirty invaders, most in leather armor covered with metal rings. This must be what's left of the men Bronau sneaked onto the plateau after dark, Aly thought bitterly. He thought he was evading raka patrols, but he hid them from the crows as well. Had they killed the raka who guarded the road to the pass? They looked like they'd had a fight of some kind, either with the raka or with Veron and his men.

"Stop!" she yelled over the noise. "Bronau is dead! Put down your arms!"

A ruffian grinned up at Aly, his face a blood-streaked mask. "If he's dead, we'll take as we like!" he shouted. "Lots of fine wenches here, and the men will be worth sommat as slaves."

"Oh, we make very bad slaves," someone announced from the main door.

For a moment there was only silence in the great hall. Everyone turned to look at the speaker. It was Nawat. He stood with a bow at the ready, an arrow on the string. Calmly he shot the man who had taunted Aly. The invader fell, in silence. Behind Nawat stood nearly thirty half-naked people, their hair and skin dotted with clumps of gleaming black feathers. Each held a crude weapon of some kind, sickles, hay rakes, cleavers, and kitchen knives.

Nawat placed another arrow on the string. "You were wrong to come here," he said, and shot a man in a chain mail shirt. With that shot the paralysis that had seized the enemy at the sight of Nawat's allies shattered. Trapped between Ulasim and his fighters and Nawat's transformed crows, Bronau's men fought for their lives, and lost them. The crow-people were fast, strong, and merciless. Ulasim and his raka battled ferociously.

Aly watched it all unfold, leaning against the wall as pain throbbed in her chest and broken arm. Only one man reached the stairs where she stood. She gazed at him with the glassy calm of shock, knowing she couldn't possibly defend herself. He collapsed with two of Nawat's arrows in his back.

When the crows and the raka finished, Aly carefully walked down to Nawat. "Ochobu," she told him. Her head was spinning. Her stomach lurched, a warning that she might throw up.

"She holds three mages at the village gate." Nawat selected three arrows with Stormwing fletchings from his quiver. "I will bring her. You sit."

Aly sat. Someone took her torch. She propped her forehead on her good hand, watching as sweat dribbled down her face to splash on the bloody stones of the floor. Here came Ulasim, bleeding from an assortment of cuts. Junai followed. She was unmarked except for a long gouge that sliced her shirt and skin from collarbone to navel. Aly mumbled, "My mother has one just like that, only it's healed."

"Shock," Ulasim said.

"This is broken," replied Junai, lifting Aly's left arm. Aly gasped as the world spun wildly. The gasp brought a stab of agony from her broken ribs.

"Is anyone alive up there?" Ulasim asked. "Our ladies?"

Aly bit her tongue to keep from fainting as Junai tied her wrist to a length of wood. "They're fine," she said when she could talk again. "It's the duke who's hurt." She looked at the open doors. Here came Nawat, supporting Ochobu. The old woman was pale under her brown skin, but no less ferocious for all that.

"Idiot luarin thought he could hold me with three mages," she grumbled as Nawat helped her over to the stair. "Is he alive to learn he can't?"

Aly shook her head and gulped. She was well into shock now, and had reached her least favorite stage of it, nausea. Her stomach fought to cast out the remains of her supper. "He's dead. And His Grace is belly-cut."

For once Ochobu did not hesitate at the suggestion that she attend a luarin. Instead she let Ulasim help her upstairs. Junai continued to splint Aly's arm.

The great hall fell silent. Everyone cleaned weapons and wounds as they listened to the sounds from the duke's quarters. It was not long before they heard the wail of a woman whose heart was broken.

"Bronau couldn't even judge wounds right," Aly mumbled. "Saying he might still live." Tears slid over her dirty cheeks.

Ulasim walked down the stairs, gray-faced. "His Grace is dead," he told the household.

Aly rested her head back against the wall, wincing as she bumped the knot on her skull. A curse on the Jimajens and their power games, she thought bitterly. A curse on the rulers of this country, Rubinyan and Imajane, who let Bronau escape them. I *will* bring them down. And I *will* put a half-raka queen on the throne if it's the last thing I ever do.

* * *

By dawn the changed crow-people had vanished, leaving only some feathers and their abandoned weapons to show they had been there at all. The feathers were set reverently aside by those who cleaned up after the battle.

They lay their own people to rest in the castle's ancient burial ground two days later, in a ceremony that lasted from mid-morning until mid-afternoon. Raka came from all over the plateau to bury their folk and to witness the aftermath of Bronau's greed.

The tally of the dead was painful. Veron had been killed as he defended the castle gate. It no longer seemed to matter that he'd been a royal spy—in his own way he had been loyal. Old Lokeij was gone, but not before he'd cut down three of the enemy with a scythe. Visda and Ekit had lost their father and older brother, who belonged to the raka patrol that had been overwhelmed by Bronau's soldiers. Two dead crows were found in the great hall. They were as honored in their burial as if they'd been human. The slave Hasui had let the enemy in; they found her dead outside the kitchen wing. It was impossible to tell who had murdered her, though Aly suspected Chenaol. The raka cook would never forgive such a betrayal. There was Mequen's body servant to bury, five men-at-arms—three of them the bandits captured on the road from Dimari—and Mequen himself. Fesgao was alive, barely. He attended the funeral on a litter. Winnamine gave him the command of her remaining men-at-arms.

The next day they burned the enemy dead near the road to Dimari. Among them were the three mages who had kept Ochobu from the castle. Nawat collected his Stormwing-fletched arrows from them before Ochobu put the torch to the pyre. Bronau had a pyre of his own. A stony-faced Winnamine collected his ashes and placed them in a box for Rubinyan.

With the funerals over, Winnamine retreated to the family's rooms to mourn her husband. Sarai and Dove took charge of their stepmother and Petranne and Elsren. The younger children were like bewildered ghosts who kept asking for Mequen. Each time they did, Sarai's eyes overflowed with tears as she hugged them and tried to explain. Dove never wept. Watching her small, set face, Aly wished that the younger girl could weep. At least Aly had Nawat to comfort her, and to comfort. Aly could endure her sorrow, having seen battles and their aftermath before. The Balitangs had not. Nawat had not. Tanair had been a peaceful place before the arrival of Bronau, and Nawat was still young for a crow.

A week passed before the duchess left her seclusion, pale but steely-eyed. The first person she summoned to her seat in the great hall was Aly. "That comes off," she said flatly, pointing to Aly's metal slave collar. "It was pointless before. It is brutally pointless now. You are free under Kyprish law as well as in your own spirit."

Aly bowed her head. For once she didn't argue. The duchess was right. All the plateau knew what she was to the Balitangs now. There was no more advantage to her pretense of being a slave. She reported to the blacksmith. He spoke the spell formula that released the collar, then pulled it open. He even gave her ointment for the red scar at the base of Aly's neck. When it was off, she visited Nawat. He had resumed his old place in the inner courtyard, sitting at his large bench as he fletched arrows in the morning sun. He squinted up at Aly. "Your metal ring is gone," he remarked.

Aly sat gingerly on the far end of his workbench. Ochobu had fixed the breaks in her ribs and arm, to a point. She couldn't heal Aly completely and still have strength to help the many other wounded. Instead Aly had to move very carefully as her bones, secured by a wrapping around her ribs and a splint on her arm, finished mending the natural way. "Yes, the ring is gone. It didn't look good on me anyway. Your clan did a wonderful thing for us. Why didn't they stay?"

Nawat bird-shrugged. "They're about—as crows. They don't like the human shape. They would rather fly."

"Well, thank them for me," Aly told him. "Without them we would have died."

"They were just looking after the wager," Nawat said, putting his arrow aside.

"That's right, Kyprioth had a wager going with the crows, too, separate from the one he's got with me," Aly murmured. "What were the crows' stakes again? I'd forgotten, if I ever knew."

"If the crows help you to live through this changing season, we get a gift from the god," Nawat answered, plainly uninterested. "Now me, I think this form is fine. These human tools interest me." Meeting Aly's eyes, he added, "And human women aren't so bad."

Aly jumped to her feet and winced as her ribs complained. "Now, don't you start. I have too much on my mind."

"I know," said Nawat, looking down at his work. His voice was meek. "And Sarai tells me I must sneak up on you."

Aly fled.

Eight days later, the crows cried the alarm. A full company of one hundred soldiers was marching onto the plateau. When Aly reported it, Winnamine ordered the men-at-arms to the village gates. She followed with a sword at her hip, a bow and a quiver of arrows in her hands. Aly, Sarai, and Dove all raced in her wake, doing their best to keep up with the long-legged woman as they climbed to the watch post over the gate.

When she saw who now stood outside, Winnamine sighed with relief. Aly peered through an arrow slit to see a face she knew: Bronau's cold brother, Rubinyan.

"We're here for my brother," Rubinyan called. "Our mages say he came to you."

"Wait," called the duchess. To the girls she said, "Well, I can't exactly shout the news, can I? They were brothers." She went out to meet him as Sarai, Dove, Aly, and Fesgao watched. Rubinyan dismounted and went aside to talk with her. When his shoulders drooped, Winnamine motioned for the guards to open the gate.

To the relief of Tanair's inhabitants, Rubinyan let his soldiers camp in a field nearby, not inside the walls. He entered the castle with only a body servant for an attendant. As he rode by, the girls could see he'd been weeping—for Mequen, not Bronau, Winnamine told the girls later.

He spent his first night at Tanair praying for Mequen and Bronau in the village's Mithran shrine. The following night Rubinyan took supper with the Balitang women in their sitting room. Aly was at hand as wine pourer.

"Come back to Rajmuat with me," Rubinyan said, his gray eyes kind as he looked at Winnamine, Sarai, and Dove. His elegant voice sounded warmer than it had in Aly's dreams of the palace. "Oron's order of exile was folly. Imajane and I want you to come home."

Dove and Sarai turned to Winnamine. They would let her decide.

Winnamine gave Rubinyan the weariest of smiles. "Truly, I appreciate the offer," she said. "And I wish to avail myself of it—but will it displease you if I wait until spring? I want to help our people through the winter. Petranne and Elsren would be so upset, uprooting again so soon after Mequen's . . . And, to be honest, we need time to mourn. You know how courtiers are when they feel you've passed beyond what they see as enough time to be sad. They act as if *they're* not sorry any longer, so why should you be?"

"They have no friends of the heart, or they might see how it is, to lose someone they cherish." Rubinyan grimaced. "Courtiers put friends on and off according to fashion. I have never been able to do so." His eyes glittered with unshed tears. He looked aside and hastily blotted them away with his napkin.

Winnamine clasped his arm and squeezed gently. "There. You understand. We will go in the spring, won't we, girls?"

Dove and Sarai nodded.

Covering Winnamine's hand with his, Rubinyan asked, "I may count on your return?"

"As soon as it is safe to sail," Winnamine said.

Rubinyan nodded. "Very good. Oh—I just remembered. We passed a merchant caravan on our way here. They have supplies for you."

He was right. The day after he and his men took the road back to Dimari, Gurhart returned to Tanair. Aly accompanied the young Balitangs to the village to look over the caravan's goods. They didn't notice the tall, broad-shouldered man who slid out of one of the wagons after they passed.

The newcomer walked to the castle and politely requested the honor of a private word with the head of the Balitang family. He emphasized his request with a gold coin to a man-at-arms on duty; another to Fesgao, who still searched him thoroughly for weapons; and finally one more to Ulasim. The footman found Winnamine to report the visitor and the size of the bribes the man had offered.

"Interesting," she said. "By all means, I'll see this Master Cooper—but in the great hall. Ask Ochobu to observe, please, in case he's a mage. Keep your people out of earshot, but arm them with bows in case he tries something. I don't want Aly to scold me for carelessness."

"Very wise, Your Grace." Ulasim smiled at his duchess and escorted her downstairs.

There she found the stranger, a man whose brown hair was lightly shot with gray. He had green-hazel eyes, a big nose, and a mobile, clever mouth. To her experienced eye his clothes looked as if they'd been very good once, but that was some time ago. They were worn but not patched or ragged. When he smiled, he was very charming.

"I am Duchess Winnamine Balitang, head of this household," she greeted him from her chair on the dais. She glimpsed Ochobu in the shadows under the main stair. Three men-at-arms, each with a crossbow cocked and ready to shoot, stood by the main door. "How may I help you?"

The man bowed gracefully. "It is good of you to put it in just that way, Your Grace," he said. "I'm here as a buyer, if you'll excuse me for talkin' business to so grand a lady as yourself. I deal in slaves. I was told your house bought one I had my eye on, down in Rajmuat. I was short on funds then, but I've come about since. I'm hopin' you'll be minded to sell. She's a little thing, about five feet six, reddish blond hair, hazel eyes. Greenish, like. Fresh caught out of Tortall she was, then. I heard she was a fighter, so it may be you'll be glad to get her off your hands."

Winnamine smiled thinly and raised her hand to stop him. "This is quite distressing, since you came all this way. I must refuse you. Aly is free. I would take it very much amiss if anyone enslaved her again. She is part of our family now."

The stranger looked at her and raised an eyebrow. "Forgive my plain speakin', milady, but that makes no sense. Slaves aren't family to nobles."

"Aly saved my life and those of my children recently. It was not the first time she had done so." Winnamine swallowed hard and added, "She was injured while trying to save my late husband. We cannot begin to pay her the debt we owe, but we made our start by removing the collar from her neck and burning her sale papers." She looked the man over. There was something familiar about him, in the raised brow, the crooked smile, and the way he seemed aware of everything around him, even though he spoke only to her. Suddenly she realized what it was, and gave him her own little smile. "But you're not *really* here to buy her, are you, sir?" She beckoned to Ulasim, who waited with her guards. The raka came over, his dark eyes suspicious as he looked on their guest. "Ulasim, please have someone fetch Aly from the village," Winnamine ordered. To the newcomer she said, "Would you like tea?"

Down by the caravan, Aly was trying to guide Sarai away from a silver-hilted sword that was more useful as jewelry than as a weapon when a footman raced up to them. "Aly, there's a man looking to buy you up at the castle," he said, panting. "Her Grace sent me for you."

"Nobody's going to buy our Aly!" snapped Sarai, brown eyes ablaze. "Who is this interloper?"

Aly and Dove looked at one another and shrugged. Apparently Sarai was in one of her imperious moods. They followed her to the castle while Aly tried to puzzle through who the visitor might be. She knew that Winnamine wouldn't sell her: she was free, and Winnamine was incapable of playing such a foul trick. But, on the other hand, the duchess had considered the new-comer's request important enough to fetch Aly from the village.

Sarai stamped into the castle's great hall. "What's this nonsense about buying Aly? She's free. She can't leave us."

Winnamine sat at one of the long tables where the servants ate, drinking tea with a man in a worn brown coat. As he turned, Aly froze in shock.

Then she threw herself across the room, shrieking, "Da! Da!"

He knocked a bench over so he could stand and grab her, lifting her in strong arms, holding Aly so tight that her not-quite-healed ribs protested. Aly hugged back just as ferociously, weeping into her father's sensible wool collar. He smelled of crisp air, wood smoke, and faintly of spices, just as he always did.

When they finally let each other go, the great hall was empty of anyone but them. The duchess had shooed her astonished children and servants away. George held Aly by the shoulders, inspecting her. "Now," he said with a frown, "what is this? Broken nose, eyebrow scar—did we raise such a savage?" His lower-class speech was gone, shed with his identity as a buyer of slaves.

"I did it on purpose, Da," Aly explained. "So nobody would buy me to pop into bed with them. How's Mother? How's the war going? Is she all right? What are Alan and Thom up to? What did Daine and Numair name the baby—the dream was over before I heard it—"

"Aly, a man can answer only one question at a time," George interrupted gently. "The war's winding down to its end at last. King Maggur's on the run—his own nobles hunt him like a deer. Your mother's to come home for a winter's rest. She's been half sick with worry for you. You'll see her, and your brothers, when you come home. Alan told us you weren't dead, but that was all he knew, and he worried. They tell me you're no longer a slave."

Aly's joy vanished, startling her. Of course he would think she was coming home now. Why did the thought of going back to the Swoop seem bad all of a sudden? What had happened to her? And if she didn't go back, how would she explain it? "Duchess Winnamine freed me, Da, but that's not why I didn't come home. I'd've done it as soon as I got here, but . . ." She fumbled for the right words. "Things are complicated."

George sat and patted the bench seat next to him. "How?" he asked.

Aly rubbed the back of her neck and sighed, then took a seat. "Oh, Da, there's a god. We had a wager, see. I was to keep the Balitang children alive till the autumn equinox, and if I did, he'd send me home and talk to you about letting me work as a spy, or bodyguard, or something. It's not equinox yet."

"A god laid you a wager?" Her father's voice was dangerously smooth. "Which god would this be?"

"Kyprioth," Aly said. "He's a local god—"

"Kyprioth," her father said with disgust. "I might have known. Show yourself, you miserable piece of Stormwing dung," he said, his voice still quiet. "I know you're listening. You're vain as a cat when anyone speaks your name."

The main doors swung open. Kyprioth entered the room in a blaze of sunlight. Today he wore the guise he most favored, the leanly muscled, brown-skinned man with short salt-and-pepper hair and a close-clipped beard. He wore a cloth-of-gold wraparound jacket today and a sarong that looked as if it were woven copper. Jeweled rings gleamed on his fingers; jeweled bracelets shone on his wrists and ankles.

"There you are, George," Kyprioth said cheerily. "How are you, my good fellow? It's been ages."

Aly's father stood and crossed his arms over his chest, his eyes glittering dangerously. "You've been hiding Aly from her mother and our mage friends," he accused.

"Of course." Kyprioth took a bench from the next table and dragged it over, unmindful of the screech of wood on the flagstone floor. Once he placed it opposite Aly's bench, he reclined on it, propping his head on his hand. "I needed her. I couldn't have you trying to rescue her all the time. Not, may I add, that she has ever needed rescue."

"You steal my daughter and then you hide her from me. Is this the way you reward my service?" demanded George. "Aly's no pawn of yours, to be whisked in and out of your mad tricks."

Kyprioth eyed one of the gems on his rings, turning it this way and that in the sunlight. It was a clear stone, cut into multiple tiny flat surfaces that threw off light like miniature rainbows. "Such fatherly wrath. I would be terrified, except, well, I'm not."

"Let's end this," George said firmly. "When we declared our association done, you swore in blood that you owed me a debt, and I might call on that. Well, here it is. I want my daughter home. Pay up, Trickster."

Kyprioth gazed at Aly. "I don't really see anything fatal coming in the time between now and the equinox, not when my cousin North Wind has decided to remind mortals of his power. We're going to have an early winter—just as effective as fortress walls for keeping bad people away from the Balitangs. Aly, I absolve you of the remaining time on our wager. You have won. George, be a good boy and put her talents to use. If you don't, I'm sure I can arrange something so that it will be *necessary* for you to make use of her. She can't be a child any longer. She has moved among adults and changed the courses of their lives, you know." Kyprioth sat up. "Well, if there's nothing else . . . ?"

From the moment he'd declared an end to their wager and Aly the winner, her brain had been in an uproar. She could go home. She could see her mother again, her adoptive family, Daine and Numair's baby, her brothers, her grandparents. She could wear fashionable gowns and toy with young noblemen. If the war was near an end, there would be a fresh crop of romantic young knights and soldiers to cut a swathe through. The lure of home was like a mermaid's song that pulled her irresistibly east. Nawat had said he would go with her when it came time for her to leave.

But.

Mequen had been kind to her, kinder than most masters were to slaves or even free servants. He'd died for the blood in his veins. The throne was held by a three-year-old and the most predatory, grasping pair of humans Aly had ever seen, while royal blood flowed in the veins of Mequen's children, making them a threat to the regents.

The raka. The fire in Ulasim's eyes as he watched Sarai practice her combat dances. The silent rows of natives that had lined the way to Dimari just to see their promised queen. Lokeij, dead because he had defended his hope for the future. Junai, patient, silent, and deadly. Sarai and Dove themselves, with their passion, intelligence, and ideals, their love for the raka and their ties to the luarin.

She had made a promise to herself on the night Mequen died.

About to surprise herself and her father, Aly hesitated—and then she saw it. "*You,*" she said furiously to Kyprioth.

He actually batted his eyes at her. "Yes, dear?"

George rested a hand on Aly's shoulder. "Lass, I don't like the look on your face."

Aly still spoke to Kyprioth. "You knew this would happen, curse you. You wove me into your festering, pustulant great trick. You didn't wager my summer. You bet that I wouldn't want to leave."

"Well, I didn't *wager,* actually," the god said modestly. "I hoped, that was all, with all the hope in my withered god's heart. You know, I do owe you a boon. I could repay it now, erase all memory of this place and these people and send you back to Tortall. No doubt your queen needs a lady-in-waiting who's good with lock picks. Or her daughter, who's now Empress of Carthak, might need you even more. Say the word, and I will let you go."

Aly scowled at him. "I'm going to make your life a misery," she informed him.

"I look forward to it," said Kyprioth.

George sighed. "I think it's very good of me to wait whilst the two of you talk in a code I don't know. I'll say this—I'm starting to dislike what I hear."

"Return his boon," Aly ordered the god. "You can't cheat and make him use it when I won't go along."

Kyprioth delivered himself of a broad, dramatic sigh. "Very well," he said, and looked at George. "I still owe you a boon, since I can't grant this one, not without her agreement." He looked at Aly. "This summer was just a trial run, and an easy one at that. Things will be much more difficult from here on. There will be more to lose, and more elements to keep track of."

Aly shrugged. "In for a garnet, in for a ruby," she said. "They're both the same to me. And it's not like I won't have plenty of help."

George crossed his arms over his chest. "You're staying? Why?"

Aly stood and hugged him. "You'd do the same in my place. So would Mother," she explained softly. "These are good people, Da. I want to keep them alive so Kyprioth can complete his great trick—putting a raka queen, not a luarin king, on the throne. You and Mother wanted me to do something with my life. Well, here it is. He—" She looked at Kyprioth. The god had vanished. I'll deal with *you* later, she thought. She looked back into her father's eyes and smiled slyly. "I'm sure Their Majesties will be interested in knowing that the raka plan to rise."

George raised his brows. "Will you spy for us here, then?" he asked drily. "Since seemingly I've no choice but to accommodate you."

Aly shook her head. "I can't, Da. The Balitangs don't know what my real family is, and I want to keep it that way. You're a merchant to them, and Mother a Player who left us after bearing me." In response to her father's shocked look, Aly shrugged. "I wasn't about to say she was dead, that's all. For now, I remain in service to the Balitangs. They would never allow me to stay if they thought I worked for a rival kingdom. No, this will be for them, and the raka. For all those with luarin blood who might die if the revolt can't be, um, *guided* into a shape that fits old blood and new." She swallowed hard. "I think Mother will understand."

George Cooper sighed. "And so she and I get what we'd wished for, only to find we don't care for the form it's taken. We asked you to assume your place in the world, to live and work as a woman. You have done so, but it's a bitter reward for us. Your mother will understand all too well. I should have known that no daughter of hers would choose the easy road." He kissed the top of her head. "Anything for a poor traveling man to eat, then?" he asked.

Aly looked around to see if a servant was nearby, or if she'd have to go beg

Chenaol for something. To her surprise, she saw that one of the double doors was open. Nawat stood there, an arrow shaft in one hand, watching her as she held another man.

"Oh, my," Aly said, releasing her father. "Um. Da, there's someone you should meet. Nawat?" She beckoned to him.

"Nawat?" George asked as the crow-man walked over to them.

"Nawat Crow, Da. He's a friend of mine." When Nawat reached her, she rested a hand on his arm. "Nawat, this is my father."

George inspected the younger man from head to toe, then looked at his daughter. Without a word he cocked one eyebrow.

She raised one of hers in reply.

George remained for three days, charming the Balitangs and talking with his daughter on long walks. At last it came time for the merchant caravan to leave, before the first snows closed the road through the pass. George went with them, waving to his daughter until he could no longer see her. Aly watched him until, even with her Sight, she could no longer see him. When he was gone from view, she wiped her eyes on her sleeve and called herself various kinds of stupid for allowing herself to be drawn into revolution.

A shadow passed over her. Instinctively she looked up. There, high over-head, a kudarung circled, riding the columns of hot air that rose from the rocky hills at the edge of the plateau. Alone it glided, chestnut wings cutting through the golden air of early fall.

"It's going to be an interesting spring," she muttered.

The air around her filled with Kyprioth's rich, merry chuckle.

TRICKSTER'S QUEEN

To Bruce Coville, divinely tricky, magically inspiring—
one of the best men I've ever known,
and
To Mary Lou Pierce,
the best Ma in the world

CONTENTS

PROLOGUE
THE COPPER ISLES

In the winter of 462–463 H.E., the brown-skinned raka people and their many allies, part-bloods and white-skinned luarin, prepared for revolution against the luarin ruling house, the Rittevons. The raka plan was to replace the Rittevons with one who had the bloodlines of both the raka queens and the luarin rulers, a passionate girl named Saraiyu Balitang.

The leaders of the raka rebel conspiracy did not spend the winter months dozing. Throughout the Isles, Crown tax collectors vanished from their beds, never to be seen again. Even more baffling, all the suspects who were questioned in their disappearances swore under truthspell that they had last seen the missing officials alive and well. Property damage on luarin estates that winter far exceeded that expected from heavy rains. Dams collapsed, sweeping away acres of rice fields. Blackrot invaded grain silos, destroying winter stores. Bridges fell. Overseers and a few nobles were murdered. When the Crown sent soldiers to kill the people of the nearest raka village, as the law required, the troops found that the inhabitants had vanished. Many people reported hearing war gongs sounding from deep within the lowland jungles.

Life for the Balitang family in the highlands of Lombyn Isle had two sides. One was that of a family that had just lost its patriarch and had to get through the winter months before they could return to the capital city of Rajmuat at the behest of the ruling family. Duchess Winnamine Balitang took solace from her two older stepdaughters, Saraiyu and Dovasary, and her own children, six-year-old Petranne and five-year-old Elsren. She conducted lessons, had snowball fights, told stories, and did her best to keep everyone from screaming with boredom. She also helped train Sarai's maid, a twenty-three-year-old raka woman named Boulaj, and Dove's maid, the former slave Aly Homewood from the kingdom of Tortall.

Beneath this comfortable domestic life lay a second, less visible and more directed. Many of the leaders of the hoped-for revolution were servants to the Balitangs. They guarded the two older girls and perfected their plans. They sent and received information through a network of mages called the Chain, who used their powers to pass messages from island to island. The members of the household practiced fighting arts, from unarmed combat to sword and spear work, in the outbuildings at Tanair Castle. They had an unusual teacher for new ways of fighting: Nawat, a young man who had once been a crow. The duchess saw this practice as much-needed exercise, and both she and her daughters joined in. To the raka's regret, Sarai refused to continue her lessons in swordcraft after she fought and beheaded her would-be lover, Prince Bronau, the night he slew her father.

Busiest of all the members of the rebel conspiracy was the newest to join, seventeen-year-old Aly Homewood. She was in reality Alianne of Pirate's Swoop, the daughter and granddaughter of Tortall's spymasters, raised from the cradle to compete in the world of international espionage. During the previous summer she had acted as chief bodyguard to the Balitang children. With the arrival of spring and the move to Rajmuat, Aly knew she would become the rebellion's spymaster. Although the Balitangs' former housekeeper, Quedanga, has remained in Rajmuat to collect information from long-standing networks of spies, Aly's specially recruited spies and those they will train have their own unique work ahead. They will collect information for the rebel leaders to use against their enemies, and conduct whatever actions of sabotage and psychological operations required to put the raka's enemies at odds with each other. For sixteen years she studied such work under her father's eye. Now she would do it herself, for the promise of better leadership for the Isles.

In preparation, Aly used the winter to build a cadre of trained spies, people among the household who could learn and use all she had to teach. The lessons of these raka and part-raka in their twenties and thirties included written and spoken codes and code breaking, lock picking, and climbing. She also taught them sign language, thorough searches, medicines and herbs, and the detection of other spies. Because she was younger than many of her trainees, Aly treated them in a teasing, grandmotherly way, while they awarded her the raka nickname of *Duani* or "boss lady." Aly also spent time with the raka mage Ochobu, creating suicide spells and magic detection charms, and with the rebels' armorer, choosing weapons for her pack and for herself.

Aly dared not tell anyone why she was so eager to take up the mantle of spymaster. To do so, she would have to reveal her true parentage. The raka would see her as a tool of the Tortallan Crown, while the forces loyal to the Rittevon king and his regents would see her as a spy. Only one being knew her true history: the deposed god of the Copper Isles, the trickster Kyprioth. It was he who had brought Aly to the service of the rebellion that would return him to his seat of power. Although responsible for her presence, Kyprioth did not speak to Aly throughout the long winter. She assumed he was hiding from the god brother and goddess sister who had cast him from his Isles: Mithros and the Great Mother Goddess.

Luckily, Aly had the crow fighter Nawat to entertain and delight her through the long months. His courtship grew more passionate throughout the winter, and he finally stopped offering her bugs to eat.

At the beginning of April, most of the household traveled south to ready the family's home in the capital, Rajmuat. The family and the remainder of the servants, including Aly, took the following few weeks to prepare for the move that would change all of their lives completely and irrevocably.

1

RAJMUAT

April 23, 463 H.E.
Rajmuat harbor, Copper Isles

As the ship *Gwenna* glided through the entrance of Rajmuat harbor, a young woman of seventeen years leaned against the bow rail, taking in her surroundings through green-hazel eyes. Despite her white skin, she was dressed like a native raka in sarong, sash, and wrapped jacket. The sarong displayed her neat, if thin, figure—one with the curves that drew male eyes. The calf-length garment also showed muscled legs and trim ankles protected by leather slippers. Her jacket, worn against the chill of the spring air, covered her muscular upper arms, while the loose areas of her clothes hid an assortment of flat knives designed for her needs. She had a small, delicate nose, inherited from her mother, just as her eyes were her father's. The wide mouth, its lower lip fuller than the upper, was all hers, with smiles tucked into the corners. Her reddish gold hair was cut just below her earlobes to fit her head like a helmet.

Aly looked the soul of repose as she lounged against the rail, but her eyes were busy. She swiftly took in the panorama of Rajmuat as the city came into view. It sprawled over half of the C-shaped harbor, arranged on the rising banks like offerings laid on green steps. Steam rose from the greenery as the early-morning sun heated damp jungle earth. Patches of white and rose pink stucco marked newer houses, while the older houses, built of wood and stone, sported roofs that were sharply peaked and sloping, like the wings of some strange sitting bird. The higher the ground, the more complex the roof, with lesser roofs sprouting beneath the main one. The roofs of the wealthier houses blazed with gilt paint in the sun. Strewn among the homes were the domed, gilded towers of Rajmuat's temples.

Above them all stood the main palace of the Kyprin rulers. Its walls, twenty feet thick, patrolled by alert guardsmen day and night, gleamed like alabaster. The rulers of the Isles were not well liked. They required the protection of strong walls.

In the air over the great harbor, winged creatures wheeled and soared, light glancing off their metal-feathered wings. Aly shaded her eyes to look at them. These were Stormwings, harbingers of war and slaughter, creatures with steel feathers and claws whose torsos and heads were made of flesh. They lived on human pain and fear. In the Copper Isles, ruled by the heavy-handed Rittevons and their luarin nobles, the Stormwings were assured of daily meals. Aly hummed to herself. There had been plenty of Stormwings when she and the Balitangs had sailed north a year before. Now there were a great many more. From the news she had gathered on their voyage to Rajmuat, she wasn't surprised. The regents, Prince Rubinyan and Princess Imajane, had spent the winter rains executing anyone who might give them trouble, in the name of their four-year-old king. Aly nodded in silent approval. It was so useful when the people in charge helped her plans along.

The Stormwings reminded her that she was not on deck to sightsee. Aly turned her head to the left. Here a fortress guarded the southern side of the harbor entrance. Beyond it, on a short stone pier, stood the posts called Examples. Each harbor had them, public display areas where those who had vexed the government were executed and left on display. In Rajmuat, the capital of the Isles, the Examples were reserved for the nobility. They were surrounded on land by a stone wall broken by a single gate. Over the gate, a banner flapped on the dawn breeze, a rearing bat-winged horse of metallic copper cloth, posed on a white field with a copper border—the flag of the Rittevon kings of the Copper Isles.

Guards streamed through the gate and onto the pier. At the foot of one of the posts men were arguing, waving their arms and pointing. They wore the red-painted armor of the King's Watch, the force charged with keeping the peace, enforcing the law, and conducting executions. Aly narrowed her eyes to sharpen her magical Sight. The power was her heritage from both parents, and allowed her to read the lips of the men and take note of their insignia. She identified four lieutenants, one captain, and a number of men-at-arms who did their best to pretend they were invisible.

Someone sniffed behind her. "Carrion crows," Lady Sarai Balitang remarked scornfully. "What, are they fighting over who gets the 'honor' of displaying the next wretch? Or just over who does the mopping?" Sarai moved up to stand beside Aly at the rail, her brown eyes blazing with dislike as she watched the men. A year older and an inch taller than Aly, Sarai had creamy gold skin and tumbles of braided and curled black hair under a sheer black veil. An excellent horsewoman, she held herself proudly straight, catching the eye of anyone who saw her.

"They seem to be missing something." Thirteen-year-old Dovasary Balitang moved in to stand on Aly's free side, and pointed. Where the Example pier joined the mainland stood a large wooden sign painted stark white. On that sign were three names and the words *Executed for treason against the Crown, decreed by His Highness Prince Rubinyan Jimajen and Her Highness Princess Imajane Rittevon Jimajen, in the name of His Gracious Majesty King Dunevon Rittevon.* The date was that of the previous day.

"What happened to their poor bodies?" whispered Sarai, brown eyes wide. "They should be here for weeks."

"Perhaps Stormwings dropped down and carried them off," Dove suggested quietly. Aly's mistress was different from her beautiful older sister, shorter and small-boned. She had the self-contained air of someone much older. She had a catlike face and observant black eyes. Like Sarai, her skin was creamy gold, her hair black, and her lips full. She also wore a black gown and veil in mourning for the father who had been killed six months before.

Aly knew exactly what had happened to the dead, because she had created a plan for anyone executed and displayed here. The absence of dead Examples was her declaration, as the rebellion's spymaster, that she would turn the Rittevon Crown and its supporters inside out. The spies she had sent ahead with Ulasim three weeks before the family's departure had been charged with putting her declaration into action.

Body thieves were expected to attack from the land. No one would expect people to swim to the pier in the foul harbor water. Her people had done just that, to remove the bodies, weigh them down with chains, and sink them in the harbor. The plan worked on many levels. The Crown officials lost the Examples they had made, and the Kings' Watch was left with a mystery. Aly knew quite well that mysteries frightened people, particularly those people who were not supposed to allow them to happen. Sooner or later word of the vanishing Examples would leak out. People would start to see that the Crown was not as powerful as it claimed to be.

"Last autumn Prince Rubinyan told Winna that there would be no more unnecessary executions," Sarai commented.

"Maybe he thinks these *are* necessary," said Dove, grim-faced. "Or Imajane does."

"Hunod Ibadun? Dravinna?" The soft voice spoke the names painted on the announcement board. The voice belonged to Sarai and Dove's stepmother, Duchess Winnamine Balitang. The girls made space for her at the rail. "They wouldn't harm a fly if it were biting them." She was a tall, slender woman, elegant in deep black mourning. "Hunod is—was—Prince Rubinyan's friend!"

"I would guess they are not friends now," remarked Dove, her voice steady.

"Winna, I don't recognize the names," Sarai told her stepmother. "They aren't the same Ibaduns who own those rice plantations on the southern coast of Lombyn, are they?"

"No," replied the duchess, wiping her eyes. "Hunod and Dravinna were cousins to those Ibaduns. They have—had—their own estates on Gempang. They grew *orchids*. Has that become treasonous?"

"It depends on what they grew along with them, I suppose," Dove said, squeezing her stepmother's free hand. "Or what *Topabaw* thought they were growing."

Aly twiddled her thumbs, as she often did when thinking. She was not supposed to protect the family this year. She was here to gather information and, through exquisite planning, destroy the people's belief in the Rittevon Crown and promote the longing for a young, sane, raka queen. Aly looked forward to crossing swords with the Crown's official spymaster, who'd held that post for thirty bloody years. She knew Prince Rubinyan had personal spies, because she had caught some of them the year before, but the master of the crown's spies, Duke Lohearn Mantawu, called Topabaw by all, was the man who bred fear. The downfall of Topabaw was to be one of her special projects now that she was back in the capital.

She was envisioning her plans for him when she heard a change in the Stormwings' shrieks overhead, from normal taunts to rage. Seagulls fled the harbor in silence, and the city's myriad of parrots stopped their raucous morning conversations. The clatter of shipping and the shouts of sailors rang overloud in the air. Aly waited, listening. Goose bumps prickled their way up her arms. Gradually she heard it more clearly, a rough sound, harsh and bawling.

She straightened with a grin. "Crows," she announced.

The crows burst into the air above the heights west of the harbor in a squalling, quarreling, soaring ebony cloud. They turned the sky above Rajmuat's palace black as activity around the harbor came to a halt. The Stormwings grabbed for height with their immense steel-feathered wings, snarling with outrage at the invaders. They darted at the crows, bladed wings sweeping out to hack them to pieces. The crows, smaller and nimbler, scattered. Wheeling, they dropped, then flew up among the Stormwings to peck at the exposed tender human flesh of their enemies. The racket was indescribable.

I wonder how many of these people know that the crows are sacred to Kyprioth the Trickster? Aly wondered. *The raka full-bloods know, but how many part-bloods, and how many full-blood luarin? Are they going to take this as an omen? I hope not. We really* don't *need omens soaring all over the city.*

Aly sighed. "I had so wished that our return would be *quiet*," she said wistfully.

"I don't believe the crows care, Aly," Dove replied.

Sarai added, "I like anything that gives those disgusting Stormwings a hard time."

The duchess took a deep breath. "Come, ladies. We'll be landing soon. Let's make sure we've packed everything." She led her stepdaughters below.

Aly stayed where she was, her eyes on the city. Things would start to move fast now. All the way here, she had picked up stories of the unrest in the Isles that had begun over the winter and still continued. Soon actual fighting would begin. The fighting, at least, was not her concern, but that of the rebel leaders who served Balitang House. Her biggest task was to make sure they had the most current information available. For this she had access to the network of informants built up by the raka, a network that drew from every skin color and every social category. She also had her own pack, the spies she herself had trained intensively over the winter. They had come south with Ulasim three weeks earlier to start training their allies in Rajmuat. They and their own recruits would gather still more information for her. Most importantly, Aly would collect information from inside the palace, to give the raka as much news of possible allies and the regents' movements as she could. Aly would then bring all the information together, study it, find connections, and get the boiled-down intelligence to the people who needed it.

She thought the odds of the rebellion's success were good. She respected the raka leaders in the household. Coming south, she had glimpsed how far their reach extended, and was pleased. They had a strong, beloved candidate for the throne in Sarai. Her attractiveness and charm would win the hearts of the more reluctant citizens of the Isles. A child sat on the Rittevon throne, governed by heavy-handed regents who were despised by many. And the rebels had been whittling away at the luarin confidence all winter. Only this morning they had dealt the King's Watch a hard slap with the disappearances of the Crown's Examples. Aly even had a god on her side, if he would ever show up.

Aly's nerves buzzed. As if he had read her mind, Kyprioth the Trickster appeared at her side. It was Kyprioth who had brought Aly to the Isles, though he was not the reason that she had stayed. Three hundred years earlier his brother, the sun and war god Mithros, and his sister, the moon and fertility Great Mother Goddess, had accompanied the luarin to the Isles and ousted Kyprioth from his throne. Now the Trickster hoped to retake what was his.

"Hello, you rascal," Aly greeted him cheerfully. "Why didn't you ask the crows to behave?"

"If I cared to clack my teeth in a supremely useless exercise, I *would* have tried to tell them to behave," retorted the god lightly, his black eyes dancing with mischief. "You'll find that not all of your allies are under your control, my dear."

The god was lean and muscled, straight-backed like a dancer. For reasons best known to him, he wore a salt-and-pepper beard and hair, both cropped short. He'd once told Aly he thought this style gave him the look of an elder statesman. Today his coat was a bright mass of yellow, pink, lavender, and pale blue squares. He jingled with a multitude of charms and bits of jewelry. His sarong, a skirtlike garment that men kilted up between their legs, was patterned in black and white diagonal stripes. He wore leather sandals studded with copper, as well as toe and finger rings made of copper and gems. For once he wore no copper earring, only a single blue drop.

Aly made a face at him. "Where were you all winter? You left me to yearn. I yearned for months, but you never so much as sent a messenger pigeon." She kept her voice quiet but teasing. The sailors looked too busy to notice her and her companion, even if they could see the god, but she liked to be careful in all she did.

Kyprioth beamed at her. "I was someplace warmer than the highlands of Lombyn," he replied. "Don't complain to me. You were having all kinds of fun, training your little spies. All *I* could do was wait. I did so in a place where I had plenty to amuse me." His gaze was fixed on the city. A will of stone showed as the corners of his mouth tightened. "I've waited a long time for this spring to come."

Aly stayed where she was, though her body wanted to flee. It unnerved her to see that depth of emotion in the dethroned god. "Well, you don't need *me,* then," she joked weakly. "I'll just take the next ship for Corus, get home in time for my mother's birthday."

Kyprioth turned to look at her. "You're just as eager to see this through as any of my raka. Don't even pretend that you aren't. Which reminds me." He reached out and pressed the ball of his thumb against the middle of Aly's forehead. Gold fire swamped her mind, making her sway.

She braced herself against the rail and waited for her normal vision to return. She dug into the folds of her sarong for the bit of mirror she kept there for emergencies. Her forehead looked much as it normally did, pale after the winter and chapped by the sea air and wind. She grimaced and reminded herself to filch Sarai's facial balm, then put the mirror away.

"What was that?" she asked him. "I thought you'd at least leave a beauty mark or something."

"I would not touch your beauty, my dear," said the god with his flashing smile. "And I would be bereft if you chose to commit suicide rather than be tortured or questioned under truthspell. No one will be able to force knowledge from your lips or your hands."

Aly raised an eyebrow at him. "Oh. So they can torture me, they just can't make me tell the truth. An enchanting prospect, sir."

His smile broadened to a grin. "I love it when you call me sir. It makes me feel all . . ." He hesitated, then found the words he wanted. "All godlike. So there's no need to commit suicide. You won't ever surrender what you know."

"Have you granted the others this splendid favor?" she asked, curious. "I wouldn't want them to be jealous."

Kyprioth leaned against the rail, his expression wry. "No one else in the rebellion has put together as much of the complete picture as you have done over this winter, gathering bits and pieces. You simply had to ferret it all out, didn't you? Ulasim can give perhaps a hundred names. Ochobu can give the names of the Chain and the main conspirators among the Balitang servants. If my other leaders die, they can be replaced."

Aly showed him no sign of the chill that crawled down her spine over that matter-of-fact "they can be replaced." He's a god, she told herself. It's different for them.

Kyprioth sighed. "But you, my dear, have learned nearly the entire thing—not the foot soldiers, but those in command and where they are, the members of the Chain. . . . You couldn't help it. It's your nature to poke and pry and gather. Even your fellow rebels are ignorant of the extent of your knowledge, which makes me chuckle."

Aly fanned her hand at him, like a beauty who brushed off a compliment.

"Besides, I've grown attached to you," Kyprioth said, capturing her hand. He kissed the back of her fingers and released her. "I would hate it if you used the suicide spell and left me for the Black God's realm. You know how brothers are—we hate to share."

"You'll have to let me go to him sometime," Aly reminded the god. "*I'm* not immortal."

"That is 'sometime.' I am talking about this summer," Kyprioth replied. His eyes darkened. "Make sure you see this through. Once battle is joined in the Divine Realms, we gods draw strength from the success of our worshippers. If you and I fail, the luarin will exterminate the raka. And I will be unable to help them, because my brother and sister will kick me to the outermost edge of the universe." He brightened. "But there, why be gloomy? We're going to have a wonderful year, I'm sure of it!"

He was gone.

For a moment Aly hoped the god was not placing more trust in her abilities than she deserved. Then she shrugged. There was one way to find out if she was as good at her task as she and Kyprioth hoped, and that was to pull off a war. "What's a little thing like revolution between friends?" she wondered, and looked ahead.

Yards of dirty water lay between the moving ship and the dock, where a welcoming party stood. "So we begin," said Fesgao Yibenu as he came to stand with Aly. The raka sergeant-at-arms swept the docks with his narrow eyes.

"No royal welcome, despite Elsren's being the heir," he remarked, settling a helmet over his prematurely silver hair. With a wave he ordered the men-at-arms who had sailed with the family to flank the rail where the gangplank would be lowered. "We are definitely the poor country cousins of the royal house." Fesgao was in charge of the household men-at-arms and the rebellion's war leader. He'd spent his life guarding Sarai and Dove, keeping the last descendants of the old raka queens safe. Now he looked at the man who commanded the twenty extra Balitang men-at-arms waiting on the dock, and saluted him. The man saluted in return, a hand signal that meant all was quiet there.

"They've added checkpoints where the docks meet the land, do you see?" Fesgao murmured to Aly. "They want to know who comes and who goes."

Aly shrugged. Soldiers could not possibly watch every inch of ground between the fortresses that flanked the harbor mouths. In the dark, a hundred raka swimmers could enter the water and no one would know. "If they're watching the docks, they're worried," she murmured. "Let's go and give them more to worry about."

Duchess Winnamine had returned to the deck, leading the two children she had borne Duke Mequen. Petranne, a six-year-old girl with silky black curls and long-lashed eyes, danced in place, excited to come home to Rajmuat. Five-year-old Elsren was his father's son, brown-haired and stoic. He hid his face shyly in his mother's skirts.

Winnamine shook her head as she looked at the dock. "This is not good," she murmured, frowning.

Ochobu, the old raka who was the household mage and healer, came up beside her. She, too, was a leader in the rebellion, responsible for the mage network known as the Chain. They had been the source of the rebels' information all winter. "What is not good?" Ochobu asked. She had a hand against her forehead to shade her brown eyes as she inspected the people on the dock. "You are a duchess, and a woman of property. You cannot walk into the city like a commoner. You must have a proper escort."

"We *have* a proper escort aboard with us," Winnamine said quietly. "Forty men-at-arms looks as if we consider ourselves important. We aren't important until the regents say we are. And half of those men are new. We can't pay more guards," Winnamine said. "I told Ulasim before he left not to hire anyone!"

"Your Grace," Aly said politely. Winnamine looked at her. "Ulasim always has good reasons for what he does, you know that. See the checkpoints? There's been trouble in the city—they didn't have checkpoints at the docks last year. Maybe Ulasim found a way to pay these men-at-arms. Or maybe they're just rented for the hour, like actors who mourn at funerals. You know, to add to your consequence."

The thought of her consequence made Winnamine chuckle as Sarai and

Dove came to join them. Overhead the Stormwings glided, shrieking like gulls.

Once the ship docked and the passengers disembarked, Fesgao and the guards circled the Balitang family and helped them into litters. Servants loaded the family's belongings into a handful of carts. Only when everything was stowed and the litters surrounded by armed men did Fesgao move the party out. The litter bearers set off into the tangle of streets that ended at the dockside.

Colors, sounds, and smells assaulted Aly, making her shrink against the litter that held Sarai and Dove. She had gotten used to the long silences of winter nights at Tanair. Street vendors shouted news of their wares, bellowing their praises of jackfruit, sweet cakes, and cheap copper and silver bracelets. Bird sellers walked among them, carrying poles laden with dozens of species of loud, unhappy winged creatures. Shops displaying goods for passersby lined the streets near the docks. Perfumes and spices filled the air with scents.

The pedestrians came in all races and colors, shrieking at those who got in the way and bargaining at the tops of their lungs. They were dressed in all kinds of styles, from luarin shirts and hose to the robes of Carthakis. Many people lined their eyes in kohl as protection against sun glare and the evil eye. Slaves and deep-jungle raka in sarongs or loincloths sported tattoos on arms, backs, and chests.

Aly took it in as she walked beside the litter that held Sarai and Dove. She had picked out a couple of watchers—people who paid close attention to their group. She also recognized a couple of her own trainee spies from Tanair. She smiled, proud as a mother whose child had taken her first steps, then glanced up to see how Winnamine and the two younger children did in the litter ahead of them. Fesgao walked beside them, talking quietly with the duchess. Rihani, the raka mage who looked after Petranne and Elsren, walked on the other side of the litter, pointing out sights of interest. Slowly they moved into the quieter, wider streets of Market Town, the city's merchant district.

There were signs of trouble in Market Town, shuttered stores with Crown seals on the doors to show they'd been seized by the law, chipped paint and splintered wood showing where people had hurled rocks. Aly saw a charred open spot where, if she remembered correctly, a temple to Ushjur, the god of the east wind, had stood. This was most certainly a slap at the luarin, who came from the east. Aly made a note to ask about it.

She had no sense of armed watchers, but she felt observed. Aly looked up. In the houses above the shops, people filled each window, their eyes fixed on the open-sided litters. Aly bit the corner of her lip. Ulasim had gotten the word out that people were not supposed to gather in the street to greet their prophesied queen, but he could not stop them from trying to get a look at her. They were drawing the attention of the spies who followed their procession.

She could see them noting the audience. Topabaw and prince-regent Rubinyan would have word of this before noon.

"Busy already, Aly?" Fesgao asked. He'd walked back to her. "Your glance darts like dragonflies on the water."

Aly fluttered her lashes at Fesgao. "I never figured you for a poet," she joked.

He smiled. "We can control the common folk only so much," he continued in his softest tones.

"Oh, I know," she replied lightly. "Her Grace was excited to see all these new warriors of ours. Did we rent them, or may we keep them? That tall one with the scar on his chin might actually be able to keep up with me for all of a day."

"You are too gracious," Fesgao replied, face straight. "You would break the poor boy by noon, and I would have to keep him in the infirmary for two weeks." He returned to the duchess at the head of the column.

"It's dangerous," Dove remarked softly from inside the litter. "They shouldn't stare so openly. Someone will notice their interest."

"Perhaps they've never seen disgraced nobility return to Rajmuat before," suggested Aly. "They could just be looking at Elsren. He *is* Dunevon's heir."

"Not officially," Dove said, meticulous as always about points of law. "The regents have to make Elsren the official heir by decree. They should—it's customary—but they may choose not to, if they think the nobles won't insist. Until then, if people know what's good for them, they won't pay any attention to Elsren at all."

Aly noted more signs of trouble as they entered the wealthier residential neighborhood of Windward: burn marks on stone, and hastily whitewashed stucco. Here no one could watch the streets from the windows of their homes, because these were set back behind walls ten feet high. Instead, people lined the street on both sides.

"The regents will hear of this," Dove added quietly. "They won't like it."

Aly patted the younger girl's thin shoulder. "Now, if they got everything they liked, they would be spoiled," she told Dove. "And nobody likes spoiled regents."

"Spoiled regents kill people and leave them at the harbor mouth," Dove said gloomily.

Aly smiled slyly and told her young mistress, "Yes, but they don't seem to be able to keep them there very long."

Dove glanced at Aly sharply, then eyed her sister. Sarai leaned against the side of the litter, watching the street. "*She* thinks the twice-royal queen is a fairy tale, you know," Dove told Aly. "Made up by Mithros and the Goddess to keep the raka quiet under luarin rule. If there is something going on, she will take a lot of convincing."

"If there was anything for her or you to know, you'd have been told, surely," Aly said. As the raka general, Ulasim had ordered that Sarai and Dove not be told of the plans being made on their behalf. "Worry about prophecies another time. Once we've unpacked and had baths, for instance."

Dove sighed. "All right, keep changing the subject," she said as she sank back against the cushions. "But I'm not fooled. You know something. You're harder to work out than Sarai, but I know you too well by now."

Aly was about to reply "Don't ask me, I have brothers," but she caught herself. Over the winter she had nearly told Winnamine, Sarai, and Dove the truth about her own background. Aly wanted to trust them. She would trust them with her life if she had to, as they had trusted her with theirs. But she could not trust them with her past, and her ties to the rival kingdom of Tortall.

She continued to watch the crowd.

There were spells written deep within the walls that surrounded the Balitang home. They appeared as a shimmering silver blaze in Aly's Sight. As the procession passed through the gate, she saw magic sunk below the stones, wood, and carvings. It was partially covered by the silvery gleam of common magical signs for protection and health that any house possessed. Unless someone else in Rajmuat had the Sight in the strength Aly had it, no one would see or sense anything but the everyday spells. Raka mages were very good at keeping their work hidden.

Ornately carved pillars lined the long front porch and framed the front door of Balitang House. The roof was layered, each lesser roof sporting upturned ends. After the summer's heat and rains, and the winter's cold and rains, with no staff to keep the place up, the house should have looked rundown. But this house gleamed. Not one clay tile was missing from the roof. The stucco was the color of fresh milk. Gold and silver leaf glimmered on the eaves and on the carved wood above the posts.

The staff was lined up on either side of the flagstone road. They wore luarin tunics and breeches or hose, raka wrapped jackets and sarongs, or combinations of styles in an explosion of colors that made Aly blink. Housemaids wore white headcloths; the men wore round white caps. They all looked to be wearing every piece of jewelry they owned.

Aly counted. Nearly sixty people were here, not including the men-at-arms. Balitang House was as fully staffed as it had been the previous spring.

The duchess could not afford this. When King Oron had exiled them, he had made them show their loyalty with gold, emptying Duke Mequen's coffers. Winnamine had drawn on her dowry to pay household costs. If Prince Rubinyan had not virtually commanded her to return to court, she would have remained at Tanair, which was affordable.

"Fesgao," Aly murmured. The man had come to stand by her elbow. "Who's paying for this?"

"Don't worry," the raka man told her. "Ulasim will explain." He went to help the duchess out of the litter.

Aly looked at the steps. Ulasim waited there, smiling. He was a hard-muscled man in his forties with the brown skin of a full-blood raka. His nose had been mashed against his face on several occasions by someone not kindly disposed toward him. A tightness in Aly's heart loosened at the sight of the head footman. He was the leader of the far-flung raka conspiracy, wise and strong at every trial. He had turned Aly's suspicion into respect. Back under Ulasim's wing, the Balitang family seemed much less exposed. Back under Ulasim's eye, Aly could turn to her specialty and leave him to deal with assassins and alliances.

The big raka bowed to Winnamine. As Aly watched, reading his lips, Ulasim told the duchess that they had not spent money they did not have. He reassured her that all would be explained to her satisfaction once she'd had a chance to eat and rest. As he soothed her, Aly identified a familiar face at Ulasim's elbow. Quedanga, the housekeeper since Sarai was born, had stayed in Rajmuat when the family left the city. She had now returned to Balitang House.

"How did they afford this?" Dove murmured as Aly handed her down from the litter.

"It will be a lovely tale," Aly replied, her voice sweet. "Some parts may even be true."

Dove looked up at Aly, smiling slightly. "You sound as if you wouldn't put it past them to have raided the royal treasury."

Aly raised an eyebrow at her mistress. "Do you think they wouldn't, my lady?"

Dove sighed. "I hope not. It would complicate things." Dove had understatement down to an art.

Hands folded in front of her, Aly followed Dove toward the house. They did not get far. A tall woman stepped onto the porch. She was a silver-haired luarin with perfect posture. Her luarin-style gown was pale blue with a high collar. Instead of the traditional overrobe, she wore a stole like the raka wrapped jacket, made of shimmering white lawn.

Sarai and Dove looked at each other. *"Aunt Nuritin,"* they whispered in shock.

Aly had heard of Nuritin Balitang—or as Sarai and Dove called her, the Dragon. Though Duke Mequen had been technically the head of the family, it was his aunt who ruled it. When he had sunk into mourning for his first duchess, it was Nuritin who had badgered him into making a new marriage and a new life. Among the Balitangs, her word was law. Among the nobles of her generation, her opinion was the first they sought.

It did not bode well that she looked very comfortable in Balitang House.

Winnamine was the first to recover. She approached the old woman with outstretched hands and an apparently genuine smile on her face. "Aunt Nuritin, it's wonderful to see you. Girls, come greet your great-aunt. Elsren, Petranne, come."

Aly looked at Ulasim and made sure the nobles couldn't see her before she hand-signed: *Does she live here?*

Ulasim nodded slightly.

Again Aly's fingers flew. *Are we safe with her in the house?*

Ulasim came over to whisper, "As safe as anywhere in Rajmuat. We're stuck with the old Stormwing, and that's that. She will learn nothing we do not allow her to."

Aly shook her head. "Well, then," she said, "we'll all just be one happy family. What harm could come of that?"

Once inside, the duchess looked at her late husband's aunt. "Lady Nuritin, may we have some time to settle in before we talk? I'm not at my best so early in the morning, and this is quite a surprise."

"Of course you need rest," the old woman said. "Go. Bathe, change, unpack, take naps if you must. We shall have our talk after lunch, and I can explain everything then."

The family headed for the stairs and the private rooms that opened off the second-floor gallery. The inside of the house was as refurbished as the outside. Teak floors glowed under fresh polish. Seashell inlays along the ceilings and floors gleamed. Frescoes were freshly colored by painstaking hands. The furnishings were influenced by raka, not luarin, taste. Flowers blazed in pottery vases as colorful as the blooms themselves. Hemp rugs with bright borders lay on the floors.

Dove and Sarai had suites of chambers connected by a shared bathing room. Aly looked around Dove's rooms and smiled. There were books on shelves on two sides of the room, books on the bedside table, and candles placed for reading. Dove had covered her walls with maps. Here was every island in the realm, as well as a large map that included the Isles, the Yamani Islands, and the Eastern and Southern Lands. The desk was set with inkwells, quills, and paper.

As Dove bathed, Aly unpacked for them both. She also searched the room, though she expected that her pack of spies had gone over every inch of the house. Mages had renewed all the common spells. She also found more concealed workings against eavesdroppers and watchers, strong ones that made her raise her brows in admiration. Aly had worried that someone might sneak something nastily magical into the house without Ochobu there to supervise, but the old mage had told her the house would be made safe.

Over the winter Ulasim had told Aly that Ysul, the Chain's mage in the Windward District of Rajmuat, where Balitang House stood, was second in rank to Ochobu herself and her equal in power. Aly looked forward to meeting this Ysul. She hoped he would be easier to work with than the cranky, luarin-hating Ochobu. Now, seeing the power in what he had done, Aly prayed he could live in the same house with the fierce old woman.

When she had finished her inspection of Dove's quarters, Ali moved into Sarai's bedchamber and study. Sarai's maid, Boulaj, one of Aly's trainees, had already begun her search of the room for spy magics and bolt-holes where someone could eavesdrop. Aly watched. Security was even more important for Sarai. She was impetuous and hot-tempered, unlike the cool-headed Dove. Since the deaths of her father and his killer, Prince Bronau, Sarai had become hard to handle. She didn't care what she said about the king who had sent them into exile or his family. Aly didn't want any rash words Sarai might let fall in her bedroom to reach palace ears.

"Very good," she told Boulaj when the woman had finished. "You must have had an excellent teacher."

Boulaj grinned, her horsy face lighting up. "She was modest, too."

Once Dove and Sarai had finished their baths, Aly had time for a wash and a change of dress. She then padded down the servants' stair to the work quarters of the Balitang servants and slaves. In the kitchen Chenaol the cook greeted Aly with a firm hug and kisses on both cheeks, then stuffed a warm meat pasty into Aly's hands and jerked her head toward one of the kitchen exits.

Junai, Aly's former guard, waited there, her face expressionless as usual. Now that Aly was to work with her spies, Junai had been assigned to the post of Dove's bodyguard at Aly's recommendation. As a fighter Junai had a place in the rebellion's inner circle, but she also had an aptitude for spy work, to the surprise of her father, Ulasim. Aly had not been surprised. For someone with no magic, Junai had often been virtually invisible when she had guarded Aly. She was a silent and accomplished tracker, with deft hands, muscles like wire cables, and Ulasim's quick intelligence as well as his sharp brown eyes. Her fine black hair was braided out of her way, and she favored the highland raka's tunic and leggings.

"You missed me so much I can't even have lunch before you sweep me up in a whirlwind of affection," Aly said as she followed the older woman down a hall in the service wing of the house, where the nobles never went. "I knew it was only a matter of time before I won you over."

Junai glanced back at her. "Some of your pack of spies are waiting in the meeting room," she said. "The men will come soon. And this is your personal office." She halted at the last right-hand door in the hall and opened it to reveal a decently sized workroom with maps and slates on the walls. Aly guessed it had formerly been used to store furniture, but now it was ready for her use, complete with a large worktable, chairs, writing supplies, and that glimmer of hidden magical spells for security.

Junai closed the door to Aly's office. "The general meeting room is here." The raka opened the door on the left-hand side of the hall.

2

DRAGONS, CROWS, AND DOVES

Aly walked in to find a much larger room, with a counter along two walls and a series of cupboards along the wall shared with the outside passageway. A number of chairs of all shapes and sizes filled the open floor. Six of them were occupied by the women of Aly's pack. All looked up at her: Boulaj, the plump sisters Atisa and Guchol, pert Kioka, lovely Eyun, and little Jimarn.

Guchol grinned at Aly. "Oh, good! Duani's here."

Atisa slipped to the floor to stretch her legs in a split. "Does that mean we may go home now?" Her black hair tumbled over her face.

Aly plumped herself into a chair. "If you want to go home, you may, my ducks, but you'll miss using the training I beat into you this winter. Where are the lads?"

"Here," a man said as seven of them entered the room. Junai closed the door as they traded greetings with the women and found places to sit.

"Gods bless us," Aly began as they quieted. "Our pack is reunited and the stakes have gone up." All of them nodded. "I trust you've been good lads and lasses and kept up your exercises when you were not under my eye?" She raised a brow as she looked around the room.

"We've been checking the backgrounds of all the new people in the house, those that weren't chosen by Ulasim before our ladies' exile," Yoyox said, smoothing his mustache. He was nearly as fine a pickpocket as Aly. "And using the gossip network set up before the family got exiled. It's good. Quedanga, the housekeeper, she's supposed to just pass messages along, but she's experienced at collecting gossip from the common folk. She gets word from servants, slaves, artisans, priests—and they're everywhere."

"Then we'll leave Quedanga to send messages and manage the people she knows best, since we'll be dealing more with the palace and the military," Aly said. "She knows she's to pass on what she gathers to me?"

"Yes, Duani," Yoyox said so meekly that Aly had to laugh. "To add to *our* ranks"—he waved an arm to include his comrades—"we have fifteen men we've been training the way you want. Most are in this house. Some belong to households on this street, so no one will think anything if they visit us often. And we've the tunnels under the house for when we don't want to draw attention to our comings and goings. Every man has been approved by Quedanga and Ysul, just like everyone who lives here."

"We have another eleven women," Jimarn added. "All in this house for the present. We have started to teach them codes, searches, and theft."

Aly nodded. This was also what she'd trained them for. Each of them had been examined by Ulasim and Ochobu before he or she was allowed to study with Aly, and she had educated them all winter. One of those series of lessons had been about choosing and teaching new recruits. Aly could not constantly look over people's shoulders here in the city, when she would have to spend most of her time gathering and studying information. She had to depend on her trainees' judgment. Now school was done, and her pack had their own work to do.

"How are your recruits doing?" she asked.

"Well," said Yoyox. "Very well."

Everyone nodded. Aly had learned that the raka already understood the demands of being a spy. In a land governed for three hundred bloody years by strangers, they had lived like spies to survive. Aly had simply taught her pack a number of new tricks, while they taught her their old ones.

"And what of Lady Nuritin's servants?" she asked. "How safe are they?"

"Safe," replied Olkey, one of the men. "Her maid is a luarin, a cousin, and devoted to Nuritin. Stays by her side, doesn't snoop. The other woman, Jesi, is more of a clerk, and writes all the lady's letters and notes. She belongs to the conspiracy."

Aly nodded. That was another worry she need not have. "Good," she said. "I'll take reports in here during the afternoon resting time. If you need me to meet one of your recruits, bring her, or him, in." As they nodded, she looked them over. "Playtime's over, children," she said with a grin. "Nice job on the Example pier, by the way. There were soldiers screeching at each other as we sailed by."

Her pack smiled or looked down, depending on their natures. Jimarn met Aly's eyes steadily. She was in charge of the Example operation.

Aly took a deep breath. "What do you have for me?"

Once her people had brought her up to date, Aly ate her cold pasty and went to the kitchen to beg another from Chenaol. As she ate that, the older woman settled in for a good talk. The cook had been Aly's first friend in the household. In her mid-fifties, plump and wickedly humorous, Chenaol had some gray in the black hair she wore in a long braid. She could flip any kind of knife or cleaver and send it straight to the center of a target faster than watchers could see, and could tell good steel from bad at a glance.

They were discussing the missing tax collectors when a messenger boy came into the kitchen. "Her Grace is wishful of you both coming to the ladies' sitting room," he told Aly and Chenaol. "She's got a cloud on her face."

Winnamine must be about to pop, wondering how we paid for all this splendor and why Nuritin is here, Aly thought as she and Chenaol followed the boy.

The room where the family relaxed during their leisure time was light and open, overlooking the flower gardens and the courtyard pool. The cushioned chairs and couches were elegant but comfortable. Nuritin sat in an armchair, facing Winnamine and Sarai, who shared a couch. Dove had taken her usual position, off to one side. Aly slid into her spot behind Dove as Chenaol, with a nod from the duchess, took a chair. Ulasim took his post next to the main door, the consummate footman. Ochobu entered and closed the door behind her.

"Aunt, I don't believe you know Ochobu Dodeka," Winnamine said. "Lady Nuritin Balitang, Ochobu." The two older women looked each other over thoroughly as Winnamine explained, "Ochobu joined the household at Tanair. She is an excellent healer and mage, so we are honored to have her. Ulasim is her son."

Aly crossed her fingers. Ochobu did not always deal well with full-blood luarin, but she would have to if Lady Nuritin was living at Balitang House. Ochobu's stony gaze was not promising. Though barely five feet tall, she gave the impression of being much taller. Her long nose always looked as if it held a sniff, particularly when she looked on luarin.

If Ochobu's stare disconcerted Nuritin, the noblewoman showed no sign of it. Instead she turned her attention to Winnamine. "You will find that many things have changed from last year," Nuritin said. Like Ochobu, her Gift showed in Aly's Sight, though Nuritin's was glowing embers compared to Ochobu's fire. Nuritin continued, "I have explained everything to the people you sent ahead"—she nodded to Chenaol—"and they certainly understood how things will be different." She looked at Sarai. "Stand up and turn around, girl."

Sarai obeyed with a pout. Nuritin looked her over as she might a horse. With satisfaction she said, "We'll have to take in the gowns I've had made. It's just as well I had Ulasim here escort the seamstresses to your rooms during lunch. You lost weight out there in the wilds—very good."

"*Aunt!*" cried Sarai, fiery roses appearing in her cheeks.

"And black makes you look sallow," Nuritin told her, adding insult to injury.

Aly ducked her head to hide a grin.

"Dovasary," Nuritin said, an actual smile on her thin lips. "Black is not *your* color, either, my dear."

"It *is* mourning, Aunt," Dove explained. "I don't think you're supposed to look becoming in it."

"That is one of the things that has changed," Nuritin said crisply. "Her Royal Highness the princess regent ordained five months ago that full mourning was disrespectful to the Black God, who takes our dead to the Realms of Peace. She ordered that all the court put off full mourning for Kings Oron and Hazarin. The only mourning permitted to any member of the court is a discreet black armband, and perhaps black embroideries or trim. No black gowns. No black tunics. No black veils. We are to wear colors that rejoice for the peace of the dead."

"Meaning Imajane looks dreadful in black and won't wear it if she doesn't have to," Sarai remarked with spite.

Nuritin nodded. "Naturally. But it is a royal decree, with the king's seal attached. You must all put off black at court, or for that matter, anywhere that the regents may appear. It has been suggested that they will regard mourning as a sign of rebellion."

"Aunt," said Winnamine quietly. Everyone looked at her. The duchess stood, arms folded. "You said you had dresses made up. You sent seamstresses up to our family rooms. And there are *these*."

She indicated two open chests. One was filled with money and topped by a clutch of parchments. Aly sharpened her magical vision to read the first of them: it was a letter of credit, issued to the duchess. Next to it was a much smaller chest that bore the crest of the duchess's own family, the Fonfalas. It, too, was open. It held jewelry: gold chains, necklaces, eardrops, and strings of colored pearls. Most were in old-fashioned or broken settings.

"The Fonfalas sent those," explained Ulasim. "They gave their permission for us to melt down the pieces and sell the stones, but we thought we should wait for you to decide."

"And the servants?" asked Winnamine, glaring down at Nuritin. "Where did they come from?"

Ulasim cleared his throat politely. Everyone looked at him. "Many of our new servants come from Lady Sarai and Lady Dove's grandfather, the baron Temaida. The servants are paid by the Temaidas, and clothed by them." He met Winnamine's startled look with a reassuring one of his own. "This is family policy among the raka nobles, Your Grace. When a Temaida girl comes of age at sixteen, she receives a staff of her own, because marriage alliances mean so much to the raka nobility. They want their daughters to appear to advantage."

"Very sensible," said Nuritin with a nod of approval. Slowly Winnamine sat again.

"Your Grace, you were Lady Sarugani's best friend," Chenaol added, referring to Sarai and Dove's mother. "You should remember it is the custom."

Ulasim continued, "They were unable to manage it last year, so they fulfill their duty to their kinswomen this year. The baron sent his regrets that he will not be coming to the city for some time, or he would call on you personally, but he knows that you will treat his granddaughters well."

Meaning last year they were afraid to help the Balitangs when they were out of favor, and this year they don't want to draw attention to their presence, Aly thought. Who can blame them? *I* wouldn't want to belong to the raka nobility of the Isles. It's like living with a knife at your throat. And Ulasim can't tell Her Grace that the Temaidas know Sarai may be queen soon. They're the ones who secretly carried the Haiming royal blood for three centuries, to give it to Sarugani, and then to Sarai and Dove.

Aly hand-signaled Fesgao, out of the Balitang ladies' line of sight: *These new people have been investigated?* Her pack would have checked them, too, but Aly was cautious.

Fesgao replied with a nod and signed, *All hand-picked.* Aly relaxed. Ulasim would have made doubly sure no one suspicious came into Balitang service.

"I can't possibly accept all this," said the duchess, sitting down once more. She was pale. "I can't ever repay it."

"You are not a fool, Winnamine," Nuritin said flatly. "Don't act like one."

The duchess frowned. Her chin came up.

"You will take all this, and you will deck this house and your children in the finest you can buy," Nuritin informed the duchess. "I am sorry—I mourn my nephew's murder, too." She smoothed a braided black armband with fingers that shook. "But politics doesn't wait, and there is work to be done quickly. I had clothes made for all of you, but they must be fitted properly *today*. Tomorrow you are commanded to present yourselves to His Majesty and the regents at court. I believe Her Highness may have intended to humiliate you by summoning you immediately, so she could make fun of your appearance in outmoded clothes. Well! She may be regent, but she cannot be allowed to toy with her nobles in this fashion. I intend for her to fail."

"Who cares if Her Highness plays games with us or not?" Winnamine's gaze was still adamant. "I certainly did not return to accept charity."

Nuritin sniffed. "My dear young woman, has the highland air made you stupid? It is an *investment*." When no one spoke, Nuritin sighed. "You must build a power base for King Dunevon's heir, goose. Elsren is next in line for the throne. He will need friends and support. Our families agreed that setting you up is worth whatever we might dredge from our coffers." She looked at Sarai. "Men will hare after *you* to forge an alliance with our family. I expect you to *remember* your family, and the interests of your family. Flirt with those men, learn their minds, and promise them nothing."

Sarai's mouth trembled. "I have not done so well in my flirtations lately," she replied softly. "If you haven't heard, my last lover killed Papa. And where were the Balitangs, and the Fonfalas, and the Temaidas, when we were in danger?"

Nuritin's thin eyebrows snapped together. "Your last lover? Do not tell me you forgot what you owe to the family by tumbling Bronau."

Sarai gasped in indignation. Winnamine rose to stand with Sarai. Dove did the same. "Sarai would never disgrace us by bedding a man of whom her father did not approve," said Winnamine, while Sarai's cheeks turned a beet color.

Nuritin's eyes were on Sarai. "Bronau deserved to die," she said, her voice flat. "You and your sister did the realm a service by killing him. You also saved his brother the embarrassment of paying an executioner." She looked at the duchess and at Dove. "Is she a fool? Better to lock her up than have her ruin things for us at court. It is not the place to stumble, not after this winter. The regents have proved to be less than patient."

"She is no fool, Aunt," replied Dove. "She just thinks the family's drawing back from us was wrong. Winna and I understood—Papa understood—the family had to save themselves from the taint of our disgrace. Sarai just hasn't made her peace with it."

"Then make your peace," Nuritin said tartly. "You have a duty to Elsren and to your stepmother, if you don't care for the duty you owe to our royal blood."

"I never had to worry about that before," Sarai retorted, her mouth mulish.

"Before there were several heirs between your family and the throne. Now there is only one. You will marry to your *brother's* advantage, which is the *family's* advantage." Nuritin inspected the faces of those before her. Then she nodded. "Come upstairs. We need to get your new clothes fitted this afternoon. And I want to see Elsren."

The afternoon dissolved in a flurry of fabrics and flashing needles. The Balitang clan had mustered an army of seamstresses to work on the ladies' new wardrobes all winter long, using Nuritin's precise memory for the Tanair Balitangs' height, weight, and measurements. The old woman was surprised to find that everyone, not just Sarai, had to have their clothes taken in. Winter had been lean.

Aly, Boulaj, and even the duchess's personal maid, Pembery, found themselves elbowed out of the way by women who sewed at a speed they could not match. Aly finally slid out and spent the remaining daylight hours inspecting the house and grounds.

Out in the garden an open-sided square pavilion glowed with extra-powerful spells against eavesdropping. Inside it, Aly could hear nothing, not even the artificial waterfall that hissed over rocks beside it. It was perfect for secret conversations.

"Come to me," a familiar voice said behind her. "The air is dead under that roof."

Aly turned and smiled. The new arrival was nearly six feet tall, with skin the color of dark sugar syrup. She hadn't seen Nawat Crow in five days, and as always when they'd been apart, she realized that she had missed him. Everything about him made her happy. He appeared to be about nineteen or twenty, with glossy black hair. His deep-set brown eyes were alert to any movement around him. The young woman who didn't follow him with her eyes when he passed was rare. The women who lingered when they got to know him were even more rare. Nawat's grasp on humanity was light, to say the least. It was perfectly understandable: despite his apparent age, Nawat was three years old as a crow and had spent only a year as a man. More often than not, he acted first as a crow might, then only belatedly and occasionally as a human.

Their friendship had begun when he was a crow teaching her the crows' language at Kyprioth's request. During those lessons Aly had fascinated Nawat so much that he had changed himself into a human, something he told her that all crows could do. Seeing him made her pulse quicken as she left the pavilion. He wore clean clothes and he'd finger-combed his damp, crow-black hair back from his face. His feet were bare. "You forgot shoes," Aly reminded him. Resting her hand on his chest, she stood on tiptoe for his kiss.

Nawat stepped back.

Aly stared at him, her hand dropping to her side. She felt almost as if he'd slapped her. "No kiss?" she asked, keeping her voice light. "I'm crushed."

"You said I must not kiss you in front of people," he reminded her. "You said they will think you are frivolous if we are kissing."

"But we're not in public," she explained patiently. "Listen. No one's outside. We could go behind a tree—Nawat, it's just a *kiss.*"

She took a step forward, reaching for his jacket lapel. Nawat took another step back. "I have been thinking," he said. "You will let me kiss you and preen you, but you will not mate with me. I think you are a mixed-up human. You think that mating is not important if you have kisses and preening. If I do not kiss you and preen you, I think you will want to mate with me. To have nestlings. To be with me all our days."

Aly rubbed her temples. Sometimes it was very hard to get a former crow to see things properly. "I didn't say I won't mate with you because we kiss and preen," she said patiently, remembering how close to mating some of that preening had gotten. "I can't be distracted. It's going to be a dangerous spring and summer. This is a horrible time to mate. We can't risk it."

"All life is a risk, Aly," he told her soberly, reaching a hand out to her, then hastily lowering it. "At any moment an archer may shoot you, or a hawk break your neck. A forest fire or a volcano will burn you. A Bronau will stab you. Risk will not end if the god gets his islands back."

Aly sighed. "No, but my task will be done, and then we can mate."

"And what if you are killed?" Nawat wanted to know. "What if I am killed? What if a Bronau steals you away?"

Sometimes a crow cannot be argued with, thought Aly, feeling a little impatient. Sometimes you only give yourself a headache if you try. He'll be stealing kisses again soon enough.

Changing the subject, she asked, "What was that display this morning? It looked as if all the crows in the Isles had decided to draw attention to our arrival."

"The crows came to win our bet with the god," Nawat replied.

Aly raised an eyebrow at him. "I thought that bet was just with the Tanair crows, and just for last summer."

Nawat shook his head. "Not just with my cousins at Tanair," he explained, his dark eyes following a Stormwing high overhead. "He wagered with all the crows of the Isles."

Aly stared at him. "*All* of them?"

Her friend nodded. "While you are here, they will help to guard Sarai and Dove. Only when Kyprioth rules again may we collect the wager, if you are still alive."

"That must be some wager, for you all to risk so much," Aly remarked. "You know, I would be so much more cooperative if I knew what the prize actually *was*."

Nawat gave a bird shrug, a lift of his shoulder blades more than his shoulders. "You would not like it," he said dismissively. "It is for crows."

For the third time that afternoon Aly felt as if she'd been slapped by someone who had never even frowned at her. In a tiny voice she asked, as she had heard girls she despised ask, "Are you angry with me?"

Nawat closed his eyes as if asking for patience. Then he cupped her face in both hands and kissed her mouth softly, lingering, holding them both absolutely still, as if only this connection between them existed. At last he released her. For once Aly could think of nothing to say.

As she stared at him, he answered her. "Never. Never, never, never." Then he turned and walked away.

Slowly everyone settled. The ladies ate with Nuritin, then retired upstairs. Before she joined them, Dove dismissed Aly for the night, reminding her that she could still take off a simple gown herself if she wanted to go to bed. Aly took a last walk around the grounds, knowing that her fellow conspirators would have to wait until most of the household had gone to bed before they could meet.

At last Aly strolled into the kitchen and down the hall to the meeting room. Nawat was there already, as were Chenaol and Ulasim. Except for Nawat, who perched on a countertop, the others had taken comfortable chairs. They shared a pitcher of the liquor called arak and bowls of nuts and fruits. They knew better than to offer the potent arak to Aly. She never drank, fearing liquor would loosen her tongue.

As Aly slumped into a chair, Fesgao arrived, then Ochobu. She brought with her a slender, young part-raka with ears like jug handles. In Aly's magical Sight he, like Ochobu, blazed with his magical Gift. This would be the mage who had laid all the fresh spellwork on the house.

"Aly, this is Ysul," Ulasim told her, pointing to the new man. "Another mage with the Chain. He will live here, to help keep our ladies doubly safe."

"He is mute," Ochobu said tartly as she sat. "King Oron's torturers did that when he was small. So don't go trying to talk his ear off just because he's defenseless."

Aly shook her head. She'd known wolverines with more diplomacy than Ochobu. Then she grinned. Ysul was using military hand-sign code to say *I'm not defenseless.*

Don't tell Ochobu, Aly hand-signed back, her movements concealed by the arms of her chair. *She's happy because she thinks she just insulted me.*

Ysul nodded gravely and settled on the floor beside one of the cupboards. The room was supposed to be a linen storeroom, but that was only in the daytime.

"Where's Quedanga?" Fesgao asked, looking for the housekeeper. "Now that we're all in Rajmuat again, she ought to join us."

"She's keeping watch," Ulasim replied. "One of us must stand guard for a third of every night, to take reports and deal with the unexpected. I have the time around midnight, and Chenaol gets the time from false dawn to sunrise."

"I'll always take that one," Chenaol said comfortably. "I have to start the bread anyway."

Nawat ate nuts, cracking them with his fingers before devouring them. As Ulasim handed Aly a pitcher of guava juice and a cup, Ochobu spoke a word that set magical signs ablaze throughout the room. They faded slowly until they were all but invisible.

Ulasim leaned in his chair. "It is good to see you all again," he remarked.

"Is it?" snapped Ochobu. "How could you allow that old woman to move in here, Ulasim? She will ruin everything."

Ulasim sighed, running his hand through his long hair. "Mother, one does not *forbid* Lady Nuritin Balitang *anything,*" he explained with resignation. "She is, as far as all Rajmuat is concerned, the head of the Balitang family with the death of His Grace. Technically this is the Balitangs' house, not Her

Grace's. It is Nuritin's signature that makes anything to do with this house possible."

"How can we keep anything in this house secret with that woman and her servants at our heart like a luarin tumor?" demanded Ochobu.

Chenaol grinned and poured out two cups of arak. She offered one to Ochobu, who ignored it. The cook gave a "Suit yourself" shrug and drank from her own cup, setting the other within reach. "Just as easily as we keep our secrets with tradesmen and messengers coming in and out all day, old woman," she told the mage. "It's far easier to do in a house like this than it was up in our mountain aerie. You let us worry about Nuritin and her servants. She's good to have on our side—connected to every family of the luarin nobility, and to one in three families among the raka nobles."

"It would draw attention we cannot afford to keep her out, and it would not be easy to arrange," added Ulasim. "Topabaw would think we had something to hide."

"Speaking of hiding . . . ," Aly began. Everyone looked at her. "I admire the way you've concealed the magics on this house. *I* noticed them, but fortunately, the Sight is the rarest aspect of the Gift. You did beautiful work here."

Chenaol looked Aly over. "Since when do you know what's magic and what isn't, mistress?"

Nawat offered Aly a nut. She took it and looked at Ochobu. "You never told them?"

Ulasim snorted. "You spent a winter cooped up with my mother and didn't see it?" he wanted to know. "She never tells anyone anything. She makes clams and oysters look slack-jawed. What is it?"

The old woman grumbled under her breath and tugged her jacket around her shoulders.

Aly popped the nut into her mouth and chewed it thoroughly. "I have the Sight," she told them. "I can see magic, or death, or sickness, or godhood. I can see poisons in food. If I concentrate a little differently, I can see distant things clearly, and tiny things in complete detail."

"So those liar's signs you told us to look for were not real?" Fesgao asked. "The looking aside, the blinking?"

"Oh, no!" Aly reassured him. "A blink, a fidget, a change in body position, those are all perfectly good measures of a lie told by an amateur." She smiled wickedly. "I just have a little something extra." She looked at Ochobu. "I spent the whole winter thinking you'd told and they didn't care."

"I *don't* care," Ochobu snapped. "It is foolish to rely on magic, any magic, including the Sight. The Rittevons have that much right, at least—they know too many people use magic as a crutch, and they are wary of it."

"So says the mage," grumbled Ulasim.

"And who would know the truth of that, if not a mage?" demanded his mother.

Nawat cracked a nut by slamming it on the counter. Everyone turned to stare at him. "Are we done with all the scoldings?" he wanted to know, his face as open as always. "Because I wish to know what use I will be in this oversized, befouled nest you call a city. I could see plain enough when I came. You have more arrow makers here than you will need." At home in Tanair, he had made arrows with special fletchings, arrows that would kill mages and arrows that flew straight despite the wind.

"But there is need for the crows," Chenaol said.

"No," replied Nawat flatly. "You have your human crows in the palace and the city and the households, picking up whatever news they have. My people cannot enter houses, and there is very little food for us here. We are here to win our wager with the god, not to sit about preening ourselves." He glanced into Aly's upturned face and away. "*I* am here to do more than preen myself."

Ulasim nodded. "He has a point," the big raka admitted. "At Tanair the crows were our watchers and patrols."

"We'll find something for him to do," Aly said impatiently. The thought that Nawat might leave made her chest go tight. "Gods help us, we only arrived today."

No one else commented. Nawat was considered to be under Aly's command. The rebel commander had agreed that winter to make their subordinates and work areas separate for the most part, though they would share any news and special requests at the nightly meetings. On occasion some areas might need to work with different ones, but those cases would be determined as they arose. It was a rebel's way to fight, rather than the way a government would do things. If the Crown captured some of them, the rest of the movement would still be able to continue the rebellion.

Aly looked at Ulasim. She knew it was pathetic to change the subject to get rid of that tight feeling near her heart, but what she had to say *was* important. "In the meantime, may we *now* bring Sarai and Dove in on this? The country is trembling on the sword's edge—we could all feel it on the way here. It's the girls' destiny at play."

Ochobu made a face. "To risk all on the discretion of a pair of girls . . . Not yet."

"I agree," Ulasim replied. "At least, not as regards Lady Sarai's discretion."

Someone rapped on the door. It could not be a stranger to the household, since the servant's wing was kept under watch. Ulasim stood to open the door and admitted Dove.

"Sorry," she said, finding a vacant chair. "It was hard to get away from my chess game. I had to let Aunt Nuritin win. I'll never hear the end of it now."

Ochobu glared at her son. "You could have said she knows."

Aly hid a grin as the big footman shrugged. "She came to me after supper to tell *me*," he explained to his mother. "It seemed only reasonable to ask her to come here."

"It's so obvious Petranne could see it," Dove said wearily. "The way the raka watched us all the way to Tanair and back, the crows, a household with all the servants but Aly who are raka full- and part-bloods, servants who used to work for the Temaidas. . . . My mother belonged to some branch of the Haiming clan, didn't she? A small one that escaped the luarin's eyes. It explains a great deal."

Fesgao smiled at her. "You are right, my lady, it does."

"The timing makes sense," Dove continued. "We have only two people with a claim to the Rittevon throne left. Dunevon is a child; his regents make Stormwings look tenderhearted. But do you mean to kill Elsren? Because Sarai and I will never permit that."

"We shall ford that river when we come to it, my lady," Ochobu said. "For the present we gather allies, identify our enemies, and look for the regents' weaknesses. There is unrest all over the Isles. It will be war by summer's end."

"Then don't tell Sarai or Winna," Dove advised. "It's quite possible Winna will have Elsren swear a blood oath not to try for the throne. She hates it at court." Dove looked around at the raka's faces. "You *were* going to tell Winna-mine, weren't you? Or is she supposed to die in the fighting?"

"We have made no decision in that area, either, my lady," Fesgao said with grave respect. "Many things must take place before we shall be forced to consider such choices."

Dove leaned back in her chair. "Tell me," she ordered.

Aly watched as the raka straightened, new life and purpose in their eyes, even Ochobu's. One after another they explained how things stood. Dove's arrival had given them something real to look at. She might have been only their future queen's little sister, but she had the same blood in her veins and the same quick wits.

When they had finished, Dove massaged her temples. "It's so much bigger than I could have imagined," she murmured. They all waited for what she would say next. Finally Dove took a deep breath and asked, "Have we a symbol? Some ordinary thing, so the common people and the middle classes will know that our country is changing?"

She's good, thought Aly with appreciation. Right to the heart of the matter. I hope Sarai does half as well.

"A symbol?" inquired Fesgao. "Like a kudarung?"

Dove shook her head. "Something more subtle. Something that looks like a message, that can be put in places where officials won't notice it."

"Something to shake the regents up," murmured Aly.

"If the regents are shaken up," Fesgao pointed out, "they will not take it kindly, I warn you."

"No, I suppose not," Dove acknowledged. "But they're already behaving stupidly. I saw all the new checkpoints in the city. It's the way the Crown chooses to deal with mindless hooligans. You know what the luarin nobility says—the raka get restless every thirty years, and have to be kicked down. We need to tell them this is no clump of restless raka. This is a movement."

"If we make the regents angry," Chenaol said, "they will slam our folk with more laws, more taxes."

"More arrests," added Fesgao. "More punishments. More executions."

"They cannot arrest what they cannot find," Nawat pointed out. "When the People, animals, claim a territory and drive rivals from it, they mark it. What if you find a way to mark your territory for all to recognize?"

Ulasim rubbed his neck as if it ached. "Please do not tell me we must go out and piss on every street corner," he said, a faintly pleading note in his voice.

"Then only the People will know it is your territory, not the Crown," Nawat replied reasonably.

"A symbol," Dove told them. "Scratched into plaster, written on a proclamation that's been nailed up, dug in the dirt, painted on a door or a shutter. Something easy—"

"An open shackle with a few links of chain attached," suggested Chenaol eagerly. "For freedom."

"Harmless enough," Ulasim admitted slowly. "Easy to spread, easy to set folk talking." He looked at Dove. "We'll do it."

"Aly?" Dove whispered in the darkness of her bedroom. Junai was still downstairs with her father.

Aly had not been asleep. She'd been expecting this. "We'll go outside. There's a pavilion the mages fixed in the garden. It's shielded from just about everything inside the walls as well as outside."

Dove and Aly wrapped themselves in robes and padded downstairs. Once outside, Aly led her mistress to the open-sided building where she had talked to Nawat. The girls sat for a moment on the couch, enjoying the cool, damp spring breeze.

At last Dove looked at Aly. "I wish you had told me."

"In all honor, I couldn't," Aly explained. "They expected me to keep my silence, and it is *their* plot. I am a newcomer."

"But the raka, the people not of our household, they know, or they guess," Dove pointed out. "It's why they always turn out to see Sarai and me. Not because our mother was raka, but because they believe Sarai is the promised queen." She rubbed her mouth with her thumb. "I'm surprised the regents haven't tried to kill us already."

"It will come," Aly said. "If they know their business, they will try nothing in the confines of the palace. They'll try in the city, if they can't get inside these walls—"

"And they can't," Dove interrupted, her words half a question.

Aly considered this. At last she said, "Not without a frontal assault, I think. And on the city streets . . . The raka have been planning this rebellion for decades. We have more allies on the streets than the regents suspect. Naturally, I'm going to do my best to make sure of what they suspect and what they don't."

"Alone?" Dove asked.

"Now you're fishing," Aly said, not in the least alarmed. "I have help, and that's all you need to know for the present. When exactly did you put it together?"

Dove began to braid a lock of her hair. "Around Midwinter, I think. Oh, Sarai and I knew the raka believed Sarai might be the promised queen before that, but it took me some weeks penned up in Tanair to see that there was an actual conspiracy among our upper servants, not the usual mutterings of hotheads. Here in the city, it's even more plain."

Aly looked aside for a moment, to do the mind trick that allowed her Sight to work better in the dark. She wanted to see the expression on Dove's face. The younger girl seemed composed, but a corner of her mouth quivered.

It is one thing to guess, and another to *know,* Aly reflected. She's starting to see the cost in blood.

"I *have* been trying to steer them away from a massacre," Aly said, deliberately adopting the tone of an elderly aunt who had convinced the children to behave. "And they have been listening. Even Ochobu, who hates the luarin more than the rest, sees that there's no profit in killing all the full-bloods, let alone anyone who's a part-blood."

"I feel so much better," commented Dove.

"And so you should," Aly replied comfortably, "seeing as how their queen candidate is a part-blood herself."

Dove laughed in spite of herself. "So the luarin's future is just a tiny obstacle, not cause for a bloodbath. You are an optimist."

"I do have a happy nature," Aly replied. "It is often remarked upon." More soberly, she added, "It will be easier with you knowing. They'll listen to you."

"But you and I need to sort out a few things, Aly," Dove told her. "The god you serve isn't really Mithros." She did not say it as a question.

Aly winced. "Um . . . ," she said, her brain racing. She had warned the raka conspirators that Dove was sharp.

"Why would my dear brother care what happens to the raka?" Kyprioth winked into view on the bench opposite them. He lay sidelong on it, his head propped on his hand. His usual motley assembly of jewels, brooches, and charms glittered in the light he cast. "And could we use actual names as little as possible? None of us will rejoice if we catch my family's attention, believe me." He smiled cheerfully at Dove. "Hello, little bird. I'm Kyprioth."

Aly had forgotten the god's effect on those with raka blood. Dove slid out of her chair and onto her knees, where she bowed so deeply her forehead touched the floor. Despite her awe, she muttered to Aly, "We are in *such* trouble."

"Nonsense," said Kyprioth. "We are getting *out* of trouble. Do sit up. You're distressing Aly."

Dove met his eyes. "There are probably dragons who don't distress Aly. Weren't you banished, or some such thing?"

Aly grinned and relaxed. Dove would let no one walk over her, not even a god.

"Details," said Kyprioth, waving away Dove's question. "A mere fluctuation of the balance of power in this part of the world. It's time to amend that."

"Don't you think you should be talking to my sister, then?" inquired Dove, very matter-of-fact for a girl on her knees. "She's the one the people love."

"I need you *both*," Kyprioth retorted. "She will be charming no matter what. We can leave her to make worshippers of this city. But you, my calculating dear, must be convinced." He threw up his hands. "Question away."

"Actually, your appearance answered the last of my questions, for the time being," Dove told him. "I always was puzzled that your great brother would choose Aly to speak for him. But she's been speaking for you. As *your* choice, she's absolutely perfect."

"Thank you, I think," Aly murmured.

Dove glanced at her. Aly noted the quiver of a barely concealed smile on the younger girl's lips before Dove returned her attention to the god. "You also explain the crows, since they've always been as much your children as the raka. One thing you *don't* explain, though. What happens when someone *does* attract your brother's attention?"

Kyprioth tapped his toe for a moment before he answered. "I will need all the victories my people can gain, to give me the strength to defeat my divine brother and sister. As the raka succeed, so will I."

"And if your brother and sister return early from their little war on the far side of the world, our collective sheep are roasted." Aly inspected her nails.

"Don't say things like that," retorted Kyprioth. "Whose messenger are you?"

Aly smiled brightly at the god who had been making her life interesting for the past year. "Sarai's," she told him. "Dove's. The duchess's. The raka's. And on down through a great, long, complicated list that ends with you."

"I'm hurt," protested the god. "After all I've done for you, giving you proper scope for your talents."

Dove cocked her head to one side. "For a follower, she's very rude."

"I wasn't even his follower. I was his conscript," Aly told her young mistress. "He press-ganged me from a dreadful pirate ship." She sniffed for effect.

"You may thank me later," Kyprioth said cheerfully. "If you're alive." He vanished.

Dove tried to rise from her knees and squeaked. She had gone stiff. Aly helped her to her feet, then back to the couch, where Dove slumped with a grateful sigh. "Does he come and go like that all the time?"

"Only when he thinks he's losing the argument," said Aly. Lips surrounded by a short, bristly beard brushed her cheek in a kiss.

Behind them Aly heard a tapping sound. She released the sheath for one of the wrist knives she wore even when she slept. The tapping approached Dove from behind. Suddenly a small, young, winged horse, known in the Isles as a kudarung, jumped up into Dove's robed lap.

"Hello," Dove greeted the newcomer softly. There was a tenderness in her voice she reserved only for animals and her immediate family. "Where did you come from?"

The tiny creature fanned his wings, then folded them awkwardly and nibbled at Dove's nightgown where it poked through the front of her robe. "That's not edible," Dove scolded, gently removing the cloth. "Aren't your parents going to wonder where you are?"

A whicker from atop a beam supporting the roof answered that question. The adult pair glided down to the floor with grace and ease. The foal watched with envious eyes.

"You'll be that good one day," Dove reassured the youngster. "You just need practice." Still keeping her voice soft, she said, "Wild kudarung in Rajmuat. *Miniature* wild kudarung. Aly, if the Crown finds out they're here, they may have to kill us."

"Ochobu and Ysul have shielded this house and the air above it. The Crown will have trouble getting a spy inside. Ulasim has cleared Nuritin's servants, and I don't see Nuritin herself sinking to that level." Aly considered this. "They'll *really* want at least one spy in this house," she murmured.

They admired the winged horses in silence until the parents got the foal to return to the beams with them. Brushing horsehair from her robe, Dove asked softly, "What are the rebels' chances to avoid a massacre throughout the Isles? And don't lie to me, please."

"I wasn't going to," Aly replied quietly, shaken from her thoughts about Crown spies. "It depends on how devoted they are to Sarai. If they love her completely, they will respect her wishes not to kill wantonly because they can." Aly bit her lip. She hated to voice unpleasant truths, but Dove would think less of Aly if she tried to give them a sugar coating. "Will there be fighting, and killing? I believe so. The conspiracy can't even control the conduct of the Rajmuat raka, let alone folk all throughout the Isles. We must simply pray that their love for Sarai will make them want to obey her rather than seek revenge. It will be tricky."

"You talk as if this rebellion were already set in stone," Dove pointed out.

"But it is," Aly replied, startled that Dove couldn't see it. "It was set in stone long before I came. With your approval or without it, the raka will rise. They've waited too long, and they are short on queen candidates. They've got the taste of hope in their mouths. That taste is dangerous. The only way we can limit the damage is to keep a firm grip on the rebellion. Even so, we won't be able to control everything."

"That's what I thought," said Dove quietly. "Thank you for telling me the truth."

Aly leaned forward and braced her elbows on her knees. "It is necessary," she explained. "Sarai can command the raka, or enough of them to make a difference, but young as you are, you have influence over Sarai and Winna. They rely on your intelligence. They'll listen to you. If you are to advise them well, someone must advise *you* well, and I think that someone must be me."

Dove sighed. "It was easier at Tanair."

"Oh, yes," said Aly, with a sigh of her own.

3

TOPABAW

The next morning Nuritin assembled the family in the lobby of the house, inspecting them as if she were a general and they her troops. No stray thread or curl escaped her frosty blue eyes, no unfortunate fold or bitten fingernail was not remarked upon. At last she smiled thinly.

"Let us see what Her Highness makes of the impoverished, newly returned Balitangs today," she told the duchess. "If she thinks she can buy you with royal favor, there is no time like the present for her to learn differently."

"Aunt, please," murmured Winnamine. "Topabaw has ears everywhere."

"He may eavesdrop all he likes. At this point, the regents need to keep us happy. They need to keep *you* happy," added Nuritin. "You'll see. Come, ladies, and my young lord," she added with a curtsy to little Elsren.

He looked up at his formidable relative and chuckled.

"Very good," Nuritin said with approval. She took his hand and led them all out to the courtyard.

The ladies had chosen to ride, though Sarai had sulked over Nuritin's decree that they ride sidesaddle. Elsren and Petranne, along with the maids who served the older ladies, and Rihani, the younger children's nurse, rode in litters; the boxes of ceremonial clothes were in a small wagon at the rear of the procession. Fesgao rode at the head of the double ring of household men-at-arms, every one of them armed and armored. Junai, dressed as a man, walked on one side of Sarai's mount, Boulaj on the other. Aly walked between Dove and the ring of guards, to be on hand in case the Crown decided life would be easier without the older Balitang girls and the rumors that cropped up wherever they went.

Fesgao moved them out into the Windward District. Despite the earliness of the hour, there were people on the streets, and still more atop walls or looking out of windows. Aly found a familiar face in the crowd, handsome Rasaj, one of her pack. The rest of Aly's spies would be watching for anything troublesome or interesting. She saw three other faces she recognized from Balitang House, and she knew her pack had taken some of their own recruits with them. That was fine. The more the merrier.

For the most part it was a quiet ride. Aly saw other signs that the winter had not been a quiet one. The King's Watch kept people from gathering in any one place for long. Aly noticed still more scorch marks and chipped wood, swatches of fresh paint, and an overall atmosphere of tension. At one intersection, shopkeepers washed what looked like blood from the ground, their expressions sullen as they eyed a nearby clutch of Watchmen.

The previous spring, even with mad King Oron on the throne, the city had been a riot of flowers, colors, and movement. Today it was as if Rajmuat held its breath, waiting for something to shatter the stillness of the air. Aly wasn't sure if the place was ready for open revolution, but she guessed it was certainly ready to explode in some fashion.

That pleased her. The people did not seem to appreciate being supervised as if they were children bent on playing pranks against their elders. Not even the luarin acted as if all was right with their worlds.

Their path rose steadily up the terraced sides of the immense crater that was Rajmuat city and harbor. By sharpening her Sight Aly could see there was a soldier posted every ten feet along the palace wall on the heights. There were no marks on the wall, so the city's troubles had yet to reach the palace. She would make sure *that* did not last. The soldiers were alert and sweating under chest and head armor. How many guards did the Rittevons lose to heatstroke? Aly wondered. Summer might be a good time for all-out war.

"I wouldn't want *their* job," she murmured to Dove, pointing at the wall. "They have to be hot up there. Do they always wear armor on duty?"

Dove shaded her eyes. "Usually they wear lighter stuff, metal plates on leather shirts. They're wearing plate armor?"

"Helms and cuirasses at least," Aly replied. "They must be cooking like lobsters."

"Idiots," whispered Dove contemptuously. "Don't they realize the whole city knows what it means when they put men in plate armor on the palace walls? Why not paint a sign that says *We're frightened* and hang it on the gates?"

"Never complain of another's foolishness, my lady," Aly said, her voice just as soft. "Not if there's a chance you might put it to use." She wondered what the city folk had been up to that winter to make their rulers this skittish? She would have to talk to her pack and catch up on the gossip.

The road entered open ground, flanked by emerald lawns perfectly cropped by slave gardeners and populated by peacocks, geese, and more than a few crows. Streams wound across the land in front of the palace walls. Bridges allowed riders to pass over the wide, deep waters where they met the road. The streams held gray and red fish with sharp, protruding teeth.

"What do they feed the fish up here?" Aly asked Dove as they rode over the first bridge. The water on either side churned as the fish swam to the surface, gathering where they heard the sound of hooves.

Sarai heard and answered. "Meat once a day, but just enough to keep them alive," she said, her eyes flashing as she looked at the stream. "For the rest, they eat whoever gets pushed in. The third Rittevon king brought them here from the rivers of Malubesang. They were to help him save money on executions. If you can make it to the far bank and out of the water alive, it's assumed you're innocent."

"How efficient," said Aly, awed in spite of herself.

"That's where the rebel's children go, when the rebel himself, or herself, is made an Example down by the harbor," Winnamine called over her shoulder. "Some years they just throw people off the cliffs into the sea, because the fish are too well fed to eat any more."

So glad I asked, Aly thought with a wince. Then a happier idea made her smile: she would enjoy putting an end to the kind of rulers who would think of such a brutal way to punish their followers, however rebellious.

At last they came in view of the main gate, called the Gate of Victory. It was set behind a deep moat, on the far side of the last of the bridges spelled to collapse if the right command word was spoken. There were no fish in this water-lily-covered moat, but crocodiles eyed the passersby. Beyond lay the gate itself. When it was open, five heavy wagons could enter abreast. Aly could see that the white marble exterior of the walls was only a facade: the core stones were granite.

Traffic here was at its heaviest. They were not the only visitors that day, but the guards bowed low to the duchess and waved her through, while they stopped the merchant who followed them to inspect his wagons. More guards joked with some riders who were leaving the palace.

Once they had clattered down the tunnel in the wall and emerged on the other side, Sarai told Aly, "That was the Luarin Wall. Rittevon Lanman started building it as he put the crown on his head. It took them three generations to finish. Maybe if the raka queens had put up something like that, instead of using softer stone for the Raka Wall, things would be different." She pointed ahead.

Before them lay an open stretch of grass. There was no place for enemies to hide. On the far side rose a wall and a second gate. The stones of the gate were faced in white marble: the rest was a coppery reddish brown sandstone. On the right side stood a giant gold statue of Mithros the Warrior. The crown of the sun blazed on his head. On the right was a giant silver statue of the

Great Mother Goddess in her aspect of the Mother, a sheaf of golden grain in one arm. Crows perched atop the statues, squalling without fear of the gods whose images they treated so casually.

"The raka didn't even have statues of the gods here," Sarai told Aly. "They believe it's unwise to draw the gods' attention."

With the Trickster for a patron god, I can see why they feel that way, Aly thought as they passed through the Raka Gate. Its tunnel was fifteen feet long. When they emerged into sunlight again, Aly halted with a gasp.

"I always forget how stunning it is," Dove murmured.

Before them lay a splendor of buildings and gardens that made the Tortallan palace Aly knew so well look like a frumpy old aunt who refused to dress for company. Aly's gaze caught and slid along curved-tipped roofs bright with gilt, pillars capped and footed in brightly polished copper. The doors were intricately carved and polished costly wood. Mother-of-pearl inlays shone on door and shutter panels.

Gardens wrapped around every structure, big and small, studded with ponds and banks of flowers that blazed with color. Trees flourished everywhere. Brightly colored birds darted overhead, the contents of a living jewel box. Aly saw a troop of woolly monkeys race along nearby rooftops and raised an eyebrow: five of them wore collars written over with listening spells. On the ground, crowned azure pigeons strutted along the paths.

As members of the Rittevon Guard came to greet them, one left their number and walked over to Aly. He blazed with a god's borrowed glory in Aly's Sight. He stopped beside Aly and stood looking at it all, hands propped on hips.

"It was the jewel of the Eastern and Southern Lands, once," Kyprioth informed Aly. "And it was *mine*." He flung out an arm, pointing to a stern granite wall in the distance. Atop it Aly saw the crenelations of a luarin fortification, like the castles and the palace she had grown up knowing. "That was the best they could do, my brother and sister," Kyprioth added. She stood with the god in a bubble of silence at the center of the household. "Build themselves and their Rittevon pets a gray stone cave where they may hide from my people. Well, that will change." The god inside the man glanced at Aly. "This is *your* chessboard, I believe, my dear."

Aly beamed at him. "So it is. And the game begins."

With an answering grin, Kyprioth abandoned his guardsman. Sounds from the real world filled Aly's ears. Other guards were helping the Balitang ladies to dismount: after a moment, Kyprioth's guard accepted Dove's reins from her. Dove slid from the saddle; Sarai, with a glare at the guard who had claimed her mount, turned, disentangled herself from the sidesaddle, and jumped down.

Stormwings circled the palace, snarling as crows darted in and out of their reach, calling crow insults. Fesgao rode back down their line, gathering the Balitang men-at-arms in his wake.

"Here we leave our ladies and the young master," he said. His bow had been directed to the Balitang ladies, but his eyes were on Aly. "We will be in the Long House by the Gate of the Moon. Send a runner for us when you are prepared to go."

Winnamine nodded graciously. Fesgao rode off with the men-at-arms and Junai.

Naturally they don't want our warriors staying with us, Aly thought as their small parade moved on. There's less chance of anyone smuggling in a rebel force that way. She smiled slyly. We'll let them find out the hard way that we already have people inside the walls. I do love surprises!

Nuritin and Winnamine led them down the road called Rittevon's Lance, which stretched from the palace to the royal docks on the harbor. Here it ended at its intersection with the Golden Road. Along the Golden Road sprawled two of the palace's most important areas, the Throne Hall, where the monarchs held audiences, and the Pavilion of Delightful Pleasures, where festivities were often set. Both structures blazed with white paint and gilt against their background of trees.

The Balitangs halted at the entrance of the Robing Pavilion directly across from the Throne Hall. Only the litters and the cart with their clothes had been allowed this far past the inner gate.

Inside the Robing Pavilion, the maids and Rihani led their charges to a small private chamber where they could change into court dress. Aly neatened Dove's many braids and helped her into her gown, shoes, and overrobe. Once the Balitangs were ready, a footman escorted them to the Throne Hall across the Golden Road. Aly followed.

Nuritin's maid; the duchess's maid, Pembery; and Sarai's maid, Boulaj, stayed in the Robing Pavilion. Pembery was to introduce Boulaj to members of the rebellion's network among the servants of the court. Both were ready to glean information from the winter's crop of gossip, news, and whispers. Aly turned down the chance to be introduced now—she wanted a view of the court. Later she would find out who served the rebellion here. Instead she entered the throne room in the wake of her employers.

Meek in her green-on-white printed sarong, her hair covered by a green headcloth, she found a place in the rear to view the proceedings. If questioned, Aly had a reasonable excuse for her presence: she had never been here before. She had come once, as Kyprioth's guest, to view Dunevon's coronation, but that visit had been one of the spirit only. Today she was able to appreciate the realities of the hall: the textures of wood and stone, the scents of flowers, and the whispers and shifting of those in attendance.

The master of ceremonies bowed deeply to the duchess and to Lady Nuritin. He stepped onto the gleaming floor of the throne room and thumped his ebony staff on the brass disk provided for that purpose. Courtiers as colorful as butterflies turned to look at him. His voice rang from the high, arched ceiling and its gilded beams as he proclaimed, "Her Grace, the Duchess Winnamine Balitang. Duke Elsren Balitang. Her Ladyship, Nuritin Balitang. Lady Saraiyu Balitang, Lady Dovasary Balitang, Lady Petranne Balitang."

The family stepped forward when he turned and bowed to them. Slowly, their chins high, they crossed the expanse of floor. Elsren and Petranne, clinging to their half sisters' hands, did their best to act as formal as five- and six-year-olds could look. Their great-aunt, mother, and sisters walked slowly so that the little ones could keep up.

Aly memorized the position of every guardsman in the room. Interestingly, those on duty here did not wear the combined sun and moon that was on the cuirasses of the Rittevon guards who patrolled the palace grounds. These men wore black breeches and chain-mail shirts, covered with an open-sided black tunic. They wore armored caps and carried broad-bladed spears. These men were the King's Guard, the personal bodyguards of the Rittevon rulers. Once more the Rittevon paranoia showed itself. Their kings could not even bring themselves to trust the guards named after them, but relied on the King's Guard instead. Aly glanced up and found black-uniformed archers with crossbows positioned on the beams from which the hall's lamps were suspended.

Aly was impressed. She had heard of the new commander of the King's Guard, a man named Taybur Sibigat. He had certainly smartened them up since Kyprioth had last brought her here. These were not bored or panicky men, as Hazarin's and Oron's guards had been. These were hard professionals, alert and attentive.

At last she turned her eyes to the dais, where the kingdom's rulers awaited the Balitangs. The dais was reached by a number of broad steps. Two steps up from the floor sat the regents, Princess Imajane and Prince Rubinyan, on low-backed chairs. Aly had seen Imajane before, first at the bedside of her dying father, King Oron. At that time she hadn't appreciated just how imposing Oron's only surviving daughter was. She did now.

The princess was an icily beautiful woman who wore her silvering blond hair in a double-domed style. Her chilly blue eyes were placed under commanding arched brows, and she sat with her chin high, like a queen. Her lips were a vivid red against her white skin, which was further set off by a pink gown under a sleeveless overrobe of white silk bordered with silver. She dripped silver jewelry with pink and gray pearls and blue sapphires.

If only someone could teach these people the meaning of restraint in adornment, Aly thought with a silent sigh. They're like newly ennobled merchants. They just *have* to show everyone they have money.

Ten feet to his wife's right sat Prince Rubinyan, the brother of the man who had killed Duke Mequen the year before. A tall, balding man with hard gray eyes and thin lips, he wore a white silk shirt and hose, and a deep blue tunic with figures of dragons in its weave. Like his wife he wore rings on every finger. His were gold set with rubies, onyx, and sapphires.

Their heads were bare even of the modest gold circle they had the right to wear as prince and princess, but they held themselves as if crowned. Aly wondered if it had occurred to them that their lives might be easier if something happened to Dunevon and they simply grabbed the throne for themselves. From the cold, shining pride that flowed from them, she was willing to bet that it had.

Five steps higher on the dais, the source of their power, King Dunevon, sat uncomfortably on an immense teak throne. He was a bit younger than Elsren, and plainly bored. Aly's heart went out to the child, clad in gold and cream silk, a small crown on his head. He was absorbed in something tucked between his side and the arm of the throne. She suspected he had a toy up there.

A man in the chain mail and black tunic of the King's Guard stood at the king's side in a relaxed posture, observing the room. Around his neck hung the gold chain and gold-framed iron disk that marked him as the Guard's captain. This would be the new man, Taybur Sibigat. Aly memorized his face and the way he stood, then turned her gaze back to the child. She wondered how long the boy had been sitting there and how much longer he would do so quietly. Elsren would have thrown a tantrum by now.

Dunevon kicked his soft leather shoes against the throne. Sibigat reached out a gentle hand and placed it on the child's knee. Dunevon's feet went still. His lower lip came out in a pout. *This is no life for such a little fellow,* Aly thought.

A chill crept up her spine. If the raka had their way, Dunevon would die. Left alive, he would be someone for dissatisfied nobles to rally around. The raka couldn't afford that.

Winnamine and the other Balitangs had stopped three feet from the foot of the dais. The ladies of the group curtsied, seemingly to Dunevon, while Elsren executed a carefully rehearsed bow. Imajane rose and clasped Winnamine's hands in hers. They kissed one another formally on both cheeks as Rubinyan stood.

"Welcome home, Your Grace, my ladies," said the princess. The room was shaped perfectly. Aly could hear the princess as clearly at the rear as if she stood in front. "Welcome to His Majesty's court."

Aly heard the tap of hard-soled boots on the floor behind her. Gloved hands grasped her elbows. One of the two men who had taken hold of her bent down to whisper in her ear, "Come quietly, wench. Draw attention and we'll make you squeak."

Aly made her eyes wide with fright, bit her lip, and nodded. When the men steered her out of the throne room, she trembled just as Aly Homewood, the lady's maid, would surely do. She was being taken captive for some kind of questioning, that was plain. How forceful would the questioning be? She would hate to *need* Kyprioth's protection against her telling the truth under torture. Out onto the Golden Road they went. The silver shimmer of the Gift wrapped around Aly and the men. Whoever had given her captors their orders did not want anyone to know who they had taken. Only one person in the realm would grab the Balitangs' full-blood luarin maid on her first appearance at the palace: Topabaw.

Letting the men half-carry her quivering body, Aly sank deep into her mind, into the liar's palace she had built in her thoughts all through the winter. Most people thought it was impossible for a Giftless human to fool truth drugs or spells, but it was not. Development of a liar's palace had been a game between her and her beloved adopted uncle Numair, Tortall's most powerful mage, a game she had studied until she could fool even him. While he could have broken her if he'd used all of his immense power, he had only tested the strength of her liar's palace against the normal truth spells. The odds were very long that she would ever be questioned by a mage of his stature.

The farther they went, the more nervously Aly behaved, giving her best interpretation of someone who expected nothing good of those in power. She was babbling questions and protests of innocence while her mind weighed her captors. Something was off about them, something that she ought to have identified already. She looked at each from the corners of her eyes, then finally realized what it was: both men were full-blood luarin. It was a sign that she had been in the Isles for some time, that she had come to expect everyone to be some shade of raka brown.

The men guided Aly eastward, followed silently by three crows. The buildings here were nondescript, despite the gorgeous landscape. These would not be state areas but working ones, where economy was considered before grandeur. When they stopped, she gauged that they were somewhere near the northeast corner of the palace grounds, right beside the Raka Wall. Her guides stopped at a building that showed only a small plaque set in the wall beside the front door: INTELLIGENCE.

Aly went from trembling to shaking in the guards' hold as they took her inside. They didn't appear to notice, but she knew they would spot it quickly if she didn't act like the others who were brought here did. Inside, the walls gleamed in Aly's Sight with spells for silence and fear. Tears began to leak from her eyes as her body was affected by the spells, but her mind worked as coolly as ever. Her father had taken most of her fourteenth year to make her accustomed to all kinds of fear magic. She would be frightened, but it wouldn't swamp her reason if she held her concentration.

This is going to be tricky, she thought.

The guards propelled her through one broad stone corridor and turned down another. Chained men and women hung from the walls. Some of these people were more than halfway to the Peaceful Realms of the Black God of death. Aly cowered from them, as she was expected to do. She wept harder, from pity, and she made certain to count every one. She would add their sum to Topabaw's and the regents' accounts when the time came to bill them.

She understood that she was meant to notice these people's pain. It confirmed the stories of the spymaster's work that had reached her ears that winter and before, at home in Tortall.

"It is just the worst possible combination," her grandfather Myles had said once, shaking his shaggy head. He was Tortall's official spymaster or, as his son-in-law liked to call him, the Target. "Duke Lohearn is a spymaster as well as a mage, and he has been at his post for thirty years. He thinks he can do everything. If he can't, he'll just kill the problem. No skill, just power."

Aly thought her grandfather might be right. If Topabaw had gotten lazy, secure in his own reputation, Aly would have an opportunity to knock him from his vital position.

The guards turned down a third hall, which ended at an open door. They pushed Aly inside. As she sprawled, they slammed the door, leaving her alone with the room's occupant.

She looked up at Duke Lohearn Mantawu: the ill-famed Topabaw. He sat on a plain chair, one hand braced on his thigh, one resting on a crude table that held a large parchment book, inkpot and quill, a three-throated lamp that smelled of cheap oil, a pitcher, and a pair of cups. Aly closed her eyes and adjusted her Sight so that the blaze of his magical Gift, added to the spells on the charms that bedecked the man, wouldn't blind her. Fumbling at her sash, she drew out a clean handkerchief and blew her nose.

Under the layers of charms, Aly saw a pallid, bony aristocrat in his late fifties. He had a razor cut of a mouth, small brown eyes, and short steel-gray hair. His cheap black cotton tunic and breeches were shabby and stained. Work clothes, thought Aly. Her Sight read the stains as dried blood and other liquids.

Am I supposed to be impressed that a luarin gets his clothes dirty? Aly wondered, lowering her gaze to the man's scuffed boots. She continued to quiver and weep.

"My dear girl, get off that floor." His voice was suspiciously kind. "It's dirty. There's a stool right beside you. Sit on that."

Aly obeyed, still not looking Topabaw in the eye.

"Isn't that better?" he asked. He opened his book to a page that was already marked. "Let's see. Your name is Aly Homewood, correct?"

Aly nodded, then scrambled to say, "Yes, my lord."

"Very good." He smiled mirthlessly, not parting his lips. "Luarin slave, given to House Balitang with the purchase of a cook on April 24, 462. Formerly a maidservant at Fief Tameran in Tortall. No bids were made for your purchase in the slave market." Icy amusement was in his voice as he added, "I think it would be very different if you were to go to the selling block at present. Some would consider you to be most fetching."

That was supposed to frighten her. She whimpered and cringed. "Please don't sell me, sir," she pleaded. "I've a good place, I'm learning to be a lady's maid—"

"Quiet," he ordered gently.

Aly went instantly silent.

"Taken into exile by Duke Mequen Balitang. Served as goatherd, then maid. Fought for your owners during a kidnap and murder attempt by our prince-regent's brother, Bronau Jimajen. Freed as a result. Now serving as maid to Lady Dovasary Balitang. You're a clever girl, Aly Homewood."

Aly bobbed her head. "Thank you, my lord, sir—"

"Your Grace," he said gently. "I have the rank of duke. Look at me when I speak to you, my dear."

Aly raised her eyes as she was commanded to, still shaking. Gazing at him openly, she realized that he did not look like the Crown's stone hammer. There were dark circles under his eyes. His skin was dry and cracked, his lips bitten and peeling. There was the slightest tremor in his hands. His hair looked greasy, as if he had not washed it for a while. This was a man who had been forced to work hard of late.

Topabaw smiled as she met his eyes. "There. Isn't that more friendly?"

She bobbed her head eagerly.

"Do you know, I am surprised they made you only the maid of the younger daughter," he told Aly. "Such a deed as you did for them, they should at least have given you the post of maid to the older girl, or to Her Grace the duchess."

Aly ducked her head. "I couldn't say, Your Grace." Then she met his eyes again, so he would think she lied, that she *had* thought of a better reward, like a higher position.

"They don't appreciate you." He nodded to a pair of cups and a pitcher on his table. "Pour us both a drink," he commanded. "Some wine will do you good."

Aly slowly rose and did as she was told. In Topabaw's position her da or her grandfather would have done the pouring, to make her feel treated almost as an equal, to flatter her. You're supposed to stroke and slap me, so I won't know what's coming, she thought, exasperated with him already. Inspecting the wine with her Sight, she found the signs of truth spells.

Taking her cup, she settled back onto her stool. It was time to call up her liar's palace. *Homewood, homewood, homewood I go,* she told herself silently, sinking into her own mind as if it were a pool of water. She surrounded herself with the mind of Aly Homewood. Part of her split off to watch and advise. The rest of her awareness filled the liar's palace. She sipped from the cup, pretending she liked the taste of the wine. She also pretended not to notice that while she drank, he did not, though he put his cup to his lips. The spell in the drink went straight to work, making her light-headed and relaxed.

"Does it not irk you, to be at the beck and call of raka?" Topabaw asked softly, more confident. "To be under the orders of that head footman, that cook, those armsmen, when your skin is as white as that of the duchess?"

"It's not my place to say, Your Grace," she said, her voice slurred from the drug.

"You may speak freely here," said Topabaw graciously. "Drink up."

She drank. "I mean, sir, Your Grace—" She giggled, then pressed her arm to her mouth to stop herself. "This is quite nice," she told him, and emptied the cup. He refilled it. Leaning forward as if this bone-pale man were her friend, Aly confided, "It was this way at home, you know. Everyone else gets the good stuff. I get the odds and ends. It wasn't *my* fault my mother left, stupid slut. And now?" She made a disgusted noise and flapped her hand as if driving something away. "Nothing for me again, ever. You know, we have these dark-skinned folk at home. Bazhir, they call themselves. Sand lice, *I* call them. Riding about like lords when *we* own *their* lands. Acting like you're dirt while they eye your bum." She snorted a laugh.

"The Bazhir?" asked the spymaster, folding his hands on his desk.

"These raka, too," she said earnestly. "They're just the same. I want to tell them, Who owns who? Seems to me we luarin beat your lot like drums, miss, so don't you go looking down your nose at me." Her internal distant watcher shook her head over the look on Topabaw's face. His contemptuous smile and satisfied pose told her that she'd said just what he wanted to hear. He didn't even respect her enough to keep it from his face.

"Tell me, where were you born?"

In her liar's palace, a door opened to show her the answer. "Ginine," she said, "north of Port Legann in Tortall. Didn't want to work there. Too many sand lice, if you take my meaning. Then I come here. Sand lice, jungle lice, they're all the same."

He asked the questions she expected. She answered all of them from her liar's palace. The girl who lived there was small and sordid, a petty servant and thief with a raisin for a heart.

"There is a way you may better yourself," Topabaw explained softly. "One that might grant you revenge on those who show you so little respect. If you will perform a small service for me, I will do one for you. Her Highness is always in search of pure-blood luarin girls for her household."

Aly sat up straight, her eyes blazing. "You'd take me from that pen of mongrels?" she asked eagerly.

"You must remain a while longer," Topabaw said, leaning forward to hold her with his eyes. "We believe there is plotting afoot in that household. Our other spies there bring us stories that hardly seem likely. I believe those spies may be compromised, or worse, that they have betrayed me. I count on *you* to find out the truth."

Distant Aly Saw that he lied about spies in the household. She also knew he wanted her to believe him, to keep her from lying to him.

"They'll cut me up if I'm caught," Liar Aly pointed out. "That's a lot of risk for just a promise of 'someday.'"

He smirked and reached into a pocket, drawing out an ordinary leather purse that clinked. "Will this make the risk more bearable?"

Aly seized it greedily and counted the coins—silver and copper, no gold, which might be suspicious if she was searched. There were listening spells on the lot of them. "This is all?" she asked.

Topabaw slammed his fist down onto the table. She jumped. "You over-step!" he barked.

Aly cringed. "Forgive me, Your Grace—I don't know why I'm so loose-tongued," she told him, kneeling on the floor. "Normally I keep my own counsel. I didn't mean any disrespect, I swear. Forgive me, Your Grace!" Distant Aly thought, You ham-handed brute.

Topabaw smiled and sat back. "Mind your place," he ordered. "You will report every third day to Master Grosbeak on Gigit Lane. Depending on what you bring to him, you will receive some manner of payment. And don't try to lie to me, wench," he said coldly, pointing a bony finger at her. "My other spies in your household will be truthful about *your* actions, if about nothing else! Get out."

Aly got out, bowing over and over until she was out of that room, then fled down the hall, bolting past the chained captives on her way to the door. Outside she raced down the path to a clump of trees. She collapsed against one, out of sight, and relaxed, feeling the last traces of the spell vanish from her body. Most such spells were short-lived, so that the person they were used on could return quickly to normal. "Homewood, homewood, homewood I go," she whispered, listening to the shriek of distant Stormwings and the calls of distant crows. Slowly her real self rose from the liar's palace, freeing her mind and concentration.

Waiting, breathing, identifying the scents that met her nose—cumin, roses, jasmine, horse urine, rust—she reassembled herself. Only when that was done did she begin to turn over the interview in her mind. He hadn't made her swear in blood. She assumed Kyprioth would protect her from the penalities for those who broke that magical oath, but Topabaw's omitting it before he'd dismissed her made her even more contemptuous of him than she'd already been.

Ham-handed *and* lazy, she thought with disgust while she stared at the leaves overhead. And sloppy. Maybe he was something once, but no longer.

With a sigh Aly got to her feet, startling a marmoset clan into flight among the trees. "Sorry," she called, and walked down the flagstone path to Golden Road. She ambled down to the Robing Pavilion, sidestepping peacocks and crowned pigeons.

She heard a boisterous call overhead. The three crows who had followed her, seeing through the magical veil over Aly and her captors, were leaving now that she was free and unharmed. She watched as they flew toward a Stormwing that soared overhead, calling insults. The Stormwing jinked in midair, then—with no other Stormwings nearby to watch his back against the crows—fled.

4

THE PAVILION OF DELIGHTFUL PLEASURES

When Aly looked into the Throne Hall, it was empty. The maids at the Robing Pavilion told her that her ladies and their maids had gone to the Pavilion of Delightful Pleasures. Aly nodded as she tucked Topabaw's purse among their boxes, grateful the Balitang party was still here. She could put off the inevitable questions about where she'd been until tonight. Casually she crossed the Golden Road to the pavilion that lay beside the Throne Hall. Aly knew better than to enter through the porch that opened onto the Golden Road. That was a stage, designed to display the court while important guests presented themselves. With the palace map in her mind's eye, she found a small bridge spanning the creek that cupped the pavilion. A well-trodden path led her to the servants' entrance. As she passed into the building, she walked into an invisible cloud of scent: lotus, rose, sandalwood, and lily as well as cherries, mangoes, and cooked chicken.

Servants pointed Aly to a gallery at the end of a long, narrow hall. Everywhere Aly saw spells for listening and seeing, but their gleam was faint. When was the last time they were renewed? she wondered, seeing glimmers of the spells. Don't they know you have to renew spells every few years? Or are they so sure their spies among the servants will report what is said that they don't bother?

In the servants' gallery the carved screen that served as one of the walls allowed servants to see the nobles beyond. They also allowed the nobles to see their own people, in case they needed something the pavilion did not provide.

Aly took the entire gallery in a second time. The mages of the Chain had been at work here. Pembery, Boulaj, and some other raka servants stood in one corner, talking. Aly heard nothing and could not read their lips. An entire corner of the servants' area was marked out with spells to counter the Crown's magic. These spells were so carefully hidden under other spells that Crown mages might not detect them. The edge of the silent corner was marked out on the floor by a line of boards held in place by a pair of pegs at each end. On this line only, the pegs were perceptibly lighter than the wood in which they were set, the only boards in the floor to show such a marking. It was subtle but effective. Aly approved. It was always nice to see a well-done piece of spy work.

It was also a powerful illustration of how the raka used their magic after the luarin conquest. Raka magic was shaped by subtlety, crafted by mages who spent their lives hiding things from other mages. To those who wielded their Gift as the mages of the Eastern and Southern Lands had been taught, raka magic seemed weak, good only for simple tasks. Its symbols were different, its spells far quieter, shaped for that effect over three hundred years of practice and development, with death for the raka mage who drew a luarin mage's attention.

As she eyed her surroundings, the other servants turned to look at her. Boulaj waved Aly over to the protected corner. As soon as Aly stepped past those marked boards, she could hear Boulaj speak clearly, when her words had been indistinct outside them. "This is Aly, Lady Dovasary's new maid. She is one of us."

The woman next to Boulaj frowned. "A luarin? She can never be one of us."

"That you must ask the god, if you dare," Boulaj informed her pleasantly. "In our household, we do as he bids us. He chose to make Aly his messenger." To Aly Boulaj said, "This is Vereyu. She represents our folk in the palace." When Vereyu protested the use of her real name and position, Boulaj said, "Ask the god about Aly's faithfulness, if you won't believe me. Go on, ask him."

Aly looked at Vereyu and raised an eyebrow. Most people of sense preferred not to call on specific gods unless matters were dire. There was always the chance the god might not care for the summons.

It seemed Vereyu was a woman of sense. She tightened her broad mouth but did not open it to call on Kyprioth. A stocky part-blood raka, Vereyu looked both intelligent and hard. Her clothing was unremarkable, but her hair drew Aly's eye. The long copper pins that secured her black hair in its coil at the back of her head housed lethally sharp miniature knives.

"You don't go near the throne with those, do you?" she asked, gently tapping one of the pins' copper knobs. "Surely the weapon alarm spells would detect them."

Vereyu swung around almost casually, reaching for the arm Aly had just used, ready to grip it and twist it up behind Aly's back. As Vereyu moved, Aly took just one step to the side, letting Vereyu's hands slide uselessly past. When Vereyu moved straight into another attack, Aly took a second step just out of range, guessing that Vereyu would lunge at her. As Vereyu did, Aly gripped a part of her collarbone that would hurt exquisitely if pressed. Vereyu went still.

"Play nicely, if you please," she murmured in Vereyu's ear. "I'm sorry I'm not to your taste. Do you want everyone to see that we know unarmed combat? Only think of how they would gossip at such undovelike behavior on the part of servants."

Vereyu considered her next move. Aly glanced at Boulaj, who was covering a smile with her hand.

Suddenly Vereyu nodded. Aly waited for a moment, alert for a trick, then let her go.

"If they knew real doves, they'd stop telling us servingwomen should act like them," Vereyu said, her voice very dry. "What is it the god uses you for, anyway?"

Aly batted her eyes at the woman. "To guard the ladies," she replied. There was no reason anyone should know her real place in the rebellion if they did not already know. "And a bit of this and that."

Vereyu snorted. "You're the god's, all right," she muttered. "You're just his sort."

Why, thank you, Kyprioth said. The sound of his voice made all the servants in the corner jump, though no one else in the gallery appeared to have heard.

Establishing my credentials with the palace raka? she asked Kyprioth silently as the servants who'd heard him bowed their heads briefly. *I was doing well enough on my own.*

I just wanted to remove any lingering doubts, he said, apparently to her alone. *Better safe than sorry.*

Aly giggled at the thought of the Trickster's ever caring about safety. When she felt his presence fade, she looked around. "I'm famished," she remarked. "Do you people ever feed a girl?"

Vereyu raised a hand and beckoned. A maid came over to them with a tray of fried dumplings and fruit. As Aly ate, she looked around the room. Servants flirted in corners, sat on cushions and chairs and gossiped, or watched their masters in the room beyond. Once she'd cleaned her hands, Aly drifted over to the screen to have a look at the nobility.

Vereyu followed her. "They are not so smug as they were last autumn," she murmured in a voice that dripped venom and satisfaction. "They have lost too many tax collectors and couriers. There have been five riots in the Downwind District of Rajmuat since Midwinter, three of them coming when the Crown sent troops to take raka mages and leaders captive. The Crown's armies have gone without pay for three months."

"I assume this means you take the god's word for me," Aly whispered in return. She had already positioned herself, and thus Vereyu, out of range of two faded listening spells. "How do you know I'm not one of his jokes?"

"Because he needs us too much to joke," replied Vereyu. "Because he needs all the victories we can win for him if he is to retake the Isles. We were great, once." She nodded toward the sprawling chamber on the other side of the screen. "All this splendor was built by *our* people. The world came to these pavilions to discover the true meaning of beauty, when our queens ruled here."

Aly looked into the gallery. Vereyu was right. The Pavilion of Delightful Pleasures was extraordinary. The walls were fashioned of pale marble and lined with arched windows that extended to the floor, the windows magically spelled to keep animals and insects at bay. A tribe of golden lion tamarins sat on the rail of the outer walkway and watched mournfully as servants passed the windows carrying fruit.

Inside, there was a raised dais at the center of the room, but Aly saw no thrones. Instead the young king sat on a cushion and directed playmates as four boys of his own age, including Elsren, moved toy soldiers and immortals into position all around an intricately carved fortress. Petranne sat beside the king and watched as Dunevon moved the castle's defenders and their weapons along its stone battlements.

Princess Imajane sat in a backless chair in front of the dais, talking to Lady Nuritin. Between them was a small table laden with food and drinks. The ladies chatted, sipped, and nibbled while raka slaves waited on them. Aly read both women's lips: they were talking of Winnamine's "magical transformation" from country lady to noble courtier. The duchess herself sat across the room, talking with other noble mothers as she watched Sarai mingle with a bright cluster of young men and women.

Aly felt Vereyu shift position. "Watch yourself," the raka whispered to Aly, and moved off. Aly could tell that someone else had come up behind her: someone large, because she felt his body heat to the top of her skull. He smelled of soap lightly scented with sandalwood and cinnamon. She pretended she did not notice him, though she kept her ears sharp for any movement that he would make, and continued to survey the large room.

She found Dove near the far rear corner, seated between two older luarin noblemen and engaged in a conversation that was every bit as animated as the ones Sarai was holding. The man on Dove's right had to be in his seventies, bald, the white hair on the sides of his head and of his beard clipped neatly short. His eyes were set in fans of wrinkles. Despite the day's warmth, he was dressed in velvet and wool. Around his neck he wore a heavy chain with a pendant that was half a golden sun face and half a white gold moon face.

"Baron Qovold Engan," a light voice said in Aly's ear. She gasped, jumped, and spun, as if she had not heard the man come over to speak to her. She stared up into the face of Taybur Sibigat, captain of the King's Guard. He was as tall as her adopted uncle Numair, who stood six feet five inches in his stocking feet. Unlike her uncle, Taybur had a solid build without any of Numair's angular gawkiness. He wore his chain mail as easily as other men wore cloth, despite the growing heat. "He's the royal astronomer, and your young mistress's former tutor in cartography and astronomy. At the moment, he's not the regents' favorite person. He's told them that there will be two lunar eclipses and a solar eclipse this summer, which some people might see as ill omens. That other fellow, next to Lady Dovasary? That's Duke Vurquan Nomru. Old Iron Bum was his nickname when he commanded the army. He was one of your lady's favorite chess partners before she was exiled. They tell me that for a girl of twelve, she played as well as any adult."

Aly could see how Dove's other companion might earn such a nickname. His nose was an eagle's beak set under two sharp brown eyes, his sensuous mouth set in a firm line. His clothing was simple bronze cotton and silk. Like the other male nobles, he wore no sword or dagger in the royal presence, but there were dents in his belt where they normally hung. For a Kyprin noble he showed uncommon restraint in his jewelry, keeping it to a single gold earring, a chain, and gold rings on his index fingers and thumbs.

"Excuse me, my lord, but why do you say such things to me?" Aly inquired, bobbing as much of a curtsy as anyone in a sarong could manage. "I'm just a maid."

"And I am just a friendly fellow," he replied. "I'm Taybur Sibigat, captain of the King's Guard." He smiled at Aly, revealing small, pearly teeth. "I wanted to compliment you on your inspection of the Throne Hall," he added. "You spotted each man I had there, including the ones on the roof beams, where no one else ever looks. And you found every exit." When Aly took a step back, frowning, he shrugged. "Spells around the dais help us to see clearly throughout the hall."

Aly gave him a trembling smile. "I've no idea what you're talking about, my lord," she said nervously, though inwardly she was fascinated. It sounded as if he'd guessed she was a spy of some kind.

"Of course you don't know what I'm talking about," he said agreeably. He was chubby cheeked like a boy. He wore his dark, curly hair cut short over his high forehead. His eyes were brown and observant, and his mouth had smile curves tucked into the corners. "Call me Taybur. We'll see a lot of each other if Their Highnesses have their way."

Aly continued to play the part of the not-very-bright country girl. "I don't know how you can say as much, my lord," she replied, deliberately neglecting to use his name. "My mistress is here today because the whole family was summoned, but she's not of an age to be going to court things. And whyever would a great man like yourself take an interest in a poor little maid like me?"

Taybur's smile lit his face and eyes. "That's very good," he remarked with approval. "I couldn't have done it better myself. Now, if I were being a nice man, one who'd let you believe I'm not suspicious of you, I would say that I like to meet all the very pretty girls who come my way. It would even be true. I'm quite fond of very pretty girls. But we both know that there is far more to you than that."

Aly looked down, the picture of the demure servant. He does suspect me, she thought. He's been trained. "My lord, you talk in riddles, I swear!"

"Very well," he said agreeably, leaning against a corner post. "You look like a girl who knows her riddles. I understand your name is Aly Homewood, and I know you were once a slave." He pointed to the faint scar around Aly's neck, the mark of a slave collar. "Today you're Lady Dovasary Balitang's maid. Your accent . . ." He cocked his head, studying her with interest. "Tortall, southeastern coast."

"I come from there, my lord," she admitted meekly. She kept her eyes down to hide her growing delight. Somehow Taybur Sibigat had recognized her for a player of the spies' game, but he didn't seem interested in exposing her. She had to try to convince him that he was wrong, but it was lovely to meet someone who spoke the language she had learned in the cradle, the give-and-take between those who sought information. Glancing around the room from the corners of her eyes, she saw that most of the servants watched them warily but without alarm. She even saw liking on some of those faces. This man wasn't as feared as the regents or Topabaw, then.

He tugged on his ringless earlobe. "I'm trying to narrow it down—you're not a Carthaki agent," he murmured, thinking aloud. "They have a, a special whiff about them, don't you agree? A well-polished one. They do unctuous better even than a courtier. Tyrans are a slippery lot. Usually they just ooze around corners. It comes of living in a swamp. But you . . ." He tipped his head from side to side. "The Whisper Man of Tortall. Are you one of his, or have you sold your services elsewhere?"

It would have taken much more than her father's nickname to make Aly twitch. She began to shake her head and continued to shake it as he asked if she served the Marenite, Yamani, Gallan, or Tusaine spy networks.

"You must believe me, I'm just a servant, my lord, just a servant, and I know naught of spying or whispering or anything like that!" she babbled. "I'm just a poor girl from Tortall, making my way in the world!" She glanced up at him from under her brows. "If you suspect me so, why haven't you arrested me or given me over to Topabaw?" she demanded. It was a risky point to make when she was supposed to be terrified out of her wits. She simply could not resist needling him a little in return.

He shrugged. "I won't do the man's work for him. Besides, Topabaw has notified me, through the prince regent, that my assistance and advice are unwelcome."

Hmm, thought Aly, I smell rivalry here. When two powerful men dislike each other, things can slip through the cracks between them.

"Besides," Taybur continued, "I'm sure you'll get to know him soon enough."

Too late, Aly thought, thinking of the purse of coins she had stowed in the Balitang luggage. Inside she grinned broadly. She hadn't realized how much she had yearned for someone who could meet her at her own level. She would be even more careful knowing that Taybur Sibigat had an eye on her. Unlike Topabaw, Sibigat did not hear only what he wished to hear. It would be much more fun to outwit someone who knew what he was doing. She'd only have to worry that the regents might give Taybur Sibigat the spymaster's job if she brought about Topabaw's fall.

Taybur leaned down until his lips were close enough to her ear that the feel of his breath raised goose bumps on her skin. "Whatever game you play at here—and let's just assume you denied it with great vigor and go about our day—please, understand. All I care about is the safety of the king. Conduct whatever games you wish on these palace grounds with my blessing. Topabaw can use the exercise. But sniff around His Majesty, and suddenly I won't like you anymore."

Oh, dear, Aly thought guiltily. He thinks I'm just a regular spy. He doesn't know what the raka are up to, or if he does, he doesn't think it will come to anything.

"You frighten me, my lord," she whispered, keeping her eyes on the ground.

"I told you to call me Tay—"

Whatever else he had meant to say was cut off by a yelp from the dais. Taybur left the servants' gallery at a swift pace. King Dunevon, not liking the way the game of storm the castle was proceeding, had kicked one of the young generals. A seasoned courtier even at that age, the boy he'd kicked knew better than to hit his king. He fell on Elsren instead, pounding the smaller child. The other two "generals" entered the fistfight. Dunevon jumped from his chair, shrieking with glee as all across the room female relatives converged on the dais.

Winnamine got there first, thrusting one boy into his mother's arms and holding another by one arm as she scooped Elsren from the pile. Rubinyan started across the room for the king, but Taybur Sibigat was there ahead of him. Gently the big man hoisted the king onto one hip like an experienced nursemaid.

When Rubinyan reached them, his face dark with anger, Taybur spoke quietly. Aly read his lips as he explained to Rubinyan, His Majesty is wearied. I'm sure Your Highness will forgive him. He missed his nap.

Dunevon, if you can't control yourself . . . , Rubinyan said angrily.

He can when he's had his nap, said Taybur, still the picture of goodwill. He walked toward the hall that led out of the building as Dunevon began to howl. Everywhere men bowed and ladies curtsied to the floor as their king passed.

Taybur walked by the screened-in servants' gallery. "I know, I know, you're tired," he told the boy shrieking in his arms. "Any normal person would be."

Aly pursed her lips. That the king's closest guardian was fond of him was a complication she could not like. Her mind knew that the odds were very good that Dunevon might be killed in the rebellion, Dunevon and maybe even Elsren. She did not want the painful cost of those two young lives on her conscience and heart.

"I hope you weren't looking for romance in that area," Vereyu said as she took Taybur's place next to Aly. "He lets nothing get in the way of his duty to the king. A number of our young ladies have sighed over it repeatedly since he left off courting them."

"I don't sigh very well," Aly replied. "And I've no idea why he singled me out." She continued to scan the room as it quieted and nursemaids came to take charge of the king's young companions. Rihani took Elsren and Petranne back to the Robing Pavilion, chatting with the maid who half carried a still-protesting lordling. Dove had not stirred from her spot between Baron Engan and Duke Nomru. Reading their lips, Aly realized they were talking about the meager winter rice crop. She shook her head. Dove had the strangest interests.

A muttering from the other servants drew Aly's attention to the corridor that led to the main entrance. An immortal made its way into the hall where the regents sat. Aly stared at the unmistakable creature visible through the carved screen as it walked over to Princess Imajane. Even the nobles were turning to stare at the basilisk, some nervously, some in wonder. He was seven feet tall, which was average for a basilisk, with gray skin as pebbly as if it were made of beads. A hint of folds at his chin told the observer that he was young, with only two or three centuries on him. He wore a chain with a loop on it around his belly, to keep his lengthy tail from dragging on the ground. His eyes were gray and wise, with a cat's slit pupils. He bowed gracefully to the princess and the ladies around her.

Aly reminded herself to gape as if she'd never seen a basilisk. This was not just any basilisk. This basilisk Aly knew as well as she knew her family.

"He is a basilisk," one of the other maids told Aly. The smug superiority on her face made it plain that she thought Aly gawped like a country bumpkin. "The monarchs of Tortall sent him with gifts to honor His Majesty's ascension to the throne and the regents' appointment. Wonderful toys that wind up and walk about, and gems for Their Highnesses. You don't see that many basilisks, even here at court." She sighed. "He's leaving soon. A pity. He's much nicer than some of the other special envoys."

"You mean he doesn't pinch your bottom, Mimisem," joked one of the other maids.

Aly watched Tkaa curiously. To uninformed eyes, the basilisk might look plump, as the pouch on his belly bulged. What was Tkaa carrying? wondered Aly. Not weapons. Nobody who can turn folk to stone with a sound needs weapons. Unless he's ill, perhaps?

Imajane smiled up at the immortal, who had deftly stopped just far enough from her that she would not get a crick in her neck as she met his eyes. She chatted with him briefly. When the basilisk went to pay his respects to Prince Rubinyan across the room, Nuritin rose and beckoned to Winnamine. Immediately the duchess walked over to Imajane and curtsied. With a graceful movement of her hand, Imajane invited Winnamine to take the seat Nuritin had just left.

Aly spared a glance for a pudgy man who whispered in Rubinyan's ear until Tkaa reached the prince. Noting how the fellow stood so that no one could see his lips moving, Aly was sure this was Sevmire Ambau, Rubinyan's private spymaster, the one who he'd asked to keep watch on his own brother. After memorizing Sevmire's face, Aly turned her attention back to Winnamine and Imajane.

"And so the Balitangs return to court," the princess said with a smile. A maid glided forward to pour out goblets of wine for the two ladies. Aly looked at Tkaa, then gave a mental shrug. He would know where she was if he needed to find her, and she was certain that he would. She didn't worry about Tkaa giving her identity away. The basilisk was one of her father's best operatives.

She continued to inspect the room. Here and there groups of people sat or stood. They talked, drank, and ate as slaves circulated with trays full of delights. It was obvious that, although they seemed absorbed in their chatter, they were equally observant of both regents. While Imajane and Winnamine talked, Rubinyan stood in a far rear corner. In addition to Tkaa, a group of noblemen attended the prince regent. Rubinyan was a listener, not a talker. He kept a gold cup in one hand, often masking his expression by looking into it.

Aly read the men's lips. They discussed pirate raids along the islands. One man accused another of taking a profit from pirates. The other told him that he would do better to mind his own pirates. The whole thing might have spun out of control had Rubinyan not put a hand on one debater's shoulder and smiled at the other, saying that he would ask the navy to step up its patrols. He handled them like an accomplished diplomat. Aly was impressed.

Forget your pirates, another noble grumbled as Aly read his lips. What I want to know is, what's being done about our missing tax collectors? The flooding this winter swept away three of the bridges in my province, and I have no way to pay for new ones! I need tax money!

You'll be missing more than bridges before the summer's done, thought

Aly. A peal of laughter drew her attention to Sarai. She stood at the heart of a group of young men and women, all of whom were applauding some joke. The men's presence did not surprise Aly: Sarai drew men like honey drew bees. Her surprise lay in the number of women of Sarai's age or a little older, women who clearly liked Sarai as well.

Many of the group were luarin who obviously didn't feel, as some of their elders seemed to, that they lowered themselves by association with a half-raka. It was too early yet to tell, but if the younger luarin were more open to friend-ship with someone of raka blood, they might yet avoid the bloody revolution that Aly feared. It was all too easy to imagine these smug, wealthy people as the dead, the smooth columns and gleaming floor marred with the bloody gouges of swords and the black sooty splashes of magical fire. It was Aly's nightmare. She just hoped and prayed Ulasim and the rebel leaders could keep the rebellion from turning into an all-out massacre.

A brown-skinned man in his twenties was bowing over Sarai's hand. He was dressed like a Carthaki, in a short-sleeved yellow tunic that hung below his knees and sandals that laced up. His black hair was oiled and combed back from his forehead, then held in a horsetail with a gold and amber clasp. He wore heavy gold cuffs inlaid with enamel and a broad gold collar set with am-ber and lapis. Aly read his lips as he told Sarai to have pity for a man smitten hard by her loveliness when he was far from home. His jewelry wasn't as bright as his lively brown eyes.

Vereyu came to stand beside Aly. "Ah, I see the Carthaki has found our lady. Let's hope he doesn't break her heart."

"I think she's guarding her heart more this year than she ever did," mur-mured Aly. "A Carthaki, you say?"

Vereyu smiled. "He's the most amazing flirt. Lord Zaimid Hetnim, the youngest mage to be made head of the Imperial University's Healers' Wing. A close friend of his emperor and some kind of distant cousin to the imperial family. He is taking the chance to learn healing techniques used in other realms before he is made the emperor's chief healer."

"He's a bold one," commented Aly. Zaimid had yet to let go of Sarai's hand.

"That's how you know he isn't from here," Vereyu said, bitterness in her voice. "He'll flirt with raka."

Zaimid released Sarai and let another man move in to greet her. On Sarai's lips Aly read the joke she cast over one shoulder to a female friend, "Have the men here gotten so much more handsome, or am I just unused to it after a year in the hinterlands?"

A young man wearing gold rings on every finger stepped close to Sarai to whisper in her ear.

Vereyu grunted. "Count Ferdolin Tomang. The family holds most of

Jerykun Isle, and that means most of the sunset butterfly trade." Aly looked at her and raised her eyebrows in a silent question. Vereyu, understanding, added, "Mages use the butterflies for fair wind and treasure spells. In all the world they are found only on Jerykun."

Against the wall near Sarai's group, a matron with young Ferdolin's eyes and nose snapped her fan open with a crack that drew glances from all over the room. Ferdolin himself never turned away from Sarai to look, even when the fan snap was followed by an intent glare.

"Ah," Vereyu said, amused. "The Dowager Countess Tomang is unhappy. No part-bloods for *her* precious darling!"

Aunt Nuritin hove into Aly's view, like a stately vessel on a cruise, pausing to exchange smiles or a word. Her course brought her to a stop at the empty bench next to Countess Tomang. She eased into the spot and murmured in the countess's ear. Nuritin's hand obscured her mouth, so Aly couldn't tell what her exact words were, but she saw the countess's eyes flick to the dais, where the toy castle still stood, then to Sarai. Her fan quivered. She closed it with a much gentler snap and used it to beckon to a maid with a tray of drinks. The two older women each took one of the delicate crystal glasses and smiled at one another, then drank.

"Well!" said Vereyu, plainly startled. "Apparently Elsren's sister is a better catch than Mequen's half-raka girl child. The year before last she did everything but send him to gather butterflies to separate Ferdy from Sarai."

"May I ask you something?" Aly beckoned Vereyu to follow her to the magically protected corner. Both of them stood with their backs to the room. Boulaj and the other maids and servants were talking casually among themselves. "Have you someone in service here that you *know* is reporting to Topabaw?"

Vereyu's brows knitted together. "How could you—"

Aly smiled. "There is always at least one," she said. "I take it you've isolated him from important information?"

"He knows nothing we do not wish him to know. Now that your ladies have returned to Rajmuat, we were going to eliminate him," Vereyu replied, clearly puzzled. "Most of us voted to dispose of him in one of the streams outside the wall at the dark of the moon."

Aly remembered the flesh-eating fish and shivered. "That would be wasteful," she told Vereyu firmly. "Where does he work?" When the woman hesitated, Aly raised an eyebrow. "The god trusts me," she murmured. "Your general"—the raka code name for Ulasim—"trusts me."

"In the gardens of the Gray Palace," Vereyu said.

Aly smiled, and wondered if Kyprioth was helping to smooth her way. "I need you to do something," she said, her mind flicking through each aspect of her idea. "Two of your people should stop near the place where this spy works.

Have you servants who work in the regents' rooms and in the places they take private meals?"

Vereyu nodded, fascinated.

"What your people will whisper, seemingly unaware that he is near, is that they have overheard the regents discuss Topabaw. They couldn't quite tell what was said, but they know Her Highness was unhappy about something, and His Highness mentioned 'new blood.' Don't let him see your people, for the sake of their lives. And then you will let him report to his master. For the present, that will be enough."

She glanced at Vereyu's face and saw astonishment there.

"You may ask your general if it's permissible, but do it quickly, if you please," Aly said. "Before Topabaw finds a way to break through our security."

"Oh, no," Vereyu replied, shaking her head. "No, there's no need to consult the general. You want Topabaw believing the regents are losing confidence in him. And best of all, it will come from one of his own spies." She smiled slowly, the expression putting light in her eyes. "I should have thought of it. I might try a few such rumors myself."

"One or two won't hurt," Aly admitted. "Don't overdo. Topabaw will be hearing more, I'm certain, and not just from the palace."

Vereyu shook her head in bewilderment. "Yes, you belong to the god, all right," she whispered. Looking sidelong at Aly, she asked, "Are you sure you're not him?"

Aly grinned. "No. My sense of fashion is so much better than his."

About to go in search of the privy, Aly halted when Imajane raised her voice. "Am I to believe my ears?" she asked, her voice brittle ice. "I grant to your stepdaughter and your son an honor that any other parent here would love to receive, and you refuse me?"

Winnamine bowed her head. "Your Highness, please. While in your wisdom you have banished mourning dress, the truth is that I still mourn my duke. His children are my mainstay. I am honored beyond all words that you invite my son to live with the king as part of his court, and that you wish Lady Sarai as a lady-in-waiting. I know how many of our friends would love such positions for their children." She swept her arm open to include the other people in the room. "Can you forgive a mother's weakness? Let me keep my children by me for a while longer?"

Imajane drummed elegant nails on the arm of her chair. "They would receive the best care, the best living that a girl and a boy could wish in our household. Sarai would be an ornament to our court and an asset to her half brother. And after all, Elsren *is* His Majesty's heir. Life is uncertain. Dunevon is healthy and strong, but so apparently was King Hazarin. Elsren will not receive the royal education he requires in your house."

Bodies shifted in the outer room. Thinking like her warrior mother, Aly realized that the ranks of nobles were changing their positions. Sarai was the first of the young people to drift over, understandably, since she was under discussion. Aly noted that Prince Rubinyan came up in support of his wife, placing gentle hands on Imajane's shoulders. Dove almost unnoticeably flanked the men who supported the prince regent until she stood at her mother's back. There was plenty of space there. The ladies who formed the princess's court had moved back as if Winnamine had the plague.

Nuritin came up, an army in her own person, to stand next to Dove. Aly was starting to fear that Winnamine had no other support when Dove's friend Duke Nomru walked briskly to stand between Nuritin and Sarai. There was a shift of color: suddenly Countess Tomang and her son glided over as if they meant to join an interesting conversation. They took positions near Winnamine.

Vereyu told Aly and Boulaj the names of other nobles who went to stand with the duchess: Lord and Lady Wesedi, Lady Adona, and Lord and Lady Obemaek. In the end, Winnamine had representatives of fifteen noble houses to support her, even if it was in silence. Baron Engan kept away, Aly noticed, as did Tkaa and about thirty other men and women. Still, those who stood with the duchess were among the most powerful families in the realm; Aly recognized their names from her winter's study. They were telling the regents that they would back Winnamine.

Imajane looked from Winnamine to each of her silent supporters. Times were uncertain enough that Imajane must be thinking hard about whether she could afford to offend these wealthy people. The princess's mouth was a thin, tight line. Aly saw the knuckles of Rubinyan's hands whiten as he pressed his wife's shoulders. She looked back and up at him, then turned and forced a smile onto her lips.

"I fear you subject your son to inconvenience, allowing him to travel to the palace and back each day, instead of dwelling here as the Lelin, Uniunu, and Obeliten lads will, but there." Imajane shook her head. "In my eagerness to have such adornments as your children at court, I forgot your recent bereavement. I hope that the wounds of your heart soon heal." She gave a razor of a smile to Sarai. "Perhaps you will grace us with your presence in the fall, Lady Sarai."

Sarai bobbed a small curtsy, veiling her eyes with her lashes. "Your Highness honors me," she replied softly. "And I thank you for your kindness to our family."

Imajane graciously inclined her head. "I trust that you, and your stepmother, and your sister Dovasary will join us at the palace the night of the lunar eclipse. Baron Engan, our astronomer, tells us that your sister is quite enamored of such things. It will be an agreeable night's entertainment and a marvel for those of us who worship the Goddess to see her veil her face with a maiden's modesty."

Oh, so that's the tale they're telling, Aly thought. Traditionally lunar eclipses were viewed as unlucky, a blurring of the Goddess's view of her daughters. Imajane was trying to rewrite centuries of belief.

You have to admire her vision, Aly told herself. She thinks big. Or maybe she's just crazy enough to believe it's the Goddess whispering in her mind.

The duchess rose. "We accept your kind invitation, Your Highness. You are too good to exiles. I do fear I am overtired. Our journey was long, and we only arrived yesterday." Her tone was as even and gracious as if she had just complimented the princess's hair, not defied her moments before. "If I may have your leave to withdraw?"

Imajane's eyes glittered like sapphires as they rested on Winnamine. "But only for the moment, Your Grace," she said with another tight smile. "We expect to have your company in the future, too, Winnamine Balitang, at our party and on other occasions. Your presence at court has been missed." She deliberately did not look at the duchess's supporters. "We need to draw you gently from your mourning, and give you other thoughts to occupy your mind."

Prince Rubinyan smiled. "In the meantime, Captain Sibigat will send troops to escort young Elsren to the palace and home each day," he said, his voice smooth as honey. "We shall care for him as if he were our own."

Winnamine curtsied deeply to them both. Nuritin, Sarai, and Dove did the same. Only when the princess nodded did they move to leave.

Aly's mind worked busily as she helped Dove to change for the ride home. That silent assembly of nobles had been most instructive. She had seen it: what might she do with it? Aly knew that everyone in that room had brought away the same lesson she had. The regents needed the luarin nobility to stand with them, united. They could not afford to offend them over something as apparently small as the appointment of a young woman to the princess regent's ladies-in-waiting.

Aly had noticed something else. Very few of the nobles who had moved to shield the duchess's back had hesitated. They had acted as if they'd been prepared to do just that, which meant they had expected something of the kind. In that group that had stood behind Winnamine, Aly had not seen a majority of the court. Those people might be a quarter of the luarin nobility in the Isles, perhaps less. The regents were in so much trouble elsewhere in the Isles that they had to tread lightly rather than punish even this small group of defiant luarin.

As the family met their horses and guards by the Gate of Victory, Aly went through the lists of nobles whose names she had learned from the raka, along with information about their interests, alliances, and political positions.

One of them had to have a weakness she could use to turn the regents against him or her, though it might take some doing, particularly if Rubinyan could control his wife's temper.

"It's like rocks," her grandfather Myles had taught her. "Many of them have what the sculptors and quarrymen call cleavage points, spots you may strike with hammer and chisel to break off slabs of stone. Communities and organizations are the same. Find the right cleavage point and you might break them in half, or even into splinters."

If I can divide the luarin nobility by working on the princess regent, I might divide her from her cool-headed prince, Aly thought as their party clattered over the second bridge that crossed the streams outside the Luarin Wall. Slipping between two men-at-arms, she let Topabaw's pouch of coins and the listening spells attached to them drop noiselessly into the water below, which thrashed as the hungry flesh-eating fish fought over the prize.

5

THE DEMANDS
OF REBELLION

All during the ride back to the city the Balitangs could hear the sounds of crows in raucous battle with Stormwings. The birds nagged the Stormwings, pecking them on their sensitive human parts, doing their best to cause the immortals to fly into one another. The crows delighted in the Stormwings' fury and in the fact that being smaller, they could escape harm by flying close to their victims. The moment one Stormwing cut another, even by accident, they turned on each other. People had to dodge falling steel feathers, all of them deadly. Aly spotted three of her pack among the passersby and signaled them to gather as many Stormwing feathers as they could find. Put to an arrow as fletching, they turned ordinary arrows into mage killers.

The only peaceful note showed high over the fray. A pair of kudarung, one chestnut, one bay, soared on columns of hot air rising over the city.

The Balitangs took another route home to avoid late-afternoon market traffic. Aly stumbled and nearly tripped when they passed through Nimegan Square. Someone had made changes to its fountain, one of the city's attractions for its carvings of climbing monkeys on stone trees. Cut into the white marble a foot apart, the open shackle symbol lined the rim all the way around.

By the time the family reached Balitang House, the sun had begun to dip beyond the palace heights. The ladies and children bathed and changed into more comfortable clothing, then took a quiet supper in the smaller family dining room. Once they had finished eating, Winnamine told the maids they were free for the evening. The Balitang ladies adjourned to their sitting room to talk.

Aly retreated to her workroom to read the reports her people had left for her. She noted each new checkpoint they listed on her map of the city; changed the pins that marked allies, enemies, and those still undecided to match her latest information; and placed a green spy marker on Grosbeak's street. Now that she had one of Topabaw's information collectors identified, she would put her people to watch the man, to mark who else reported to him for Topabaw. She meant to turn the spy-master's network of agents inside out, leaving the regents virtually blind to what actually went on in the city.

"Are you coming?" Nawat leaned against the doorway, his arms crossed over his chest. "Everyone's there but you."

Aly put her papers aside. "I wasn't sure if we'd meet early or not." She walked past him, expecting him to kiss her, but he seemed determined to keep to his new hands-off rule. She almost reached out to touch him, only to remember that the raka were waiting. She had some fast talking to do if she meant to finish the night alive.

She poked her head into the meeting room. "Let's go to the Pavilion of Secrets," she suggested pleasantly. "I could do with some evening air."

Chenaol and Ochobu complained, Chenaol because her feet hurt, Ochobu because she just liked to complain, but everyone followed Aly and Nawat outside. Only when they were safely within the pavilion's magical protections, and the miniature kudarung who nested in the roof beams had settled down, did Ulasim look at Aly and raise his eyebrows. "I assume you did not have us troop out here for so much nice, warm, damp air," the big raka said drily. "Even if the spells do keep out the mosquitoes. Do you fear the security spells in our regular meeting place have been breached?"

"No," Aly admitted, "but they won't prevent our people from hearing you shout when I break my news, and I'd hate for them to witness an argument from our wonderful commanders." She beamed at all of them and perched on a railing. From here she could see all their faces despite the twilight shadows.

Dove rolled her eyes. "Aly, just once, forego your love of drama and spill whatever surprise you have. Otherwise I'll go back and listen to Sarai growl about how nobody at court cares about anything that matters anymore."

Aly looked at them, noting suspicion even in Nawat's eyes. Kyprioth, you'd better be ready if they jump me, she thought at the god. "Well, I have good news and better news," she told them. "The good news is that Topabaw has a spy in this household." As they stiffened she quickly added, "The better news is that it's me."

Ulasim had chosen to lean against one of the pillars that supported the roof. "And that's *good*?"

"It's not just good, silly," Aly said affectionately, "it's necessary." She looked at each of their faces. Ysul struggled with silent laughter. Chenaol began to wave a palm fan as Quedanga examined her nails. Fesgao and Dove waited patiently for her to continue, as Nawat looked at Aly and gave his bird shrug. It stands to reason Nawat doesn't understand, Aly told herself. Crows don't sneak into each other's nests and pretend they belong there. "Think about it," she continued. "Topabaw *must* have people in every important household in the city. He's had his job long enough to do it. How do you think he would feel if he kept failing to get someone on the inside here? You've already held him at bay for three weeks. He'd think we were up to something smoky, and he would be right. It's *much* better to have someone report to him regularly, and the fact that he recruited me just makes it easier. As it is, we still need to look for his spies in other households to do the odd search when they visit us. Topabaw will want to be sure I'm telling him everything."

"Doesn't he trust his own spies?" Nawat asked. "Why have them if he can't trust them?"

"Because it's how the shadow world works," Aly explained, her eyes on Ochobu. The old mage was glaring at her. "No spy trusts another. The only thing they expect is a mix of truth and lies. They protect themselves first. Topabaw would be a fool to believe every word I send him; he'll check my reports out of reflex."

"How can you be so certain?" demanded Ochobu. "How can a country maid from Tortall know so much?"

Aly grimaced. "Your god picked me," she reminded the old woman, not for the first time, she thought, and certainly not for the last. "In your shoes, I would expect him to arm me for my post. Do you think the raka could have gotten away with half of what they've done this winter if Topabaw were young and fresh? He believes his own legend. He's been doing this so long that he thinks he can't be tricked. We can use that certainty for many interesting bits of work, and we shall. We will turn his system against him."

"Are you all *mad*?" barked Ochobu. "He could be listening to every word that's said here at this moment—or she'll tell him what we say when she reports to him!"

"If you weren't so disagreeable, Mother, you'd just put a spell on her and find out right now," Ulasim told Ochobu.

His mother glared at him. "I've worked magic all day," she snapped. "If you're so clever, *you* do it."

"That's very nice, Mother, except I'm no mage," Ulasim retorted.

Ysul shrugged and threw something that blazed like a white veil in Aly's Sight. She let it sink into her skin, though it itched. He inspected Aly, then frowned at Ochobu and shook his head.

"No listening spells?" asked Fesgao.

Ysul hand signaled, *None.*

Aly smiled at Ochobu as if the old mage were a favorite elder who was getting peculiar with age. "Ochobu, if *you* couldn't crack my liar's house, what makes you think Topabaw can? And I doubt his successor will be any better."

That startled them. "Successor?" whispered Chenaol.

Aly nodded. "Well, he'll have one. Too much is slipping through his fingers for him to keep his post much longer. Unless he moves first, of course. Once he knows the regents are losing their faith in him."

Quedanga blinked. "They are?"

"So he will hear," Aly informed them. "As the regents will hear that Topabaw is unhappy with their treatment of him. When people who like control feel that they are not *in* control, they tend to react with a hammer, not a needle. If you keep them feeling things are out of control, believe me, there will be a change in many positions at court. Perhaps even the top positions. Either you trust me, or you do not," Aly reminded them patiently. Her father had taught her that spies spent much of their time explaining themselves to those they worked for, and that any spy must accept such explanations as part of the work. "If you do not," she continued, "then you are already destroyed. I've had ways to send word to Topabaw for nearly a month. Since you are here and breathing, and no member of the family decorates the harbor posts, I suggest that you stop fussing and see to your own projects. We are nowhere near a victory."

"I bet she gives Topabaw even more headaches than she gives me," commented Chenaol. "I could almost feel sorry for him."

Ysul stared at Chenaol, plainly shocked.

"You haven't known her as long as we have, lad," the cook told him kindly. "When you do, you'll understand."

Aly looked at Dove, who smiled crookedly. "I tend to be of Chenaol's mind. Now. What else have we to discuss?" Dove asked, looking at Ulasim.

Later, as their gathering broke up, Aly called, "Nawat? I have something for you to do."

His eyes lit up. "You do? Something real?"

"Something important," Aly assured him. "Come back to my office."

"Did Topabaw hurt you?" Nawat asked as they went inside. "Did he frighten you? I will hurt him if he did."

Aly ushered him into her office and closed the door. "I was as scared as I needed to be," she said, resting a hand on his arm, noting in spite of herself the shift of his wiry muscles under cloth and skin. "You need to be afraid some in a spot like that, or the questioner can tell something isn't right about you." She sat at her desk and produced a sheet of weathered parchment from a drawer. From another drawer she got out ink and an expensive pen. "This will be tricky. I need a crow to drop this in a very specific location."

Nawat sat in one of her chairs, looking at her. Glancing up at him, Aly couldn't tell what thoughts ran behind his deep-set eyes. "It doesn't seem important to you, perhaps, but trust me, Topabaw won't like it one bit."

"You wish me to send a messenger for you," he repeated, his voice flat. "Or better, maybe, *I* should be your messenger."

Aly beamed at him. "It would be lovely if you did it, if you can. I'm not sure the crows here will understand me like the Tanair ones did."

"They will," Nawat said, still expressionless. "The god wagered with all the crows of the Isles, not just the Tanair flock. We serve you and keep you alive, and we win the wager. They learned to speak with you just as you learned to speak with us."

"That must be some wager, that all the crows of the Isles want to win it," Aly remarked, shaking her head. "What is it—eternal life? Unlimited chances to heckle Stormwings?" She forgot her question almost as soon as she asked it, bending her head over her work. Carefully she wrote in an elegant, properly bred lady's script:

He says he wishes new blood, and new methods, but he also remembers years of service. Still, I think with a bit more discussion, he will appoint you to a post that will certainly restore all of our family's fortunes.

Aly waited for the ink to dry, then crushed the weathered parchment several times. Next she ripped pieces off, making sure that none were so large as to destroy the central message. Kneeling on the floor, she briefly rubbed each side of the paper against it, until the parchment looked mauled. She offered it to Nawat.

"It must be dropped near the door of Topabaw's offices, but not too near." She opened a palace map and showed Nawat the spot she meant. "He works and does his torturing there. The reports are that he starts his workday not too long after dawn. He'll be watching the ground out of habit, so don't leave it in the open where anyone can see it. Put it under a bush or something, so he'll just glimpse a corner."

"And stay to be certain he takes it," Nawat added. "I am not a man as Ulasim or Fesgao is, Aly, but I have a mind."

He walked from the room, leaving Aly to stare after him. What had he meant by that? she wondered, baffled. She hadn't said she thought him stupid, or lacking a mind!

He's so touchy anymore, she thought, biting her lower lip when it dared to quiver. *He's the only real friend I have here, the only one I can trust not to turn on me if I don't do all the right things. If* he *doesn't like me . . .*

She refused to finish the thought. She had work to do. Opening a box, she drew out clothes and put them on: a black hood that left only her eyes uncovered, a black suit that covered her from chin to ankles and wrists, black gloves, and long slippers that laced up over the legs of the suit. The entire thing was made of oiled cloth to repel water and spelled to make anyone who looked at her forget she was there. For the moment she let the hood dangle at her back, so that her own people could see her when they arrived.

They came as the watch called the midnight hour, all dressed as Aly was, carrying robes, gowns, and cloaks. Aly herself had put on the hat, veils, and loose overrobes of a Carthaki woman of noble blood. Small, dark-faced Jimarn wore the same disguise over her own black suit. Fegoro donned a Tortallan Bazhir's robes and headcloth. Lokak wore a southern Carthaki's full-sleeved shirt and billowing trousers under a cloak and turban, posing as Jimarn and Aly's escort. Yoyox dressed in the all-covering black hood and habit of the Black God's priesthood, having sacrificed at the god's shrine that afternoon in repentance, in case the god should decide he was being impious. None of them was worried: of all the gods, the Black God of death was the most forgiving.

From a secret basement under the laundry house, they took a tunnel that led under a block of wealthy houses, emerging in a shed where the slaves who tended the nearby public garden kept their tools. Walking casually, stopping to buy treats from late-night street vendors, the "Carthakis" and the "Bazhir" strolled down to the part of Dockmarket that stayed open late. Yoyox was already there, having taken a different route: a watchman's shack at the landward edge of one of the merchant docks. A soldiers' checkpoint was set at the end of the dock, but it was empty, as were others set to guard the landings. With the harbor's mouth blocked by a protective chain at night, there seemed little point in soldiers' waiting for ships that would not land until after dawn.

The watchman was a friend. He left for a walk as Aly and her people removed and folded their disguises, tied hoods and gloves in place, and checked that measuring cords were wrapped securely around their waists. Once they were ready, Yoyox opened the hidden trapdoor at the rear of the shack, revealing a ladder down to the edge of land under the docks. Silently they all climbed down into the stench and ooze of the harbor's edge. Here the boulders that lay against the earth were covered with a dark slime, which made the footing very tricky. Jimarn, who knew the harbor's reeking edges better than anyone after nearly a month of removing bodies from the Examples pier, led the way. They stayed connected to one another by a length of rope. The spells that kept them safe from observation made it impossible to see each other. Their only lamp was a small crystal globe that threw off enough light to show their path north and east along the shore, under the docks that supplied those who imported and exported goods to and from Rajmuat.

At last they came to a halt under one of three docks separated from the merchant docks by a fine chain net, the farthest edge of which was anchored well past the end of the wooden piers. It did not quite reach the boulders, which meant that Aly and her people could slip into the gap between land and net. Only there did they slide their hoods from their heads so that they could see one another. They didn't have to worry about drunken sailors stumbling through here and catching a glimpse of them. This stretch of the Dockmarket was guarded at street level. The three docks that served the slave markets were set between two nets designed to stop any slave desperate enough to jump ship and try to escape.

Quickly they separated, Yoyox and Jimarn to the farthest of the three docks that supplied the slave markets, Fegoro and Lokak to the second, and Aly to the first, and shortest, of the three: the one where the ship in which she had been a slave had moored. Working quickly and memorizing their results, they took the measurements of the length, width, height, and thickness of all the wood that made up the docks. Once they had mapped the area thoroughly, they gathered on the other side of the net, covered their heads and faces again, and returned to the watchman's shack. There they resumed their disguises for the trip back to Balitang House.

Only after they had all written down their measurements on a map that Aly had made did they return to the laundry house. Guchol, Atisa's sister, waited for them there. Guchol took charge of the stinking suits and thrust them into a large tub of specially treated water to soak, while Aly and Jimarn cleaned up in a second tub filled with soapy water, and the three men scrubbed themselves in a third.

"A good night's work, my lambs," Aly told them as she dried herself. "And a better night to come quite soon, I think."

"Yes, Duani," her pack mates chorused.

Before Aly went to bed, she stopped in the refitted storage room that served Ochobu and Ysul as a workroom. Picking up a slate and chalk, she wrote a request in code for twelve pots of the sticky, flammable paste called blazebalm.

Trotting downstairs the next morning to get more of the soap Ochobu made specially for Dove, Aly discovered a number of servants were already at work, taking bouquets of flowers out into the public areas of the house.

"They know Lady Sarai's back, all right," Boulaj told Aly as she carried a delicate arrangement of orchids up to her mistress's rooms. "Ulasim says it's worse even than the year before they were exiled. And there are some for Her Grace and Lady Dove."

"I know Dove will be pleased," Aly said, straightfaced. "She lives for admirers." As Boulaj snorted and continued up the stairs, Aly went in search of one of her pack. She found plump Atisa arranging a bouquet of bird of paradise flowers in a vase inside the large, formal sitting room.

"Good morning, Duani," Atisa said cheerfully. "Are you still dazzled by the magnificence of the palace?"

"I was more dazzled by the idea of man-eating fish," Aly replied, helping to position greenery around the orange blooms. "Atisa, you help Chenaol with the market shopping, don't you?"

"Every other day," Atisa said with a nod that made her pinned brown curls leap free of her rolled hair. "When she goes to the fish market. She likes to take Hiraos or Rasaj to the meat markets."

Aly grinned. The two men of her pack chosen by Chenaol were the most handsome ones, which Aly suspected was the reason Chenaol requested their help with the heavier meat. "You can't say where you heard it, mind, but tell one or two people Topabaw is cursing the regents for not being firm enough with these rebellions on the outlying islands. Have you identified the best market gossips?"

Atisa pressed a hand to her bosom, shocked. "Duani! The first thing we did was mark out who talks and who is heard around town. We knew you'd never let us forget it if you came and we didn't have sources ready!"

"I feared you'd be so busy beating these city boys off with sticks that you'd forget your old Duani," replied Aly. "But I see how I have wronged you. Pass the message down through your recruits, will you? They should spread some form of rumor that Topabaw is critical of the regents, or their generals, or their laws. Make sure everyone tells a different tale—if it's always the same one—"

"They'll know it's planted," Atisa recited. It was a lesson Aly had taught often over the winter. "Do you want me to pass it to the rest of our pack?"

Aly shook her head. "They'll get their own rumors. We'll ensure the regents and Topabaw have plenty to worry about here at home as well as in the outlying Isles."

"Will talk really bother them?" Atisa asked quietly, her black eyes serious.

Aly patted her on the cheek. "It's hard to ignore talk that's just talk," she said, and smiled. "It's funny, though, how gossip can burrow under the skin. You can't make it go away, and you can't answer it. The target goes frantic, trying to find where it comes from."

"And frantic people make mistakes," Atisa replied, once again quoting Aly. "I'm glad you're on our side, Duani."

Aly grinned at her and went to fetch her mistress's soap.

While the family took breakfast together, Aly ate hers in the servants' mess hall. She was nearly done when Nawat came to sit across from her. "Your message is delivered. I watched him pick it up myself. He did not like what he read."

Aly nodded. "Thank you," she told him. "He'll suspect it was planted, but he'll have other things to consider soon. Do you think the crows will help us send more things like that?"

"They will if you call them," said Nawat quietly. "They will even like being messengers. Talk to them in your dreams, and they will do as you ask. Just as I do as you ask. You don't need me to speak with them."

Aly raised an eyebrow. "Are you vexed about something?" she asked softly. He was saved from having to answer when Ulasim and Fesgao sat next to him. "Good morning, Nawat," Ulasim greeted him. To Aly he said, "Boulaj says you had quite a conversation with the captain of the King's Guard yesterday."

"Captain Sibigat is interesting," Aly replied. "Sharp." Wanting to needle Nawat for being so distant and contrary, she added, "Handsome and charming, too."

Nawat traced the grain of the wood in the table, not appearing to listen. Fesgao whistled silently, while Ulasim raised his brows.

Aly sniffed, and despised herself for acting like a total lackwit whose nose was out of joint. "He was probably just flirting."

"Don't get attached to him," Fesgao warned. "He is devoted to his little king."

"Ulasim!" Fesgao nudged his friend and pointed at the door. Two of their men-at-arms had arrived, half-carrying a young part-blood who wore only a loincloth. He was caked with dust. Chenaol came over with a pitcher and a cup as the guards helped the youth to sit next to Ulasim; Fesgao moved to the end of the table, where he could see the youth's face. Chenaol filled a cup and handed it to the lad. He gulped as if he'd had nothing liquid in a long time, water streaming from the corners of his mouth. Chenaol refilled the cup as the men-at-arms left. As the boy drank the second cup, Ochobu joined them. Finally the messenger set the cup down.

"I was sent by Inayica, captain of the *Ombak*," he said, thin chest heaving. "She bids me first tell you that the swans are crows."

Ulasim nodded. The phrase was a code to designate that the messenger carried important information. "Go on."

"We're not anchored in the harbor, but in Moriji Cove," said the boy. "The cap'n sent me 'acos I'm the best runner."

Aly folded her hands on the table. Moriji Cove was on the far side of the hills that circled the harbor on the southwestern flank. This boy had run ten miles uphill and down, somehow evading the checkpoints and the city guards. She was impressed.

The boy closed his eyes and spoke as if he recited from memory. "On the Jimajen lands, the Birafu estates on Tongkang," he said. "The raka there have risen. They killed their guards and overseers and have cut the chains from the slaves. Governor Sulion of Tongkang had his mage far-speak to the regents' mages asking for soldiers, but my captain says the first message was caught in the links of the Chain."

From the way he said it, Aly knew that he didn't realize the chain was a human one fashioned of mages. Many of them had been set to watch each isle's governor as protection against this kind of event. She also knew that when no messages came back from the regents, the governors would know their pleas weren't reaching the capital and would try other ways to call for help, ways the Chain couldn't stop. The regents would not be able to ignore the message when they got it—Tongkang was too close to the capital, and the lands the boy had named were Prince Rubinyan's. He had inherited them when his brother Bronau had died.

"How many of our people are on the Birafu estates?" Chenaol asked.

"Two hundred–odd slaves," said Ochobu, "five hundred villagers, and thirty-four upper servants. And it is Jimajen land, has been Jimajen land since the Conquest."

"Is there more?" Ulasim wanted to know.

The youth opened his eyes and shook his head. "That's all the captain said, *duan*," he answered. "They burned the farm, though. We could see the smoke at anchor."

"Come," Chenaol said. "Let's get you a meal and a bed." She helped the youth to his feet.

"I need to get back to the *Ombak*," the youth protested as she led him toward the kitchen. "They'll sail without me!"

"Tongkang hotheads!" whispered Ochobu when he was gone. "We told them to wait!"

Ulasim stroked his small beard, lost in thought.

"It's hard for people to wait when their blood is up," Aly pointed out. "If they've heard of the other revolts, it would be even harder. Everyone says the Jimajens are cruel masters even for luarin."

"It would be good if the rebels simply disappeared," Ulasim remarked calmly. "If they just vanished, under the regents' very noses, so to speak. We need to get word to any of our people close enough to help. We'll take the rebels to Malubesang and let the army hunt them on Tongkang until their feet bleed." He stood. "Let's see who we can shift. Mother, we'll need you to speak with the mages."

Aly also got to her feet. Dove had said she wanted to visit some friends that morning, which meant she would require both her maid and a guard. Nawat remained where he was, hands fisted on the table before him, frowning.

Aly touched his fists. "I miss my cheerful crow man," she whispered.

Nawat refused to look at her. "I miss having a place where I fit."

Aly drew breath to argue, then shook her head and walked away. It was her experience that even the best of men had to indulge themselves with fits of moroseness. She would think of something to cheer him up once he'd had a chance to get bored with gloom.

Dove was ready for her outing. Elsren, too, was ready to go. He sat on the hall bench in his best luarin clothes, scowling as he slumped against the wall. Standing with him was his manservant, Gian. Aly smiled at him. Gian was one of Olkey's trainees. He had brought them interesting tidbits gathered when he attended Elsren at King Dunevon's court.

Dove sat next to her half brother. "Is that the face you show His Majesty?" she teased gently.

Elsren shook his head. "No. I must only show him a smiling face. That's what Aunt Nuritin says. But it's hard. Sometimes he's mean and I can't even hit him."

"Hitting the king would be very bad," Dove said with a nod. "But you could hit pillows instead."

"But pillows don't make me angry," complained Elsren. He looked up at Gian. "If I am good with the king, Gian and the guards let me gallop until we get to the city."

Dove kissed him on the top of his head. "Well, since I know you are always good, with all that practice, you'll be able to outrace Sarai one day soon."

Elsren grinned at her. "She'd be *furious*."

"My lord," Gian said politely, "the guards are here."

Aly glanced through the open front door as Elsren got to his feet. There indeed was a squad of the King's Guard riding into the courtyard. The hostlers waited there with Elsren's pony and Gian's horse.

"Remember, you want to beat Sarai one day," Dove told Elsren as she straightened his tunic.

He flung his arms around her neck in an enthusiastic hug, then trotted outside, Gian at his back.

As soon as Elsren's party had left the house, the number of uniformed guards Aly had commandeered for Dove's trip, led by Junai in men's clothes, assembled there. When Dove saw them, she scowled, very much as Elsren had. "I don't require nursemaids," she snapped.

Junai, inspecting the six men-at-arms, looked at her. "You are the half sister to the king's heir," she said, using more words than she ever did with Aly. "You have your consequence to think of."

Dove glared at the men-at-arms, who stared straight ahead, fighting smiles. "If you scare my friends, I will dismiss you," she told them. "Before, Papa only made me take two guards."

"In those days, you had plenty of people between your menfolk and the throne," Aly said. "Now there aren't. And dismissing them is a choice you don't have."

Dove frowned. "Sarai's the one who likes consequence, not me," she reminded Aly. "Let's go."

As the men formed a loose ring around Dove, with Junai in the lead, Aly took a position on the outside. On their way through the gate they passed the royal messenger with the beribboned copy of the Balitangs' invitation to the eclipse party, which made Dove scowl harder. "I hate parties," she told Aly as they turned down Joshain Street, "but Engan's got this marvelous new spyglass that gives a closer view of the moon, and he'll have it there. Otherwise I'd get vilely ill for the evening."

Few people but servants were out and about yet. Aly spotted three of her pack ranging ahead of and behind them in different disguises. Hiraos was a student, chubby Olkey a toy seller, Kioka a player. The rest of the pack and their recruits would be spread over the city right now, gathering information.

Dove headed straight for the Dockmarket. The guards had to constantly move aside as she was greeted by a storyteller, an herbalist, two fishmongers, and a potter. As they wandered down the lines of stalls, Aly noticed a thing or two: someone had carved the open shackle symbol into a doorpost. Four soldiers were posted at each point where a main street opened onto Dockmarket Way, in addition to the soldiers' checkpoints at the docks themselves. All of the soldiers looked bored.

That will change, thought Aly as Dove admired a glassmaker's new baby.

"How do you know all these people?" Aly asked as they waited for a wagon full of kegs to move out of their path.

Dove gave her cat smile. "I'm very quiet," she explained. "Once my nurse thought I was at my lessons, or reading my books, she'd go visit with the staff. I'd make sure she was gone and take one of the tunnels outside our walls. Then I just wandered where I felt like it. Ulasim always managed to find me before I was missed. And I like to know things. It's funny how much people will tell you if they know you're interested. I can blow a glass ball, or I used to be able to. And I can gut and filet fish."

"Did Sarai know?" inquired Aly.

"Yes, but since she liked to sneak off to the stables and the horses, we worked things out," Dove replied.

"Didn't your father mind?" Aly wanted to know.

"For a long time he was grieving for Mama," Dove explained. "And then he was courting and marrying Winna. I think Winna figured out what I was up to and was trying to decide if she ought to stop me when we got exiled."

The wagon moved out of their way at last. "Don't try anything of the kind on me," Aly told her mistress with a sweet smile. "I won't take it well."

Dove giggled. "I think you'd find me quicker than Ulasim ever did," she replied as they walked on. "Besides," she added softly, "there's more at stake now."

They had come to the poorer end of Dockmarket, where the stalls sold used materials for sarongs and sashes. The sandal and slipper makers were replaced by peddlers who sold used footwear, as well as dented pots, chipped dishes and mugs, and knives that had already been sharpened so often they were just thin strips of metal. Here a few beggars approached them, to be sent along by Dove's guards. Most didn't even try to come near, only watched them with hollow eyes.

"There weren't so many before," Dove whispered to Aly, her thin brows knit in disapproval. "Not nearly so many." She fumbled at her belt-purse. "Have the rest of you coins? I'll pay you from my pocket money when I get home."

The beggars surged out of corners and alleys. Junai put up a hand in warning. "My lady, this is not a good idea."

"Just the children," Dove called, making her voice carry over the racket of the Dockmarket and the pleas of the beggars. "We haven't enough for all of you, I'm sorry!"

The adults fell back, some more readily than others. A few glared at Dove and her guards, all of whom had their hands on their swords. Junai was lazily turning her long staff in a circle in front of her. One twist of the carved grip at the center and long blades would spring from each end of the weapon.

Kioka and Hiraos closed in subtly, until they stood on either side of the opening the guards had left between Dove and the nearest child. The other children came around there, grimy hands outstretched. Aly watched the crowd. Merchants and customers alike turned to look. On their lips she read Dove's name, and Sarai's. Crows descended to perch on stalls, flicking their wings and tails to warn interlopers that this was their territory.

Aly heard the tramp of boots with nailed soles before she saw the wearers. Two squads of soldiers converged on them, knocking people out of the way. Children screeched as adults tried to run, knocking them down. Dove and two men-at-arms grabbed several youngsters, hauling them into the ring of guards as it closed around Dove. Aly slid slender blades from her sash, holding the grips in her palms and lining the blades up against the insides of her wrists so that the soldiers would not see them.

"Go on, get about your business!" snapped a soldier, pushing a slave out of his path. "No assembling, remember, you ignorant swine?"

The lieutenant with the other squad halted in front of Junai. "Let me pass, in the king's name," he ordered her.

Junai stared at him, her dark face without emotion. Aly and Dove traded glances; Dove moved forward, urging the guard at Junai's right to move over so that the officer could see her. "Somehow I doubt the king is concerned with gatherings in Dockmarket," she said icily, drawing herself up to the full height of her five-foot-four-inch frame. "When I saw him yesterday, he was far more interested in playing with toy soldiers, not real ones who strike unarmed people."

The lieutenant stared down his nose at Dove. "And who might you be"— he glanced at Dove's guard and their excellent weapons—"my lady?"

"You address Lady Dovasary Balitang," the guard beside Junai told the man.

"By what right do you knock people about?" Dove wanted to know, her voice quavering slightly.

"The right of the regents to decree that assemblies of more than ten folk are banned, my lady," said the lieutenant. "There have been too many brawls in this part of town of late, and we are charged by the regents to keep order. It would be most helpful for the maintenance of order, *my lady,* if you returned home. They don't get nobility much down this way, and you being here may incite them to rob you."

Dove stared at him briefly, then turned and walked down the street toward the Windward District. Aly lagged behind: the lieutenant had grabbed Junai's arm.

"Mind your place, raka bitch," he told Junai softly. "Before someone cuts your throat in an alley."

Aly rushed forward before Junai forgot herself and showed the man what she was capable of. "Lokeij, please hurry!" she cried, playing the fussy maid, laying hands on Junai's free arm. She had used a dead friend's name so the guard would not have Junai's true identity. "My lady says you have the perfume she bought, and she wants it right away." She looked up at the lieutenant sidelong, fluttering her lashes, making it plain she thought the sallow-faced luarin attractive. "She's that particular, is Lady Dovasary, and I told her to let me carry the perfume, but she says I'm all thumbs. . . ." Talking as frivolously as she could, she managed to draw Junai away from the soldier and down the street. At the first chance Aly turned Junai to face forward properly and said in the softest of whispers, "Don't ever confront them like that again! Ever! You have no right to throw your life away by being disrespectful to some armed lout, not when Lady Sarai needs you. We're not on Tanair anymore, and the regents rule by the fist. Do you want me to tell your father you were stupid, or do you want to promise me you'll never be so foolish again?"

Junai drew her arm out of Aly's grip. "Careful," she said, also keeping her voice low. "People hear you talk like that, and they may start to think you care."

Dove glared up at Junai when they rejoined their group. "Don't ever do that again, Junai. *Ever,* do you understand me? Risking your life in a Dockmarket brawl with a soldier when you owe your life to us!"

Junai looked down at her young mistress, amused. "So it will seem, Mother." She looked at Aly. *"Duani,"* she added with emphasis. "I will be a good girl and try not to get gutted in the market." She moved up into the lead once more.

Dove stalked on, her small face grim. Once they were back at the house, she dismissed everyone, including Aly, and locked herself in the library. Aly waited long enough to hear the crash of a thrown object and Dove's cry of *"Brutes!"* before she left Dove to her rage in peace.

Aly sat on a bench in the main hall, closing her eyes to think. Did the regents understand how much they revealed by ordering their men to break up gatherings? Surely they'd been around government long enough to know it was a bad idea to let people know you feared them in groups that were not even very large.

Ulasim found her there and sat next to her. Aly opened her eyes. "I was plotting," she told him.

The big raka looked uncommonly grim. "I have no doubt that you were," he pointed out. "I believe you plot in your sleep. I have something to tell you. I want you to hear it from me. You may recall that we were trying to think of a way to get quick aid to the people on Tongkang."

Aly frowned, puzzled. Why did he tell her this? That was the military side of their duties, not the spy side. "I'm sure you'll do whatever's right."

"I believe I have," replied Ulasim, resting a hand on her arm. "At his request, I sent Nawat and some of his crows."

For a moment Aly's ears buzzed. Then her entire body went cold, as if she had been dunked in snowmelt. "Nawat?" she whispered through numb lips. "He's no warrior. You can't be serious."

"He and his cousins fought well when Bronau attacked Tanair last year," Ulasim reminded Aly. "He wants to do something, Aly. A man needs something of his own, just as a woman does. And he and his crows can get messages to far more people on and around Tongkang than my mother and all the mages of the Chain. They can watch for warships and soldiers. He thinks he can even divert an armed party. His reasoning is sound. I approved it."

"He's a *crow*," Aly whispered, clenching her hands. "A crow who spends time being a man—that doesn't make him one. You had no right to use him for this!"

"He's not your pet," Ulasim said gently. "It is time that he learns if he is a crow or a man. As long as he sits in your shadow, he cannot be certain. And his stake in this is far higher than yours. He and his people are the raka's cousins. You are only an imported luarin."

Aly flinched. What was wrong with her? She was on the verge of tears. "You should have asked me."

"*He* asked *me*, as was his right," Ulasim replied without mercy. He looked her over with the gaze of a commander who saw a weakness in one of his soldiers. "Must I worry about you? Are you going to pout and mope and ignore our work?"

Aly stiffened at the verbal slap. He'd as much as accused her of not being professional. "No!" she said, outraged.

"Nawat is intelligent. He has the ears and eyes of his fellow crows," Ulasim told Aly, his eyes direct. "This is a chance made for him. He is as safe doing that as any of us are safe." He put a big hand on Aly's shoulder. "This has nothing to do with whatever games you play together, and everything to do with our cause. Have I made myself clear?"

Aly bit her lip. He was treating her as if she were a silly girl who could think only about her sweetheart. Worse, he was right. Just so would her own father speak to her about neglecting her job. Hanging her head, she nodded.

"Then I do not want to hear of this again," instructed Ulasim. "There is work to be done." He got up and strode off down the hall.

6

SPIES

As the family rested and the household prepared for that day's callers, Aly met with her pack. They watched as she tapped the map and the pin that marked Grosbeak's shop. "This is Grosbeak, on Gigit Lane in Middle Town. Topabaw uses him to collect reports from spies in the city. Now we gather information from Grosbeak."

"All of Topabaw's people report to him?" asked Guchol, fascinated.

Aly shook her head. "I doubt it, not with the number of spies Topabaw must have in the city alone. But Grosbeak is a place to start. Guchol, you'll handle this. Put your recruits on him day and night. Everyone who goes there, I want to know who they are and where they live. And don't be surprised when I come there. Topabaw recruited me yesterday."

Unlike the rebellion's leaders, these people had learned their spy craft from Aly, including the tricky work of double agents. If they doubted her ability to protect herself from Topabaw or anyone else, none of them showed it.

"Was it fun?" asked Olkey. "Or did he hurt you?"

"Does the general know?" Kioka inquired.

"Did Topabaw pay you anything?" demanded Lokak.

"He paid me in coin loaded with listening spells, so I got rid of it. The general knows, Topabaw didn't hurt me, and don't get too attached to him," replied Aly. "We'll be dealing with someone new before long, if I have anything to say about it. Once we know who reports to Grosbeak and where they live, we will send them a token of our regard. I was thinking that baskets of rats left beside beds would give our regards that personal touch."

A number of them snorted. Lokak only frowned.

"Yes?" Aly asked.

"Why don't we just nail rats to the door, like the old raka rebels used to do?" Lokak wanted to know. "It's cheaper."

"But not so thoughtful as a basket of them," Aly said. "And leaving the basket in their bedrooms provides an intimate note."

"We're saying we can get at them as they sleep," remarked Eyun, her eyes filled with the discovery of some new twist she had just uncovered.

Aly smiled benevolently while thinking, And this way my aunt Daine doesn't come flying over from Tortall wanting to know why I'm killing animals for no good reason. "Tell me what you have learned from your people so far."

By the time they had finished their reports, the city's bells were chiming the end of the rest period. Aly dismissed them and went to help Dove to dress for the afternoon. The duchess had told Quedanga to open the reflecting pool court and the large sitting room. Afternoon was the usual time for callers, and she expected quite a few.

Aly stood behind a carved screen inside the house to observe the young noble visitors as they flirted, talked to Sarai, accepted treats carried on trays by maids, and gossiped. The younger ladies were watched by their maids, who had taken positions against the walls of the courtyard. Nuritin and Winnamine had chosen to stay indoors, in one of the large, formal sitting rooms, to greet the callers who came to see them. Dove joined them there, after muttering to Aly that she refused to have her brain filled with puffs of scent and flirting, as it would be if she stayed with Sarai.

Talented Eyun made friends among the maids and talked animatedly with them as she gave the men servants sidelong glances. Ukali and Olkey, two of Aly's male agents, were making themselves known to the nobles' servants as well. Pert Kioka was out in the stables, listening to the guards who rode with the noble guests. At some point during the afternoon, talking in strictest confidence with their new friends, all of them would pass on some bit of gossip that would sit ill with those who collected it for the palace. The rest of Aly's pack, and more of the people they had recruited, were out performing the same service. Little of it would go straight to Topabaw or to Rubinyan's spymaster. People who worried about the stability of the government chattered constantly, the threads of gossip twisting as they passed from one person to the next. By the time they reached those who were most interested in holding power, the strands would be so tangled that no one would be able to trace them back to a handful of sources.

Gossip was a realm's lifeblood, Aly's da had told her repeatedly. She intended to make this realm bleed with it.

She let her eyes roam over the crowd, reading snatches of conversation on the lips of their company. Everyone wanted to tell Sarai the winter's news, away from the watchful eyes of their elders. Count Ferdolin Tomang, the Carthaki healer mage Zaimid Hetnim, and the heirs to the Lelin and Obe-maek houses wanted to court Sarai. She kept them dancing around her, pout-ing at one, teasing another, ignoring a third, and urging her female friends to do the same. She seemed cruel to Aly, as if she didn't care if she hurt the feel-ings of the young men. *Was I that bad?* Aly wondered, remembering the days when she lived like Sarai. *Picking them up and dropping them, whether they deserved it or not, just because I could?*

I can't do it anymore, she realized, startled. *Even if the god were to dump me into such a gathering at home. It's small to promise a man something, even without words, if you never intend to give it to him, whether it's kisses or your heart.*

She didn't like where that trail of thought led her: Nawat. Rather than dwell on him, she looked into the formal sitting room. Here there were older ladies and men alike, deep in conversation with Nuritin, Winnamine, and even Dove. They kept their voices low and watched the maids who served refreshments, talking only when they were out of earshot. Reading the nobles' lips, Aly saw that they spoke of missing officials, uprisings, and the vanished bodies of those executed by the Crown. Dove was engaged in a conversation about copper exports with a noble couple at least three times her age.

Aly eased her way out of the room. She was about to go to the servants' hall when one of the household runners found her. "Chenaol says tell you, one in Her Grace's private study, one in Lady Saraiyu's bedroom. She asks if you have ever been a poacher, since you knew where to set traps."

Aly smiled. "Thank you. Tell Chenaol I'm on my way."

Aly climbed the stairs and entered the ladies' private study. There Win-namine, Sarai, and Dove read and wrote letters and kept their personal ac-counts. It was one of the first places a spy would look for incriminating correspondence, which was why she had recommended that the raka mages plant a spy trap there. When Aly walked into the well-lit, comfortable room, she saw a part-raka maidservant, locked in place with her hands in a desk drawer. The woman shimmered under the magical net that had captured her. Ysul sat on a chair watching her, his almond-shaped eyes unreadable. Ulasim, too, was present, as was Junai. They nodded as Aly came in.

She went to the chair across the desk from the captive and sat, resting her hands on the chair's arms. The maid glared at her.

Aly eyed her. "Was she searched for death magic?"

Ysul nodded and held up three fingers. He had removed three spells that would have killed the woman if she tried to speak the truth.

"Three?" Aly asked. She looked at the captive. "If someone were to put three death spells on me, I might wonder if they trusted me at all. Such persons would be less than careful about giving you assignments that might cost your life. *I* would not reward service in such a manner."

She inspected the captive. She was a part-raka woman in her late twenties, dressed in a blue gown, probably a mistress's castoff. She wore her brown hair pinned up, with enough hairdressing ointment on it to ensure that no loose hairs would fall on anything she searched. There were white silk gloves on her hands. Through the magic that held the maid captive, Aly could see that the gloves were spelled to keep her essence from sticking to anything she handled. On the desk lay a set of lock picks—good ones, Aly saw with approval.

Aly raised a hand, lifted a finger, then bent it. Ysul lowered the spell, freeing the captive's lips so she could speak.

"I don't understand!" she cried. "I was just looking for a bit of paper—please don't tell my mistress, she'll be furious, but they always count the paper in our household and I just wanted to write a note to my betrothed. . . ."

Aly held her finger to her lips. The maid's words trailed off.

Ulasim leaned in and sniffed the air around the maid. "You stink of Topabaw," he informed her, his voice thick with scorn. "You were spelled to die before you named your true master—that's spy work." He nudged the lock picks. "These aren't needed to steal paper. If you were a slave, you would pay for these with your life. As it is, you won't look so good with a thief's brand on your forehead."

"I swear, I swear, those were here when I came in!" protested the maid.

"And the gloves?" inquired Aly. "Spelled to leave no trace of you?"

"They belong to my mistress!" cried the woman. "I just borrowed them, you know, to make my hands softer, like hers!" She started to cry.

Aly let Ulasim and Junai question her for a while, listening with appreciation. The woman had been well trained. When Aly judged the time was right, she laid a gentle hand on the desk in front of her. Everyone stopped talking. Aly let the silence linger for a moment, then asked gravely, "What is your name?"

The maid drew breath to speak.

Aly raised the index finger of her hand. So frightened—and so clever—was the maid that she saw even that tiny gesture. She clamped her lips shut.

"I will know if you lie, and I will be displeased," Aly said.

The woman hesitated, apparently considering whether she dared lie in any case. Aly smiled, and the woman reconsidered. "Vitorcine Townsend."

"Very good," Aly replied. "What household employs you?"

Head hanging, Vitorcine murmured, "Obemaek. I am Lady Isalena's maid."

Aly nodded. "Well, then, Vitorcine Townsend. Perhaps we need to summon Lady Isalena. By your own admission, you are a thief." She saw Vitorcine's shoulders relax slightly. *She probably has something she can blackmail Isalena with if she should get caught,* Aly thought. *I would, in her place.* "Better still, perhaps the young lady will thank us for pointing to Topabaw's spy in her household."

Vitorcine's skin went dead white. She swayed. Only the spell around her hips and legs kept her upright. "I beg you, no," she whispered. "I will do anything you ask. Only do not tell."

"Why should we not?" Ulasim wanted to know. "You have taken advantage of our mistresses' hospitality and defiled this house with your prying." He stepped closer until he loomed over the woman, his eyes fixed on hers. Vitorcine could not escape the fact that he was large, well muscled, and full-raka. In the city, there were feuds based on how much raka blood someone had. Vitorcine had a drop, no more. Used to the city, she would expect full-bloods to be hostile to part-bloods.

Aly leaned forward, drawing everyone's attention. Even Vitorcine looked at her as she cringed from Ulasim. "What has your mistress to fear from Topabaw?" Aly asked softly.

"It may be paltry," the woman babbled, more broken by her own terror than anything the rebels had said. Aly had seen this before with some of her da's agents. She fought to keep her face bland. She knew she had just hit treasure.

"Is it arms?" she asked, her voice gentle. "Or is it correspondence?"

The woman bit her lip. "The Obemaeks will kill me," she said at last. "As Topabaw will kill me if I am found out."

"A moment," Aly interrupted gently. "*Both* of your masters would kill you?"

Vitorcine nodded. "I have not told Topabaw. It could be nothing. What I have gathered is only hints. They write letters in code. It may only be family gossip. I did not wish to inform Topabaw until I have the key to the code. When I find it, I will have to tell him. I have no proof until then, so they are safe from me."

Aly's nerves sang with excitement. Two gifts had dropped into her lap. Vitorcine obviously knew those communications would mean bloody trouble for the Obemaeks should Topabaw learn of them. Yet she was trying to protect her mistress and her family. Whatever Topabaw had used to frighten Vitorcine into spying for him, it wasn't strong enough yet to overcome her loyalty to the Obemaeks.

"You are brave, to take such risks," Aly told Vitorcine kindly, signaling Ysul to free the maid. "A chair, I think." Ulasim brought it over and helped the frightened woman to sit. "Would you like tea?" Aly asked. "Something stronger?"

Vitorcine shook her head. From the sudden grim twist in her mouth, she knew as well as Aly that it was very bad for spies to take spirits.

"I believe we may help each other," Aly continued. This young woman required a velvet touch. Aly would have to be teacher and mother figure. She put an elder's authority into her voice. "Will you do this for me? Copy those coded letters and bring the copies here. We shall see if there is even anything in them that would interest Topabaw." She caught Vitorcine's gaze. "In addition, you report to me what you report to Topabaw. You will also report to me what Topabaw says to you, do you understand?"

"He'll kill me," whispered the woman.

"Then you must be very careful," Aly told her, still kind. "He is not as all-powerful as you may think. I heard somewhere that he is losing his grip on the realm and will soon be replaced."

Vitorcine met Aly's eyes with her own. "Is it true?" she asked breathlessly.

Aly smiled. "Keep it in mind." From the front of her sarong she drew a small, thick book. In it she kept pledges of obedience, signed in blood. Opening it to a clean page, she drew a small dagger she kept in her sash for these occasions. "This is just a formality," she assured Vitorcine. "Write here—you can write, can you not?"

Vitorcine nodded.

"Write that you will serve Balitang House and keep its secrets," Aly explained, setting out an inkpot and pen. She unsheathed the dagger. Its blade was the length of Aly's little finger, and razor sharp. "Then you will sign in blood." As Vitorcine shrank back—the breaking of a blood oath meant the oathbreaker died with the blood boiling in her veins—Aly leaned closer and held Vitorcine's deep-set brown eyes with her own. "You will swear, or they will find you floating in the harbor tomorrow," she whispered.

Vitorcine swore, as Aly knew she would. Everyone thought they could get out of a bad situation if they could just buy some time. Vitorcine was no exception. Besides, Aly had promised to help her with the coded letters.

Once her oath was given and Ysul had put healing balm on the small cut in the maid's finger, Aly went in search of their second captive, another of Topabaw's agents. Ochobu stripped this one, a footman, of any death magics before Aly began her questions. The man had no pearls of news like Vitorcine, but Aly knew better than to expect two such windfalls in one day. Ochobu took the footman's blood vow, giving Aly two agents who would report both on the activities of their noble masters and on Topabaw's orders.

A good day's work, Aly told herself. Da was right. With careful handling, and plans laid in advance, I *can* pluck my enemies' spies like ripe plums from a tree.

While she had worked, new guests had arrived. A glance into the salon where the older men and women met showed her that Duke Nomru sat in quiet conversation with the duchess, Nuritin, and Lord Obemaek, whose daughter Isalena was one of Sarai's friends. Aly's fingers prickled. She would have loved to know what they said, but she was in the wrong position to read their lips.

You can't hear everything all the time, Aly thought as she went to see what was happening with Sarai. But it's so *frustrating*. It occurred to her that she was trying to fill her brain with anything but Nawat. She banished the thought.

There were more new guests in the courtyard. Dove had left the sitting room to speak with two of them. Aly found her mistress seated between Baron Engan, the astronomer, and Tkaa the basilisk.

Aly didn't think Tkaa had come to visit the Balitangs. She gathered up a tray of drinks and circulated, drifting toward Dove and her company. When she reached them, her tray was empty. She placed it on a table and ambled into the house. There she turned down the corridor and out into a separate garden where lovers could talk unseen. She was wondering how often Sarai came here when she heard the click of claws on the flagstones.

Like the rest of the house, the courtyard was spelled to protect it from eavesdroppers. Aly felt no qualms about beaming up at the basilisk as he arrived and saying, "Of all the people I thought to see here, none of them was you!" She hugged him, careful of his bulging pouch.

"I was fortunate enough to be chosen to bring the monarchs' greetings to the new king and his regents." For so large a creature, Tkaa had a soft, whispery voice. "I also bring greetings from your family. The Scanran War is done. Your mother has returned to court, and your father with her. Your brother Alan is squire to Raoul of the King's Own, your brother Thom continues his mage studies. Your grandparents, your uncle Numair, and your aunt Daine send their love, as does your immediate family. Prince Roald's bride, Princess Shinkokami, awaits her first child. Your aunt Daine expects a second child. And Daine has also sent you a gift."

Tkaa opened his pouch. A glossy black glob about twice the size of Aly's head dropped to the ground with a plop. There it began to wriggle. A round piece broke off, then another, and a third, until thirty-six small blobs sat before her. Despite their similar appearance, many held visible differences inside their bodies: a piece of ribbon or stone, lace and honeycomb patterns, streaks of bright color or light.

The first to break away from the main mass had made its glossy surface resemble Tkaa's beaded hide. Now it produced a neck and a head. "Hello," it squeaked. "I am Trick."

Aly knelt, staring in wonder. "I'd heard of them, but I never saw one," she whispered. "You're darkings, aren't you?"

The blobs produced their own heads to nod. Aly rocked back on her heels. "But I thought you lived with the dragons." One of her favorite Daine stories was about these creatures, made of blood and magic. Aly had always been disappointed that they had stayed in the Divine Realms rather than live in the mortal world with Daine.

"Dragons are boring," announced a darking with a bit of clear quartz at its center. "Dragons study and peer and eat and sleep."

"And talk," Trick added. "For days and days and days."

A number of tiny heads nodded agreement and chorused, "Boring."

"Some stay," said Quartz. "Gold-streak stay. Olders stay. We go."

"Aunt Daine said all but one of you was killed in the Battle of Port Legann," Aly murmured, thinking aloud.

Trick shook its head. "More that Daine not meet in Divine Realms," it told her. "And more born as we split in two."

Aly scratched her head and looked up—far up—at Tkaa. "Why bring them to me?" she asked.

"Daine said to tell you, what one darking knows, all will know," Tkaa explained. "And they are very good at getting into places where humans cannot."

To illustrate, the one patterned like lace flattened itself into a thin sheet on the ground.

"I stay with you," Trick squeaked. "They tell me, I tell you. Sometimes show." Spreading itself thin, it presented a view of the garden where they now stood from the ground.

"Not boring," added one that had blue ribbon inside itself.

"Fun," chorused the others. "Funfunfun."

For once, Aly had nothing to say. In a moment, she knew, her mind would be whirling with ideas, places to send these creatures where the discovery of a human would result in a spy's or Aly's death. And unlike her human spies, these creatures had no tasks they were supposed to be about, so they might hide, and listen, day and night.

"But I'll have to train them so they know what to listen for," Aly mused. "So they can tell what's important or not."

"No," peeped the tiniest of the creatures. "Whisper Man teach us before we come. We know secret. We know trouble. We know rumor. We know fact."

"And murder," added another darking.

"And poison," said a third.

"We know allies and enemies," a fourth darking said. "Between dragons and Whisper Man, we know plenty."

The one called Trick oozed over to Aly. Producing small limbs or tentacles, it began to crawl up her sarong-covered thigh until it reached her sash.

Stretching itself cord-thin, it wriggled until only its head showed above the cloth. "Fun," it reassured Aly. "Mortals are always doing things."

After long thought Aly murmured, "Such a delightful gift. And it isn't even my birthday."

After more news from home, she said goodbye to Tkaa and went in search of a covered basket for the darkings. Carrying it, and them, into her workroom, she realized she could tell no one of her new guests. The darkings were too odd. Once Ulasim or the other rebel leaders saw them, they would start to ask questions that Aly dared not answer.

"I'll just say I developed new sources," she decided as she set the basket on her desk. "This will have to do for the present," she told her new spies. "I'll be taking you places later on. Actually, if two of you would join me? I'd like to settle you right away."

The darkings started to bounce like eager children. She chose one that contained a bit of lace in its depth and one that had patterned its skin like bird feathers. "There will be fun enough for all of you," she told the rest as she tucked Lace and Feather into a pouch she could hang from her sash. "Do you need anything? Food? Water?"

The darkings shook their heads. "We get our own," Trick assured her. "No one will see. Mortals don't *look*."

Since Aly had frequently observed that most people didn't pay attention to the details of the world around them, she was inclined to agree. "No one should be able to come here once I lock the door," she explained, "but if someone does, *hide*."

Every darking nodded. Aly looked at them helplessly. Darkings, she thought. In Tortall she was used to living among legends. After a year in the Isles, she had fallen out of the habit of expecting the extraordinary. As she locked her door and entered the meeting room, she wondered if Kyprioth had anything to do with this.

As if he'd been eavesdropping, the god spoke in her mind. *No, but they are* quite *delightful. Maybe I can recruit them to my service when this is done.*

Lucky darkings, thought Aly as she took Lace from her pouch. "You stay here," she told the darking. Its cocked head managed to convey complete attention. "Some people will come in from time to time. I may be with them, so don't say hello, or nice to see you, or even wait till I tell you what I heard. Just listen, and pass things on to Trick."

Lace nodded, and dropped from Aly's hand to the floor with a plop. Off it rolled, making an inspection of its new quarters.

Aly went out around the house until she came to the window of the room where the older guests had met that afternoon. Most of them were already gone; the rest were preparing to leave. Aly gave Feather the instructions she had given Lace, then held the darking so that it could trickle through a gap in the carved wooden screen and down into the room. The others she meant to place at Grosbeak's and the palace, but she was interested in that group of older luarin nobles who gravitated toward Nuritin and the duchess. Their movement to silently take Winnamine's part at court had been done with such grace and speed that it looked practiced. Something was going on there. With Feather's help, she would learn what it was and if she could use it. As for Lace and its position in the leaders' meeting room, it never hurt to know what her fellow conspirators were up to. Probably she wouldn't have gotten word of Nawat's commission from even a darking in time to stop him from going, but she wanted no more surprises.

Nawat. The thought of him plunged into a war zone jammed a hot fist of anger and fear under Aly's lungs. Until now she had managed to put off thinking about him. She hurriedly crossed the small garden to one of the lovers' nooks, where she could get her heart under control. She didn't know what to think or say about his departure; she feared so much what she *might* say that she would have to try not to speak of him at all.

She clenched her hands. She knew what damage a sharp tongue could do from her long years with her mother. Aly could not exercise it on Ulasim, or on Nawat if he came home safe. It would be cruel to ask Nawat who he thought he was, to dive into human battles. It would be cruel to point out to him that the household message runners knew more of war than he did. No, she would calm down and get a grip on herself. She would have to handle him properly so that he would stay where he belonged once he returned, if he returned.

That night, when Aly walked into the big meeting room, she found the leaders already present. Ulasim, Fesgao, and Ochobu stood, looking down at a good-sized wooden chest. The others were seated, their chairs pushed well back from the chest as they, too, eyed it.

"There are no spells on it," Ochobu said. She looked at Aly as the girl closed the door behind her.

Ulasim nodded to Aly. "Come have a look," he invited. "This was found on the doorstep of Temaida House this morning, with a label that read *For the Twice-Royal.*"

Aly nodded. In the prophecy that spoke of the freeing of the Isles, the main person mentioned was the twice-royal queen. The conspirators and the rebels believed that was Sarai, who was Rittevon on her father's side, Haiming on her mother's.

"They had it conveyed secretly to us. Need I say the Temaidas were very frightened?" the big raka asked Aly.

She smiled crookedly. For a house that had secretly raised the last descendants of the Haiming line for three hundred years, the Temaidas as a whole were terrified of their own shadows. Then she reconsidered. Perhaps that very skittishness was what had enabled the Temaidas to survive.

"Ochobu and Ysul say there is no magic on it," Fesgao pointed out. "Yet we are not sure about a box that has come to us from someone unknown."

Aly knelt and inspected it closely. It was a plain chest, banded in iron and locked. She got to her feet and went to her workroom to fetch her lock picks. Little Trick thrust its head out of her sash as she picked up the rolled cloth that held her tools.

"Fun?" it asked.

"Probably not," Aly murmured. "Someone is playing a game, but I'll bet my sarong it's just to send a message. No fun. Back into hiding, you." Trick pulled its head under her sash with what sounded very like a sigh.

In the meeting room, Aly peered into the keyhole of the box and saw no magic. By the time she had inserted three lock picks, she knew the lock's mechanism as well as she knew her own name. Two more picks did the trick. The lock sprang open. Aly tucked it into her sash as a memento and shoved back the lid. Inside were bags, each with a round wax seal on the drawstring. Aly picked one bag up. It was heavy with clinking metal. The thick seal, in bright blue wax, was glossy on one side and dull on the other. Her heart was pounding. She had always loved presents from home.

She reached up under her sarong, where she wore fine cotton breeches to keep the knives strapped to her inner thighs from chafing her bloody. Drawing the right knife, she reversed it in her grip and smashed the pommel onto the glossy side of the wax seal. The top layer shattered, as it was meant to do, laying bare a second seal. A metal emblem was pressed into the blue wax of the true seal: a tin sword thrust through a tin crown. The drawstring loosened, revealing a bag full of silver and gold coins, mixed in age and origin so that they would be impossible to trace.

Aly held out the bag, the seal facing up. Ulasim took it from her with a frown.

"It's the Tortallan national emblem," she told her companions. She smashed the outer seal on each bag to reveal the same hidden seal. "All this money is a love token from the Tortallan king's spymaster." She looked at Ulasim. "They're giving you funding for any mischief you care to concoct. Their spies believe you are preparing to stir this country up. They want to help."

The raka went very still. Finally Chenaol, white under her bronze skin, whispered, "If the Tortallans know, the Crown's spies know. Topabaw knows."

Aly shook her head, busily constructing a story they would believe. She couldn't tell them the truth, that her father, one of Tortall's spymasters, had wanted to be sure his little girl had the coin for whatever she was up to. She got to her feet and stretched, grinning impishly at them. "You may thank the god for this, I think."

They stared at her as if she'd grown a second head. "What do you mean?" Fesgao asked at last.

"The god mentioned once that he was the patron of one of Tortall's highest-ranking spies," Aly told them. It was not completely a lie. Kyprioth had been her father's patron god for years, though George Cooper's family had been unaware of the alliance. "I imagine he whispered a word to that spy that things were unsettled here. There's enough bad blood between the Tortallans and the Rittevon kings that no doubt Tortall would be happy to do the Rittevons and their supporters an ill turn. Promoting rebellion among the raka is a way to do it while still claiming friendship with the Copper Isles." The raka continued to stare at her. Aly shook her head. "You had a princess nearly twenty years back, Josiane. She was being groomed as a future queen of Tortall, except that the heir to the throne didn't wish to marry her. She took it badly. Well, she *was* a Rittevon. She was killed in an attempted takeover, and things have not gone well between your realm and mine ever since. King Oron lost two sons, didn't he, in the attack on Port Legann nine years ago? The god knows the Tortallans would love to pay off an old grudge, and rebellions always need money."

"The god told you this?" Ulasim wanted to know.

"I will ask him," Aly said truthfully. She suspected that her father had pieced together her story during his visit to Tanair the previous autumn, and that he had commissioned Tkaa to deliver the money to the Temaidas without being seen. "But I know he has a connection with Tortall."

"We should send it back," said Fesgao. "I do not like it that they think to buy us."

Aly beamed at him. "Very sweet *and* very silly, Fesgao. They are *buying* mischief. Face it—unrest in the Isles means the regents will be too busy to pay fake pirates to raid Tortall's shores this year. The Tortallans aren't putting any names to it, and they won't expect you to pay them back." She propped her hands on her hips and looked at them one by one. "Countries do this to each other all of the time, you know," she explained. "Meddle in one another's affairs. Look for the tiniest bit of advantage over their neighbors. You don't have to *marry* the Tortallans, just take their money. If I thought you could trust any Carthakis, I'd suggest you approach them for extra funding."

"But we can't trust the Carthakis," said Chenaol.

Aly gathered up the lock picks. "Well, you can't trust anybody, but if the money's all clean of spells, there's no reason for you to refuse it. They've done it this way so it can't be traced back to them. So if someone from here was to accuse the Tortallan monarchs and their spymaster of sending money to support unrest, they can say, 'What money?' and not be caught in a lie." She settled into a chair and began to slide her picks back into their pouches. "Now what else have we to discuss?"

Ulasim shook his head. "You were born a spy, Aly."

She smiled cheerfully. "No, but I'm a *very* fast study."

7

PUTTING DARKINGS TO WORK

The next morning, Aly woke before dawn because her nose itched. She crossed her eyes to see the cause. It was the darking Trick, who had produced a thin tentacle to tickle her with. Aly groaned quietly—Dove was still asleep, Junai gone—and retreated to the privy closet. "What is it?" she whispered.

"Look," the darking told her. It leaped to the shelf that lined the wall and stretched until it formed a thin snake nearly thirty inches long. Then it changed shape until it looked like a long string of black beads. Rising and turning, it made itself into a continuous necklace. Sticking up the bead that seemed to be its head, it told Aly, "Neck more fun than sash."

Aly twiddled her thumbs. Finally she asked, "Where did you get this idea?"

"I snoop," Trick said proudly. "Dove have beads. Sarai have many, many beads. Duchess have beads. Rihani have beads. Chenaol—"

Aly raised a hand for silence. She had the idea that the enterprising creature would have told her the contents of every jewel box in the house if she had asked. Trick stopped talking. "Do you ever sleep?" Aly asked.

"Sometimes," Trick replied. "After we split to make new darking."

Which could be useful, Aly thought. Spies that seldom need rest. "Have you any information from Lace or Feather?"

"Feather say there weapons under house and barn and stable and dairy and in tunnels under house," Trick replied promptly. "Lace say Ochobu and Ysul magic on workroom and bedroom hurt. Lace can't go in there."

"And the others? What do they say?" Aly wanted to know.

"The others explore Joshain Street. Lord Asembat next door snores in night. Lady Asembat meets young man in room by dock. Spies outside Balitang House from Topabaw and Carthak and Tyra bored. They say nothing happens here. Raka man stabbed soldier and other soldiers kill him. Lady Yendrugi in pink stucco house expects baby. Guards in Kadyet House across street owe Fesgao fifty silver gigits over dice. They tell Fesgao their master say Duke Nomru must watch step with regents. Daughter in Kadyet House is kissing her maid. In Murtebo House—"

Once more Aly raised a hand to halt the flow of information spilling out of her darking necklace. "I have to get some of you into the palace," she murmured. "If you learn all this in just one night, I'll be deluged with what you can learn where it matters."

"Kissing maid not matter?" asked Trick.

"No," Aly said. "But the stabbing and the news about the duke matter." She nibbled her lip, then said, "Once I'm dressed, you go back in my sash. Dove will want to visit the market—I'll find an excuse to break away, report to Master Grosbeak, and leave one of you with him. When I return, I'll wear you, so everyone will think I bought you at market. While we eat breakfast, get about four of you into that small red pouch I left in my workroom—the place where I put the others. You're all back, aren't you?"

"Yes," replied Trick. Its bead head hung, somewhat forlorn. "No more fun today?"

Aly smiled and stroked the creature's head with a finger. "Don't worry. All of you will be having more fun than you can stand by week's end, I promise."

She gathered up the darking and quietly went into the other room to dress. Junai's pallet was already folded and stowed. Dove slept with her light coverlet over her head. Once clothed, Aly tucked Trick into her sash and went downstairs.

In the stable courtyard, working by the pale early-morning light, all combat-trained members of the household practiced their skills, with Ochobu and Ysul's spells to keep the sounds of their training from escaping into the air outside the walls. Aly joined them and soon found how rusty she had gotten since the family had left Tanair to come south. When Fesgao dumped her on her back in the dirt and leveled a spear at her throat, Aly noticed a trickle of darkness flow away from her sash. It seemed Trick did not care to be smashed. Aly swiveled her legs, twining them around Fesgao's as she gripped his spear, then yanked his feet from under him while gently touching his throat with the spear's butt. She rolled to her feet as Fesgao lay on the ground and cursed, turning to guard herself as Ukali came at her with double daggers.

When the sunrise bell rang out over the city, everyone dusted themselves off and checked one another's bruises. Fesgao tousled Aly's hair with a grin and ambled off with the other men-at-arms to change into uniforms. Aly scrubbed herself and combed her hair in the laundry, then went to her office. Trick was already there, exchanging sniffs with a miniature kudarung on Aly's windowsill.

"There seem to be more of those things every day," she remarked, picking up a sheaf of reports.

"They come careful," said Trick. "They don't all come at once. They can take darkings to other places."

"We might do something with that," Aly said absently, absorbed in her reading. Merchants who dealt in crops were saying that the price of rice would shoot up that summer, which meant poorer folk would be forced to eat millet. It was edible grain, but not by much.

She was halfway through the stack of paper when Junai stuck her head in the door. "You missed breakfast, and Lady Dove wants to go to Market Town," she informed Aly.

"I rejoice," Aly replied, setting her reports aside. "Nobody even saved me a sago cake?" She didn't love the palm-starch cakes, but they were filling.

"I saved two," Junai said, placing them on Aly's desk. "Hurry up. You're supposed to be a lady's maid, remember?"

After she left, Aly hung her red pouch, with its five darkings, from her sash. She then hurried to dress her mistress for an expedition to Market Town. This time Dove and her guards followed Joshain Street to Susashai Way. After three blocks of eyeing the seamstresses' shops that lined Susashai, they turned down Ratechul Avenue. Dove knew many people here, too—flower sellers, door guards, and booksellers. Having learned the day before that Dove could spend an hour chatting with just one person, Aly asked to leave the group for a short time. She knew Dove would be well watched in her absence.

Dove nodded permission as a bookseller came out of his shop, beaming. Aly nodded to Dove's guards and left.

From here, it was nine blocks to the building that Topabaw's man Grosbeak used as his workplace. Aly walked through his door into a large waiting room, where faded bolts of cloth were displayed on counters.

Seated at a table, with an account book, reeds, and ink before her, was a hard-faced old woman. She glared at Aly but said nothing. Aly looked about as if for a friendlier face, though no one else was there. She wrung her hands to complete the picture of nervousness, then bent down and whispered, "I'm here to see Master Grosbeak. I have messages."

The old woman sniffed. "Don't you all." She got up. "Follow me." She led Aly down a narrow, badly lit hall to an office. There were bundles of paper stacked everywhere, on shelves and on the desk at the center of the room. There was no chair for visitors: Aly suspected that few people would want to linger.

Grosbeak himself was a part-raka with wiry black hair. Aly fumbled with her hands, then her sash, wondering if he'd been trapped into this like Vitorcine or if he liked his work. She noticed the large emerald ring on his left hand as he opened the ledger and decided not to care about Grosbeak. Topabaw had made him rich.

"You're new," he said, his black eyes memorizing her face. "Name?"

"Aly Homewood, your lordship," she said, voice shaking.

"Where do you work? And it's Master Grosbeak, wench. I don't hold with mockery." His voice was as tight and flat as his mouth. He picked up a writing brush, dipped it in ink, and began to copy her particulars into his ledger.

"Please, Master Grosbeak, I'm maid to Lady Dovasary at Balitang House." Aly had tucked a darking with a peony inside it into her sash on the way to Grosbeak's. Now she smoothed her hands over her sash, as if drying her palms. "I wasn't mocking, sir, truly." Rubbing the sash was her cue to Peony. The darking flowed out the back of her sash and down to the floor. Aly stepped closer to the desk so that Grosbeak could not see her below the hips.

"Have you anything to report? Treasonous talk against the regents or His Majesty, letters and messages from mysterious sources, private chats between nobles without the servants to hear? Gossip from the servants about making trouble in the streets? Rumors of unrest, or traitors?" He scowled when she didn't answer right away. "This is Rajmuat, *wench*. Someone always talks loosely."

"Well, but, sir, we've only been back in the city less than a week, and first my ladies had to go to court, and folk are calling, and there's dresses to be made, and my lord Elsren comes and goes from the palace, it's really all very confusing. They were sad when they saw some people from the Ibadun family had been killed when we came, and Lady Dove was scared bad when a fight broke out near us at Dockmarket yesterday. . . ."

She nattered at him until he tired and dismissed her, with orders to listen to more conversations between noble guests. Aly curtsied as much as the sarong allowed, to ensure that Peony was tucked under Grosbeak's desk. When she saw that glint of flower, she knew the darking would manage well, and retreated. The old woman scowled at her in the front room, while a newcomer turned her head so that Aly could not see her face.

Aly was smiling as she turned into an alley two doors down from Grosbeak's. By the time she visited the man again, she would know a great deal more about who was loyal to the regents and who was not. Then she could do her best to direct Grosbeak's—and Topabaw's—suspicious eyes toward their own supporters.

In the alley, she stepped into a dark corner between buildings. "All right, Trick," she murmured. "If you want to spend life as a necklace . . ."

The darking poked its new bead-head out of her sash. "See more," it explained.

"Very true," said Aly. She gently lifted the Trick-bead string from her sash and draped it over her neck. It felt like cool drops of water rolling over her skin as Trick arranged itself in two loops of shiny beads. Under her right ear, one bead joined with another as a kind of clasp, giving Trick a slightly bigger head to speak from, where Aly could easily hear it.

Once she was freshly arrayed, Aly went in search of her mistress. Dove had moved on from the bookseller's where Aly had left her group, so Aly walked along until she saw Dove's unofficial guards. They pointed out the three household guards stationed at the entrance to the largest shop on Dori Way: Herbrand Edgecliff, Bookseller and Importer.

"How long has she been in there?" Aly asked the man-at-arms positioned by the main entrance.

"Long enough for my feet to hurt," drawled the man, an ex-bandit and devoted family servant.

Aly smiled. "Then I believe I'll wait out here. How many books can one person read?" she joked, with only a little, well-hidden wistfulness for long winter afternoons spent curled up, reading until her eyes began to blur.

The man-at-arms grinned. "Don't ask me—I can't read anyway." Then pride dawned on his face. "But my daughter can. Her Grace's maid's been teaching the little ones."

Aly smiled. She understood a father's pride. "She's a clever girl," Aly told him. "With luck she'll go far."

To keep from distracting him, she wandered along the storefront, part of her mind on the talk around her, part on what she had planned for that evening, and part on the bookseller's display. He had a very expensive front window, made of small panes of costly glass, the better to show off his wares. The books looked gorgeous, even through the warps and bubbles in the glass.

Something caught her eye. In the lowest right-hand pane in the corner, someone had scratched a design. Aly sharpened her magical Sight. The emblem of the open shackle was cut into the window. More importantly, it had been done from inside. Someone working in the shop, perhaps Master Edgecliff himself, supported the rebellion.

She yawned. "Maybe I can hint that it's getting toward lunchtime," she told the guard, and ambled into the shop, switching her behind like a lazy servant girl. When the door closed behind her, she reached into the bag that hung from her sash. It was like reaching into a bowl filled with lively cool liquid. A ball of it moved up into her palm. Gently Aly brought out a darking and, while looking at a wall of books, deposited it on a bottom shelf. There was an inch-wide gap between shelf and floor: the darking slid into it and vanished.

Pleased with her morning labor—she would place two more darkings on the way home, one at the checkpoint on Joshain and Trade Winds Street and one near Topabaw's spy outside Balitang House—Aly went to find Dove.

* * *

As the household napped, Aly returned to her workroom to talk with her pack and their recruits. They were training more people, teaching them how to gather information and where to send it. And there was news: Vereyu had sent a note from the palace. It seemed that the night before, Topabaw had been forced to interrupt the regents' supper with the news that the luarin governor of Ikang Island had been murdered. Servants had been present to hear both Topabaw's admission that he had no information as yet and Imajane's enraged reply, "Then what good *are* you?"

Aly smiled with pleasure. Already the relationship between the princess-regent and her spymaster was fraying and they had foolishly, or arrogantly, shown it before witnesses. "We must do our best to ensure that Topabaw continues to look unable to manage his work," she murmured, going through new reports on her desk. At the bottom of the stack was a slate with code signs written in chalk: Ysul's notice that her requested pots of blazebalm were ready for use. Before her pack returned to their own jobs, she said, "Those of you who were with me two nights ago, I'll require you at midnight once more." They nodded and left.

Ulasim stuck his head in the door as the last of Aly's pack filed out. "The guests have begun to arrive," he said. "And the young eagles have decided they wish to go riding to Lady Weeps Park."

Aly raised an eyebrow in silent question.

Ulasim answered it. "Her Grace says they will all go, including Lady Dovasary." He gave his thin smile. "Dove is not pleased. She has new books to read. Her Grace says His Grace of Nomru *particularly* requests his young friend's company."

Well, that's that, Aly thought, getting to her feet. It's not as if she can turn down one of the ten most powerful nobles in the realm.

She had asked Dove two nights ago, as she prepared her mistress's hair for bedtime, why she talked so much with a man old enough to be her grandfather. Dove had replied, "He's one of the few people who can keep up with me, and I with him. It's a pleasant change from having to slow down to deal with most people."

Aly, looking at Dove in the mirror, raised an eyebrow.

Dove smiled. "Not *you*, silly. I have trouble keeping up with *you*. Where everyone else sees a straight line, you see a maze, and when I'm done talking to you, the maze starts to make more sense."

"Thank you, I think," Aly had replied then. Now she amended her thought. Dove *would* risk offending one of the realm's most popular nobles if she didn't actually like him.

With Nuritin in command of household social functions, it was less than an hour until they were ready to go. Sarai's court of young men drew straws for the honor of riding at her side. Aly noticed that the Carthaki Zaimid did not choose to compete. Instead he rode with Nuritin, keeping pace with the duchess and her father, Lord Matfrid Fonfala.

Sarai's court supplied all the color and liveliness their parade could want, laughing and joking. At last the park appeared at the end of their road, the entrance graced by curved palm trees. Five wild kudarung soared overhead on the day's heated air. Even the younger riders stopped to watch, awed. When they entered the park, they did so quietly.

Aly and the other servants ended up in a pavilion set near the gate and the stables. Those nobles who chose not to ride left their mounts and wandered among the flower gardens, eating delicacies sold at small pavilions. Sarai and her companions rode on the park's horse paths, racing each other, Sarai determined to beat them all. She lost only to Zaimid.

After the racing, the horses were led to the stables to be cared for by the hands who worked there. The young people then joined the older ones for rest, food, and conversation. Aly wandered into the stables, admiring the horses and flirting with the hostlers, while she slipped a darking each into the saddle blankets of Duke Nomru, Lord Fonfala, and the Dowager Countess Tomang. She had talked to the creatures about what they were to do and questioned them enough to know that they understood her quite well. Though the darkings did not care to be elaborate with spoken language—perhaps because speech was a tricky affair for them—they were very intelligent.

Once the mosquitoes came out, it was time to return. Pembery, Boulaj, and Aly repaired their mistresses' appearances with degrees of success. Pembery and Aly did well enough because their ladies had spent the afternoon talking. As soon as Pembery finished, Winnamine went to see if the horses were ready to go. Boulaj had more of a struggle. Sarai had lost every one of the hairpins that had kept both her straight and her curled locks in place. She shook her long mane free. "Don't pin it, Boulaj," she ordered. "Whose idea was it anyway to make us torture our heads?"

"It's not seemly," protested Boulaj. "Young ladies are supposed to wear their hair up."

"Aly, there's a sheer scarf in my bag," Dove murmured. "Somebody should have thought to tell Boulaj that Sarai's old maid always carried spare pins." She looked at Pembery, eyes narrowed, as Aly searched out the scarf Dove had mentioned. "You were friends with her," Dove told her stepmother's attendant. As senior maid, it was Pembery's job to help Boulaj, as Dove well knew. "Perhaps you might tell Boulaj the different tricks to dressing my sister that she knew."

Pembery recognized a command even when it was phrased as a request. "Yes, Lady Dovasary." Dove didn't look away until Pembery gave a small bow of her head.

Aly produced the scarf, a gold and red length of silk that covered Sarai's hair enough for everyone but sticklers like Nuritin and Countess Tomang, who sniffed at the same time. Aly restrained a giggle and Boulaj covered a grin.

The party was quiet from weariness as they rode back down the stepped rises that lifted the different levels of the city above the harbor. Though it was still spring, the day had been warm and sticky, a hint of summer to come. Nomru and Matfrid Tomang spoke idly of moving to country estates for the summer. Zaimid told his companions, Sarai, Dove, and Sarai's friend Isalena Obemaek, that he wouldn't miss the dampness at all when he returned to hot, dry Carthak.

The closer they went to the heart of the city, the more Aly's skin prickled. The sidewalks were unusually crowded, even for this time of day, and few people on them were moving. Instead they stared at the noble riders. At Sarai.

Aly eased along the line of guards until she found the commander of the Balitang men-at-arms. Junai moved in from the other side of the thin ring of men to listen to Aly. First Aly counted, then wished she hadn't. The Balitangs had sent five soldiers. Most of the other riders had brought one, maybe two, guards, not anticipating trouble on an afternoon's ride to the park.

"You've got your cautious face on," the guards' commander murmured. "What is it?"

"Too many quiet people who are just staring," Aly replied. "And we know who they're staring at, too. Is there any way we can avoid the next army checkpoint?"

"I would think you'd *want* soldiers to handle the crowd," he replied.

Aly and Junai both shook their heads. "Oil on tinder," Junai explained. "The soldiers itching for a fight and the people itching to get at soldiers."

"It might not be too inconvenient to the regents if the very popular Balitang sisters got hurt—or accidentally killed—in a fight between a mob and soldiers. Things get so confused in street fighting—"

"Too late," the commander interrupted, "here's the checkpoint. I'll pass the word for everyone to look sharp." Ahead, the road crossed with Rittevon's Lance, the street that went from the palace down to the docks. The soldiers at the checkpoint warily eyed the people, who outnumbered them, but did nothing to send them away or to hinder the nobles. It was five blocks farther down that the mob swept out of the side streets to surround the riders. In eerie silence, many of the new arrivals ragged and dirty, they tried to force their way through the guards, reaching for Sarai.

"Whatever you are doing, this is neither the time nor the place." Duke Nomru had a thundering voice when he cared to use it. "You will bring grief upon yourselves with this display. Return to your homes!" He wheeled his mount, forcing the people nearest him to back away.

Ferdy Tomang had stronger feelings. "Raka dogs!" he cried, lashing the nearest member of the crowd with his riding crop. "Back to your kennels!"

Oh, splendid, Aly thought, rolling her eyes. Our hero.

The eerie silence broke with a roar. Half of the mob turned on the young count. Ferdy spurred his horse to rear. The other noblemen and Matfrid Fonfala did the same, urging their mounts to turn on their hind legs, showing everyone the crushing power of those raised front hooves.

Balitang House's people had been trained for this, even if the guards with them had not. Junai and a man-at-arms collected the duchess and Nuritin. They drew them and the other noblewomen onto the sidewalk to put a building at their backs and take them out of the physical movement on the street. Aly gripped Sarai's and Dove's mounts, forcing them toward the same wall.

"Sarai, don't!" cried Dove. Aly looked up.

Sarai had her riding crop raised; her target was Aly. "Let me go!" she ordered. "I have to stop them before they kill people—before we kill more raka!"

Aly held Sarai's eyes with her own. She did not say it, but she thought it: if Sarai hit her, Aly would teach her a lesson Sarai's supporters would not like.

"Don't be a fool!" snapped Dove over Aly's head. "Get the wall at our backs, and get our servants behind us!" Boulaj was already ranging among the maids' horses, drawing them together and moving them to the rear, speaking softly as their riders kept very still. Aly was grateful that maids seldom chose lively mounts.

"This bad," Trick murmured in her ear. "Four-leggers mashing two-leggers bad."

Above the cries of the mob Aly heard the sound she'd been dreading: the tramp of boots. "It's about to get worse," she muttered. Here came the King's Watch, stern, hard men in red-painted breastplates, metal helmets, and boots with nails in the soles and metal pieces that covered the toes, making any kick the soldier gave a bloody one. They were armed with short swords, clubs, and shields, and used all three to drive the mob, cutting their way through to the nobles. A raka woman moved to scoop two children out of the way of their mounted captain, diving between the Balitang guards into the protected inner circle. It was Eyun, one of Aly's pack. She bore a scratch down one creamy cheek. She looked at Aly, who nodded that she'd done well, then turned her attention to the shrieking children. One looked to be a merchant's child. Her gown was luarin-style cotton, unfaded and unmended. She yelled for her nursemaid while the other child screamed over his broken arm. He looked like the worst dregs of the slums, ragged and filthy.

"Here." Winnamine knelt beside Eyun, a flask of water in her hands. To the girl she said, "I'm sure your nurse is fine." She offered the boy a drink from her silver flask. The boy blinked at her, then took the flask and drank. He might have then tried to run with it, but light flashed from Nuritin at Winnamine's side. The boy's eyes rolled up and he collapsed, Nuritin's sturdy old hands catching him before his bad arm hit the stones. Aly had heard that the old lady had been rough and ready in her day. It seemed she could still muster a bit of power at need. "Well, I couldn't leave him feeling all that pain," Nuritin said, meeting Winnamine's look. "And softhearted as you are, I suppose we'll need a healer who will tend him."

"That depends on the healer, surely." Zaimid dismounted. He knelt in the street, apparently unaware of the war being fought on the other side of the protective line of men-at-arms and noblemen on horseback. "It's quite a simple break, and luckily, it's not pierced the skin." Gently he wrapped long fingers around the broken limb, his head bent, his brown face closed and thoughtful. In Aly's Sight silvery fire spun a thread from his blazing magical core down through his arm and into the boy's.

He's got wonderful control, thought Aly, impressed. Of course, he would. They wouldn't put a noble idiot in charge of the Carthaki emperor's health.

Zaimid released the boy's arm. The marks of his hands showed pale at first, then faded. The boy stirred, then grabbed his arm. He looked at it, agape, then at Nuritin, who had recovered Winnamine's flask, then at Zaimid.

"You'll do better here until this ends," Zaimid said. "No good sending you out to get something else broken."

Dove nudged Aly and handed over plums that had survived the nobles' meal. Aly gave them to the boy. He began to devour them, his wondering eyes still on Zaimid.

Beyond their circle of safety, the royal soldiers dispersed the mob with brutal speed. Sarai was still trying to fight her way between Ferdy Tomang and Duke Nomru, screaming, "They weren't hurting anyone! Leave them alone!" She finally gave up when the soldiers had driven the crowd so far down the street that none of them could hear. She glared at Duke Nomru, tears running down her cheeks. "They weren't going to hurt us!"

The older man raised his stern brows. "And do you think that would stop the kind of men they have in the King's Watch? Their orders are to disperse gatherings." He looked down the street, with its litter of bodies. "This one is well and truly dispersed, whatever its intention was." He looked back at the ladies. "I propose we return to Balitang House at all speed, before the animals hired for the Watch return."

Winnamine and Nuritin mounted up.

Aly moved in close to Eyun. "Stay here. Learn what you can, maybe get this little one home?" The little girl had sobbed herself into silence in Eyun's hold.

Eyun nodded and hand-signed, *They wanted to touch the twice-royal. That's all. Just touch her, to know she is real.*

"So much beauty shouldn't be marred," Zaimid said over Aly's shoulder. He brushed Eyun's cheekbone with his fingers. Her cut healed before their eyes, as if the work of several weeks had been put into a breath. There was not even a scar. To Nomru he said apologetically, "Your Grace, my ladies"—he looked at the older women next—"forgive me, but I am needed here. I bid you all farewell." To Sarai he added, "I'll make sure these two children are looked after." He was already unbuckling saddlebags from his horse. Draping them over his shoulder, he asked the boy, "Will you hold my reins?" He passed them into the child's hands. Aly thought he was being overcharitable, giving the reins to a boy who had meant to steal the duchess's silver flask, but it seemed the boy held the healer in too much awe to steal the horse at present.

Aly mounted her pony. Sarai might have pulled away from her group, but her grandfather Matfrid came up beside her as she urged her horse forward, and took the reins. "Granddaughter, you are overwrought," he said quietly, holding her dark eyes with his gray ones. "Allow me to escort you."

They rode off, picking their way around the fallen—Aly was pleased to see a few soldiers groaning in the road—the men and the guards in a ring around the ladies and their maids. Aly looked back between two guards. Zaimid, saddle-bags on the ground beside him, was engaged in turning over a woman who resembled a bundle of rags, unaware or uncaring that she'd left a bloody handprint on his white lawn sleeve.

At the house, the gathering broke up quickly. Sarai announced that she had a headache and needed to lie down. Without her to hold them together, the young nobles chose to go home. The gloss had been stripped from the afternoon.

Only when the guests had gone did the Balitang ladies and their maids ascend to the family quarters. They entered their private sitting room to find Sarai and a litter of overturned chairs and decorative tables. Gazing at the mess, Aly thought it was just as well that the second-best furnishings went into this room, which was for comfort, not style.

"Have you taken leave of your senses?" asked Nuritin. Her back was as stiff as a poker, her voice chipped ice. "This is not the behavior of a properly bred young woman, it is the behavior of spider monkeys!"

"After seeing all those 'properly bred' people just sit there while people were being thrashed, I'd *rather* live with spider monkeys!" cried Sarai, eyes swollen with furious weeping. "Every last one of us—every last one—just let it happen! Ferdy was *glad*—he called them raka dogs, I heard him!"

"A riot cannot be controlled, Sarai," Winna said calmly, setting a table upright. "All we could have done was get pulled from our horses and savaged. Soldiers can lose control in those circumstances. They don't care who they batter—and they can always claim they didn't realize we were nobility when we were among the commoners. It's happened before." Dove, Aly, and Pembery began to help the duchess pick things up. Nuritin continued to stare at Sarai as if she were a badly trained housemaid.

"It's happened *here*," Sarai shouted. "It happens *here*, because soldiers believe the poor are a disease, not people. And they get that attitude honestly—it comes straight from the Throne! It always has and it always will, and people who are supposed to be noble in nature will *let* it happen, for fear of their own lives! Only one of us showed any decency today: Zaimid! The foreigner! He actually cares about people, whether they live in kennels or not!" She stormed out, yanking the door open so hard it chipped the stucco wall.

There was a long silence. At last Nuritin said tartly, "Well! I am not charged with her upbringing, Winnamine, but in your place, I would slap her for addressing elders in such a way."

"She was upset, Aunt," Winnamine replied wearily. "There was blood running in the gutters."

"Screaming and shouting will not change that," snapped Nuritin. "Getting enough power among ourselves to *force* the Crown to change how it rules the people, that is the way to change."

Well, it's one way, thought Aly, collecting the pieces of a broken vase.

What Nuritin had just said sounded very close to treason. If Aly really did belong to Topabaw, she could get all kinds of favors from him for that tidbit alone. She wondered if Countess Tomang—certainly not her son!—Lord Matfrid, Duke Nomru, and Baron Engan, Dove's astronomer friend, held the same view that the Crown must be controlled.

At the conspirators' nightly meeting Aly reported on the fight. Ochobu was not present. The moment she'd heard the news, she had packed her bag of medicines and gone to offer help. No one suggested they would pray for any member of the Watch who made the mistake of trying to stop her.

There were more reports to give and to hear. At last the conspirators separated, most bound for their beds. Aly went to her office. Ysul came in not long after with three packs, setting them on the floor very carefully. He was dressed as an itinerant worker, the kind of fellow people expected to see around the docks. In a cloth bag carried like a bedroll on his back he had his waterproof and sight-proof disguise. Aly dressed in her own suit, then in her Carthaki noble's disguise. Fegoro came again as a Bazhir, Lokak as a southern Carthaki, Jimarn as another Carthaki noble, and Yoyox as Death's priest. Aly, Jimarn, and Yoyox hid Ysul's packs under their flowing clothes.

"Fun?" whispered Trick in Aly's ear. "Meeting not fun. Fight in street and house stupid."

She followed the others to the laundry and down into the tunnel, whispering softly inside her veils, "It depends on what you think is fun. It will be loud."

"Loud maybe fun," said Trick. "You think fight in street and house stupid, too?"

Aly was about to ask how the darking could judge what was stupid for humans when she stopped herself. She had to remember, these creatures were intelligent. They learned ferociously fast. They already knew every member of the household by face and voice. And they had lived nearly ten years among dragons. Surely that counted for something, since Daine had also mentioned dragons were less than patient as a whole. Aly grinned wryly as they emerged from the tunnel.

"Fights were stupid," she said. Then she and Jimarn each took one of Fegoro's arms as the rest of their group cut over to other streets.

As before, the King's Watch had abandoned the checkpoints for the night. The afternoon's unpleasantness had taken place in Middle Town, not at the dock. It was habit among the city's guardians to decide that a violent outburst kept the lower classes quiet for days, which meant they were off their guard now.

Their watchman friend was absent. They entered his shack, removed their disguises, then redistributed the packs. Quietly they descended the ladder to the meeting places of stinking piers, stinking water, and stinking boulders. The noise from the dockside merrymakers was as loud as ever, a jangle of music, singing, debate, and the occasional fight. It covered any slips they made on the rocks. At last they came to the metal net and passed into the slave market piers.

Aly adjusted her Sight as the three teams split up. Beside the piers she could see ships at anchor—seventeen in all. They should be close to empty. Even with the net, slavers didn't like the risk that some desperate swimmer might yet escape. Slaves were always taken to the market's pens as soon as their vessel docked. Aly hoped there would be crew aboard but knew the likelihood was small. They would be out, spending the profits of other slave sales.

She led Ysul out to the farthest left pier of the dock she had kept for herself, the dock where she had disembarked as a slave. As he treaded water, she took a small clay globe from his waterproof sack and jammed it into an opening between boards. Back and forth they went, careful to let no water leak into the sack of globes. At last all six were placed. As they waited, Ysul left the waterproof bag close to the nearest globe. It would be incinerated when the globe was set off. It was always important to get rid of any trace of the mage who did a piece of work like this. If Topabaw's people were good enough, they might track any remnants back to Ysul.

Aly and Ysul returned to the net to wait for their companions. The others arrived, their own bags left behind. Swiftly they made their way back to the watchman's shack and changed out of their waterproof clothes into their disguises. As they left the shack, they took the bundled suits over to one of the many fires that lit Dockmarket and burned them. Then they mingled with the crowds.

They reached the end of the night market, a good four blocks from the slave docks and pens. Wooden barriers were set there, manned by rock-muscled freemen with iron-studded clubs. The slave merchants liked to guard their property.

Aly, Jimarn, and Fegoro reached the barriers, inspected the guards by eye as if they too may be for sale, then turned to look at the fading gaiety of the Dockmarket. Ysul was watching a juggler nearby. When he glanced at Aly, she raised two gloved fingers.

She saw the silver flash of Ysul's magic. At the corner of her eye she noted an orange flicker; fast behind it came the roar as the blazebalm ignited, blowing their cheap clay globes into dust and setting the slave docks on fire. Aly turned when the other merrymakers did, to see a vision that made her shiver in delight. Columns of flame clawed the night sky as fire raced over the docks. Within moments their fire was reaching for the ships. A handful of men threw themselves from a few vessels and swam for shore: watchmen, left behind while their mates toured the city.

Like the rest of the Dockmarket crowds and the guards on the barriers, Aly and her friends stayed to look on as ship after ship caught fire and alarm bells began to sound in their part of the city. Only when they heard the ominous thump of marching feet did they mingle with the rest of the crowd and flee, splitting up as the crowd did, to find their way home by separate routes.

Aly went to bed feeling drained but pleased. When she had been brought to those docks and the slave markets beyond, she had promised herself that everyone who had fetched her there would come to regret it. It might take her years to find the actual pirates who had captured her, but the docks, and the vessels of some providers of captives for sale, made for a very fine start. She rather thought her mother would approve.

8

PLOTS HATCH

Once again Aly was roused by a tentacle tickling her nose. She cracked one eyelid, to see it wasn't quite dawn. "Trick, I *need* sleep. I know you don't," she croaked after pulling her cover over her head so she wouldn't rouse anyone. "But *I* do."

The darking said, "Sleep or big news? Pick!"

Aly's eyes flew open. She was wide awake. "Big news. And it had better be big."

"Nomru arrested," Trick told her. Aly smothered a gasp of shock. "Nomru at party at palace when messengers come and say docks burn," the darking continued. "When princess say punish many people for this and other trouble they make, Nomru say people afraid. He say, kindness do more than hurting. He say, help to buy food, take less taxes. Princess say, arrest him. Take him to Kanodang. Flame with Nomru still. Flame say Nomru say many bad words. Flame say guards afraid to hurt Nomru."

"I should think so!" Aly whispered. Imajane had misstepped badly. "Why didn't Rubinyan stop her?" she asked.

"Prince try, Flame say. Princess not listen."

I need to get more darkings into the palace, Aly thought. Then she remembered: "Was Quartz there with Countess Tomang?"

Trick nodded. Although the cover shut out the light, such as it was, Aly's Sight still let her see the darking's featureless but somehow expressive face. It had opened up from its necklace shape so that it could watch her—or could it?

"Can you see in the dark?" she asked.

"Nothing dark to darkings," Trick replied, matter-of-fact.

Aly pressed that into her memory, then inquired, "So what does Quartz say? Was the countess there when Imajane ordered the arrest?"

Trick nodded. "Quartz say, countess drink too much rotten grape juice. Countess vomit twice on way home."

Of course she did, thought Aly. Sometimes you don't have to be an oracle to read the omens of your own doom. "Back into place, please, Trick," she whispered. "We're getting up. Tell Flame to try to come home as best as it can. I can learn nothing from Nomru in prison that's useful right away."

As soon as her "bead necklace" was secure around her neck, Aly tossed off her coverlet. As usual, Junai was already gone and Dove was sound asleep. Quickly Aly put her pallet bed away, got dressed, cleaned her teeth, and combed her hair. She raced down to the ground floor and out to the practice ground. Ulasim was exercising his longsword skills with Fesgao, but the moment he saw Aly he put up a hand to stop the match. Fesgao drew up and looked over his shoulder to see what had distracted the big footman. Ulasim handed the practice sword off to Boulaj, then advanced on Aly, his muscled chest sweaty despite the early-morning chill. Aly wondered how long he'd been practicing when he grabbed her by one arm and towed her toward the house. "Lovely to see you this morning," he said, his voice filled with false cheer. "Might I have a moment of your time for a chat? I knew you would agree." Into the house they went, and down the hall to the meeting room.

Aly tried only once to tug her arm from his grip—it was like wearing a shackle on her bicep. "Why the enthusiasm?" she asked, trotting to keep up with his long stride. "I was coming to see you. There's something you ought to know."

He thrust her into the room and followed her in, closing the door behind him. "I'm sure there is a great deal I ought to know, but first, there is something you *will* know," Ulasim said, facing her. "Just *what* were you thinking of last night?"

Aly crossed her arms. "We agreed that, unless it was necessary, we were to keep one another uninformed about exact operations done by our individual groups. It's to everyone's advantage in case we're questioned." He reminds me of someone—who? she wondered.

"Yes, we were to keep one another uninformed about particular operations," Ulasim retorted, scowling. "I do not object in the least to your strategy, your target, or your methods of achieving your goal. I *do* object—gods curse it, woman, must I ask Mother put a watcher spell on you, to let us know where you are if you go off these grounds? What I *do* object to is *you* taking the command yourself."

Aly winced. Suddenly she knew what had puzzled her about his stance and his speech. Just so would her own da chew out the leader who led a raid on his or her own.

"I allowed it because I knew the source of your interest in that area," he informed her. "I can understand it all too well. I also had Fesgao send some of his people out to keep an eye on you, in case things went awry."

Aly had noticed familiar faces in the crowd. She had simply assumed that members of the household had taken a night to enjoy themselves. Idiot! she scolded herself. That's the kind of slipup that can ruin everything! If you hadn't been so fixed on your stupid revenge, you would have asked why our people were out so late!

"You could have been trampled when the crowd ran," Ulasim went on sternly. "You could have been taken by the King's Watch."

Aly couldn't help it. She snorted.

"Well, even slaves can get lucky once," Ulasim admitted. It was an old Kyprin proverb. "But you endangered your people by being there. You endangered us. And you endangered our ladies. Do you understand me? No more heroics, Aly. I know better than you how frustrating it is to stay behind while others strike a blow. But it's necessary. We know too much, and there are ways to get around suicide spells."

About to explain that the god had made her immune to telling what she knew through torture or magic, Aly changed her mind. Instead she bowed her head. "I'm sorry. You're right. I was foolish."

Ulasim frowned. "Don't toy with me, girl. I'm not in the mood."

Aly shook her head and showed him her real face, which expressed rueful acknowledgment. "I'm not, Ulasim, honestly, for once. You're right." She raised an eyebrow at him. "You knew beforehand?"

Ulasim nodded.

Aly collapsed into one of the cushioned chairs. Since it was impossible for him to loom over her without making himself look silly, Ulasim picked a chair for himself. "And you let me do it anyway," Aly went on.

The big raka smiled crookedly. "I understood. But it cannot happen again, Aly. You are too valuable to take such chances."

Aly nodded. "But I'll have to do it once more," she pointed out. He scowled. "It'll just be me, a quick job. It's something you really don't want to know about." As if I dared explain about setting darkings to listen inside the Gray Palace, she thought. To Ulasim she added, "I can't trust it to anyone else, and it's vital. After that, I'll move to the rear, just as you do. I swear by the gods." Again she raised an eyebrow at him. "Are you done scolding me?"

Ulasim began to lever himself out of his chair. "I am done," he replied.

Aly put a hand on his arm and pressed down. "I told you I have news of my own, news you'll want to hear."

Ulasim sank back into his seat. "Will you make it quick?" he asked.

"I'll make it quick," she teased, "but once I'm done, you might be caught up for longer than you think. Last night Duke Nomru spoke unwisely to Princess Imajane. He presently enjoys the Crown's hospitality at Kanodang."

Ulasim's jaw dropped. "*Nomru?* Are they mad?"

Aly shrugged. "His Highness, I don't believe so. *Her* Highness? We still await the magistrate's ruling in her case. Now, they've jailed him. The Prince at least will see that if Nomru was an honest critic before he was arrested, he will in all likelihood be an enemy if they let him go."

"They *have* to let him go," whispered Ulasim. "He's the most powerful noble in the realm after Topabaw. And he's one of the wealthiest. . . ."

Aly let him turn the idea of Nomru's wealth over in his mind. After a few moments she said, "Topabaw won't like Nomru as an enemy of the Crown. I doubt Her Highness would ever forgive the duke for implying she rules the Isles badly." She smiled. "And if His Highness is ever said to have a flaw, it is that he desires more wealth than he has. I don't think he's mad, not that I've heard. But greedy . . ." Her eyes sparkled. "I love greedy regents, don't you?"

"Aly, you are a wicked creature," replied Ulasim. The corners of his eyes crinkled. "You are right. Her Highness may have made the mistake, but the prince will not wish to make it worse by freeing Nomru. Even if he considered it, he will not be able to forget the Crown's ability to seize the lands, goods, and wealth from suspected traitors."

Aly traced the edge of a lotus printed on her sarong. "It sorrows me that you think I am wicked," she said wistfully. "I fear you are right. I really must change my ways. Eventually." She sighed, then continued briskly, "Have we people at Kanodang?"

Ulasim gave her a look full of pity. "My dear, we have people everywhere."

Aly scuffed her sandaled foot on the polished floor. "*Inside* Kanodang? Not prisoners, but jailers? Cooks?"

"Everywhere means *everywhere*, Aly Bright Eyes," Ulasim pointed out. "And I will endanger none of our people for a single luarin."

Possibilities raced through Aly's mind as she examined all angles of her idea.

Ulasim waited. "That look in your eyes makes me *very* uncomfortable," he finally said. "You look like the god when he has a horrendous piece of mischief in mind."

This is all I would need, Aly told herself. This would disgrace Topabaw utterly. It would show just how weak the regents really are.

She beamed at Ulasim. "I have an idea, if you're interested. Something no one's prepared for. A fast stroke, it'll have to be. Really fast. But oh, so lovely in the results." She began to whistle a little tune.

"Suddenly I am *very* worried," Ulasim said. "I have visions of islands sinking under the sea because of your 'something.' Spit it out."

Aly looked at the ceiling. "Break out all the prisoners we can, luarin and raka. Use the eclipse. The people think it's unlucky. So use the night when a shadow lies on the Rittevon line"—the ones assisted by Mithros and the moon Goddess, she thought, but did not say, in case the gods were near—"to deal a blow against the ruling family."

Ulasim stared at her.

Aly folded her hands demurely. "We have an opportunity, or so it seems to me."

"What of the risk to folk who know nothing of this? To our own people, to the entire city? The Crown has ordered entire villages slain—what makes you think they'll stop at slaying every raka in the Downwind District? Of all the—"

Aly raised an eyebrow. "Why should they suspect the raka?"

Ulasim took a breath to shout his answer, then stopped.

You have it, thought Aly. Just below her ear she heard a tiny voice say, "Fun."

"They won't suspect the raka," whispered Ulasim. "Nomru's wealthy, he has powerful friends with money and household men-at-arms. The Crown will search the city—they must. But the stroke will fall heaviest on the *luarin*, the very people who are the regents' base of support. Their men will be so busy chasing escaped prisoners and trying to find out how it happened that we will get away with scores of preparations for the actual fighting." Ulasim frowned and stroked his bearded chin. "You are an evil girl child."

Aly ignored this pleasantry. "You'll shake up the luarin nobility. They're already thinking that if the regents will jail Nomru, who will they turn on next? The duke himself will be in our debt, when the time comes." And you'll force that limp luarin conspiracy to develop a backbone, she thought. Fear for themselves will drive them into planning rebellion instead of just talking.

Ulasim rested his elbows on his knees. "There will be deaths of people who knew nothing about it. They'll torture anyone they think might be involved."

Aly crossed her arms. Knowledge of what she suggested closed over her shoulders like an enemy's arm. She had grown up aware of the deaths of many people her parents had known during an attempt to take the throne. They numbered friends and enemies alike: the uncle her brother Thom was named for; her mother's teacher and companion, the supernatural cat Faithful, for whom her mother still wept; the Shang Dragon, the queen's and her mother's friend; Duke Roger of Conté, the king's cousin; a princess of the Isles, King Oron's daughter, who had been killed in the fighting. Aly's family knew the price of revolution, though she couldn't say as much to Ulasim.

"People died in the street yesterday," she told him. "People who just wanted a look at Sarai. Is this a war or not?"

Ulasim was nodding before she even asked her question. "We free only

Kanodang's political prisoners. Unless you mean to loose rapists and murderers on the city?"

Aly shook her head. "They can stay in their cages. I won't mind that. And it will reinforce the idea that it was luarin. They free Nomru, so they figure releasing the other political prisoners will confuse the trail."

Ulasim sat back with a groan. At last he said, "Send me Fesgao and Ochobu. Anything of interest that your people turn up, come straight to me. It's two days until the eclipse—we have to move fast. We'll strike after Her Highness's party."

"It's a good thing you've been sneaking warriors into the city since last autumn, then, isn't it?" Aly inquired.

Ulasim glared at her. "How did you— Never mind."

"Will you be needing my spies?"

Ulasim shook his head. "Where we must go, we have them."

Aly went to find Ochobu and Fesgao. "No fun for us," Trick muttered in her ear.

"Oh, we'll have fun," Aly assured her companion. "I always do." She wandered into the female servants' dormitory. There she hand-signaled to a woman of her pack who was awake: *Bring the girls to the meeting room soonest.* She left and went to the single men's dormitory. Sadly, she encountered Ukali before she could enter the big room. Aly sighed with regret: she knew most of the men slept in loincloths, and she would have enjoyed the sight. Accepting the disappointment, she gave her message to Ukali and went back to the large meeting room.

It wasn't long before every chair was occupied. Some of those without chairs leaned on the walls; others sat on the floor. When they were all settled and the door was closed, Aly said, "My dear ones, I have something for you to do on the night of the lunar eclipse. Alas, it will not include me. I'm afraid our general has told me that I am quite naughty and will no longer be permitted to do such things."

"He's right, Duani," Olkey remarked as he peeled a mango with his knife. "You can't go risking yourself. What if Topabaw had gotten word of last night's celebration? *You're* the one who told *us* if we're caught, it's trouble for everyone else once the torturers and the mages get done with you."

Aly raised an eyebrow, not sure that she liked having her student quote her warnings back to her. "This was personal," she replied.

Guchol was working a comb through her tangled hair. "You told us we can't ever let anything be personal, Duani."

"Sometimes personal is too important for rules," Jimarn said, her cold voice cutting through the room like a blade. "Sometimes personal has to be taken care of." Her flinty eyes met Aly's. They both smiled. Jimarn was a runaway slave.

"Well, I'll be good and not do it again, which means I leave this next bit of deliciousness for those who volunteer," Aly said. She pointed to the map of Rajmuat and its surroundings. On the northeast side of the harbor were the slums of the Downwind District, with the human garbage heap called the Honeypot highest on the slope to the ridge. It was no more than wood cabins on stilts, lean-tos, tents, and shacks. Kanodang was on the far side of the heights. There were only two good things about Kanodang, said the wits. It was upwind of the stench of the Honeypot, and it was a nicer place to live.

At the end of the ridge that split the two was the northeast fortress that guarded the harbor mouth. The Lesser Fortress was two simple towers surrounded by a wall. Aly placed a finger on it, then on the complex that guarded the harbor's far side. The Greater Fortress rose on high ground, dominating the harbor. The display grounds for Examples lay below the fortress's stone ramparts.

"Two nights from this, well after midnight," she explained, "we need fires to start in both fortresses and in the barracks. Ysul will help you with blaze-balm. If you set afire all that will burn in both, I will bless you before your ancestors, but I will rest contented if you just keep a large number of soldiers busy for a time. Can you do it?"

"Well, there are the tunnels through the ridge that will get us up into the Lesser Fortress," Rasaj pointed out.

"But they're not safe," objected Hiraos. "They're centuries old, they could collapse any time."

"But they haven't, have they?" asked Lokak. "And the word is they're open still."

"You'll trust 'the *word*'?" demanded Hiraos. "Probably sent in by some old rock rat who wouldn't know if a tunnel dropped on his head, it's happened so many times. . . ."

"So go look for yourselves," Jimarn told them scornfully. "We've got two whole days." She looked at Aly. "There's a pretty big sewer from the Greater Fortress that we can use, if people can stand it. We'd need those special files that cut through iron."

"I know where they're stored," Junai said. To Aly she pointed out, "There's only so much of those things that will burn, you know. They're mostly stone."

"I don't care how much of them burns, only that they burn brightly enough to catch a lot of attention," Aly muttered, rubbing her fingers over her "necklace." She had discovered that Trick vibrated when happy, a sign of contentment as soothing as, and more silent than, a cat's purr.

The room went silent. Aly looked up to see all their eyes on her.

"You want a diversion," Atisa said, grinning. "A big, noisy, attention-getting diversion."

Aly shook her head. "If I'd thought you were stupid, my children, I wouldn't have bothered to train you. Can you do it?" They all nodded. "Well, then, you don't need me. Bring your plans around during the rest period, and we'll have a look. Think it through. I need you all in one piece."

As she walked down the hall on her way back to the kitchen, she asked Trick quietly, "What does Lace report? What are Ulasim, Fesgao, and Ochobu talking about?"

"Getting horses and small sailing boats for escape," replied Trick promptly. "There is cove north of Kanodang where they hide boats. People inside prison will let fighters in. Fesgao must pick out force. They will get word today for people at Kanodang to be ready. We go?" it asked wistfully.

"No," Aly consoled it. "We're going to a party instead."

"Party fun?" asked the darking.

Aly smiled. "It could be."

Once more Dove insisted on a morning walk to see her merchant friends. Elsren was leaving for the palace when they reached the front door. He insisted on hugging his "favorite sister," as he proclaimed to the guards. Aly noted that a number of the black-armored men of the King's Guard turned their heads or brought up their hands to hide smiles.

Once Elsren's party had left, Junai and their escort of men-at-arms emerged from the side courtyard. Dove began to scowl, then sagged. Tacking a proper smile to her face, she greeted everyone by name as they formed up around her. Aly's people slowly collected ahead, to the sides of, and behind their group as they walked down Joshain Street. Today Kioka, Eyun, Hiraos, and Ukali went as secret guards. While Dove visited with her friends, they could deal in rumor.

The walk to the business part of town was not as relaxed as it had been before. Knots of people stood at corners, talking in soft voices, unless soldiers of the King's Watch came to send them on their way. The poorer the gossipers were, the more kicks and blows they got from the soldiers.

"Slime," murmured Dove as they passed one man whose nose was clearly broken and bleeding. Without a word she offered him her handkerchief.

"Stop somewhere and tilt your head back," a man-at-arms advised kindly. "Just wait till the bleeding stops."

The raka muttered his thanks and went into an alley.

"I hope when the time comes things will be done about behavior like that," whispered Dove. "We'll never all live together if the luarin don't accept anyone whose skin is brown."

Her pleasure that day was to stroll down Green Street. Respectable cooks and their assistants shopped here, or they were supposed to. Many stood in tiny groups, whispering. Pairs of men in the scarlet uniform of the Watch paced everywhere, their eyes shifting in the frames made of the face plates of their helmets.

As they passed a small group of civilians, Aly heard a luarin woman with a dusting of flour in her hair whisper to two raka, "Rats, I tell you! My best tenant wakes us all screaming in the dead of night. There was a basketful of rats by his bed! So what does he do but open the door to his room, so they can get out into the house *and* my bakery, if you please! Well, I told him . . ."

Dove and her companions, including Aly, walked out of earshot. Aly smiled. Looking around, she saw the words *Nomru* and *slave docks* on a number of lips. It wouldn't take long for Dove to hear the news.

They halted at a spice seller's stall, with its baskets of seasonings. Dove greeted the woman who was accepting payment from a customer. Aly observed that one seller of garlic, leeks, and onions had hung a decoration at the corner of her booth. Four bulbs were braided together, connected to a broken circle of leeks tied to a wooden frame. It was a very subtle open shackle.

"You're sure?" Dove asked sharply. Aly turned. Her mistress was gripping the spice seller's arm. "There's no doubt?"

The luarin woman shook her head. "My husband was making a delivery to His Grace's house. There's a seal on the gate and everything. The family's inside—they may come and go, but they're terrified."

I should have told the Balitangs this morning, Aly thought, then shook her head. They would have wanted to know where she had gotten her information, and she could not tell them.

A cluster of Mithran priests brushed past their group without so much as an apology. The priest in the lead sported a bite on his cheek. Two acolytes whispered that the temple's master of the flame had been assaulted by rats. Aly rubbed her hands together. People wrote down their secrets, or had a temple scribe write for them, and gave the folded scraps of paper to the master of the flame. It would not be difficult at all for a man in that position to keep the scraps and sell whatever useful information he collected to Topabaw.

They'll be scrambling like an upended basket of rats themselves when Topabaw falls, Aly thought.

"We're going home," Dove said abruptly. "Aly, come along." The guards closed in as Dove said farewell to the spice seller. Once she was ready, they began to hurry back the way they had come. When Aly came up beside her, Dove said quietly, "Duke Nomru was arrested last night, *and* someone blew up the slave docks."

"Did they?" Aly asked innocently. "Fancy that. And we saw His Grace only yesterday. He didn't say he was on the outs with the regents."

"I'm worried about Nomru," said Dove, biting her lip. "He's too mule-headed to beg the regents for anything. And why the slave docks?" she asked with a frown. "Why the ships? There will be more."

"Perhaps as a hint that there should be no more, my lady," suggested one of the guards. "The first thing built after the conquest was a bigger slave market."

Aly glanced at the man. As far as she was aware, he was simply one of Fesgao's warriors, picked for his loyalty and his skill with arms. From his light skin, if he had a slave ancestor or ancestress, it had been some generations ago.

"But we've always had slavery," Dove reminded him. "Even before the conquest."

"They used it as a way to bring the raka to heel," replied the soldier. "Here it became a weapon. Wise as you are, Lady Dovasary, surely you know, if any members of your family are accused of crimes against the Crown, it is the Crown's right to sell any of your household with raka blood. That would include you and the lady Saraiyu."

Dove glanced at Aly. "Not one word," she said.

Aly shrugged. "I wasn't going to say a thing." She put her fingers under her Trick necklace to touch the scar where her slave collar used to be. Dove made a face.

"If the Crown abolished slavery, it would beggar the great nobles," she told the man-at-arms. "They would turn to treason before that."

The man shrugged. "I was just mentioning it as history, my lady. If you please, I am forgetting my duty. I must not converse, or I will be distracted from your safety."

Passing a basketmaker's booth on their way out of Market Town, Aly saw an ornament displayed on the edge of the awning. Palm fronds were woven into the shackle-and-chain design.

They want to join, Aly thought, awed. Not just the raka. The merchant luarin. They want to rid themselves of the Rittevons. But will they fight?

"Trick," she murmured, so quietly that only her necklace darking might hear, "what has Peony to report from Grosbeak? Anything?"

Trick extended a very long neck up until it could loop itself around the back of Aly's ear and dangle its head by her eardrum. "Peony says woman called Lutestring come from palace for daily report from Grosbeak. She takes papers and what Grosbeak says. Grosbeak tells her mysterious new sign of four circles then broken circle appears in more places every day. He say half reports he gets say Topabaw turning against regents. He say other half say regents want to replace Topabaw. Grosbeak is shaking. Grosbeak does not tell Lutestring that he is taking all of his money out of money-changer accounts and packing a bag if he must run. He already send wife and children into country today."

"Thank you," Aly murmured as they walked through the Balitangs' gate. "I'd hate to lose Grosbeak, though. At least, right at present." She stopped, thinking, nibbling her lip as Dove went into the house and the guards returned to their barracks. Aly's unofficial watchers would return to their listening and rumor-spreading throughout the city.

"Why stopping?" Trick inquired.

"Ah," Aly said. The sound of Trick's voice practically inside her head gave her an idea. "Does he take a nap during the rest period?"

Trick waited for a moment, then told Aly, "Every day."

"Peony must wait until he's sound asleep, then whisper that Grosbeak should stay to help Topabaw. Tell him that gods are smiling on Grosbeak." Bless me, I'm starting to talk like them, she thought. Aloud she told Trick, "Ask Peony to tell Grosbeak he will be rich if he stays to help Topabaw. Keep repeating it until he is almost awake. Peony must be careful and speak softly, positioning itself like you are doing. The longer Grosbeak stays and works for Topabaw, the more of his agents we'll catch."

Trick was briefly silent, then said aloud, "Peony say, fun."

Aly smiled. "Well, I did promise *all* of you some fun."

The footman in the front hall told Aly that Dove had headed straight for her stepmother's room. Lady Sarai still lay abed. Aly nodded her thanks and proceeded through the house on the way to her workroom, where she was sure a stack of reports awaited her. They had regular deliveries from the rebellion's other agents, chosen and working long before Aly had even come to the Isles, people like Vereyu at the palace. Like Grosbeak, these people gathered information from their spies and sent it to Quedanga, who made sure that everyone who should see it did, including Aly. There were also reports from those agents Aly's people had recruited and trained, in addition to those of her own packs.

Passing the mages' workroom, she saw that the door was open. She looked inside. A footman who served in Kadyet House across the street was seated on a stool. His breeches were dusty, and he sported a swollen gash over one cheekbone. His shirt was off, revealing a spreading bruise over his ribs. Ochobu worked at the counter behind him, mashing herbs and oils in a mortar as silver wisps of her power rose from it.

"Bacar, what happened?" Aly asked, leaning against the doorframe, turning slightly so that her sarong hugged her curves. She knew this man well enough to flirt with him. "From the look of it, somebody doesn't like you."

He looked at her and winced, trying to cover his face with one hand and his ribs with another. "Bright Eyes, I hate your seeing me when I'm not at my best," he complained. "Couldn't you come back after Duani Ochobu here makes me presentable?"

Aly smiled. "Even bruised, you're a treat with your shirt off. So what happened?"

He let his hands drop into his lap. "I said the wrong thing to one of the King's Watch at the barricade to the slave docks. They burned, you know. The docks and fifteen ships. They might be able to repair the other two ships. *Might*."

Aly widened her eyes. "Who would be mad enough to do such a thing?" she asked. Since they both knew the other worked for the rebellion in some form, he knew she was joking. "So what did you say to the Watchman?"

"The same thing you asked. What happened? For that I got a double kiss from those cursed clubs they carry, and the threat of Kanodang hospitality if I didn't carry my lazy rump elsewhere." He smiled, his eyes dreamy. "You should see it, Bright Eyes. All three docks and all those ships, burned right down to the waterline. Whoever did it was an artist." Quietly he added, "There's a fifty gold lan reward for information leading to the capture of those who did it."

Ochobu turned with a handful of glop and motioned for Bacar to raise the arm on the side of his bruised ribs. Bacar did so, wincing. Ochobu spread the mixture on the man's torso.

Aly whistled at the reward amount. It was more than any five families in all Middle Town made in a year. "They're dreadfully excited for just a loss of wood."

"Well, the ships' captains are screaming to be paid for their vessels, but that's not it." Bacar lowered his voice. "See, somehow the slaves in the market got wind of the fire. They rioted. Some made it out of Dockmarket before the collars choked them till the catchers found them. And they killed three guards, mauled five more. I got it from some lady friends who work near there." He and Aly smiled at one another. Both knew what kind of "lady friends" Bacar would have near the slave markets. If the information came from them, it was accurate.

"Anyway, the ladies patched me up enough so I could come back here without the Watch arresting me, and I knew my master would have plenty of questions if I came in all battered. Thank the gods for Ochobu here."

The mage spread more of her glop on Bacar's face. Ochobu said, "It'll fall off when it dries, and you'll be good as new. Go beg some food from Chenaol. It'll be dry by the time you're done eating."

Bacar hopped down from the stool. "Thanks, Duani Ochobu," he said. "You just saved me some unpleasantness with my lord Kadyet."

He advanced on Aly, the arm on his undamaged side snaking out for a grab. She let him get just close enough, then swung out of his reach. "Naughty," she teased. "Besides, Lady Dove tore out her hem and I have to mend it before the callers arrive today."

"But what about my being shirtless?" he asked, woebegone, as she sauntered down to her workroom.

Aly looked back over her shoulder at him. "I got an eyeful," she replied, and winked. Strolling into her office, she closed the door and went to her desk. As she'd expected, it was piled with slates and paper.

She picked up a report verifying that there had been a revolt in the slave pens, as Bacar had said. There was more, the writer being employed at the slave pens. The brokers had sent a hysterical delegation to the harbormaster, begging that they be granted ships to carry their current lot of slaves to Carthak. The harbormaster had said he would send the request on to the minister of trade.

Aly smiled, a very different smile from the one she had given Bacar.

9

REPORTS AND CONSPIRACIES

During the afternoon rest, Aly took reports from anyone who came into the meeting room. Between guests, she read the information that was piled on her desk across the hall. She also consulted with Trick, who had news from the darkings. The one Aly had left in the shop of Dove's bookseller friend, Herbrand Edgecliff, revealed that the bookshop was a nest of raka sympathizers, including Herbrand himself, who never had fewer than three fugitives from Crown law in the shop's basement. Edgecliff and his wife, both pure-blood luarin, belonged to the raka conspiracy, which made Aly happy. Every instance that luarin could work with and help the raka was a brick in the wall between quiet coexistence and massacres. All of the darkings buzzed with word of people's reactions to the duke's arrest and the burning of the slave docks. So much of it was the same that Aly asked Trick to tell her only important things she hadn't heard yet.

There was no word from Tongkang or from Nawat. It was much too soon. Even flying, it would take time for him to reach the island and find the rebels. They wouldn't get reports from him for another day or so. Aly tried not to dwell on it. You told him you had to concentrate on the rebellion—well, concentrate on it, her reasonable self said.

The resting time was nearly gone when a recruit who worked for seamstresses in Middle Town came to the meeting room to speak with Aly. She was a slender young raka woman who wore a baby in a sling on her back as she carried a basketful of dye powders. "The cockerel crows at noon," she said, giving the code phrase for the tier of agents recruited by Aly's pack.

"Then it's the cockerel's time to be put in the pot." Aly gave her the counterphrase that meant the recruit could pass information to her safely. She hadn't seen this young woman before. It was possible she didn't even know who Aly was, except that she was in the right room, and she knew the right countersign.

"Late this morning, when the King's Watch came to arrest Duchess Nomru and her family, they were gone," the seamstress said. "There was no sign of them. The servants and slaves were gone, too, every last one. The Watch took what valuables were left, but the lady's jewels and the family coin were all missing."

"Is there anything else?" Aly inquired.

The seamstress nodded. "Five arrests, two of 'em luarin accused of selling books on poisons and death magic to raka, one for taxes, one a printer who had funny pictures of the regents hid away to be placed about the city later, and one of the raka nobles, Meipun Kloulechat. No one knows why. The paper for his arrest has the black seal on it."

Aly knew what that meant: the noble had been arrested on a royal warrant obtained with information from Topabaw. Delivery of such a warrant gave the recipient a chance to kill himself honorably rather than suffer the humiliation of questioning and the execution that usually followed.

Maybe this will teach the raka nobles they might lose everything if they *don't* become involved, she thought. "Is that all?" she asked her informant.

The woman nodded and shifted the sleeping baby. "That I know of. But the city's crawling with King's Watch, all in a vicious mood, and the regents have ordered a company of the Rittevon Lancers to patrol Middle Town and Market Town. Stay out of their way if you see them. They like getting us to move with their riding crops."

Aly had noticed the red welt on the woman's arm. "Two doors on the other side of the hall from me, on your way back, is our mages' workroom," she said. "They'll give you something for that."

The informant shrugged. "I get worse if I fray the material I sew. May your troubles fly away on the wings of crows." She touched her fist to her forehead in a raka salute and left the room.

Aly sat back, considering what she had just learned. Nomru's family and household not only had knowledge of his arrest, but they'd managed to flee the city, or to hide within it in full daylight. They were connected in no way to the raka, so someone else had warned them. She suspected it was a noble who'd been present when the princess had called for Nomru to be locked up, which meant that the warning must have come from a luarin.

The city's bells rang out, signaling the end of the quiet time. Aly went to dress Dove for the afternoon.

Guests descended on Balitang House once again. There were more today, a number of young men and women and their parents. The heirs of three noble families made for Sarai, while their mothers draped themselves between Nuritin and Winnamine.

At first everyone gathered in the big sitting room or at the pool courtyard just outside. Despite the nobles' apparent quiet and lassitude, tension hummed in the air. Every time a young man's voice began to rise, a parent's fan opened with a loud snap of warning, and the errant son went quiet. The girls chattered a little too much, except for Sarai. She remained cool and gracious, as if a man they'd all thought untouchable were not in prison. She had to know as well as anyone that Nomru had helped her mother to resist Imajane's request that Sarai and Elsren move to the palace, but she acted no differently than usual.

Not long after Winnamine's father, Matfrid Fonfala, arrived, the duchess stood. "My friends, I believe the Teak Sitting Room may be somewhat cooler. I am sure our young people would prefer that we were elsewhere. I should think their attendants would be chaperons enough, wouldn't you?"

Idly, as if only the promise of a breeze tempted them, the older members of the gathering followed the duchess. Aly watched as they left. She was fairly certain those people were the core of the luarin conspiracy. In any case, she would soon know for certain, because the darking Feather occupied the Teak Sitting Room.

Aly had expected Dove to follow the older nobles, but she didn't. Instead she talked with Zaimid, who, with a kind man's sharp eye, had noted she sat alone while Sarai's friends jockeyed around her. Once again Aly added a point to the Carthaki healer's score. Zaimid and Dove were soon so deep in a discussion of the emperor's creation of charity hospitals that Aly would have bet that Dove noticed nothing else. She would have lost. When the footman announced Imgehai Qeshi, a priestess of the Black God who served at the city's biggest temple, Dove politely broke off her conversation to introduce her to Zaimid. The priestess wore her habit, but her hood was off, indicating she was not there on spiritual business. After she, Zaimid, and Dove had chatted for a few moments, Dove excused herself and the newcomer to Zaimid and led the priestess away. Aly watched Zaimid's gaze follow them, his brown eyes alert and interested. Then he managed to step out into the pool courtyard in time to be at Sarai's side as she left the sitting room for the garden.

A moment later Trick murmured in Aly's ear, "Feather say Dove and Imgehai have come." Aly twiddled her thumbs. The priestess stood high in the temple hierarchy. She would be a powerful ally.

It was funny. Old King Oron had banished the Balitangs on suspicion of treason. Everyone had thought it was one of his mad ideas. It seemed he'd been right all along. Still, he had to have been mad to consider their group a threat, thought Aly. Obviously they've been talking about this for a while, and they haven't done anything. That will have to change, she decided. If they're to be of any use at all, they'll have to stop talking and start doing.

Ferdy Tomang's raised voice caught her attention. ". . . can't forget who guards their backs!" A number of his friends begged him to lower his voice.

"Don't worry," Sarai told them airily. "There are so many secrecy spells around this place you could start a war in here and the Crown mages would never know."

Aly winced. Apparently it had not occurred to Sarai that secrecy spells were best left secret. If Topabaw had any spies among her friends, he would know by sunset that the place was more than usually well guarded. She reminded herself to warn Ochobu and Ysul and thanked the gods that Sarai did not know about the plans made on her behalf. And Aly was forced to think her more than a little foolish for speaking as she had. Anyone with any sense of self-preservation in the Isles knew better than to speak so carelessly about the Crown unless that person was *very* sure of the listener's loyalty.

Ferdy lowered his voice, but only slightly. "It's time we taught them a lesson," he said, looking at the young noblemen who stood around him. "I say we wait until tonight and ride to Kanodang. Everyone knows that if you spend enough in bribes you can get inside."

"We can break out Nomru." Druce Adona's cheeks were flushed.

Another young man added, "Show the regents they are nothing without the luarin nobility."

"Teach them a lesson," said another. "And if we have to fight our way out, we will." He set his hand on his sword hilt.

Idiots, thought Aly as she listened to them rant, working themselves into a state of fury. These men were filled with youth's righteous anger, ready to start killing anyone in their path. Only Zaimid said nothing, but stood there, arms crossed over his chest, with the courtier's expression of polite interest. The young noblewomen's faces were a study in contrasts, from those who showed fear to those filled with the men's enthusiasm.

At first Sarai showed polite interest, her expression like Zaimid's. She nodded when comments were addressed to her, smiled when anyone looked at her. Then, as the men began to discuss meeting places and who else they might recruit, a new look crossed her face, one that was half slyness and half contempt. It was replaced by lowered eyelashes, a subtle step on the back hem of her cream-colored gown so that it pulled tight to emphasize her figure, and a pouting lower lip.

"That's all very well and good," she murmured. "But *I* think it's very silly, and useless, and tiresome."

"But we're standing up for one of our own!" protested Ferdy. "He's a luarin, a noble! They can't treat us this way!"

Sarai pouted even more. "I bet Their Highnesses expect it. I bet they'll have hundreds and hundreds of soldiers inside the walls, waiting for something just like this."

Good point, Aly thought. But Ulasim and Fesgao will make sure of that before they go. They're too sharp to miss something that obvious.

Sarai continued, "You'll all be arrested, and maybe even put on display at the harbor mouth, and *then* who will be my escort to the Summersend Ball?"

"Or mine?" added one of the sillier noblewomen.

The realization of the likely consequences slowly dawned in the young men's faces. When Sarai reminded them of arrest and execution, they began to lose their enthusiasm. It took a little more work, but in the end Sarai had cast their feverish excitement to the four winds.

Out of curiosity's sake, Aly looked at Zaimid. The Carthaki watched Sarai and the noblemen, the tiniest of smiles on his lips. He knows what she's doing, Aly told herself. And he's not surprised by the results.

When talk turned to a riding party the day after the lunar eclipse, Aly ended her watch on the nobles and returned to her workroom. There was more to do, and she had better ways to use her time than by listening to airbrains chasing butterflies. She smiled. *Airbrains chasing butterflies* was a phrase her mother often used.

Aly resumed her walk. "Maybe Mother was more right about such things than I thought," she murmured.

"What such things?" asked Trick.

"Oh—the way those fools were talking, and how quickly they changed their minds," Aly replied.

She could not see if the darking nodded, but she did hear its contempt when it said, "Stupid."

One of the household runners came to Aly's office, bearing a message from Chenaol. Aly's first double agent awaited her in Chenaol's private sitting room—Vitorcine, Isalena Obemaek's maid. Aly went to see her. Vitorcine paced in Chenaol's sitting room, her hands white-knuckled as she clutched a small basket. Once Aly had closed the door, Vitorcine thrust the basket at her. "I made copies of everything," she whispered as Aly leafed through the papers in the basket. "Topabaw has seen none of it."

Aly looked into the maid's worried eyes. "You know Topabaw will reward you well for information he can use against the Obemaeks. And yet you put off telling him, at the risk of your own life, to keep your masters from trouble."

Vitorcine blushed and looked away. "Lord Obemaek has been a father to me. Lady Isalena is a fine mistress. She's never hit me like some of the other ladies do." She wrung her hands. "I don't *want* to betray them, but Topabaw . . ."

A twinge of something like guilt for putting Vitorcine in such a spot pinched Aly's heart. She ignored it. She would do anything to protect the Balitangs. If that meant blackmailing the powerful Obemaek family, Aly would do so. "Is there anything else?" Aly wanted to know.

"No. Not information, but—I must report to Topabaw's man tomorrow night," Vitorcine explained. "What should I say?"

Aly had expected this. "Tell him that there is great unrest over the detention of Duke Nomru, which is true enough," she said. "The hotheads rant, but they fear Topabaw too much to act. Say also that people are afraid they will be next. Tell him you fear Lord Obemaek suspects you, and that you must be very careful until you think your master has decided you are no danger. That should fill his tiny belly for the moment."

"And Topabaw will accept that?" Vitorcine asked, her cheeks pale.

"Practice it in a mirror until you can say it convincingly," Aly told her, just as an elder who cared for Vitorcine might say it. "Topabaw has seen this kind of thing before, after all. The city will be talking of the arrest for days. You're no good to him if your master leaves you dead in an alley somewhere. The excuse will wear thin after a time, but I trust that by then we'll have something else he can gnaw on."

Aly left Vitorcine to collect herself before she rejoined the other servants, and walked down the hall to her office. Stepping inside, she closed the door and whispered, "Trick?"

She felt her necklace stir. "Scared lady," Trick remarked, sticking a head up next to Aly's ear.

"She has every reason to be scared," replied Aly as she sat at her table. "Ask Feather what they're talking about."

Trick instead released itself and trickled down Aly's sarong to pool in her lap. There the darking spread to become a circle with a shiny surface. An image appeared, and with it sounds. It took a few moments for Aly to identify what she looked at, because the angle was extremely odd. She finally realized that Feather must be seated atop a cabinet, looking down at the nobles assembled in the room.

Aly raised an eyebrow, then leaned back and listened to the luarin conspirators. She was still listening when someone rapped hard on her door. "Trick," she whispered. "Sash."

Grumbling softly, the darking folded itself up so Aly could tuck it away.

"Enter," she called.

Atisa stuck in her head, grinning broadly. "Your traps have caught three more spies, Duani," she said. "Do you want to make them our spies yourself, or should one of us convince them?"

Aly got to her feet. "I shall do it," she told Atisa. "But you come and watch. I cannot be everywhere, and things are heating up." She strode down the hall in Atisa's wake, her thoughts flying in a dozen directions. As conspiracies went, she didn't think much of the luarin's, but it gave her something to work with. They might stiffen their spines if they allied themselves with the raka, though getting the two groups to agree would be a trick and a half.

*   *   *

That night, in the conspirators' meeting room, Aly told her companions what she had learned that day. Not once did she look at Dove or mention that Dove had been meeting with the luarin conspirators.

When Aly finished, Chenaol snorted. "That dried-up bunch of twitter-pated worrymice!" she said scornfully. "They've been whispering for years, without anything to show for it."

"Maybe it's time to give them something to show," remarked Ulasim.

Quedanga spat on the floor. "Deal with luarin? I'd as soon boil my hands and head."

Aly looked at the ceiling.

"I don't think it's worth it," said Fesgao. "They do not have the best security, if our Aly could ferret them out before she'd been here so much as a week."

"And what will you do with them if we win?" Dove wanted to know. "Kill them? Kill Sarai's friends and their parents? Kill the people she studied dancing and riding with? Kill Winna and her family, and the Balitangs?"

Ysul hand-signed, *Better to be allies. Many old raka houses are gone. Not all luarin are bad luarin.*

"Because I can tell you, just from reading Saren history," Dove said quietly, "once the killing between peoples who share a country begins, it is very hard to stop. The lowland whites and the K'mir tribesmen have been killing one another for centuries. The only way to avoid that fate is to decide we must live together, and then do our best to ensure that we do. We can do as Rittevon Lanman and Ludas Jimajen did when they came here, and reap a bloody harvest of our own, or we can call a halt to it."

"Easier for you than for some of us, Lady Dove," Chenaol pointed out.

Dove's eyes flashed. "I didn't say easy. I said *necessary*."

The door popped open. Ochobu was there, her gray hair straggling out of its pins, sweat rolling down her face. Ulasim, closest to her, guided his mother into his chair while Chenaol poured a cup of mango juice.

Ochobu gulped it down, then said, "News from the Chain. The people of the Birafu estates are now gone, traveling over land or by ship. The crows managed to bring in some merchant galleys along with fishing boats. There is more." Her face was alight with triumph and malice. "Governor Sulion of Tongkang was found dead on his balcony this morning. He'd been shot with three crow-fletched arrows."

Aly looked down, quivering. She knew, just as surely as if he'd shouted it in her ear, that Nawat had been the archer.

"The Crown will go berserk," Fesgao said, his eyes burning. "The governor of Ikang and the governor of Tongkang killed within a week of each other? Never has such a thing happened, not after the Conquest!"

"And more," said Ochobu. "Just this last, so let me finish. The Velochiru raka on Imahyn have burned the homes of the overseer and of the family. The governor there has sent a call for more troops."

Ulasim rested a hand on her shoulder. "You're done, Mother," he said kindly. "Rest awhile. What did you do, speak with every mage on the Chain tonight?"

She glared up at him. "I'm not senile," she snapped.

Ulasim gave his crooked smile. "Ysul, will you reach the Chain mage closest to Nawat? Ask him to ask Nawat if he will take a look into the situation on Imahyn?"

Ysul nodded and left them.

Dove looked after him, then at Ulasim. "Do all the mages of the Chain know hand signs?"

Quedanga was mending a sarong. "Ysul writes the message and shows it to them. General, if we don't get atop this storm, it's going to roll straight over us," she warned. "I don't know if the god arranged it this way, or if it's just a dam bursting, but we need to take control of it."

Ulasim leaned against the wall. "We'll have a way soon to make contact with the would-be rebels among the luarin," he remarked in an even voice. "I expect more fights in the city over the next week. It seems clear enough to me that the Crown cannot control this city and the outlying islands, too. If the regents send more troops away from here, we may have an opportunity to announce ourselves—we shall see. In the meantime, Aly will continue with her work. Fesgao and I have a project or two, as have Mother and Ysul. Quedanga and Aly, make certain everyone hears of what has taken place on Tongkang and Imahyn. Chenaol—"

"Crow-fletched arrows," said the cook, who was also their armorer. "It would be easy if I had a ready supply."

"I'll ask the crows," Aly said. "I'm sure they know where they've lost feathers. Have they been bringing in Stormwing feathers from their brushes with them? Nawat asked them to before we came here."

"I find a pile of them by the kitchen well every evening," replied Chenaol. "And since we've no longer got Nawat to cut them up and use them on arrows, my girls have found a way to turn them into throwing darts and set the shafts in hilts so they become knives. Pity the beasts aren't cleaner," she mused. "The feathers would be perfect for tissue-cut raw fish, but we don't know where those feathers have been. Even after boiling I don't trust them."

"There will be more," Quedanga said. "They and the crows have been fighting all over the city. I saw the most astounding thing yesterday as I shopped. Stormwings lined up in the air wingtip to wingtip and darted at a group of crows to cut them in half."

Aly snorted, guessing the result.

"The crows split and got them on the backs and chests as they passed," Quedanga said. "One of them even managed to dump a load of dung on their queen's head."

All of them shook their heads over the audacity of crows and the frustrations of Stormwings as their group broke up. Dove waited until she and Aly were climbing the stairs to the family quarters before she made Aly stop.

"If you know what they talked about, you know I was there," she said quietly, looking up at her face. "Why didn't you tell?"

Aly shrugged. "It wasn't my secret to tell. You'll let our group know when you feel it's time." She felt the urge to add something but was not sure it would help. "Your ladyship, I know you're just thirteen and all, but—and don't bite my nose off for it—I trust your judgment more than that of some older people I know." They both knew she meant Sarai; Aly could see the awareness in Dove's eyes. "Others I might question, but I know you're not a fool. We opened the door to the luarin in there tonight, that was the important thing."

When they entered the ladies' sitting room, they found the duchess on the floor with Elsren and Petranne, telling a story, as Sarai read a book. Winnamine used her long, elegant hands as the raka storytellers did, making them form shadows on the wall that looked like figures from the tale. Rihani, Pembery, and Boulaj had sewing in their hands, but they were as entranced as the children, watching each shadow. Even Sarai spent more time watching than she did reading. Dove and Aly sat quietly in their regular spots, Dove folding her hands in her lap, Aly taking up the sewing she kept in a basket by her chair.

The story ended. Pembery and Boulaj began to stitch as Winnamine got to her feet. Elsren was asleep, worn out by another day with Dunevon. Rihani scooped him up and waited as Petranne kissed her mother, Sarai, and Dove good night. Once the children and their nursemaid were gone, Sarai gave up even the pretense of reading.

"Winna, when will they let Nomru out?" Sarai asked. "They can't just keep him in Kanodang forever."

"I doubt it," said the duchess. "I imagine that he will be out—one way or another—by the end of the week. In the meantime, we have the eclipse party tomorrow night. Have you decided what you will wear?"

Sarai ignored this distraction. "If only we knew some men with *spine*," she complained. "You should have heard them this afternoon, planning 'the great rescue of Nomru.'"

"I hope you discouraged them," said Winnamine. "Don't they understand they could die that way?"

Sarai smiled bitterly. "Relax, Winna. All it took was a pout from me and they were happy to give it up. I can't think much of their courage if they care more about escorting me to the Summersend Ball than they do about the life of a great noble like Nomru." Suddenly she jumped to her feet. "How can you stand it? How can we live among so many cowards?" she demanded, pacing the room, a tigress in cream silk. "To watch what they do to people—all kinds of people, not just the raka!—and say nothing, and simper, and take another stitch, and pretend the world's all lovely?"

"Because I have patience," Winnamine said quietly. "And because I like to sew."

"Patience?" cried Sarai. "The luarin nobles haven't done anything in centuries, and they're not going to. It makes me sick. In other countries, rulers can't just do as they like. Zaimid told me Emperor Kaddar set it up so that for *anyone* to be arrested in Carthak, their accusers must give evidence before a magistrate. The magistrate has to write out a warrant for the arrest, based on proof of wrongdoing. If Duke Nomru lived in Carthak, he'd be heard, not tossed into a cell."

"Emperor Kaddar got that idea from the Marenites," Winnamine pointed out.

Sarai shrugged. "As I say, other monarchs have to respect their people. You don't see Tortallans sneaking around, afraid to speak their minds. In fact, they're a little too zealous about that, especially when they visit us."

Aly raised her brows.

Sarai smiled and flapped a hand. "Not you, Aly. But some of your people have been painfully frank about what they think of the Kyprin way of life."

Aly, who knew someone who was painfully frank about more than that, looked at her needlework.

Winnamine leaned forward and caught Sarai's arm. "You're certain your men friends aren't going to try something? If need be, I'll send notes to their parents—"

Sarai shook her head. "That lot? They're gelded already. They'll do what the king stallion tells them to do. I wonder what it's like to live in a country where there are more stallions than geldings."

"I doubt they'd come running when you flutter your lashes at them," Dove remarked, her voice very dry.

Sarai smiled. "Oh, a challenge! That would be new." She collapsed into a chair and looked at her stepmother. "Winna, Otaviyu Lelin and Rosamma Tomang have invited me to go riding tomorrow morning."

The duchess rested her needlework in her lap. "And their brothers?" she asked delicately. Dove smiled.

Sarai shot her sister a glare. "*And* their brothers, and the rest of our crowd, and Countess Tomang, and Otavi's mother. Boulaj will be with me, if she can keep up."

"I see no problems, then," Winnamine replied slowly. "Genore Tomang has a spotless reputation, and she is known for her skill as a chaperon." She grinned wickedly at Sarai, whose shoulders drooped.

Dove asked, "You haven't seen Boulaj ride, have you, Sarai? I mean, like you like to ride?"

Sarai glared at her. "No."

Dove chuckled. "She will be on you like a tick on a howler. Try slipping away with her on your tail!"

"You're being a brat, O wonderful, uncontroversial, educated sister of mine," Sarai retorted. She asked her stepmother, "So I may go?"

"You may go," replied Winnamine. "And if I hear of one escape attempt or of bad behavior, the only person you will be allowed out of this house with is Aunt Nuritin."

Sarai winced. "I'll be so good you'll hardly know I was there. Good night, dear Winna." She kissed her stepmother's cheek, and the top of her sister's head. "Good night, brat." She waved to Pembery and Aly, who murmured their own good nights, and left the room.

Once she was gone, Dove scowled at her stepmother. "Does she even *care* what becomes of this country? Of us?"

Winnamine leaned her head back. "Patience, Dove," she said wearily. "I think she still hates herself for her father's death, just as she hates the houses that produced King Oron and Prince Bronau. I think she feels that people *meant* to stand up for us when we were exiled, until something distracted them. She thinks because things have always been this way, they will always *be* this way."

"Well, they won't," said Dove, getting to her feet. "And when they aren't, she had better live up to all those nice, shiny ideas about equal laws for everyone." She kissed Winnamine on the cheek and left the sitting room.

Aly followed her without a word.

10

ECLIPSE

Aly woke before dawn once more, although no tentacle tickled her nose.

"Are you sleeping late or something?" she asked Trick.

"Not sleeping," replied the darking. "Listening. Reportsreportsreports. All city mostly same report. Scared. Everyone scared. If people die just to look at her, what happens when she asks for throne? Most of the ones who want to know are raka or poor, or poor *and* raka. If duke in Kanodang, who next? some say. If Topabaw falls, who next? some ask. Most of those who ask are nobles or soldiers. If king die, if regents die, who rules? Most asking that one are nobles. More Stormwings come from north. Flame came home from Kanodang. All darkings in house back in Aly's room before warriors come to practice," Trick added mournfully. "They ask, when do they get to do real work? Boring, staying in house all day."

"Tonight," Aly whispered. "Most of you will go to the palace tonight, and those who go will stay there."

"But not me," said Trick.

Aly grimaced. She knew what it was like to be penned up all day, not allowed to go out and have what she thought of as fun. "Trick, if you can train someone to do for me what you do, you can stay at the palace," she whispered. "You deserve some fun."

"No!" squeaked Trick. "I was fooling!"

Aly considered that, grinning. "So where did you learn how to tease?" she asked.

"Like I say, you more fun than anybody," Trick replied, lightly tightening its beadlike self around Aly's neck in something that felt like a hug.

Aly leaned her cheek against the darking. "Nawat would like you," she murmured, missing her crow-man.

"Then I meet Nawat one day," replied Trick.

Aly got up. She practiced with the warriors, then took a complete bath. Once she had dressed Dove and sent her to breakfast, she threw open the shutters and looked outside. It will be perfect for an eclipse if the weather holds, she thought, watching Stormwings bait a lone crow in the cloudless sky. The crow flew lower and lower, until it nearly touched the treetops of Middle Town. An army of nearly one hundred crows exploded from the trees, going after the Stormwings.

The crows reminded her of a duty. Tilting back her head, she voiced a hoarse caw. Three crows, idly watching the Stormwings streak toward the palace, came to perch on the windowsill. Aly was asking them to gather their dropped feathers as they did those of Stormwings when one tried to grab Trick. The darking wriggled and turned itself into a cobra with its cowl fully extended, striking at the crow. The crow squawked and fell off the ledge.

"I teach *him*," Trick said proudly, and turned itself back into a necklace. The other crows were too busy mocking their disgraced comrade to take offense. When they calmed down, they agreed to leave their feathers where Chenaol could find them. Then they spotted a five-man squad of the King's Watch marching in patrol on Joshain Street. They flew off saying, if Aly understood them correctly, that they would give the soldiers "wet face surprises."

Dove went out with Aly and her guard, visiting a maker of fine chessboards, a seller of Yamani goods, and a beggar on the steps of the small temple dedicated to Gunapi the Sunrose, the Kyprin goddess of war and flowing lava. Waiting for Dove and the beggar to finish an involved discussion about the rice crop, Aly kept her eyes on her surroundings. People were starting to add the open shackle to the embroideries on their clothes. She saw it on shop steps and the sides of wagons. If the people knew what it meant, the rebellion had more support in Rajmuat than she had thought.

When they returned to the house, Aly felt tension in the air, humming like a plucked bowstring. There was nothing she could do to ease it. After all, she wasn't supposed to know the details of the Kanodang escape, though thanks to the darking Lace she had everything but Nomru's boot size. By now she knew the raka conspiracy's true reach and numbers in Rajmuat, particularly in the city's jails, including Kanodang. She was impressed. They've been holding out on me, Aly thought. How sneaky of them!

She envied the spies of her pack. They were keyed up but able to joke as they passed on their day's gatherings of information. They, at least, would be having fun as Trick termed it.

Stop that, Aly told herself. You'll have a quiet bit of fun yourself tonight. It won't be as enjoyable as watching bad things burn, but life is imperfect that way.

By midafternoon the Balitang ladies were ready to leave. The evening's festivities included a banquet before the eclipse party, with the regents and a chosen few dozen. Invitation to the feast as well as to the party was a gesture of condescension from the regents to the Balitangs, and they were all keenly aware of it.

"I think she's trying to be kind to us," Sarai muttered to Dove, reading over the letter of invitation one last time. "So people will say how charitable she is."

"What do you care?" asked Dove, snatching the letter from her. "All your puppy dogs will be there, panting after you—Ferdy, Druce, Zaimid . . ."

"Zaimid is hardly panting after me," Sarai told her younger sister. "And Ferdy is too conscious of his wealth to pant. Drool a bit, yes, but never pant."

For this trip to the palace, the dress boxes in the wagon held dinner gowns and party ones. Aly, Pembery, and Boulaj had gone over every stitch with exacting care, making sure their ladies would be perfectly dressed that night. In packing Dove's box, Aly also managed to slip in a garment of her own, a fresh suit from Ochobu that would cause anyone who saw Aly in it to forget they had done so. Aly hardly believed she would be so sloppy as to be seen, but there was no point in taking risks. Under the forgetting suit was a pouch full of very excited darkings. They squeaked with pleasure as Aly tucked them away, and assured her they would have no problem breathing in the box because they didn't breathe.

Once the boxes were stowed, the ladies' maids took their positions. Pembery and Lady Nuritin's maid, Dorilize, rode in the wagon. Boulaj walked beside Sarai, Aly beside Dove. Dove, cross at having to socialize at dinner as well as the eclipse party, read as she rode. If she noticed the people in the street or in upper-story windows who watched as their company passed, she gave no sign of it. At a nod from the duchess, the men-at-arms drew closer to their party. Aly checked the crowd often, noting her spies and their recruits mingling, spreading doubts about Topabaw and his standing with the regents.

The ladies changed for dinner in the Robing Pavilion. The duchess wore a dark maroon undergown and a sheer black silk overgown, her jewelry equally modest. Sarai gleamed in pale amber silk under creamy gauze, her jewelry simple as well. Dove had chosen dark amber under black gauze. All three wore sheer silk veils secured to their neatly done hair with jeweled pins. As they walked to the Rittevon Enclosure, Aly felt her heart swell with pride. They made the other nobles look overdressed.

Inside the wall they found the towering stone L that was called the Gray Palace. As they walked its halls, they saw countless goods the invaders had looted from their raka subjects on display. They included copper statues turned green with time, gaudy silk rugs and tapestries, figures carved of gemstone, and jewelry made of copper and gold, polished to a brilliant shine. It was all set up to present a message: to the rulers of the Isles, the raka would always be the conquered, not equals.

Royal servants separated the guests, escorting the men to one salon and the ladies to the next. Here maids gave their mistresses' appearances a last going-over. As Aly tugged a fold here and straightened a sleeve there, she placed a darking on top of one of Dove's shoes. The darking was to remain in the dining hall when Dove left there.

With their ladies gone, the maids settled to wait, in case their mistresses tore out a hem or stained their clothes during the meal. Later the servants could relax at the Robing Pavilion. For the time being they ate their suppers as they chattered with acquaintants. Aly nodded to Boulaj and opened Dove's dress box. Casually she drew out her forget-me suit and the pouch of darkings, tucking both into the large cloth bag that held a maid's necessities. When Aly had everything she needed, she went in search of the privy.

The nobles' servants not only had a separate privy at the Gray Palace, but one with stalls, for privacy. Aly entered one and bolted the door. She stripped off her clothes until she wore only her Trick necklace, a breast band, and a loincloth. She pulled the suit out of its bag and was nearly blinded as the spells on it, made by Ochobu, left spots on her magical Sight. She slid the garment on and secured it as her vision cleared. Then she donned the gloves and shoes, tucked the darkings' pouch into an opening in the suit, and pulled up and tightened the hood until only her eyes were visible.

Aly put her sarong and sash into the bag and closed it. She listened to make sure no one else had come in, then left the privy. Carrying the bag low, where few might notice it, she returned to the salon. Most of the servants were still at the food tables, loading their plates. Boulaj sat near their ladies' dress boxes, a full plate in her hands. Aly set her bag behind the boxes. Boulaj would not remember seeing her, but she knew what the bag meant. If anyone came looking for Aly, Boulaj would send them in all the wrong directions.

Thanks to the raka conspirators among the palace staff, Aly had memorized the map of the Gray Palace. Thanks to her magical Sight, she saw and avoided the alarm spells. The vision spells that littered the rooms and halls slid uselessly over her suit, not recognizing it as anything more than empty cloth. Moving silently, Aly placed two darkings in the small throne room of the inner palace. They chittered their glee and began to explore their new home.

Walking onto an outside terrace, Aly eyed the rough stone of the walls, then began to climb. It was simple enough. The Gray Palace's builders had been in such a hurry to build a defensible stronghold that they had not smoothed the stones, and their approach to mortar had been haphazard. Cracks between the blocks gave a determined climber hand- and footholds. Once again she had her palace informers to thank. Masters here had no idea that their servants and slaves clambered up and down the walls to spy or to steal.

Moving as quickly as she dared, Aly released darkings in Imajane's and

Rubinyan's rooms. She placed two darkings in the private audience chamber where the regents discussed delicate matters with favored subjects, one in the informal dining room used by the regents, and others in the clerk's office, Rubinyan's study, and a map room. One darking went to the office next to Rubinyan's study, where his personal spymaster, Sevmire, worked. She sent four in search of the kitchens and the servants' quarters. She even left a darking in the king's bedroom, just so she could say she had done it. She hardly expected anyone to discuss royal policy with Dunevon, but the regents might say something interesting to the King's Guard in a moment of irritation.

Feeling pleased with herself, she changed back into her normal clothes and returned to her fellow maids. The thinner pouch of darkings stayed with her as she left two more where the servants awaited their masters.

The banquet ended eventually. The nobles went back to the Robing Pavilion to change out of dinner clothes and into those considered appropriate for viewing an eclipse. The maids then completed the last touches on their ladies' hair and makeup. Vereyu presided over them all, taking in everything. She and Aly had exchanged nods when Aly had followed Dove into the ladies' side of the pavilion.

As the women worked and chattered, many part- or full-raka maids volunteered to do any service for Sarai or Dove. Aly shared what duties she could, ignoring Dove's request for people to stop fussing. Boulaj stood back and let other maids tend Sarai if they could do so without their own mistresses' noticing. Observing that Nuritin watched this with a frown, Aly shifted her position to block the old woman's view. She wasn't sure how far to trust Nuritin or her secretary and maid yet, if she could trust them at all.

Sarai was oblivious to the quiet war for her attention. She smiled at everyone and gossiped with her friends. Aly let three darkings slip to the floor as she listened.

"It's not right," a young woman complained. "At least *five* men are jostling for your favors! You could share!"

Sarai giggled. "You could have most of them with my blessing. Really, some of these fellows must think we're no more intelligent than sheep. The only one who treats me like I've a brain in my head is the Carthaki."

"Does that mean Ferdy is out of contention?" one of Sarai's friends inquired, inspecting her lip color in a mirror. "I'll take him if you let him know you're not interested."

Sarai smiled at her. "And will you take that female Stormwing who gave birth to him?"

Isalena shuddered at the thought of living with Lady Genore Tomang. "Into every life some rain must fall. Besides, I don't want to *keep* him, just *use* him for a month or two." She sighed. "He has such lovely muscles!"

A footman wearing Obemaek livery appeared in the door to the outside and beckoned to one of the Obemaek maids. He had the air of a man with important news. All of the women fell silent and watched, while Aly's belly cramped. Had something gone wrong? Had the prison break been discovered before it had even begun?

The footman left. The maid turned and saw that all eyes were on her. "Oh, my," she whispered. Then she straightened. "There is news. The raka on the Velochiru estates of Imahyn Isle have risen in revolt. They have burned the overseer's home and the Velochiru's family home there. The governor has sent to the regents for the army."

Oh, *that*, thought Aly with disdain. We knew about *that* last night.

Most of the women present made the star-shaped Sign against evil on their chests. Any slaves with raka blood retreated to the rear wall of the pavilion; raka and part-raka maids stepped back, wary eyes on their mistresses. All around the room noblewomen shifted, their hands and feet restless. Their eyes were unsure, their voices soft. They were frightened. Some had turned their eyes toward the raka. More were looking at the door to the Robing Pavilion.

Winnamine thanked Pembery and got to her feet. She looked at the other nobles and smiled. "It could simply be a rumor." She looked at Nuritin, who nodded. "I will inquire of Their Highnesses." She swept from the room before anyone could say a word against it.

"What has gotten into the raka?" asked a noblewoman, her voice quavering with anxiety. "This is the second rising this month. Do they forget what they owe to us?"

Those of raka blood in the room, all servants or slaves, looked carefully at the glossy boards of the floor, doing their best imitation of women who could not hear. Aly shook her head. People always believe what they want to believe, not what's true, she thought with disgust. They never use their eyes and see the world around them.

"These will be wild raka," said a woman in her sixties, one of Nuritin's friends. "Or slaves on some huge rice farm, ruled by a paid overseer. This is the ill that comes of not looking after your own lands. Those who farm for you can't feel a servant's affection for someone who is not there."

"Forgive me, Lady Ankoret," began Sarai politely, addressing Nuritin's friend, "but there are brutal owners as well as overseers. Some bitternesses come not from bad present usage. They come from seeing others profit from the lands where your ancestors are buried. Have you seen how the raka in the big rice farms and in the mines live? I don't understand how we can treat our people so."

"Saraiyu Balitang!" cried Nuritin. "Apologize at once and speak with respect for your elders!"

Sarai got to her feet. "Forgive me if I offended, Great-aunt, Lady Ankoret," she said proudly, her chin raised, "but I think also of the elders who work in the fields and the mines." She swept out of the room like a queen. Aly heard a worshipful sound, though it would be impossible to identify the ones who had made it.

Dove made a face. "Idiot," she murmured. "We need to put a muzzle on her."

Aly, kneeling beside Dove, raised an eyebrow.

"Don't look at me," protested Dove. "I'm going to marry Baron Engan and have my own personal observatory. Someone else can muzzle Sarai."

Aly couldn't help it. She giggled softly into her hands, then murmured, "Until the excitement of being married to you kills him, anyway."

She heard the whisper of silks and brocades in movement and rose instantly to her feet. The other maids and slaves, trained to notice such tiny clues, also stood as Princess Imajane swept in, Winnamine at her elbow. The maids and slaves bowed low and stayed that way. The noblewomen and young ladies rose and curtsied to the princess regent. Imajane was a sight to inspire awe and fear. She wore her hair braided and coiled on her head like a crown. Her large blue eyes, lined with kohl, blazed in a pale, tight-drawn face. Her mouth, red with color, was tight as well. Her hands clenched and unclenched in the folds of her ice blue silk gown and white silk overrobe.

"I see that news travels fast," she said, her voice cutting through the heavy spring air. "I assure you, ladies, the situation on Imahyn is trifling. We must not give it more attention than it deserves. The Goddess has blessed us with an unusual event tonight as she veils her face. We would not forego this for something of importance, let alone the unrest of a small rabble. Come. The Jade Pavilion awaits us. Baron Engan, His Majesty's own astronomer, has a new spyglass that I think is quite extraordinary. Lady Nuritin, Lady Ankoret, you would honor me if you gave me your arms."

With the two oldest ladies in the room, the princess left the pavilion. The other ladies trailed after her, Sarai at the center of a tiny knot of younger women, and Dove with her mother. Aly straightened from her bow along with the rest of the servants and slaves.

Whatever else you can say about the princess regent, she has the royal manner, Aly thought wryly. *Once I'm rid of Topabaw—maybe even* before *I'm rid of him—I need to work out a way to drive a wedge between the regents.*

Many of the servants settled in for their evening's wait. The male servants drifted over from the men's side of the Robing Pavilion to gossip or flirt. A few people had brought cards and dice. Some of the maids did embroidery or bobbin lace. Others went for a walk on the palace grounds as the day's heat faded. Aly, too, went out, stepping around a pair of crowned pigeons. She idled along the Golden Road until she entered the gardens at the southwest corner of the palace. Slowly she walked along, listening to other passersby as they speculated about the news from Imahyn, the rebellion on Tongkang, and the boy king's health. When she reached the path that followed the edge of the pond, Aly halted. Taybur Sibigat looked as if he'd been waiting for her. There was a broad smile on his boyish face. He stood casually in his black mail, one hand tucked into his breeches pocket.

"Do you know, I thought I might find you around here," he greeted her, his words pelting her in his usual rush to get them all said. "A wonderful evening for an eclipse, isn't it? How goes the contact-making process? Have you recruited anyone in the Gray Palace yet?"

Aly widened her eyes in fear, though inside she was delighted. She needed a playmate while Nawat was away. She could serve both the rebels and herself if Taybur held that position. "My lord—"

"Oh, please," he interrupted. "Spare me. Pretend that you've said the 'I don't know what you mean' speech and we may both continue our evening with more time for a proper talk. I've been dealing with dolts all day and I have a headache. And they're keeping His Majesty up past his bedtime, even though they know it makes him cranky." He held out the hand he'd kept in his pocket and opened his fist. It contained a darking: the one named Spot, because it was about half the size of its fellows. The one she had left in the king's bedroom.

Aly took a big step back.

"It's the most curious thing," Taybur said. "I briefly left the king in his room, and I return to find him bouncing on the bed with this little fellow. He's rather sweet, whatever he is. He even said hello. Dunevon said he caught him rolling around the walls. So I asked him what he is, and he said—"

"Darking," interrupted Spot, putting up its head so it could look over its blob shoulder at Taybur.

"Yes, that was it. So I asked his name, and he said—"

"Spot," the darking told him. "Dunevon like Spot. Spot like Dunevon."

Aly wanted to knock her head slowly and repeatedly against the nearest tree. Approached the right way, the darkings could be fatally friendly. Spot was younger than the rest, which was why she had used it in the king's bedroom. She honestly hadn't thought Spot would learn anything important, but the darking had been so depressed to see Aly collect most of its fellows that she couldn't bear it. *This is what I get for being sentimental*, she told herself.

"The thing talks," said Aly, playing the timid maid still. "It's not natural."

Taybur ignored this. "And then I asked Spot what he was doing in the king's bedroom. First he said . . ." With a nod, he indicated Spot could fill in.

"Nothing," the darking supplied.

"So I asked again, and this time he said . . ."

"Playing," Spot responded.

"And I asked him why, and he said . . ."

"Secret."

"Secret," agreed Taybur, smiling. "I've known the folk who poke their noses through the palace for years. Even the new ones are all alike. They use the same tools, corrupt people in the same positions, use the same codes. Then you arrive, Aly Homewood. You are *not* what I expect. And then I find another thing I do not expect, and I'm sure it's no accident that you're in the Gray Palace at the same time. I imagine you may have sowed these little creatures—"

"Darkings!" Spot insisted.

"These darkings in the hope they will gather information for you," Taybur said, closing his fist to hide Spot as several parties of nobles passed by on their way to the pavilions. Aly thought it over and mentally shrugged. If he'd meant harm to her, she would be in shackles. When the nobles were gone, she crossed the path to stand closer to Taybur.

As if he'd never gone silent, Taybur opened his fist and continued speaking. "I don't care if you've left darkings from the dungeons to the rooftops of the Gray Palace. If you've left one in my office, prepare for disappointment. I discuss nothing important in there. Topabaw has papered it in listening spells. Eavesdrop on palace gossip all you like, though if you can afford medicine for migraines, I'd invest in it. It's like eavesdropping on vipers. But this"—he patted Spot's head with a finger—"no. Dunevon is a little boy who deserves silence and consideration. And he is my charge. Please don't go into his bedroom again . . . though don't mistake me, I'd love to know just how you did it." He thrust the darking at her.

Aly knew she'd get nowhere if she argued. Instead, keeping an eye on Taybur, she reached out and took Spot. "It's warm," she said with surprise, as if she'd never seen one before. Holding Spot up to her face, she spoke to it as if she might a very small child as she asked, "Now, confess, little fellow. What were you doing in the king's bedroom?"

Spot looked at her, or at least, the position of its head-blob showed that it looked at her. It remembered this part of its instructions, that it was to act as if it had never seen or heard Aly before. "Secret," it told her.

She looked up at Taybur, still acting the part of an ordinary maid. "Can't His Majesty keep it? It seems harmless enough." She gave him a shy smile.

He grimaced. "Because I work very hard to keep those rooms like a proper child's home, and because he deserves a place where he can be himself with harm or advantage to no one *but* himself. Because I think someone should be able to cry himself to sleep in privacy."

Aly petted Spot with her finger, thinking about Taybur's approach with her. Many spies could be erratic. All her life she had dealt with her father's agents and with the agents of other countries, and she could testify that this was so. Some of them, however, knew the reality of the world. Her instincts told her that Taybur understood that spies were inevitable. If she did no harm to him, he would do no harm to her. She was under no illusions. If he'd been in Topabaw's place, guarding the kingdom, she would have been on the next ship to someplace nasty. But she couldn't see this man having a person killed just for doing their work unless it hurt someone. If he thought she meant harm to Dunevon, she would not be surprised to find herself dropping into a deep stream filled with meat-eating fish some night.

A child's furious "No!" cut through the summer air. Taybur shook his head. "If they let him eat soursop fruit again, I swear, I'll shackle the regents in the dungeon. It *always* makes him sick." He turned and hurried away. Aly sat on a bench tucked between hedges to think.

Point one, she thought as Spot climbed up her shoulder to be consoled by Trick. Dunevon has a devoted guardian. A devoted, clever, *attentive* guardian. One with very good instincts. Point two. What will the raka do with Taybur when they rebel? He won't let them murder his king without a fight. Three. How wide does Taybur cast his net? Does he know about Kanodang and Nomru?

That one was easily answered. If he had legions of spies at his beck and call, he would have set a few on Aly at Balitang House to understand her better. He was too relaxed for someone who knew the raka plans to open up Kanodang and steal its treasures. He probably kept most of his people inside the palace, where they could watch Dunevon and anyone close to him.

She nibbled her lip. She needed a plan to get Taybur out of the country without killing him, if possible. He was no fool, and he guarded a Rittevon king.

Even the rebels had an affection for the big man. Ulasim and Fesgao had mentioned that the new captain of the King's Guard treated raka as if they were luarin. The main problem would be getting him away from his charge.

That was the other problem: his charge. Aly had always thrust away the knowledge that Dunevon and Elsren would probably be killed for the crime of possessing Rittevon blood. She couldn't thrust it away now, not if she wanted to avoid killing Dunevon's diverting guardian, and not if she didn't want children's blood on her hands.

What if we let him *take* Dunevon? she asked herself. Ulasim and the others would kick at leaving the boy alive, but if Dunevon and Elsren both swear in blood they will never try to take back the Crown or the Isles, it might work.

It was a dream. Part of her knew that, the part that had been raised in the brutal schools of history and royal politics. She refused to listen to it.

Aly continued her amble toward the water. Crystal globe lamps shone on two of the water's three pavilions: the central one was dark. Shifting her Sight to see better over distance, she found Baron Engan's immense spyglass there, where the globe lights would not make it impossible to view the sky. Dove stood at his side, chatting, as did Winnamine and some other nobles. Aly hoped that Dove had stopped at the Jade Pavilion before she had joined the astronomer, so that the darking Aly had set on her mistress's shoe at the Robing Pavilion could eavesdrop. Not for the first time she thanked the gods the creatures were so light. Had Dove noticed it, she would have asked questions that Aly dared not answer.

From the Jade Pavilion Aly heard Sarai's infectious laugh. The regents were visible, seated in open-backed armchairs, surrounded by their cronies. A third empty chair with an extra cushion on the seat, obviously meant for the king, stood between Imajane and Rubinyan.

Taybur strode down the path that led from the Jade Pavilion with two guards at his back and a shrieking four-year-old in his arms. He nodded to Aly as he passed, then halted abruptly. Turning Dunevon to the side, he positioned his charge so he could vomit into a clump of bushes.

Aly had helped to care for Elsren for over a year. The minute she heard the king gurgle she stepped down to the water and quickly soaked the extra handkerchiefs any lady's maid carried for emergencies. She peeled off a wet linen square and offered it to Taybur.

"Soursop fruit?" she asked as he cleaned Dunevon's face. Another handkerchief went to cool the boy's forehead, a third the back of his neck. Gently Taybur smoothed damp black curls from the child's face.

"They don't know," he replied with soft savagery. "They weren't really watching him, since they knew the guards wouldn't let him off the pavilion and the walls on it are too high for him to climb. He could have eaten anything." He glanced at the vomit. "Oh, splendid—soursop fruit *and* curry. Excuse me." He strode down the path, the guards hurrying to catch up, the boy king sobbing quietly on his shoulder.

Aly frowned. She didn't enjoy liking those she was supposed to bring down, like Dunevon and his large protector. They stood between the raka and their freedom. Something had to be done, but the thought of killing either of them made her grind her teeth.

In soaking her handkerchiefs, she had spied a bench placed just by the water, one that gleamed with magical discouragements to insects and snakes. Though sheltered by a willow, the seat gave Aly a clear view of all three water pavilions. She settled there, hoping that no one chose this hidden place for a lovers' encounter, though it was clearly designed for that. The sounds of flutes, harps, and soft drums floated over the water through air like smooth balm.

Watching darkness fall, she considered the night's activities. Her own people would be taking positions on either side of the fortresses. Ulasim's had been seeping into Kanodang for the last day, locked up as prisoners until they could guide the freed captives to horses, boats, or hiding places.

"This is *taking too long.*" Kyprioth, dressed as a raka and tinkling with charms, appeared in front of Aly's nose.

Aly shrugged. She had been watching Rubinyan and two of his nobles discuss horse racing. She had already seen that no one on the Jade Pavilion dared to speak of the newest rebellion. "An eclipse party does have to wait for the eclipse to happen. You're blocking my view."

"I didn't mean the eclipse," snapped the god. "I can't distract my brother and sister forever, Aly."

She raised her brows. "We've done quite nicely for rebels who have only been back in town for a month. I would like to point out that this week will be quite eventful, thank you so much." She cocked her head and looked at him. "We need the luarin, Kyprioth. Unless enough of them come to our side, we'll fail. You need strength to battle the others? You say you get that from victories. We haven't won that many yet. Though it sounds peculiar, we short-lived creatures need time." She leaned back against the bench. "The country's coming to a boil. Once we convince those who are unconvinced that the regents are not good rulers but vicious ones, that this isn't just a matter of the raka bringing up old grievances, it will be war, and you'll have your victories."

Kyprioth tugged the emerald earring that glinted in the light from the pavilions. "Every day it takes to drive these people along, we are a day closer to my brother and sister's return. So it's vicious rulers you need? Maybe I can work at that." He vanished.

"If you use your power now, your brother and sister will know anyway," Aly told the empty air.

"There is power, and there is *power*, my dear," she heard him whisper. "My power can be vast, in the right places."

Aly shook her head. They moved forward as fast as they could, the conspirators in Rajmuat and the ones on the outlying Isles. Since she couldn't control any of them, she could only wait and do her own work. She remained on her bench, her Sight locked on the nobles on the Jade Pavilion. Most of them spoke of social matters. Officers of the royal navy complained to Lord Matfrid of strangely choppy seas and difficult voyages. Ferdy tried to tell the Carthaki Zaimid that nobles did not raise horses themselves. Sarai shoved him with one hand and told him he was stuffy.

Each time Aly tired of reading one conversation, she turned her gaze to Topabaw. He was always easy to find. His array of magical amulets and the glare of his magical Gift burned in her Sight.

Topabaw was restless. He fiddled with his charms, changed position, and rubbed the nape of his neck. For a while he paced around the edges of the pavilion, until Prince Rubinyan shot him a glare that made the spymaster halt.

The next time Aly could read Topabaw's lips, he was assuring a couple of nervous men that the winter had simply made the raka crazy, and it would wear off. Another time he refused to discuss Duke Nomru's arrest with Count and Countess Tomang. More than anyone else, he kept glancing at the regents, his jaw muscles clenched. Topabaw was nervous. And he was nervous about his masters.

Aly smiled.

The moon had begun to rise when she heard steps on the path. She stiffened, then relaxed: the steps were Taybur's. The big man walked straight down to the water's edge without hesitation. He pushed aside trailing willow limbs and entered her enclosure.

She looked up at him and raised an eyebrow as he sat beside her.

"Fear not, gentle maiden. I have no intentions on your virtue."

"You're no fun," Aly accused. If she'd thought for a moment he had such intentions, she would have made it plain she was uninterested. Once she would have worried more that he gave no sign that he thought her attractive, but these days she didn't care. She had changed from who she'd been in Tortall, but she refused to ask herself how.

Taybur leaned back and thrust his long legs out, crossing his ankles as he folded his hands on his chest. "Any other night and you'd have to fight for this spot, you know," he said blithely. "It's popular with lovers. But with the news from Imahyn, the servants not on duty are hiding, and the nobles want the regents to see their smiling, loyal faces." He sighed. "People don't know how to appreciate a spring night anymore. By the way, according to my agents, there is no family named Homewood in service at Fief Tameran in Tortall."

Only years of training kept Aly from betraying shock. Instead she yawned, keeping her eyes on the Jade Pavilion. Beyond it, on the dark Lapis Pavilion, Baron Engan adjusted his spyglass as Dove and a few young scholars looked on.

"If you're worried about Topabaw, don't," Taybur said lazily. "Look, there's the first firefly. Make a wish. Topabaw is so used to people being afraid of him that he's gotten lazy. My people visited Tameran at a certain risk to themselves. I don't want to share their reports with a man who thinks torture gets honest answers. You *can* speak, can't you?"

Aly looked down. Her mouth quivered with amusement.

Spot emerged from its silent conversation with Trick, rolling along the back of Aly's neck to sit on the shoulder closest to Taybur. He offered his palm to the darking, who created four legs for itself and walked across his fingers.

"In case you're thinking I'm lazy, I did give my mages a chance at this little fellow before I returned him to you. Their magic just bounced off." He idly tossed Spot into the air.

"Whee!" cried the darking. It spread out two wings to slow its descent onto Taybur's palm.

"You are easily pleased," Taybur informed it. He passed Spot back to Aly and glanced up through a break in the leaves. "The Goddess begins to draw her veil. If you'll excuse me?" He stood, then seemed to think of something else. His face was shadowed as he looked down at Aly. "Things can't be easy for a full luarin in service in a household with so many raka. If you ever need a friend, come to me." He strode out of the willow's shelter, then turned back again, almost giving Aly a fit of the giggles. He was *very* good and had the timing of an actor. "Have you seen how edgy Topabaw's been lately? Wouldn't you love to know why?"

This time he continued on his way to the Jade Pavilion. Soon after his arrival the light globes winked out to allow the nobles a clear view of the darkening moon.

The eclipse was predicted to last nearly until dawn. Once the moon's face was covered, however, many nobles, including the Balitang ladies, said their good nights. Dove followed her mother and sister reluctantly, glancing up at the hidden moon.

Seeing them on the path, Aly trotted back to the Robing Pavilion, grateful that they would be home long before the alarm was raised at Kanodang. She had not liked the risk of being near the palace when the regents learned of the prison break.

"I was down by the Lily Water. Many of the lords are preparing to leave," she announced to her fellow servants. Immediately the men returned to their masters' side of the pavilion. Cards were put away, sewing packed up, boxes opened for a change to clothes better suited to riding or litters. Pembery sent a runner to alert the men-at-arms and the hostlers that it was time to go. When the ladies arrived, the maids helped them change clothes.

They were part of a large group of nobles riding into the city. Ferdy and Jevair Ibadun urged their horses to either side of Sarai, glaring at one another behind her back. Zaimid joined the Balitangs at the last minute, riding a spirited mare whose grace made Sarai's eyes shine. Instead of jostling with the other two men, he rode with the duchess and Nuritin, talking about the evening and politics in Carthak. Dove rode just behind them, listening.

Party by party, the nobles left the main group to finish the trip to their scattered homes. The Balitangs' companions, including Zaimid, turned away when they reached Joshain Street. They assured the ladies they were going straight to bed, but no one was fooled. There was plenty to interest lively young men in Dockmarket at that hour.

Once Aly was brushing out Dove's hair in the girl's bedroom, Dove glared at her in the looking glass. "*Now* will you tell me what's got you on pins and needles?" she whispered. She didn't want to rouse Junai, who'd gone to sleep the moment she lay down on her pallet. "You hide it well, but you've been too alert all day. It's the same with Ulasim, Fesgao, and Ochobu these last two days. I asked Quedanga, but she says that the chiefs in different areas don't talk about special projects with anyone who isn't involved, just those who help them to pull things together."

Aly shook her head. "It's better for those of us who don't take active part to hear as things happen."

"So when anyone asks if we knew what was going on, we can say no, and it will read to a mage as the truth," Dove said, making sure that she had understood it correctly.

"If you're so clever, what do you need me for?" teased Aly, putting the brush aside.

Dove sniffed. "Two clevers are better than one." She turned on her stool to look at Aly. "But you know, don't you? Even though you aren't supposed to, you already know what's going on, because that's what you do. Ulasim told me once that he wouldn't be surprised if you'd found ways to listen to them when you aren't about. He thinks you probably know the shape of everything, the entire rebellion, throughout the Isles. I think so, too."

I could sometimes wish she were a bit less intelligent, thought Aly. No wonder most of her friends are adults.

"As long as I do no harm with what I've picked up, I don't see why anyone should even care," she assured her mistress. "Don't we each have enough on our plates, without adding more?"

"Except that it's your job to collect more for your plate," Dove pointed out, then yawned. She got to her feet and went to bed. "Good night, Aly."

Aly hesitated, watching Dove get comfortable. "I am sorry you missed the rest of the eclipse," she whispered.

"There will be a solar eclipse in August," Dove murmured sleepily. "Half the court says it's a grand omen, the other half claims it's troubles on the rise."

Aly said, her voice breathless and panicky, "But, lady, with these raka up to mischief, the gods are obviously trying to warn us. We could be murdered in our beds!"

"You will be if you aren't quiet," grumbled Junai.

Aly waited until both Dove and Junai fell asleep, then slipped out of the room.

11

A FEW CHANGES

Aly found company in the kitchen. Ulasim, Fesgao, Quedanga, Chenaol, Ochobu, and Ysul all sat around the table in their nightclothes. Idly they played at dice, chess, or backgammon. Chenaol poured Aly a cup of arak and shoved a plate of fried dumplings at her. It was a mark of the cook's distraction, because everyone knew Aly hated arak. Aly set her basket of sewing on the table and watched the others' faces. She had wondered if Ulasim or Fesgao would choose to break their own rule and go on the Kanodang mission. The temptation must be overwhelming, after months of doing nothing but creating plans. She thought the better of them for staying out of it, but then, she had known they took their revolution seriously. If they made a mistake, it would not be any of the obvious ones.

"So *now* will you tell us what goes forward?" Chenaol demanded wearily. "Now that all the chicks are in their coops? Aly's little pack of wolves never so much as showed up for supper."

"No," Ulasim and Fesgao said at the same time.

After a moment Ulasim said, "You will know when it is done. It is not yet done."

"If I die of curiosity before it is done, I will wait in the Peaceful Realms and ensure that you do *not* find them peaceful," Chenaol warned. She looked at Aly. "All's well at the palace?"

Aly smiled. "They got word of the rising on Imahyn. They pretended it meant nothing. And Topabaw does not look at all well. Nor does Prince Rubinyan appear to regard him with any pleasure at all."

"I hear from a thousand sources that Topabaw plans to overturn the regents, or the regents plan to dismiss Topabaw," said Quedanga with a yawn. "They speak of it even at the palace, where such things are usually left in silence."

That was the extent of their conversation for some time. The watch was calling the fourth hour of the night when Ysul raised a hand for quiet. Everyone went still. Ysul had the best hearing in the household, but Aly already knew what he'd noticed. A moment later the others heard it, the tiniest ghost of an explosion down by the harbor. They ran through the servants' gate into the street, looking. A dull orange glow showed in the sky to the southeast. Aly knew as if she had seen it that her agents had set the kegs of blazebalm on fire in both fortresses. So much blazebalm, tightly packed in wax-coated kegs, would explode when it burned.

"Don't look at me," Fesgao said, holding up his hands when everyone turned to stare at him. "This isn't my doing."

Alarms sounded all around the harbor. Aly crossed her fingers and prayed that her people were safely away from the damage they had done. Servants from nearby houses emerged in their bedclothes, curious about the uproar. Word finally reached them via the other servants and householders who lived between there and the harbor that the Greater and Lesser Fortresses were on fire, as well as the soldiers' barracks behind the Greater Fortress.

Aly finally complained of cold feet and went back inside. Her people would be careful to make their way home, using the web of tunnels to enter the grounds unseen. Just in case, she went to her workroom. There they were, everyone who had undertaken the night's diversion, using oil to clean off the soot that turned their faces to shadows. They were laughing and joking with relief. Only when Aly held a finger to her lips did they remember that most of the household was abed.

"Don't tell me you worried about us," one of the men said with a bold grin.

"It was the easiest thing." Guchol used a bit of cotton to remove a last streak on a friend's face. "We didn't lose a single recruit, and you can see we all came back in one piece."

"The silly clunches store all their blazebalm in one armory," Kioka said with a sniff.

Rasaj was combing out his long hair. "Both fortresses, they did it that way. We hardly needed to do anything more."

"But you did," suggested Aly.

"We stuck wedges under the barracks doors and the sally ports," Lokak told Aly with grim pleasure. "We disabled the drawbridges and the portcullises."

"It will take them all day to get out," said Jimarn quietly. "By then they'll have sampled their food and drink. They may not have enough alive in the Lesser Fortress to open the gates at all."

"They're not idiots," protested Olkey. "Once they realize all the places we hit, they'll have to check the food before they try it."

"*You* said nobody would be stupid enough to keep all their blazebalm in one spot," one of the women pointed out.

Aly caught the whiff of sewer that clung to her pack even after they'd discarded the clothes they'd worn. "Baths," she ordered. "Get that smell off you." She went around the room and kissed each pack member's forehead. "You've done beautifully," she told them with approval and pride. "Let us pray all our adventures fare as well." She caught an especially strong whiff from Jimarn. "Bathed and dressed by dawn. And need I tell you—"

"No word to anyone, not *anyone*," they chorused, having heard it from her often enough.

Aly grinned at them and returned to the kitchens to take up her mending again. She'd expected to feel sleepy once she was sure her pack was safe, but her nerves still hummed. Her thoughts passed over the Windward District, across the harbor, up along the tenements of Downwind and the pretenses of dwelling places in the Honeypot. Over the ridge and there it would be, gray stone Kanodang, with its thick walls and strong towers. What was happening there?

Soon enough the light turned the pearl gray that came before dawn. The household came down for the morning's exercises, Aly and the chief conspirators joining them after they'd changed into day clothes. As they practiced with and without weapons, the sun began to rise above the same long ridge of the Kitafin mountains that hid Kanodang from view. Ulasim and Fesgao both took bruises they normally would have avoided, because they kept looking northeast, toward the prison. After Ulasim took a staff hit that turned his left cheekbone purple, Aly dragged him aside.

"Were they going to burn it?" she demanded softly.

He glanced at her, startled. "Of course not," he replied. "Rapists and murderers, remember?"

"Then stop looking up there like you expect a column of smoke," she said. "We'll know if the warning bells—"

Ysul stopped in the middle of throwing a man-at-arms, turning his face northeast. His victim struggled and protested, unable to break his captor's hold as Ysul listened. Then the others heard the toll of a bell from the far side of the harbor. Another bell took up the call, then others.

Above the booming of the bells came the thin, raucous screeches of Stormwings. More than a hundred of them flew overhead from the direction of the palace, sun dancing off their metal wings as they sped toward the source of the alarm gongs.

"Will you look at that," Aly said with a brilliant smile for Ulasim. "Whatever could have stirred them up so?"

He hugged her hard enough to make her squeak, then released her. To Ochobu he said, "You see, Mother? And you were all fretful."

Ochobu raised her eyebrows. "It is unseemly to gloat, boy," she told her forty-five-year-old son.

Aly sauntered back into the house. She did not delude herself. She would get the formal reports later, but she guessed they might have killed between two hundred and five hundred at the harbor fortresses, if some of the wedged doors had been those in the barracks. With Kanodang she could not be sure, since Ulasim had told her they had people who worked inside, but she could guess a death total of fifty to one hundred. She owed a debt to those ghosts. The Kanodang breakout had been her idea, as had the attack on the fortresses. This was what her parents had done all their lives, racked up lists of those who could thank them for their deaths.

No wonder Mother gets cranky when anyone asks how many people she's killed, Aly thought, washing her face before she went upstairs. I've lost count of every war and skirmish and raid she's fought in, not to mention the duels as Champion. That's why she never wants to talk about them. She'll have to remember the lives she has taken.

There were people who had killed so often there was little humanity left in them. Aly had met plenty like that, helping her da with spy work. She knew a few of them among the household guards here, and in Topabaw she'd found someone who couldn't even remember what it was like to feel regret, or pity for the families of the dead. Her parents fought to hang on to their humanity, and Aly had never valued the struggle more.

I'll make it up to them when I go home, she promised herself as she trotted up the back stairs to Dove's room. I'll be a better daughter.

Dove was opening the shutters on her window: the night had turned chilly as they'd come home from the palace. The younger girl looked fresh and alert, not like someone who had reached home after midnight. "Alarm bells and gongs," she said as Aly changed into clean clothes. "And Stormwings," added Dove. "A *lot* of Stormwings." She turned to look at Aly. "Is there something I should know?"

"Oh, my lady, don't worry your head about these things," Aly said as she took out Dove's clothes for the day. "I'm sure some nice man will explain in terms you can grasp."

Dove raised her brows. "That big, is it?" she asked dryly.

Aly, her arms full of clothes, bobbed a curtsy. "It's not for me to say, my lady," she replied, her voice prim. It was wonderful, how she rarely had to explain things to Dove. "Will my lady be wishful of a bath this morning?"

The sounds had took up a particular rhythm: bong bong *bong*, bong *bong* bong, bong bong *bong*. The duchess, wearing a robe over her fine lawn nightdress, swept into the room and helped Aly open the rest of the shutters. "That's the alarm at Kanodang," she said grimly. "The prison. There's been an escape. Aly, get Fesgao. Have all the guards mustered and close the gates, *immediately.*"

Aly ran to obey. For now all they had to do was lock the house down and wait for news. Since news could take time to reach the city, Aly thought she might get to catch up on the sleep she'd lost. That would have to wait, though. First she wanted to get to her office, to hear what her darkings could tell her. Sleep would come later, after they made all the motions of a house full of innocents.

She found Fesgao seated at the kitchen table, watching drowsily as Chenaol and the maids rushed to prepare breakfast. He blinked at Aly as she rested her elbows on the table beside him and leaned down so he could speak privately to her. "Seko's back," Fesgao murmured. "I thought it would please him, as a former bandit, to crack a prison. He says that they got more than a hundred and ten political prisoners out, including His Grace of Nomru. They are dispersed, by ship or horse, to the other islands."

Aly smiled. "Very good work," she said with appreciation.

Fesgao looked up at her. "Do you know, with any other girl of your age, if she spoke thus to me, I would give her latrine duty for a year. But from you?" He shook his head. "I am complimented beyond words."

Aly winked at him. "And that is as it should be," she told him. Before he could come up with a retort, she said, "Her Grace heard the alarms. She wants all the gates locked, with guards put on them right away."

Chenaol passed a chunk of cooked pork and two sago cakes to Fesgao. As he took them, he told Aly in a normal tone of voice, "Inform Her Grace it will be done immediately." He left the kitchen, as brisk and alert as if he had spent the night in his bed, sleeping well.

Ulasim leaned against the kitchen doorframe, grinning. "The guards at Kanodang are worse than we thought," he said when Aly and Chenaol gave him questioning looks. "They didn't realize there had been an escape until the morning guards came for their duty. No one else checked on the place. It means those who got out had more time to get away than we could have hoped. Thank you, Bright One!" he added in tribute to Kyprioth.

"What about our people in the prison?" Chenaol inquired. "The ones who stayed?"

Ulasim shook his head. "They're safe. Our folk were disguised, and those who were to remain knew nothing of the plan. When Crown mages question them, our people will truthfully say they were captured and sent to sleep along with the other guards and prisoners." He straightened. "I'd best see Her Grace. She will have orders for me for today."

Not long after the family had finished their morning meal, servants from the nearby houses came to see if the Balitangs knew anything about the alarm. They were followed by hastily dressed masters and mistresses, who asked the same questions of the duchess. It wasn't long before someone realized that Elsren's escort of King's Guards had not arrived. He was left to kick his heels in the downstairs sitting room for a time, before the duchess decreed that he could change to more comfortable clothes and play with his sisters.

It was almost noon when they heard the tramp of feet outside the walls. The King's Watch had come in force. Their captain ordered everyone to return to their homes and remain there. When Winnamine's noble neighbors protested, he told them that they could walk back or be carried, again by order of the regents.

Their guests left. After lunch, the Balitang ladies dismissed their maids and retired for naps. Nearly everyone in the household did the same. Usually there was some activity during the afternoon rest time, but with no one permitted outside, most of the household except those on guard chose to relax.

Aly went to her office and closed the door, then closed the shutters on her windows and locked them in place, putting the spells in the wood up as a barrier to all eavesdropping. Only then did she allow her two-strand bead necklace, which currently sported anchoring beads on each shoulder, to reshape itself into Trick and Spot.

"You have a new name," she told Spot. "Secret."

"Secret," it agreed, and nodded. It plainly liked either the name or the idea, Aly wasn't sure. She looked at Trick. "What is happening in the palace?" she asked it. "What do our friends up there have to tell you? Wait." She found slates and chalk. "Go ahead."

What the darkings had to say fascinated Aly. Between the attacks on the fortresses and the escape from Kanodang, Imajane was furious. She was spending her day writing warrants for the arrest of the warden and his lieutenants in the case of Kanodang, and dictating instructions for the storage of blazebalm for the army and the navy, since the commanders and their staff at both fortresses were among the dead. Trick passed on the names on the warrants: none was a member of the raka conspiracy. Ulasim had issued orders years before that his people within the prison were not to be promoted beyond a certain level, because the Rittevons were notoriously fond of executing people in charge when things went wrong.

Rubinyan's darking told them that the prince had taken over the investigation beyond the grounds of Kanodang. He ordered the captain-general of the King's Watch to hunt down fugitives and question his informants about the jailbreak. He was also to lift the ban on people in the streets. Both men knew it was risky to keep a population indoors for more than a day. The prince called for the commanding general of the Rittevon Lancers and gave orders for the horsemen to search for fugitives outside the city walls. He then tripled the Rittevon Guard's security at the palace. He was cool and crisp, giving each man he spoke to the impression that he was in control of the situation.

He then commanded the chief herald to put his scribes to two tasks. The more important job was a proclamation to be read at every crossroad, with copies sent to each person on a list of the noble houses and the city's wealthiest merchants. He decreed that there had been pirate attacks at the harbor's mouth during the eclipse, fought off with heavy losses to the Harbor Guard. There had also been the prison break from Kanodang. The people were asked to watch for twelve fugitives, five of them full-blood luarin. There would be a reward of two gold lans to anyone who gave information that would lead to the fugitives' arrest.

"That's sweet," Aly remarked cynically. "That way, if he gets any tip-offs, he can say someone else already reported them, so they got the reward."

"Cheating," Secret commented with disapproval.

The second proclamation was to go out through the Isles. It offered a hundred gold lans each for a list of ten men, one of them Vurquan Nomru, formerly a duke, whose lands and holdings were now Crown property.

Aly's hand cramped, she wrote so much as darking after darking passed her information the rebellion could use. It was Rubinyan's darking once again who provided Aly with the tastiest bit of information of all, as the late-afternoon light streamed through cracks in her shutters. When Aly heard it, she had to savor it, but she had the self-discipline to wait until she had given all of her darkings one last check.

She praised each of them through Trick and asked if they were having fun. All of them agreed they were most definitely having fun. They weren't sure what they liked best, the people whispering, throwing items, or jumping at noises, but all agreed these things were amusing. Aly suggested to them that they might try some of their own whispering, throwing, and noisemaking, and left them to it.

Then she sat back, crossed her hands on her stomach, propped her feet up on her desk, and savored. Back and forth she wavered: ought she to tell the conspirators or not? In the end, she decided to let them learn without hearing it from her. For one thing, Ulasim and Ochobu at least would like to know how she'd found it out, and she was not ready to tell them about the darkings. For another, she wanted to see the look on each face when they realized she had done what they had thought impossible.

She wished she could tell Nawat.

Realizing the time, she went in search of Dove, in case she had instructions for Aly. She found the ladies of the house in the nursery, Nuritin embroidering as Winnamine, Sarai, and Dove played with Petranne and Elsren. It was something they'd done all winter, but not as much since their return to Rajmuat. Aly left them alone. This might be the last time they could relax for weeks.

She spent the afternoon and the early evening reading reports from the palace. The chief armorer did not like the Rittevon Guard, who treated their weapons badly. The captain of the Rittevon Guard thought the armorer was a penny-pinching old fool. One of Imajane's ladies-in-waiting appeared to have an eye for Prince Rubinyan. Reading this in a report from Vereyu, Aly chuckled. *Now* she had a wedge to drive between the regents, if she could make the lady-in-waiting's interest obvious to Imajane.

There was more, from all over the city. Reading paper reports, Aly marked out who might be shifted to the rebels' side, given incentive, and made a list of rumors for her people to spread. The shakier the regents looked, the more eager people would be to do things they would not dare if the Crown appeared strong. There was the personal gossip— Rubinyan's possible involvement with one of his wife's own ladies-in-waiting—and the more ominous news about what had really happened at the fortresses. Rubinyan's personal spymaster, Sevmire, had told him, with Aly's darking to hear, that more than three hundred and twenty men had died at the fortresses, burned or poisoned. Rubinyan had ordered him to keep that number to himself. If Rubinyan heard that people knew the correct number of the dead, he might think Sevmire or his subordinates had been indiscreet. It could also be that by the time Rubinyan's spies heard the city gossip, the number of dead soldiers would be vast, amplified by gossip as it passed from one person to the next. She relaxed in her chair. It had been a very nice day for her.

Her pack sought her out shortly before supper, to see what orders she had. She handed over the list of rumors. They assured her that they would continue to pass on gossip about Topabaw and the regents. Aly only nodded.

Supper came and went. The ladies retired to their sitting room with their maids, sewing, reading, and talking softly, without once referring to the reason they had not gone out all day. At last Winnamine sent everyone to their rooms, though she and Nuritin remained where they were. Dove and Aly went downstairs to meet with the conspirators, where Dove and the others heard the details of what Ulasim, Fesgao, Ochobu, and Aly had pulled off among them to bring the city to a standstill.

"Gods bless me," whispered Dove when they were done, "we might just do this."

There were more plans to discuss, and then the conspirators broke up for the night. From the looks on Quedanga's and Ysul's faces, they had thought of some fresh ploy. Chenaol stayed with Ulasim to talk about a shipment of bows and spears that was scheduled to arrive soon, and where they would be stored.

Dove and Aly were halfway up the stairs to the family quarters when Dove turned and faced Aly. "They'll think the luarin did it," she whispered. Just because the house was spelled and watched for outsider spies was no proof that someone inside might not lose their nerve, or try to get a reward for what he or she knew. "They don't believe the raka have money, resources, mages, or the will to organize and fight. They'll think the luarin set Nomru free—and the others, to hide Nomru's trail. Topabaw will be watching the luarin more closely than ever, and with his usual touch. He'll turn more luarin nobles against him that way than if he'd just hanged their full-raka slaves."

"Don't mistake Topabaw for the regents," Aly advised. "Do you think they would act differently with another spymaster?" She took a step up, so that her mouth was on a level with Dove's ear, and she whispered, "We had to force that feeble luarin conspiracy of yours to *act*. So far, they're just an association that meets to complain about the government. You can't play with rebellion, Dove. You're either in it, or you're dead."

A small, strong hand fastened on Aly's arm. Dove towed Aly down the stairs, through the house, along the garden paths, and into the Pavilion of Secrets. "You don't understand the pressure they're under," she whispered fiercely.

Aly sank onto a bench. "I understand that this country's rulers have gotten away with things that are unthinkable in Tortall. They get away with it because their nobles haven't stood up for those in their care. I'm just a simple country girl. I rely on what people *do,* not how much they whisper."

"I can't tell the nobles about the raka," Dove said, slumping on the bench next to Aly. "I swore."

Aly stretched. "No. But you can tell them your market and merchant friends have whispered of other conspiracies in the outlying Isles, people who are prepared to do more than just talk. Let them chew on that for a time. And if you don't mind, I mean to retire for the night. I'm *exhausted.*"

"You're supposed to wait until *I* come up to bed and undress *me,*" Dove said as Aly got to her feet. They walked together into the house. "You're a terrible maid that way."

"You could always get rid of me," Aly replied, yawning so widely she half feared the joints in her jaws would give way. "But then you'd miss my charm and wit."

Aly was asleep the moment she lay down on her pallet.

Early the next morning, a herald came with the announcement that people could leave their homes. The family had just finished their breakfast when the news came. Rihani and Gian, Elsren's manservant—now a spy recruit—had to scurry to prepare Elsren for his daily visit to the palace. They were still dressing the boy when the squad of ten King's Guards arrived. As they waited, their sergeant was happy to talk to Quedanga. He'd noticed on earlier visits that the housekeeper was a handsome woman always willing to give a soldier a cup of tea and a bite to eat. He assured her that things were almost normal. There were more checkpoints on the streets, and folk wouldn't want to idle as they went about their day's business, but the regents had the city well in hand.

"He's not bad, for a luarin," Quedanga told Aly as the duchess and Dove waved goodbye to Elsren.

"Let him know," Aly said. "He might be useful." She trudged upstairs.

Despite permission to leave home, Nuritin advised the duchess not to allow Sarai or Dove to go out and about just yet. "The regents *have* to let people buy food and do business unless there is an army at our gates," Nuritin told both girls. "That does not mean we have no dangerous criminals running about. We should answer all those invitations that have collected on Winnamine's desk. It is more personal when one of the ladies of the house replies." Aly, Pembery, Boulaj, and Dorilize rolled their eyes at one another. For them, this meant a morning of needlework.

The morning was advanced when a sound made Aly look up. Wayan, a house message runner, peered at her around the doorframe with eyes as wide as saucers. As soon as Aly saw her, she fled. A few moments later, a footman did the same thing. Like Wayan, he stared only at Aly. A pair of kitchen maids followed him. Their whispers roused Nuritin from her concentration on the letter she wrote. She turned on her chair and scowled.

"Have you business here?" she demanded.

The maids shook their heads.

"Then get back to your work!" As the maids fled, Nuritin shook her head. "Silly young creatures, no more sense than finches. When *I* was a girl . . ."

This time Winnamine, as well as the other women, rolled her eyes.

It was almost time for lunch when Ulasim rapped on the doorframe. "Your Grace? My ladies?" he asked, his face locked in formal, senior-servant blankness. "I bring important news."

Winnamine beckoned him forward as everyone but Aly looked at him. Aly, sensing what news he bore, kept her attention on her needle.

Ulasim bowed. "Your Grace, my ladies, I . . ." He paused for a moment, so oddly for him that the ladies looked worried. Ulasim was the ideal manservant and never fumbled. "It's Topabaw," he said at last. "He's— They made an Example of him. By the harbor mouth."

Nuritin jerked, dumping a bottle of ink on her desk and herself. As the maids rushed to stop the ink's spread and to save the old woman's dress, the duchess stared at him.

"Ulasim, this is a very poor joke," she whispered.

He looked at her not as a servant looked at his mistress but as one human being looked at another. "Your Grace, I did not believe it, either. I have just come from the harbor. I have seen it with my own eyes. Topabaw is dead." He looked at Aly, his eyes holding a shade of the awe the maids had showed. "There is no proclamation of his crime, but the royal seal was placed on his chest. Burned into it, actually."

Nuritin stopped trying to clean up the ink and half-collapsed in her chair. "I know there was a time before Topabaw," she murmured, "for I lived and bore children in it."

"It must have been the prison escape," said the duchess, folding hands that quivered. "I've heard rumors that he was losing his grip, that the regents had come to think he was too old for the work. . . ."

"Who cares?" snapped Sarai, jumping to her feet. "They didn't kill him for all the people he's had murdered, did they? They killed him because he let Nomru escape! They only care about luarin lives around here. They always have and they always will!"

Winnamine's eyes flashed. "Do not forget you are half luarin, mistress, whether you like it or not."

"How can I forget?" demanded Sarai. "It's the only part of me people are interested in." She stalked out past Ulasim, skirts flaring around her.

Dove set down her pen and corked her ink bottle. "Things will be different," she observed quietly. "He kept all of the work of the intelligence gatherers in his own hands for years. He never replaced the assistant spymaster when the man was assassinated five years ago."

Nuritin frowned. "I'd forgotten. He never did, it's true."

"Whoever takes up his post won't know everything he did." Dove looked at her mother, then her great-aunt. "They won't know his files. They won't know his agents. And his agents won't be sure if they aren't next, or if the new man isn't there simply to hand out more blame. His networks will be all chaos for a while."

Suddenly Winnamine remembered the maids and Ulasim. "All of you, it's almost lunchtime. Go wash up. Ulasim . . ."

"Yes, Your Grace?"

"Tell our people, *Mind your tongues.* Say or do *nothing* that might look wrong to the regents," Winnamine insisted. "We don't know who will be taking notes for them."

Ulasim bowed to her again. "Your Grace is always wise."

12

MEDDLERS

There was no rest period that day. All of the servants watched Aly as if she were god-touched. Her own pack, when it met in her workroom, had that same look of awe mingled with fear. Aly was glad when callers descended on Balitang House. At least none of them stared.

For once the young nobles talked quietly about things other than themselves, though the young men were careful to tell Sarai she might count on them, just in case. They did not say in case of what. The only man of Sarai's circle not present was Zaimid. Sarai made the mistake of asking Ferdy where the Carthaki was.

"Caring for rioters over on Soursop Lane," the young count informed her with contempt. "The Watch had taken care of them as they should be cared for, and off goes our healer to tend the wounded. I'll be glad when we see the last of that sanctimonious face!"

"At least he helps," retorted Sarai. "At least he's doing something *for* people, instead of living off them and ignoring them when they need him."

"Lady Sarai, helping troublemakers only encourages them," Ferdy said gently. "Look at Topabaw. He got slack. Now we've had a prison break, attacks on the fortresses, and uprisings all over the Isles. It's time we had new blood to set the realm to rights."

Chenaol touched Aly as she watched the young nobles. "Vitorcine Townsend, Lady Isalena's maid, wants you," the cook whispered in Aly's ear. "She looks like she's in love. You'll find her in my rooms."

Aly raised an eyebrow and went in search of the housekeeper's private sitting room. Chenaol was right. Vitorcine looked as if she had shed years of her age or a great burden. Aly lowered herself into a chair. "You heard the news of Topabaw, then?" she asked Vitorcine.

The young woman nodded. "There's more. Grosbeak! Grosbeak is gone! I report to him as I run errands for my lady, and I was late, close to the noon bell. His shop is locked up, doors and shutters! I . . ." She looked down, blushing, then met Aly's gaze. "I picked the lock. The books, papers, all of it was gone. And everything was a mess, as if he'd packed in a hurry. So I took a chance and went to his home." In response to a question Aly hadn't asked, she rushed to say, "I tracked him there once, just . . . just in case."

Aly tapped her chin, fascinated. She hadn't thought Vitorcine had that kind of gumption. Perhaps she could find something better suited to her talents than simply reporting on the activities of the Obemaeks. Aly had decoded the information Vitorcine had brought, to discover correspondence about the things she already knew, that Lord and Lady Obemaek belonged to the luarin conspiracy.

"What did you find at Grosbeak's home?" she asked.

"Gone, him and his family," Vitorcine said eagerly, giddy at being free of Grosbeak and his master. "And they must have taken only what they could carry. The smith who lives next door said they went around dawn." She reached out and gripped Aly's hands. "Please, will you not free me of my vow? The Obemaeks are so good to me. I hate watching them!"

Aly looked at her meaningfully, as a mother might look at a daughter who had not thought a problem through. "If Topabaw kept records, his successor may yet come back to you," she reminded Vitorcine. When the maid's face fell, Aly patted her hands. "But there. Why borrow trouble? For the time being, do not fret over thoughts of spies."

That night, when the raka leaders met, all of them, even Ochobu and Dove, stared at Aly when she entered the room. She expected it. They had built Topabaw up into something more than human for years. Learning he was now an Example must have made them feel as if the earth had turned sideways. She helped herself to mango nectar. "I said it could be done. Remember, I'm an outsider. He'd been in power for so long that the people who live here forgot the man was human, and the regents more human still. Humans get jealous. That we can use, whether it is between Topabaw and the regents . . ." She paused and looked them over. "Or between Imajane and Rubinyan."

They were startled, as they'd been when Aly had suggested that Topabaw was vulnerable. This time, however, instead of denying that such a thing could be done, the conspirators appeared thoughtful. Aly let them turn it over in their minds, then asked Quedanga, "You'll make sure people know *we* created this, yes? That it is no coincidence that so soon after our return, the regents turned on their spymaster?"

Quedanga opened her mouth and drew in air, but nothing came out. She gulped from her cup and tried again. "Are you certain you are not an aspect of our Bright One? Because you begin to worry me in the same way."

"No, just a loyal servant," Aly reassured her, stroking her Trick-and-Secret beads. They hummed softly against her collarbone. "Things will be a mess in the spy service for now," she told the others. "Rubinyan put his private spymaster, a man named Sevmire Ambau, in charge. He was born on the Jimajen estates, got recruited as a spy at the university in Carthak, and came home to do intelligence for the army. That was when he came to Rubinyan's attention. He's worked for the prince for years, watching the king, Topabaw, even his brother. Sevmire's competent, but he was never a part of Topabaw's organization. He'll be scrambling to find and decode Topabaw's files. He'll try to grip Topabaw's spies, which will be like trying to get control of a runaway team of hurroks." Hurroks were the kudarung's less likeable, clawed and fanged kinfolk. "Some of you know people who worked for Topabaw. This is a good time to suggest to them that the new man is green. He's never had a network bigger than a few islands, or more than a hundred people, to run. He'll get into trouble fast. The more commotion we can stir up throughout the Isles before he can learn his job, the more overwhelmed he will be."

Ulasim stroked his small beard. "I can think of a few . . . possibilities."

Aly looked at him, then at their two mages. "Should something happen—should they fear the worst—Their Highnesses might well start calling in their best generals and mages. It would be nice if some, if not all, of them were unable to respond."

Ulasim chuckled. "We *were* at this before you came, Bright Eyes. Our plans in those areas already move forward."

Aly smiled back. "Then I won't worry, unless you tell me to."

The meeting went on as the raka discussed all they had learned that day. When they finished, Aly went to her workroom and shut the door. She lay on the cool wooden floor with relief. A muffled squeak made her sit up quickly as Trick and Secret dropped away from her neck. Only when they were free did she lie flat again. The two darkings trickled up her shoulders and onto her chest. If Aly tucked her hands behind her head, she could just manage to see them, ink against shadows in the dark.

"I take it you are not offering yourselves as a new, more fashionable breast band?" she asked softly.

"What is—" began Secret, and halted. Aly suspected that Trick had explained in that manner the darkings had, because Secret then said, "Oh. No."

"Bean get bored in eating room," Trick announced. "Bean explore in Gray

Palace. Bean follow Sevmire to new workplace. Bean sitting under Sevmire desk now."

"Ah," Aly said. "Very good. What has Bean to say?"

The venturesome Bean confirmed what Aly had suspected: Sevmire could not find many of Topabaw's files. He knew his predecessor's code, but translations took time. Then Trick relayed something that made Aly pop up so fast the darkings tumbled into her lap. Sevmire was issuing writs for his people to kill Topabaw's principal agents throughout the Isles, and to take their places.

"Never blame an enemy for his stupidity," Da and Grandfather had often told her. Aly didn't blame Sevmire at all. She would have kissed him, if she kissed stupid men. Sevmire was doing to his agents what Rubinyan had done to him. He was placing them in jobs much too large for them.

The next afternoon the nobles came to call, more composed than they had been the day before. With Sarai's friends and their parents came Baron Engan and the priestess Imgehai Qeshi. They disappeared into the study with Nuritin, Winnamine, and Dove.

Once again Aly used her spyhole to watch the young nobility. Ferdy Tomang had thought to buy his way back into Sarai's good graces with an offering of an armful of blue-violet flowers. She simply thanked him and handed them off to a footman to put in a vase. It was only when he proposed a riding party the next day that she smiled at him. Then her smile faded. "Not if Winna and Aunt Nuritin have anything to say about it."

"Mother is talking to them," Ferdy assured her, unaware that his mother might go aside with Sarai's female relatives for more serious purposes. "She says the sooner we show people we're back to our daily lives, knowing the regents are in control, the sooner people will feel better. And maybe we'll even get Zaimid to come. If he doesn't have another emergency. I told him, you'd think we don't have healers in Rajmuat, but he only says this is the kind of healing he won't be able to do once he's the imperial physician."

"Ferdy, what do you mean?" demanded one of Sarai's female friends. "Zaimid left again today?"

"He got word of sickness over in the Honeypot and ditched us on our way here," complained Ferdy. "He said he'd come by and pay his compliments if he had time."

Sarai tossed her head. "Well, I'm not one to get worked up over a man who finds some Honeypot kennel more attractive than *me*."

Her friends laughed. Aly didn't. She knew that trick. Sarai was hurt that Zaimid had been absent two days in a row, and was going to show she didn't care. She flirted outrageously with all her young men, leaving even her female friends tapping their toes.

Feeling sorry for Sarai—Aly knew what it was like to miss one particular man—Aly turned away. She had a table full of reports to read, and the darkings' news to hear. Perhaps she could find some crows to talk with later.

The next day Winnamine reluctantly agreed to a riding party, but no farther away than the closest park, which had only simple horse trails and no room to gallop. At least Ferdy had been right about one thing, Aly thought as she and Dove watched the young nobles ride off. The prospect of riding—or the lack of emergencies—had even brought Zaimid back to Balitang House.

If the Carthaki's presence sweetened Sarai's mood, it was not evident when she came home. She slammed into the family sitting room. Dove and Nuritin were there, fanning themselves as they discussed preparations for Matfrid Fonfala's birthday party and for the king's birthday celebrations. Aly, passing in the hall with a load of Dove's gowns to be pressed, heard Sarai's outraged shout after the door slammed: "Five times! Five times they stopped us, and asked us—*us!*—our business, even after we *told* them who we were, and they poked in our saddlebags!" Aly leaned against the wall to eavesdrop as Sarai continued, "And then they did it to us again, on our way back! The same soldiers! 'Am I a Tomang or not?' Ferdy asked them, and they said it didn't matter who he was, it was the regents' orders!"

Nuritin's brittle voice cut the air. "Sarai! You forget yourself! Are you a lady or a shrieking Dockmarket trollop?"

"Neither, apparently, according to the regents!" Sarai replied, her voice a little quieter. "And it's sad when people who are related to the royal family aren't allowed to express opinions! In Tortall the monarchs *must* listen to the Councils of Lords and of Commoners. In Carthak the emperor has created an assembly of nobles. Landholders matter there, but not here. We are just going to rot from within."

The family was at supper when a Crown messenger arrived. Word spread through the house that Princess Imajane had requested Duchess Balitang's company the next morning when Elsren went to join the king. Winnamine accepted, puzzled. "Unless she wants to press her case to have you join her ladies-in-waiting," she remarked to Sarai as the ladies, children, and maids whiled the stormy evening away in their sitting room. Elsren squeaked each time lightning flashed and thunder boomed, and Petranne giggled.

"If she does," Winnamine continued, nudging Petranne and Elsren with a slippered toe, "I shall tell her I cannot allow you to join her at present, for the sake of the family's honor. You're not fit to serve in polite company anymore, Sarai."

"Because I'm not blind and complacent?" demanded Sarai bitterly. "Because I get angry when common people are treated badly and no one of our class tries to help? Or because I resent being pushed around by a bully in armor? A girl wanted to give me a flower on our way back, and a soldier shoved her away. He knocked her down! Zaimid cared for her—while Ferdy and the others looked on—but still, Winna, how can we stay in such a place? No one can live a decent life here anymore. Look what happened to Topabaw. He gave a lifetime of service, and they made an Example of him."

"*Definitely* not fit for polite society," Nuritin commented, her voice dry as she pushed a needle through silk.

The duchess, accompanied by Pembery and Yoyox, who looked most respectable in a footman's livery, joined Elsren and his escorts from the King's Guard on their morning ride to the palace. A squad of household men-at-arms fell in step behind the guards, the duchess's protection when she chose to return.

Dove waved goodbye until the house gate closed behind them, then turned to Ulasim. "I think I'll go visit Herbrand Edgecliff," she told Ulasim firmly. Looking at Aly, she added, "I had better request an escort of men-at-arms before it's forced on me."

Ulasim smiled at her as he might at a favorite niece. "If Lady Nuritin says you may," he replied. Dove scowled at him, for the moment an ordinary girl deprived of an amusement, then flounced into the library. She knew that Nuritin would not allow her out of the house with a hundred guards, not so soon after the prison break.

Aly watched her go. "You might want to put watchers on all the tunnels out of the grounds," she suggested.

"I shall," Ulasim answered, "but Lady Dove is too wise to try it. Lady Sarai I would have to shackle to a post. Lucky for us that it takes until noon for Lady Sarai to wake up all the way." He rested a hand on Aly's shoulder. "I received a communication this morning. It sits on your desk."

Aly, curious, went to see what had come. She found a grubby note, written by Nawat.

I am busy but I did good on Tongkang. Now I am at Imahyn. There is war smoke almost everywhere we fly over. Our cousins the raka are mobbing the soldiers everywhere. The sparkly is for you.

Aly looked. Beside the note was a small, many-colored piece of glittering rock. She held it in her hand as she reread the note, then kissed the paper and tucked it into her sash. She kept the stone in hand as she began to read her usual stack of reports.

The duchess returned at noon. She found Nuritin, her daughters, their maids, Petranne, and Rihani in the courtyard, mending clothes or reading. All but Nuritin rose as Winnamine hurried toward them. Her face was bone white.

"Aunt, Sarai, Dove, let's go to our sitting room. We will have lunch there,

Boulaj, if you will tell Chenaol and the maids." Rihani was already taking Petranne inside, though she had to stop so the girl could give her mother a kiss. At a nod from Nuritin, Dorilize gathered all of her things and left. Boulaj, too, went to execute her orders. Only Aly remained.

"Are you still the god's messenger?" Winnamine asked.

Aly was worried. The duchess was trembling from top to toe. "I have always been, Your Grace," she replied, though she knew Winnamine thought she was Mithros's messenger, not Kyprioth's.

"Then come with me," said the duchess. She looked around the pool courtyard, distracted, then strode into the house, Aly trotting to keep up.

Once inside the ladies' sitting room, they spoke of Lord Matfrid's birthday. It was simply a way to pass time. The day was already so hot that the duchess closed and locked the shutters to provide shadowy coolness. No one touched their food, though they continued to talk as the maids left. The duchess locked the door behind them.

"Why does *she* remain?" demanded Nuritin, pointing a bony finger at Aly.

"It's a long story, Aunt," said Winnamine, taking a seat. She began to twist her handkerchief in her hands. "I haven't time to tell it at present. Just accept that I trust Aly as if she were family."

"Goddess bless, Winna, what did Imajane *say* to you?" demanded Sarai, resting a hand on her stepmother's arm. "You're shaking!"

The others waited, their eyes on the duchess.

"I met with the regents." Winnamine spoke slowly. "In their personal quarters . . ." She looked up at them and took a deep breath. "They have noticed—they've been told—how much attention you girls receive from people in the street," she said. "How they like to do things for you. They believe it is because you are half raka and yet close to the throne. They have made us a proposal. I said we need time to think. We have until the king's birthday." She turned to Sarai. "The regents propose a marriage between you and Dunevon," she explained. "The contracts are to be signed quickly, 'to give the people confidence in the Crown,' Rubinyan told me. I protested; I reminded them you were cousins. They reminded *me* you were second cousins, which is not as serious. There are precedents, in Carthaki, even in Kyprin history. The royal line of Siraj came from marriages between siblings or half siblings. They would ask you to move to the palace when the contract is signed, to convince the people of their sincerity. But they say it would bring peace and hope to the raka. And, when Dunevon comes of age, the Copper Isles would have a queen again."

Nuritin struggled with a lifetime of caution and lost. "Are they *mad*?"

"They are worried," said Winnamine, without taking her eyes from her stepdaughter. "The country must seem unstable, between the rebellions on the other islands and the escape from Kanodang. I think they want more support in case Nomru rebels. They know they will have serious problems if he does so, but if they can set your marriage against that, they might be able to preserve order."

"You *approve?*" Sarai asked, her voice tiny.

"I understand their reasons. I did not say I approve." Winnamine grasped Sarai's arm. "I can advise you, but the choice must be yours," she told Sarai earnestly. "Marriage to a child is no guarantee of stability. It does not comfort me that Imajane refers to him as 'the brat.' Rubinyan is an honorable man, and he loved your father. That does not mean he would hesitate to take the throne himself, if he thought the nation required a strong adult king."

"I cannot imagine that Imajane has ever forgotten that under the old laws of the country, *she* would have inherited when Hazarin died," Nuritin added. "She would have her own reasons to advise Rubinyan that the country would be stronger with them on the throne."

"Don't give them an answer yet," Dove advised. "Let them think you're considering it, but you can't decide. Find reasons to put them off until after the king's birthday—that's two weeks from now. They offer the Crown like a bauble—play with it, and with them."

"Buy time," Nuritin advised, nodding. "Dove is right. Promise nothing."

"Things change so fast," Dove went on. "Look at just this last week. And Sarai, once they get you in the Gray Palace, you won't ever be able to escape."

"But you all think I should do it," whispered Sarai.

"We didn't say that," Winnamine told her. "We present our ideas, and you consider them. You make the choice." She looked up at Aly, eyes pleading. "What do you say?"

Aly admired the regents' boldness. There were so many different ways this plan could be changed. It gave them a hundred options, some of which might even work. At the very least, if Sarai accepted, the people might well think it was a sign that a raka queen would reign again. Plenty of queens had seized power from much younger kings, and not just in the Isles or Carthak.

"I can say nothing, Your Grace," Aly remarked slowly. "I have no guidance in this."

"What?" demanded Nuritin with a frown.

"We'll explain later," Dove said hurriedly. "Sarai, *think.* We can *use* this. There are so many ways to manage it. All you have to do is pretend."

Sarai got to her feet. "I need time," she said quietly, not looking at them. "At least give me until after Grandfather's birthday to give *you* my decision. And ask them to wait until after the king's birthday for a reply, please." She looked at the duchess. "You must see that I can't possibly answer, not right away. Who would have imagined they'd make such an offer? I'll tell you by the end of the week."

Everyone nodded.

"After we come home from Grandfather's," Sarai told them. "I promise I won't discuss it with anyone but you." She left the room.

The raka conspirators were not happy when Aly and Dove told them of the regents' latest move. Even Ulasim lost his temper and shouted that the raka would fight in the streets before they allowed such a thing. It took Dove and Aly hours to calm them down. It was not official, the girls reminded the conspirators. It might never *be* official. All anyone could do until she reached her decision was to keep the rebellion going forward. They were due to leave for the three-day celebration of Matfrid's sixtieth birthday. Sarai wouldn't voice a decision until they returned.

"Things could change," Dove and Aly said over and over. "Things are changing already."

Two days later word came of a fresh uprising on Ikang Isle. The Crown sent a division of soldiers to crush it. Nawat wrote that he would go there with his crows and see what they might do. To Aly he sent a griffin feather. She kept it on her desk. She also reminded herself to tell the truth in her workroom, in case one feather had the same effect as an entire griffin, in whose vicinity no one could lie.

That night Aly was just going to sleep when a familiar, glowing shape knelt beside her pallet. Junai and Dove slept on, oblivious to Kyprioth's blaze in this form.

"I have an idea," he told Aly, "something to distract my brother and sister for a time. They really shouldn't have left their sun shield and moon shield in the Divine Realms, where some dishonest person might stumble across them."

"Perhaps they thought the Divine Realms wouldn't have that many dishonest people running about," Aly said with a yawn. It seemed Dove and Junai couldn't hear her, either. If they could, Junai would have been on her feet with weapons in her hands. "Except for you, of course."

"You wrong me," Kyprioth said in hurt tones, pressing a bright hand to the glowing area that was roughly the spot where a heart might be. "I am crushed. You think me no more than a low creature, and I a god. See what *you* get for your Midwinter's present from me! Besides, they would know I'd been there. I did, however, find myself a most enterprising young thief among the horse nomads east of Port Udayapur. He'll collect the shields if I guide him. There's an elemental who owes my beloved brother an ill turn or two. She will hide them well."

Aly yawned again. "Is this going to be a legend, or a hero tale, or something?"

"It's a diversion," said Kyprioth. "My brother and sister are about to return from the other side of the world. This will keep them busy for a time, though not forever. Tell Sarai that I have said she will never marry any Rittevon or Ji-majen."

"If I get the chance," Aly said. "She's always with her friends, or her maids, or the family. And I think she ought to at least pretend she'll do it for the moment...."

Kyprioth vanished.

"I've known mayflies better able to pay attention," Aly mumbled as her eyes closed.

The next morning the servants packed for the three-day celebration of Mat-frid Fonfala's birthday, at his estates on the other side of the harbor's southern ridge. All of the Balitangs were going, which meant trunk after trunk went into the wagons.

Boulaj nearly went mad as Sarai dithered over what she would take. "She gets fussier every day," Boulaj confided, packing nearly everything Sarai owned. "And when she doesn't keep changing her mind about what to bring, she broods. I'm always relieved when her friends come—let *them* put up with her moods for an afternoon!"

Aly was preoccupied with a series of reports she had gotten about troop and ship numbers around the capital. She only nodded in response to Boulaj's complaint.

Dove shook her head. "It's this marriage thing," she told Boulaj. "She doesn't seem to realize that it's not real until the vows have been made. I keep telling her, there's no reason why she can't say yes and hold them off until something happens, but she's not listening to me." She smiled wryly. "Not a very good omen of my influence with her as a counselor when the time comes."

All three of them knew what "the time" was.

"She'll calm down," Aly murmured. "She's not a fool."

The afternoon was perfect for riding, the recent heat broken in a storm that had lasted all night. For once the air was warm and only slightly humid. The sole blot on the ride was the soldiers at various checkpoints who searched their wagons three times before they had left the city. Sarai was rude, despite warnings from Winnamine and Dove. It took a flat order from Fesgao to si-lence her.

Sarai remained quiet all the way to the Fonfala estate. There they caught up to another party, including Ferdy and Zaimid Hetnim, who charmed her out of her gloom. At supper, when the political situation came up, Zaimid found a way to distract Sarai from the conversation. He had her laughing by the time the second course was served.

"If he'll wait till I'm older, *I'll* marry him," Dove told Aly as she brushed her hair before bedtime. "We could use allies in Carthak, especially the emperor's personal physician."

Aly frowned. "Do you know, I think you're right," she said, considering it. "It won't do for Sarai—her husband should be from the Isles, and the queen can't live in another country. But I wouldn't sneeze at a Carthaki alliance."

The next day the celebration began at noon. Fonfala servants directed their guests to the areas of the estate they would most enjoy. For the younger family members, the Fonfalas had decorated the old nursery with enough toys to tempt the most fretful child. The doors at the side of the formal sitting room were open and tables were set on the veranda, perfect for the older adults. The library was available for the more studiously inclined. Dove settled in there with a chessboard and Baron Engan, though by midafternoon she had a score of other opponents, including her aunt Nuritin. Aly thought it funny that Dove had as many chess opponents as Sarai did dance partners.

Winnamine, her brothers and sisters from the family holdings on Malubesang, and Sarai and her companions went riding. They took their lunch together in a grassy clearing beside a small waterfall. Afterward they had an archery contest and a riding contest. Everyone changed clothes for supper, then again for the dancing. After she had set the last hairpin in Sarai's braided and curled hair, Boulaj came to Aly. She was sweating.

"Rihani, Dorilize, and Pembery are ill. So am I," she told Aly, sitting on Dove's bed. "I'm afraid the chicken sambal may have been off."

Aly had not had the popular dish at the servants' supper. She had tried sambal once and avoided the spicy dish on principle ever since. She had gotten accustomed to Kyprin spices, she liked to say, but never *that* accustomed. She told Boulaj, "I keep saying that stuff will kill you."

Boulaj gave her a tight smile. "No, but at least this time it makes it difficult to stray far from the privy. I should have listened to Lady Sarai—she said she thought it tasted odd. Can you look after Her Grace, Lady Nuritin, and Lady Sarai as well as Lady Dove? Our ladies are all dressed. We could manage that much, at least."

Aly smiled. "Go to bed. I think I can tend our ladies on my own for one night. It's not like they come rushing in to fix their clothes over and over." The Balitang ladies were the most self-sufficient noblewomen Aly had ever met.

"Gods bless you," said Boulaj gratefully. "Excuse me." She left.

Aly escorted the ladies to the ballroom. Dove headed for a chair next to Nuritin and Baron Engan and was welcomed into their conversation. Sarai and her female friends sat with the young men. Winnamine found a chair with the mothers.

Aly strolled into the gallery where the servants could observe their masters. Once she had explained the absence of Pembery, Dorilize, and Boulaj, she took up a position by the carved screen through which she could see the ballroom. For the first time in months she felt a pang of envy as she watched Sarai, glorious in a white lawn kirtle and doubled silk ivory gown, come down the lines of dancers with a different young man for every dance. Once that might have been Aly herself.

But the colors would have been different, she told herself firmly. Less . . . insipid.

She knew that was jealousy whispering in her ear. She couldn't help it, any more than she could help thinking how she and Nawat would look, properly dressed, going through the steps. Nawat danced beautifully, she had found out at Midwinter at Tanair.

A pang shot through her; her eyes burned slightly. First I start missing his kisses, then I miss him at a party where we wouldn't be allowed to dance anyway. What's wrong with me? she asked herself. She did not try to answer. Instead she tried to pick out who among the young noblemen might be a good partner, if she were allowed to dance. The only one she liked was Zaimid. He was handsome, graceful, clever, and he had a good heart. But he lacks something, Aly decided. Directness, perhaps. An odd sense of humor. He would never send a girl a shiny rock or a griffin feather as a token.

She was getting up to check her ladies again when brightness—the white-hot blaze of godhood—struck her eyes. She clapped her hands to them and retreated, then did complex things with her Sight, making herself better able to see through that fire. Had Kyprioth returned?

"Aly?" asked a Fonfala maid. "Are you all right?"

"Dust in my eye," Aly replied, blinking. "Yes, that's better." She looked up.

The source of the fire was just vanishing through the door to the hall outside. Aly slid between the other servants and stepped outside. An old brown-skinned woman in a black and orange headcloth and sarong hobbled away from Aly, a tray in her bony hands, godhood shimmering around her. Aly called, "Grandmother, wait."

The old woman glanced at her. She grinned, the essence of mischief in her expression. Then she turned the corner, moving more quickly than Aly would have expected of someone of her age.

"Uh-oh," Trick whispered. "Gods not good. Gods sly."

"I know," Aly replied softly. "But we need to know what brings a god here." She followed, tracking the old goddess by her glowing footprints.

She had a very bad feeling about this. Might this be the Great Mother Goddess, who had returned to the Isles in her aspect as the Crone? Aly prayed it was not as she went on into the gardens. If the Goddess had come, she would uncover Kyprioth's plans. The war between the Great Gods would start with Kyprioth still unprepared.

Finally Aly saw her quarry on a bench near the estate's temple. Aly adjusted her Sight to allow for the dark as the woman shook off her headcloth. Only gray stubble covered her head. There was a scarred socket where one of her eyes had been. When she grinned, Aly saw gaps in her teeth.

"Bad. Wily. Careful." That was Secret, quavering from Aly's shoulder.

The goddess squinted at Aly. "Ah," she said in a cheerful voice. "You've little tattlers on your shoulders. How sweet. They will be silent for the time being." She pointed: white light swarmed over Aly. Trick and Secret immediately went still. Worried, Aly touched them. Their bodies in her necklace were warm, but she felt no heads.

"They're alive," the goddess assured her. "I just don't want them meddling."

And I don't need *you* meddling, Aly thought, though she said "Good evening" politely. From long acquaintance with her mother and her Aunt Daine, she knew it was wisest to be polite to strange gods. "I never thought the Fonfalas were so remarkable that they might draw a god to their house."

"But I like playing servant, dearie, just like you," the goddess told her. "People think you're furniture. They hardly notice. You can have all kinds of fun without them realizing who's doing it, but you already know that. I love to see their little lives collapse in flames. It's even more amusing when they start blaming each other as things go wrong."

Goose bumps crept over Aly. There was something familiar about this goddess. "Are you a raka god?" she asked, still cautious.

"Gracious, no. Don't they have enough troubles with my cousin mucking about? Just be thankful his sister the Jaguar Goddess is locked up, and all the others are small gods," the goddess told Aly. She snatched at the air, grabbed a firefly, then popped it into her mouth. "Mmm, I like these. I wonder if I could get some at home."

Aly remembered where she'd heard of a goddess much like this one. Daine had told her about the Carthakis' quirky patron goddess. "You're the Graveyard Hag."

The goddess beamed at her, revealing all of seven teeth. "Aren't you the clever boots," she said with pleasure. "I'd heard that you were, but 'Count on it,' I told Gainel—that's the Dream King to you, dearie. 'Count on it,' I told him, 'they're always *said* to be quick, but it turns out to be all smoke.' No," she cautioned as Aly took a step back. "Don't run off. That wouldn't be polite, and I'm not done with you."

Aly could not move her foot—either foot, for that matter. Or her hips. Or her arms. She tried to open her mouth to scream and failed.

The goddess nodded. "Every bit as clever as my cousin says. Mind, I don't want to ruin Kyprioth's game. I just want to tweak it a little. Besides, I'm doing a favor for one of my own lads. Such a good one, he is. He built me a shrine—paid for it with his own money, too! One good turn deserves another, and he's in love."

Aly released the breath she'd meant to use to scream through her nose. Suddenly her mouth could move again. She could talk, but she also knew better than to try to call out. "May I ask questions?" she inquired. "Since I'm going to be here for a time?"

The Hag chuckled. "Oh, you are a treat. Well brought-up, even with a mother who's a violent bumpkin."

Aly ignored the insult. Her mother had been called worse things. "This worshipper must be very devoted, to bring you all the way here. Surely it would be easier to favor him at home. Unless you have other business?" She kept her voice light and sweet.

"It's more personal satisfaction than business," replied the Hag. "Normally I could give duckmole's dung about the Isles, but Kyprioth is annoying even for a god. He gloats. He's been saying we lesser tricksters couldn't fool Mithros and the Goddess . . . as if we don't know what we're doing. He deserves a lesson." She seized another firefly. "And I can do my worshipper a favor while I'm at it."

Aly raised an eyebrow.

The Hag grinned. "Besides, I owe Kyprioth. He's gotten the better of me twice. I mean to repay him."

Aly picked through the Hag's words. Aunt Daine *said* gods talk in riddles, she grumbled to herself.

The Hag replied aloud. "Naturally," she said with glee. "You mortals are so adorable with your faces all screwed up when you're trying to think."

Carthaki, Aly thought, shooting a glare at the Hag. A worshipper from there . . . "Zaimid Hetnim?" she asked.

The Hag chortled. "Bright girl." She stood, dusting off her hands. "By the time you can free yourself, my boy will have his heart's desire, Kyprioth will have his comeuppance, and *you* will have some work to do." Wriggling her fingers in a mockery of a wave, she vanished.

Aly didn't like it, but there was nothing she could do. The Graveyard Hag had sealed her lips. Her mind raced frantically. Stupid! she told herself over and over. Stupid, over-confident, *blind* . . . Why did I not see it coming with Sarai and Zaimid? Sarai's not good at hiding how she feels. I've been trained to spot intrigue in every form! But no, I was smug about Topabaw and creating more spies. And while I was being so festering clever, a girl in love cooked something up right under my nose!

She berated herself without mercy, remembering clues that should have been obvious, including Sarai's conviction that nothing in the Isles would ever change for the better. She remembered how quiet Sarai had been after Imajane's offer of marriage to the boy king. Despite everything her advisors told her, Sarai had appeared convinced that she would have to marry her royal cousin.

At last the spell that locked Aly into place began to thaw, like ice on a sunlit pond. It faded bit by bit, driving Aly half insane as she waited. Somewhere, she knew, the Graveyard Hag was enjoying her frustration. At last she was free.

"This bad?" asked Trick, once he and Secret were also able to move again. They settled back into their bead necklace shapes, with the two connecting medallions that were their heads on each of Aly's shoulders.

"It's not good," Aly told the darkings. "And I am an idiot." She didn't even bother with the servants' gallery, but ran into the ballroom itself. When she stumbled to a halt at the room's center, everyone turned to stare. Aly ignored them, scanning every face in the room. Sarai and Zaimid were not there.

She ran into the servants' gallery. Zaimid's attendant was gone. She told herself not to panic yet, then bolted outside. As the Fonfalas' daughter, the duchess had been given her own pavilion separate from the main house, where she and her stepdaughters slept with their attendants. Petranne and Elsren shared the nursery in the main house with the other children. Aly knew that Boulaj, Pembery, and Dorilize would be in the household infirmary, wherever that was.

She raced to the duchess's pavilion. Inside, a lamp was provided for the Balitang ladies' return. In the flickering light it cast, Aly could see that Sarai's trunk—the one into which the vexed Boulaj had simply thrown all her mistress's personal items as Sarai kept changing her mind—was gone. Moreover, there was a folded and sealed document on the duchess's bed. Aly went to look at it. The note was addressed, in Sarai's curling writing, to *Winna and Dove.*

Aly was sitting on the pavilion steps when the duchess arrived. "Aly, what's going on?" she asked, her sweet, deep voice concerned. "Papa said you burst into the ballroom looking as if the dead marched on your spine. . . ."

Aly held out the letter Sarai had left.

"Oh, no," said Winnamine. She hurried into the pavilion without taking the letter. Aly stayed where she was.

Soon more footsteps slapped the flagstone path. This time it was Dove. "Aly, have you seen Sarai? Ferdy Tomang is searching all through the main house, and he's saying he'll kill Zaimid or Druce or Vedec if they've sneaked away with her—" She cut herself off abruptly. "Aly?"

Winnamine walked onto the steps and sat next to Aly. "She left a letter for us," she told Dove, and broke the seal. Using the light from the torches that marked the pavilion's entrance, she read the letter to the girls in a leaden voice.

"*Dearest Winna and Dove,*

"*I can only beg your forgiveness a thousand times for running away like this.*"

Dove sat in the walkway with a thump, ignoring the damage to her clothes.

"*I am so very sorry. By the time you read this Zaimid and I will be sailing for Carthak. There is a ship waiting for us at Moriji Cove.*"

The cove lay five miles downhill from the estate. It was a favored raka smuggling port because it was not readily visible.

The duchess continued.

"*I can no longer watch as good people are taxed into poverty, jailed, beaten, or killed. It makes me sick, the never-ending executions, the despair, and the fear. Neither will I marry a boy thirteen years younger than me, to be a puppet for the regents. I know you cannot fight them and win, and once they have won, I would not give a copper's chance in a volcano for Dunevon or for me to live to old age.*

"*Please tell Dorilize, Pembery, Boulaj, Rihani, and Junai that I am sorry I made them sick. The herbs will wear off by dawn. I knew they would stop me.*

"*I would have done none of this if I were not truly, deeply in love. Zaimid is kind and gentle. When people are hurt, he helps them. We can't bear to be parted. And neither of us can stand to see more people hurt where we can do so little. With him I can have the life I want, raising horses and our children, and helping him to build hospitals when he takes his post as the emperor's healer. Like me, he begs your forgiveness for our stealing away. I will write more when we are settled. Please try to understand, I did not do this on impulse. I have known I loved him for some weeks. The thought of marrying a child cousin was bad in itself, but it was so much worse when I compared it to marriage with Zaimid.*

"*I love both you so much, and Elsren and Petranne, too. I hope that you will wish me well. Zaimid has already said that our first boy will be named Mequen.*

"*Your devoted Sarai*"

13

A CHANGE OF PLANS

After hearing Sarai's letter no one had anything to say. They just sat in silent gloom on the steps.

Finally Nuritin came to see where they were. "What is it?" she asked sharply when she saw their faces. Mutely, Winnamine handed the letter to her.

While Nuritin read, Aly walked around the guesthouse to inspect it for listening spells. She found only a number of strong charms to keep any listening spell from taking hold there. There were similar protections all over the Fonfala buildings and grounds. The Fonfalas, she decided, loved their privacy. When she finished her search, she stopped herself from going to tell the ladies it was safe to speak here. She had been too overconfident for too long. Carefully Aly went over the place again. She even sent the darkings under the house to check there. When they returned to report they had found nothing, Aly then went back to find the ladies.

"There are no listening spells here that I could see," she told them numbly, sitting next to Dove. "And no spies."

Nuritin, rereading the letter, looked up with a frown. "What makes you certain of that?" she demanded sharply.

"She knows, Aunt," Winnamine replied, weariness in her voice and face.

"Hmph," Nuritin said, still glaring at the seated Aly. Aly propped her chin on her hand and returned the old lady's look. She was tired and depressed. She was not about to stand because Nuritin thought her a servant. It was the older woman who looked away.

"Silly chit," Nuritin commented, giving the letter back to the duchess. "She obviously didn't believe that she could keep Imajane at bay on this marriage." Nuritin looked at Dove. "You will not make that mistake, though, will you?"

Dove blinked at her, startled. "Will the regents offer it to me? They're probably going to think Sarai as good as slapped their faces, doing this. I'm thinking maybe we should run for Tanair before they arrest us all."

"They dare not," Nuritin told her flatly. "You girls are too popular. Imajane admitted as much when she offered the marriage to Sarai in the first place. She needs to offer it to you, and you must do as we advised Sarai." Nuritin's abrupt smile was thin and frosty. "You're vexed that she didn't tell you," she added, glancing at Dove and Winnamine. "She did it to me, too, and I was as much her chaperon as anyone. She planned this under our very noses, the minx. She hid her interest in the Carthaki by including him with all her young men. She was good at slipping off for private assignations before you went to Tanair. Obviously she got better at it."

Aly, thinking of the raka and what this would do to them, shifted impatiently. It drew Nuritin's attention.

"And she gave *you* the slip, watchful as you are," Nuritin said, that smile razor sharp. "That must gall you." When Aly, Dove, and Winnamine all stared at her, Nuritin rolled her eyes. "Even apart from mysterious hints about this one being more than just a maid, I've noticed how very attentive she is. I don't know what she's up to, and I don't want to. When I must know, I'm sure one of you will tell me. For the time being, it's important that we deal with this, first here and then at home. The regents will have the news by the time we get there, if that new spymaster knows the least bit about what he does. It will still be important to let them know in person. They will be outraged for a day or two, and then they will make their offer to our Dove. Mope about here if you like, but I am going to bed, and I advise you to do the same. There is nothing more to be done tonight." She looked at Aly. "Since Sarai made certain that Dorilize would be in no condition to stop her, I require you to undress me." Standing, she shook out her skirts and marched inside.

Aly stared back at her with admiration. "I want to be *her* when I grow up," she murmured.

"Let's work on growing up first," Dove replied, her voice and face glum. "Then you can be anyone you like."

"Nuritin is right," said Winnamine, exhaustion in her voice. There were tears rolling down her cheeks. She appeared not to notice them. "It's too late to do anything but sleep."

Aly passed a handkerchief to her. When the duchess stared at it, not understanding, Dove touched her cheek. Winnamine angrily swiped her eyes. "I thought she trusted us," she whispered. "I thought she trusted *me*."

"Except that you would have asked her to do her duty by her family and country," Dove said gently, her own eyes full. She did not cry, though. "You would have made her feel she was selfish to want her own freedom and happiness when others depend on her for so much. And you would be right. She knew that, too. So she ran away."

"Girl!" an imperious voice called from inside the house. Aly scrambled to her feet and went to assist Nuritin, thinking that Dove had the right of it. As she prepared all three ladies for bed, she berated herself. She had been over-confident for the last time, she hoped. She would pay for that. Only she and Dove knew that the raka and Kyprioth were not going to take Sarai's elopement well.

The duchess asked her to let the family know that Sarai, too, had felt unwell and had left the party early. Aly returned after delivering her message, but she did not sleep. Her mother had a rich vocabulary of curses, as did her father. Aly used all of those words first on herself, then on Sarai and Zaimid. Trick and Secret, understanding that she needed to think, kept quiet, though they hummed gently against her skin, offering comfort.

When she ran out of bad words, Aly decided that the joke was on her. Only a year before, she might have helped Sarai to marry her love rather than be trapped in a political life. At the very least, she would have loved Sarai's boldness. Aly's mother had done as Sarai had, chosen the life she wanted over the life that was expected of her. My, how I've changed, Aly thought ruefully. These days I *care* about duty to those who look to one to lead. These days I care less about fun and more about work. Though at least *my* work is fun.

Shaking her head, she began to prepare for the consequences of this night. Kyprioth had not appeared, which meant that he was still arranging for the theft of the sun and the moon shields. She would need all her arguments marshaled when the god returned, and when they brought the news to the raka conspirators. She wondered if the conspiracy wasn't to blame for not telling Sarai what they intended. Then Aly shook her head. If Sarai had known of their plans, she would have fled all the sooner.

The next morning Winnamine sent Aly for the ladies' maids. They had recovered, but they could tell that something wasn't right. "It's for Her Grace to tell you," Aly said, leading them to the duchess.

As they helped their mistresses dress for the day, Winnamine explained what Sarai had done. For a moment, hardy Boulaj looked as if she might faint.

"She dosed you," Dove said quickly. "She dosed all of you. She said so in her letter."

"She must have put it in the sambal," Aly put in. "Boulaj, remember? She tasted the sambal and said she thought it might be off, but she couldn't tell, and neither did you. That's when she added the herbs to make your bowels run. She knew she'd get most of you, because Chenaol makes dreadful sambal, and you all eat it at every house we visit."

"How did she escape Aly?" demanded Pembery, her voice sharp but her hands steady as she pinned up Winnamine's hair. "Aly was supposed to be looking after our ladies." Dorilize, doing up Nuritin's buttons, shook her head.

"Aly was lured away and locked up," Aly said absently, her mind churning with plans and questions. "If one of the Fonfalas' maids hadn't needed a night-shirt for a guest who forgot his, I might still be locked up." She wasn't about to mention the Graveyard Hag, not yet. She had already concocted a story for those who might not accept the truth. "One of Zaimid's servants brought a message saying you wanted to tell me something, Pembery. I knew you were sick, so I went running, and that's when they grabbed me." Even the hint that she might have been involved would stop Pembery from digging further into the mess they were in.

Winnamine shook her head. "We must put our best face on this," she told the maids. "To our men-at-arms and the rest of the staff. The thing is done. We all knew Sarai was more interested in her heart than politics." She got to her feet. "Let's show proud faces to the world, shall we? It will take some time to live down this shame. Give no one the satisfaction of seeing we are hurt. I must explain things to my parents, and let the rest of our people know we are leaving today rather than tomorrow."

As soon as she had left the house, Pembery and Boulaj pulled Aly out onto the porch. "How could you let this happen?" cried Pembery, tears running down her cheeks.

Boulaj, too, wept. "Can the god—?"

Aly put her finger to her lips. She motioned toward the house: Nuritin and Dorilize were within earshot.

Dove had followed them outside. "We can talk at home. Why don't you two start packing up, please?"

The women moved to obey as Dove turned to Aly. "Walk with me. I don't have that much to pack."

They strolled out into the misty air. It was cool. Howler monkeys pro-claimed their territories; crows shrieked in reply. Aly walked at Dove's elbow without mentioning that her feet were soaked. Sandals were inadequate cover for early morning grass. They halted by one of the many streams that crossed the property. Aly looked around. There was no sign of magic anywhere.

"They act like it's the end of everything." Dove's soft voice sounded ten-tative.

"But it isn't," Aly replied. "It could be the beginning."

Dove looked at her, eyes ablaze in her small face. "How may I convince them?"

Aly thought about it. "Work," she said at last. "You're farming, that's all. The ground's been tilled and prepared and it's ready to take the seed. If one batch of seed gets moldy, we find another batch."

"One less vulnerable to mold," added Dove. "Will you help me?"

Aly held out her hand. Dove clasped her by the forearm. After a moment's hesitation, Aly clasped Dove's forearm.

"I don't need a maid," Dove said. "I need a friend."

For a moment Aly found it hard to breathe. It had been hard to get passionate about Sarai as queen, as the raka had been. But Dove . . . Dove was no stranger to emotion, Aly knew, but it didn't govern her as it did Sarai. Dove understood duty to those who needed her. Dove could be trusted to keep a clear head. She was one of the most ferociously intelligent people Aly had ever known. Aly had seen it the night before: they must put Dove on the throne.

"I will be your friend until the end of time," she told the younger girl.

The ride home was silent. All along the way the raka who came to watch them pass saw that Sarai was not with them. Aly studied their faces, her mind busy. At the city's outskirts she saw members of her pack, as uneasy as the bystanders over Sarai's absence. To each query they made by way of hand-signal Aly replied: *When we meet at home.* She didn't want word getting to Balitang House ahead of them.

While Dove and Aly had settled the focus of the rebellion between them, Aly knew some raka conspirators would require persuasion. They were used to seeing Dove as Sarai's intelligent, bookish, quiet sister, a fine counselor, but not the kind of person who could rally the passions of her followers. Dove would have to show them they were mistaken.

When they reached Middle Town, Dove greeted many soldiers at the checkpoints by name. Vendors and shopkeepers waved and called to her; Dove waved back with a smile. Aly was instantly reassured. Dove *did* have charm. It was quieter and less flashy than Sarai's, but it was there. Aly also thought that once the people remembered they still had one twice-royal girl, their first concern would be to put her on a throne. Afterward they could fret about her ability to win the crowd.

As the riders clattered into the courtyard before the house, servants ran to take their horses. Ulasim trotted out the front door, bowed to the duchess, then pulled Aly down until she could hear his whisper: "Nawat and his crows got every one of the raka who rose on that Ikang estate off the island. Every one! He and his crows drove the army mad while our people made it to the escape ships. More than two hundred raka, safe thanks to him."

Aly's heart lifted at the sound of Nawat's name. She nodded her thanks and dismounted as Ulasim moved clear of her. Now that he'd unburdened himself, the big footman noticed there was something wrong with their company. He took the sleeping Petranne as Rihani handed the girl to him, but his eyes were busy reading their faces.

Suddenly they widened. Aly knew he'd realized who was missing.

"Ulasim," the duchess called. He went over to her, still holding Petranne in his arms. "Open the ballroom and summon the household," Winnamine ordered quietly. "Lock the gates and bring all the household in, even those who are off duty. We have news that everyone must hear."

It was not long before all but Rihani, Petranne, and Elsren, who had gone to the nursery, had assembled in the great ballroom. Aly stood just below the dais where Winnamine, Nuritin, and Dove sat, waiting. From the faces of the household she could tell they knew only that Sarai had not come home with the duchess. The maids and guards who had been at the Fonfalas' had told them nothing, leaving it in their mistress's hands.

Maybe, thought Aly, they were afraid of how people would react.

Everyone stared at the duchess, their eyes flicking from her to Dove to Nuritin and back.

"Good morning," Winnamine said. "Forgive me if I am blunt, but I know of no easy way to say this. Lady Saraiyu eloped from my father's party last night with Master Zaimid Hetnim, the Carthaki." She smiled grimly. "We shall be apologizing for what she has done for months, I think. Do not blame our maids for not looking after her. Sarai made arrangements to get them all out of the way. No one knew until Sarai was long gone."

The members of the conspiracy within the household stared at Aly with disbelief or outright suspicion. Aly made a note to herself to ask Ulasim to let them know about the Graveyard Hag. The conspirators had to learn Aly had not betrayed them, or she would find herself in very hot water.

Winnamine continued, "On Sarai's behalf I apologize to you. We must be happy for her. She wrote that she loves Master Zaimid. While we could have wished her to love closer to home, we had no choice in the matter. She was very sure to make it look as if Zaimid meant no more than her other suitors."

The duchess rubbed her temples. "We must write to people, explaining what has happened. Ulasim, I will require every message carrier you can spare, and a footman in livery to take a letter to the regents." She noticed that the servants were disturbed by this move and explained, "Lord Elsren is in the line of inheritance, and our girls are of royal blood. Their behavior is a matter of state." She smoothed her skirts with her hands. "Thank you all again. I am sorry to bring such tidings. Those of you on gate duty, see if any visitors will return another day. Only admit them if they insist."

Slowly, murmuring to one another, the household dispersed. Dove watched them go, then hugged Winnamine. "I'll help you with those notes, Winna," she said.

"As will Jesi and I," Nuritin said.

Dove looked at Aly. "I believe we'll need tea in the ladies' study."

Chenaol grabbed Aly in the kitchen, but Aly shook her head. "Tonight," she said quietly. "Things will be a shambles today. We'll have company as soon as word gets out."

Chenaol gasped. "Gods, yes. Here." She stocked a tray with fruits, cheeses, flatbreads, and luarin-style sweet biscuits. "I'll need an assistant cook if all this entertaining keeps going on," she muttered. Thrusting the tray of food into Aly's hands, she said, "I'll send tea as soon as it's ready. Start heating oil," she ordered the kitchen maids. "Get out what bean curd we have. I'll need three of you to go to market, and if anyone so much as *breathes* word of what's happened, I'll filet her, understand?"

The footman returned from the palace around noon with a note granting the duchess a private audience the next morning, when Elsren went to attend Dunevon. In the afternoon the Balitang cousins came on the footman's heels, followed by Countess Tomang still dressed in riding clothes: she too had left the Fonfalas' early. She demanded a private conversation, but did not stay long. Aly, listening outside the Teak Sitting Room, heard Ferdy's mother shout that Sarai had made a monkey of her son, and that blood would tell. Winnamine did not answer. Aly knew the duchess probably agreed.

Nobody else came after the Countess and the Balitang relatives left. Apparently no one wished further contact at Balitang House until they knew how the regents would jump. Winnamine and Dove wandered through the rooms, talking to servants and slaves, showing themselves as steady and unshaken. Aly unpacked Dove's things, took her dirty clothes to the house laundry, and retired to her office to work. Two days of reports awaited her, as well as the darkings' news from the palace.

"Trick," she asked, "what do you hear from the regents?" Instantly her bead necklace turned into Trick and Secret, who stuck heads out of their blobby bodies to look at Aly.

"Yesterday morning regents in private audience chamber when head of shipwright guild ask for talk," Trick informed her. "He makes ships for king and navy. He is angry because man sail little ship to royal dock and show him a paper with Rubinyan order, saying put little ship there. He say little ship is for king's birthday. Guildmaster say guild and navy should make little ship for king. Rubinyan say he have man who build little ship for *his* birthday make one for king, so man feel useful. Rubinyan writes paper so navy shipwrights build six more ships right away and get three ready to sail. He says shipwrights here needed for serious work to send ships to kill rebels. Guildmaster go away.

"Then messenger come. Messenger say slaves on Rittevon estate, north Gempang, kill overseer, then kill Imajane's old nursemaid. Imajane very angry and say, kill all slaves on estates. Rubinyan sends order to army fort in north Gempang to kill slaves."

On and on the reports went. Aly realized that more estates throughout the Isles were experiencing violent upheavals. She set pins with red ribbons at every spot on the map where Trick reported trouble. They showed her a deliberate pattern. The rebellions began on the estates nearest the sea, closest to the lands and towns that would be the first on the island to get help by water.

Army fortresses had also come under attack, even if the mischief was as subtle as the disappearance of patrols into the jungles, or the constant illness of the men.

Among the reports passed on by Trick were appeals for help by landowners. The palace darkings had also heard Rubinyan and Imajane talk about how many remaining soldiers, cavalry, pikemen, fighting ships, and sailors they had. They had sent companies of soldiers and cavalry all over the Isles to back up troops already assigned there. Their reserves of men in the city were dwindling.

Aly saw it, as plain as day: *This* was Ulasim's grand plan. Bit by bit, the rebels were drawing protection away from Rajmuat. Ulasim had not lied when he'd said he had not ordered the first uprisings. But would I see a lie on him if I asked him about that now? Aly wondered. He knew his people. He may even have sent agents last year to whisper ideas to the raka who lived closest to the coast, where ships could unload men and supplies.

Rittevon Lanman had demoralized the raka three centuries ago. He had overrun the most powerful of the Isles, then captured Rajmuat, already torn by bloodshed in the royal family's never-ending feuds. He'd executed the queen and her remaining family. Then the still-feuding raka had come down from the inner lands to be fought, killed, or enslaved. Now the reverse was happening. The inland raka were drawing the Rittevon forces up onto their ground, taking them into the jungles. It was so devious that, unless Rubinyan and Imajane had grown up around maps of trouble spots, they might not realize how thinly they were spread. This was no accident. This was planned by Ulasim.

Aly was silent, awed. Years of preparations by Ulasim's predecessors had gone into the picture she saw here. They and he had built it up bit by bit, deciding who needed instruction, and who could be trusted to exercise their ancient hatreds of the invaders at just the right time.

She wanted to help. Someone should point out to Ulasim that more damage would result if the Crown's troops were weakened by hunger. An attack was a thing the enemy was prepared for. People driving wagons filled with supplies that arrived on schedule were another matter. It could be arranged for some of those supplies to be drugged, or for some of those wagons never to arrive at their destination.

What could she find for her own people to work on? The army was not the only group with storehouses. Wealthy merchants kept their goods in warehouses in Downwind and Market Town. After the attacks on the fortresses and on the slave docks, the waterfront and the royal and naval docks were under extra guard, but the storehouses were not.

It was late afternoon when the darking Bean reported the reaction of the court to news of Sarai's elopement. After Trick finished passing on Bean's report, the supper bell rang. Nuritin, Winnamine, and Dove went to the nursery to eat with Elsren and Petranne and try to explain what had happened. After the children were put to bed, Nuritin and Winnamine retired to their own rooms. Dove and Aly went nervously down to the conspiracy's meeting room.

Everyone was there: Ulasim, Fesgao, Ysul, Chenaol, Quedanga, Ochobu. As soon as Dove and Aly came in, Ochobu threw up the room's magical shields and glared at Aly. "How could you let this happen?" the old mage demanded. "You're the clever one, you're the spy—"

Aly shook her head. She was in no mood to be verbally whipped. "I was unable to stop it," she said. "You see, I had a bigger problem. The Graveyard Hag paid us a visit. She's the patron goddess of Carthak—of Zaimid. And while she's fun in a perverse way, she is no easier to cross than your Bright One. When was the last time *you* argued with a god?"

Ochobu scowled. "A likely story!"

Reproachfully Aly said, "You have forgotten I like to tell lies that will be believed."

Chenaol's mouth twitched in spite of her distress. "She's got you there," she told Ochobu.

Aly continued, "Kyprioth got the better of the Hag on a few occasions. She wished to pay him back. And yes, I made an immense mistake." She leaned against the wall, taking care not to smash her darking necklace. "I was so busy watching the world outside the house, I neglected to keep an eye on things inside. Can you possibly kick me harder than I'm kicking myself?"

"We have to get her back," said Chenaol. "Some of us will have to go after her. And at least one should be a mage, in case this Graveyard Hag is hanging around."

Ysul hand-signed, *You can't chase Sarai to Carthak. We don't have people or time.*

From her chair Dove said quietly, "Sarai isn't the only one with royal blood from both sides of the family."

Aly saw them all turn to look at Dove, and then her world went black. Aly was whipped through an immense, howling darkness. Trick and Secret keened in her ears. Everything around her roared, until she landed on her behind with a painful thump.

She sat in a pavilion house that looked bigger than the palace. She could have sworn there were clouds among the ceiling beams. Jewelry dangled along the walls in crazy ranks. Enormous pillows were strewn over piles of gaudy rugs. A number of large crows pecked through the contents of dishes on the floor.

Beyond them stood Kyprioth, his dark eyes blazing. "What have you done?" shrieked the god. Aly clapped her hands to her ears. He roared, "It's all ruined! Ruined! You bumbling, blind, oblivious *mortal!* How could you let her slip away? I leave to do one little thing and I return to find everything in ruins. *Ruins!*"

Thunder rolled in the ceiling clouds. Lightning bolts raced over the god's jewelry.

"I thought you'd be gone for a while," Aly remarked, as if this were another casual talk between them. "I thought you were preparing a trick of your own."

Kyprioth glared at her. An invisible force pressed Aly against the nearest marble column. "Give me one good reason why I shouldn't cook you where you stand," the god snarled. "You, the clever one, and you can't keep an eye on one lone, lovesick chit!"

"The way you're carrying on, I'd say you were in love with her yourself," Aly said lightly, her stomach in knots. "Isn't she a little young for you? Not to mention boring, but that could just be me."

"You mock me," he said, coming closer. He'd begun to blaze with light.

The crows suddenly rose in a thunder of wings. They glided through the air until they landed beside Aly.

"It's not like you're making it easy to have a proper conversation," Aly pointed out to Kyprioth as she shaded her eyes. What could she do but talk back? He was a great god and could do as he wished with her. If she was going to die, she wanted to die arguing. "Honestly, Kyprioth, how long would it have been before that lovesick girl lost the throne you schemed so to get her? How long before she got angry and insulted someone, or married the wrong noble and started the Haiming rebellions all over again?"

He pointed at her. "That's it. You die."

Aly forced a merry tone into her voice as she replied, "You'll lose your wager with the crows. You never said the bet didn't count if it was *you* who killed me, so you'd still have to pay them. And I know you hate to lose wagers."

"This is what I wagered," Kyprioth snapped.

A long necklace detached itself from a wall and flew at Aly to strike her full in the face. She yelped in pain and pulled it off. Blood dripped from a number of cuts on her skin. She had never seen anything uglier. It was made of gold and silver beads, gem beads in all colors, and gaudy glass beads. "You mean to tell me the crows were helping me for *this?*" she demanded, indignant.

One of the crows walked over and grabbed the dangling end in its beak. To Aly's surprise, little Secret rolled down her arm and wrapped around the end of the necklace that Aly still held, securing it to her hand. "Not yours," Secret told the crow. "You didn't win it. Help her."

The crow cocked its head, looking the darking over. Trick flowed down Aly to cover Secret and twine itself with a foot of the necklace beyond Aly's hold.

Dropping the necklace, the crow turned to look at Kyprioth. "How can she fail if she was tricked in turn?" the crow demanded sharply. Somehow it sounded male. "Ask the Graveyard Hag where she was that night the girl ran away."

"The—" Kyprioth said, his face dark with fury. There was a pop. Air rushed to fill the space he had occupied.

Aly knelt so she could be face to face with her defender. "Thank you."

Another crow walked over to take a lock of her hair in its beak. It gave a hard tug, making Aly wince, then let go. "Save your thanks," the crow advised in a voice that was the female version of the male crow's. "You're not back in the Mortal Realms yet."

Aly had guessed she was in the Divine Realms. She'd never heard of a human dwelling with clouds under the roof beams. "So you're the Dawn Crow and Sky, the crow goddess?" she asked. "But what are they?" She pointed to the others.

"The first flock," Sky explained. "I must say, I see why our cousin Nawat feels so strongly about you."

"Oddly," said the Dawn Crow.

"*Strongly,*" retorted Sky, fixing her mate with a beady stare. When he did not answer, she told Aly, "Not every mortal could talk back to Kyprioth when he's in one of his tempers. His nasty streak is *very* nasty."

"I've certainly enjoyed myself with what he's shown me so far," replied Aly.

"I do not approve of one of our kind changing his shape just for a mortal," the Dawn Crow remarked stiffly.

"You must ask Nawat if he cares," replied Sky. "He is free as all of us are free, to fly as he wishes and to steal as he may."

Aly smiled and ducked her head, suddenly shy. "I miss him," she found herself admitting to the goddess. "He—"

The air boomed with a sound that was hard to recognize at first: an old woman's laughter. It made the pavilion house shudder. It was followed by an immense shriek of rage. Both sounds grew fainter. Shivering, Aly gave the necklace a fresh inspection. "Kyprioth wagered my *life* on this thing," she said, aghast. "I've probably seen uglier, but the shock has driven them from my mind."

"Actually, he wagered one of them for each of us who helps you," Sky explained. "They are very sparkly and colorful. They are well worth our mortal cousins' efforts."

Aly looked at the necklace. "If you say so, goddess, then I must believe you," she said reluctantly. "It certainly is, um, sparkly."

Time passed. She itched to get back to the raka, but she was stuck in Kyprioth's home until he returned. The crows might have had the power to send her, but they told her it would be rude. She was Kyprioth's guest, which meant it was up to Kyprioth to send her back.

She talked with the crows a while, then took a sudden nap as all the fright she'd felt in dealing with the god came home to her. When she woke, he was still nowhere to be seen. She explored the house, ignoring the part of herself that constantly reminded her time was passing. The crows brought her berries and a melon, and told her stories of all the other trickster gods in the Divine Realms.

Aly refused to think that she might not return home. If she didn't, then she didn't, but in the meantime, why waste so many uninterrupted hours with no one to call on her and no reports to read? Planning what she would set in motion for Dove, she dozed off again.

When she woke, Kyprioth sat next to her. "You were right," he told her, back to his cheerful self. "The old girl admitted to it readily enough. And I managed to remind her who is the boss Trickster around here. So. Do you really think Dove can win the people?"

"I think at the moment a howler monkey could win the people," Aly said. "They will rally to Dove because she is what they have. And they will be glad they did so, because she is everything Sarai is not, from cool head to cool heart. And she knows how to talk to different kinds of people so they feel she thinks of them as equals. Sarai's friends were all that young noble crowd. Dove is friends with beggars and street vendors, spice merchants, cobblers, booksellers, the royal astronomer, priests, priestesses. . . . Even that milky luarin conspiracy group that's been meeting with Winnamine and Nuritin listens to her ideas with respect."

Kyprioth's black eyes caught and held Aly's. "You've sworn to her already," he remarked, his crisp voice soft.

"Oh, stop that," Aly said crossly. "What's important is that Dove will do the thing right. She'll not only get your Isles back for you, but she'll *keep* them for you."

Kyprioth patted her cheek. "I would have been very sorry to have killed you. You are the most amusing mortal I've dealt with in ages."

Aly gave him her sweetest smile. "All that flattery is going straight to my happy, unkilled head. May I go back? I've left Dove there all alone, convincing the raka she will be worth their support."

"Cheer up," he ordered. "She convinced them, without you. And you have convinced me. We shall continue. And it is time for you to . . ."

"I think she's waking up." That sounded like Boulaj. "Where's that pitcher of water? Wayan, go tell Lady Dove and Her Grace that Aly is coming around."

Aly heard bare, running feet, then the gurgle of water poured into a cup. She fought to open her eyes. "The god had me," she croaked.

Arms helped Aly to sit up: Chenaol's. "Drink," the cook ordered, putting the cup to Aly's lips.

Aly drank, thinking, The last time the god took me, it was Nawat who was there when I woke. She blinked rapidly to keep her eyes from watering.

"How long?" she asked.

"Three days, but they've been quiet ones," Chenaol said as Boulaj poured a second cup of water.

Aly looked at the older woman. There was a smug tone to her voice and a smug smile on her lips. "Quiet?" she asked.

"It was Atisa's idea," Boulaj explained. "She said if folk were going to be unhappy about Sarai's departure, they should be allowed to be unhappy. Quietly. Very quietly."

"Stop dancing," Aly said crossly, struggling to sit up. She was in Ochobu's infirmary, on one of the low beds. "What did Atisa suggest?"

"Shutdown," said Chenaol. "Except for the luarin households, most luarin businesses, and the palace, the entire city has stopped work and has gone indoors. It took us a day to get the word out, and it started at dawn yesterday morning. It's a beautiful thing, and there are too many people in it for the regents to kill everyone."

Aly chewed a hangnail. "But what if the Crown holds reprisals? All they have to do is see what businesses and houses are open and which are not."

"That is a risk they must weigh." Ochobu stood in the open doorway. "But the regents must first consider where to exact vengeance first. The royal governors of Imahyn and Jerykun Isles are dead, shot near their homes with crow-fletched arrows."

Chenaol winked at Aly. "What do you call four dead governors?"

Aly blinked at her, her mind still trying to catch up. "I don't know."

Chenaol grinned a wolf's grin, all teeth and predatory intent. "A good start."

14

OOVE AMONG THE NOBLES

Aly woke in the dark, with a dark shape seated by her bed. She sat up with a gasp. She groped for knives—taken from her when she was put to bed in the infirmary—as she adjusted her Sight. The figure got up and opened the door to the torchlit hall, but Aly had already identified her visitor: Nuritin Balitang. Aly waited as the lady took a lamp from a niche in the hall. She placed it on the table at Aly's bedside and resumed her seat.

"You needn't rise," the old woman said. "I just wanted us to have a quiet chat. The family and the servants are at their supper."

It's not that late after all, Aly thought. It's just there are no windows in here, so no one can spy on Ochobu and Ysul. "I'm at your ladyship's service," she said cautiously.

"Winnamine says that your service is in fact the god's. Mithros's." Nuritin's eyes were sharp as she looked at Aly. "She has also said you know all our secrets. Is this true?"

Aly shook her head. Nuritin was every bit as sharp as the duchess, Dove, or Ulasim. "I'm only one person, my lady," she replied. "I couldn't possibly know *everyone's* secrets. It's a big household. I do know some."

"Don't toy with me, girl. I am out of patience with anything that crosses my path after Sarai's disgraceful behavior—which you *also* appear not to have known about."

Aly hung her head. "I'm not very happy with that myself, my lady. I would have stopped her, had I known." Would I? she wondered briefly. Really, would I?

Nuritin continued. "Do you know what is discussed in the Teak Sitting Room?"

Aly scratched her nose, considering. Let's see how far she wants to play this, she told herself. To Nuritin she said, "I do, my lady."

"And you have told . . . ?"

"No one," replied Aly. "Forgive my saying so, but it's not much of a conspiracy. It's more a complaint society."

Nuritin pursed her lips. "It is hard to get comfortable people to do anything when it might cost them their comfort. And only a fool takes on the Crown with a handful of allies."

Aly thought carefully. At last she remarked, "There might be allies, somewhere. It would help if your complaint society members showed they were earnest in some way."

Nuritin raised her brows with elegance. "And I suppose you have a suggestion?"

Aly shook her head. "Even chosen by the god, I am just a servant girl. But, do you know, with the city and the people so unsettled, your friends might consider bringing more men-at-arms, or even mages, to Rajmuat. Finding housing for them, and so on. If the men had extra weapons, they might even bring those. Just in case."

She waited, looking at the lady's face. Aly was taking a risk, but it was time to take a few. It was time for the luarin conspiracy to prove if it had what it took to be proper allies to the raka when the time came. There was a darking in Tomang House. Aly would ensure that darkings reached the other conspirators' houses. If she had guessed wrong about Nuritin or her friends, the darkings would warn her in time to stop the luarin from reporting to the regents.

It was an acceptable risk, Aly decided. Having listened as Feather passed on what was said by the luarin conspiracy, Aly knew they were frightened and angry. The regents should not have killed Topabaw without a trial. Duke Lohearn Mantawu had been a luarin noble before he was the spymaster Topabaw. Imajane and Rubinyan had killed yet another member of the class that would normally support them, without even a pretense at legality. That, the executions of the Ibaduns, and Nomru's arrest had told the luarin nobility that their bloodlines no longer made them safe. If the regents could be pushed to do something even more extreme, the luarin conspirators might throw their lot in with the raka. And Aly knew Dove would be able to talk the raka into joining hands with these uneasy nobles, if the raka accepted her in place of Sarai.

"You have given me food for thought," Nuritin said at last, getting to her feet. "I will broach the matter with my fellows, without mentioning you."

"Oh, please don't," Aly begged, glowing with false sincerity. "Thank you ever so, my lady. Such great persons would not care for ideas from the likes of me."

"You are an impertinent minx," Nuritin said drily. "Take care someone does not shorten that clever tongue."

"I do, all the time," Aly assured her earnestly.

Shaking her head, Nuritin left the infirmary, shutting the door behind her. Someone had left fresh clothes on the bench at the foot of Aly's bed. Her bead necklace lay on top of them. As soon as Nuritin had gone, Trick and Secret thrust heads up from their large connecting bead disguises. Aly set them gently on the bed, kissing each tiny head quickly.

"Thank you for helping me up there," she told the darkings softly as she put on a breast band and began to wrap her sarong around her body. She checked the seams. All of her thin, needle-like knives were in place.

"Had to help," Trick said. "Crow gods annoying."

"But fun," Secret pointed out.

"But fun," agreed Trick. "Kyprioth fun, too. Wailing and howling like Elsren and Petranne."

Aly grinned at them as she lifted her folded sash. It was heavier than it looked, because it held still more knives. Carefully she settled it around her waist, ensuring that the hilt to each blade was where it was supposed to be.

"What news from the palace?" she asked Trick.

"Regents say bad things about Sarai," the darking replied instantly.

Aly waved the comment away. "Sarai opened us to that," she replied grimly. "What else?"

"Imajane want to arrest people in every third house that is closed," said Trick. "Imajane shake all the time now. Too many noises in the night, she complains. Too many people talking but she cannot tell what they say. She tells maid she will feel better if people who make her nervous die. Rubinyan say killing many people make others angry. Imajane throw a vase at him. They not share bedchamber last night." It stopped talking for a moment, then told Aly, "She shouts at him about it now. She say with mages saying two more governors are dead, Examples must be made. She say death only thing raka understand. She say, burn rebel villages and hang headman or headwoman of every town near rebel villages." For a moment Trick stopped, tiny mouth agape in wonder.

"Tell," urged Secret. "Tell, tell."

Trick raised its head as if meeting Aly's eyes with its own invisible ones. "Rubinyan say *they dare not*. Rubinyan say, soldiers spread too thin." Trick rose up to look Aly more closely in the face. "This good, yes?"

Aly smiled. "Let us but stretch them a wee bit more," she told the darkings, not aware that she sounded much like her father. "Just to be thorough."

"Thorough good," said Trick, nodding.

"Thorough fun?" Secret asked.

Aly put on her sandals. "We shall have to see."

* * *

Aly went to her workroom, braced for the heap of reports from her pack and their recruits that she would find there. To her surprise, the heap was smaller than she had expected after three days' absence: the more people her spies recruited, the more reports had come. Then she saw the thick notebook next to a stack of reports. Opening it, she found notes in Dove's precise handwriting. They were in the proper code and condensed the reports into vital information including the informant, date, and anything that might be of use. Dove had even adopted Aly's way of sorting which of the conspiracy's leaders could most benefit from a particular bit of intelligence. Being a cautious Dove, she had left the reports in a wooden box to the side of Aly's desk, each with a number that matched its location in the book. Aly read through both the notebook and the reports rapidly, and realized that Dove had done as good a job as she could have herself.

With a lighter heart—it was always nice to have help—Aly reviewed the newest pack reports, condensing them and writing information onto sheets for each leader at the nightly meeting. The light outside her office faded. At last she heard the raka conspirators come down the hall to their meeting room. Aly gathered up the information to be passed on and went to join them.

Ulasim smiled at her. "I take it the god was displeased." He looked as if he lazed his days away, rather than conducted a small series of battle campaigns in secret.

Aly returned the smile, glad to see him. "And *I* take it you all agreed a nice, three-day work stop throughout Rajmuat was just what the healer ordered."

Fesgao chuckled. "It gave our people something to do. Hotheads in the Honeypot were all for burning the city down around our ears over losing Sarai. Then one of their old grannies got up and said, 'You act as if Sarai is the *only* one who is twice royal.' They still required persuasion, but after my lads dented a head or two, the idiots decided to see how Dove manages."

"In case I fall flat on my face," remarked Dove with a yawn. "How's the god?" She patted a seat next to her.

"Feeling better since he's had a chat with the Graveyard Hag," Aly said, taking the offered seat. "I confess, I was a bit worried that he might go off in a pout. Not enough to give me wrinkles, but a bit. I talked him into giving you a try." She looked around. "And from the looks of things, I take it you have convinced our friends."

"It's not like we have a choice," said Chenaol as Ochobu sniffed.

"Well, it would be a waste of all this planning, and all these dead governors," Aly replied, falsely helpful. She looked at Dove. "Her Grace formally told the regents?"

"They knew already, of course, but she still had to tell them in person," Dove said. "They made remarks that weren't very nice, along the lines that blood will tell. Winna came home and broke those two big vases in the front hall."

"Those vases were ugly anyway," Aly commented, thinking the regents must have said *very* bad things for the duchess to lose her temper. She began to pass out the reports to those who could best use the information in them as their usual meeting began.

They were nearly done when Dove announced, "The day after tomorrow I'll start my walks again. People are worried. They wanted Sarai, and she's gone. They'll be happier if I remind them I'm still here."

"Absolutely not," snapped Fesgao.

"It doesn't look right, you being the heir's sister," added Chenaol.

Dove looked at Aly, who shrugged. "She needs to show the people that being the hope of the raka hasn't gone to her head, and she needs to show the Crown's spies that she hasn't changed her routine. You'll need more guards," Aly said. "I'll see who my pack recommends for mingling with the crowd. Fesgao, maybe another ten fighters not in livery?"

"It's mad," Ochobu announced. "She is all we have."

"There are still hotheads in the Honeypot," replied Dove, leaning forward to make her point. "They need a real candidate to look at. I'm not beautiful, I'm not elegant on a horse, but I talk to people. And there are others I should speak to, people who could be of use to us. The only way I can do that is to continue visiting the marketplaces."

"Ysul wants to say something," Aly noted.

In hand-signs the mage said, *I will go with Lady Dove, too.*

"Yes," said Ulasim. He saw Dove's frown and said, "No complaints, and no tricks."

Dove thought it over, then nodded.

As the meeting broke up, Aly asked Fesgao and Ulasim to stay a moment. When the others had left, she told these two, in charge of the combat troops, about Rubinyan, the coming arrests, and the regents not daring to expend more soldiers to punish the raka. Ulasim and Fesgao looked at one another and smiled, their eyes alight. They could use this information to direct their fighters to the Crown's softest spots and to halt arrests.

When Aly turned to go, Ulasim said, "Wait."

She looked at him, raising an eyebrow.

"How can you be so sure of what you've just told us?" the footman asked. "You speak as if it's fact, not rumor, and you've been unconscious for three days."

"Because it is fact," Aly assured him. "Ulasim, didn't your mother ever tell you to leave a girl some secrets? I was picked by the god, and this particular information is real. If Rubinyan thinks they dare not punish the villages and estates that have already rebelled, what will he do if more rise up? He'll have to send someone, and at the moment, all he has are the reserves in Galodon. Wouldn't it be dreadful if he were having problems with the reserves? With food, say, or good water?"

She left the men to their planning, fluttering her fingers at them as she walked out and closed the door. Before it shut, she heard Fesgao tell Ulasim, "Old Lokeij used to say she'd never say a thing straight out if she could come at it from the side. He never mentioned the headaches you'd get listening to her."

Aly found Dove in her workroom, calmly going over reports. "Just the person I wanted to see," Aly remarked, locking the door. "Thank you for sorting those out while I was . . . away. You did wonderful work."

Dove put down her quill. "Honestly? I don't know how you keep up. I thought I might go blind." She nudged at the quill with a finger, her face shadowed. Finally she asked, "Aly, what if it goes to pieces because I'm not Sarai? Because it really should have been her?"

"It won't go to pieces," Aly told her. "The last piece is finally where it's supposed to be—that's you. The raka have planned this for generations, and planned it well. The only change is Sarai. Now we have you instead. Sarai may have gotten all passionate about the people and how they're being trampled, but you're the one who *knows* the people. Go to bed, my lady. We have one more day of the halt to work here in Rajmuat, one more day of peace for us to settle our plans. If you don't go get some rest right away, I'll come up to prepare you for bed. Maybe put lotion on your face for you to wear as you sleep. Oh, and I'll brush out your hair a hundred strokes. . . ."

"Stop it!" cried Dove. "I'm going, I'm going! Don't follow me! I can undress myself!"

Aly watched her go, thinking, a little sadly, *And when you are queen, you will have proper ladies-in-waiting who will do all of those things for you. You will not be able to dismiss them for fear of offending their powerful families. So enjoy dismissing me while you can.*

She locked the door behind Dove and returned to her work. There was more news from the palace darkings as well as more reports to read. Near midnight a darking posted in Rubinyan's chamber gave Trick a message that made Aly grin. She found Ulasim and Fesgao still in the conspirators' meeting room. She told them what she had learned and invited them to her workroom to talk.

She then gathered her pack's most determined members: Fegoro, Yoyox, Eyun, and Jimarn. They joined Ulasim and Fesgao. *It's good to be home,* Aly thought.

* * *

In the morning a palace messenger arrived with an invitation to a lily-viewing party the next day. Nuritin, Winnamine, and Dove were included in the invitation, which was not a request but a demand. Winnamine sent a note of acceptance. The house was quiet as everyone caught up on chores. It was during the noon resting time that the King's Watch swarmed into the city to arrest a third of those who had taken part in the three-day stop of work. By then Ulasim and Fesgao, forewarned by Aly, had hidden any important rebels from the searches. Those unfortunates caught by the Watch were sent to the slave market's pens, to be sold in Carthak as soon as vessels were ready to take them. The Watch expected to ship them out in two days. Aly prayed that Jimarn, Yoyox, Eyun, and Fegoro would concoct a suitably firm surprise for the slave markets before then.

Word of the arrests reached Balitang House in the early evening. Dove, furious, came flying into the workroom as Aly met with her pack. Aly smiled at her young mistress as sweetly as she knew how.

They understood each other. Dove did not need to ask if Aly had known about the arrests. Aly did not need to tell her that she had the matter in hand. The girl turned and walked out again.

"Where were we?" Aly asked her pack as she viewed her notes once more.

The ride to the palace the next afternoon was quiet, though not as quiet as it might have been. Rajmuat was simmering over the arrests. The regents had obviously expected this response. Rittevon's Lance was heavily guarded, with soldiers at each major crossroads and square and guards in pairs on every block.

As always, the men-at-arms left them at the gate. The ladies were to meet the regents in their private audience chamber. Aly assumed they would offer Dove the marriage they had Sarai. As she waited, Aly spent her time in the Robing Pavilion investigating something the darkings had relayed. According to them, the regents distrusted their mages. Aly had to confirm this, not because she didn't trust the darkings, but because she could hardly believe it. Someone had once complained that in the Tortallan palace it was hard to turn without stepping on a mage. Except for Topabaw and his staff, the monarchs here preferred to send their mages to support soldiers outside the capital, and to man the harbor fortresses. The servants Aly asked about it waved off the question with a reply that boiled down to, "Everybody knows that!"

How have they stayed in power this long? Aly wondered as she flirted with servants on the men's side of the pavilion. Were they smarter at first, and the intelligence got bred out of them, or were they simply lucky at the beginning?

At last the Balitang ladies came to the Robing Pavilion to change. As Aly helped Dove to remove her overrobe, Dove hand-signed to her, *They offered me the marriage.*

Aly slid a lightweight sleeveless silk robe over Dove's shoulders, then signed, *And?*

"I dithered," Dove murmured. She didn't care if this part of the conversation was overheard. "It was so sudden, and such an honor after Sarai. . . ." She shrugged. Aly smoothed her young mistress's hair and shared a smile with Dove in the looking glass.

Aly kept an eye on Nuritin and Winnamine. At last they rose, ready for the party. "Dovasary?" called Nuritin.

As Dove stood, Aly bent close, fussing with the line of her overgown, then followed them out. She had already talked this out with Dove. Pembery and Dorilize would remain in the Robing Pavilion; they always did. Aly would go with her young mistress and fan her. The Lapis Pavilion would be warm, and other maids would be there performing the same duty. Winnamine and Nuritin had looked askance when Dove had told them what Aly would be doing, but they had not argued, though they believed in fanning themselves. They both understood Aly was not there just to show how spoiled Dove was.

Down the Golden Road they walked, nodding and bowing to nobles they passed, until they reached the trails around the Lily Water. If they heard the whispers about Sarai that began before they were out of earshot, they did not speak, though crimson flags burned on both Winnamine's and Nuritin's cheekbones. Dove showed a calmly smiling face, even after the nobles could no longer see her.

"You do that very well," Aly said with approval after they had bidden farewell to an especially annoying dowager.

"They only talk about it because they're thinking, 'There but for the blessings of the gods I go,'" Dove said thoughtfully. "Lady Merani"—one of the women they had just left—"has a sixteen-year-old daughter who's a handful. And her husband drinks."

"It's no excuse," Nuritin said in a low voice that shook with fury. "They should have sympathy, and keep their mouths shut."

"This is why my lord and I always hated this place," added Winnamine softly. "Because everyone is encouraged to bite and pinch and cut at one another with words, until the words are so real the courtiers end by trusting no one. It's a poisonous life. Frankly, I'm envious of Sarai."

The two older ladies moved ahead as the path narrowed. Aly waited until they could not hear, then asked Dove, "Tell me, do you know *everything* about everybody here?"

"No, but it's easy enough to get information. The merchants keep track of the nobility because they affect their lives." Dove's mouth curved in a tiny, impish smile. "You know a lot of my friends are merchants."

"I had noticed," Aly said, trying not to smile herself.

Dove clucked to a marmoset, offering the tiny creature a grape she had tucked into her belt-purse. Gingerly the animal, who had a magnificent white mane, leaned down to accept the grape. Once it snatched the fruit, it fled back into its tree. Dove continued, "Besides, I like gossip." She smiled shyly. "I like knowing what people are doing and why. It's just so interesting."

"I always thought so, too," Aly said. They left the shelter of the garden and emerged onto the open ground. Nuritin and Winnamine had already climbed the steps of the Lapis Pavilion and walked over to curtsy to the regents. The pavilion was a roofed stone square set in the water and approached by a short stone bridge. Around it floated water lilies, lotuses, and swans.

Inside the pavilion, the group of ladies seated closest to the bridge was commanded by Princess Imajane. She looked ethereal in white, almost transparent silk with gold embroidery. Aly wasn't sure if it was decent, but then, she still felt half dressed in a sarong with her shoulders bare. And the day was impossibly hot. Maybe Her Highness is the wisest of us all, Aly thought as sweat trickled down her spine.

Nuritin and Winnamine, having saluted the princess and received a nod from her, drifted over to the prince and his companions. Aly saw why as she and Dove curtsied to Imajane: Countess Tomang sat next to the princess. Ferdy's mother looked as if she sucked on a lemon.

"Lady Dovasary, welcome," said Imajane lazily. "I am honored. With your brother attendant upon His Majesty, all the Balitangs but little Petranne are here." She indicated the group of boys at the far corner of the pavilion. Dunevon and his small court stood on the steps that led down to the water, each boy with a wooden sailboat in hand. "As you can see, His Majesty minds the sun less than we fragile adults," she drawled, causing the ladies seated with her to chuckle. "Though we had to supply a mage so the children might have a breeze."

Sure enough, a young man whose hands sparkled with his magical Gift crouched on the lowest step to the water. Tiny puffs of power pushed at the sail of each little boat to the boys' gleeful yells. Aly wondered if the mage heard Imajane, and if he had studied magic so his Gift could be spent on the amusement of children. Admittedly, her experience of mages was extraordinary, but even such confident mages as her mother, Aunt Daine, and Uncle Numair did not appreciate being slighted.

Imajane flicked her fingers at the woman who sat on her left. She obediently got to her feet and curtsied to the princess. As she left the company, Aly looked for Nuritin and Winnamine. They were still talking easily with Rubinyan and his friends.

Dove curtsied to the princess again, then moved to the vacant seat. She sat gracefully, apparently unaware of the glare that Countess Tomang leveled at her. Aly wondered if the princess knew that the last meeting between the countess and the Balitangs had not gone well. From the creamy, self-satisfied smile on Imajane's mouth, Aly would happily bet that she did.

Dove snapped her fingers. "You may fan me," she ordered Aly, nearly as haughty as the princess. Aly installed herself behind Dove. She took the woven palm-leaf fan a maid passed to her and began to wave it gently.

Imajane placed a graceful, well-cared-for hand on Dove's arm. "We had no chance to talk about your sister's elopement earlier," she said archly. "Your mother says you did not know, but I fancy I may know a little more about young girls. Tell me honestly, Dovasary, did you not have some *tiny* hint of what Lady Saraiyu intended?"

Dove lowered her head, shamefaced. "Your Highness, I would never be so foolish as to tell you a falsehood," she said quietly. "Besides, Sarai is five years older than I. Girls with suitors have little interest in talking to sisters who are bored by them." She picked at her skirt. "And she knew I'd tell Winna—Her Grace," she amended herself artfully, "she knew I'd tell, to keep her from disgracing our name."

Aly wanted to hug her. Thirteen, and already aware enough to maneuver around a question about the duchess's watch over her stepdaughters. In the games played at palaces, the whisper that Winnamine could not keep her family under control might cause Elsren to be dismissed from court. By that game's rules, Elsren's position in the king's group of playmates was the kind of thing families used to gain advantages. Even Aly wanted Elsren to be one of the king's companions. It meant the Balitangs were invited to more palace events than most nobles, so there could be more trades of information with palace rebels. The darkings couldn't be everywhere.

"These young girls," one of the ladies across from Dove remarked with a sigh. "No patience. I'm certain Lord Zaimid's family would have accepted Lady Saraiyu if they had gotten married in the proper way. Carthakis are so . . . cosmopolitan about their marriages."

Aly felt the breath desert her lungs at the implication that brown-skinned Carthakis didn't care if they married half-raka girls. Her gentle waving of the fan did not falter. And why do you care what's said of Sarai? Aly asked herself. You're the one who thinks her running off with Zaimid was for the best, even if it *was* a black eye for your ability to watch members of the household.

She was relieved to see that Winnamine and Nuritin were wrapped up in their conversation with the prince. How many such darts had the two women taken since Sarai eloped?

"Oh?" Dove asked politely, as if she discussed a change in fish prices. "Cosmopolitan. How wonderful that sounds! Have you been to Carthak, Lady Uniunu?"

The lady smiled at her. "Actually, I have not."

Dove raised her dark brows. "Have you visited Tyra, then?" she inquired.

The lady shook her head.

Dove pressed. "Tortall? Scanra?"

With each shake of her head, the lady looked less and less pleased.

"Oh," Dove murmured, tracing a design in the embroidery on her sleeve. "But travel is what *makes* us cosmopolitan, or so I was taught." She looked up and smiled girlishly at Lady Uniunu. "But perhaps our own cities count? Have you been to Fajurat on Malubesang? I hear the water is so clean there you can view coral reefs from a ship's deck. Or Ambririp? Or Yimosuat on Gempang?"

The lady had stopped bothering even to shake her head. Her hands, tucked into her lap, were white-knuckled as she clenched them into fists. "Our lands are here, on Kypriang," she said, her voice trembling. "I have learned all I know of what is cosmopolitan right here, Lady Dovasary."

Back off, Aly thought to Dove. She's gotten your point. Drop it, before she becomes your enemy.

As if she heard Aly, Dove gasped and put her hand to her lips. "I hope you didn't mean I thought . . . ," she said, her face dismayed. "Please believe me, I meant only that I am eager to learn of other places." She hung her head. "I have spent my entire life here in Rajmuat, or at Tanair, on Lombyn." Glancing up, she made a face. "Tanair was not in the least cosmopolitan, I'm afraid. We were all living in the keep last winter, because a keep was all the holdings Tanair has. Well, that and outbuildings."

The woman, who had started to fluff like an irate pigeon, slowly resettled. "You are young, and no doubt unschooled as to the proper form of conversation among grown women," she said graciously. Dove hung her head even lower.

"Tell me," began another lady, "do you know why those people were always staring at your sister?"

Dove's lower lip protruded slightly. She looked the spirit of the pouting thirteen-year-old. "I suppose because she's so beautiful, your ladyship," she said, clearly unhappy. "Aunt Nuritin said my looks will improve, but it seems to be taking a long time."

This produced polite laughter from the ladies. The talk moved on to other things, such as the boy king's approaching fifth birthday. "I have an invitation on its way to your home," Imajane told Dove. "There is a separate invitation for Lord Elsren," she explained, leaning closer to the girl. "You see, my dear, His Majesty has been asking for a true ship of his own. On His Majesty's birthday, he and his little friends will board his very own ship, the *Rittevon*."

Dove bowed her head. "We're all honored by His Majesty's invitation to Elsren," she said with just the right amount of awe in her voice. Inclusion in such a party would tell everyone that Imajane and Rubinyan meant to keep Elsren in Dunevon's household, making him a veritable brother to the king.

Aly continued to fan, listening and reading lips. A group of ladies and nobles talked about the hottest part of the summer, when everyone would move to their country estates for a month. Some of the young men in Rubinyan's group urged him to let them go fight the rebels. Winnamine pretended to be interested in the conversation. Nuritin did not.

Aly sensed him behind her before Taybur Sibigat leaned down to speak into her ear. "Do you rest easier since Topabaw has been replaced by a complete nincompoop?"

Aly turned slightly, never allowing her fan to stop its movement, to whisper, "Which nincompoop would that be, my lord captain?"

"Tease," he said, amusement in his eyes. "Sevmire. His Highness took him from a fish pond and tossed him into the ocean. I'll wager you he doesn't last till September."

"I never wager, my lord," Aly murmured flirtatiously. "Particularly not with the nobility. It's so hard to collect."

"What a charming little creature you are," he said with frank admiration. "Really, you're wasted among the Balitangs. You'd have more scope here in the palace."

Aly coughed to hide the giggle that almost escaped her. "I have scope enough, sir," she replied demurely. Behind her laughing face lay a bleak thought: This man might die in the storm to come, and I like him.

And that's your first mistake, lass, said the part of her that sounded like her da. You can't afford to like one of the enemy in this game, and he *is* the enemy.

Raucous shrieks cut through the humid air like knives. Along with the rest of the people on the Lapis Pavilion, Aly turned to find the source. Over the Lily Water, Stormwings and crows battled for possession of the sky. At last one female Stormwing escaped the battle to land on the waist-high balustrade around the pavilion. She was a handsome female, despite the claw marks on her flesh. If her broad, steel-toothed grin was any indication, they didn't bother her.

"More fun for you mortals," she announced in a musical voice. "Remember the Imahyn revolt? Five estates along the Susashain River are burning.

Over two hundred dead, or so my nest-kin tell me. Each human smells different to us, you know. All that lovely fear." She ran her tongue over her teeth. "Keep serving them up, Your Highnesses! We accept all contributions of terror and rage, we're not picky!"

"Konutai, you're being a bore," Taybur drawled, wandering over to her. "And you'll make His Majesty throw up in the Lily Water."

Dunevon did look rather pale. He was certainly downwind of the Stormwing.

"Be a good girl and gloat elsewhere," Taybur continued. "I'm sure we'll get proper reports in due time."

The Stormwing cackled wildly and took to the air, heading for the battle between Stormwings and crows over the water. This time it ended with the crows in retreat. Aly crossed her fingers in the hope the crows would go unhurt.

"Don't believe them, Highness," Countess Tomang said to Imajane. "You know how the ugly beasts like to start trouble."

Imajane looked at Taybur, her eyes blue ice. "Which is it, Sibigat? They like to start it? Or they like to live off it?"

The big man bowed to Imajane. "Far be it from me to instruct Your Highness in the behavior of Stormwings," he said quietly. "I am certain that you were as well schooled in that as you are in other things pertaining to the Crown."

Imajane showed a razor's edge of smile. "Your nimble tongue has led you out of a potential situation yet again, Captain Sibigat. I fear you are too clever for me."

As the other ladies protested that no one could be more intelligent than the princess, and Dove chimed in a beat behind them, knowing what was expected of her, Aly met Taybur's gaze. For a moment she thought she saw fear. Then it was gone, replaced by Sibigat's boyish smile.

The talk resumed once more on a false, light note. No one wanted to admit that they had believed the Stormwing. Imajane herself seemed determined to carry on as if everything were normal. Slowly the ladies began to relax, though the young knights were begging Rubinyan once more to let them sail north and fight. Rubinyan calmed them, insisting the army had matters well in hand. Aly's admiration for his ability to lie soared. She knew that this man had only recently told his wife they dare not send more soldiers.

He must tap his reserve forces in Galodon, Aly thought. And then he'll have next to no one to defend Rajmuat. He may even have next to no one to send, if Ulasim and Fesgao mess with their stores soon.

Why does he send his young knights? she wondered. That's what the hotheads are for, Grandfather always said. Then she saw it. He fears they will get beaten, she told herself, and their parents will turn on him. Either that or he fears they might be good enough to come back and get rid of him.

A shift of silver and gold at the corner of her eye made her look at Imajane. The princess regent had turned slightly to look at her husband. Her crimson mouth was tight. She had seen Rubinyan smile at Duchess Winnamine.

If I don't get overconfident again, if I don't make any more mistakes, we might well do this thing, Aly thought. We might bring these people down. There are so many ways they can be led astray that I'll be hard-put to choose.

At last the Balitang ladies begged the princess's indulgence so they could go home. Not only did Imajane grant it, but she gave them leave to take Elsren with them. Taybur was already talking to the boys about going inside to dress for supper. The ladies and Aly collected Elsren and left the Lapis Pavilion.

On the way home they found the streets were clearing. Above them faces in the windows stared at Dove, looking for a sign that she was kin to Sarai and their hope for freedom was not misplaced.

"My lady," Aly murmured as they put three blocks between their group and the palace checkpoint, "please look at the folk in the windows. Smile, at least, and nod. Don't wave. We don't want these soldiers taking news back to Sevmire that you are encouraging the raka's fascination with you. But a smile never hurts."

A flush rose in Dove's bronze cheeks. "I forgot," she admitted. Hesitantly she smiled up into some second- and third-story windows, then looked at the people nearest her. A woman stood with a cluster of children. Dove slowed her mount and bent down to look at them. Finally she smiled at the woman. "Not all yours, I hope?" she asked.

The woman hesitated, unsure of Dove's intent, then saw the smile. She grinned. "Gods, no, lady," she said with as much of a curtsy as she could manage with the attached children. "I watch them all while their mothers work in the shops."

Winnamine rode over, Elsren seated before her. "Dove, we must go home," she murmured, with a cheerful nod to the woman. After a moment she thrust her hand into her belt-purse and fished out some coins. "I'll wager you wouldn't mind a treat," she told the children with a smile. She offered the coins to the woman. "Because I have little ones of my own," she explained.

The woman turned crimson and curtsied again. "And you love them, I can see that," she replied, beaming at Elsren, who was half asleep. "Goddess bless you, ladies."

As they rode on, Dove said, "Winna, you didn't have to do that."

The duchess kissed the top of Elsren's head. "I wanted to have something good to remember about today," she replied quietly. "Something that wasn't petty and mean. Sometimes you have to provide such moments yourself."

As they passed through Rittevon Square, Aly wished that lightning would strike the first king's immense bronze statue, rising above the flat dish of water that surrounded it. She was about to look somewhere else when a detail caught her attention. An anonymous carver had made an addition to the statue's belt line. A deep-cut open shackle shone brightly around the weathered bronze of the statue's waist, above the dip of the sword belt.

Aly grinned, and followed her mistress to the next checkpoint.

15

REBEL PREPARATION

The ladies and their maids retreated to their rooms to change after the hot ride home. Aly was about to help Dove with her buttons when a knock sounded on the door. One of the house's runners stuck her head into the room. "Excuse me, lady," she said, bobbing a curtsy to Dove, "but Chenaol says Jimarn and her folk need to talk to you in the meeting room."

Aly looked from the runner to her mistress. She ought to help Dove to change clothes, but Jimarn, Fegoro, Eyun, and Yoyox were operating on a time limit. The Crown would start shipping the captives in the slave pens the next morning. She sighed, trying to make up her mind.

"Let me help?" asked Boulaj. "I liked being a lady's maid. It's very soothing," she told Junai defensively. "There's no reason why I can't do her hair and clothes and protect her at the same time."

"Go on," Dove ordered Aly. "We'll sort it out. I *do* know how to remove my own clothes," she protested yet again.

Aly followed the messenger to the servants' stair. It occurred to her that she had less and less time to attend Dove as the rebellion began to pick up its pace. She didn't mind being Dove's maid, but she was needed to deal with the material from her spies. Is it always like this? she wondered as she trotted downstairs behind Wayan. The more successful your work, the more it shoves other things to the side?

She wondered what her mother had given up when she had become the King's Champion. Da had given up being an outlaw as he'd made the transition from thief-king to spymaster, but what had Mother surrendered?

I'm going to have to let Boulaj take over, she realized. I'm more use to the rebellion getting information out to people as quickly as I can. But I'll miss talking to Dove.

When Aly reached the conspirators' meeting room, Jimarn let her in. Aly nodded to the others who sat in the room. She recognized five from households nearby, but six she did not know at all. Eyun, Yoyox, and Fegoro waited behind them, frowns of worry on their faces.

Aly went to an available chair and sat. "What is it, my dears?" she asked. "Surely you have not come to tell your old Duani they have shipped the captives already."

"The slave pens are a harder knot than we expected," Yoyox admitted ruefully. "We can whittle that stick down a day or two, but they're moving both faster and slower than we expected."

"They have about five hundred people to ship," explained Eyun. "And the head clerk told me the regents have ordered them to get as many out of the Isles as they can, as soon as they can." She smiled slightly. "The clerk has taken a liking to me. He says the regents want to free up the soldiers who guard the slave pens, because they're needed elsewhere. They expect an attack from the kinfolk of those they arrested, so they won't be reassigned until there's less danger."

"Getting to their kitchen is tricky," admitted Fegoro. "I won't have a shot at it tonight, not if they're loading slaves." He pointed to a chunky young luarin. "Tell her," he ordered.

"Three ships leave for Carthak tonight from Fifth Dock," the young man explained. "They'll load at midnight and sail at dawn. All of the other ships have cargo in the hold, or are off-loading cargo and taking new cargo on. We won't be able to save those who get shipped tonight."

Aly shook her head. "Children, children," she told them in a sorrowful voice. "The solution is right under your noses, if you would but look. Yes, they have three ships scheduled to sail, only three ships, all due to sail at dawn. There is no law that says they must be *able* to sail."

The conspirators looked at her, mouths agape. Then Yoyox struck his head with his palm. "We focused on the pens and the guards. We didn't think to look at the ships."

"Such vulnerable things," Aly remarked. "All that wood and tar—it's a fire hazard. I tremble to think what would happen if, oh, a ship lost its rudder or its masts." She looked at them from beneath raised eyebrows. "Need I go on?"

They shook their heads, suddenly eager to get back to mischief.

The heavy luarin chuckled.

"Share the joke, Callyn," ordered Yoyox.

"I work at the harbormaster's," the bearded man explained. "We're still wading through bills submitted to the Crown for payment for the ships that burned when the slave docks did. That's one of the reasons they could only find three ships right away—their masters are nervous about cargo from the slave markets. If something happens to these three, I bet they won't be able to find *anyone* at anchor here who will take on slave cargo. In fact, they might decide they've taken on enough goods and sail anywhere, as long as it's not Rajmuat harbor."

Jimarn smiled. "Thank you, Duani," she said.

"Shall you require a mage?" Aly wanted to know.

The bearded man shook his head. "No, see, Duani, the last seven or eight months we've had these twin hedgewitches hiding out in the Honeypot. They have this spell that cuts clean through a piece of wood. In October Her Highness went to inspect a new royal navy ship named for her, and she leaned on the rail, and she'd've gone straight into the harbor if the prince hadn't grabbed her. If the girls can do a rail, they can do masts just fine."

Aly nodded. She would have liked to see that.

"We could use some bows and arrows," one of them remarked. "But not for the slave market. For Downwind. So the folk there can have them."

Aly looked at Jimarn, who nodded. "Then speak to the armorer," she said. "Get crossbows—they're easier for inexperienced archers. Is that everything?" she asked. When they said nothing, she went on, "Very well. Go forth, with my blessing." When they were gone, she ran her fingers over Trick and Secret.

"Stupid?" asked Secret.

"No," Aly replied. "My children are not stupid. But sometimes you can stand too close to a thing to see it. It takes a fresh set of eyes to tell you where to find the cracks." She went to her workroom and assembled paper, ink, and a quill. "What happens in the palace?" she asked.

That night, the raka conspirators had plenty of news to report, particularly Ochobu. Aly had not known that the mages of the Chain had been laboring to eliminate any mages who had worked magic on the Crown's behalf. So far they had killed seven of the most powerful.

Chenaol would call this count of the dead another "good start," Aly thought grimly. This crude business of counting up lives taken struck her as a bad idea. It took the horror from death. When Ochobu named four mages on Lombyn who had been killed in the streets of their towns, it was about numbers, not lives.

Maybe this is how you become a Rittevon, she thought. You get used to the dead being described as numbers, not fathers or daughters or grandparents.

She turned to Dove when Ochobu finished. "Don't ever be like this," she urged. "Don't think that it doesn't matter if you only hear of murder as a number. If you keep it at a distance."

"They serve the Rittevon Crown," growled Ochobu. "They have killed in their numbers, too. We must even the odds between us and the Crown, and the mages matter. It was the mages who destroyed us when Rittevon invaded."

"They and our own feuds," Dove said quietly. "That's why we have to make peace with the luarin who agree. So we aren't so torn that we are easy pickings for some of the Carthaki malcontents."

Everyone winced. While it had been eleven years since Emperor Kaddar had taken power, he continued to struggle with his western nobles, all of whom thought they would make better emperors that he. It was all too easy to imagine them turning their attentions to easier pickings in the Isles.

As the meeting broke up, Aly drifted over to Ulasim. "How go things at Galodon?" she asked, curious, though if he refused to answer, she would ask Trick to query Ace, the darking who hid under the chair Ulasim normally used.

Fesgao stood and stretched. "All we did today was ensure that the army's provisions for the next five weeks were delivered and neatly stored. We'd hate for them to run short."

Aly grinned and left them. She worked for a while before she went to bed. As she slept, she dreamed of the whispers of the darkings, and the endless black scrawls of reports.

It was nearly dawn when she was roused by the clang of alarm bells sounding down by the waterfront. Aly smiled as she sat up on her pallet. "I could get very fond of that sound," she commented as Boulaj and Junai sat up as well.

"Aly?" Dove asked warningly. "What have you done?"

"I, my lady?" Aly said, holding her hand to her breast as if she were unsure of Dove's meaning. "I have done nothing whatsoever. I was here all night, and I was at the palace with you yesterday, if you recall."

Junai listened at the window. "It's coming from Dockmarket or the wharves," she said after a moment. "Forgive me for saying so, my lady, but if it is, you won't be having your walk again today."

Dove scowled and rang for her wash water to be brought up. It took some time, enough that Dove, who normally did not press the servants when she knew they would also be busy with the others, rang a second time. Soon after, a pair of kitchen maids practically tumbled into the room, hot-water jugs in their hands.

"Forgive us, my lady," said one as she filled a basin, "but Fesgao was telling us the news. He likes to drill the men before dawn, you see, and when they heard the alarm—"

"Does he know the cause?" Dove interrupted.

"Oh, my lady, such a shocking thing!" said the other girl, who filled the servants' basin. "Three ships destroyed, right at the wharves! One sank, one burned, and one had the rudder and the masts and the anchor chain and the mooring ropes just cut, Fesgao said!"

"They meant to ship out some of the folk they arrested because they stopped working," the first maid said, shadows in her eyes. "They meant to ship them to Carthak. But now they can't, and there are no more ships."

To say there were no more ships was an understatement. From Jimarn's recruit Callyn and the palace darkings, Aly learned of furious arguments as Rubinyan and Imajane tried to order other captains in port to put off their loads and ferry the newly enslaved to Carthak. Some claimed they needed hull work done before they could sail. Others showed their master's papers, each with a clause that they not transport slaves. Some captains sailed before the harbormaster could order the harbor mouth barred. Then there were the officials who complained the harbormaster had been suspiciously slow to close the entrance.

Aly was taking darking reports midafternoon when the second blow came to Rubinyan. A thousand of his reserve soldiers, and more than half of the sailors, were confined to their beds with violent dysentery. The darking present when the prince regent heard this news was so impressed with Rubinyan's language that it copied him, earning the name Foul.

The news arrived just before word came that a company of soldiers had been lured into the mountains of northern Kypriang and massacred by renegade raka. Imajane demanded the deaths of everyone in the village closest to the fight. Rubinyan was forced to tell his wife that the soldiers were too ill to move.

That night, when it came Aly's turn to report to the raka conspirators, she asked, "What happens if the army and navy have food shortages? If, say, they have to replace poisoned stores? Who handles the emergency supply, at least until more food can be brought from outlying islands or even overseas?"

The conspirators looked at one another. It was Dove who said, "Local merchants are invited to share warehoused provisions with the Crown, who pays them . . . something. Not full value. Full value when there's a shortage is higher than full value in good times. The merchants who are asked to share with the Crown will see their other friends make money hand over fist while they're forced to practically give food away. But that hasn't happened in ages."

Aly twiddled her thumbs. "But it *could* happen?"

"They would approach the merchants and remind them of their obligations," replied Dove. "And they're already pressed, the merchants. It's been a dreadful year, and the harvest doesn't look good. Nobody's that far away from debt bondage, Aly. The regents might as well ask them to empty their pockets. They . . ." She stopped, her eyes wide.

She sees it, Aly thought.

"No, we can't trust these regents to be careful, can we?" Ulasim asked softly. "They might annoy the merchants. They might turn the merchants into—"

"Enemies," said Fesgao, his eyes bright. He looked at Aly. "You'd thought of that when you suggested it would put a dent in Rubinyan's reserve troops to poison their food."

"You flatter me," Aly said shyly.

"Here I just thought you would deal with information," Ochobu remarked slowly, her eyes on Aly. "But you understand a thing or two about war, don't you?"

"As much as any girl reared under the sign of the Trickster would," Aly replied smoothly.

Ulasim smoothed his beard. "You are a gift and a marvel to me," he said. "What are you doing at the slave pens?"

"Me?" inquired Aly. "Nothing. I sit here and interpret reports. My bottom is going flat from all the sitting I do."

Ulasim shook his head. "Very well. Keep it to yourself. If you require assistance, only ask. Now. Through the Chain we hear that the raka of southern Lombyn have risen up against their masters. And the governor of Lombyn is dead, as is his chief mage, as is the general in command of the army posts on Lombyn, all shot with crow-fletched arrows. Nawat and his people are helping the Lombyn rebels retreat into the highlands, where the new general may hunt for them until he encounters a ribbon snake. Or a hundred."

The next morning Dove finally persuaded Ulasim and Winnamine to let her take a walk to the Dockmarket.

"I'm going mad in here all day," she informed them. "And Fesgao has got layers of protection on me that an onion might envy. I swear, the moment anything untoward happens, I'll trot right home. But seriously, Winna, Ulasim, I'm going to rend the next person who speaks to me if I can't go out for a time."

Pressed, the duchess and the head footman gave way. Aly, too, was grateful for the chance to go out, though she thought she ought to deal with reports. Information was pouring in at a rate she was hard-put to manage. A walk will do me good, she told herself firmly.

At the Dockmarket people went about their business, but they kept one eye on the soldiers present. The ship that had lost its masts had drifted to the center of the harbor. Men were out in rowboats, securing lines to bring it in. The ship that had burned had also drifted when the fire devoured its hawsers. No doubt it would be sunk: it was only a charcoal shell. There was no sign of the third ship, which had sunk.

She could see Dove taking note of the changes, though she said nothing. No one could miss the increased guard around the royal dock where the king's birthday present rode at anchor, its colorful sails furled. There were even men on its decks, watching no doubt for whoever could navigate the harbor waters well enough to burn the slave docks and destroy three merchant ships, in case they turned their attention to the king's ship.

As Aly looked around, Dove crouched to talk with the old raka who sold good-luck charms. She had known the woman since she was small, she had told Aly, and the charm seller always knew the best gossip. As they talked, a part-raka woman who carried a basket of seaweed approached the girl. Aly hand-signaled the men-at-arms to keep to their places. The woman lingered until Dove kissed the old charm seller on the cheek and stood. When Dove looked at her inquiringly, the woman blurted out "Good morning" and fled.

As Dove walked on, a sailor came close enough to tell her that she looked well that day. He was followed by a gaggle of well-wishers, all of whom were happy simply to say hello or to venture an opinion about the weather.

Aly led Dove's group in another direction when they neared the part of Dockmarket where soldiers in the armor of the Rittevon Guard and the King's Watch protected the slave pens. Several of those guards did not look at all well. Jimarn and her cohorts finally got into the slave market kitchens, Aly thought.

A little girl ran up to Dove to show her a dirty rag doll, obviously much loved, then ran away.

"I don't understand," Dove murmured to Aly as they finally left Dockmarket. It was almost noon. Normally Dove would have visited friends at some of the nearby shops, but that was before it had taken her the entire morning to go from one end of the markets principal to the other. "They don't queue up to say hello to anyone else."

"But you let them," Aly pointed out. "You're walking down here with street muck on your sandals, asking what the squid is like today and how business is doing. They'll have heard from your friends that you're not the kind of girl who rides by with a smile and a wave. You understand business. You don't want a fuss. You just want to learn. And they need to see for themselves if your friends have spoken truly." She looked back at the market. A number of the people there were staring in Dove's direction. When they saw Aly turn, they hurriedly went back to work.

"But I'm no warmhearted people lover!" Dove protested softly. "I like to know how business is doing. I'm interested in things like who's importing and who's exporting, who buys and who sells. I like to try and figure out trade, that's all."

Aly shrugged. "Even if they did know that, it would probably only make you more of a real person to them. Don't forget, their fortunes rise and fall with the tiniest drop of the squid-fishing industry. A blight among sheep, and prosperous merchants are selling their old clothes to make some money." She leaned in so that only Dove would hear. "They will look at you, as you ask them questions about how they manage to earn a living, and they'll compare you to people who tax them without asking if they can pay."

Dove's eyes were startled as she stared at Aly. At last she said, "Care to wager on how many days it takes before the regents hire someone to kill me?"

Boulaj and Junai heard, and moved closer. "Just let them try, my lady," Junai assured her. "We'll send whoever takes the job back to the Gray Palace in pieces."

That night Jimarn and her crew killed the brokers' guards who were still healthy enough to fight. The former slave and her companions raced through the slave pens with keys to open the locks, and baskets of weapons. Every captive who could lift one took it—sword, axe, knife. Most raced through the shadows to the Honeypot and up over the ridge, vanishing into the forest that lay on its northern side. Others were given places to hide in the city.

Many returned to their old homes in Downwind. Once they had reached their district, they scrambled to lay wagons, tables, benches, even stable doors on their sides to block streets. As they did so, Yoyox, Fegoro, Eyun, and their cohorts scattered, to bring out crossbows and quivers of bolts they had hidden away. Jimarn remained, helping people as they blocked the streets, reinforcing the wood barriers with cobblestones and pavement flags. When word got out, soldiers would comb the area. They would quickly learn that for every person who had fled, five had stayed to fight.

Too anxious to sleep, Aly waited until the house had been quiet for a couple of hours, then climbed to the second-story room where the family placed winter things and ancient keepsakes. The door was locked with a hasp and padlock. As a professional, Aly was offended that someone of her skill was taken so lightly. As she chose her lock picks, she felt Trick and Secret put up heads to watch.

"What that?" whispered Secret, always curious.

"It's a lock, and I'm opening it," Aly whispered back. The lock sprang open easily.

"That not a key." Secret understood keys. Quedanga wore a bunch of them on her sash.

"No, it's a lock pick. Actually, both are lock picks. You need different kinds."

Aly stepped into the storeroom. It was huge, but everything from Tanair was near the door. She spotted the trunk she needed immediately. It too was locked. At least this was more of a challenge. She went after it with her picks. It resisted her a little longer than the padlock had.

Opening the trunk, she found Duke Mequen's correspondence going back three decades. Here were bundles of letters from Winnamine, tied up in scarlet ribbon, and letters from Sarugani, his first duchess, in gold. He had letters from family members and friends. Then Aly found what she needed, a bundle of letters in bold, slashing handwriting, with a distinctive signature: Rubinyan.

Carefully she replaced everything but Rubinyan's letters and did up the lock. She dusted the floor to hide the marks left by her knees, then dusted off her knees. After making sure all was in order, she left as quietly as she had come, doing up the padlock. Then she carried the letters downstairs so she could practice the prince regent's handwriting.

She found Kyprioth at her desk, sandaled feet on top of a stack of reports, hands locked behind his head as he leaned back in her chair. Aly squinted at him. Had he grown larger?

"What a wonderful night this is," he told her, his black eyes dancing. "How such small mortals like you and Ulasim cause so much damage . . . I tell you, it fills me with a sense of wonder. It truly does."

"And if it were just us, you'd be right to wonder," Aly said. "We have good people and we trust them to trust their training. I take it you've been down by the slave pens."

"A work of art," the god replied. "I'm beside myself." For a moment there were two of him.

Aly cringed. "Please stop that," she begged. "The thought of two of you makes my head ache."

"I understand. It would be too much glory for your poor mortal body to withstand. When do you rise? When does the rebellion begin?" he wanted to know.

"When the regents give us an excuse," Aly said, taking a chair. "You know, you're getting marks on my papers."

"I'll take them off. I *am* a god, you know."

"So you keep telling me," replied Aly. "Why ask when we rise? Are your brother and sister on their way?"

"Not yet," said Kyprioth, polishing an emerald bracelet on his wrapped jacket. "Why wait for them to push you forward? The regents?"

"Because we're supposed to be the heroes, rescuing the Isles from oppressors," Aly explained. "It never looks good to other governments if we rise up against a lawful monarch."

Kyprioth smiled. "I thought that might be it. Perfectly sensible, of course. I'm sure it will all work out in the end. Get ready, Aly."

"Are you bigger?" she started to ask, but he was gone.

Aly waited up for her pack to return. They were tired but content, and complained only from habit when she insisted that they scrub every trace of blood from their persons before they went to bed. Only when they were tucked in did she go to her pallet. She was certain she had just nodded off when the alarm bells sounded, rousing the entire household. Someone had found the ruins of the slave pens. It would not be long before they also discovered that when they went to search for fugitives in the city, they would get a far warmer welcome in Downwind than they expected.

Aly followed her morning routine, then cleaned up Dove's room. Boulaj went over the girl's dresses. The day before, an invitation had come for the three Balitang ladies, asking them to a riding party in the palace parks. Aly suspected that Imajane meant to press Dove on taking her place among the regent's ladies-in-waiting, where she could persuade Dove to accept Dunevon as her betrothed.

Aly hoped they would not have to cancel their outing due to those alarm bells. She wanted to pass some incriminating bits of paper to Vereyu to be placed where Imajane, or someone stupid enough to inform her, would find them.

Their plans went unchanged. Two squads of the Rittevon Guard came to escort the ladies and their maids to the palace. Their group had just reached Rittevon Square when they saw that people stared and pointed at the northeastern part of the city. Columns of smoke rose from Downwind; the Honeypot itself was blanketed with it. The King's Watch had discovered the barricades, and fighting had broken out.

Imajane greeted her guests as if there were no fighting on the streets of Rajmuat and led them away to ride with her. Aly sat outside the Robing Pavilion, watching the sky. The crows reigned supreme over the palace. The Stormwings had gone. They've plenty to feed on today, Aly thought.

Suddenly she drew in her breath. Above the crows soared a golden kudarung, great wings outspread. It was the most beautiful thing she had ever seen.

She was dozing off when Vereyu poked her. "Late night?" she asked, sitting next to Aly.

"Only because I worry too much," Aly replied. "Here." From the front of her sarong she drew some battered, dirty scraps of paper with bold black handwriting on them. One read simply *meet tonight*, another *must not know*. A third mentioned *your blushing lips*, a fourth *cannot live with this secret for much longer*.

Vereyu looked them over with a frown. "That's the prince's handwriting."

Aly smiled. "Certainly that's what we want the princess to think. Over the next week can you leave these in places where he might drop them? His dressing room, for instance, or the hall outside Her Highness's door, or their private dining room."

"She may not even see them," Vereyu told her.

Aly wrapped her arms around her legs and leaned her chin on her knees. "You've known Her Highness far longer than I," she murmured. "Do you honestly think she never slips into his rooms when he's not around?"

"But who is this foolish woman, if that's what you mean Her Highness to think?" asked Vereyu. "Who would be mad enough to get involved with His Highness?"

"If you can get samples of her handwriting for me, Lady Edunata Mayano," Aly replied.

She watched Vereyu's face as a flinty light filled the raka's eyes. Lady Edunata was infamous for having taken a raka lover and then claiming he'd raped her.

"It will be our pleasure," said Vereyu. "I think I can lay hands on some of the lady's writing right now. Wait here."

Ah, revenge, Aly thought drowsily as she listened to peacocks cry. People never lose interest in it.

She stood, stretched, and returned to gossip with the other servants at the pavilion. Only when she saw Vereyu at the servants' door did she leave off flirting with a boastful manservant to talk to her. With the ease of long practice Vereyu slid papers into Aly's hands. Aly in turn rolled them casually and tucked them into her sash.

Imajane seemed determined to incorporate the Balitang women into court life. They rode to the palace nearly every other day over the next week and a half. The regents did their best to pretend the fighting in Downwind was minor, but Aly knew of their real worry from the darkings. The rebellion was spreading like wildfire: for each rising that was put down, two more broke out elsewhere.

"Rubinyan say they maybe need mercenaries," Trick told Aly two nights before the king's birthday. "Princess say can they afford? Prince say they can't *not* afford."

Aly smiled. Mercenaries were always such a problem. If they weren't paid on time, they got unhappy and did damage. If they were without work, they often looked for trouble out of boredom, burning villages and robbing travelers for their amusement. People feared them as much as they respected the need to hire them. The luarin nobility would also see mercenaries as Rubinyan's attempt to build an army that would answer to him alone.

While the princess entertained the ladies, Aly supplied Vereyu with incriminating scraps in Edunata's handwriting. These were hidden in Rubinyan's chambers and study. One of the prince's earrings also found its way into the sweet dreams bag that Edunata, like many luarin women, hung over her bed.

Sooner or later Imajane would find something to make her uneasy, in her husband's or in Edunata's rooms. When she did, Aly was willing to bet that the roof would come off the Gray Palace.

16

DUNEVON'S BIRTHDAY

The day before King Dunevon's birthday, the regents sent an announcement throughout the city. The "unpleasantness" was over. The criminals who had barricaded themselves in the Downwind district had been captured and killed.

Aly wondered if the proclamation fooled anyone. The truth was that the rebels had set fire to the Honeypot, then melted away, into the city via sewers and tunnels or up and over the ridge, into the mountains. The Watch had killed some, but the victory was not as great as the regents claimed it was. That same afternoon the bodies of the King's Watch night commander and its captain were placed at the harbor mouth. Aly chuckled grimly when she heard of it. Once again the regents did her work for her by putting men unaccustomed to the job into positions of authority.

The king's birthday dawned bright and hot. The Balitangs were already awake and dressed, as were their servants, ready for the first ceremony of the day. Elsren was sleepy and irritable in blue silk and white lawn. Winnamine held him in front of her as the family rode out of the house; Dove had Petranne, who was tired of being left behind. Servants and masters wore their best clothes. They joined party after party of nobles, all on the way to the broad green lands around the palace walls.

They did not have long to wait before the royal party rode out to meet them there. For the occasion the regents had assembled all the pomp that should attend a king, from the Rittevon Lancers to the King's Guard. King Dunevon was not allowed to doze against a friendly breast like his cousin Elsren. Dressed in scarlet, half asleep in the saddle, he rode his pony between the regents. Taybur Sibigat led the pony, one hand behind the little king's back. As the royal group passed, Dunevon's attendants and their families rode into place behind them.

Behind them came the other luarin and raka nobles, all in their finest day clothes. Down the broad avenue lined with soldiers they rode. People waved from their windows and cried birthday greetings to Dunevon. It was impossible to hate the little boy, even if he was a Rittevon. Banners and garlands hung everywhere, their colors as bright as the parrots that flew overhead. Even the Stormwings could be seen as decorative, the sun glinting from their steel feathers as they idly circled in the air.

Through the city they rode, and down to the royal docks, where the *Rittevon* was moored. Taybur excused himself as he turned Dunevon's reins over to Rubinyan. The ten men of the King's Guard dismounted as one and followed their captain aboard the pretty boat, spreading out to inspect it for the third time in two days. Everyone waited, getting warmer and sweatier. Only when Taybur reappeared at the top of the gangplank and nodded did Rubinyan look down at his charge.

"Your Majesty," said Rubinyan, his voice carried on the breeze, "from Her Highness and me, to you, with love, we give your first sailing vessel. For the king of an island kingdom must have his flagship, do you not agree?"

Dunevon bounced in the saddle, applauding. Everyone around him relaxed, taking honest pleasure in his happiness. He dismounted and strode up the gangplank, chest thrust out with pride. Taybur, his men, the captain, and the sailors lined along the rail bowed deeply to him.

Imajane rode over to the four boys waiting with their families and smiled at them. "Lord Elsren, Master Huldean, Master Gazlon, Master Acharn," she said teasingly, "I do believe that if you do not hurry to board, His Majesty will order the ship to sail without you."

The boys bowed to the regents in their best courtly fashion, then to their families. Well-coached, they did not run to board, though they did walk very quickly.

Funny, Aly thought, Elsren's the only real lord of Dunevon's little court. The rest are younger sons.

The gangplank was drawn up, the boarding gate secured. Aly grinned to see the captain at the wheel behind his king, clearly allowing Dunevon to steer as tender boats guided the craft out into the harbor. Sailors raced to unfurl canvas as the *Rittevon* was turned to catch the breeze. The sails filled. Off the boat sped, all other shipping kept back as the king took his maiden voyage.

Imajane yawned politely behind one hand. "Anyone of a mind to go back to bed?" she asked the nobles around her. They even laughed.

Imajane and Rubinyan left the dock for the ride up to the palace. The mothers of Dunevon's companions waved until the boys leaning over the stern rail, also waving frantically, could not see them. Then they said their farewells for the day, promising to meet that evening for what one of them described as "the mariners' triumphant return." With her own bodyguards, Winnamine returned home.

To no one's surprise, Dove set out along the dock, Ysul, Boulaj, and Junai around her, with an outer guard of household men-at-arms. Other guards and Aly's spies, dressed in everyday clothes, spread through the crowd as her invisible protectors. Aly followed as Dove greeted her friends and asked how they did. She did not linger in Dockmarket. Except for the food sellers, shops had closed in honor of the king's birthday. Instead the shop workers decorated their windows and doors, while day laborers prepared the flowers and garlands for that night's grand celebration.

Dove eventually drew her mare to a halt and dismounted. She sat on a silversmith's doorstep and asked the shopgirls there if she could help. Nearby workers stopped to look at her.

Aly crouched beside her as Dove tried to braid vines. "If you joke about your lack of skill, they'll like you better," she whispered. "I know it's hard to admit you're not perfect—ouch!" she cried as a thin elbow caught her in the side. Aly rose, wincing. "I was only telling you what folk might say, my lady!"

Dove took the braided garland she'd just finished and placed it on her head. It promptly fell to pieces, startling a laugh from those who watched. Just as instantly they stopped laughing and drew back.

She pelted them with vines. "And *that* for making fun of a poor, fumble-fingered country girl!" she told them with a smile. Laughter went through the onlookers. A couple of them ventured to give Dove hints on how her work might be done better. Dove looked at Aly from the middle of a cluster of advisors.

Aly gave her a pleased thumbs-up.

It was nearly time for Dove to return home when a sudden cold burst of air slapped Aly's face. Startled, she looked at the sky. The clouds that boiled there were blacker and lower than those that usually wet down the city in the afternoon. They moved quickly, a yellowish green glow collecting in the air below them. Flickers of brilliance caught Aly's vision. She stood in the street, staring, trying to get a better look. Was it lightning?

Dove stood. "I suppose the farmers are right. You only make a fool of yourself trying to predict weather," she remarked as the shopgirls hurriedly gathered their materials. "It's a good thing the king has an experienced captain."

Thunder rolled; lightning flashed. The wind flattened everyone's clothes around their bodies, chilling them. Aly frowned. "We're going home," she told Dove, "if you please, my lady." Aly wouldn't put it past the regents to arrange for Dove to be struck by lightning. The darkings couldn't be everywhere and hear everything. Aly's job was not to work only with those things she was sure of. She also had to consider the things she did not know, as Sarai had taught her.

Dove said quick farewells to the shopgirls. A gesture from Aly brought the men-at-arms in close, forming a ring around Dove. The wind whistled around shutters and signs, making them flap. One sign was yanked from its moorings. It missed Ysul by an inch as it cartwheeled down the street. Off the group of them went, dodging people who raced to the harbor to secure their ships. Tree branches flew through the air, ripped from their trunks. The wind yanked at shutters, dragging some from their mountings. Dove and her companions were only halfway home when the skies opened. Within a breath all of them were soaked.

At last they entered the grounds of Balitang House by way of the servants' gate. Maids descended on them with umbrellas and blankets. Inside, Quedanga ushered Dove upstairs to a waiting hot bath. Aly changed into fresh clothes, patted her darking necklace dry with a cloth, and went in search the mages. Ysul sat in Chenaol's kitchen, wearing dry clothes, a bowl of water in front of him. It shone with silvery magic in Aly's Sight.

He turned as she reached out to touch him. "This isn't your doing, is it?" she asked him in words and in sign language. "To sink the king's ship?"

Ysul emphatically signed back, *And kill other people at sea? No!*

"Very well," Aly said, not even bothering to apologize. "Where is Ochobu?"

Workroom, signed Ysul, as two kitchen maids and Chenaol said, "The mages' workroom."

"What are you so excited about?" Chenaol demanded. "It's just rain."

"With cold gusts that rip up trees and signs?" demanded Aly. "On a day when the court mages said the weather would be as usual?" She turned and ran to the mages' workroom—no Ochobu. She found the raka woman in the infirmary, grinding aromatic herbs in a mortar.

Aly stopped just inside the door. "Tell me you had nothing to do with this storm," she told the old mage.

Ochobu turned, her brown eyes suspicious. "What?"

Aly pointed to the window. Though the shutters were secured against the outside of the building with hooks, they clacked as the wind tugged them from their moorings. Overhead, thunder boomed.

Ochobu dropped her pestle and went to the window, where she stared at the storm-swept kitchen garden. The plants had been flattened by the hard rain. "This is not right," Ochobu muttered. "There is magic in it."

Aly rolled her eyes behind Ochobu's back. I don't need a mage to tell me that, when it's the wrong weather for Rajmuat! she thought, impatient. This is like a *winter* storm!

"We are taught to leave weather alone." Ochobu was talking more to herself than to Aly. "It is ungovernable. It is likely to turn on the spell caster or to exceed its limits." She glared at Aly. "And I never would have done it this way, either. Five of our people that I know of are on that ship. And there are raka and part-raka out in their boats, fishing. Do you think they will go untouched? A storm this strong will scour the harbor and the coastline for miles. Once a weather spell is begun, there is no way to stop it." From beneath her wrap-around jacket she drew a leather cord. On it dangled a circle of obsidian, set in silver. She murmured something, passed her palm over the circle, then gazed into it.

Aly Saw the flare of magic as Ochobu tried to scry for what happened at sea. Waiting, Aly realized that Trick and Secret were shivering. Gently she ran her hands over their living beads. Sweat began to roll down the raka mage's face.

Aly bit her lip. One of the first lessons she had learned was *Never interrupt the mage.* She was about to try it anyway when the old woman straightened and jammed the disk back under her jacket.

"I see nothing," Ochobu snapped. "*Nothing.* My vision of the sea is blocked, and by the magic of luarin mages."

"How can you know that?" demanded Aly. "Magic is magic. It's not luarin or Carthaki or anything."

"In the Isles it is," Ochobu replied wearily as she sat. "Luarin magic hurt us the most during the Conquest. Raka mages began to devise ways to hide our work. You often say our magics look odd—so they should. We shape them to be done in plain sight, without detection from the luarin. What I scryed is pure *luarin* magic. That is to say, *Crown* magic, because any other mage with sense learns how *we* work. Why do you think Zaimid Hetnim came here? It wasn't to be called 'brown dog' behind his back by the regents."

Aly grimaced. "Very well," she replied. Distant thunder got her attention. "Will you be all right? Will you ask other members of the Chain if they can see anything?"

Leaning on the window ledge, Ochobu nodded.

On her way to see Dove, Aly heard a commotion at the front door. Ulasim stood there, arms spread wide to block the way out. Before him stood the duchess, tension in every line of her body. She was wrapped in an oiled cloth cape against the rain. Nuritin, Dove, Pembery, Dorilize, Boulaj, and Junai stood behind her, also in rain gear.

"Ulasim Dodeka," Winnamine was telling him in a voice that shook, "you have been a friend to me, and I know you think you are being my friend now, but as the gods are my witnesses, you will either stay behind or carry my umbrella, but you *will* let me through that door. I want to be on the royal dock when they come home. You know—" Her voice cracked. She swallowed, then went on, "You know that Elsren does not care for lightning. He will be frightened. He will want his mother."

Aly signed Ulasim that she would get men-at-arms. He nodded, then told the duchess, "At least wait until your guards are here, Your Grace. And then I will be happy to hold your umbrella."

Fesgao led the men-at-arms himself. Aly also called for Ysul and three of her spy pack still in the house as she found her own waterproof cape and broad-brimmed hat. She fell back with her spies as Ysul joined Dove and Winnamine.

"Get to the marketplaces, wherever you find people," Aly murmured to them. "Say this is an uncanny storm, and too convenient with His Majesty at sea. Go." They went, as Aly followed the Balitang ladies, biting the inside of her cheek. She knew what had happened, but she could not say it, not to these people. They would want to put off hearing the truth as long as they could.

Aly caught up with Dove. No one spoke as they walked. Winnamine didn't seem to care that her feet were soaked, any more than Nuritin or Dove cared. The duchess and Nuritin held hands, like children.

When they reached Dockmarket Way, Winnamine looked at them. "It's the wrong time of year," she said, indicating the street and the harbor. "The wrong time for such damage. And this is the snuggest harbor in all the Isles. What did it do outside in the open sea?"

Aly saw what she meant. There were tiles, ribbons and flowers that had been torn from decorations, a few signs, and the collapsed remains of stalls all along the waterfront. The ships were tangles of torn sail and spars. Small boats had been driven against the pier and smashed.

When they reached the royal docks, the guards at the wrought-iron gates let them in. Winnamine led them to the berth where the *Rittevon* was supposed to drop anchor. Sailors rigged a canvas awning to shelter them from the downpour and pulled up a bench. Nuritin sat, looking older than she had at dawn. Winnamine and Dove stood, looking toward the mouth of the harbor, veiled by rain. The duchess's lips moved in silent prayer. Dove began to pray and stopped. Aly wondered if her mistress had been about to call on Kyprioth and had stopped herself, either because she didn't want her stepmother to hear her address a raka god, or because she wouldn't like what he might say.

Aly had no such compunction. She wanted information; she wanted it immediately. *Kyprioth!* she shrieked silently. Show yourself! Is this *your* doing?

The god remained silent.

Aly stepped back to question the palace darkings. They reported that Imajane was supervising the arrangements for Dunevon's party that night. Rubinyan met with officials and officers of the army and navy about the newest revolt on Malubesang. Aly's ears pricked when Trick whispered the holder of the lands in rebellion: Duke Nomru. Trick added that Rubinyan had snarled at his absent wife for arresting the duke in the first place. Aly nodded. All was not well with the regents. As she had observed in the case of her parents, it was hard for a man to silence a too-frank wife when she spoke in front of company. Da was usually amused, but then, the pricklier her mother, the happier her father. Aly had never understood it. She did understand that Rubinyan had to keep the peace with Imajane. She was the source of his power.

Let's see what he does when the source of his power goes bad, Aly thought, returning to her ladies. Let's see how he feels when she turns that Rittevon gaze on *him*.

The mothers of the other three boys in Dunevon's court came to the docks as the rain eased, to join Winnamine's vigil. The sailors found more benches. By late afternoon, the rain and the cold had moved on. A normal summer's heat dropped on the city like a wet coverlet. Their wet clothes began to steam. The king's ship was supposed to return by sunset. People were drifting out to line the harbor walkway and the docks around those reserved for the Crown, keeping a mostly silent watch.

The Balitangs should have gone home to change—the other mothers wore their court costumes under their oiled capes in case all was well—but the duchess refused to move. Both Dove and Nuritin had to persuade Winnamine to drink a cup of tea. More tea was fetched for the other ladies. When they had finished it, Nuritin and Dove sat on either side of Winnamine, Nuritin holding Winnamine's hand, Dove keeping an arm around her stepmother's shoulders. The other mothers did not talk with each other or the Balitangs. All of them were fixed on the harbor's mouth.

"They really should dress and meet the regents for the procession down Rittevon's Lance," Ulasim murmured to Aly. "Her Highness may not be pleased to find our ladies here, not attired for the festivities. At least the others are properly clothed."

Aly looked up at him. She stifled an urge to swear at the regents and instead replied, "Do you mean to drag her?"

Ulasim shrugged. His face was impassive as he stared out at the harbor. Aly was not fooled. She knew that he had been in the Balitang household since before Elsren was born.

"He is half Rittevon," she said. She knew him well enough to be sure that he, too, believed the boys were dead.

"I know that. Don't you think I know that?" Ulasim's voice was a harsh whisper. "But we could have worked something out, for him at least. . . ."

Aly didn't have to say that he fooled no one. She felt only a small, hard knot beneath her breastbone tighten as she looked at Winnamine, Dove, and the other boys' mothers, or when she looked at the harbor mouth. Someone was going to pay for this, she promised herself. She meant to present the bill herself.

The city's shadows spread across the harbor, which grew dark while the heights still lay in the sun. Along Dockmarket Way people cleaned up debris and brought lanterns to light the watchers and the dock workers. When sailors tried to light the royal docks, the duchess asked them to wait. Light would make it hard to see the harbor mouth.

The regents arrived in gala dress, surrounded by their households. Rather than dismount, they rode halfway onto the dock. Their noble companions dismounted from their horses and walked out in their wake, dressed in their finest and followed by the rest of the court. Two of the other mothers who waited instantly rose to greet the regents. The third was urged by her servants to go to them. No one dared say a word to the duchess.

Rubinyan was the first to notice the small group of Balitangs waiting by the *Rittevon*'s mooring-place. After a whispered conference with Imajane, he sent one of her ladies-in-waiting to approach the duchess.

"Your Grace, my ladies, what is this?" the lady asked, smiling. "You are not prepared for the evening, you did not meet Their Highnesses with the rest of us. . . . Her Highness is concerned."

"As are we," Nuritin said, her voice a croak after long, tense silence. "You *do* remember that storm today, do you not? It was quite severe." The lady nodded, still apparently puzzled. "We fear—Her Grace, Lady Dovasary, and I— we fear that something has happened to that ship. Our family has had more than its share of trouble of late. Should the *Rittevon* dock at the appointed hour, we will submit ourselves for the regents' forgiveness and make haste to dress and come to the palace. But we shall remain here until we are certain His Majesty and Lord Elsren are safe."

The lady favored them with a stately nod and returned to the princess. When she whispered her report, both regents nodded in understanding. Prince Rubinyan dismounted and came to see the ladies. "Winna, surely you are overreacting," he said when he was close enough, his elegant voice warm. "It was a storm. Our best seamen crewed the *Rittevon*. And our weather mages predicted fine weather for this first sailing. Violent storms in the spring rarely have much reach." He took Winnamine's free hand in his and chafed it. "So cold! My dear, you shouldn't do this to yourself."

Aly glanced at the princess. Had Imajane's face gone pale? She spoke to one of her guards, who helped her to dismount. As graceful as a swan she came to join them.

"My dear," Rubinyan said, turning to show Imajane Winnamine's white hand. "She feels like ice!"

Dove got to her feet so that the princess regent might sit. Imajane inspected the bench, then settled into place next to Winnamine, taking the hand Rubinyan had held. "While I am not a birth mother, I think I know your feelings," she said graciously. "The chance that anything may have happened to our dear little boys . . . My own blood runs cold at the thought."

After that, she kept silent. Aly was grateful. She wasn't certain that Winnamine had even heard either regent, her eyes straining toward the shadowed entrance to the harbor, but Aly had seen sparks in Nuritin's eyes. If Imajane had continued to talk, Aly wasn't at all sure that the older woman wouldn't have slapped the princess regent.

By the time the city watch cried the candle hour past sunset, people all along the docks shifted nervously. The king should have returned. When the watch cried the second candle hour past sunset, they were restless. Rubinyan walked away from the group of women and servants, beckoning to the guard captain assigned to the royal docks. Once the man trotted to his side, Rubinyan began to speak. They kept their heads close together. Between that and the flickering light it was impossible for Aly to read their lips, but it didn't matter. There was only one way for the regents to proceed if they did not want to appear guilty.

Soon horsemen galloped down both sides of the harbor. Galley drums began to pound. Sailors in the uniform of the royal navy raced to their ships. Aly was impressed by how quickly they were able to board the vessels and cast off.

At the half-candle hour, the twin beacons at the Greater and Lesser Fortresses went from gentle gleam to blazing light: they had been the destinations of the horsemen. As the mages who worked the beacons brought them to full power, Aly closed her eyes. She gave her Sight the twist that would keep her from being blinded by either the beacons or the magic in them.

When she looked again, she saw a small, two-masted ship slowly moving through the harbor's entrance. It was not the *Rittevon*. When Aly sharpened her Sight, she saw that this craft had taken a battering. One mast was broken in half; the sails were tattered. A handful of men slumped on the deck. Others worked slowly and painfully around them.

A small hand clasped her gently by the elbow. "Is it the king's ship?" Dove asked as Ulasim, Fesgao, and Junai looked at them.

Aly shook her head.

Two naval galleys moved in to bracket the mauled vessel. They were too far away for those on land to hear what was shouted between them and the newcomer, but they could see when the galleys' oars were shipped and gangplanks were swung across the distance between the vessels. Men, carrying weapons, trotted across the gangplanks to inspect the vessel. Aly nodded. That was sensible: something nasty might lurk in the hold. The navy would not allow the ship farther into the harbor until the galley captains were sure that everything was as it seemed.

At last the sailors roped the newcomer to their own vessels and returned to them. The galleys towed the ship straight to the place where the *Rittevon* was supposed to dock. Aly heard footsteps and turned. Here came the court, looking properly worried. The mothers of the other three boys gathered around Winnamine, helping her to stand or drawing strength from her, it was hard to say. Princess Imajane and Prince Rubinyan stepped up to be the first to meet the little ship. They, too, looked prepared to face bad news. Beyond the dock, on the street, the crowds waited in utter silence. The only sound in the soft night air was the mild slap of harbor waves against the land.

Finally the battered ship was tied up. The first man to come down the gangplank, bearing a small, motionless form in red satin, was Taybur Sibigat. His eyes were red and swollen. His mail was gone, his clothing ripped. There was a long gash over his left temple, and the entire right side of his face was one purple-black bruise. He limped as he carried Dunevon's corpse to the regents.

People in the crowd moaned. Someone shouted, "He's just a boy!" and was silenced.

Behind Taybur came a raka sailor. In his arms he carried one of Dunevon's court, Acharn Uniunu, very much battered but alive. He wept as he strained to reach his noble parents. They ran to him, his father seizing him while his mother wept and kissed him. Aly recognized three other men who came down from the vessel that must have rescued them, two of the *Rittevon*'s sailors and one man of the King's Guard, helped off by two raka seamen. He'd lost half of one leg. One of the royal sailors had a bandaged head; the other had an arm in a sling. The rescue ship's sailors were in no better condition.

Taybur turned away from the regents and came over to the families of the other three king's attendants who had not returned. He didn't seem to realize that he still held the dead king. Looking at them, his eyes overflowed. "I'm sorry," he whispered.

"What happened?" asked Lord Lelin as his lady and daughter began to weep.

"The storm came out of nowhere," replied Taybur. "Gale-force winds, waterspouts . . . It was a ship killer. We weren't the only ones caught out there." His voice broke. "Forgive me. My boys and I tried to save them all, but . . ." He looked at the boy in his arms, then at the mothers of the other three lads. "We couldn't even find their bodies."

"I, too, am sorry, Captain," said one of the noblewomen who had lost a son, her voice cracking. Her husband put an arm around her and led her away.

"We must go home." Winnamine stood very straight, her brown eyes wide in a face that had gone dead white. "We must . . . tell our people. . . ." She reached out with hands that shook. Dove took one, Nuritin the other.

Without saying farewell to the regents, the Balitangs left the pier, the servants and guards in a tight cluster around their ladies. Aly brought up the rear. When she glanced back, she saw something that looked like contempt on Imajane's face, and heartbreak on Taybur's. Rubinyan's face showed nothing at all.

*   *   *

Somehow they broke the news to the household and fumbled their way through changing clothes, trying to eat, and getting the ladies to their beds. Finally Aly could slip away into the flattened and littered gardens. The moment they were out of the house, Trick and Secret spread themselves out blanket-like over her shoulders and tightened. "Is this a darking hug?" Aly asked with a sad smile.

"Is a friend hug," Trick said. The pair had left only their heads out of the embrace, leaning them against Aly's cheek. "No crying, but sad, Aly."

"It was a decision I didn't want to make. You'd think I'd be happier that it was made for me, but I'm not." She found a bench by a lily pond and sat down. As she did, miniature winged horses crowded around, nuzzling her.

"I'm sorry," Aly told them softly, petting one after another. "If Nawat were here, he could tell you what's wrong. I just don't speak kudarung."

A small winged mare braced her front hooves on Aly's leg and fluttered her wings. That much kudarung Aly knew, at least. She bent down to pick up the mare, cuddling her in her arms.

Secret shifted, pulling together to flow down to the bench next to Aly. There the small darking rolled and moved, shaping itself as a miniature kudarung. When the shape settled, Secret jumped down among the other miniature winged horses and went muzzle to muzzle with the stallion who governed them, to tell them what had happened to the Balitangs.

Aly looked up at the sky, blurred slightly through the spells that covered the house and grounds.

"Kyprioth," she said, running her hand over the mane of the winged horse in her lap, "I want you, my dear. And not in a happy, let-me-kiss-your-grizzled-cheek way, either."

"My grizzled cheek may wither of neglect." The god was there, seated on the rim of the lily pond, dabbling his toes in the water. "You've been very noisy in your calls for me, I would like to point out. If I got headaches, you would have given me one."

"If you knew I was calling, why didn't you come?" she demanded.

"Because I knew you would scold, and scoldings bore me," he replied. "As if they do any good after the fact."

"Was this your work?" she asked softly, gently, that hard place under her breastbone scorching the inside of her skin. "Did you murder those little boys?"

"I? Please. I'm busy preparing for battle, mustering my fellow tricksters. I refuse to worry over what mortals are up to," he said carelessly. "And I won't do everything for you. It's bad for your character."

Aly shifted until she had a clear view of that clever face. "What did you do? It's not like you to be evasive about your tricks. Bragging's more your style."

Kyprioth looked at her. Aly felt his power as he tried to overwhelm her. She closed her eyes and fought. "Stop it," she told him stubbornly. "You've already tried this with me, and it ages *very* fast." The force of his godhood slacked off enough that she could breathe.

"I told you, my brother and sister are near to their return to the Isles," he said, as if she were not very bright. "You and my raka have given me some of my old vigor, but it won't be enough. The only way I will be strong enough to fight my brother and sister is if you stop tiptoeing around the king and take this country back. Since you could not seem to reach that point, I made a few suggestions here and there." He eased up on his power completely.

Aly took a breath and ignored the sweat that trickled down her face. The little kudarung in her lap whickered and licked up the salt. "What kind of suggestions?" Aly wanted to know.

Kyprioth inspected his rings. "I mentioned to the regents that it's a shame they must bow to the whims of a four-year-old, when they have more experience and intelligence than any Rittevon boy king. Ludas Jimajen—Rubinyan's ancestor—"

"I know," murmured Aly.

Kyprioth grinned at her, white teeth flashing in the dark. "*He* was supposed to have been the next king, or his son." He began to juggle balls of gold light. "That was the agreement he made with Rittevon, so that both of them could claim the throne. But Jimajen was killed supposedly by a raka assassin after Rittevon's second wife gave birth to twin boys. Amazing how these things work, isn't it?"

Rubinyan Jimajen had no children by his marriage to Imajane, but he did have sons from his first marriage. He even had grandsons. Had Imajane ever wondered if he didn't want to take the throne and make the next monarch a Jimajen king?

"I love to watch you think," Kyprioth said. "Your face gets so agreeable."

"Was the storm yours?" she asked.

He shook his head, as if disappointed. "Why should *I* need to brew one?" he inquired patiently. "They had mages who can do it. Mages who care only that they keep their untrusting master and mistress happy."

"Is that all you did with the regents themselves, then? A suggestion?" she wanted to know, eyebrows raised in casual interest.

"Well, I reinforced it with repetition," the god admitted. "Whenever he had a tantrum, whenever he shouted that he hated them, as children so agreeably do when they are crossed. Aly, you aren't usually so dense. Dunevon was in the way, as was Elsren. They had to go. If I waited for you tenderhearts, my brother and sister would return and wrap me in chains, then kick me off the edge of the universe. I didn't care to wait."

Aly looked at him, a mantle of cold settling over her skin. Twice she had erred very badly. The first time was when she had been too cocky to think Sarai might surprise her. The second time was at present. She had forgotten that Kyprioth was not a wildly eccentric, magically powerful human. She looked into his face and saw that those lives meant nothing to him. He was a god. He might care for a few chosen humans. He might even enjoy their company. But in the end, he could no more feel as humans did than could Stormwings.

She got to her feet. "I'm sorry you can't grieve for those people," she said quietly. "You don't know what you miss." She set her dozing miniature kudarung down and returned to the house. Once she reached her workroom, she put her head on her table. "Tell me about the dragons," she whispered to the darkings. As they talked of burning sands and fields of stars, she tried to imagine them and nothing else, particularly nothing to do with the sea.

She woke in the morning slumped across her worktable. Her head felt as if it were stuffed with cotton. Somehow she cleaned herself up and made herself eat, a ghost in a household full of ghosts. Conversations were quiet and kept to the basics. The ladies retreated to the nursery to tell Petranne and to mourn for the second time in less than a year. Finding herself unneeded, Aly retreated to her workroom. Automatically she busied herself with information, starting with the darkings.

She expected the news they gave her: The regents had summoned the chief Mithran priest to crown them, with their luarin cronies as witnesses. The official coronation, with all its pomp, would be held the day after the coming eclipse of the sun, in celebration of Mithros's victory over the dark, Trick said.

Aly turned a silver coin over in her fingers, walking it across their tops, then under them. "They have to put it that way," she said quietly. "It's that or admit their god is vulnerable for a day."

She assembled more reports, taking in information and writing it up for the raka leaders. Even if they had been able to meet that day, she couldn't have borne it. She had told Elsren stories, changed his clothes, taught him to somersault. She did not want to think of him cold and alone in Kyprioth's uncaring waters. Instead she lit a stick of incense to the Wave-Walker, the merciful sea goddess, in the hope that she would see Elsren properly to the Peaceful Realms. Aly did not know how she would attend the memorial service held when there was no body to bury, but she knew that she must.

It was almost noon when the clamor of crows drew Aly out into the garden. A cloud of them flew overhead, calling to each other, telling the native crows that they were allies, come from the north. Aly watched them, numb. *Tomorrow I must get to work,* she told herself. *There are opportunities now, with the Crown unsettled. I must not sit here like a lump, or allow my people to do so.*

At least she had custom on her side. With the announcement of the emergency coronation had come the proclamation of a week of mourning for the Isles, a week when all but the most necessary work was to be set aside. Aly did not mean to idle that entire week away, but she needed at least one day to collect herself. From the shock on all the other faces of the Balitang household, she could see that everyone felt the same, even Ulasim. Even Ochobu.

She returned to her workroom and to processing information. Someone had left a stack of reports for her while she'd been roaming. Most of her pack and their recruits had been out and about, listening to what people had to say. Except for Boulaj and Junai, they'd had little or nothing to do with Elsren. His death had less of an impact on them, and in Dunevon's death they saw an opportunity. Aly had expected them to: she had trained them for that, as she herself had been trained. It was just very hard to get excited over the opportunity when that knot of fire under her breastbone had turned to ice.

Someone opened her door without knocking. Aly looked up from her work, scowling, and froze. It was Nawat, sun-bronzed, bearing a scar on one cheekbone, wearing a loose cotton shirt and breeches, and tired boots. He set a bow and a quiver of crow-fletched arrows by Aly's door and came toward her, an odd look on his face.

It was a look she would have known on any other man's face as he greeted the love of his life. She had seen it blaze in her father's eyes, King Jonathan's eyes, and Uncle Numy's eyes, but never in Nawat's. It was there now.

Aly jumped to her feet and threw herself into his arms. It was no crow-turned-man who caught her up, but a man, confident in who he was and what he wanted. Aly had time to emit one squeak before he covered her mouth with his. She clung to him and lost herself in warmth and a melting in her belly and legs that went beyond desire. Nawat drew back, took a breath, and kissed her again, his lips sweet and moist, his arms hard with muscle as he lifted her off the floor. Aly's hands explored the muscles of his back and the softness of his black hair, but her mind could escape his mouth for only a second before it came back to his kisses. Nawat carried her to her worktable and sat her on piles of reports so their faces were at the same level.

Trick and Squeak dropped from her neck, where they were being mashed. Aly didn't see them watch with interest as Nawat kissed her forehead, her cheeks, and her palms. Finally she tugged away and rested her forehead on the V of brown flesh that showed in the collar of his shirt.

"We were fifty miles away when we got word of the nestlings," Nawat whispered. "I had to come ahead faster. I knew you would need me."

Aly looked up into his eyes. She felt her chin quiver. All she could do was hide her face against his shirt again as the tears came in a rush. Nawat held her close and preened her hair with his fingers as Aly cried herself out. She didn't even try to apologize as her head slowly cleared. She knew he understood.

"They were a problem," she whispered at last. "But I never wanted it solved like this."

"Good," Nawat replied over her head. "I would not wish you to drown our nestlings."

She laughed and sobbed at the same time, then pulled herself away. Taking a handkerchief from her sarong, she mopped her face. "I got your shirt wet," she pointed out. Then she looked at him. "If you came the fastest way, did you steal those clothes?"

Nawat's smile made her heart do funny things. "I hid some of mine away in case I should have to come home this way," he explained. "My clothes fit better than stolen ones. There are little creatures on your table."

Aly half turned and saw the darkings. "They're darkings," she explained. "And my friends. That one's Trick, and that one's Secret."

"Is this lovemaking?" Secret inquired.

"No. It is kissing. Lovemaking comes after kissing," Trick replied.

"That is true," Nawat said. There was a look in his eyes that made gooseflesh ripple over Aly's body. "Please go away, little friends of Aly."

The darkings plopped to the floor and rolled out of the room. Nawat went over and locked the door. Aly watched him with a mixture of nervousness and anticipation.

"I don't think this is the best time to do what I think you want to do," she pointed out.

"There will never be a good time until Dove is queen." Nawat walked over to put his arms around her again. "We might be dead by then." He kissed her temple, then his lips drifted until they found hers again. This kiss was long, slow, and sweet, the kiss of lovers who had all of time.

At the end of it, Nawat held Aly's face in his hands. "I am no longer a crow who turned into a man, Aly Bright Eyes," he told her soberly. "I am a man who can be a crow at need, but I am still a man, and I love you. I have seen so many people die since I left you. I do not want to wait for priests to say words or for you to want chicks. If I go to the Peaceful Realms tomorrow, or the day after, I want to go with the taste of you on my lips."

He kissed her again, slowly, folding her into an embrace that left her breathless. Aly had time to gasp when he pressed his mouth against the tender skin on her neck and collarbone. Dizzy, she suddenly realized that he'd undone her sash.

"Um, wait," she said, her voice wobbling.

"No," he replied, gently placing the sash, and its cache of knives, out of their way. "No more waiting, Aly."

"I didn't mean that kind of waiting, exactly," Aly told him, holding him at arm's length. Nawat lifted the arm, kissing the inside of her wrist, then the inside of her elbow. I had no notion those areas were so sensitive, she thought giddily. "Nawat, stop. There's, um, a thing, for us females. . . ." He was kissing her palm. It was very distracting. "Nawat, we can't bring chicks into the world, I'm not ready, we're not, and well, there's a thing women wear, only I haven't got one." Babbling again, observed that cool corner of her brain. "Until we have a safe nest, I can't—not without that charm."

Nawat smiled and pulled something from his pocket. It shone gold and shimmered silver with its touch of magic. "My fighters told me," he explained as he draped the anti-pregnancy charm around her neck. "It is a thing women put on, until they want chicks," he said, laughter in his dark eyes.

"Oh," Aly said weakly. "That, well, that changes some things, definitely—"

Nawat kissed her again. This time his free hand worked at the tie of her sarong. Aly couldn't help him. She was too busy undoing his belt.

"I want to always have the taste of you on my lips," Nawat whispered as they sank onto the floor.

Aly slept, the first deep sleep she'd had in a long time. She woke to find Nawat setting a pallet on the floor beside her. He'd brought a lamp and a blanket as well. Eyeing the lamp, she murmured, "It's night?"

"Nearly midnight. Ulasim said to let you rest." Nawat knelt beside her and cupped her cheek with his hand. "I did not think it would hurt you. Lovemaking."

She smiled at him. "It often hurts the first time, when you're a girl. So I've been told."

"Only the first time?" Nawat asked.

She kissed his palm. "I think so."

"Then perhaps we should try again," Nawat said gravely, bending down to kiss Aly.

She nodded vigorously until their lips met.

17

MOURNING

Aly opened her eyes. She was curled inside the curve of Nawat's body, his arm over her waist. On the floor next to their pallet was an audience: a few miniature kudarung and five crows, all watching with fascination. Warm lips met the back of her neck, raising goose bumps on her body.

"What time is it?" Aly inquired drowsily.

A crow made the sound for "before the sun rises."

"If the sun is not awake, *I* am not awake," Aly said. She turned under the blanket to burrow her face into Nawat's shoulder.

"Go away," he told the others.

It only then occurred to Aly that the crows and the kudarung could not have entered through closed shutters or a closed door. She sat up quickly. The door was open, but the frame was not empty. A number of weary yet fascinated faces—Ulasim's, Junai's, Yoyox's, Boulaj's, and Kioka's—looked down at them. Aly was grateful that Nawat had left her in the blanket as he proceeded to dress.

She raised an eyebrow at their audience. "Enjoying the view?" she inquired.

Yoyox grinned. "Actually, yes."

"I enjoyed the other view," said Kioka, watching Nawat pull on his shirt.

Aly glared at her. "I know a hundred different ways to make you disappear," she warned the young woman.

"This is all as beautiful as the flowers of spring," observed Ulasim. "Nawat, where are your warriors?"

Nawat kissed Aly gently, then straightened. "Thirty miles north, sir," he replied, a soldier in answer to his general. "I brought two hundred and fifty, as many as could be spared. They should be on the outskirts of the city by tonight."

"Come give me what news you have," Ulasim ordered, beckoning. "You may settle romantic matters later. The regents have decided they no longer need a Rittevon male to rule." He shooed the others away from the door and led Nawat across the hall. Nawat closed the door. Aly scowled at it, remembering it should have been locked. "This is the problem with training people to open locks," she complained as she dressed. "They can turn what you taught them against you." As she picked up her darking necklace, Trick and Secret poked out their heads. "Human lovemaking looks silly," Secret told Aly.

"Darking way more sensible," added Trick.

Aly settled them around her neck. "Our way is more fun," she replied absently, her mind on the rebellion. Getting up to wrap her sarong, she stared at the map that marked the path of the war. As soon as her sash was arranged, she set a pin for Nawat's warriors, on their way to Rajmuat.

What had possessed the regents to kill those boys? she wondered. Now, when they are stretched so thin? They will lie and say it was the storm, but who will believe them? Do they think people will accept them on the throne? They'll have to fight, and they haven't got the soldiers.

The numbness of the day before was gone. Her heart still ached for Elsren and the others, but she could wall it off to consider her next move. Sitting at her desk, she began to pore over the reports she had not yet reviewed, looking for signs of weakness and for ideas. It took the breakfast gong to break through her concentration. She was ravenous.

She could not have forgotten their loss even if she had wanted to. In the servants' mess hall she saw black armbands everywhere, and eyes still red and swollen from weeping. Talk was kept quiet. Chenaol had retreated inside herself, dishing out food as if she didn't even care what it was. Aly simply accepted her bowl and did not try to distract the cook. When Nawat came to eat beside her, they slid together until their legs touched and ate in silence.

Once the meal was done Aly went upstairs to get clean clothes. "She slept on a trundle bed in Her Grace's room," Boulaj said when Aly asked for Dove. She was shaking out black clothing for Dove to wear. "So did Lady Nuritin. I'm glad Nawat came back."

Aly, caught as she wrapped a clean sarong around her, blinked. "I know *I* am, but why are you?" she asked, startled.

"You seemed a little lost after he left," Boulaj explained. "Not lost as a spy, but lost as a woman. As if he'd taken a piece of you away that you needed. He has changed."

Aly tucked her fresh sarong, remembering that man's look, and those very male kisses. "I, um, hadn't noticed. Much." She began to wrap her sash. "How is Her Grace?"

"Her Grace is livid," Winnamine said coldly from the door. Aly turned to face her. Dove and Nuritin stood behind Winnamine, watching her. "Her Grace wants to know why the god sent you to this house, Aly."

Aly swallowed. You should have expected this, she told herself.

Winnamine continued, "Where is our great destiny that was promised by the god? Can it be the god *meant* my husband and son to die? That my little boy had to drown so the regents would take power and the throne would be strong? Was *that* it?" Her eyes were overbright, but no tears fell. Aly was certain that the duchess had no tears left.

Gently Aly said, "No, Your Grace." The sight of her pain made her stomach knot. "There is no greatness in what happened to Elsren, or to the duke. I'm afraid the gods don't care what makes their servants happy. They see only what they desire. We are tools to their ends."

"You speak knowledgeably about gods," the duchess said bitterly. "You know a great many, do you?"

"I have seen the god-touched in Tortall, Your Grace," Aly replied, thinking of her parents and Aunt Daine. "They did not look entirely happy. They looked—driven, at times. As the god drives me."

Winnamine turned, nearly colliding with Nuritin and Dove. They moved out of her way just in time and followed her back to her rooms.

"That's the problem with luarin," Boulaj observed softly. "They think gods have rules and follow them. They should dedicate their lives to the Trickster, as we do. They would not be comfortable, but they would not have this illusion that life is supposed to make sense, either."

"Thinking of trying for the priesthood?" Aly wanted to know. She blinked rapidly. She would not cry, not for the duchess, or the Balitang family, or herself. The time for tears was over.

"To be a raka under the luarin is to be a priest of the Trickster," replied Boulaj. "Will you help me fold this sheet?"

Aly and Boulaj straightened Dove's chambers, then Aly went back downstairs. She met Quedanga in the hall that led to her workroom. "I left the night's gleanings on your table, and I rolled up your pallet," the housekeeper said. "The city is quiet—there is little to pass on. I think we are all in shock."

"Thanks, Quedanga," Aly said. "It won't last, you know."

"I know." Quedanga's grin showed a wolfish number of teeth. "And then the raka's time will come."

And then the raka's time *may* come, Aly replied silently. Imajane and Rubinyan have opened the door for it, but it is not yet set in stone.

She went to her table and began to make her way through the heap of news Quedanga had collected from her own network within the city. Aly wasn't sure how long she worked before the runner Wayan rapped on the frame of the door. When Aly nodded, she came over to lean against Aly affectionately. She opened her hand to show a folded piece of paper, sealed with a blank circle of wax.

"A man at the servants' gate gave me this for you," she said. "He said it was from his master."

"Is he waiting for a reply?" Aly inquired. She inspected the note to see if the wax had been tampered with. She had taught her people ways to remove wax seals, but she also knew how to tell if somebody had been playing with one. This note had not been opened.

Wayan shook her head. "He gave me a silver gigit and left."

Aly kissed the girl's cheek. "Then you don't need a tip from me. Scamper."

Giggling, Wayan left. Aly got to her feet and locked her door before she heated a thin knife and slid the hot metal under the seal. The note popped open.

That boat came apart in the first big wave. They didn't need a storm that sank a number of other ships, too. Whatever it is that you intend to do, I am your man. —T.S.

Only one T.S. that she knew of would send her such a message: Taybur Sibigat. The regents—now the monarchs—had made a stupid mistake in killing the boy king he had loved. Aly was certain that Sibigat had been meant to drown, and just as sure that he had noticed that.

Aly ran her fingers over her darking necklace as she tucked the message back into her sash. She would keep this to herself for the present. The time would come soon when she would ask Taybur to make good on his promise. At this point, they both needed him to remain where he was and do his job. History was rife with palace revolts spearheaded by the very fighters who were there to protect the rulers.

They never should have killed his king, thought Aly as she returned to her work.

Two quick raps and an open slap on her door told Aly she was wanted in the meeting room. She locked her workroom and went in. Her pack, from Boulaj to Yoyox, waited there for her. They all watched her with bright attention, that look of hounds who had at last caught the scent.

Aly closed and locked the door, then settled in a chair. "We're in mourning," she stated.

"We would like our own way to mourn," said Jimarn. "Guide us, Duani."

"You've been doing this for a while," Aly pointed out. "Surely you don't need me."

Atisa rolled her eyes. "You're being aggravating."

"Sometimes aggravation is the irritant that forces a result," Aly replied quickly, then sighed. "My goodness. You young people are so impatient."

"We know *you*," Olkey explained patiently as he popped a snow pea into his mouth. "Knowing you, we decided you probably have a list of things to tidy up in that clever head of yours. Lazy children that we are, we'd rather you did the thinking, and we handled the details."

Aly twiddled her thumbs, staring at the ceiling. This was what she had been working for since the fall before: the time when their minds and hers would work to reach the same place at the same time. I've done well with them, she told herself. It's time for them to see what they can do.

"I don't know how this can be, but the naval shipyards are a mess," she remarked at last. "All that wood and tar, all those ships being repaired. What if company comes to call?"

"That's a big one," said Guchol. "That will take work." Aly raised an eyebrow. Guchol responded to her unspoken question. "We can *do* it," she said hurriedly. "There are some knots to untie, though."

"Come to me if you need help," Aly said.

"I don't want to burn ships," Junai snapped. Like Boulaj, she had been closer to the family than the others, which meant that she had known Elsren. "I want them scared."

"People are very scared by bad things that seem to have come out of nowhere," Aly observed, her gaze back on the ceiling. "Things like a basket of rats in a closed bedroom. Or a dead rat." She looked at Junai and Boulaj. "A dead rat appears on the streets of the Windward District, where folk think they are so safe . . . it frightens them."

Boulaj and Junai exchanged bright-eyed glances. "We can do that," Boulaj said. "At night, once the house is abed."

"What about the regents?" demanded Lokak, dark eyes hard. "When do we strike *them*?"

"Giant-killing is tricky," Aly replied, knowing Lokak had spoken for the pack. "If you go for his eyes, he kills you by stepping on you. Instead you cut his legs from under him. With a weak army and navy, the new monarchs will struggle to protect themselves. Duke Nomru's estates have risen on his behalf against the Crown. His New Majesty needs more troops, but he doesn't have enough for Malubesang *and* the other rebellions. He'll have to scramble. As he does, he and his queen will be vulnerable. Our general can see that day come. He'll let us know when it is time. For now, we help him by doing what we have trained to do."

Most of them gathered around Guchol. As they whispered, Aly returned to her workroom. It would be foolish to suggest anything to them, when she didn't know the shipyard and they did. She *would* leave the list of Sevmire's spies in the Windward District out where Junai or Boulaj could find it. If they could pick her lock to see who had kept her in her workroom all night, they could pick it to find the list, too.

Back at her worktable, Aly set her darking necklace on its surface. "What happened while I was—occupied?" she asked them.

"Royal tax collector for all of Lombyn is dead," Trick announced. "Royal governor of Malubesang is missing."

Aly nodded. "Very good. Is that it?"

"For yesterday, with Rubinyan and Imajane," said Trick.

"What of my friend Sevmire?" Aly wanted to know.

"Bean say he draws up list of possible enemies," piped Secret. "Balitangs on it. Also Fonfalas. Also Engan."

"Also Obemaek," Trick added. "Sevmire asleep now."

"He drink too much wine," Secret explained. "He drools on desk."

"Bean ask, can he take list away from Sevmire?" Trick relayed.

Aly stretched. "Sevmire will just make another one."

"But he will wake up with dry quill and open ink bottle and no list," explained Secret. "Bean say, he will search everywhere, and then he will think someone took it."

"Bean say, Sevmire will twitch and drink and suspect his people," added Trick. "He will think they try to take his place with Rubinyan. Bean say— says," it corrected itself, to Aly's surprise, "that Sevmire worries all the time about everything. Bean says, if he worries more, he trusts people less."

So not only have I taught them to be spies, but it seems they're also learning to speak more like human beings, Aly mused. I wonder if this is a good thing or a bad one? "Tell Bean that by all means it should take the list if it can," she said. "And if Bean can think of more things to do to Sevmire *without* getting caught, it shouldn't worry about asking, just go ahead." I do it for my pack, she told herself. I can surely let the darkings off the leash as well.

After a moment Trick said, "Bean is very happy. He takes list into Sevmire's dung room."

"He will drop it in the dung pit," explained Secret.

Aly nodded. She loved their term for a privy. And a dung pit is where Sevmire himself belongs, she thought. Where they all belong.

She worked on papers until her belly reminded her that she had missed lunch. Out she went, in search of cold meat, bread, and some fruit. Once she had her meal in her hands, she went out into the garden to the Pavilion of Secrets. She wanted some time alone, to think in privacy of the wonderful things that had happened the night before. She knew moments like that were stolen from time, and she did not want to forget any of it. Leaning into a corner of the pavilion, she closed her eyes to remember, and dozed. When the food tumbled from her hands to the ground, the miniature kudarung swooped in for the feast.

She woke to their whickering and a shadow that loomed over her. Her senses identified a large body between her and escape. Aly was on her feet with two knives in her hands before she realized it was Ulasim.

He crouched to pet the clamoring kudarung around his legs and looked at Aly with appreciation. "That was very quick for someone who just woke up," he remarked. "It is as I always suspected—you sleep with one eyelid cracked."

"Only sometimes," Aly replied with a sheepish grin. She put her knives away. "If I slept that way all the time, I'd be predictable, wouldn't I?"

"Very true," Ulasim said, the corners of his eyes crinkling in his secret smile. "Nawat went out to see to his people. He said he would return for supper. Have you new information for me?"

Aly nodded and told him the news from Lombyn and Malubesang. "Nomru's people rising against the monarchs, that's bad."

Ulasim nodded. "Nomru is the chief landholder on Malubesang."

Aly bit her lip. She wanted him to look beyond the raka. "Call it a hunch, but I bet the Fonfala estates won't be far behind," she suggested, watching his face for his reaction. "They were friends, before the duke's escape. They're neighbors on Malubesang. The lands are held by Her Grace's brother. It stands to reason."

Ulasim's thin smile hooked to one side. "And the Nomrus and Fonfalas both belong to that pathetic luarin sewing circle," he added. "Why should I deal with them now, when they have been good for nothing before?"

"Because Dove is one of them," Aly informed him. "And—I think they are ripe to actually do something."

"I shall consider it," replied Ulasim. He hesitated, then grinned. "It is good to see you are not *completely* distracted by . . . other things."

Aly made a face at him. The sight of the black armband he wore punctured her good mood. "I wish I could stay distracted. I need to get one of those."

"Don't feel guilty because you are alive," he counseled, wrapping an arm around her shoulders as they walked back to the house. "I feel guilty enough for twelve people."

"Because the choice of what to do about the Rittevon heirs was taken from your hands?" she asked.

The arm around her shoulders tightened, then relaxed. "That," he admitted.

"We can and will all feel guilty about that," Aly consoled him. "And we can share our feelings with our new rulers."

Nawat returned, as promised, in the late afternoon. Aly heard the bawling of amused crows and translated that they were laughing at him for changing shape and putting on uncomfortable clothes. When he emerged from the stable loft where he had changed, she was waiting for him. They kissed, and then she asked, "Would you talk to your friends for me?"

"So we are back to that," he commented, shaking his head. "My only value to you is as a crow."

"Nawat!" she cried, grabbing his shirt. "That's not true, I . . ." She saw the glitter in his deep-set eyes and gaped at him. "You're *teasing* me?"

He kissed her. Even when their lips parted, he kept his arm around her waist. "You look beautiful when you are shocked. It is sweet," he said, a man's grin on his face. "This is more fun than dragging Ochobu's clothes in the mud."

Aly pushed him away lightly, not hard enough to make him let go. "I swear she still expects you to do that," she said. "And I have some fun for your kindred, if you would like to explain it to them."

He tipped his head back and called in something far better than Aly's clumsy crow-speech. Immediately three of the birds came flapping down to land in the branches of a nearby tree.

"I was thinking," Aly began, "that winged messengers come and go from the palace all the time. It would be nice if your people could force them to lose their messages or even drive them to the ground."

One of the crows admitted, in caws and clicks, that this *could* be interesting.

It would require more skill than tormenting Stormwings, Nawat replied in the same language.

The crows flicked their wingtips and took off, already calling the news to the other crows within earshot.

"So they'll do it?" Aly wanted to know. "Or will they just talk about it?"

Nawat held her close. "It amuses them. They'll do it," he said with a grin.

That night the rebel leaders gathered in the meeting room to hear the news from all over the city and the realm. This time Nawat joined them to report what he'd been doing as a warrior and what news he had gathered from the crows. Once more Aly was awed by the change in him, from ill-at-ease bird in a human's body to confident young man. Ulasim was thanking him when suddenly their world went a bright, roaring white. The air boomed as if they sat inside a monstrous kettle drum. That vast roaring sound filled Aly's ears until she would have screamed to drown it out, except that she feared she was already screaming.

The roar stopped abruptly. Outside, thunder crashed directly overhead.

Kyprioth appeared next to Aly's chair. "This is where I leave you all," he told them as he looked apprehensively at the ceiling. "My brother and sister have returned." He kissed Aly's cheek. "Good luck. Victories, remember!" He vanished.

They didn't even wait to discuss what they were doing: all of the leaders raced outside to look skyward. Pale white flames spread from the moon, which shone full at a time when it was only supposed to be a quarter full. Bright orange waves of light spread across the sky in sheer curtains. Lightning flashed everywhere and faded.

"And so the fun begins," murmured Ulasim. He clapped his hands together and rubbed them. "Come, my friends. Let's see how much trouble we can cause."

Aly and Nawat spent the night on a pallet in the Pavilion of Secrets, talking through much of it. When dawn came, they went outside to join the fighters for morning drill. Everyone watched for dawn when they weren't actually facing off against one another. When it came, they could see the gods were still locked in battle. The sun shed light and heat as it always did, but its rays were far longer than normal, dark orange pennants around the gold disk. White, fiery veils that had to represent the Goddess drifted in the morning sky, while everywhere the sparks that showed Kyprioth and the lesser tricksters winked in and out, points of color that never stayed the same hue for more than a moment.

Aly shivered and concentrated on her staff work. It was unnerving to see a sky so different from normal. She didn't like it at all, and she was nearly certain that the others felt the same. It was a relief to go into the laundry with Nawat and take a long bath together. Afterward he left on errands for Ulasim, while Aly went upstairs to see if Dove needed anything. Once again she found Boulaj gathering up Dove's washing. The bed was freshly made, the room aired out, the water basin dumped and cleansed. "What's this?" Aly demanded with a frown. Dove's night table had been straightened. So had the stack of books next to her bed.

Boulaj faced her, determination on her long face. "Aly, you're needed for other things," she said. "I trained to be a maid as well as bodyguard for Lady Sarai, and I like it."

"She's right." Dove emerged from the dressing room she had once shared with Sarai. "Things will heat up now that Imajane and Rubinyan rule us. You're needed to do what you do best. Boulaj and I manage nicely as mistress and maid."

Aly was a little hurt that they had come to an understanding without her. The moment she recognized the emotion, she thrust it away as meaningless. Dove and Boulaj were right, and that was that. What mattered was her own ability to pass information quickly to the rebel leaders. She needed to concentrate on that and on the kind of mischief that would drive their new rulers into a rage.

Boulaj yawned. Aly looked at her and raised an eyebrow. "Late night?" she asked wickedly.

"We got *some* sleep," Boulaj replied. "And the work itself was satisfying."
She caught Dove's curious glance and said, "Spy stuff."

Aly held up a finger and went to the window. Something, some sound,
made the shutters quiver under her palms. She opened them. In the distance
she heard a roar of noise from the direction of the market districts and Downwind. She glanced above the nearby trees and saw smoke in the distance.
Without a word to the other two she raced downstairs.

Outside the front door stood Nuritin, Fesgao, and a sweat-bathed Olkey.
His eyes registered Aly's arrival as he told the other two, "It was the gods fighting that set them off, my lady, sir. Over in Downwind, folk were weeping in
the street over the little boys' deaths. They've got three songs written about it
already, and one of them calls it *murder*. And then there was last night, and
they all waited for the dawn, and saw all the lights and colors. . . . They went
mad. They're rioting in Downwind and the Honeypot, and the folks in Dockmarket are closing up. It's just a matter of time before they call for a lockdown
of the city."

"Secure the gates," ordered Nuritin. "Put more guards on them."

Fesgao saluted her. "Very good, my lady," he said.

Here in the open Aly heard the distant calls of horns and the clang of
alarm gongs. She went back inside to see what her people knew.

The regents kept the city under martial law for three days, not caring if
people had enough food to eat. Those foolish enough to challenge the King's
Watch found themselves hustled off to local jails. If the Watchmen got very
annoyed, they sent the offender to Kanodang. The fires were put out; a number
of rioters were hanged. There was nothing anyone in Balitang House could do
but wait it out. People crept in and out using the tunnel system, but they had to
be careful. Aly nearly lost Atisa and Ukali of her pack to the Watch, until the
pair's recruits spotted them and swarmed their captors to help them to escape.

The flow of information into the house continued, courtesy of the darkings, the crows, and the mages of the Chain. Through them the household
learned of riots all over the cities and towns of the Isles. It was too much for
the people to take, coming all at once: word of the little king's drowning, the
informal coronation of two new monarchs, and the gods' battle overhead.
Most riots were put down savagely. Others burned themselves out by the end
of the week.

Seven days after the boy king had drowned, memorial services for him and
his three dead companions were held in the Black God's temples. The people of
Rajmuat came to pay their respects in numb silence, mourning not just the children but the hundred-odd others who had drowned with them, their boats cap-
sized or their homes crushed by falling trees. After the prayers to the god
ended, the faithful carried flowers down to the harbor and tossed them into the
brown, soupy water. In silence still, everyone returned to their homes.

At noon that day, the regents lifted martial law, though soldiers were everywhere. Roaming the city streets, Aly took note of the damage, most of it in the poor districts of the town. Trudging back to Balitang House, she wished the people would turn that wrath on the sources of their pain rather than on their own homes. *We need more rumors about the monarchs and their plans for the kingdom,* she told herself. *The poor need to hate the monarchs as much as they fear the gods. This time it was the gods who drove them to riot, I think. Next time it must be Imajane and Rubinyan.*

During that hot afternoon's rest time, a number of people visited the house. Aly joined those who had come to see her in the meeting room. There she found members of her pack who were not out in the city and a number of trusted recruits who had been approved by Ochobu or Ysul. Vitorcine Townsend was present as well. Aly had decided she would make a good addition to her spies.

Nearly everyone had written reports for Aly, information that had piled up while it had been so difficult for their contacts to get to them. They placed the reports in Aly's hands. A representative of the rebel spies in the palace was present, this being his normal free day. He too gave a sheaf of reports to Aly. She glimpsed at the topmost one. The first line read: *I. went into a rage over a scrap of paper.*

Aly nodded and yawned. That plan seemed to be unfolding nicely. Folding her hands on her belly, she looked at the packed room. "Has anyone anything special for me?"

The man from the palace raised a hand. "Lord Sevmire dismissed three of his secretaries this morning. He says he refuses to work with those he cannot trust. And there is an armed guard at the mages' house. Stormwings roost on the roof peak. No one is allowed to leave."

Aly whistled silently. "An interesting development."

Bacar, the footman from across the street, raised his hand. "The housekeeper at Murtebo House was found with her throat cut. There was a paper pinned to her clothes that read *Spy.*"

A ragamuffin wearing only a loincloth spoke. "Up on Junoh Street, they found two like that, a footman and a maid. Dead the same way, both wearing *Spy* signs. That's what the folk who found them said."

"Any more?" Aly inquired. They all shook their heads. She nodded. "Very well. You already know the rumor that the storm that sank the boys' ship was not a natural one. And here's another thing—a source I trust says the boat went to pieces suspiciously fast. Add also that the mages who serve the Crown appear to be under house arrest. Those are interesting bits of news, aren't they?"

Her listeners nodded.

One of the Obeliten maids asked, "Duani, everyone knows the Crown mages have been known to meddle with weather before, though they know they can't control it." There was a chorus of yesses and calls of "She's right." Emboldened, the maid continued, "And isn't it strange how the one child saved belonged to a family known to be great friends of the regents?"

Aly thought that was more luck than attention to that particular boy's life. At the same time, she had not forgotten that the only heir to a family title on the *Rittevon* had been Elsren. Dunevon's other three companions had been younger sons unlikely to inherit the title. Their families could afford to lose them, a fact of which the new rulers had been aware.

Aly nodded. "Those also are good points to make with those you talk to," she told her people. "Ask your particular friends on the streets if Mithros and the Goddess are not angry because they are represented by monarchs with the blood of children on their hands. Especially the Goddess, as children are her care." She noticed their startled glances: they had not thought of this. "One more thing. The royal fortress at Galodon has lost at least half of its soldiers and sailors to bad food. The strongest fighting force in Rajmuat is now only the Rittevon Guard." She waved them out. "Be watchful, and take no unnecessary chances," she warned as they prepared to go. "We are going to make our new monarchs very unhappy, and for that I need you all."

A number of them touched the arm of Aly's chair on their way out. "Gunapi the Sunrose guard you, Duani," some whispered. Others remarked, "The luck turns our way."

Aly waved them off, not sure of what was going on, uncomfortable with the awe of her in their faces.

18

CONSPIRACIES

Supper was quiet. Aly ate at her worktable, reading over reports and making notes. She was sweating as she burned the reports she had condensed when Fesgao knocked on her door and looked in. "We're gathering," he told her.

Aly nodded and collected her papers that the other leaders might use. In the meeting room, she saw that everyone was present but Dove.

"Perhaps we should begin?" she asked Ulasim. "I think at the moment Dove wants to be with the duchess."

"No doubt you are right," Ulasim agreed. Quedanga closed the door as Ysul woke their security spells.

Aly had just finished passing out the reports when a knock sounded on the door.

"She came after all," Quedanga murmured, surprised, as she opened it.

In walked Dove, followed by Winnamine and Nuritin. The conspirators started to their feet, all but Ulasim, who measured the two haggard women with his eyes. In this room he was the raka general, who stood at attention for no one.

"I thought it was time," Dove told him, a mulish set to her mouth. "*Past* time."

"The rebellion—if that's what you are about, I want to be part of it," said Winnamine, her voice quavering. "I've known—my lord and I knew—there was something going on, but we let it go. We did not much care for our laws and hoped that a good fright would lead to better government. You were all so careful that we could not see how anyone might discover you. And . . . I want to help."

"As do I," said Nuritin, folding her arms over her chest. "There are others, just as appalled by this child murder as we are. Others who can bring arms and finances and fighters to this cause. In fact, one of them is at my house in town."

Ulasim looked from Dove to the two older women. "You see me in a delicate position."

"You're going to have to trust my judgment at some point," Dove reminded him. "I think that now would be a good time. I won't be a puppet, Ulasim. If I rule, I *rule*."

Ochobu poked Nawat with a finger. "Give the Lady Nuritin your chair," she ordered. To Nuritin she said, "Who is this guest?"

"I have sent Jesi for him. She knows to be careful," replied Nuritin, lowering herself into her chair.

Ulasim gestured for the duchess to take Aly's seat as Dove assumed her usual place.

"We just let them in?" demanded Quedanga. "And when members of their families die, what is to keep them from running to the monarchs with all they know?"

"Members of this family *have* died," snapped Nuritin. Quedanga looked down.

"If we were going to go to the Crown, we would have done it long before this," said Winnamine, her voice tired. "While we still could walk away from you with our own skins intact. No one will believe we were ignorant of your activities all this time."

"We'd like to avoid a bloodbath," Aly told Quedanga. "So unsightly, and it will give entirely the wrong impression to any greedy foreigners who are watching us. That means coming to terms with some luarin."

"You think the great lords will give up their lands and titles to the raka?" asked Nuritin.

"They will have to give up *some* of their lands," replied Fesgao. "But let us face it, many of the raka families who held those titles originally are long dead. Unless a luarin has been cruel to his or her people, or has supported the Rittevons and all they did, we must be ready to negotiate."

"How can we trust *your* allies?" demanded Quedanga. "Those luarin you plot with? Any of them could be an agent of the Crown simply waiting for you to pose a real threat before he reports you—or she reports you."

Aly cleared her throat. "With regard to the main members of their group, *I* can vouch for their loyalty," she said modestly. "I've had them watched." With normal spies she would have waited for them to observe their quarry for months before she could say with near-certainty that they were loyal to their fellow conspirators. With the darkings able to follow those who met in the Teak Sitting Room, she was certain that none of them was in communication with the Crown. Not only had her small allies watched the heads of those families, but they had inspected their desks, their wardrobes, and even their diaries.

"They could have hidden something from you," argued Quedanga.

Aly shook her head. "You must trust me."

"What good might you do us?" Ulasim asked the duchess and Lady Nuritin. "You are formidable allies in your own persons, but we need fighters, and weapons, and horses. We need ships, and crews. We need money."

"All of which we have," said the duchess.

"What if your warriors choose not to obey your wishes?" Chenaol asked, curious rather than hostile. "What if they report you to our new rulers?"

"Remind them of Topabaw's fate, and that of two commanders of the King's Watch," said Dove. "Remind them that Imajane and Rubinyan are less than loyal to those who serve them."

"You might also want to mention those dead persons who have appeared with the word *spy* on their clothing recently," Aly murmured. "And those who will be found tomorrow, and the day after. I think we'll have the Windward District fairly well cleared by then." She gazed at them under her lashes. Everyone had turned to look at her. She added, "After that, we'll start on the rest of Rajmuat. District by district, that's the best way to handle these things."

"And only think, she is on *our* side," Fesgao said at last.

Nuritin smiled frostily at Aly. "Or we need simply to remind such would-be traitors that the Crown will not believe they were innocent while their fellows conspired."

Aly grinned. "That will work, too."

Someone rapped on the door in the rebels' signal. Aly went to open it, to find Guchol outside. "Lady Nuritin's secretary, Jesi, is here with two priests of the Black God."

Aly looked back at Nuritin, who nodded regally. "Bring them," she ordered.

"*Here?*" asked Guchol, startled. "But . . ." One look at Aly's raised eyebrow changed her mind. "Right away, Duani." Guchol trotted off down the hall.

"Duani?" Aly heard Nuritin ask. Aly remained in the doorway, listening to the talk as she watched the hall.

"She is our spymaster," Ulasim explained. "Her people call her that."

"And how did a maid from Tortall become a spymaster?" demanded Nuritin, outraged.

Aly flapped her hand for silence as people came down the hall, Jesi in the lead. She nodded when she saw Aly, and stood aside to let the priests go ahead. When they walked into the room, Imgehai Qeshi put back her hood, revealing her pale luarin face lit by amber eyes. With a nod to Winnamine and Nuritin, she leaned against the wall as Aly locked the door. The other priest looked around the room from the shadow of his hood, then pushed it back. Aly recognized the eagle nose and short-cropped gray hair of Duke Nomru. Some of the raka murmured in surprise.

You sly thing! Aly thought, beaming at Nuritin with approval. All the realm's soldiers and spies are hunting for him, and you've had him tucked away in your vacant town house! She bowed to Nuritin to show her appreciation.

Winnamine and Dove stood to kiss the renegade duke on the cheek. Nomru's eyes swept the room, lingering on some faces, then settling on Ulasim. The raka met the duke's gaze with one of equal strength. Ulasim would make sure these people, normally luarin masters, would learn right away who was in charge here.

After a moment the duke asked Ulasim, "May I join you?" Ulasim nodded.

Secret stretched a long neck up from its place in Aly's bead necklace to whisper to her.

"Excuse me," Aly said. She went into her workroom for privacy, locking her door behind her. Taking off her necklace, she held it in her hands as it reshaped itself into her two darkings. "Say that again?"

They conferred. Finally Trick said, "Servants took food to house of mages inside Gray Palace walls, took food to guards on watch. A man of Rittevon Lancers comes to say fresh guards come soon, but guards eat now because mess is closed. Guards eat. Dark come. Guards start to fall. They try to breathe, but breath not come. Their faces swell. They lay down, no breath coming. They stop trying to breathe."

"How do you know?" asked Aly, her mind ticking away. "All the guards? They're all dead?"

"Peony go to mage house, after Grosbeak run away," explained Trick. "Peony not want to go with Grosbeak, and we think darking should watch mage house. Darkings know mages. They stir things up. Peony stays at mage house."

"Oh, dear," Aly said ruefully. "I didn't even try to find Peony."

Trick and Secret shook their heads. "Darkings here to work. Aly can't do everything," Trick said. "We think of some."

"No, I do not remember everything. And I should have taken you more seriously," she admitted.

"Darkings learn," Trick said with pride. "Peony check all guards outside mage house. All dead. Peony go inside mage house. Five mages there and families. All dead."

Aly felt her bowels tighten. Were the new rulers *mad*? "What else?" she asked.

"Wagons coming to mage house," Secret continued. "Men packing up dead mages, dead guards. Rubinyan send them. He say, give the dead to meat-eating fish. He wants no one but trusted guards to know what happened to them."

Aly shuddered. It was a fate she would not wish on anyone. "What are the king and queen doing now?" Aly wanted to know. "Are they, I don't know, slumbering the sleep of those without cares?"

Both darkings shook their heads.

"Imajane screaming and throwing things at Rubinyan," replied Secret. "Bottles, brushes, mirrors. She says Rubinyan . . ." It cocked its head as if listening. "She says he is tumbling a lady?"

"Ah," Aly replied. "It means he is making love with a lady. If Imajane is throwing things, she believes he is in love with some other woman. Is she still throwing things?"

"She has nothing to throw unless she picks up chair," said Trick. "Uh-oh."

"She picked up chair," Secret explained.

Shaking her head, Aly returned to the meeting room, interrupting an intense discussion of numbers of household men-at-arms. She waited for a lull in the conversation, then announced, "I have some interesting news." She looked at Ulasim, who nodded for her to speak. "Someone—I suspect Imajane—has poisoned the court mages. Either a natural poison was used, one no one would notice in food, or they didn't look at their supper properly."

They stared at her. Nomru was the first to speak. "My dear young woman, not even Imajane is so mad. For that matter, how can you possibly know this?"

"She has means that we do not," Chenaol told him.

Aly knew Chenaol probably thought the god had told her. That was good enough for the time being.

"Imajane would certainly be that mad if she were getting rid of evidence," said Nuritin. "Everyone knows the storm that sank the *Rittevon* was no accident. The Rittevons have been wary of mages since that cabal that worked for Carthak was uncovered fifty years ago and since Oron's mage killed his father. And the Crown does have a reputation for doing away with their tools, once used."

"Rubinyan is no Rittevon," Imgehai Qeshi remarked.

"Rubinyan didn't know," Aly told her. "She ordered their deaths without consulting him. He is quite upset."

"And so he should be!" Nomru said. "Letting a woman decide a matter of state . . ."

He looked down at the strong brown hand that gripped one of his arms, then up into Fesgao's eyes. "Perhaps we have not made ourselves entirely clear," Fesgao told him mildly. "We are not in this to put another luarin man on the throne. We are here to reclaim our homeland and set a proper queen of our own blood to rule."

Nomru took a breath, as if to argue, then halted, and released it. "I confess, we have done poorly with our charge," he admitted reluctantly. He looked at Dove. "Of course. The one who is twice royal." He fell silent, then nodded.

"I am an old dog, but I believe I am still able to learn. Dovasary might do very well for us all."

The next day callers returned to visit the duchess. That night Duke Nomru moved secretly into Balitang House. One or two or three at a time the luarin conspirators, starting with the Fonfalas, learned they had new allies, people who were not prepared to allow them to take over. It took little to persuade most, particularly because Aly urged the duchess, Nuritin, and Dove to let them know what had happened to the court mages, their families, and the men set to guard them. The luarin conspirators could work it out for themselves that Imajane had done all this to cover up some dreadful act like regicide.

Two days after Matfrid Fonfala visited his grieving daughter, Trick told Aly that the Fonfala estates on Malubesang, next to the Nomru lands, had risen against the Crown. They were led not by servant and slave rebels, but by Winnamine's brothers. That same day word came from Malubesang of the discovery of the royal governor's body, hanging from the cliffs that overlooked Fajurat Bay.

When a twentieth Crown spy turned up dead, courtesy of Boulaj and Junai working from Aly's lists, Rubinyan and Imajane instituted a twilight curfew throughout Rajmuat. Even with the curfew, neither spies nor the night patrolmen themselves were safe from the rebels. From her sources Aly cheerfully reported growing unease in the warehouses commandeered for use as barracks and in the barracks proper for the army. The men complained that death in battle was expected; simply disappearing from the street was not.

Two nights after the curfew began, the chief conspirators, including Duke Nomru, the priestess Imgehai Qeshi, Winnamine, and Nuritin, met outside at Aly and Nawat's suggestion. Certainly it was stifling indoors; the garden was cooler by far. Urged by Nawat, the miniature kudarung came out to meet the four luarin, who were charmed and awed. No kudarung had come voluntarily to Rajmuat in over two centuries. Aly thought better of the stern Nomru when she saw how gently he handled a small piebald foal that tried to eat the trim on his tunic.

The curfew gongs were ringing when the southeast horizon flared orange. Aly pointed it out to her companions as a big explosion thudded in their ears. Nomru started to his feet, the ladies and then the raka beside him. Over the southeastern wall of the house the orange glow expanded. Where the white light-veils and the multicolored sparks shifted over the sky, the orange glow kept its place on the horizon. Soon they heard the now-familiar clang of the city's alarm bells.

Nomru frowned. "That looks like it comes from the naval shipyards," he said.

Aly sighed happily. "It does. My little ones do such wonderful work."

"Their Majesties will start executing people over deeds like this," Nomru warned.

"They would do it sooner or later in any case," replied Ulasim. "They must, to show they have control. They will find it is not so easy to kill rebels here. And while they search for people to execute, they will force those who did not want to choose between them and the rebels to pick a side."

Aly pointed upward. The multicolored points of light scattered across the sky blazed more strongly than ever. "So nice to know our work is appreciated," she remarked.

The next morning, when she went to her workroom, her pack was already there, freshly washed and wearing clothes that did not smell of blazebalm.

"Very good work last night, my lambs," she told them as she flung herself into her chair and laced her fingers on her stomach. "Very inspiring. What is left?"

Jimarn unfurled a small, deadly smile. "Very little. No wonder it's a death sentence for a raka to possess blazebalm. It's very useful stuff."

"What next, Duani?" Olkey wanted to know. "We have ideas for our recruits, of course, but do you have anything special in mind?"

Aly tugged an earlobe. She would have loved to get to work inside the palace, but the raka there were too easily trapped. For the time being she named four people in the city as targets. All were the prince's cronies, placed in high offices when he became regent. It was even more galling that the lone raka among them was in charge of the Crown prisons on Gempang and Kypriang, where the prisoners were also mostly raka. If he felt anything for them, he had yet to show it.

"You might advise these four that it's a mistake to support the current government," she said. "They should be allowed to live. But they should remember they cannot hide from us. Indulge your imaginations. Be mindful of their children. Many times children grow up to make different choices than did their parents. Jimarn, you might want to visit the Crown warehouses on Josefa Street. They are packed with grain. Wouldn't it be nice to hide it someplace so we can share it with those in need this winter? Do as you like with the empty warehouses."

"Duani, remind me to stay on your good side," Hiraos commented, shaking his head. "You really know how to hold a grudge."

"*And* she makes it painful," Guchol remarked soberly.

Aly waved goodbye and watched them go. Their tasks would keep them occupied for a few days. By then she ought to have some ideas for the palace in general, and the Gray Palace in particular. The darkings had already mentioned that their noisemaking and item-throwing had increased the tension of all who lived there.

As soon as the pack was gone, Trick told Aly that Imajane was sending

Lady Edunata home to her family covered in bruises. The morning after Edunata left, Imajane woke to find that two more ladies-in-waiting had left her service in the night. They did not want to risk Imajane's jealousy.

That same day Rubinyan brought Varwick Jimajen, his oldest son by his first marriage, to court from his home estates. Aly passed on to the conspirators that Rubinyan confided to Varwick his fear that he could not control his queen. It worried him that she had ordered the deaths of the mages without consulting him. He rightly asked himself what other orders she might give.

Nawat expanded the work of the crows. They had already put a stop to the Crown's attempts to communicate with the outer Isles by winged messenger. The only reliable ways to get news or give instructions were through messengers on the ground or by mage. Since the queen trusted what her new mages told her no more than she had the old mages, the newcomers were a jumpy crew. Nawat then made sure that it was not safe for a noble or soldier on the open palace grounds. When Imajane tried to do a day's hunting just outside the walls, Nawat and his friends mobbed the falcons, driving the royal party back to the Gray Palace.

Seventeen days after Dunevon's death, Kioka raced into Aly's workroom. "I just came from the docks!" she announced, panting. "You won't believe it! They posted it on the docks while their messengers delivered the letters to the palace. They're calling their ambassadors home!"

Aly drummed her fingers until Kioka caught her breath. "I would share your joy more quickly if I understood what to be joyful about," she said gently.

"I'm sorry, Duani. It's the Tortallans, and the Carthakis. They say their mages discovered the storm that sank King Dunevon's ship was magical, and they traced the magic back to the Gray Palace. They say they will not trade with king-slayers! Every Tortallan and Carthaki ship in port is weighing anchor, even if they don't have cargo. Even if they're half unloaded! Olkey says the Tyrans are debating cutting their trade with the Isles, though he isn't sure they'll do it. Tyrans are less choosy about where they get money."

Aly stopped drumming her fingers. She hadn't expected this. Tortall and Carthak had just put the Isles under a trading ban until the king's murderers were caught. With a bad harvest and national unrest draining the royal treasury, this was a heavy blow. How would the monarchs cope? They would have to find someone to take the blame. A pity that Imajane had been so quick to kill the mages, but Aly supposed the princess had decided she couldn't be certain that the mages would keep quiet about who had issued their orders.

Would the Crown try to hold the Tortallan and Carthaki ambassadors here in Rajmuat? Aly hoped so, but surely Rubinyan and Imajane wouldn't be that stupid. If they did try, they could expect the Tortallan and Carthaki navies within the week.

"It's good, right?" Kioka asked, brushing her hair back from her eyes.

Aly sighed. "Think how distressed Their Majesties must be," she said. "And shouldn't the people know our two richest, most powerful neighbors have stopped trading with us?"

"Got it," said Kioka. She raced from the room, squeezing past Nawat.

Aly raised her eyebrows. "You left me to sleep the rest of the night alone," she said.

Nawat grinned. "I was helping to steal soldiers who couldn't keep up."

"What do you do with them?" she asked, curious. "I haven't heard of bodies being found."

"Nor will you," Nawat informed her, sitting on a corner of the worktable. "They were still alive when we gave them to my warriors at the edge of the jungle." He picked up Aly's hand and laced his fingers with hers. "My warriors will be able to say *they* last saw the missing soldiers alive, when the troops went on a visit to the jungle."

Aly walked her free fingers over their entwined hands. "But why would Crown soldiers visit the jungle?"

"They didn't think they would at first," Nawat admitted. "So my warriors show them the beauties of the deep jungle. They take away all the things the soldiers have of the civilized world, such as clothes and weapons and armor, so the soldiers will appreciate the jungle with their entire bodies. But my warriors have seen jungle before, so they get bored and leave. The soldiers stay longer."

"Like the tax collectors," Aly whispered, awed by the beauty of what he described. "Take away all they have and leave them to survive the jungle. If you're questioned under truthspell, you can say they were alive when you left them. And the only way they could survive naked out there . . ." Nawat was shaking his head. Aly nodded. "I take it you don't leave them near any trails."

"They are there to appreciate the jungle that has been untouched by humans," Nawat told her, a teacher to a student who did not quite understand.

Aly sighed. "I am limp with envy," she told him. "Simply limp."

Nawat raised the hand still entwined with his and kissed it. "I knew you would be." He got to his feet.

"You're leaving?" Aly asked, dismayed.

Nawat bent down and kissed her thoroughly enough to make her limp again. "I am bored with nobles and soldiers who hide," he explained. "The flock that watches the palace will keep them busy. I thought the city flock and I could play for a time. But I will come back." He cupped her cheek in one hand. "I promised myself that I would not let any day go here when I did not see you once, and not just for kisses." He tweaked her earlobe and left her there among her reports.

She propped her chin on her hands. There was a great deal to be said for having a former crow as a lover, she decided. They kissed as if they meant it to last. They kissed as if you were the only one they had ever kissed or would ever want to kiss. And this one . . . there were no two ways about it. He was a man.

"I won't be able to push him around anymore," she observed aloud.

"You have work," Trick reminded her. "Do not let kissing distract you."

"I don't, not for more than a moment or two," Aly replied. She glanced at the darkings. "You know, my mother always told me you had to seize the bright moments, because you never know when they will come again." She smiled dreamily. "The older I get, the smarter she seems."

"Rubinyan visits Sevmire," Trick told her. "Sevmire is drunk."

Aly glanced out her window. "It's barely noon."

"Rubinyan is very unhappy," Trick added. "Rubinyan knocked Sevmire down."

"Well, the man's drunk when he's supposed to be on duty," Aly remarked. She looked at them, sitting up a little straighter. "I suppose you could say the same of me."

"You are happy," Secret told her. "That is nice. You don't have many nice times."

Aly smiled. "I believe that is changing. Is Rubinyan going to get rid of Sevmire?" She wasn't sure she wanted that, not now, when Sevmire was doing such a terrible job.

"Sevmire promise not to drink," Trick told her. It straightened, then quivered. In a flash it joined with Secret to become a two-stranded necklace again. Aly was putting them on when Boulaj poked her head into the workroom.

"Our ladies have received an invitation," she told Aly. "The new queen invites us to a late breakfast tomorrow morning. She wishes to consult with 'certain valued friends' about the coronation ceremonies."

"Oh, splendid," replied Aly, reaching for reports. "Has she said how they will pay for those ceremonies?"

"Not in the invitation," Boulaj said with a shrug. "Is the treasury really so low?"

Aly nodded. "They have to keep the armies and navy happy, which is to say, paid. There's not much left over. They're discussing an invitation to the merchants and the nobles to contribute to the ceremonies as a proof of loyalty. I'm sure everyone will be delighted to hear they must beggar themselves to confirm the new king and queen."

"No doubt," Boulaj replied. "Anyway, Lady Dove asks if you will come with us."

"I wouldn't miss it for the world," Aly assured Boulaj.

The conspirators, particularly the luarin ones, were not as eager as Aly. That afternoon, they protested when the duchess told them about the invitation.

"I don't like it," Lehart Obemaek declared. "Bringing so many of our ladies together at the palace—what if they mean to hold them, to ensure the lords' obedience? Because it's not just you and Nuritin and Dovasary, Winna. My wife and daughter have been invited."

"As have Rosamma and I," said Countess Tomang.

"Lehart, I have never thought you overburdened with sense." Baron Engan looked dry and frail, but he did not sound it. "But even you must perceive that they dare not offend us—and there *are* far more of us in the outlying estates, who won't be meeting with Imajane. They need us if they mean to survive."

"If you please, my lord Obemaek," Aly said politely. "My palace sources say that His Majesty—"

"Faugh!" interrupted Nuritin.

Aly bowed to her. "His Majesty keeps Her Majesty under constant watch. *She* is the uncertain element. He has told his people they must bring her orders to him. He also understands that his power base is shaky. For the present he grips the reins. My sources tell me nothing sinister is planned for tomorrow morning."

"I find it hard to have faith in intelligence garnered by a young woman, and a foreigner at that," Genore Tomang announced with a sniff. Matters between her and the Balitangs were stiff, Sarai's insult still raw, but the Tomangs were still willing members of the conspiracy. They had been heavily taxed for the third year in a row as one of the wealthiest families in the Isles.

"I could make myself up as a raka man, if that will appease you, my lady," Aly offered. "I think it would be a waste of my time, but I live to serve in any small way that I can."

Even Duke Nomru's mouth twitched at that. "Stop it, Genore," he told the countess. "Have you forgotten this young foreigner brought about the fall of Topabaw?"

"So we are told," said the countess.

"So we *know*," Ulasim said flatly.

"So *I* know," Dove added, soft-voiced.

Her comment brought silence. Many of the luarin conspirators still were not quite sure what to do about their future queen, though Nomru, Engan, and Qeshi addressed her as an equal, as did Winnamine and Nuritin.

Aly sat back as Quedanga began to pass on what her people had gathered. Aly did not want to tell the luarin conspirators that Imajane and Rubinyan had taken to walking in the gardens at night, out of earshot of her darkings and well away from any of the raka spies. It could be something as basic as Rubinyan wanting to calm his excitable wife and to reinforce their affection after the problem of Lady Edunata. They could also be deliberately discussing plans someplace where it would be hard for a spy to hide, and where it would mean death for the mage who put a listening spell there. Aly could not be sure.

In any case, Aly wanted their party to be ready for everything. The breakfast with Imajane was to be held in the Jade Pavilion. Breaking out of the main palace enclosure in an emergency would be easy enough. Some of Fesgao's people would enter the grounds in the morning, driving wagons of foodstuffs through the Gate of Carts. Dorilize and Pembery would remain at home, allowing warriors Jimarn and Junai to play at being ladies' maids. They had the crows to interfere if the rulers planned treachery. And Fesgao would come, disguised as a footman, bearing a small gift for the new queen from the Balitangs. He knew where the Haiming Tunnel was, the secret exit from the palace that had allowed Dove's forebears to escape with their lives. The rebels hoped those precautions would be enough to keep Dove safe.

The luarin conspirators left at last. Aly looked for signs of the darkings she had placed with them but found none. She didn't expect to. Some days they journeyed with their people to Balitang House, but they also spent much of the time exploring their new homes and reporting to Trick. They had understood when Aly told them to watch for spies in the conspirators' household as well as traitors among the nobles.

Dove waited in Aly's workroom, glancing at her maps. "I feel so useless," Dove complained. "It seems like all anyone will let me do is look promising. All this important work is being done, and you won't even let me visit Dockmarket anymore."

"I know, and I am sorry, but the risk is too great," Aly told her. "It's a bad idea to remind Their New Majesties how popular you are, particularly since they can no longer use a marriage to Dunevon as a leash on you. Though if anything happens to Imajane, Rubinyan might come to your door with a gift of flowers."

Dove grimaced. "I'd as soon sleep with a ribbon snake," she told Aly. "Not that I think I'll be offered the marriage. We're nearly ready to move, aren't we?"

"Nearly, yes. As ready as anyone can be in a fix like this," Aly said. "The night before the day of the solar eclipse. They might expect something the day of the eclipse, and certainly they expect trouble on their coronation day."

"And while everyone else does something real, *I* get to be protected," said Dove bitterly.

Aly put an arm around Dove's shoulders. "If all goes well, you'll have the hardest task," she said quietly. "Bringing a country together. Making sure your reign isn't marked by bloodletting, which should be an agreeable change around here. It's a scary task, but you have good people to advise you—Her Grace, Lady Nuritin, Ulasim, Fesgao, Ochobu—"

Dove looked up at her. "Will I have you?"

Aly blinked at her. You should have expected this, her brain clamored, seeking a quick answer. You should have had your story all prepared. Lie, idiot, lie! Tell her you'll be there! You've lied millions of times, so do it now!

Dove pulled away from Aly's arm. "That's what I thought," she said, and left the room.

Aly started to follow, and stopped. Catching up to Dove would only work if she were ready to lie, and she wasn't. She couldn't. Not about this. If she survived, and she wasn't entirely certain that she would, she had to go home. The daughter of Tortall's spymaster had no business so close to the Kyprin throne.

By late afternoon people were bringing news of the crows' latest rampage through the skies over Rajmuat. Aly listened to the reports with admiration and envy. Nawat and his friends had sprinkled Crown officials and soldiers with urine and dung. They attacked soldiers at the checkpoints as the men inspected carts and saddlebags, using their claws and beaks and, as a last insult, more dung. Any shop that carried the emblem of supplier to the Crown— something that was no longer a guarantee of more business—soon had a doorstep piled with crow dung, and no customers. The crows drove them away.

At supper she was picking at her food, thinking about information, when a very warm presence thumped onto the bench next to her. A man's hard thigh pressed hers. She looked up into Nawat's eyes.

"You forgot about me," he told her, shaking his head. "My heart is broken forevermore."

Startled, Aly pulled back, then recognized the twinkle in his deep-set eyes. "You're *teasing* me again," she said, outraged. "And I could hardly forget you, with all the ruckus you stirred up today."

"You are no longer the one who does all the tormenting," Nawat informed her, reaching across her for a bowl of rice. She forgot what she was about to say in the brush of his arm against her breasts. Warmth flooded her veins. Nawat looked into her face and smiled as he slowly brought the rice bowl over to his plate. "I have learned to torment, too."

You have indeed, she thought, tearing a piece of bread in half.

Others came to sit with them, applauding the latest behavior of the crows. Aly listened with a smile, shaking her head, without forgetting Nawat's warmth against her side.

She excused herself, her meal half-eaten, and clambered out from between Nawat and Junai. Nawat smiled up at her and continued his conversation with Chenaol.

Aly met with some of her spies and their recruits after supper, taking in the day's reports. The wider they spread their net, the more information she had to sift for nuggets of real worth. These nuggets were what she wrote out and handed to the other rebels in the house. Once the humans were gone,

Trick and Secret passed on their most recent gleanings from the palace and the homes of the luarin conspirators.

This is why Da spends his days at a desk, Aly told herself as she worked. It's why he jumps at the chance to meet with an agent. Because sooner or later all you can do is review information and pass it on to those who will use it.

At least when I'm done for the day, I have Nawat, she thought. Suddenly the night ahead looked much brighter.

19

RITTEVON SQUARE

When they rose before dawn to train with the warriors, Nawat made sure to kiss Aly thoroughly once more before they left the Pavilion of Secrets. They had both agreed not to show too much affection for one another before their fellow conspirators. Neither wished to be accused of not paying attention, Nawat because he had discovered he enjoyed command over his human warriors as much as that over the crows, and Aly because so much depended on the rebels seeing her as reliable. "Another day," Nawat said, looking up at the pearl gray sky. The moon was veiled by the colorlessness of the sky. Only the Trickster sparks continued to show, winking on and off, never the same color or in the same position twice. Kyprioth continued to hold his own.

"My kin will be in the air to watch over you today," Nawat said as they walked toward the stable yard where everyone practiced. "And my warriors and I will be near, at the edge of the jungle."

Aly smiled up at him. "I love you," she replied. "If you get yourself killed, I will be very unhappy with you."

Nawat grinned. "I have loved you since I became a man, or even before that," he reminded her. "You must try to stay out of trouble, too."

Between breakfast and the summons to court, the house was bustling. Aly put on fresh clothes in the dressing room off Dove's chambers. Boulaj added the finishing touches on Dove's appearance as Aly emerged with her hair combed and tucked under a sober headcloth. Boulaj winked at her over Dove's head.

"Why do you always wear that same old bead necklace?" Dove wanted to know. "I have dozens that are prettier that I never wear."

Aly heard a muffled squeak from the double bead on her right shoulder. She stroked the darkings quiet with a smile. "They have sentimental value for me, my lady," she explained. "If you'll excuse me . . ."

She trotted downstairs, ignoring the outraged squeaks from her necklace.

Outside she reviewed the guard chosen to escort the ladies. Fesgao had assembled twenty men-at-arms in livery. Half were armed with spears and short swords, half with swords and the shield-stick called a tonfa, a good weapon for trapping an enemy's blade by edge or point. Some members of Aly's pack and their recruits lounged near the gate. They would range out along the streets, watching for potential trouble as the Balitang ladies rode. The soldiers of the King's Watch would be vexed at so heavy a guard for an ordinary palace ride, but there had been unrest in the city, and the Balitangs were not about to tell them that they distrusted Crown troops more than Downwind rioters.

As their party moved out, Aly walked on the side of Dove's horse closer to the double ring of guards. Boulaj walked on the inside. Fesgao, in a footman's livery, walked just ahead of Nuritin's and Winnamine's mounts, the small wooden box that held their gift for Imajane under one arm. He stood just behind the corporal who was supposedly in command of the men-at-arms. When he gave the signal, their company moved out, the wagon with the ladies' court dresses bringing up the rear.

It was still early enough for traffic to be light. They soon joined other ladies on their way to the palace. Aly watched the crowds. It made her uneasy to see this many people outside, all paying attention to the noblewomen as they negotiated their way past the soldiers' checkpoints along Rittevon's Lance. They were everywhere, in the windows and on the roofs that gave them a view of the ladies. Of Dove.

Go away! Aly thought. Go home, go to work! Stop drawing attention to us!

Shrieks sounded overhead. The crows had come to play with the Stormwings. They arrived in hordes, scattering the immortals as they darted among them. The Stormwings shot toward the relative safety of the distant palace, the crows in pursuit.

When they reached the green belt outside the palace, Aly gave an internal sigh of relief. She'd never thought she'd be so happy to see those streams full of meat-eating fish. Crossing a bridge, she looked off to the side, but the water was too murky to allow her a view of them. Was it possible they were still full from the feast of dead mages, families, and guards? Or had the poison that killed the humans also killed the fish? She didn't have time to see for certain as their party moved on.

As before, their men-at-arms parted from them inside the Gate of Victory while the ladies and their maids rode to the Robing Pavilion to change. When Aly bent to place the wooden box with their riding dresses against a wall, her darking necklace dropped from her neck onto its lid. Trick and Secret nodded to Aly, then dripped into the shadow. They were off to make contact with the other palace darkings.

Once the ladies set forth for the Jade Pavilion, Aly followed at a distance like any disinterested servant on a stroll, careful to step off the garden paths when other noblewomen passed. Aly turned at the edge of the Lily Water and wandered into the shelter of a familiar-looking willow. As she had suspected, Taybur Sibigat sat on the hidden bench. He put his finger to his lips for silence, then rose and walked off down a lesser path, back into the gardens. Aly waited for a party of ladies to go by, then followed him.

He led her to a semicircle of hedges that framed another bench, affording a view of the water and some black swans as they glided by. There were spells here, but not for listening. They would damp the sounds made around the bench, luarin version of the spells that guarded Balitang House from eavesdroppers.

"It's safe to speak here," he told her, digging his hands into his breeches pockets as his mail jingled. "Not that I've much to say. I have to swear my allegiance in blood on the day they are officially crowned, you know. All of the Guard must. Those who wish to stay."

Aly looked up at him. "You're certain the ship was tampered with?"

He nodded. "Plenty of good ships went down in that storm, but only after the winds and waves knocked them about for a while. The crew didn't even have time to furl all the sails before the *Rittevon* crumpled like rice paper."

"I'm sorry," Aly told him. Her eyes stung as she remembered Elsren's glee as he had marched aboard that vessel. "I truly am."

"Thanks," Taybur said. "Have a care for your young lady—her popularity is noticed." He hesitated, then added, "I suppose the next time I see you, we'll be at the gate to the Gray Palace." With a nod, he strode off down the path.

He'd given Aly a new concern. If Imajane and Rubinyan had decided to do something about Dove's popularity, they would be idiots to try it inside the palace, where no one would believe they were blameless. After the jailbreak at Kanodang, they would be reluctant to imprison another popular luarin. Aly would lay odds their attack would come on the street.

Taybur had also let Aly know the part he was ready to play once things came to a fight. I'll keep him to myself, just in case he changes his mind, she decided. No one *needs* to know what he'll do, if he chooses to.

She returned to the Robing Pavilion to sit with Vereyu. They "talked" about hidden stores of drugs and weapons by writing on a slate and passing it to each other. There was no corner safe from eavesdroppers in the Robing Pavilion. When their conversation was over and they were picking through a plate of dumplings, Fesgao—still dressed as a footman—wandered into the ladies' side of the pavilion. "Pretty Aly, will you walk with me?" he asked, offering his arm.

"You want to watch this one," Vereyu warned Aly. "He's got a wife who's a trapper on Imahyn."

Aly fluttered her lashes at Fesgao, the image of an empty-headed flirt. To Vereyu she said, "It's only a *walk*. What could happen on a walk?"

Fesgao leered and led her down the Golden Road to the Pavilion of Delightful Pleasures. "This was the old Haiming palace," he murmured, for all intents looking like a man who whispered secrets in his sweetheart's ear. Aly giggled as she clung to his arm. "They tore down the New Palace to build their gray stone monster," Fesgao continued, "but the old one was still used for celebrations and guests. And the old escape tunnel is still here, kept up by generations of raka." Slowly they wandered around the side of the Pavilion of Delightful Pleasures, Aly stopping to smell a flower as a squad of the Rittevon Guard marched by on the Golden Road. Once the soldiers had passed, Fesgao led her around the pavilion's side, between the bubbling stream and its veranda. Marmosets cheeped to each other in warning from overhead, while brightly colored finches peered at them from the trees. Aly looked up to see a dart of light from a Stormwing's feathers, then the shifting white veil in the sky that marked the Great Goddess's war with Kyprioth.

When they could see the pond that lay behind the pavilion, Fesgao drew Aly across a bridge over the stream, to a small building set behind a screen of trees. Aly flinched and put up a hand to shield her eyes. Raka magic might be hidden to luarin mages, but not to anyone with the Sight. The building and the ground at its rear wall blazed with it. "You people are lucky no one with the Sight came near this place," she informed Fesgao, blinking to twist her vision so she would See the magic, yet not be blinded.

"Raka prefer not to trust in luck," the man replied. "This place is watched, and not by mages. Had you crossed that bridge with anyone but me, or walked down the other side of the building, you would soon find polite gardeners to turn you back. If you are stubborn, they can be less polite." He knelt and ran his hands through the grass behind the building. He stopped at what looked like a trailing vine and yanked hard. The grass and its bed, several inches of earth, lifted as if it were hung on oiled hinges. Fesgao raised it only a foot, to show Aly a wooden door below. At its center was a ring of steel to use as a grip.

"Now you know," Fesgao said. "That makes five of us: you, me, Ochobu, Ulasim, and Chenaol."

"I don't know where it opens out," Aly reminded him. "Beyond both walls, I assume, but not where. Why haven't the raka used this way to attack the luarin from inside?"

Fesgao raised his brows at her as he lowered the grass mat again. "Because we were told to wait for the one who is twice royal," he told her. "Because there were too many luarin, and we were too beaten. And because the kings before Oron liked mages and kept them around. Then Oron talked a mage into killing old King Hanoren so Oron might take the throne. No one of the royal family has trusted mages since. Besides, we needed the god."

"All right," Aly said, holding up her hands in surrender. "You had plenty of reasons." *I still would have tried it,* she thought as they walked back toward the Golden Road, once again arm in arm.

"You will be shown how to enter soon," Fesgao murmured. "When it is time."

Aly spent the rest of the morning with the maids, waiting for her ladies to return. The main thing she learned from the servants was that they were too frightened to talk of anything important. As they spoke of the coming eclipse and coronation, their voices sounded false to Aly, as if they forced themselves to sound eager for the holiday. They chatted of weather, dress, and hairstyles, and of places where they found the best bargains.

I'll be happy when Dove's on the throne and I can go home, she thought as a maid came to say the ladies were returning. *I'm tired of living with fear and fearful people. Of course, first we have to get Dove* on *the throne.* Opening the box of riding dresses, she found her darking necklace waiting for her. Carefully she slid it over her head.

"Enjoy yourselves?" she murmured.

"Rubinyan says he must take soldiers from Imahyn and Ikang and some from Gempang to fight rebels on Malubesang," Trick whispered by her ear. "He says they must retake Imahyn later. He says he may have to use soldiers from Lombyn to defend north Kypriang. Imajane not know Rittevon estates on north Kypriang all in revolt."

Aly whistled softly as Jimarn, Boulaj, and Junai took the riding dresses from the box. Having lived among warriors, Aly knew it was a sign of weakness to give an enemy one position in order to hold another. Rubinyan might as well have shouted that his armies were spread too thin.

She shared that news with Fesgao as the Balitang ladies dressed. She also passed on to him, Boulaj, Junai, and Jimarn the word that Dove's popularity no longer sat well with the Crown, though she didn't name her source. Fesgao went to tell their men-at-arms they were leaving, and to pass on the order to watch for trouble on the way home. The wagon would follow outside the ring of men-at-arms this time, so that they made a tighter double circle around the women.

Down Rittevon's Lance they went, the servants on foot beside their mistresses. Boulaj kept her hands tucked into her sash: she wore cestuses, leather gloves with iron plates sewn across the knuckles. She was adept with the cestuses and could even deflect sword blows with them. Junai carried her spear, a weapon that, when the grip was twisted, presented a blade at each end. Jimarn and Aly had their knives within quick reach.

Though their ladies must have noticed the warlike preparations—Fesgao had produced his own longsword from the wagon—they said nothing. Instead they let their maids walk between their mounts and the two rings of guards, and drew their horses closer together. They could not ride three abreast on Rittevon's Lance, so Nuritin changed places with Dove, allowing her to ride beside her mother, closer to more men-at-arms.

As they left the green belt for the city, Aly noticed immediately that there were more civilians outside. There were also more soldiers, placed in lines along the pavement as well as at the checkpoints. The streets were packed, as were the buildings on either side of their route.

Something red fluttered in the air above them. Aly flinched, but it was a flower, tossed from someone's window. Another flower dropped on them, followed by more. Soon they were passing through a rain of blossoms.

Aly ground her teeth. Civilians. If the new monarchs had wanted proof that someone in the Balitang family drew the crowds, they had it. They could, if they chose, lock up the entire household on suspicion of rebellion with nothing more than this.

They neared the intersection and checkpoint at Rittevon Square. The great bronze statue of the first Rittevon king was now covered with open shackle insignia, each showing gold through his weathered bronze skin and clothes. As they entered the square, the Balitangs moved out of the range of the flower throwers. It was then that Aly, her head swiveling, saw a crossbow poke through a third-floor window into the open, crowded square.

"*Down!*" she yelled, shoving Dove toward Winnamine, out of range. The bolt struck a man-at-arms in the shoulder. His knees buckled; another man kept him on his feet.

Winnamine stood in her stirrups. Dove was already off her horse, standing on the ground, shielded by the two mounts. "Soldiers of the Crown," the duchess cried in a voice any field general might envy, "protect us!"

The men of the King's Watch did not move from their positions. Fesgao dragged Winnamine from the saddle and beckoned for Nuritin to dismount. On foot, they were less visible targets.

Aly put a foot in the stirrup of Dove's horse, gripped the saddlehorn, and pulled herself up, balancing for a look over the men-at-arms' heads. The line of soldiers parted in two places, one on either side of their group. Men in rough laborers' clothing armed with knives or short swords darted through. Aly yelled, "There! And there!"

The men-at-arms faced the invaders, weapons up. Aly glanced at the squad of the King's Watch at the checkpoint. They lazed at the barricades, no expression on their faces. They already knew they were not to interfere.

Aly didn't see the first rock fly. She did see it strike a soldier's helmet, just as she glimpsed the dent it left before the soldier went down.

"They're killing her!" someone screamed. "They're killing our hope!"

Suddenly the men of the Watch were the targets of a rain of flowerpots, pans, stones, and chamberpots both empty and full. People held back by the soldiers shrieked and surged forward, clawing at their old oppressors. The soldiers fought for their lives. They killed and killed, but they could not kill everyone. Thrusting his sword into one civilian, a soldier would be swarmed by five more armed with belt knives, stones, or fingernails. The crowd boiled through the gaps in the lines as soldiers began to fall.

The assassins pushed past the men-at-arms, where they collided with Junai, Jimarn, and Boulaj. Jimarn leaped onto an assassin's back and clawed at his eyes. Boulaj killed one man as Junai accounted for a second. The horses fidgeted, eyes rolling, wanting to panic. The three Balitang ladies hung on to their reins for their lives. In these crowded quarters, the horses might kill the very people they served.

A crack opened in the doubled ring of household fighters in front. Aly saw the assassin pair slip through, one engaging Fesgao as another came at Dove. Aly pushed off the saddlehorn, swinging her legs over the restless horse's rump, smashing into the killer with both feet. She was down on him with a knife in each hand, taking his life before he even understood where he was. Trick and Secret screeched their disgust as blood struck them.

"Sorry," Aly told them, panting. She mounted Dove's horse properly so she wouldn't need to use a time-wasting jump like that a second time. Everywhere she looked she saw chaos. People streamed in to fill the square, many carrying weapons. Others fought to escape it. Some failed and were trampled. The square filled with a roar of sound: screams, furious yells, battle-voiced commands. Above that animal sound was a high, warbling trill. The Stormwings had come to feast on the pain and fear.

A little girl, shrieking, tried to climb the statue to escape the mob. A boy who might have been an older brother pushed her from behind, trying to get her to the top, the only safe place he could see. A handful of other children splashed through the fountain. One of them was pushed into the water, toward that bit of safety, by a woman who fell then beneath a man's club.

Light blazed from steel. Down came two Stormwings, deflecting the rare arrow with a sweep of deadly wing. The first seized the girl in her claws; the second grabbed her brother. Others came for the remaining children, carrying them up to the balconies that overlooked the square.

Aunt Daine wasn't joking, thought Aly in awe. They *do* like children.

A rotting melon struck the back of her head, jolting her. A moment later a rock flew past her nose. Aly dismounted in a hurry, remembering her grandfather Miles's adage: "A spy is not a target. A spy *points out* the targets." Moments after she touched the ground, an arrow caught her mount in the withers. Dove's horse screamed in pain and reared. The men-at-arms tried to get out of the maddened animal's way as it yanked its reins free. A flying hoof caught one man's shoulder with the crack of breaking bone as the horse plunged into the crowd.

Their remaining men-at-arms instantly closed the gap. Once more they placed themselves as a living fence between the mob and Dove.

"Soldiers come," Trick shrieked in Aly's ear. She looked around, hearing nothing but the crowd and the Stormwings. Then, in a break in the overall noise, she heard the tread of heavy boots. At the far end of the square a stallion neighed. From Middle Way came a company of the King's Watch, half wielding clubs, half with short swords. From Shield Way on the southwest side of the square Aly heard the clatter of hooves. She adjusted her Sight and strained for a look. It was a company of Rittevon Lancers, armed with swords and spears. They cut a route through the mob.

Suddenly the Lancers' disciplined line of riders bent outward, then split. Organized columns of raka and part-raka in leather tunics stitched with metal rings plowed into the horsemen. Ulasim's secret troops carried small round shields and longswords, and they hammered at the cavalry. Once the lancers' lines were broken and the mounted soldiers were fighting in groups of twos and threes, the raka warriors, men and women alike, surrounded them, striving to cut away their saddles and bring them to the ground.

The men of the King's Watch on Middle Way slammed into the mob, which turned on them. Those civilians who had been fighting each other now had a better target, one that wore a uniform. They swamped the new arrivals, grabbing weapons that fallen guards had dropped, wielding them with enthusiasm if not expertise.

Slowly the group that guarded Dove moved out into the open square, trying to make it to a side street. Instead the battle forced them forward, though they fought to hold their ground. They would be crushed against the fountain.

A gap opened before Aly. A soldier had grabbed a club. He was about to bring it down on the skull of a toddler who clutched his knees, screaming. Aly lunged out, knifing the soldier in the back as she yanked the child away with her free hand. Another soldier descended on her with a roar of fury. She slung the toddler toward the Balitang group and blinded the soldier before she cut his throat.

"I know it's nasty," she told the darkings, panting as she wiped her blades, "but this is the not-very-fun part."

Trick and Secret didn't answer. Both of them leaped from Aly's neck to cover the faces of two soldiers who were headed for Dove. As the men fought to breathe, a raka woman with muscles like rocks bashed one with a piece of stone. A luarin woman thrust a short sword home through the other soldier. Trick and Secret leaped to Aly as the two unknown women continued to fight soldiers, shoulder to shoulder, falling back until they filled the gaps in the line around Dove. Aly stayed behind them, in case this was a ruse to let assassins get close to her mistress. The ladies paid attention to nothing but the people who smashed into them.

Aly looked around in despair, wondering how they were going to escape. The riot was growing. It would help no one if Dove got crushed.

Crows and miniature kudarung rained down, shrieking and gouging, biting and blinding, driving everyone from a space in front of the fountain. In their wake came a much larger shadow, one so big that even those who battled around Aly's companions looked up. Everywhere else the insanity raged. Here there was a moment of quiet as a bright chestnut kudarung stallion spiraled down to land in the open space. As regal as any king, he walked over to the Balitang defenders, who moved aside. At last he stood before Dove.

Slowly, gracefully, the great creature furled his batlike wings and knelt on his forelegs, a plain salute to the girl.

Aly was the first to recover. "Don't just stand there, climb on!" she cried, yanking Dove's arm so she would advance. "Fesgao, your sash!"

"But . . . a saddle," Dove murmured, stroking the chestnut's muzzle. "Where do I, um, mount?"

Aly envisioned the messenger who had come to Tanair the year before on a captive kudarung. "Behind his wings," she said. Fesgao thrust his sash into her reaching hand. "Excuse me," Aly told the great creature. "It's demeaning, but necessary." She tied the sash around that powerful neck, and passed its ends to Dove. She hesitated, then slung the toddler she had rescued up in front of Dove. "If you don't mind?" she asked the kudarung.

He straightened his forelegs. Then he nodded.

"Balitang House?" she asked.

Again the kudarung nodded. His hindquarters bunched, and he jumped, massive wings opening with a snap. Up he soared, scooping at the air until he was above the houses. Then he flew into the distance, toward Balitang House.

The afternoon was half over when the rest of them came home. Footmen and maids waited for them beside the guard at the locked gate. They took charge of the worst hurt, carrying or helping them to the infirmary. All were bruised, scraped, and bloody. Petranne shrieked to see her mother and her great-aunt disheveled and carrying the red-bladed spears they had grabbed to help in the fight. The duchess passed her spear to Nuritin and scooped up her daughter, hugging her until Petranne yelped. Nuritin placed one spear on the front hall bench and, taking out her handkerchief, began to clean the blade of the one she held.

Chenaol had followed them from the gate. She grinned at Nuritin and collected the other spear. "If you want me to take that, my lady, I'll clean it properly," she said, nodding toward the weapon Nuritin still held.

Nuritin looked at the spear, then at Chenaol. The old woman trembled from top to toe, but her voice was firm and clear as she replied, "I thank you, but I will clean it myself. I suspect I may need it again. My father said a good blade should always be seen to by the one who uses it."

Chenaol scratched her head for a moment, then offered, "Would my lady like to see our armaments, and choose something more to her taste?"

"I would," Nuritin replied stoutly. "This is a bit heavier than I can manage easily." As the two women walked to the back of the house, carrying spears, Nuritin added, "And since we are to be comrades in battle, we had best do away with this 'my lady' nonsense."

Dove was seated at the foot of the stairs, her arms wrapped around her knees. When Aly looked at her, Dove said, "Next time, I want a saddle."

Fesgao and the rest of their group, who had been catching their breath until now, knelt as one and bowed their heads to her. Aly followed suit.

"Mama, why did they do that?" asked Petranne. "They're only supposed to bow like that to the king."

Winnamine turned, Petranne still in her arms, and saw their escorts and Dove. She set Petranne down. "Because Dove is to be the next king," she replied, and curtsied deeply.

Petranne did the same, as well as her six-year-old coordination would allow her. Despite that, she said, "But Dove can't be king. She's a girl."

Dove rose and walked over to them. She said, her voice shaking, "And this girl isn't going to be that kind of king. Get up, all of you, please. I never want to see any of you on your knees again, for anyone. Winna, please, don't. You're my mother, Petranne's my sister." Her chin wobbled. "Please don't close me out." She looked at Aly. "That applies to you as well."

Winnamine rose and hugged her stepdaughter. Kissing the top of Dove's head, she said in a mother's croon, "It's all right. We're all home and safe."

Safe for the moment, thought Aly. The riot in Rittevon Square had not diminished once Dove had gone. If anything, it had intensified, spreading north and east through Middle Town. The household had lost three men-at-arms, killed in the fight. Five more were seriously hurt. Boulaj had dislocated her shoulder.

"If you will excuse me, I need more information," Aly told the others, and headed for her workroom. Passing a door that opened out to the pool courtyard, she saw the great chestnut kudarung there, drinking sedately. Three full-sized mares and a handful of miniature kudarung cropped the grass that grew outside the tiled court.

So much for secrecy, Aly thought tiredly, and walked on. She ducked into her workroom to collect herself. Nawat was there, to her surprise, caught in the act of placing a lotus on her worktable. He swept her up for a hard kiss and embrace. "My kin told me you were well and fighting your way home," he said, "or I would have come for you. Were you pleased when they came to help

Dove? I didn't even ask them to, or the little kudarung. They did it because they wanted to."

Aly pressed a hand to his mouth. "I'm *very* grateful," she said. "Is anyone in the meeting room?"

"Many of your spies, and Ulasim, and Fesgao, and Quedanga," replied Nawat. "They have information for you, as have I, from my kinfolk."

"Information is good," said Aly as they crossed the hall. They could barely fit in, so many sat in the chairs and on the floor. She managed to wriggle her way through to a counter along the wall. Sitting there, she had a view of everyone's face. Nawat remained by the now-closed door, leaning against the wall. Guchol took a few slates from her lap and handed them over; Atisa provided a lump of chalk.

Aly murmured her thanks, nodded to Ulasim and the other senior conspirators, then looked at her pack and their recruits. Placing a clean slate on her knees, she said, "Very well, my children. Since we all have much to say, let us be organized about it. Who has word from Downwind and the Honeypot?"

She released them to go learn more once they had emptied their budgets of news. She noted that Fesgao and Quedanga came and went, pursuing their own duties. Dove arrived at some point, followed by Nuritin and Nomru. The last three stayed, as did Ulasim, while still more messengers arrived. Dove even took over the note-taking briefly so that Aly could ease her writing hand and eat something.

Aly took a short walk to unwind and visit the privy, then stepped out into the garden and looked up. Was it her imagination, or were the multicolored sparks that represented the Trickster now brighter?

When she returned, she reviewed the notes for what she had missed, then began to take things down again. Finally Ulasim called for lamps. Aly hadn't even noticed it was growing dark; she had simply shifted her Sight so she could work without interruption as the light grew dim. Knocked from her concentration, she looked up and around. Winnamine had come, as had Baron Engan, Ferdy Tomang, and Lord Obemaek. Nawat returned soon after lamps were lit. As Aly stretched her neck to ease a cramp, Imgehai Qeshi arrived, her black priestess's robes disordered, her hood shoved back.

"The fighting has reached the middle of Market Town," she told them, panting. That was where her temple was located.

Aly looked at Ulasim. "There's been no dwindling of the riot since we got home," she told him wearily. "It's spread. And don't ask me how I know this bit, but Rubinyan has sent two hundred of the Rittevon Guard and four decades of Rittevon Lancers out. Their orders are to beat the fighting back to the lower edges of Middle Town, but they're stalled at Rittevon Square. The Honeypot is burning again. Who knew they had anything left? The King's Watch is trying to contain another riot in Downwind. With a little help from people who know what they're doing, their lines can be broken there, if you are in the mood. That riot's spreading to Dockmarket and up to Flowergarden. That is the state of affairs in Rajmuat at this time." She massaged her neck. "What are your orders?"

Ulasim sat, his eyes going from one conspirator's face to another's, ending on Dove's. For a very long, still moment the big raka said and did nothing. At last he made a face. "I think it is plain to all of us that the war has begun ahead of schedule," he said drily. "Any child knows it is better to swim with the tide than against it. We attack in force at dawn."

20

BATTLE JOINED

Messengers left the house with orders for the fighter groups hidden all over the city. Members of the luarin conspiracy sent their loved ones, with some guards from their own households, to the Balitang home. Lord Obemaek told Fesgao that if worse came to worst, the families could flee Rajmuat from the house closest to the docks. Aly thought it sweet, though unrealistic. If Crown troops showed up in the Windward District at all, it would be because the rebels had been beaten, and no ship would be able to sail.

Ochobu made certain that everyone who entered Balitang House first had to submit to truthspells wielded by Ochobu, Ysul, or the handful of Chain mages who had entered the city, or to questions under Aly's Sight as she looked to see if they lied. Those who failed the test of loyalty were locked up rather than executed. It was time to start changing their old policies, Ulasim had told the conspirators. If people who were not on their side were spared when possible, it might create goodwill after the fighting was done.

As everyone bustled about in the hours after midnight, Aly sought a private moment with Ulasim. "You'll see Nawat later," he said before she could open her mouth. "He and his fighters will meet you and Chenaol." When Aly did not leave, he sighed. "That's not it? Well, can the rest wait?" he asked, trying to tie back his hair and write at once.

"It cannot," Aly said, taking control of his hair. "Believe me, I'm not here to waste your time." She did an efficient braid and tied it off.

Ulasim finished his document and handed it to a waiting messenger. "Close the door," he ordered her. As the door thunked shut behind her, Ulasim looked up at Aly. "What is it?" he demanded.

Aly crouched and held out a hand. "Lace," she called. "It's time."

The darking had been hiding under Ulasim's chair. Now it rolled forward onto Aly's palm. Aly picked it up and showed it to Ulasim.

"This is Lace," she told her general, whose eyes had gone wide at the sight of the odd creature. "I cannot tell you how I came to know it, or where it comes from. You would *really* dislike the answer. Lace is a darking. Say hello to Ulasim," she instructed.

Lace stuck up a neck and head. "Hello. What one of us knows, we all know. We can even show sometimes, if you are not in a hurry."

Aly offered the darking to Ulasim. "I mean to give one to Fesgao, Ochobu, Chenaol, Nomru, Her Grace, and Dove." Gingerly Ulasim accepted Lace. "They're all I have left," Aly continued as he rolled the darking on his palm. "The others, but for my personal darking, are at the palace. You keep yours by you, as I always keep mine by me. Say hello, Trick."

Trick put its head up from its necklace shape. "Hello," it said. "It is a fine thing to say hello to you people at last."

"How long have they— No," Ulasim corrected himself as Aly raised a finger. "No questions. But can we trust them, whatever they are?"

"We have kept your trust for weeks," Lace informed him. "We have heard everything, and we have told only Aly."

Ulasim started to speak, then stopped. He looked at their surroundings, the conspirators' meeting room, then at Lace. "For weeks," he repeated, his voice very dry. "And you reported only to Aly."

"We do not *lie*," Trick said in reproof. "Not much."

"Lies are boring," added Lace.

"A good thing we never planned to betray *you*," Ulasim told Aly.

Aly smiled at him. "Now you're being silly," she replied. "The best place to wear one is around your neck. That way they can speak in your ear."

Lace rolled up Ulasim's arm, raising goose bumps on the man's skin. It shaped itself like a band around his neck. "I tell you what is happening around other darkings," Lace explained.

Ulasim hitched his shoulders. "It is the strangest feeling," he remarked. "Bright Eyes, it is always something new with you. Fesgao, Mother, Nomru, Chenaol, Her Grace, and Lady Dove?" Aly nodded. Ulasim smoothed his bearded chin. "And you. Very good. The Crown's mages can interfere with the communications of our mages. Will that affect these creatures?"

"No," said Trick, authority in its tiny voice. "We are not shaped from the Gift of mortals, but by Stormwing blood and magic in the Divine Realms."

Ulasim looked startled.

"It will go better if you treat them as people," Aly said gently. "With their own minds and thoughts. Treat them as you would any message runner. The only differences are, these never leave you, and they get news from widely scattered forces more quickly than any runner." She raised her eyebrows. "Have I permission to give one to the others?"

"I would be a fool to stop you," said Ulasim. "Though if your sources are limited, I would keep one back for Nawat. He will be meeting Chenaol's party."

"Quartz," suggested Secret. "Quartz came with Countess Tomang. Quartz doesn't want to stay while we hunt."

"Good idea," Aly told it.

Ulasim gazed at Lace with a frown. "These . . . darkings . . . are in the palace?"

"We hear things and we tell Aly," explained Lace. "Fun."

With his free hand Ulasim rubbed his eyes. "I bless the day the god sent you to us, Aly." When Lace squeaked in indignation, he added, "And you darkings. I hope the god has no more surprises left. I have had all the surprises I can wrap my mind around." He flapped a hand in dismissal.

Aly had similar conversations with Fesgao, Ochobu, Duke Nomru, Chenaol, and Winnamine as she introduced them to their darkings. She made sure to talk to each of them alone. It would be a bother to explain her small friends to even more members of the conspiracies. As it was, Ochobu threatened her with blisters for keeping them to herself.

The last person she sought was Dove. The girl sat on the edge of the courtyard pool, little kudarung tucked and slumbering all around her, the big stallion and his mares dozing nearby on the grass. Though there were no torches lit in the garden, Aly could see Dove's face plainly. It was the face of mutiny.

"If you've come to say I serve best by waiting here . . . ," she warned as Aly approached. "'Stay safe,' they tell me, while people are dying in my name. What kind of queen sits around eating guava while her people are in danger?"

"A creative one," Aly told her, kneeling beside Dove. "I have someone I want you to meet, my lady. Secret."

There was a squeak from her left shoulder. While Trick, on her right, had spoken up with its own firm opinions as Aly introduced the others to their darkings, Secret had shriveled against Aly's skin, making itself smaller and smaller. Secret had believed it would have to stay with Aly.

"I have to meet someone secret?" asked Dove, confused.

"No, someone *named* Secret," Aly said, holding out her left arm and open hand. Secret rolled down her arm and into her palm, producing its head the moment it came to a stop. "I kept you back for Dove," Aly explained to the darking, which shivered with excitement. "I wasn't going to leave you out." She made her introductions and explanations and transferred Secret to its new friend. It gave her a pang to part with the little darking, but she could tell from the way Secret wrapped itself around Dove's slender neck that it had badly wanted work of its own.

Aly got to her feet, her heart pounding. She kept her voice even as she said, "It's important that you stay safe. Without you, we have nothing to secure any kind of victory with. But there's safe and there's *safe*, if you take my meaning." Dove stared at her, then frowned. Aly continued, "True, it would do the fighters good to *see* you, but not if it will bring you within arrow-shot." She bowed to Dove. "My pack and I go hunting at dawn," she said. "If I don't see you again, I just want you to know, I would have worked for you gladly even without the god's involvement."

Aly left the garden, thinking, If she takes the hint, Ulasim will kill me. She grinned. Though he'll have to dethrone Imajane and Rubinyan first. I can live with that.

Her pack and their recruits assembled in her workroom while Aly changed into a specially made sarong that included hidden sheaths for her thin, flat knives. The sash also had a few surprises in its folds. Breifly she envied her mother, able to tuck herself into armor with a number of weapons at hand. Aly felt virtually naked. There was nothing more she could do apart from settling a length of chain in her sash. Her work was different from Mother's, that was all.

"We've been taking orders from a girl who's younger than *any* of us?" cried a recruit who had never met her.

Boulaj and Junai fixed him with stony eyes. "She is the god's gift," Boulaj said in a voice like ice.

"I have a *daughter* her age," protested a woman who loaded grain at the Dockmarket as she gathered information for Eyun.

"I am ancient in treachery," Aly said with an agreeable smile. "If you're going to whine, you may stay and tend the real children here."

Someone whispered, "She brought down Topabaw. She said she would do it, and she did."

"He still rots out by the harbor," added Vitorcine, Aly's first double agent. "I haven't had to betray my masters since he got dead. I'll follow her wherever she likes."

After that, there was no more discussion. They all checked weapons and each other's clothing. Chenaol arrived as they were doing a final count. The cook was also dressed to fight, a cutlass belted at her waist. In one hand she carried a heavy ax. Light slid along its curved, sharp edge.

"Let's go, my dears," she told them. "We have to cross the city by dawn."

Getting to Flowergarden, the district west of Downwind, took them triple the time it would have taken if conditions had been normal. Royal patrols that numbered twenty and thirty grim-faced men roamed the streets. They did not submit to the rain of garbage and stones that fell from the buildings, but killed anyone foolish enough to be caught outside. Any fighter who shot at people who threw things went down the next moment with an arrow in his throat.

After her people's fifth plea to help those attacked by the soldiers, Aly asked Chenaol for a quick halt and gathered them close. "We *cannot* stop and fight every fight along the way," she told them softly, firmly, keeping anger and nerves out of her voice and face. They had to see her calm and in control, these people who had only ever known the pack member who had recruited them. "If you want to drop out and die foolishly, do it without argument. The rest of us have a mission, a vital one. We can't afford distractions, however many old ladies douse the King's Watch in night soil. Either leave or be silent."

After that, they kept silent. Aly wasn't sure if it was her words or the glares of those who had recruited them. Either way, no one left their group. They moved on through the night, through tunnels, alleys, and sometimes up stairs and over rooftops, any course that would keep them clear of the patrols and the pockets of fighting scattered throughout the city. North and across Dockmarket, Market Town, then Middle Town they followed Chenaol, who seemed to know exactly when to hide and when to advance. As they crossed the city, Trick whispered in Aly's ear. Ulasim and his fighters had met Crown troops on southern side of town. These soldiers came from the Greater Fortress. They were hesitant and inclined to run. As the survivors of the deadly raids and fires at the fortress, they lacked the spirit of other men who had come to battle on the Crown's behalf. Ulasim told his darking that he thought these soldiers felt that they'd had enough raka fighting the night the two fortresses had burned. They would be remembering that there should have been more of them, and that many of them should have been whole and strong, not marked with burns.

Fesgao's soldiers collided with nearly one hundred men-at-arms in service to loyal luarin families on the northeastern edge of the Swan District, where it met Market Town. The luarin troops were outnumbered but fighting well, his darking reported. Fesgao was far short of his destination, but Ochobu, hearing of his delay, sent two Chain mages to his aid. Three more mages joined Ulasim, while Ochobu herself led a small group of mages, hooded and cloaked like the Black God's priests, up Rittevon's Lance, straight into the fighting on the square. They started to blast their way through the soldiers of the hated King's Watch.

Nomru and his fighters cut across the city at an angle to Rittevon's Lance, driving across Middle Town and into the Swan District, attacking guards at the checkpoints and any household troops foolish enough to get in his way. He gave the same rough treatment to anyone on the edges of the riot if they did not move when he ordered.

Everyone had plenty of light. The Honeypot was ablaze again, its fires spreading into Downwind. Isolated fires burned in Dockmarket, Market Town, and Middle Town. Aly and her group heard the roar of the riot and the shrieks of the injured. Over it all rose the eerie trill of feeding Stormwings. Lit from below, they looked like monsters from the realms of Chaos.

Once Chenaol's group reached the border between Market Town and Flowergarden, they followed the ground as it began to slope upward. There were fewer soldiers to interfere as they cut across the house and temple gardens that gave the district its name. Aly frequently glimpsed a steady flow of warriors that came from the ridge where Flowergarden met the jungles at the city's back. These people stayed clear of Chenaol and her companions. Their faces—male and female, raka and luarin—were grim and eager in Aly's Sight as they flooded into the city to do battle.

Higher Chenaol's group climbed, through a maze of cottage gardens where people grew vegetables for the city's markets. At last they crested the ridge, halting where a dirt road ended in a small shrine to the Jaguar Goddess. As they stopped to drink from their water bottles, each member of their company tossed a small token—a button, a flower, an arrowhead—down the deep well at the heart of the shrine. Even Aly contributed a flower. It was her philosophy that it never hurt to be polite to strange gods.

She heard the rustle of branches, and a crow fledgling's unmistakable call for more food, followed by the call for "friend." Chenaol responded with a soft howler monkey call.

"You do that well," Aly whispered as warrior shadows approached from the shelter of the trees. The sky in the east shone with a pale gray light that just touched the edges of plants and weapons.

"A misspent girlhood in the jungles of Gempang," the cook explained.

Nawat reached them, flanked by a hard-faced raka woman and a thin, whipcord-lean man who looked as if he might be related to Nawat. He had the same nose and floppy black hair, and he sported a knot of crow feathers at the crown of his head. Also like Nawat, he carried an unstrung bow and a fat quiver of crow-fletched arrows. Without making a sound their companions drew up around Aly's group. There were nearly two hundred of them, all wearing clothes that showed signs of hard use, under mismatched and battered armor. All carried bows and quivers of black-feathered arrows, just as all carried swords, from the sailor's heavy cutlass to longswords in nicked sheaths. Like the other groups of raka fighters Aly had seen, this one was composed of both men and women.

Mother would love it here, Aly thought, then shook the notion out of her head. When preparing for combat, it was a good idea to concentrate on that and nothing else.

As the new arrivals crouched to wait with Aly's pack and their recruits, Aly beckoned Nawat aside. From her pouch she took the last darking, Quartz, and introduced it to him. Once they had reached an understanding and Quartz had settled around Nawat's neck, Aly looked at the eastern horizon. The sun was coming. Already the extra-long rays that indicated the god was locked in battle thrust into the sky over the horizon.

Positioning himself so that no one could see him do it, Nawat kissed her fingers. Aly smiled into his eyes. They said or did nothing else, but for them, that was enough.

"We go in first," Chenaol told Nawat's assistants, her voice soft. "Then you. We'll be out doing our work for a time before we call you in—Aly will signal Nawat. Then you must come through and attack anything in a uniform."

"Try not to kill any more than you can help," Aly reminded them. "Particularly among the servants. It's time to start trying to live together. Tie them up or lock them in somewhere, if you get the chance."

"What about the Gray Palace?" asked Lokak. "There are no tunnels there. How will we take the place?"

"Leave the Gray Palace to your old Duani," Aly told him. "We haven't come so far for nothing." Nibbling her lip, she looked at them all. She wanted to tell them to capture Imajane and Rubinyan, not to kill them. It would be nice if the new queen could show neighboring countries that the deposed monarchs had gotten a fair trial. Inspecting their faces, she realized it would be better to hold her tongue. She'd often heard her mother and other warriors say, "Never give an order if you are not sure it will be obeyed." She wasn't sure that her position as Duani gave her the authority to issue orders at all, let alone that one, just as she knew from the grim faces around her that she would not be obeyed if she gave it. She settled for "Don't take trophies from those you slay. They never look as good as you think they will."

A wave of soft chuckles passed through the group.

"The sun comes," Nawat said, raising his face to its rays. "Mithros is angry."

They all turned to look. The sun was the sun, shedding light and heat as it always did. Its rays streamed like dark orange pennants around the disk, whipping and rippling as if a hard wind blew them. The white veils of fire that had marked the Goddess in the daytime lengthened to cover the parts of the sky left to it by the sun, rippling like the sun's rays. Everywhere overhead the sparks that showed the Trickster's fortunes had expanded to the size of greater stars.

On the slopes below their position, the rebels could view the city. The Rittevon Square riot still went on. Pillars of smoke from burning buildings rose all over town.

"Let us vex the sun god some more," said Jimarn. "Or do we wait until we die of old age?"

"No one wants to live forever," added Yoyox.

Aly had already seen the suspiciously sturdy vine that twined around one of the shrine's pillars. Chenaol beckoned for one of the bigger fighters to help her. They hauled together on the ropy vine, teeth clenched, sweat soon gleaming on their faces. Two of Aly's pack went to help. Slowly the square of a doorway became visible in the ground. A handful of Nawat's people circled it, using blades to cut away the bush and grass roots that had woven themselves into the door's cover in the years since this exit had been used. With a last, long rip, the grassy hood pulled free. Those hauling on it dragged it back to rest against the shrine, then tied ropes around the ring in the door below. It too had settled into the ground and was reluctant to leave its bed. Growling, the warriors pulled it up.

"The one at the palace didn't give so much trouble," Aly murmured, watching.

"We make sure of that. We've had to use the palace entry as a hiding spot. There used to be other exits," said Chenaol, panting. "But this one is so isolated, it's hard to get at. And there's no way to keep people from coming on you here without warning."

The door was up. Someone struck a flint to light the torches they had brought. Aly looked at the steps that led into the ground. "It's going to be nasty down there," she whispered.

Nawat looked at her and gave his bird shrug, as if to say, Nasty is as nasty does.

"Trick, what news?" Aly wanted to know. Warriors went into the tunnel with torches and swords, clearing away cobwebs and roots. Aly, Chenaol, and Nawat followed them, ignoring the muttered comments from their people about the accommodations.

"Nomru at Rittevon Square," the darking said as the rebels passed along the tunnel, "catching soldiers between him and Ulasim. Fesgao's fight done. They are near the edge of Flowergarden. Fesgao says Fonfalas wait for signal to attack the Grain Gate." Aly nodded. The Grain Gate and the Gate of Carts were the side entrances to the palace, where supply wagons brought in ordinary goods for those who lived there. Ulasim and Nomru meant to attack the Gate of Victory once they combined forces.

It seemed like hours until they reached the tunnel's end at the stair that opened next to the Pavilion of Delightful Pleasures. The rebels hesitated there. If Vereyu hadn't got the message Ulasim had sent to her during the night, they might come up among Crown soldiers, who would be able to hack at them at will. Nawat beckoned one of his people forward, a small, perky young luarin with a headful of red curls, bright blue eyes, and a whip-weal that divided her face in half. As she climbed the stairs toward the closed door, the silvery fire of her magical Gift streamed upward to wriggle through cracks in the wood.

She was nodding to Nawat—friends waited outside—when Trick whispered into Aly's ear, "Dove *flies.*"

Aly grinned. She wished she could see it: Dove astride the big chestnut kudarung as its great wings caught the air, carrying her over the battles in the streets. It was a risk. A well-placed arrow might ruin everything. But Aly's heart lifted at the thought of Dove in the sky, running risks so that her people might see her. If Aly were out there, fighting for the freedom of her native land, that sight would inspire her like nothing else.

Trick added mournfully, "Secret flies too. Not me."

Aly moved aside so that some of the fighters could get under the tunnel door to push. "I'll make it up to you," she whispered as the warriors thrust at the wooden barrier. Hearing the noise, those outside helped to raise it. Climbing the stairs, Aly looked up into Vereyu's face. "Lovely day, don't you agree?" she asked, stepping into the open air. "Perhaps we'll have lunch on the water pavilions later."

Vereyu's face was grim and set. "Only you would make jokes at a time like this," she told Aly.

"If not now, when?" Aly wanted to know as she brushed off her sarong, trying not to look at its bright colors. It only reminded her that she couldn't wait for the fight to be over, so that she could wear luarin quiet colors again. Eyun of Aly's pack, Vitorcine, and several of the full- or nearly full-luarin recruits wore similar clothes, the kind meant to attract attention. Two of the women who waited with Vereyu were dressed the same way. All of them had been chosen for their looks and their pale skin.

Vereyu and her companions had set a number of shallow open baskets on the ground. Most were loaded with fruit, bread, and rolls filled with slices of meat. Two baskets were full of water flasks, and had handles on either side so that they could be carried by two people.

"We did our best with breakfast in the mess halls," Vereyu told Aly. "Plenty of the men on duty have already run to the privy. I took your advice—I didn't drug everything, so they may not suspect you. Get off the wall if they realize their problem lies in the food." She looked down into the tunnel, where Nawat and his warriors waited. "How will we know when to turn these folk loose?"

Aly smiled at Nawat, who stroked the band around his neck that was the darking Quartz. He'd discovered the darkings' relaxing purr. "They'll know," she said. "I hear Her Majesty has company." The Gray Palace darkings had been announcing the arrival of loyal, panicked nobles since early the night before.

"All the rotten eggs together," Vereyu said, and spat on the ground.

I suppose it would take an extraordinary degree of hate to serve here, day in and day out, in the hope that sometime you would be able to tell your masters what you really think of them, Aly thought. Her respect for Vereyu, already high, doubled. She would tell Dove's spymaster to make good use of Vereyu. Bringing peace to the outlying Isles would be a long, hard job once the capital was won. Vereyu would be good for the distance.

"Any parting words of cheer?" Aly inquired.

Vereyu grinned. "Get stuffed. And send anyone who needs care to the Pavilion of Delightful Pleasures."

Aly nodded and looked at those who were playing royal servants, come to help the soldiers on the Luarin Wall as they stood guard in the hot sun. The soldiers would welcome their burdens of food and water, not realizing the annoying or, in enough quantities, deadly secret in many of the fruits, rolls, and flasks. "Ladies, shall we?" she invited.

They strolled down the Golden Road, past the servants' mess hall, and out through the Gate of Carts. That gate was nearly closed, those who kept watch on it fidgeting nervously. The Grain Gate, one hundred yards from the Gate of Carts, was shut and barred. Wagons had been rolled in front of it as an extra barrier.

Aly and her girls reached the stair to the watch posts on the Luarin Wall and began to climb. They braced their baskets on one hip, a position that ensured the bearer's gait would have a little extra sway. Once they reached the top of the wall, Aly fluttered her lashes at the tough-looking sergeant who waited for them beside the steps. "Something to wet your throat, Captain?" she asked, thrusting her basket of fruit at him with one hip. Men always liked it when a girl promoted them. The sergeant grinned and took his time selecting a star fruit. Aly's companions passed food and water to the men who watched the green belt through the crenels at the top of the wall.

"Tell me, Captain, should we be afraid for our lives?" Aly inquired, her eyes lingering on the man's face. "I've heard these wild raka are no better than animals." He swelled with pride and self-importance, never asking why a girl like this appeared so interested in a blue-chinned fellow whose arms and legs were covered with tattoos.

"Just rabble, girlie," he told her. "Rioting, burning up their own homes. Half crazy with snake fever, if you ask me. And make no mistake. His Majesty will come down hard on them. They'll never get the city fixed up in time for the coronation." He tried to snag Aly around the waist.

Nimbly she stepped just out of reach, glancing at him sidelong from under her lashes. "I've work to do, sir!" she said, and put her nose in the air. Apparently relenting, she smiled and added, "Perhaps when I come round again."

He guffawed as she ambled down the walkway. You keep laughing, she thought amiably. Things will be different when you see me next.

Slowly they worked their way around the broad stretch of wall, distributing their offerings, until they reached the Gate of Victory. Here they found a surprise. Aly did a fast count. One hundred and fifty Lancers waited on the ground by the gate, men and horses alike in battle armor. If they rode out, that would leave only fifty Lancers to help defend the palace. Behind them stood three companies, or three hundred men, of the Rittevon Guard, drooping with heat and boredom. They too were dressed for battle and stood in combat formation. The captain of the Guard and the commanding general of the Lancers conferred with each other and with messengers in the shadow of the gate. Obviously they were waiting for orders.

Aly asked Trick to pass the information to Ochobu, Ulasim, and Nomru, who were supposed to meet where Rittevon's Lance entered the open green lands around the palace. They would have to deal with these fighters. Once Trick finished, Aly crossed over the gate on a walkway, her girls behind her. There were whistles and called remarks of appreciation from the bored men below, until their officers silenced them. The young women giggled or laughed, and offered their drugged goods to the rest of the men on the wall.

Vereyu's people met them with fresh supplies by the Gate of the Sun, the closest gate to the Gray Palace. This Gate had been closed and blocked with stone, hastily laid but solid. No one could enter and leave the palace there. Aly and her women continued around the wall, joking with bored sentries whose posts overlooked little but cliffs or jungle behind the palace as they passed them food and water. The women had almost reached the Grain Gate when Trick said, "They come. Fesgao, Nomru, Ulasim, they come all together. They are on the grass."

Aly looked at the Crown's men around the Gate of Carts. Faces were already missing, the guard smaller by a third. "Tell Nawat to come," she whispered to Trick. To the women who followed her she hand-signaled, *Retreat. Get off the wall.*

On she walked with her empty basket, coming up beside the sergeant who had been so complimentary earlier. He had gotten none of the drugged food, she guessed, since he still looked hearty enough, though he sweated in the day's remorseless heat. Aly handed him a flask of water. He took it absently, scanning the merchants' road with a spyglass. "I feel like there's more to all this than a riot, even if it's just a riot close to us," he murmured. "It's more than a herd of ragged beggars crazy with the summer sun."

She sharpened her Sight. The Fonfala men-at-arms emerged from the jungle in the distance. With them were armored raka warriors, bearing a crest on their breastplates: a chest topped with a copper key. She had seen that emblem on things that Sarugani had left Sarai and Dove. It was the coat of arms of the Temaida family, the shadowy relatives who lived on other islands and waited for their last hope to become real.

The sergeant put down his spyglass and surveyed the men around him. "Where's Hessken? Mayce? Rufert?"

"Privy, sir," called another man. "Something off with breakfast, I think. I'm not so well myself."

"Breakfast, or . . ." The sergeant turned to look at Aly, the picture of innocence with her empty basket. The sweat on his face was heavier, the drops rolling off his cheeks.

"Let me help you, Sergeant," she said, hooking his feet from under him with one of hers. He collided with the wall and slid down until he sat, his eyes fluttering as the sleep drug took him. When he gave her a last glance, she said kindly, "I'll look after things up here."

"Help me!" she cried to the closest men. "His eyes just rolled up and he fell." She went down on her knees as if to help. Two soldiers turned to come to her, only to sprout black-feathered arrows. They toppled from the wall to the ground outside the wall.

Aly ran for another stair to the ground rather than get in the way of Nawat's people as they scrambled to the wall. A few more arrows whizzed past her. She wove from side to side to throw off the Crown's archers who could still aim. Once on the ground, she raced for the cover of the trees as a storm of crows descended on the wall's defenders. In the distance Aly heard men roar as the rebels swarmed onto the green belt. She saw them in her mind's eye, carrying gates they had removed from buldings on the way here to use as bridges over the streams and their deadly occupants.

"Gate of Victory opens," Trick informed her as she trotted down the path to Sevmire's headquarters. "Rubinyan comes with soldiers. He leads Guards and Lancers out to fight Ulasim, Fesgao, Nomru."

"I love it when warriors get noble," Aly said as she yanked open the door to the spymaster's building. "They get themselves killed with hardly any help from us. It's the best time-saver." Here was the corridor where the spymasters hanged the victims of recent tortures to frighten people like Aly Homewood. Sadly, each pair of shackles held a captive. In one bloodied, broken-armed wreck Aly recognized a cook whose dumplings were one of Dockmarket's main attractions.

Running to Sevmire's office for the keys, Aly halted when Vitorcine emerged from it. She held a bloody knife in one hand. Behind her something cast flickering orange light through the door. She had set the place on fire.

Aly brought out her lock picks. "I don't suppose you thought to get his keys when you lit him up?" she called, running back to the captives. Starting with the one closest to the hall where the fire burned, she got to work on the padlock on his chains. A moment later a grimy hand thrust a ring of keys under her nose.

"Why do you think I went in there?" asked Vitorcine.

Aly looked the keys over and singled out the one that opened the shackles. "Catch them as we take them down," she told Vitorcine as she began to undo locks. "You know, Sevmire wasn't worth killing."

Vitorcine gently helped the cook to stand. "He wasn't worth leaving alive, either, Duani."

Aly shrugged. "You have a point." She glanced at the end of the hall. The fire was brighter. "Let's get them outside," she suggested. "I'm sure they'd be happy for sunlight, and we don't want them getting all crispy in here."

Vitorcine nodded and began to escort people out of the building. Aly freed the last prisoners as flames began to crackle beyond Sevmire's office. Some of the captives could walk. They and Vitorcine helped the rest outside.

Aly followed them into the open air. "See if you can get them to the Pavilion of Delightful Pleasures," she told Vitorcine. "And nice work." Moving off toward the Golden Road she asked, "Trick?"

"Nawat's friends put wedges under barracks doors to trap soldiers who sleep," Trick replied obediently. "Ulasim attacks Rubinyan from the left, Fesgao and Nomru from the right. Ochobu, Ysul, and Chain mages come up Rittevon's Lance with their spells hiding in the air and in the ground. Luarin mages not looking at air or ground, only at Ochobu and Chain. Ground is eating luarin mages and their horses. Air is pushing other mages under soldiers' horses. The crows attack soldiers on the wall. Dove says more royal soldiers come to protect Gate of Carts from Fonfalas and Temaidas."

Aly looked up. Overhead circled the chestnut stallion with Dove in a saddle on his back. Outside the walls, she heard a deep-throated roar as men and women cheered the girl's appearance. With Dove looking on, they plowed ahead without letup, battling their way toward the Gate of Victory.

21

WORK

"Uh-oh," said Trick.

Aly, her eyes on Dove, said, "What oh?"

"Soldiers on horses ride up from city," Trick replied. "Secret sees them. Soldiers and archers. And archers climb to walls near the Gate of the Sun."

Aly cursed. The nobles who had taken refuge with Imajane in the Gray Palace must have left men in the guest barracks. If they were so healthy, they couldn't have eaten the food Vereyu's people had poisoned. Perhaps they'd brought their own rations? She'd find out later, if there was a later.

"Tell Nawat of the archers on the walls," she ordered Trick. "Tell Fesgao that an attack comes up behind Ulasim. Nobody else, understand? Just those two."

A squad of soldiers wearing the crest of a luarin noble house came toward her at the trot. As they swerved around Aly, she reached into her sash for a small packet of sleep dust. Suddenly a soldier screamed and went down, a crow-fletched arrow in his eye. Other arrows flew from a clump of trees, followed by the archers: Nawat's people, bows set aside and swords taken up.

"Stop!" Aly yelled. Everyone, the soldiers and Nawat's warriors, turned to stare at her. "Wouldn't it be nice to be able to trust the person on the throne?" she asked their enemies. "To not have to live wondering each day as you wake if your family is safe, or if your master is rotting by the harbor?"

Nawat's people waited.

"Do you really want to die for the Rittevons?" Aly asked more quietly.

Three soldiers raised weapons and fell, shot by Nawat's suspicious archers. The rest hesitated. Then one of them, a sergeant by the bright red bands on his breastplate, set down his sword and dagger. When he straightened, one of his own men tried to attack him. Two other luarin soldiers grabbed the attacker and wrestled him to the ground. He lay there, killed quietly by one of his fellows. They in turn dropped their weapons. Others followed suit.

A woman with crow feathers in her hair shrugged and took a coil of thin rope from her belt. "Our brother said if they surrendered, bind them and move on," she said. She looked at the surrendering soldiers and grinned, teeth flashing in her lean face. "If I meet you again in battle, I won't be so nice," she warned them.

Aly moved on. "Trick?"

"Crows drive archers from the wall and knock some off," Trick replied. "Some crows are shot dead. Fesgao fights soldiers who attack Ulasim from behind. Nomru leads his people forward against Rubinyan's. Mages fight each other. Ochobu is saying many bad words to them."

On and on it came, a flood of information. Aly finally had to stop helping her people, Nawat's, and Vereyu's clean out pockets of resistance in the greater palace. She hid in a corner of the Robing Pavilion and sorted out who needed to know what piece of information. Trick pooled in her lap, allowing images to form inside it. Now Aly could see what the darkings saw when she asked Trick to focus on each of them.

Dove and Secret gave Aly a view of the entire battle that raged all around the Luarin Wall. They pointed out breaks in the lines of enemy soldiers where Nomru, Fesgao, Ochobu, and Ulasim could swamp them, and when an attack came at them from the sides or the rear.

Dove told Aly that fifty of Nawat's people had cleared and opened the Gate of Carts and the Grain Gate, allowing the Fonfala and Temaida fighters to stream into the palace. Secret showed her Nawat and another band of his people, picking more defenders from the walls of the Gray Palace with arrows. Quartz, riding around Nawat's throat, showed Aly the front of the Gray Palace. The gates were shut and barred. It was finally serving the purpose for which it was built, a last stronghold for the luarin Crown.

Ochobu's darking reported that the old woman was ill, tottering as she pulled up all the strength she had in one last spell. Her heart burst as she flung it out, taking five luarin mages to the Peaceful Realms with her. Aly cringed as Ochobu's darking fell to the ground with her, seeing it all as the darking did. Keening its grief, the creature moved promptly to Ysul, who took command of the Chain. There was little he *could* command, as Trick and Aly could see. His cohorts were locked in their own battles. Ysul used his power briefly to direct them to new targets as they each finished wrestling one enemy mage to powerlessness or death. When the mages were occupied again, Ysul looked for a project of his own. Trick and Aly looked with him.

Behind Rubinyan and his troops loomed the Gate of Victory, shut tight, locked with heavy timbers, written over with spells of protection. Ysul's darking told Aly that he was "up to something." While it could feel magic course through the raka mage, that was a sensation it couldn't pass along to Trick or Aly. Instead the two looked around, prepared to warn Ysul if someone was about to attack him. No one was. As if they sensed the power Ysul summoned, the people who battled near him left him alone at the center of a rare open space. Once Ysul sent his magic out into the ground, hidden like most raka magic, Aly could See it course through the earth. It passed under the fighting men of both sides. The luarin mages didn't even notice it, hidden as Ysul's spell was. His magic streamed up into the Gate of Victory. Aly held her breath. Suddenly the dense, bespelled wood of the gate burst into white devouring flames.

Lace broke in, showing its views of the battle. Ulasim, wielding a longsword, had cut his way through the last of Rubinyan's protectors. Aly and Trick watched as Rubinyan closed with Ulasim, hacking at him from horseback. Lace dropped from Ulasim's neck to batten onto the cinch strap on Rubinyan's saddle. For some moments all Aly could see were Ulasim's straining legs. Then the saddle slid. Down tumbled Rubinyan, twisting to fall on his back. In lunged Ulasim, his blade passing through an opening in Rubinyan's armor to cut deep. Rubinyan, grimacing, rolled and thrust his sword through Ulasim. For a moment the two men stared at one another.

Then Ulasim looked up. Dove swooped in on her kudarung, venturing close to the enemy's archers in her need to save him.

"Look!" Ulasim bellowed, pointing up to her. His voice rang over the clash of weapons and the shrieks of warriors and Stormwings. "Look at her! There! See our future? See how we can be great?"

He swayed and fell as his darking keened. Beneath him lay Rubinyan, already dead.

Aly didn't realize tears streamed down her face as she told Fesgao's darking what had befallen their general. Fesgao didn't hesitate. He plowed through the warriors, crying for them to follow him, in the queen's name. As the raka, howling, surged forward, the Gate of Victory collapsed, burned to cinders by Ysul. Behind it, the Raka Gate, too, burned.

Ysul dropped to his knees. When the Raka Gate fell to ashes, he lay down. Two rebels ran to pick him up. His darking told Aly that Ysul was alive, but worn out. The creature went to the next mage to take command of the Chain.

From Dove's position Aly saw that the fighting had slowed in many places close to where Ulasim now lay. Seeing that Rubinyan was dead, a dozen or more luarin warriors raised their hands in surrender. The other Crown troops, mauled by the attacking Fesgao and his fighters, had borne enough. They turned and ran through the destroyed gates. Nawat's warriors and the Fonfala and Temaida troops met them there. Caught between Fesgao's rebels and the forces that had taken the palace grounds, the luarin soldiers fought or surrendered, as they preferred. The more soldiers farther back who saw them put up their hands, the more surrendered.

Aly wiped her eyes, gathered up Trick, and began the weary trudge from the pavilion to Rittevon's Lance. They weren't finished yet. Chenaol caught up to her. The cook and her weapons were smeared with blood. Silently they joined the rest of their people, watching as the last of the Crown's forces inside the walls gave up. Soon Nawat, sweat-soaked and disheveled, came to stand with them. The Fonfala and Temaida warriors stripped the weapons from those soldiers who had surrendered and herded them against the wall to be held under guard.

At last Fesgao strode through the gate, Nomru behind him. They joined Aly, Chenaol, and Nawat, looking with dull eyes at the ruin that surrounded them. None of them was unmarked. Even Aly had picked up a handful of cuts, though she couldn't remember when. Fesgao looked them over and nodded, as if they'd just met in the marketplace. As soon as those mages of the Chain still able to work caught up, he turned and led the way to the wall that surrounded the Gray Palace. Nomru, Aly, Chenaol, Nawat, and the rebel warriors followed him, weapons in their hands.

High above Stormwings shrieked in ecstasy. Seeing the bulk of the soldiers were surrendering, they began to swoop down, to plunder the dead. Nawat raised his voice in a raucous crow bawl, a sound that told other crows a hawk had come to steal from them. Cawing in one thunderous voice, hundreds of crows rose into the sky above the palace and turned, heading for the Stormwings.

Aly looked at Nawat. "I could not bear for Stormwings to touch the old woman," Nawat admitted, his eyes bright with unshed tears. "Or Ulasim."

Aly touched his cheek, her own lips quivering. "If she thought you cried over her, Ochobu would just throw magic at you again."

"That is why I waited until the death god had her to do it," replied Nawat.

At last they stood before the granite walls of the Gray Palace. Aly looked at their heights and blinked. There was no guard in view. For a moment Fesgao waited, unsure of what happened now.

"Trick?" Aly asked. "What do the palace darkings say?"

"Surprise," Trick replied. Extending a tentacle, it pointed to the top of the wall.

"We need to make a ram," Fesgao said wearily. Nomru nodded. Aly stepped up to them and put a hand on each man's arm. When they looked at her, their eyes reddened from the dust, she pointed to the wall. Taybur Sibigat stood there at parade rest, hands clasped behind his back. He looked down at them and nodded, his face expressionless.

Slowly the gate to the Gray Palace swung open. Soldiers in the black clothes and mail of the King's Guard, all of whom looked the worse for heavy fighting, lined the flagstone road that led to the residence with dead men all around them. It was four of the Guard who had opened the gate.

"Those troops still loyal to the Rittevons are locked up. So too are those noble families and servants who remained loyal," Taybur called, his voice and face as emotionless as if he read a marketing list. "I surrender the Gray Palace to your war chief. Queen Imajane is being held."

"Does he lie?" Fesgao asked Aly without taking his eyes from Taybur.

"No, sir," Aly replied. "He tells the truth."

A long shadow fell over them. Everyone looked up, then backed away to clear a space as Dove's mount slowly descended. At last the kudarung stallion stood on solid ground, its sides streaked with sweat. Fesgao strode over to help Dove from the saddle.

At the corner of her eye Aly registered a wave of motion. She looked around. First those of raka blood went to their knees. Slowly the luarin troops, even stubborn Duke Nomru, followed suit. Aly knelt slowly. At last only Nawat and those who looked as if they had recently been crows stayed on their feet.

Dove saw them and grinned, her small face lighting up. "Cousins," she said with a nod.

The rattle of chain mail drew Aly's gaze to the men of the King's Guard on the flagstone road. They, too, knelt and bowed their heads. Taybur, who had descended from the walkway overhead, knelt at the center of the open gate.

Dove looked at him. "Imajane?" she asked, her voice steady.

"In her rooms," Taybur replied. "Your Majesty."

Aly glimpsed a flutter of pink high on the side of the residence, on a balcony that overlooked its small garden. "There's a balcony outside her chambers," she said, refusing to look at that spot with her close-in Sight, amazed her voice did not quaver at what the deposed queen was about to do.

"I know," replied Taybur as the bit of pink plummeted from the balcony rail.

"At least we don't have to pay to house and try her," Jimarn murmured from somewhere behind Aly.

Fesgao pointed at the sky. The white veil that showed the Goddess's battles with Kyprioth and his allies was shrinking. The long, swordlike rays that framed the sun, Mithros's sign, were shrinking, too. The brilliant sparkles that had shown the Trickster's growing power flew together to form a single multicolored globe, with a handful of brilliant stars scattered around it: the lesser tricksters, Aly thought. The Goddess's veil and Mithros's rays did not vanish.

There's still work to do, Aly thought. We haven't won, not completely.

In the weeks that followed, Aly learned the truth of something both her parents said: cleaning up always seemed to take much longer than the fighting.

She would have told them it only seemed that way because everyone was tired, except that she was too weary to write a letter home.

The Islanders buried their dead quietly, with services held for a week in the temples of the Black God. Dove insisted that Ulasim have a grave beside the steps to the Throne Hall, covered over in malachite and bronze, with a white marble marker stating his name, dates of birth and death, and the simple epitaph THE STRONG ONE. Ochobu was buried on the far side of the steps from her son, her grave covered in lapis and bronze. Her epitaph read THE WISE ONE. In time, Fesgao would join them as the warrior of the old prophecy. Aly knew where she fit in, but she wasn't sure that she wanted a marker on her grave that read THE CUNNING ONE. It seemed to her most fitting that no one know where she was buried at all.

Ulasim and Ochobu were not their only losses. Vereyu was alive but would limp all her days; Imajane had slashed the tendons behind her knee when Vereyu went to take her prisoner, and the healers had not reached her in time to completely mend the damage. Of Aly's pack, seven had been killed in the fighting: Lokak, Hiraos, and Ukali among the men, and Guchol, Eyun, Kioka, and Junai among the women. Aly mourned them bitterly where no one could see her. Junai had watched her back all that summer at Tanair. The others had been her pack. Only Nawat understood how cruel it was to lose them, just as she understood his grief for sixteen of his flock-mates, as he called the humans and transformed crows he had led.

The priestess Imgehai Qeshi had perished in her burning temple, Lord Obemaek in the fighting. Countess Genore Tomang was dead, killed helping to defend Balitang House. Her son Ferdy lost an eye in the battle before the palace gates. Aunt Nuritin had kept looters from breaking through the servants' gate at the house before a stroke felled her. She was working now to speak again, but the healers said her left hand would never regain its strength.

Once the fires were put out and the palace secure, Dove met with the captive luarin nobles. Chenaol, the duchess, Quedanga, Ysul, and Duke Nomru were present to advise her. From those who surrendered and acknowledged her as queen, she required a blood oath on the spot. She did not ask for one from Taybur.

"They murdered his king," she explained to her council of advisors. "As far as he was concerned, their authority over him ended there. I will trust him."

Her elders argued. They told Dove that, having betrayed one set of monarchs, Taybur could never again be trusted, but Dove would not be swayed. Aly said nothing in front of the others. She had already convinced Dove that Taybur deserved a chance.

Dove also sent out messages to the commanders of the Rittevon forces in the outlying Isles, and to the rebel raka. She received replies in trickles, promises of surrender or vows of resistance. A number of noble luarin hurried to court, anxious to convince their unofficial new queen that they deserved to keep their wealth and lands. Dove told them, every time the subject came up, that property would be redistributed. The luarin could be content with less wealth than they had possessed before, or they could leave the Isles. Most chose to stay, particularly as the Nomrus, Balitangs, Fonfalas, Obemaeks, and Tomangs began to divide their own lands with those who had a legal claim.

For the challenges to her rule, Dove sent out troops led by Fesgao, Nomru, and others. Nawat, who wore a multicolored, incredibly gaudy necklace these days, as did every crow Aly saw, also went out to persuade the fighters to stop. As summer deepened and began to wane, crops were far more important than battle. By the end of August most of the Isles had decided to see how they'd manage with a half-raka queen. Only Ikang and parts of Malubesang and Lombyn continued to resist.

Aly worked even harder than she had before the fighting. Rubinyan's old study, with its well-executed maps and many useful books, became her office. Soon she had to clear rooms on either side to make space for her deputies, Vitorcine, Yoyox, Olkey, and Atisa. They took in the information that arrived each day and rendered it in a form that could be presented to Dove and her counselors. When she could leave things in their hands, Aly ventured out into the Isles, turning the spies of the raka conspiracy into her agents. She chose people from every walk of life. By the start of September she had broken the Kingdom into districts and appointed an agent to take charge of each.

One September morning she woke up—she had fallen asleep on her desktop again—to find Trick squeaking in her ear and Dove settled in a chair in front of her desk. Aly, her brain muddled, struggled to push herself to her feet.

"Stop that," Dove said crossly. "When was the last time you slept in a bed, not at your desk?"

Aly yawned. "Recently, Your Majesty."

"When was the last time you saw Nawat?"

Aly grinned. "Very recently, Your Majesty." She touched the antipregnancy charm he'd given to her. She wore it on a chain long enough that she could tuck it into her breast band under her sarong.

"Better. When are you getting married?"

"Before I lay eggs," Aly said, awake at last. "Why is Your Majesty asking me these questions?"

"Do you plan to nest here or at home?" Dove wanted to know. "Because of all those I have worked with, you are the only one who hasn't sworn to me. Are you going back to Tortall?"

Aly bit her lip. Why couldn't Dove have started this after Aly had spent a night sleeping in a bed? At last she replied, "I wouldn't sell your secrets to other realms, Your Majesty."

"That isn't why I'm asking," Dove snapped. Secret squeaked from its position around her throat. She and the small darking had been inseparable since their first meeting, just like Aly and Trick. "I'm sorry, Secret. But really, Aly, one moment you're braiding my hair and the next you're at least a table length away, giving reports. It's not the same." She looked down at her bronze silk lap. "I thought you were my friend," she added quietly. "I still need a friend."

Aly sighed. It was time to make choices about her future. "Taybur would do very well as your new spymaster," she said, shuffling papers. "He's got the right shifty turn of mind."

"Until the Isles are at peace, I need Taybur with the Queen's Guard," retorted Dove. "He's thorough. If I'm to visit some of the Isles next week, I want him preparing the way. I want *you* for spymaster."

Aly looked at her sadly. "There are things about me you don't know," she told Dove, her belly clenched with tension. "Things that make it impossible for me to be your spymaster. Things that as your permanent spymaster I *must* tell you."

"Oh, stop bouncing and say it." Kyprioth appeared in a window seat, dressed in a jacket and sarong like woven copper, jangling with jewelry. "You know you want to."

Aly scowled at him. "I thought you were going to be really large if you won."

"I am large," retorted the god. "This is only the part you see. I imbue this palace with my essence, every stone and every drop. My visit will do wonders for the flowers."

Aly propped her chin on her hand. "So does manure," she observed.

Kyprioth chuckled. "Whyever would you want to leave me, my dear? We're *made* for each other, in a god-to-servant way." He looked at Dove. "I see you're removing those statues of my sister and brother outside." His face lit with anticipation. "Will you have them melted down?"

"Perhaps *you* can afford to offend them," Dove replied. "I can't. They're going to the temples of Mithros and the Goddess in Rajmuat, as is proper. Do you want me to put up a statue to you? Our custom says it's very unlucky."

"Put a statue up of me? Nonsense," scoffed the god. "I am multitudes. You see but one of my faces. I am—"

"Vast," Aly interrupted. "Yes, you've mentioned it."

"So when's the big day?" Kyprioth asked Dove, unmoved by Aly's sarcasm. "When is my queen to be crowned?"

"The day after Midwinter," Dove replied, a smile tweaking her mouth. "So my official reign begins with the rebirth of the year."

"With the rebirth of the sun," the god corrected her. "Not that I begrudge him, poor fellow. He still hasn't gotten his shield back. That thief I got is truly talented." He raised an eyebrow. "Ah. A summons." He looked at Aly, black eyes dancing. "If she's crowned at Midwinter, the foreign delegations will have to come by the end of October and stay the season," he pointed out. "Your monarchs are sending their very favorite people. You had better hurry up and tell her." He vanished, leaving a thin layer of copper sparkles where he'd sat.

"What did he mean by that?" Dove wanted to know.

Aly had a very bad feeling. "I'd like to tell Winna at the same time, if I may," she said wearily. "I think you both should hear it from me. Trick?"

Trick sat up on her shoulder. "She comes," it said. Like the other darkings given to specific people, Winnamine's had chosen to remain with her as the duchess took over the running of the domestic side of the palace. She had long since ordered Aly to call her by her nickname.

Waiting for her, Aly and Dove talked over plans for Dove's visit to the nearby Isles. The chief problem lay in finding ways for her attendants to keep up, since she would be riding the winged stallion she had named Kypry. "I just won't land until I know the place is safe," she was telling Aly as Winnamine swept in.

The duchess had set a new fashion, wearing her darking as a glossy band twined throughout her hair. Other ladies of Dove's new court were trying the same style, without success, since a darking could grip better than a satin ribbon. "Midget says you two want to discuss something with me," she said as she settled into a chair. "It's not bad news from the outer Isles, is it?"

"You should wait," said Trick. "Fesgao and Chenaol come, too. We told them."

"Why?" Aly wanted to know.

"The darkings are right," said Dove. "They were with us at the beginning. They should hear whatever it is, too."

Aly changed position, hiding the fact that she was making sure the knives in her sash and under the top of her desk were ready to hand. Sheer self-preservation had made her flinch from telling members of the old raka conspiracy. Of all the people Aly had dealt with since her arrival in the Isles, she felt they had the most right to be vexed when they learned the truth about her.

"While we're waiting," the duchess said, pulling a folded parchment from a pocket. Dove and Aly recognized the bold writing right away.

"Sarai!" cried Dove, and grabbed the letter.

As Dove read greedily, Winna told Aly, "They married when they reached Carthak. Sarai is expecting a child next spring." She smiled, her lips trembling. "If it is a boy, they do mean to name him Mequen. They won't be here for the coronation, but they promise to visit as soon as it's safe."

Chenaol arrived from the kitchens, her arms covered to the elbows in flour. Dove had pressed her to accept a more important position, but the raka had refused flatly. Her place was in the kitchen, she'd told Dove. If people wanted to talk weapons, they would find her there.

Fesgao was not far behind the cook. As commander of the queen's armies, he kept an office at the headquarters building near the Rittevon enclosure. He had settled into his work, spending his days like Aly, sorting through papers to decide what mattered and what did not. He'd told Aly that he looked forward to Dove's trip as a break from documents.

When the door was closed behind them, Aly took a deep breath. "Your Majesty, friends," she said quietly, her hands resting on her sash, "I cannot be your spymaster. I am the daughter and granddaughter of Tortall's spymasters, and the daughter of Tortall's King's Champion. The god did not teach me most of what I know—I learned it at my father's knee. I am *not* working on Tortall's behalf. Kyprioth claimed me after I'd foolishly left my home, and set me to work with you. That is the truth of it." She looked down, listening for the slightest hint of movement. The knives in her sash were the quickest to reach, but if it was Fesgao who came for her, she'd need the sword secured under the desktop.

For a very long moment, much too long for Aly's taste, no one spoke or moved. Then Chenaol hoisted herself to her feet. "If that's all, I've got two wagonloads of flour coming from Digger Brothers' mill. I want them to explain how I found gravel stitched into the bottoms of the bags last time. Then I need to decide how much I'll take out of them in blood."

Aly stared at her. "That's it?" she demanded, shocked. "Or will I find you waiting for me in some dark night with one of those thousand and three new carving knives you bought for the kitchens?"

Chenaol rolled her eyes. "Half for the kitchen, half for the armory," she explained. "Why *should* I care? The god picked you. How many times do you have to prove whose side you're on? Oh, I remember—you've already done that." She stomped out.

Fesgao called after her, "Wait." To Aly he said, "She's right, you know. The god wouldn't saddle us with someone who worked for a rival country. I wonder what happens now. Will your father spank you for playing with the neighbors?" He followed Chenaol. "I thought I asked for a *thousand* knives for the armory," he told her.

"Five hundred is what you get with the treasury in the mess it is," they heard her reply. "Talk to Quedanga, if you want to hear her moan about all the money spent on food supplies for those whose crops didn't make it."

Aly blinked, then looked at Winna and Dove. "Maybe the god's recommendation is good enough for you, Your Majesty," she said to the queen. To the duchess she respected she added, "But, Your Grace . . ."

Winnamine smiled and rose to her feet. "Chenaol is right. You have more than proved who has your allegiance, Aly." She came over and leaned down, in a puff of lily-of-the-valley scent, to kiss Aly's cheek. "I would hate to force you to choose between your family and us, but it goes without saying that we need you more." She smiled at Dove and left them, gently closing the door behind her.

Aly looked at Dove.

"Are you going to be my spymaster or not?" demanded the younger girl. "Winna's right. We need you more. We met your father, didn't we? Last year, at Tanair. Only he said he was a merchant."

"Your Majesty, he lies," Aly said, shaking her head with regret. "He lies all the time. I think sometimes he lies just to stay in practice."

Dove smiled and stood. "And to protect his daughter, alone in the enemy's country," she pointed out. "Will you be my spymaster, please? I still do need a friend."

Aly got up and walked over to her, then knelt, took Dove's hand, and pressed her forehead against the younger girl's fingers. "I will serve you all my days, Your Majesty," she told Dove softly, meaning it with her whole heart. Then she looked up. "You're wearing five rings. You promised you'd never wear more than three."

Dove giggled. "Boulaj says they look nice." The young woman had decided that she liked the post of bodyguard-maid and kept it.

"She's Kyprin," Aly scolded. "They think twelve necklaces on one neck is nice."

Dove pulled a ring off, a gold band with a piece of basalt set in it. Embedded in the smooth, matte black stone was a small copper kudarung. "Then here," she said, holding the ring worn by her personal household to Aly. "You wear this one."

For once Aly had nothing to say. She could only nod, and slide the ring onto her index finger.

Someone pounded on the door. "Your Majesty!" called Nuritin, pronouncing each word with care. "You have an audience in the Throne Hall this morning. Will you be late to your own audience?"

Dove grimaced and walked out to meet her obligations.

Aly looked at her jumbled desk. "Well," she said wearily, "if I'm staying, I'd better recruit some more help."

The day after the end of Midwinter, the Throne Hall of the royal palace blazed with the light cast by a thousand lamps and candles. It glittered on gold and silver jewelry, hoards of gemstones, silks and satins, and in the hundreds of pairs of eyes that were fixed on the dais. Incense rose to form clouds against the high ceilings, scenting the air. Chimes tinkled as breezes moved through the hall.

Taybur Sibigat, captain of the Queen's Guard, knelt on the second-highest step of the dais, holding a cushion above his head. On it shone gold shaped as a crowned headdress at the front, with a spray of copper sprigs at the back, each dangling gold drops. Copper drops hung from a forehead plate. Dovasary Haiming Temaida Balitang, dressed all in silver satin patterned in black, reached for the Crown, made from old descriptions to look like the original Crown of the Isles. With hands that trembled, she raised it for her audience to see, then carefully lowered it to rest on her own head. It was how the Kyprin queens had always been crowned, since no one wanted to offend their peculiar god by claiming his priesthood.

The onlookers, noble and common born, sent up a thunder of applause and cheers that startled the small winged horses from the beams overhead. They swooped around the new queen, who stood there patiently, waiting for quiet.

To the side, tucked into the shadow of a pillar, her spymaster leaned against Nawat Crow with a happy sigh.

EPILOGUE

At the Kudarung Inn
Rajmuat in the Copper Isles
April 2, 464 H.E.

In the morning the Tortallan delegation would sail home, with reports for their monarchs on the new queen and her government. For this occasion some of its members had taken a private room for a very private dinner. Their two local guests came separately, one as a crow who changed into human form once he reached his father-in-law's chambers. Aly came disguised as a Carthaki lady, complete with veils.

She and Nawat sat at the table with her family, everyone full of good food and busy with lively talk. Aly, whose morning sickness extended sometimes to evenings, had contented herself with a mild broth and fruit juices. She looked frequently at the slight swell of her belly, mystified by the thought that another human being was taking shape beneath her navel.

She sat between her father, George Cooper, baron of Pirate's Swoop, and her mother, Alanna the Lioness, lady knight and King's Champion of Tortall. From that position she could look at her brothers. Alan wore a squire's gear. His knight-master had allowed him to carry word to his parents that it was time to come home, and to attend his twin's wedding before he returned with them. Thom was bouncing Sarralyn Salmalín on his knee, explaining to the two-year-old the difference between a star and a moon, while Sarra beamed up at him. Next to him Veralidaine Salmalín, known as Daine the Wildmage, gently rocked baby Rikash and talked softly with the crowd of darkings assembled on the table before her. Her husband, the mage Numair, was deep in conversation with Aly's grandfather, Tortall's official spymaster, Myles of Olau. Eleni, lady of Olau, discussed bird lice cures with Nawat.

"Well, I never thought you would do it," Alanna remarked as she sat back in her chair.

Aly gave an inward sigh, certain she was about to get a speech in how she ought to behave. "Do what, Mother?" she asked, keeping the impatience from her voice. *It's the last time I'll see her,* she scolded herself. *I can take a little lecture from her, surely.*

"Find a cause that caught you up and gripped you in your very veins," Alanna replied quietly, her eyes on the raka tapestries on the walls. "Find some passion that would consume you. Make you a fool with the rest of us fools."

"I'm *hardly* consumed," Aly began to say. Then she looked at her mother, at the lines at the corners of her mother's famed violet eyes, at the blue pearl drops hanging from her ears, Aly's Midwinter gift, at the callused and scarred hands that Alanna had folded on the table. Slowly Aly's sense of reality overcame her. Her mouth twitched. Her mother was right. Aly *had* found something to consume her, even if she didn't show it as her mother did. "Have I ever mentioned that I hate it when you're right?" she asked instead.

Alanna shook her head. "No, I don't believe you have. As far as I could tell, you never thought I was right."

Another bubble of vexation fizzed up out of Aly's belly and popped. She could see a smile tugging her mother's lips. "Since you mention it, no. Except now, Mother." She offered her hand.

Alanna took it and kissed Aly on the cheek. "Goddess bless you each and every day," she whispered. "The Great Mother is surely too wise to hold a grudge simply because you helped her brother."

Finally Aly and Nawat had to go, or fall asleep on the table. Aly took leave of her family, hugging everyone hard, fixing their faces in her mind. She saved her father for last. Standing on tiptoe, she whispered, "Da, I'd like all of your agents out of the Isles by the end of the month. Elsewise I'll arrest them and ship them home."

George looked down at his daughter, his eyes lighting up with amusement. He raised an eyebrow at her.

Aly knew what he meant by it. He would simply recruit new people in the Isles, because that was his job. Smiling wickedly, she raised one eyebrow of her own.

Back in their palace quarters, Nawat watched as Aly walked onto the veranda. The late-night air blew around her, molding her light nightgown to her body. "You will find ways to see them, and they to see you," he called to her. "They are not lost to you, or you to them. They will always be your flock."

"I know," Aly called, looking up at the sky. The sliver of the moon and the dots of the stars were as they had been in the months before the gods had waged their battle in the Divine Realms. Kyprioth had reclaimed his true throne in full, and Mithros and the Goddess were still searching for their shields. "I know. There's no reason we can't see each other, if we're discreet. Though we're going to be frightfully busy."

"There is much for us to do," Nawat agreed. "But there must be time for fun as well. Fun, and sparklies, and nestlings, and all the other things that make life interesting. For example, you could make my life interesting right now, if you chose."

Aly laughed. "And where would you be if I didn't choose?" she asked, walking inside once more.

Nawat smiled at her, the smile of a man who loved a woman. "Right here," he said confidently. "I would wear you down."

Aly was drifting off to sleep when a familiar, crisp voice whispered in her ear, *There's a girl. You get some rest. The Isles will give you all the interesting things you can stand.* Kyprioth added, *And so will I.*

CAST OF CHARACTERS

Acharn Uniunu	boy noble, member of Dunevon's court
Adona	luarin noble house
Alan of Pirate's Swoop	Alianne's twin brother, a page
Alanna of Pirate's Swoop and Olau	the King's Champion, lady knight
Alianne of Pirate's Swoop	daughter of Alanna the Lioness and George, baron of Pirate's Swoop
Ankorek Obeliten	noblewoman at regents' court
Arak	herding dog
Athan Fajering	disgraced luarin nobleman
Atisa Libo	pretty, plump, Guchol's sister, one of Aly's spy pack
Bacar	footman for a Balitang neighbor
Bean	darking placed in the palace
Bonedancer	living Archaeopteryx (dinosaur bird) skeleton
Boulaj	raka warrior, maid to Sarai, one of Aly's spy pack
Bronau Jimajen	non-royal luarin prince of the Copper Isles
Buri (Buriram)	former commander of the Queen's Riders

Callyn	spy recruit, works for the harbormaster
Chenaol	free raka servant and head cook for the Balitangs
Cinnamon	Aly's chestnut mare
Coram Smythesson	baron of Tortall
Daine (Veralidaine)	half-goddess, called the Wildmage for her skills with animals, Aly's adoptive aunt
Darkmoon	Alanna's horse
Dilsubai Haiming	last raka queen of the Copper Isles
Dorilize	Nuritin's maid, member of raka conspiracy
Dovasary (Dove)	Mequen's half-raka daughter from first marriage
Druce Adona	nobleman, one of Sarai's suitors
Dunevon Rittevon	boy king of Copper Isles
Ekit	Visda's brother, Tanair herdboy, raka
Eleni of Olau	Myles's wife, Aly's grandmother
Elsren Balitang	Dunevon's heir, luarin son of Mequen and Winnamine
Eyun	part-raka warrior, determined, member of Aly's spy pack
Faithful	supernatural cat, Alanna's former companion
Falthin	part-raka bowyer at Tanair

Feather	darking placed in Teak Sitting Room, Balitang House
Fegoro	hard raka warrior, member of Aly's spy pack
Ferdolin Tomang (Ferdy)	one of Sarai's suitors, count, wealthy luarin
Fesgao Yibenu	raka man-at-arms who protects Sarai and Dove
Flame	darking placed to spy on Duke Nomru
Gary (Gareth the Younger)	heir to fief Naxen, King Jonathan's principal advisor
Gazlon Lelin	boy noble, member of Dunevon's court
Genore Tomang	dowager countess, Ferdonlin's mother, member of luarin conspiracy
George of Pirate's Swoop	Alanna's husband and Aly's father, baron and second-in-command of his realm's spies
Gian	Elsren's manservant, spy recruit
Grace	herding dog
Graveyard Hag	trickster and primary goddess of Carthak, Kyprioth's kinswoman
Grosbeak	Topabaw's spy, collector of information
Guchol Libo	plump, good-humored, Atisa's sister, one of Aly's spy pack
Gurhart	part-raka merchant, caravan leader
Haiming	former raka ruling house

Hanoren	son of King Oron's second marriage
Hasui	part-raka kitchen slave and royal spy
Hazarin	King Oron's half brother
Herbrand Edgecliff	luarin bookseller, member of raka conspiracy
Hessken	soldier, Rittevon Guard
Hiraos	handsome raka, member of Aly's spy pack
Huldean Obeliten	boy noble, member of Dunevon's court
Hunod Ibadun	noble executed by the regents
Ianjai	wealthy raka merchant family
Imajane Jimajen	born Rittevon, King Oron's half sister, princess regent
Imgehai Qeshi	priestess of Black God of death, member of luarin conspiracy
Imiary VI	second-to-last raka queen
Imrah of Legann	lord, knight-master to Prince Roald
Inayica	female ship captain
Isalena Obemaek	luarin, one of Sarai's friends
Jafana	former luarin nursemaid to Petranne and Elsren
Jesi	Nuritin's secretary
Jevair Ibadun	noble, one of Sarai's suitors

Jimarn	former slave, deadly member of Aly's spy pack
Jonathan of Conté	King of Tortall
Junai Dodeka	raka daughter of Ulasim, Aly's guard
Kaddar Iliniat	emperor of Carthak, patron and cousin of Zaimid Hetnim
Kadyet	noble house, Balitang neighbor
Kioka	pert raka, one of Aly's spy pack
Keladry of Mindelan	called Kel, lady knight
Konutai	female Stormwing, Taybur's friend
Kyprioth	trickster god
Lace	darking placed in raka meeting room, Balitang House
Landfall	Tortallan spy in Scanra
Lehart Obemaek	luarin lord, member of luarin conspiracy
Lelin	luarin noble house
Lohearn Mantawu	Topabaw, duke, Crown spymaster
Lokeij	raka hostler for the Balitangs
Ludas Jimajen	second-in-command of the luarin invasion of the Copper Isles
Lutestring	Topabaw's agent and information gatherer
Maggur Rathhausak	Scanran king and warlord

Matfrid Fonfala	Winnamine's father, lord, member of luarin conspiracy
Maude Tanner	housekeeper and healer at Pirate's Swoop
Mayce	soldier, Rittevon Guard
Meipun Kloulechat	raka baron
Mequen Balitang	exiled luarin duke, head of the Balitang family
Merani	luarin noblewoman
Murtebo	Balitang neighbor
Musenda Ogunsanwo (Sarge)	training master of the Queen's Riders
Myles of Olau, baron	head Tortallan spymaster, Aly's grandfather, Alanna's adoptive father
Nawat Crow	a crow who turned himself into a man
Numair Salmalín	powerful mage, Daine's husband
Nuritin Balitang	Duke Mequen's luarin aunt
Obeliten	luarin noble house
Ochobu Dodeka	raka mage and mother of Ulasim
Olkey	chubby, thoughtful, one of Aly's spy pack
Oron Rittevon	deceased king of the Copper Isles
Onua Chamtong	horsemistress to the Queen's Riders
Oron Rittevon	mentally-ill king of the Copper Isles

Otaviyu Lelin	one of Sarai's friends, parents are members of luarin conspiracy
Pembery	part-raka, slave of the Balitang family
Peony	darking placed to spy on agent Grosbeak
Petranne Balitang	Mequen's first child with Winnamine
Pilia	Pochon resident, watches Ochobu's house
Qovold Engan	baron, royal astronomer, member of luarin conspiracy
Quartz	placed with Countess Tomang
Quedanga	Balitang housekeeper, head of communications, member of rebel leadership
Raoul of Goldenlake and Malorie's Peak	lord, Knight Commander of the King's Own, Tortallan hero, known as the Giant Killer
Rasaj	handsome raka, member of Aly's spy pack
Rihani	raka healer, nursemaid to Petranne and Elsren
Rikash Salmalín	Daine and Numair's infant son
Rispah	baroness of Trebond
Rittevon Lenman	leader of luarin invasion
Roald of Conté	prince, heir to Tortallan throne
Roger of Conté	King Jonathan's deceased uncle, rebel
Rosamma Tomang	one of Sarai's friends, Genore's daughter

Rubinyan Jimajen	luarin, husband of Princess Imajane, Bronau's older brother, prince regent
Rufert	soldier, Rittevon guard
Saraiyu (Sarai) Balitang	Mequen's oldest daughter, half-raka, from his first marriage
Sarra	Daine's mother, now the minor goddess The Green Lady
Sarralyn Salmalín	Daine and Numair's daughter
Sarugani Temaida	Mequen's first wife, raka, mother of Dove and Sarai, died in a tragic riding accident
Sevmire Ambau	Rubinyan's personal spymaster, luarin
Shinkokami	princess, wife of Prince Roald, heir to Tortallan throne
Spot (now Secret)	darking first placed in king's bedroom, then with Aly
Sulion	royal governor of Tongkang
Taybur Sibigat	captain of King's Guard
Temaida	raka noble house, keepers of the Haiming bloodlines, Sarugani's family
Thayet of Conté	Queen of Tortall, co-ruler with her husband, King Jonathan
Thorn of Pirate's Swoop	Aly's eighteen-year-old brother, a student mage
Tkaa	basilisk, immortal and friend of Aly's family

Topabaw	people's name for Duke Lohearn Mantawu, Crown spymaster
Trick	darking who stays with Aly
Tulpa	miller's daughter at Tanair
Tyananne	widowed luarin noblewoman
Ukali	wicked, dangerous, one of Aly's spy pack
Ulasim Dodeka	free raka servant and head footman to the Balitangs
Uniunu	luarin noble house
Vedec Golzai	young luarin noble
Vereyu	raka servant, head of raka conspiracy at palace
Veron	luarin sergeant in command of the Balitang men-at-arms
Visda	raka niece of Chenaol, goat herder
Vitorcine Townsend	double agent, maid to Obemaek family
Vurquan Nomru	duke, luarin, popular, member of luarin conspiracy
Wayan	raka child, message runner at Balitang House
Wesedi	luarin noble house, friends of Winnamine's
Winnamine Fonfala Balitang	exiled duchess, Mequen's second wife
Wyldon of Cavall	lord, district commander of Nortall's army in the north

Yoyox

cheerful, bold raka, member of Aly's spy pack

Ysul

mage of the Chain, mute, member of raka conspiracy

Zaimid Hetnim

handsome Carthaki healer, friend of the Carthaki emperor

Zeburon

royal council member, enemy of Rubinyan

GLOSSARY

Ambririp: harbor on northern tip of Imahyn Island.

arak: distilled palm-sap liquor.

Azure Sea: body of water between Imahyn, Jerkun, Ikang, and Lombyn islands, known for its clam, bright blue waters.

basilisk: immortal (cannot be killed by old age or disease), lizard-like creature, can be seven to nine feet tall, walks erect, is skilled with languages, possesses a shriek that can turn its targets to stone.

Bay Cove: village one day's sail southeast of Pirate's Swoop.

Bazhir: collective name for the nomadic tribes of Tortall's Great Southern Desert.

Birafu: estates on Tongkang belonging to Jimajen family, in rebellion.

Black God, the: the hooded and robed god of death, recognized as such throughout the Eastern and Southern Lands.

blazebalm: sticky, paste-like substance that clings to everything it touches and burns very hot.

Carthak: slaveholding empire that includes all of the Southern Lands, ancient and powerful, a storehouse of learning, sophistication, and culture. Its university was at one time without rival for teaching.

Chain, the: network of rebel mages, mostly full and part-raka, spread throughout the Copper Isles, with members on every isle, including one posted especially close to the isle's royal governor. It has been in existence over one hundred years. Its present commanding mage is Ochobu Dodeka.

centaur: an immortal (cannot be killed by old age or disease), half horse, half human; attitudes to mortal humans vary.

Conqueror's Laws: laws enacted by the luarin conquerors of the Copper Isles, exacting heavy penalties (seizure of lands and monies, slavery for rebel families, executions of leaders of any rebellion, mass executions where a noble luarin is killed) paid by members of the subject raka peoples should any harm befall their luarin masters.

Copper Isles: originally named the Kyprish Isles, once ruled by queens of the Haiming noble house, presently ruled by the Rittevon dynasty. The Isles form a slaveholding nation south and west of Tortall. The lowlands are hot, wet jungles, the highlands cold and rocky, Traditionally their ties are to Carthak rather than Tortall. Kyprish pirates often raid along the Tortallan coast. There is a strain of insanity in the Rittevon line. The Rittevons hold a grudge against Tortall (one of their princesses was killed there the day that Jonathan was crowned).

Corus: capital city of Tortall, on the banks of the River Olorun. Corus is the home of the new royal university as well as the royal palace.

darking: creature made in the Divine Realms that has evolved into an independent being; small, blob-like, able to manipulate shape, reproduce by splitting, capable of thought and learning; some reside in Dragonlands in Divine Realms, others have returned to Mortal Realms.

Dawn Crow: male god of the crows

Dimari: eastern harbor town on the island of Lombyn

Divine Realms: home to the gods and to many immortals

Dockmarket: section of town defined by Dockmarket Street along wharves; open-air markets for food, spices, various products; includes warehouse, slave market.

Dominion Jewel: magical artifact presently held by the Tortallan kings, a round purple gem that draws those under its influence to form tighter national bonds and tighter connections between the wielder of the Jewel and the land that forms the nation under its influence.

Downwind: poorer section of Rajmuat.

duan: raka word for old man, boss.

duani: raka word for old lady, boss.

Eastern Lands: name used to refer to those lands north of the Inland Sea and east of the Emerald Ocean: Scanra, Tortall, Tyra, Tusaine, Galla, Maren, Sarain. Original home of the luarin nobility and kings of the Copper Isles.

Ekallatum: one of the most ancient kingdoms in the history of the Southern Lands, now part of the Carthaki Empire.

Emerald Ocean: body of water west of the Eastern and Southern Lands, containing the Yamani Islands and the Copper Isles, among others.

Examples: Kyprin term for nobles and wealthy people who are executed by the Crown and displayed on posts as a warning to others.

Fief Tameran: neighboring fiefdom to Pirate's Swoop.

Flowergarden: district north and west of Downwind, contains lower-class residences, also district of brokers of domestic animals, fullers, tanners, blacksmiths.

Frasrlund: Tortallan port city at the mouth of the Vassa, straddling the border with Scanra.

Gainel: god of dreams, with one foot in the Mortal Realms and one foot in the realms of Chaos.

Galla: country to the north and east of Tortall, famous for its mountains and forests, with an ancient royal line. Daine was born there.

Galodon: housing town for military and royal navy fortress and reserves.

Gempang: island in the Copper Isles, on the opposite side of the Long Strait from Kypriang.

Gift, the: human, academic magic, the use of which must be taught.

Gigit: smallest coin of the Copper Isles: 10 copper gigits equal 1 silver gigit; 50 copper gigits (5 silver gigits) equal 1 copper lan; 1 copper gigit will buy a cup of tea, a bun, or an orange.

Grand Progress, the: a two-year circuit (457 H.E.–458 H.E.) of the realm of Tortall made by the monarchs King Jonathan and Queen Thayet, accompanied by their heir, Roald, and his betrothed, Princess Shinkokami, of the Yamani Islands. The Progress included tournaments; festivities; scholarly, medical, and legal research; aid for areas afflicted by nature or attack; meetings with immortal residents; and appraisal of worsening military relations with Scanra.

Gray Palace: Eastern Lands-style castle built inside a separate wall on the palace grounds, to house the Rittevon family.

Great Mother Goddess: chief goddess in the pantheon of the Eastern Lands, protector of women. Her symbol is the moon.

Greater Fortress: citadel that guards the southeastern approach to Rajmuat harbor.

griffin: feathered immortal with a cat-like body, wings, and a beak. Males grow to a height of six and a half to seven feet tall at the shoulder; females are slightly bigger. No one can tell lies in a griffin's vicinity (a range of about a hundred feet). Their young have bright orange feathers to make them more visible. If adult griffin parents sense that a human has handled their infant griffin, they will try to kill that human.

Gunapi the Sunrose: raka warrior goddess of volcanoes, war, and molten rock.

Haiming: name of the former line of raka queens, supposedly wiped out during the Luarin Conquest, with members who survived in secret until the present.

healer: a health-care professional with varying degrees of education, magic, and skill.

his realm's spies: network of a kingdom's agents, charged with gathering intelligence at home and abroad; spies in service to a particular country.

Honeypot: worst of the Downwind slums.

hostler: one who cares for horses: their feed, medicine, grooming, cleanliness, saddling.

Human Era (H.E.): the calendar in use in the Eastern and Southern Lands and in the Copper Isles is dated the Human Era to commemorate the years since the one in which the immortals were originally sealed into the Divine Realms, over four hundred and fifty years previous to the years covered by *Protector of the Small*.

hurrok: immortal shaped like a horse with leathery bat-wings, claws and fangs.

Ikang: island to the southwest of Lombyn (the northern-most island).

Imahyn: island just northwest of the Long Strait and Gempang.

Immortal: creatures from the Divine Realms who cannot get sick or grow old. They can be killed, but otherwise they live forever.

Immortals War: short, vicious war fought in 452 H.E., named that for the number of immortal creatures that fought, but also waged by Carthakis (rebels against the new Emperor Kaddar), Copper Islanders, and Scanran raiders. These forces were defeated by the residents of the Eastern Lands, particularly Tortall, but recovery is slow.

Inti: westernmost village on Tanair estates on the island of Lombyn. Inti is astride the road leading down to the west coast of Lombyn.

Jaguar Goddess: feral and bloody goddess native to the Isles, overthrown by Mithros and the Great Mother Goddess during the Luarin Conquest and chained below the earth until she should be freed. Sister and sometime consort of Kyprioth, who also prefers that she stay chained.

Jerykun Isle: smallest of the Isles, situated between Imahyn in the south and Ikang in the north. Virtually all of Jerykun is held between the Tomangs, who have grown rich from the trade in sunset butterflies (a source of precious blue dyes and magical ingredients), with smaller estates held by, among others, Sibigat House.

Kanodang: prison to the northeast of the Downwind slums, over the ridge of the Kitafin mountains that runs between Rajmuat and the coast.

Kellaura Pass: opening on the Dimari Road through the Turnshe Mountains on Lombyn, leads to Tanair and other estates.

King's Council: the monarch's private council of advisors, made up of those people he trusts the most.

King's Guard: small contingent of soldiers/bodyguard responsible for the safety of the ruling monarch of the Copper Isles, presently led by Taybur Sibigat. Their armor is chain mail painted black.

King's Own: cavalry/police group answering to the king, whose members serve as royal bodyguards and as protective troops throughout the realm. Their knight commander is Lord Sir Raoul of Goldenlake and Malorie's Peak. Their ranks are filled by younger sons of noble houses, Bazhir, and the sons of wealthy merchants. The Own is made of three companies of one hundred fighters each, in addition to the servingmen, who care for supplies and re-mounts. First Company, a show company, traditionally provides palace body-guards and security for the monarchs. Under Lord Raoul, Second and Third Company were added and dedicated to active service away from the palace, helping to guard the realm.

King's Watch: patrol group that polices Rajmuat, wears armor painted red.

K'mir: brown-skinned nomadic horse tribes of Saraine, expert at guerilla fighting against the Saren ruling class of lowland whites. Queen Thayet of Tortall is half K'mir on her mother's side and has been responsible for a mi-gration of K'miri, who now work for the Tortallan Crown.

kudarung: Kyprin (raka) term for flying horses.

Kypriang: capital island of the Copper Isles, holding the capital, Rajmuat, and its harbor. Location of the Plain of Sorrows, site of the last great defeat of the raka by the luarin.

Kyprioth: the Trickster, greatest of the trickster gods, former patron god of the Copper Isles, overthrown by his brother Mithros and his sister the Great Goddess, now relegated in the Isles to rulership over the seas that surround them. Cousin to the Carthaki goddess the Graveyard Hag.

lan: largest money coin in the Isles: 1 gold lan equals 10 silver lans; 1 silver lan equals 10 copper lans; 1 copper equals 5 silver gigits, or 50 copper gigits.

Lesser Fortress: citadel that guards the eastern arm of Rajmuat harbor.

Lombyn: northernmost island of the Copper Isles, home to the Tanair estates of Lady Saraiyu and Lady Dove Balitang, the legacy of the their mother Saru-gani. The location of the Turnshe Mountains, Kellaura Pass, Dimari town and harbor, and the villages of Tanair, Inti, and Pohon.

Long Strait: the narrow, tricky body of water between Kypriang and Gem-pang Islands.

luarin: raka (native of the Copper Isles) term for the white-skinned invaders from the Eastern Lands, now used in the Isles to indicate anyone with white skin.

mage: a wizard, male or female

Malubesang: largest and most southern of the Copper Isles, notorious for streams that are home to meat-eating fish. Home to the most prosperous estates of the Isles, particularly those of Nomru House. The extended Fonfala family also has lands bordering the Nomru ones.

Maren: large, powerful country east of Tusaine and Tyra; the grain basket of the Eastern Lands, with plenty of farms and trade.

Market Town: pricier market district west of Dockmarket.

Mastiff: fort that serves Lord Wyldon as command post during events in *Lady Knight*.

matcher: a slavebroker who deals in matching experienced slaves with owners who will pay top price for them; some owners insist that matchers only sell slaves to buyers who will treat them well. Many are also talent spotters, operating schools at which they groom slavers for particular tasks before they are sold at a higher rate than the slave would have gotten originally. Some matchers have magical Gifts that help them to spot talent, both magical and non-magical.

Middle Town: district that is part residential for middle class, part shopping area, includes Rittevon Square.

Midwinter Festival: seven-day holiday centering around the longest night of the year and the sun's rebirth afterward. It is the beginning of the new year. Gifts are exchanged and feasts held.

Mithros: chief god of the Tortallan pantheon, god of war and the law. His symbol is the sun.

Moriki Cove: cove on the southern coast of Kypriang near Fonfala estates.

network: group of spies or other persons who exchange information among themselves.

pavilion: an outdoor structure that can be open on its sides, walled halfway up its sides, or fully walled in.

Port Udayapur: port city-state on the northeast corner of the Great Inland Sea, entry gate to the mountains called the Roof of the World.

Plain of Sorrows: site of the biggest and last defeat of the Copper Isles' native raka people by the white, or luarin, invaders (opportunists from the Eastern Lands). The battle that broke the power of the Haiming royal line and of the great noble houses of the Copper Isles, and set the Rittevon kings on the Isles' throne.

Pohon: village on the northern border of the Tanair estates on the island of Lombyn. The raka of Pohon are notoriously inhospitable to their luarin overlords.

Port Caynn: port city that serves the Tortallan capital of Corus.

Port Legann: the southwestern port city of Tortall, ruled by Lord Imrah and his lady.

Queen's Riders: cavalry/police group that protects Tortallans who live in hard-to-reach parts of the country. They enforce the law and teach local residents to defend themselves. The basic unit is a Rider Group, with eight to nine members. Rank in a Group is simply that of commander and second-in-command; the head of the Riders is the Commander. They accept both women and men in their ranks, unlike the army, the navy, or the King's Own. Their headquarters is between the palace and the Royal Forest.

Rajmuat: capital of the Copper Isles under both the raka and the luarin.

raka: brown-skinned natives of the Copper Isles, under the lordship of the luarin arrivals from the Eastern Lands for nearly three hundred years.

Rittevon Guard: guard that covers the palace grounds and walls of Rajmuat; combined sun and moon engraved on breastplates.

Rittevon Lancers: light cavalry military force of the Copper Isles. They generally carry lances and swords as weapons.

Rittevon's Lance: major street of Rajmuat and the palace, running through the center of Rajmuat and up through the Gate of Victory to the center of the palace enclosure. Ends in the palace street called the Golden Road.

Royal Forest: vast forest that blankets land south and west of Corus for several days' ride.

sarong: for women, the wrap-around garment that extends from under the arms to the calves. For men, a skirt-like wrap-around garment that can be kilted in the middle to make rough breeches.

Scanra: country to the north of Tortall, wild rocky, and cold, with very little land that can be farmed. Scanrans are masters of the sea and are feared anywhere there is a coastline. They also frequently raid over land. In recent years, their Great Council (formerly the Council of Ten, expanded in the disruptions following the Immortals War), made up of the heads of the clans, elected the warlord Maggur Rathhausak to be their king. The war with Tortall began in 460 H.E. (the events are covered in *Lady Knight*) and has moved into its second year, though Scanra is visibly weakening.

scry: to look into the present, future, or past using magic and, sometimes, a bowl of water, a mirror, fire, or some other device to look through.

shape-shifter: one who can take the shape of an animal or another human. Those who shift into immortal form are unable to change back.

Sight, the: aspect of the magical Gift that gives its holders certain advantages in matters of vision. It can be erratic, showing holders only lies, illness, magic, or future importance. In its fullest form, it can allow the holder to see clearly over distance, see tiny things in sharp detail, and to detect illness, lies, godhood, magic, death, and other aspects of life.

Sky: the crow goddess, consort of the Dawn Crow.

slave broker: one who buys and sells slaves

Southern Lands: another name for the Carthaki Empire, which has conquered all of the independent nations that once were part of the continent south of the Inland Sea.

spidren: immortal whose body is that of a furred spider four to five feet in height; its head is that of a human, with sharp, silvery teeth. Spidrens can use weapons. They also use their webs as weapons and ropes. Spidren web is gray-green in color and glows after dark. Their blood is black, and burns like acid. They favorite food is human blood.

Stormwing: immortal with a human head and chest and the legs and wings of birds, with steel feathers and claws. Stormwings have sharp teeth, but use them only to add to the terror of their presence by tearing apart bodies. They live on human fear and have their own magic; their special province is that of desecrating battlefield dead.

Swan District: residential neighborhood for the newly rich, north and west of Dockmarket, Market Town, and Middle Town.

Tanair: Lombyn Isle estates that form part of the inheritance of Lady Saraiyu and Lady Dove Balitang, granted to them by their mother, Sarugani Temaida. Estates include Tanair castle and village, and the villages of Inti and Pohon.

Thak: language of old Carthak, used as a magical language in present times.

Tongkang: island to the south of Gempang, between Gempang and Malubesang Isles.

Tortall: chief kingdom in which the Alanna, Daine, and Keladry sagas take place, between the Inland Sea and Scanra. Home to Alianne of Pirate's Swoop and her family.

Trebond: birthplace of Alanna the Lioness, now held by Baron Coram and his wife, Rispah.

Turnshe Mountains: central mountains of Lombyn, stretching from the northern point of the island to the southern point. Travel in northern Lombyn is through the Kellaura Pass on the Dimari road.

Tusaine: small country tucked between Tortall and Maren.

Tyra: merchant republic on the Inland Sea between Tortall and Maren. Tyra is mostly swamp, and its people rely on trade and banking for an income. Numair Salmalin was born there.

Vassa River: river that forms a large part of the northeast border between Scanra and Tortall.

wild magic: magic that is part of the natural world. Unlike the human Gift, it cannot be drained or done away with; it is always present.

wildmage: mage who deals in wild magic, the kind of magic that is part of nature. Daine Sarrasri is often called the Wildmage, for her ability to communicate with animals, heal them, and shape-shift.

Wind: Kyprioth's cousin, a god.

Yamani Islands: island nation to the north and west of Tortall and the west of Scanra, ruled by an ancient line of emperors, whose claim to their throne comes from the goddess Yama. The country is beautiful and mountainous. Its vulnerability to pirate raids means that most Yamanis get some training in combat arts, including the women. Keladry of Mindelan lived there for six years while her father was the Tortallan ambassador.

Yimosuat: capital of Gempang Island, known for its many temples.

NOTES AND ACKNOWLEDGMENTS

Aly's story is a pair of books instead of a quartet thanks to J. K. Rowling (I haven't met her!), who taught adults that American kids will read thicker books, which means I don't need four books to tell a complete story.

My thanks, I think, also go to my beloved editrix, Mallory Loehr, who suggested both that I write about a spy and that I write a character who is laid-back and easygoing, not driven. One day I will find the proper manner in which to express my appreciation of an exercise that made a Moebius strip of me for the last three years. Sarai's fate is her idea as well. My gratitude also goes to my Australian editrix, Margrete Lamond, for her very provocative pointers on pomp and on the behavior of gods.

Thanks as ever to the home team, those who gave me help with so many of the problems that cropped up in the *Trickster* books: my excellent Spouse-Creature, Tim Liebe, who gives me so many plot ideas and twists, and also supplies necessary photographs; my best friend Raquel Starace, fashion consultant on flattering colors for everyone who is not a fair-skinned redhead like me, and the progenetrix (through her discussions of making an inanimate object animate and her analysis of the differences between human and computer animation) of the darkings; my wonderful assistant, Sara Alan, for her proofreading and for her reassurances with regard to my feminist credentials as well as for her tolerance of major author flake-outs; my agent, Craig Tenney, he of the watchful eye and the sound advice; Peter Glassman at Books of Wonder for shoring up my faltering courage; and the excellent Christina Schulman and the National Aviary for crowned pigeons and tropical woods mood enhancement.

I bow also to the *Law & Order* franchise, World Wrestling Entertainment, *National Geographic*'s photographs of people around the world, and photographer Joyce Tenneson's *Wise Women* collection in thanks for their inspiration for a number of characters; to the novels of John Le Carré, particularly *Tinker, Tailor, Soldier, Spy* and *Smiley's People* for insights into effective spycraft, as well as to the innumerable books by innumerable experts I have read on the art of guerrilla warfare.

For musical inspiration I have turned to sources that may appear odd and unrelated, but aren't: Alan Lomax and the singers of his collection *Negro Songs and Work Calls,* performed by Southern blacks in the 1930s and 1940s; pianist Glenn Gould and his classic recordings of Bach's "Goldberg Variations"; composer Ottorino Respighi and his incredible "Pines of Rome," of which I have at least three recorded versions with three different orchestras and conductors; and "Two Cries of Freedom: Gypsy Flamenco from the Prisons of Spain," sung by José Serrano and Antonio "El Agujetas," Reachout International Records, Inc.

Those interested in the historical sources of some of my ideas and conflicts may want to examine Alexander the Great's conquest of Egypt and his placement of the Greek Ptolemies over the native Egyptians; William the Conqueror's arrival in England and its centuries of consequences; American slavery; the history of Tudor England during the childhood of Edward VI and the beginning of the reign of Queen Elizabeth I; and the history of any power that invades a country that is not its own and attempts to keep it. As the Rittevons and Jimajens learn, it's hard to completely pacify a country when the bulk of the people who live there are opposed to being pacified.

TAMORA PIERCE captured the imagination of readers more than twenty years ago with *Alanna: The First Adventure.* As of September 2004, she has written twenty-two books, including three completed quartets—The Song of the Lioness, The Immortals, and Protector of the Small—set in the fantasy realm of Tortall. She has also written the Circle of Magic and The Circle Opens quartets. Her books have been translated into many different languages. Some are available on audio from Listening Library and Full Cast Audio. Tamora Pierce's fast-paced, suspenseful writing and strong, believable heroines have won her much praise: *Emperor Mage* was a 1996 ALA Best Book for Young Adults, *The Realms of the Gods* was listed as an "outstanding fantasy novel" by *VOYA* in 1996, *Squire* (Protector of the Small #3) was a 2002 ALA Best Book for Young Adults, and *Lady Knight* (Protector of the Small #4) debuted at #1 on the *New York Times* bestseller list. *Trickster's Choice* spent a month on the *New York Times* bestseller list and was a 2003 ALA Best Book for Young Adults.

An avid reader herself, Ms. Pierce graduated from the University of Pennsylvania. She has worked at a variety of jobs and has written everything from novels to radio plays. Along with writer Meg Cabot (The Princess Diaries series), she co-founded Sheroes Central, a discussion board about female heroes, remarkable women in fact, fiction, and history, books, current events, and teen issues. She now sponsors Sheroes Central and Sheroes Fans, helping to run it with her beloved Spouse-Creature and an administrative team of adults and teens.

Tamora Pierce lives in New York City with her husband, Tim, a writer, Web page designer, and Web administrator, and their five cats, two birds, and various rescued wildlife.

For more information, visit:
www.tamora-pierce.com

Sheroes Central at:
www.sheroescentral.com